ENOUGH GOOD MEN

Enough Good Men

Charles Mercer

G. P. Putnam's Sons New York

TO ALMA
With Love and Gratitude

Contents

Book One
THE YOUNG ONES
Page 11

Book Two
PROCLAIM LIBERTY
Page 115

Book Three
LONG RETREAT
Page 183

Book Four
THE LION'S MOUTH
Page 273

Book Five
BIG LAND YONDER
Page 411

ENOUGH GOOD MEN

Book One

THE YOUNG ONES

I

A MIGHTY clap of thunder over west, beyond the Ohio, awakened Micah Heath, the bound boy. As it died away in a long drum roll, the spruce began to sough, and then the rain came, pattering across the river and rattling on the shellbark roof. The death of summer, Micah thought, and slept again.

Later, when he came fully awake, it was still dark. There was no sound except the *drip-drip-drip* of spent rain from the big hickory. Then, gradually, he became aware of many sounds. A green log creaked and field mice scampered in the cabin loft; a porcupine dragged its quills across the clearing and a small bird chittered. The world was whispering out there, night hunters slinking away and the day awakening. Somewhere a cock turkey raised his bubbling cry; five times he called before a hen fluted her answer. It was morning.

Micah rose from his leaf bed, working his feet into elkhide moccasins as he fastened the belt of his deerskin shirt. Padding across the hard-packed dirt floor, he unbarred and opened the door. Gray light shafted the eastern sky while here below a white mist smoked from earth. Rain and then clear; cold now and a warm day, turning cold again at sundown; weather making and season changing as October waned.

Again the turkey raised his proud, watery cry.

Micah slung pouch and powder horn over his shoulders, picked up his long rifle, and went quietly down-wind until the spruce swallowed him. Soon he turned south, a shadow among innumerable shadows, feet falling silently on the brown needles. The cock turkey called again, and this time the hen replied immediately. Over there. He knew the place, in the red oak bottom, where they would be scratching and picking for mast. He moved on silently as the invisible sun rubbed at the sky and shapes emerged from shadows in the land between the river and the ridge.

At the next call, close by, he halted and removed the deerskin lock cover from his rifle and poured powder into the muzzle and the priming pan. Placing a patching and ball in the muzzle, he rammed them home with his thin hickory stick. He opened the setscrew on the hammer and turned the flint to a fresh side, and then he noiselessly stretched prone behind a log on which he rested the long barrel.

The day grew while he waited, patient and unmoving. Blue banners of light sprang up the sky and the ground mist lay down slowly, revealing the bright splash of fall up yonder on the ridge. Elbows resting on the earth, he stared across the log until, at last, he saw a movement fifty yards away among the red oaks. The movement became the strutting shape of a big cock turkey. He waited until the head, raised, was directly in his sights. He pressed the trigger. There was a blinding white flash in the priming pan, a deafening crash, and his shoulder was jolted sharply. Springing to his feet, he ran forward. He had not missed. The ball had plowed through the turkey's head.

He walked home through the dawn, strutting a little, as had the heavy turkey he now carried by limp claws. Hunter Heath. He held his rifle handily in the crook of his left arm, unlike the careless way that Fogarty carried a gun. Today or tomorrow Fogarty would come back from Pittsburgh and then it would be fetch this and tote that and fix t'other. All day long it was "Boy, boy, boy!" except when Fogarty let him go off to bag them fresh meat or run his short trap line. Well, come Christmas Eve he'd be eighteen years old, and three years from then he would be free. It was said that a child born on Christmas Eve had a prophet's vision, and though he'd had uneven luck in prophesying anything, he knew for a fact that his indentured servitude would be ended forever when he was twenty-one.

Crossing the small clearing, he entered the cabin which he had helped Fogarty build two years ago. "Fogarty's Post," the trader had said proudly. "Fogarty's Post on the Ohio, b'y. Afore ye know it this'll be Fogartytown here." But it was mighty short of being Fogartytown. The river *plock-plocked* along as empty as ever and all around the silent woods pressed in and swung out as far and dark and quiet as you could wish. Daniel Twillow had brought out his wife and two young ones and built a cabin a couple of miles up-river. But that was as much as Fogartytown had grown in two years. It suited Micah. Movers like the Twillows spoiled a country and scared off the game.

Outside, bluejays began to cry raucously. He went to the doorway and saw nothing unusual. His belly growled in hunger and he broke off a piece of last night's corncake. Picking up the big iron kettle, he went out and around the cabin to the run, munching the corncake as he went. He lay down on the flat rock and buried his head in the cold, swiftly running stream and drank deeply under water. Raising his dripping head, blinking and gasping for breath, he heard the changed pitch in the cries of the jays, his watchdogs. Something was afoot.

He filled the kettle quickly and hurried to the cabin. Setting the kettle by the chopping block, he listened intently, his gaze traveling the edge of the clearing to the mist-cloaked river. The river went its way, *plock-plock-plock*. And then, faintly he heard a *ka-plock, ka-plock*. The sound, he knew, was of quiet paddles.

Stepping inside the cabin, he loaded his rifle. When he came out, two—three—four Indians were filing up silently from the river mist. Reaching behind him, he shut the cabin door. "Keep off all Injuns," Fogarty had told him eight days ago when he and Red Deer, the old Mingo, had left for Pittsburgh with a canoe-load of skins. Well, he would keep them off. But he wished, as he counted ten—eleven—twelve Indians coming out of the mist, that there were not so many of them.

They were strangers to him, on their way to war somewhere. Their faces and bodies were blackened, their eyes smeared green and encircled with red, and across their bare chests they had daubed the vermilion paths of war. Two carried trade muskets and the others carried bows. Fifteen—sixteen of them, spreading out now and advancing slowly toward him.

Letting his right arm hang loosely at his side, he swung the rifle laid across his left arm up and down easily by light pressure on the stock. They halted, staring at him and the hint of menace in the rifle which they saw he handled as deftly as if he were a full-grown man. Then one, who wore an eagle feather war bonnet and the silver armbands of a chief, stepped forward and raised his right hand, palm out.

"Young brother," he said in the Delaware language, "we come in peace to trade with you. Do you understand?"

"Brother," Micah said, "I speak your tongue."

He let that sink in. He was mighty proud of his power with the Delaware talk; it was not muskrat Delaware, but the true language that he had learned from Red Deer and many others in the past two years. It had come easily to him, as naturally as all of this life in the woods, and it had greatly enhanced his value to Fogarty, who never could remember more than a few words of Delaware.

"Young brother," the chief said, "we come to trade for guns and powder and bullets. We go to war against our ancient enemy, the Catawbas, who have slain numbers of our people only a moon ago."

"Brother," Micah said, "if you would trade, show me your pelts. Bring them out and set them on the ground before me, as your people do when they come here to trade."

The chief spat on the ground and turned his back. "We do not trade with babes," he said. Then he faced Micah. "We spoke with the trader, who will stay away many more days, and he sent a message that you give us what we want."

Micah's mouth felt dry. So they knew that Fogarty was away; they had been scouting him and they knew he was alone.

"Brother," he said, "the trader returns today. If he sent a message, show me the paper."

Fingering his belt, the chief strode forward. When he had walked three paces without showing a paper, Micah swung the rifle to his shoulder. The chief halted, his large brown eyes glazed over with thoughts of death as he stared at the ivory foresight of the rifle aimed steadily at his head.

"The message, brother." Micah wished that his voice did not sound so high and piercing.

Silently the chief backed away and then turned and strode to the edge of the clearing where the others clustered around him.

He began to feel pretty good as the sun climbed above the ridge. He'd faced down those Indians like a grown man. Fogarty should be proud of him when he learned what he'd done, though Fogarty never would say so. Still, Fogarty must know that he'd driven a good bargain away back east in Chester County nearly two and a half years ago when he bought him from Timothy Murdoch. Fogarty had paid fifteen pounds for him. At the time Micah had been rather proud of the fact that he, then a boy of fifteen, was considered worth fifteen pounds. But now, in this autumn of 1771, thinking of his worth and the three years and two months he still must serve Fogarty, he sighed. He was worth much more. . . .

Across the clearing the Indians had broken off their talk. But they were not going to their canoes.

His heart gave a great bullfrog plop and he licked his lips. They were fading into the woods, not filing away, but simply fading like the mist. Then they were gone. There was no sound except the angry hawking of the disturbed jays. They were gone, but they were not gone. They were working around through the brush to torment him. He was tempted to rush into the cabin and bar the door. They wished he'd do that. Then they could smoke him easily by setting a fire and waiting for him to dash out, coughing and blinded. The place for him to stay was here.

Kicking the chopping block nearer the closed door, he sat down. The morning sun was hot. He wanted a drink of water from the kettle, but it would be a sign of weakness to the watching eyes. He wished he'd remembered to put on his foxtail cap and cover his great thatch of tawny hair; it would make him look more like a man and less a boy. Stealthily he fingered the hard muscles of his left arm. Oh, he was strong and lean and tall, and he was slippery as an eel when he wrestled the Delaware and Shawnee boys who came with their fathers to trade.

The Indians began their turkey talk, warbling and fluting back and forth, trying to set his nerves on edge. After a while it made you want to jump up and leap into the river and swim straight across it. But the trick, he knew, was to think of nothing while you remained aware of everything, like the time last spring when he'd chopped his foot and had managed not to whimper while Fogarty sewed it up.

When a pebble thudded on the cabin roof, he did not start or turn his head; it was only a pebble, he knew. Fogarty might come down the river at any time now, bringing Red Deer with him unless the old Mingo had gone on a big drunk in Pittsburgh again. But he mustn't count on Fogarty; he must not count on anybody or anything except his own skill and luck.

There was a whirring sound and a thud behind him. Glancing around, he saw an arrow fast in the door. Another shivered into the chopping block beside him, telling him, Run, boy, run. If they meant to kill him, he thought, they wouldn't need to warn him. Drawing his skinning knife, he began to pare his grubby nails with elaborate care. Maybe he shouldn't do it, but his hands were itching to do something and all he could think of was to pare his nails like a Philadelphia dandy.

An arrow rang against the kettle. He sniffed something musky and an arm closed around his throat as the knife was struck from his hand and his rifle clattered to the ground. He twisted, straining his shoulder muscles against the musky arm, thinking that his one error had been to show off by paring his nails. Then he plunged down a deep well into darkness. . . .

He was rising from the well, up through a piny smell into daylight, his head and neck throbbing painfully. Blinking, he found himself lying on his left side, hands bound behind him around the slim trunk of a young spruce. His rifle was propped against another spruce nearby and his pouch and powder horn were hung from a bough. The Delawares swarmed into and out of the cabin like bees working a hive. They squabbled over the trade guns and one pranced out with a bolt of red calico unwinding over a shoulder while two others lugged the powder keg.

Micah closed his eyes at the thought of Fogarty's ruin and groaned when he thought of his wrath. He remembered how he and Fogarty had brought this plunder all the way from Germantown by pack train, walking and climbing and wallowing the hundreds of miles to Pittsburgh where Fogarty sold his hammerheaded horses and hired Delawares and canoes to bring them seventy-five miles around the big bend of the Ohio to this place. Oh, Fogarty was a pushing, hard-laboring man who never said die. But when he sees the ruin of his trade, Micah thought, he'll take a block instead of a stick to me and never listen to how I tried to save his plunder.

Staring up the empty river, he began cautiously rubbing the deer-thong bonds against the spruce at his back. The thongs were tightly tied; it might take him most of the day to free himself. Why didn't Fogarty come?

Maybe Daniel Twillow would wander in from his slashing up-river. But he wouldn't be any help. The Delawares would truss him up faster than greased lightning. Daniel Twillow didn't belong out here; he belonged away back east among the Quakers. He wasn't much of a hunter or trapper, and he wasn't much of a farmer either. Somehow he'd taken up rights to land out here on the Ohio. He'd pushed west from Bedford with his poor gaunt wife and their two scrawny young ones and their big sure-footed ox, slipping and creeping the forty miles of woods trace from Pittsburgh. Sometimes, when you looked at Daniel Twillow and his careless ways, you reckoned he was a man with one foot in the bury hole.

Micah wished he hadn't thought of the bury hole as one of the Delawares came toward him, tomahawk drawn. Today he might die. Fear struck his belly like an icy blast of winter air and strength drained from him.

But he gathered his legs under him and worked his back up the spruce trunk until he stood, facing the Delaware. The large, brown, cruel eyes stared fixedly at his, then shifted upward slightly. The tomahawk flashed and buried in the spruce so close above his head that his scalp chilled. The Delaware grinned and then he laughed. He felt Micah's lean arms and slapped his face, hard but almost affectionately. Drawing his tomahawk from the tree, he strutted away.

The day warmed. Sweat beaded Micah's face and rolled down his flanks as he stood with his back against the tree working at the thongs. The Delawares loaded muskets and bullet molds and lead bars into their canoes. From the powder keg they poured powder into two deer bladders, carelessly spilling the precious black stuff and treading it into the black earth. What, Micah wondered, are they going to do with *me?* Suppose they took him with them?

As he imagined them passing on down the Ohio through the endless wilderness he thought that it would be more tolerable to go with them than to face Fogarty's wrath. Thinking of the black forest that rolled far west, as wide as the sea, he stopped sawing at his bonds. Out there a man would be eternally free while his feet turned the earth under him on its great northern icicle pole.

Suddenly and distinctly, he heard a voice calling.

"Hooo—eee, b'y!"

Fogarty!

Raising his head, he shouted, "Foo—garty! Help!"

The Delawares raced toward their canoes. Before they reached them, however, Fogarty came in sight around the piny point of land a hundred yards up-river. Red Deer had not returned with him; he was alone in the stern of the big canoe which lay low in the water under the weight of the goods he had floated from Pittsburgh. Behind came Daniel Twillow and his wife, Mary, in the little shellbark canoe which Red Deer had made for them. They must have hailed Fogarty as he passed their clearing and followed him down to eye the new trade goods.

"Fogarty!" Micah cried.

Fogarty's paddle grew still as he stared at his bound boy tied to the tree and the Delawares scrambling into their canoes. Daniel Twillow's head was lowered in his customary oblivion to everything as he chopped his little canoe along awkwardly. But Mary Twillow, seeing the Delawares, and Micah tied to the tree, cried out piercingly. Fogarty suddenly dug his paddle and swung the big canoe broadside to the current.

"Fogarty!" Micah could not believe that he was trying to run away. Yet he was. Fogarty was afraid. "Fogarty!"

Fogarty dug his paddle frantically while the big canoe yawed on the current. Then Micah shouted wordlessly as Daniel Twillow clumsily drove into Fogarty's broached canoe and Daniel's paddle slipped from his hands. Daniel and Mary were trying to stand up; their wail of terror came across the water. Arms flailing, Daniel toppled backwards into the river and Mary flung herself forward, grasping the lip of Fogarty's heavily laden canoe. Screaming curses, Fogarty struck at her hands with his paddle. She clung on as the big canoe slowly tilted and began to ship water.

"Fogarty!"

He did not know how to swim. Screaming in fear, he was going down slowly with his plunder and his canoe and the terror-stricken woman who was trying to save herself. The river swirled around his shoulders and his arms thrashed a white foam. Slowly he sank from sight.

The river purled along emptily, twirling the overturned little shellbark canoe.

The Delawares had halted when Fogarty started to flee. Unmoving, they still stared at the place where the unbelievable cowardice and clumsiness had occurred. One suddenly gave a great *whah* of laughter and slapped his thighs. Then all were howling with laughter, some rolling on the ground in ecstasy at the unbelievable: the white people who lived by water but could not swim in it, the two armed white men who were frightened at sight of a boy bound to a tree, the loud and boldly swaggering trader who obviously had lived in fear.

Micah, his head lowered, felt numbed. At the sound of lightly padding feet, he looked up. The chief stood before him, stroking his knife on his left palm, staring at him unfathomably. I wish, Micah thought dimly, that I'd been born an Indian. He raised his chin defiantly.

Stepping behind the spruce, the chief slashed his bonds. He sheathed his knife and walked away.

Silent now, the Delawares launched their canoes. The sternmen set the rhythm with a quick "Hyuk!—hyuk!" and then they disappeared from view. There was no sound except the Ohio *plock-plocking* toward the unknown country.

He knew at once what he should do. But he passed nearly an hour thinking of the things he'd like to do. He'd like to find and stock a canoe and float down the river, far down beyond the forests where there was said to be a golden grass country teeming with game. And then maybe he'd swing up north to the big lakes after winter had passed. He could do it, he could take care of himself anywhere in the woods.

The trouble wasn't with him. The trouble was what Timothy Murdoch used to call legal. Legal-wise he wasn't free, even though Fogarty was dead. Legal-wise he reckoned that until he was twenty-one he would belong to Murdoch, who had bound him out to Fogarty. Legality was strange. He lacked, for instance, the legal right to take a thing that had belonged to Fogarty, and the fact that Fogarty had been a yellow-dog coward who had treated him unjustly made no difference. Legality should take account of justice, but it did not. A man could handle justice himself. But legality was legality and it made your head spin. Justice-wise he felt able to look out for himself, he felt that he'd earned the right to stock a canoe with plunder and go down west. But legal-wise he reckoned that he was supposed to foot it clear across Pennsylvania back to Chester County and Murdoch.

Well, he'd see about that in time. For certain, though, he had to go to Pittsburgh and report what had happened. That reminded him of the Twillow young ones. Yes, he'd tote them back to Pittsburgh and hand them over to the sheriff to be found by relatives or bound out to strangers. He wouldn't leave them out here for the wolves and panthers to lick their bones, even though two young ones their age tied a powerful millstone around your neck.

While he pondered the things that he'd like to do and the things that he must do, he walked far down the riverbank hunting for the bodies. At last he paused, realizing that the river was keeping its dead. As he stared across it to the silent wilderness on the farther shore he wished there was a preacher or someone on good terms with the Almighty Lord who could stand here and say a few words in behalf of the three souls. Yes, for Fogarty too, the yellow dog, who must now be roasting in the torments of hell.

Maybe it was better to try to forget him and not judge him. Maybe it was better to remember him as when he'd first seen and rather liked him, a grinning, bandy-legged little brown man leaning over the worm fence that spring morning at Murdoch's farm and watching Micah corner and bridle and mount the stallion. "Ye've a hand with horses, b'y," Fogarty had called. Yes, he had a hand with horses. When he rode the stallion bareback to Fogarty, the trader stared up at him shrewdly and asked whether he'd like to work for him. He was at that moment outfitting in Germantown to go trading on the western frontier, Fogarty said. Micah, dispirited for several days since Murdoch had put his services up for sale, was elated at the thought of going west. "My services are for sale," he told him. "Go up the lane to the stone house yonder and ask for Mr. Murdoch. He came from Philadelphia last night and he's eating his breakfast now." So Fogarty went up to the big stone house and bought him.

At the last moment he'd dreaded to leave the farm. It was the only home he remembered, the place where his mother had worked as a bound servant and died of the fever. But he had to go. Kathy Murdoch had seen to that. It made no difference that Murdoch's farmer, John Tout, and his wife, Martha, had pleaded to let him stay. Kathy's wish was always her father's command. Once he was on his way, however, he decided that it was far better to go west than to be bound out to a Philadelphia barber or a Germantown tanner.

Now, as he returned to Fogarty's cabin, he thought, I'm glad I came west and I'll never go back east. I wonder if Kathy still thinks ill of me?

Making himself a pack of two blankets, he rolled up a good-sized bag of meal and a small bag of salt and a few pounds of jerked venison and the little kettle and the small ax. He loaded his pouch with balls and cloth patchings and flints and his horn with powder and he checked the grease box in his rifle stock. At the last minute he remembered his legal paper which identified him as Micah Heath, born in Dumbartonshire on the twenty-fourth of December, 1753, ward of Timothy Murdoch of Chester County in the Proprietary Province of Pennsylvania, and bound out to John Fogarty until he should be twenty-one years of age. Taking it from the keeping-place under the hearthstone, he put it in his foxtail cap and pulled the cap low over his ears.

He shouldered his pack, which was heavier than he wished, and, glancing around the cabin once, he went out and shut the door behind him. The sun was a quarter down the afternoon sky. He strode toward the faint trace that wound north to the Twillows' slashing and he did not look back.

At the edge of the slashing he paused, wondering what he would say to Philly Twillow and her little brother, Tom. When nothing came to mind, he walked on into the ghostly gray light cast through the dying giant white oaks which Daniel Twillow had girdled. Poor Daniel Twillow. Every fool knew that white oaks grew on sour land, yet he had settled among white oaks—and giant white oaks at that. Furthermore, his cabin by the river was carelessly built. Then he remembered that Daniel Twillow was dead and he was sorry that he'd thought ill of him.

For a moment he could not believe the events of this day. It was like a bad dream from which he'd awaken presently as he walked among the dying oaks. But here he was and over there was the river, sucking at the bones of Daniel and Mary Twillow as it rolled past the bone-white slashings of the place where they'd tried to make a home.

"Philly!" He paused at the cabin doorway and looked inside. "Tom!" There was no answer.

Behind him he heard a faint rustle in a brush pile. Then Philadelphia Twillow chanted, "Bound boy, bound boy, fly to me now. I mought be in heaven or under the plow."

"Well, now," Micah said in a voice that she could hear, "where might she be? I can hear her, but I can't see her."

"Bound boy, bound boy," piped Tom Twillow and fell silent when Philly giggled.

"Come on out," Micah said. "I want words with you."

The brush pile shook and Philadelphia Twillow clambered out. She was thirteen years old and she wore a faded short skirt that caught her bare, brown, straight legs well above the knees. Under a wild tangle of chestnut hair her face was small and serious.

"Ma an' Pa went to the post, Micah. Trader Fogarty come by an' he sung out he bringed tradin' things from Pittsburgh."

Micah swung off his pack and sat down on the chopping block as Tom, a foot bandaged, hopped out of the brush pile.

"Come here, the both of you, and set beside me."

Philly shook her head shyly. But Tom limped to him and sat down and asked, "You got salt lickin's?"

"I got salt," Micah said, "but first you listen to what I say. Something bad happened. Your ma and pa ain't coming home. Their canoe turned over and they drownded."

"Drownded?" Philly's lips trembled. "You mean they drownded dead?"

Micah nodded. She came to him and placed her hands on his knees, her gray eyes brimming with tears. Tom, seeing her tears, began to wail.

"Now listen here," Micah said, putting an arm around each. "You listen, Tom. How old 're you?"

"He were seven middle o' summer," Philly said.

"You're a man." Micah squeezed his shoulder. "You got to shift for Philly and her for you." He ruffled her tangled hair. "We all shift together because Fogarty drownded too. We're all going to Pittsburgh."

"Hoo!" Tom leaped up excitedly and then winced when his weight came down on his bandaged foot.

"Ma," Philly whispered, rubbing at her tears, "an' Pa, they ain't even been laid out or had a bury hole. I mought better stay here lest they come back."

"They ain't coming back," Micah said. "I saw their canoe hit Fogarty's and I saw them all drown."

He wished that he knew an easier way to put it to her. But there was no easier way. They were dead and she had to know it and live with it for a spell and then try to forget it as quickly as she could.

"Try not to think about it," he told her. "They went quick and easy."

He did not mention the Delawares, for he did not want to rile their minds with fear. Although he was not afraid himself now, he suddenly wished that they were not so close to the river which seemed to sound a throaty glug, like a man choking on a bone.

"Tom," he said, "what ails your foot?"

"A fawn bit me."

"He means a thawn," Philly said.

"A thorn? Let's see it."

When he examined the suppurating cut on the sole of Tom's left foot, he wanted to groan. The child could not walk a half-mile, let alone all the way to Pittsburgh. And they had to walk it. Even if he had a canoe, he could not push the three of them up-river against the riffles. He could carry Tom, but who would carry his pack and rifle?

Philly stared at him solemnly. "Tom can ride on Angus. I reckon Angus can carry Tom an' the beddin' too."

Now that he thought about it, he liked this little mite Philadelphia

Twillow. If she ever grew up she'd make a sensible woman. She suddenly found herself an orphan, but she wasn't having a fit about it. She was *thinking*. Her thinking wasn't much good, because he'd be hanged before he'd crash through the woods with the two young ones and Angus, that big blue ox of the Twillows. But at least Philly put thought instead of tears to their troubles.

"Angus!" she called shrilly. "An—gus! Gee-haw—gee, gee, gee!" She looked at Micah. "He hears me. He's comin'."

Sure enough, he heard a rustling in a moment and Angus swayed leisurely around a brush pile, licking his lips. He was a big one, blue-and black-spotted, with a long, grave, white face and a mighty neck. Below his flaring horns his liquid blue eyes were friendly. He strolled up obligingly when Philly leaped onto the chopping block and called him. Her arms strained over his great shoulders and she squirmed onto his back, tugging down her short skirt.

"Set Tom up," she said to Micah. Tom squealed with delight as Micah swung him up behind her. "Lookee!" She slapped Angus's flank; the big ox sighed and lumbered off. "Lookee!" She pulled Angus's right ear and he turned to the right. "Lookee!" She pulled his left ear and he turned to the left.

An obedient ox, and smart about his footing. It would be hard to kill him because he was as sociable as a person. But better to kill him than leave him to varmints. For Angus was not going to Pittsburgh with them; he was too big and awkward and slow for the dangerous trail.

In any event, they weren't leaving for Pittsburgh this evening. He told Philly to blow up the fire and fetch water for boiling. Clutching Tom about the waist and sliding off Angus's back, she hastened to obey him.

Near the river he found a gum tree and cut off a small chunk of resin. He pulled a handful of fresh oak leaves and carefully honed his knife on his pocket whetstone. When he returned to the cabin, Philly had water heating.

Reluctantly Tom stretched on his belly in the doorway at Micah's bidding. Sitting on Tom's bottom, Micah hooked his leg back and dipped a clean rag in the kettle of hot water which Philly placed beside him. Gripping the foot tightly, Micah lanced the sore with the point of his knife and pressed out pus and the broken head of a thorn. Tom screamed and Philly began to sing "Old Sir Simon the King" in a quavering voice. Grasping Tom's foot more tightly, Micah rubbed salt against the flow of blood. Tom screamed louder and Philly, clutching his head tenderly in both hands, sang faster. He placed the leaves on the cut and took from under his shirt the resin blob which he'd been warming in an armpit and worked it over and around the poultice. Then he bound the foot with a clean rag and rose and tapped Tom's bottom and said, "Now you get your salt lickin's and mind you lay still a spell."

Tom licked on a small chunk of salt and eyed Micah morosely until his salt craving began to be satisfied.

The Twillows hadn't left their young ones much rations. The bag of parched corn meal was low and there was only a bit of dried deer meat. Philly said that her pa had forgotten to run out his fish lines last night and that he'd never had much luck with snares. Thinking of her ma and pa made tears come to her eyes again as she helped Micah mix up all the Twillows' meal in a big mess of johnnycakes.

"What we goin' to do when we git to Pittsburgh?" she asked as they sat down to the hot johnnycake and deer meat which Micah had fried in coon grease.

He didn't want to think about that yet. "You shouldn't talk when you're eating," he said. "It ain't polite."

After they'd eaten their fill and she was scouring the wooden plates with river sand, he said, "Where's your kinfolk at, Philly?"

"We ain't got kin," she replied, "since Uncle William an' his wife was took off with the pox."

He felt troubled. It was true that he lacked kin and hardly ever thought about it any more. It was true that they'd learn to get along without kin too. Still, it would take Philly a while to forget her ma and pa.

"I had a pox," Tom said. "Philly had a pox. Where's Ma and Pa at, Philly?"

"You hesh," Philly said. "They's in heaven."

"It's luck to have the smallpox young," Micah said. "I had it. You live it through, you don't get it again."

"Where's heaving at?" asked Tom.

"Higher'n the sky," Philly told him. "Ma an' Pa went up thar today an' I reckon they et a fine supper. Ma told me onc't the rations is fine in heaven. Beef an' pork an' real bread all the time an' poke greens the year 'round, winters too."

Tom yawned. "Let's go to heaving."

"You hesh," Philly said. "You shouldn't never talk 'bout heaven that way."

She followed Micah outside. "Tom don't ken what happened. He don't ken much he's such a young un. I got to learn him about our Lord an' His Son Christ our Saver an' heaven an' such. Ma was too tuckered most the time to learn him."

Looking down at her face staring gravely up at his, he thought what a woodsy she was. She needed somebody like Mrs. Tout to raise her and teach her the King's English. Back in Chester County they'd laugh at her woodsy talk and ways. But she'd never see the County. It was too far for her to go, as it was too far for him.

He ruffled her tangled hair and said, "You take along your haw-comb and lye soap too or settlement folk'll laugh at you for a woodsy." There, he'd hurt her and he hadn't meant to. Her face fell. Such changeable expressions as she had, light and shadow and gloom, like an April day when sun and clouds chase across the young earth.

She turned and marched off, her back as rigid as ice. In the same way, he remembered, Kathy Murdoch used to make her back as expressive as her face when she was displeased. Girls were a trial.

He followed her to Angus's lean-to where the big ox was munching the grass which the children had pulled earlier in the day. The sun was sinking beyond the river now, casting up red cloud streamers above the black forest. Somewhere a timber wolf howled.

Angus raised his head, sniffing. Philly passed her arms around his thick neck and kissed his forehead loudly. She whispered in his ear. Perhaps he really understood what she said to him, for he brushed his nostrils across her face.

"Dear Angus!" she cried passionately. Looking up at Micah, she said, "I telled him we all's goin' to Pittsburgh an' he says he'll tote us."

II

THEY were ants lost in a great field of tall grass, Philly thought. Here in the thick woods of huge oaks there was no sun. It was dark, even at noon. The black trunks of the trees rose up and up, their branches lacing and twining in a high yellow ceiling. Up there somewhere low gray clouds raced before a wind that was just a whisper of tossed branches to them far below.

It gave you a mighty shut-in feeling. If you closed your eyes on this warm and tossing raft that was Angus's broad back you got to feeling dizzy. So she remembered to keep her eyes open, and she remembered not to look back as she rode with arms around Tom before her. It was a powerful temptation to keep looking back because it seemed, here in the twilight of the forest, that there was always something behind you, something with eyes that bored holes in your back.

At sunup, as they left the slashing, she'd looked back at the cabin, her eyes filling with tears when she thought of Ma and Pa and the great lorn emptiness into which she plunged without them. Micah had said, "Don't look back, Philly. Don't never look back."

"Why?" she asked him through her tears.

He scratched an ear, a habit of his when he wasn't rightly sure of something. At last he said, "The Bible's against it. There was an old man named Lot and the Lord told him to get out of a settlement name of Sodom and not look back. So he got out with his wife and young ones. But his wife looked back. You know what happened to her?"

"What?"

"She was turned into a pillar of salt."

"Eeee," Tom murmured.

Since it was written in the Bible, the Lord must have turned Lot's wife into salt. But she didn't believe He would do it to her if she looked back. Still, she didn't look back again because Micah had told her not to.

What a wonder he was and what a blessing. It was like the Lord had sent him after taking Ma and Pa. Watching him walk ahead of Angus made her feel warm and singy. He was sure and easy and as clever as a man, even though he was only a bound boy. He was cleverer than Pa; coming out the trace from Pittsburgh last spring Pa had got them lost time and again—as any mortal easily could in these thick woods where every tree looked like another. But Micah found the way without trouble.

The day grew colder as they left the river behind them and passed deeper into the woods. It grew darker and a misty rain shook through the high tree ceiling. There was no sound except the distant wind up yonder and the slough of Angus's hoofs in the thick woods duff. Here they were on Angus, a little log of sound floating down a broad Ohio of quiet. It shut you in and blew a great sap gum bubble in your belly, swelling bigger and bigger until it popped words into your mind. And the words sang a tune of their own. Hugging Tom to her, she began to croon softly.

> "Ol' wind hesh yer blowin',
> Ol' rain hesh yer fallin',
> Listen fer a sound o' folks.
> Ol' snow hesh yer snowin',
> Ol' wind hesh yer—"

"Philly!" Tom squirmed. "That ain't singin'!"

There was a sudden crash that seemed to shake the earth under them. She clapped a hand over her mouth to still her yelp of fright and

Angus bolted into a trot, nearly shaking them off his back until they hollered at him to hold up.

Over left, through the black wall of oak, the earth seemed to belch smoke. It was duff and rot dust, she knew. Another tree had fallen, but the woods did not mention its death. Not a bird flew up, nor an animal scurried away. There was no sound, not even the slough of Angus's hoofs, for he had halted, head lowered and legs braced. A single yellowing leaf spiraled down. Surely, Philly thought, it would hit earth with a crash. But it settled silently, lost in the dun and russet of the forest floor.

A shadow moving in the motionless shadows up ahead made her heart knock. Then she saw it was only Micah standing there, gazing back at them through the gloom. Angus, shaking his horns, began to turn slowly. She tugged at his off ear, but he paid her no heed. He continued to turn until he was facing the way they had come.

"He smells somethin'," she whispered, hugging Tom so tightly that he protested with a loud yell.

Micah was beside them.

"They's somethin' back thar," Philly whispered. "I kain't see hit but I kin feel hit."

Micah pressed hard against Angus's shoulder, trying to turn him, but he would not budge. "Get off and lead him, Philly," he said in a low voice. "Go on up the hill."

She slid off and grasped Angus by a horn. He turned reluctantly, snuffling his discontent. As she led him ahead, she looked back at Micah. He stood behind a great oak, his rifle ready.

As the hill grew steeper, Angus moved more slowly and Tom was hard put to cling to his back. There was a trick to finding the weathered blazes on the trees, Philly soon realized. You had to watch the trees instead of the ground. On the ground your eyes imagined paths, but the way led by the trees.

At last she halted Angus. Calm now, he nibbled ferns. It seemed that Micah never would appear. When he did, he startled her, for he emerged silently from the woods ahead of them instead of the direction they had come.

"You give me a turn," she said crossly. "You mought let a body know ye're comin'."

He almost smiled at her. "I circled 'round. There's nothing human back there or near about. Wind's with us, so maybe Angus scented something that couldn't scent us—a bear or painter going about his business."

"Painter!" Tom exclaimed.

"Painter won't harm you 'less you cross 'em," Micah said. "They're just curious about humans. Red Deer says sometimes a painter'll follow along behind you for the best part of a day, just curious." Tom shivered and Micah frowned. "Don't pay any mind. That's just one of those stories Red Deer tells. Up you go, Philly." Taking her by the waist, he swung her lightly onto Angus's back.

They came after a while to the crossing of a small creek which flowed over mossy rocks. Micah peeled off his pack and rested his rifle against a tree. She was happy to see that he was smiling gravely.

"Stage stop," he sang out. "Stop for the Pittsburgh stage. Travelers get down."

"What a stage?" asked Tom. "What a traveler?"

"You hesh," Philly whispered. "This a stage an' you a traveler."

As they slid to the ground, Micah said, "Welcome, travelers, welcome to the Sign of the Burnt Bear Paw."

He could play-act after all when he had a mind to, Philly realized with delight. "Mister Stage Man," she said to him, "we uns hungry fer our dinner. What you got today?"

"We got roast beef and roast pork. We got ham and chicken and turnips and taters. The preserves is mighty good and so's the pickle. You try our deep cherry pie with cream cheese on it. And . . ."

Her eyes boggled at the strange and tasty things he described while Tom's mouth fell open and a little saliva drooled onto his chin. Finally, when Micah took from his pack the morning leavings of cold johnny-cake and venison, Tom howled in anger and stomped his good foot on the ground. That was just old breakfast, he cried.

"No, it ain't," Micah replied mildly, breaking off a piece of johnny-cake. "Owoo!" He tossed it in a hand. "This roast pork's so hot I burned my fingers." He popped it into his mouth. His cheeks bulged, his eyes glazed in pleasure, surely fresh pork grease trickled down his chin. He swallowed and rubbed his stomach. "Ha!" He broke off another little piece. "Some sweet melon pickle'd set mighty good on that."

Tom, clutching upward, cried out for some. Philly allowed that she'd have the roast beef and turnips. It *did* taste like roast beef and turnips, she thought, whatever they tasted like. What a lark this was, here by this creek that Micah said was flowing rum. It made you forget that a cold, misty rain was falling and the world was dark at midday. While they ate, strolling around and play-acting, Angus browsed among the ferns.

Tom asked when the Pittsburgh stage got to Pittsburgh.

"I reckon we come five mile this morning," Micah said. "I reckon we've got three more days after today."

"How d'you reckon it?" Philly asked.

"It's forty mile to Pittsburgh. If we make ten mile a day it'll take us four days to get there."

"You kin figger?" There was envy in her tone.

"I can figure," he said proudly. "I can figure and I can read and I can write some."

"Philly kain't," Tom said.

"I kin *too!*" she lied, sudden anger at Tom shaking her.

"You kain't *not!*" Tom shouted. "I 'member Ma sayin' ain't it a pity Philly kain't read or write or figger."

She struck wildly at him and glimpsed his bewildered expression as he collapsed on the ground before her fury. Shame gripped her, shame at having such a little de'il for a brother, and then shame at being so put out by him, and—finally—deep shame at herself, a big old thing who'd soon be fourteen years old but couldn't read or write or figure, a woodsy born free who couldn't curb her tongue to talk proper even as this bound boy did. Whirling, she dashed away blindly until she found herself in waist-high ferns. There she plopped into a cold damp world as dark as her thoughts.

Oh, the Twillows were fine old country Presbyterians, she silently keened. My Grampa Twillow had a cabin with a winder light back east an' my Pa was oncet a soldier of the King. Hard times come on the Twillows an'—

She heard Tom calling her, but she did not answer. Then Micah called that they were leaving without her. Let them go. She'd weave herself a caterpillar nest and in the spring she'd be a butterfly. She heard Angus ploshing in the stream and the receding suck of his hoofs. By hokey, they were going without her! Raising her head above the ferns, she looked around. By hokey day, they'd up and left her! Let them go, if that was all they cared about her. Still she'd better tag along, keeping them in view, and just mind that she never spoke to them again as long as she lived.

Which side of the creek had she been on? Why, she'd been on both sides in her foolish play-acting. But which side had she been on *last?* Angus's hoofmarks came and went in both directions. She stood still, listening. There was no sound but the purling creek. Then she heard a faint *thup-thup-thup,* as of feet running on moss. She spun around quickly, all the way around, and then around again until the closely pressing trees whirled dizzily. Something was moving out there, something blurred. Panther! Screaming piercingly, she turned and ran as fast as she could. The *thup-thup-thup* grew quicker and louder. Dimly she realized it was her heart.

"Philly!"

Micah's voice, loud and harsh, was close behind her. She stopped and turned, gasping for breath.

"You gnat-wit, Philly!" He scowled at her. "I should whop you hard."

She wished he would, it was so good to see him. A sob worked up her throat and wet her eyes. Springing to him, she flung her arms around his waist and pressed her face against the good leather smell of him. He rested a hand on her head, letting her wail out the torment of death and loneliness and the endless silent woods.

When she stopped crying, she raised her head. "You whop me good, I dasarve hit. I lied to ye. I kain't read er write er figger."

"You'll learn," he said, still gently resting his hand on her head. His voice became gruff. "There's things harder to learn. Like not heatening up your anger and letting it bile your wits. I speck you t'do what I say till I get the both of you to Pittsburgh."

"I will, Micah, I will." She gazed up at him, thinking that she never could bear to let him out of her sight again. "Micah, we git to Pittsburgh, be you aimin' to leave me an' Tom?"

"Philly"—he sounded powerful mad—"you get up that hill and climb on that ox!"

As Angus lumbered on through the waning afternoon, she began to ache with fatigue and to imagine uneasily that something was following them again. Micah ranged farther ahead. She wished he wouldn't leave them so far behind, though she knew he was hunting game.

Once, while walking beside them for a spell, he said, "I do believe there ain't so much as a thin gray squirrel in this country."

Lord send him fat gray squirrels, she thought. She purposely didn't address heaven directly because she'd lied today and she reckoned the Lord was in no mood to listen to her. She pondered delivering a prayer asking forgiveness for her terrible lie and temper, but if she followed *that* prayer with *another* requesting game she knew that the Lord would realize she was trying to wool His eyes. It could make Him so wrathful that He might send panthers or Indians after them, or at least call Ma and Pa up to the throne and ask them how in heaven's name they'd managed to raise such a bad young one. And *that* would trouble Ma, who probably was already troubled enough wondering how it fared with her two young ones left alone down here . . .

"Whoa!"

Micah, halting Angus by grasping a horn, brought Philly wide awake as she started drifting heavenward in a pleasant dream.

The woods had finally opened, revealing a sky that was as moistly pink as Tom's tongue. Here the trace dropped steeply among huge boulders to a little valley of chestnut trees. They'd stay the night in yonder valley, Micah said, but they'd have to walk down.

Keeping a shoulder against Angus's, he led the way slowly. Angus moved with caution, picking his way as sure-footed as a cat. Once, when a stone rolled under him, Micah grasped him by both horns. Legs braced, boy and ox strained backward while the stone rolled on. When they reached the valley floor, where the chestnut trees grew thick and tall, sweat was streaming down Micah's face and Angus's breath bubbled hoarsely.

Micah started to speak and paused, his mouth open, listening. Philly heard it then, a sound like distant thunder rolling toward them. She moved close as Tom tensely gripped him by a leg. Over east the wet, pink sky was darkening faster than any wind-driven storm. There came a throbbing tumult of wings and cries, as if, Philly thought, the heavens had split like a ripe fox grape and spilled out a host of clamoring angels. She closed her eyes as the world grew dark and the thunder of wings enclosed them.

"Glory be!" Micah shouted and Tom squealed wordlessly.

Here I be, Lord, she thought, take me up easy. She opened her eyes and saw pigeons, more numerous than the leaves of the chestnut woods. They settled in the trees with strange cooings of pleasure. The trees turned gray, and still the pigeons settled. Boughs bent, snapped and fell under the weight of the foolish birds which fluttered earthward or merely plunged and lay on their backs, still cooing, with plump breast and limp claws raised to the sky. From the birds that remained gorging themselves in the chestnut trees white droppings fell like rain.

Micah and Tom and Angus were smeared with droppings. Brushing at her hair, Philly stared in disgust at her filthy hand and cried, "Let's git out o' hyar."

Micah paid her no mind. He walked among the pigeons with a stick, clouting heads and gathering up the dead. "Come here," he called, "the both of you." But the de'il was in Tom. Whooping madly, he hopped among the birds, striking at them wildly and jumping on them with his good foot as if they meant him harm.

Walking to him, Micah whacked his bottom so hard that he fell down. He stared up, too dazed to cry. "I told you to come here," Micah said. "Now take a dozen of these dead ones and get back out of this mess. Philly!"

She went to him and he filled her arms with dead pigeons. Their wet ammoniac smell sickened her and the soft feathered breasts she clutched to her own suddenly reminded her of the puppy she'd loved long ago back at Bedford. She wanted to drop the dead birds and run. But she held them, trying not to look at them, because she knew that she must do as Micah said.

After he had knotted a thong around the claws of a dozen pigeons and flung the string over a shoulder, he scouted their way around the chestnut woods. It was growing dark when they returned to the trace on the farther side of the valley where a small creek flowed quietly. Behind them the pigeons in the chestnut trees sounded like a constant wind in buffalo grass.

"We're too nigh them birds," Micah muttered, "but we got to stop. There's water here and grass for Angus. Philly and Tom, you fetch all the driest wood you can find after we wash some of this mess off ourselves."

While she and Tom gathered wood, she frequently glanced at Micah working swiftly. Kicking open a dead stump, he dug out a handful of dry punk and dropped it between two stones which he'd placed midway of the creek and a clump of three large maple trees. Dusting powder from his horn onto the punk, he primed his rifle lock and cocked the hammer. Then he laid the rifle across the stones with the lock close to the punk and snapped the flint. The pan flashed, the punk flamed; he fed it carefully with twigs.

"Philly," he called, "build this fire and fill the kettle here. Set it on these stones. Tom, dig a deep hole handy to the fire."

He stood for a moment, rubbing a grease rag over the rifle lock and hammer with great concentration before he loaded the gun. Then he was gone into the gathering night and there came, in a moment, the quick *k'chuck-k'chuck* of his little ax. Next Philly knew he was laying boughs between two of the three closely clumped maples. He left off that when she called that the water was boiling. His knife flashed swiftly as he cut off the pigeon heads and dropped them in the hole. Holding each bird in turn by its claws, he dipped it in the boiling water and then plucked its feathers easily. After a quick lance with his knife, he drew the guts in a single three-fingered scoop and pull. The claws he snapped off with a cracking sound that made Philly wince. Feathers, guts and claws he dropped in the hole. Next he rubbed each naked white pigeon with a little salt and coon grease from the gourd of fat which he'd told her to bring in her bundle. Piercing each with a green stick, he drove the stick into the ground at an angle so that the bird hung over the fire. She counted ten pigeons, which was as high as she could count, but there were many more nodding and hissing in a circle around the fire before he stamped the last claws in the hole and filled it carefully and treaded down the dirt. All this time, while she and Tom watched him with wide eyes, he had not spoken.

"He says ary word," Tom whispered. "He mought be mad."

His expression still set in thought, Micah cleaned and greased his knife and walked out of the ring of firelight. In a moment they heard the sound of his ax. Over the fire the birds nodded and sputtered on their roasting wands while Angus munched grass nearby and out yonder in the night the countless pigeons began to quiet their rustle. It made Philly drowsy. But she felt she should make herself handy. Emptying the kettle, she filled it with fresh water at the creek. After the water came to a boil, she took the kettle off the fire and dropped in some of the sassafras and dittany root shavings which she'd brought in her bundle. The steeping root shavings smelled mighty sweet. She was proud that she'd remembered to bring dittany tea makings, for Micah had not mentioned it.

When he'd finished the little lean-to in the three maples, she could not withhold a cry of pleasure. It was such a snug little house, open to the firelight, with two slanting walls leading to the mighty back maple. He had roofed it with boughs and covered its floor with a thick bed of fresh leaves. You could crawl into it and sleep forever.

"Hit's pert," she told him. "Thankee fer buildin' hit, Micah."

He merely grunted as he came to the fire and pinched the breast of the first pigeon which he'd started roasting.

"Done," he said, pulling the stick from the ground and handing it to her. "Mind you don't burn your tongue." He pulled the next stick and handed it to Tom. Taking the third, he sat down, legs folded under him like an Indian, and sank his teeth in the pigeon.

It was mighty fine eating, she had to admit, tender and sweet with a juicy tang of coon grease and salt. Micah ate quickly and tossed the bones into the fire. Rising lithely without touching his greasy hands to the ground, he pivoted all the sticks away from the fire.

"Eat your fill," he said as he tore off another pigeon leg. "You may be hungry tomorrow."

Suddenly, above them, there was an unearthly shriek. Philly's heart leaped in fright. Tom dropped his bird and cowered against her.

"Screech owl," Micah said through a full mouth. "You must've heard a screech owl before."

"Screech owls is different 'n screech owls back home," she said. "To home thar's roof atween you an' 'em."

Somewhere another owl screeched and then the night was loud with their shrieking. The ebbing rustle of the pigeons began to rise again.

"Owls like pigeon meat," Micah said. "There'll be some fat owls here-about come morning."

Off in the night there was a high-pitched squeal.

Tom edged closer to the fire. "Painter?" he asked.

"Rabbit," Micah said. "Owl got himself a rabbit. Painter is—" He cocked his head and his right hand crept toward his rifle propped on his blanket roll. Philly heard and recognized the sound then: the soft flop of a deer's tread. Old night coming alive, she thought. All day it sleeps, waiting for us to sleep.

The sound was gone, the deer had passed. Micah's hand left his rifle. "Deer meat makes better rations than pigeon," he said.

Far off there was a faint scream.

"Now that's painter," he said.

She knew it was; a panther cry always seemed to press ice against the nape of her neck.

"Painter always sounds like"—he gazed blankly across the fire for a moment—"like a woman. It—Philly, take hold there and help yourself to another bird."

"I et my fill," she said.

Nearer now, a panther screamed and owls shrieked as the echo died away. Angus shuffled closer to the fire, shaking his head and licking his lips. He sighed and, folding his legs under him, ponderously lowered himself to earth.

Close by a timber wolf howled; another answered.

"That's a varmint I can't abide," Micah said, rising. He strode into the darkness and they heard the sound of his ax for some time. When he returned, he carried a huge pile of wood.

He ate another pigeon and drank a cup of dittany and pronounced it fine. Before they slept, he said, they had to wash. He went with them to the creek and made them wash their feet, as well as hands and faces, cold though the night was. He washed his feet too and inspected their soles for bruises and blisters. When they crawled into the lean-to, he showed them how to fold their blankets and bundle together warmly.

"Ain't you comin' in too?" Philly asked him.

"I'm going to set by the fire a spell and mend a moccasin," he replied. Eventually, she slept.

When Micah crept into the lean-to and awakened them, the world outside was gray in rain. By the faint light she saw that his thin face was tired, his blue eyes bleared from wakefulness.

"Eat," he said, holding out two cold roast pigeons. "We're going on."

She made up a song about the sun, but it wouldn't rhyme. In her song droves of menfolk came into the dark woods and cut down the trees and let in the sun. There were cabins everywhere and dogs barked and the land was full of cattle. She could see it, but she couldn't make the words rhyme. It never would happen anyway, she thought, because there were so many trees and not enough men.

About noon, as they crept eastward along the trace, the sun did come out. It warmed the forest roof and, here and there, streamed down in golden barrels of light. Where it touched sumac, the leaves blazed red as fire. She sang happily then while Tom, playing he was a drummer, beat the rhythm. Oh, it was a happy land, with the promise of perpetual sun ahead somewhere if they went just a little farther.

Once they paused in a tiny island of sunlight where fox grapes hung from twining vines in great purple clusters. They broke them off, staining hands and faces as they gulped the sour fruit, unmindful of Micah's warning that they'd get the bellyache if they didn't stop.

Late in the afternoon, when Micah had been out of sight ahead for a spell, they came on him staring at a muddy stretch. "Look." He pointed down, frowning. "Movers, most like. A pair of big feet and a pair of little feet coming west since morning. A man and a woman." He nodded, still frowning. "Movers. They turn off north here." He looked around. "You can't tell if they had a mind to go off here or missed the trace and went off losted."

Philly stared north, half expecting to hear the sound of voices or an ax. There was no sound. If you listened hard enough you could hear the blood singing in your ears—and that was all you could hear. She'd like to follow those foot tracks until she found the man and the woman, and then they'd sit together and gossip the whole night through.

She said, "We mought—"

"We might just not," Micah cut her short. He slapped Angus's flank and they moved eastward along the trace.

That evening he did not build them a lean-to. It would not rain tonight, he said, as he spread fresh leaves between the high-ridged roots of a giant beech near a brawling creek. In the blaze of their fire the beech rose whitely above them, with widespread limbs like naked arms and a cleft above like a frowning face. Philly took care not to look up at the face of the beech towering above them as Micah cooked johnnycake, which they ate with the last of the cold pigeons. He had not found game. Before darkness fell he'd located a rabbit trot along the creek and set a few twitch-ups tied from the precious horsehairs he carried in his bullet pouch. There was no game, he said glumly, but with luck they'd have fresh rabbit meat for breakfast. Then, draping his blankets loosely around him and leaving his arms free, he lay down on the leaves beside his rifle and was asleep instantly.

Philly and Tom bundled together in their blankets, pressing close against him. She set herself a doze dream that would waft her into sleep, a dream about a land of sun and cattle and dogs where she and Micah and Tom and Angus wandered happily. But sleep did not come. Opening her eyes, she bit her lip to stifle a cry of terror.

Beyond the dying fire an Indian stood as motionless as a tree. She could not make out his face in the shadows, but there was no mistaking that a man stood there, an Indian wearing deerskin breeches and a blanket. Then she almost cried aloud when she realized that Angus was gone. If anyone harmed Angus, she'd— Cautiously, she reached around and touched Micah's shoulder. He started slightly.

"Injun," she whispered.

He did not move, but she could feel his muscles gathering. The fire popped. Why did Micah take so long? Then, in one sudden flowing movement, he sprang to his feet with rifle raised. The Indian shouted something and his arms shot up.

"Red Deer!" Micah exclaimed.

Sure enough, she saw now, it was that old Indian of Trader Fogarty's stepping into the firelight. "Red Deer," she called, "whar's Angus at?"

Neither he nor Micah paid her any mind as they came together, jabbering Indian talk as if Red Deer didn't know a word of English. "Angus!" she cried. "Gee-haw—gee, gee, gee!" She startled Tom, who began hollering for Angus before he was fully awake. In a moment she saw the big ox strolling into the firelight.

Red Deer sat down by the fire after Micah built it up. His voice rolled and he gestured grandly. But there was no expression on his ugly, pock-marked face. He paused and Micah spoke. Then they both turned and looked at Tom and her.

"Speak plain," she said. "A body kain't tell what ye're sayin'."

"I told Red Deer what happened," Micah said to her. "He feels sorry for you. But the English talk has left him. He won't speak it again. They treated him bad at Pittsburgh, him and some Delawares. Not the English soldiers, but *our* people. They got him and the others drunk and stole their pelts and flung 'em in jail and then they flung 'em out of town. They're walking home down west. Red Deer saw our fire from where they're camped up ahead."

Red Deer spoke again.

Micah rose and gave him the cold johnnycake that remained from supper. Turning to them, he said, "You young ones get to sleep. Have no mind to worry. Red Deer says he'll go back part the way to Pittsburgh with us."

He went nearly all the way. Philly understood why soon after they started early the next morning.

Red Deer had left well in advance. Micah did not range ahead but walked slowly beside Angus through the misty morning light. He carried his rifle across his left arm with the stock in his right armpit, as he did when stalking game.

After a while they heard a cock turkey call somewhere in the mist ahead. To her wonderment and Tom's delight, Micah fluted a hen's answer. Soon afterwards Red Deer appeared silently. He nodded, turned, and led the way. Micah slipped three rifle balls into his mouth and fell behind Angus.

"Sing, Philly," he said, rolling the balls under his tongue. "And don't look back."

It seemed that no song could keep time with her racing heart. Only her own song came to mind. Her voice piped and she told Tom to beat the rhythm.

> "Angus is our ox,
> Smarter'n a fox,
> Oh, Angus is a frien', frien', frien' . . ."

The silent, mist-soaked woods were almost more than her voice could bear. When Angus hesitated, shaking his head from side to side, her voice faltered and died.

Micah prodded Angus with a knee and said, "Sing, Philly."

Angus stumbled on and her voice caught at her song. She did not stop, even when she glimpsed five Indians standing off the trace. They stood erect, arms folded, staring at her, and in the eyes of one she read a powerful hatred. But she did not stop singing and she did not look back as Angus lumbered on.

She and Tom grew tired and sore from the roll and pitch of his broad back, but Micah would not let them pause. Whenever Angus slowed his pace, he whacked him with a stick. Although Micah never did explain the danger to her, she understood it. Without Red Deer's help they could not have passed unharmed through those angry Indians. The old Mingo had gone ahead and spoken to his friends for them and led them through the danger and on toward Pittsburgh.

That night he and Micah sat talking by the fire for a long spell. She didn't understand what they said, but it appeared to her that Red Deer was arguing him to do something that Micah already had half a mind to do anyway. It troubled her, for it made her wonder what would happen to them in Pittsburgh. Then, hopefully, she told herself that Micah, she, Tom and Angus could not be parted now; where one went, all would go.

In the morning she expected that Red Deer would turn back west. But he went on east with them until late afternoon when he spoke quickly to Micah, nodded to Tom and her, and suddenly disappeared in the woods.

"What's he up to?" she asked Micah.

He did not answer her. Reaching out, he broke a branch of scrub oak. "Pittsburgh's yonder," he said, slapping Angus's flank.

The woods thinned in slashings. They came to an honest clearing with stumps and an empty cabin that made her laugh aloud in pleasure. Above, fat clouds rushed before a west wind. There was a patch of blue and a sudden blinding glare of sun that made her blink despite her will to look old sun square in his shining eye. And then, quite suddenly, the land dropped away before them.

"Hooo!" Tom cried. "Pittsburgh!"

There it was, between the two rivers that became the one big western river. The huge five-sided fort that lay at the point of land filled her with awe. Beneath the British flag fluttering from a staff the fort seemed to scowl across the river at her and say, Go back, Philadelphia Twillow. And such a mortal smoke as came from the log houses sprawled out in streets along the Monongahela; you'd have thought the town was on fire until you recollected that most folks here burned coal instead of wood.

They came, at last, to the riverbank. There, wedged in a cleft pine tree, was a long horn made of basswood. As Micah reached up for it there came a mighty cannon crash from the fort across the river and the flag fluttered down. They heard, then, the roll of drums and the sweet tones of a bugle.

Grinning suddenly, Micah raised the basswood horn to the sky and blew for a boatman. His blast, long and loud and somehow mocking, drowned the sweet bugle tones in the fort where the flag had disappeared.

III

A CANOE shot toward them paddled by a thin, gray-haired man wearing a foxtail cap and fringed buckskin.

"Who be ye young uns?" he called.

"I'm Micah Heath, bound to Trader Fogarty at the Cross Creeks 'round the Big Bend. These are Daniel Twillow's young ones."

"You had trouble with red varmints?"

Micah shook his head slowly, thinking that he'd best wait and tell the whole story to the sheriff. "The Twillows' and Fogarty's canoes turned over and they all drownded."

The thin man spat a jet of tobacco juice into the river. "Don't know the Twillows. But *Honest* John Fogarty at the bottom o' the Ohio ain't any much loss." He cast his dark little eyes over Micah shrewdly. "You walked it by the trace with that 'ere ox, eh? Ain't bad fer a boy. Boys these days ain't what they was." He spat again. "Name's Fergus. Ye mought ha' heard o' me. I ain't in the ferry business hyar, but I seen yer foxtail acrosst the river an' I knowed ye weren't one o' these settlement folks. Git in."

"Thankee," Philly said to him, "but we mought better tarry fer a boat that'll take Angus." She patted the ox.

"Then ye'll tarry maybe a year, young miss," said Fergus. "How'd that 'ere ox git on this side the river?"

"He swummed hit," Tom said.

"If he swummed over," Fergus said, "I reckon he kin swum back. Git in."

Tears sprang to Philly's eyes and she looked up at Micah appealingly. When he pointed to the canoe, she and Tom climbed in slowly with their blankets and bundle. Micah put his rifle, powder horn and pack in the canoe, and then, grasping Angus about the neck, he led him into the water. The ox resisted while Philly and Tom wailed encouragement to him and Fergus stared at them blankly.

Micah, waist-deep in the river, wrestled with Angus until Fergus backed his canoe close and said, "H'ist yerself in, an' don't spill us. That 'ere ox'll follow 'long now."

Micah climbed over the bow. Philly and Tom started to rise as they called to Angus swimming behind the canoe.

"Set down," Fergus told them, " 'less you want to j'in yer folks. An' hesh yer caterwaulin'. Man kain't hear hisself think." The dark skin crinkled over his gaunt cheekbones when he looked at Micah slicking water from his breeches. "I've a mind ye was givin' the sons o' bitchin' English at the fort the jackass hee-haw with that 'ere basswood horn back thar."

Micah smiled faintly. He did not like the English soldiers, as he did not like the Quakers. Nobody in this country liked either the English soldiers or the eastern Quakers. Nor did anybody like Indians. When you got to the drulix of it, nobody liked anybody very much out here.

Fergus pointed a dripping paddle toward the fort. "In '63 I was forted up there. Snuck in from up country with my coattails afire. *We* uns held out. If *we* hadn't been thar—" He spat in the river and talked obscenely of the English soldiers.

Micah understood about *we*. *We* included *him* because he wore a fox-tail cap and carried a long rifle and came from over west. *We* inherited the earth without owning an acre of it because we dared it and fought over it. Like me, he thought, some of us ain't even free. But it's our land and it don't belong to anybody but us, not a bag-wigged whey-faced Philadelphia Quaker nor a bloody lobsterback of His Majesty the King. *They* own the land, but *we* inherit it.

"Two comp'nies," Fergus was saying sarcastically, "two comp'nies of the 18th, the R'yal Irish Reg'ment of Foot, commanded by Cap-tain Char-les Ed-mon-stone. That's the gar'son. That's fer the hull west far as the lobsterbacks care."

Micah stared at the dim bulk of the fort in the fading light. Surrounded by a moat, palisaded on the three sides which fronted the rivers and bricked on the two landward wings, it suddenly struck him as a useless place.

"*They* want *us*'ns to go *back*," Fergus said to the fort. "They'd give it all back to the red varmints an' send us all clean to Lancaster. An' mind my word, hell's nigh bustin' out its britches. The red varmints is all stirrin' up an' folks don't know if'n their land claims is any good an'—" His tone changed. "What you goin' t'do, young feller, now that *Honest John Fogarty's* on muddy bottom?"

Micah shrugged and looked beyond Fergus at the sunken red sun line above the western shore. He knew what he was going to do, but he wouldn't tell this stranger Fergus who was a mite too talkative even though he was one of *us*. Once he'd turned the young ones over to the sheriff, he was streaking back west. Red Deer and he had agreed on a plan last night. They'd outfit themselves from Fogarty's plunder and go partners far down the Ohio to a place Red Deer knew where he said you couldn't walk without stepping on beaver. They'd make their fortunes in one winter, they would. The old Mingo was waiting for him over there. Tonight or tomorrow morning at latest he'd slip back across the river and they'd head west, free, his servitude ended forever.

"Legal-wise," he said, "I reckon I'm still bound to Mr. Murdoch back in Chester County. Fogarty bought me from him."

"Legal-wise!" Fergus's tone was scornful. "Ass-wise! You kain't go *back!* I warrant ye any lawyer west o' Lyttleton'd hold ye're free."

"Would they now?" Micah asked hopefully. "I'll speak of that to the sheriff."

"We ain't got a reg'lar sheriff," Fergus said slowly. "We got a dep'ty we didn't elect 'cause Pitt Township's under jurydiction o' Bedford County. The County wuz formed last winter spite o' the goddam Phil'-delphia Assembly. The sheriff's in Bedford. His dep'ty hyar ain't no 'count. He sucks up to the English."

"What's his name?"

"Sam Snook. But I don't reckon I'd speak on anything to Snook. He might figger he owned a piece out'n yer skin too. An' don't dibble with lawyers, young feller, er *they*'ll own a piece 'f ye. There ain't many law-yers west o' Lyttleton anyways, an' them as is you'd better stay shut of. Jes' take my word ye're free. I'm fixin' myself to go up country fer beaver an' I kin use a handy young feller. Learn ye all the tricks, boy. You *must*'ve heard o' me, Harry Fergus, best trapper west *er* east o' the Juniata. You come 'long with me."

And have *you* own a piece of me, Micah thought. What a torment it was not being free. Fergus appeared to be the kind of man he thought he wanted to be. Yet Fergus probably had been one of those who skinned Red Deer and flung him out of town. Red Deer waited trustingly for him across the river, and yet Red Deer was an Indian—and a man like Fergus, a man like he wanted to be, would say that you never could trust an Indian.

He could not make out clearly the faces of the children before him. But he could feel their eyes straining up to his as they listened, and he thought, What about *them?* Well, what about them? They'd have to learn to shift and do for themselves, as he had. Still, they tugged him power-fully each time he looked at them. Philly, especially, tugged him. He'd see to it that they found a good home, that's what he'd do.

"I'll think on your offer," he muttered to Fergus as the canoe ground ashore. "I'll think on it."

Here was Pittsburgh, a smell of coal smoke and sound of voices in the twilight. He didn't want to be here, but here he was. A year had passed since he'd returned to the town with Fogarty for supplies and, for all he cared, ten more could pass before he saw it again.

Fergus went with them, up a rutted street stinking with refuse, between cabins where the smell of grease and smoke reminded Micah that they were hungry. There were loud voices everywhere, cursing and laughing and wrangling. It made him uneasy. The first to laugh at sight of the woodsies and their muddy ox would feel his fist, he thought. But no one paid them any heed in the darkness.

Fergus led them, at last, to a big log house where candlelight shafted dimly from an open doorway. On one side were empty stocks, on the

other a pillory. Thrusting his head in the door, Fergus said, "Evenin',
Mis' Snook, the dep'ty sheriff t'home?"

"Be he ever?" She complained, profanely and at length, on the lot of
a deputy sheriff's wife.

Micah, peering over Fergus's shoulder, made her out in the dim
candlelight: an enormous woman wearing a dirty short skirt and sprawling on a stool beside a keg on which was set a gourd of rum and a wooden
cup. Her thick, purple-veined legs and feet were bare, her gray hair
tangled over a bloated red face.

Glimpsing Micah, she ceased her complaining and grinned toothlessly.
"Who's yonder yaller-haired young un, Fergus?"

"He's workin' fer me," Fergus said. "He brung in two young uns from
over west to be bound out. Their ma and pa drownded."

"Bound out, ye say?" Mrs. Snook heaved her heavy body forward
from the log wall, as if she intended to rise. Then, as if she thought better
of it, she drained her wooden cup. Smacking her lips, she said, "How
auld air they? What they weigh? Come in hyar, young yaller hair." She
grinned at him as he stepped in reluctantly. "How'd ye like t'be bound
out t'me?"

"Not *him*," Fergus said, "he's workin' fer *me*, I telled ye. These uns."
Turning, he shouted to Philly and Tom, "Come here, young uns!"

The low-ceilinged room stank of human feces. There was a long
counter and a couple of stools. In one corner was a stilt bed with dirty
blankets rumpled over a cob mattress. Through a barred door across the
room suddenly came the high-pitched wail of a man's voice.

"Yonder's the jail room, dearie," Mrs. Snook said to Micah. "We put
in Ol' Charley agin today. He's—" She tapped her head. "Thinks he's the
Bonnie Prince hisself agin. Thinks it's Mar's Year an' the 'forty-five.
An' we got two drunk Injuns in thar. Wot's yer name, dearie?"

"Micah Heath." His tone was almost a whisper. The room seemed
to press him like a vise. He watched Philly and Tom creep in, gripping
each other by the hand and staring with horror at Mrs. Snook.

Looking at them, she moaned, "Oh sweet Jesus Christ! They ain't
worth two pound the two on 'em t'gether. Nary soul'd have 'em. They's
only good fer eatin' up a body's vittles an' there's ary lick o' work in 'em."

Tom whimpered. Philly gripped his hand more tightly and whispered,
"You hesh."

"Lookee now, Mis' Snook," Fergus said, "yer man's th'ap'inted dep'ty
sheriff an' the law says he's 'sponsible fer watchin' out fer orphans till
they's found by kin er bound out. If'n—"

Mrs. Snook remarked obscenely on the law and then said, "They kin

have a bite o' cold pone an' sleep the night yonder." She nodded toward
the barred door.

"In the jail room?" Micah exclaimed. "With a couple of drunk Injuns
and a crazy man?"

"That's the place orphans alus sleeps, dearie."

"Mrs. Snook"—his voice rose—"where's your husband at?"

"He mought be at Semple's Tavern er agin he mought be at Dowelson's. But—"

"Come on." He pushed Philly and Tom out the door as Fergus and
Mrs. Snook called after him.

They walked through the darkness, Philly holding his right hand and
Tom clutching the stock of his trailing rifle, while Angus ambled behind
them. Micah's belly felt cold, as it always did when he was roused in
anger. He wasn't certain what had angered him. Perhaps Fergus, perhaps that filthy Mrs. Snook and her filthy jail. Maybe Pittsburgh itself.
But Pittsburgh was like the world he knew outside of the woods. Except
for the farm, he thought. He mustn't think of the farm, however. It was
too far away and he never could return to it. Yet he couldn't put from his
mind the clean kitchen and kindly ways of Mrs. Tout, who had taught
him to read and write and figure and speak in the manner of gentlefolk.
Philly here, and Tom too, deserved the love and care of a good woman
like Mrs. Tout. But it was too far for them to go and it was the wrong
direction for him. His way led west, across the river where Red Deer
waited. Yet how, he asked himself, can I leave these young ones to root
in the dirt for themselves like animals?

"Lookee, Micah." Fergus was walking beside them again. "Ye take
the young uns back to Mis' Snook. She's legal-bound t'look a'ter 'em
an'—"

"Mr. Fergus," he said, "I'd be obliged to you for directions to Semple's
or Dowelson's where I might find the deputy sheriff."

"Wal," Fergus grumbled, "he'll be at Dowelson's. Sam Semple's put
out with him."

When he opened the door on the broad, low-ceilinged room that was
David Dowelson's Tavern, a mighty roar of talk and laughter engulfed
them like a torrent from a broken dam. Philly and Tom retreated before
it and he was half of a mind to flee himself. But he stood his ground as
Fergus pushed ahead of them. The din that rose from a throng of men
at a dozen long plank tables surely had forced those cracks in the ceiling beams. Grasping Philly by a hand and shoving Tom with a knee,
he went in and shut the door.

At one end of the room was a huge fireplace with two wide boards
angled before it. Through the fog of tobacco and candle smoke he saw

that one was laden with gourds of tree syrup and wooden platters of cold venison hams, coon sausage, pressed buffalo tongue, hot roast turkeys and fried mush and cornpone fingers. Behind it a red-cheeked girl kept tally of those who heaped wooden trenchers with food. The board was not as well attended, however, as that where a bald and sweating man wearing a long leather apron tied about his throat served drinks from kegs of rum behind him. He was a tall, heavy man, yet he seemed to move as gracefully as Kathy Murdoch dancing, Micah thought. In his left hand he held six wooden gill mugs and in his right hand four wooden quart mugs by their handles. Men crowding around the planks shouted their orders, by dram or gill or quart, and dropped their money in a hollowed pumpkin shell before leaving with their drinks. Whirling constantly between plank table and kegs, turning the spigots with flashing elbows, the big man filled each order accurately, spilled not a drop—and seldom took his eyes from the pumpkin shell.

"Thar's Snook," Fergus shouted, pointing to a fat man pounding a table with his mug while he harangued a man beside him.

Micah barely glanced at Snook and looked again at the table of food. Philly and Tom were staring at it too, he observed, their mouths hanging open and Tom beginning to drool. "Mr. Fergus." He raised his voice. "Would you stake the young ones and me to a bite?"

"Wal." Fergus scratched his jaw thoughtfully. "Be ye goin' to work fer me?"

Not until hell froze, Micah thought bitterly. Now nor ever. Now he'd turn and walk out of here. But Philly and Tom still stared at the food. "A man's a stout log and each time he lies an ax bites him," John Tout used to say. "Enough lies and he's just burning wood." If you did not lie, you always had honor, more precious than a storehouse of beaver skins. Still, Philly and Tom stared at the food.

"Be ye?" demanded Fergus.

Beside them a man said, "Go to yonder table with the children, boy, and help yourselves. Say you are the guests of William Dawkins." Micah looked up at a tall, middle-aged man whose lank black hair hung straight from under a broad-brimmed felt hat. He carried a trencher heaped with food and wore the long drab shad-breasted coat of a Quaker.

"Be damned, ye bloody Quaker!" Fergus shouted at him. "These young uns is wi' *me*."

The Quaker nodded soberly to Micah and passed on. When he sat down at the end of a long plank table, men scowled at him, muttered to each other, and hitched their stools away from his.

"Set down yer rifle an' pack," Fergus said to Micah, "an' he'p yerselves. I'll speak to Dowelson."

The red-cheeked girl behind the table of food smiled at Micah as he sliced deer ham and jellied buffalo tongue for the children and himself. She heaped their trenchers with coon sausage and mush and cornpone.

Shouts pierced the clamor rising from the rough boards set on wooden trestles where men leaned forward, pounding their fists, or sagged back as they raised their mugs to drink. On each table was a wooden water bucket with a gourd dipper. Occasionally, after a man drank, he gulped a little water from the dipper to cool the fiery liquor.

Philly and Tom, clutching their heaped trenchers in both hands, followed him wide-eyed as he searched for an eating place. An easterner would have thought some of these shaggy-haired smoke-blackened men in buckskin shouting at each other meant to cut throats with the long knives sheathed in their belts. But they were only being sociable, Micah knew, as they raked over important matters. Land claims. Beaver. Indians. Parliament. The Philadelphia merchants and the Pennsylvania Assembly. Such matters of sacred concern were wrenched profanely from the throats of men accustomed to long silences, while yonder, at a small table in a corner, two subalterns wearing the scarlet of His Majesty's Royal Irish Regiment of Foot stared with drunken vacantness on this bear's den at the limits of the Empire.

"I tell ye," roared a bearded man whose right ear was swollen shapelessly, "*they* aims to shet us out o'all that kentry." His hairy paw prodded the man next him. "I tell ye *thet!*"

The man who was being prodded spat over a shoulder and shouted angrily, "I *knows* they does."

They glowered fiercely at each other and then nodded slowly until the bulbous-eared man's blue eyes gleamed happily and he smiled somewhere under his beard with the pleasure of having said something important on an important matter in this sociable gathering. He began slowly banging his mug on the boards while he pondered what he'd say next.

They found vacant stools at the table opposite Deputy Sheriff Sam Snook. He did not seem to be a popular man. Down the table a stocky German cursed him.

"Samuel, you are not so nice what you used to be. At the fort what do you do each day? One thing more I say to you . . ."

Snook ignored him. His eyes, so heavily lidded that their color was indistinguishable, fixed on Micah and Philly and Tom. He slowly scratched the huge, mounded belly that protruded from his unbuttoned leather waistcoat and drank lengthily from a quart mug. Tap his veins, thought Micah, and he'd squirt a watery pus instead of blood.

With his knife he cut up the meat on Philly's trencher on his right and then Tom's meat on his left. As the children began to eat with their fingers, a man seated beside Snook sneezed violently, showering their plates.

Micah looked up, scowling, and the man said, "Damn!" His nose, large and red, dripped like a leaky tap. His small eyes appeared red, too, and swam with tears. His hair, unpowdered and tied back in a queue, was also red. He was, it seemed, a red man, for his coarse, snuff-flecked and greasy coat had once been dyed a bright red. He sneezed again, showering them, and said, "Damn!"

"Mind your manners," Micah told him.

The man stared at him stupidly. He was, Micah realized, very drunk.

"An' mind yer own, young coon," said Snook, " 'less ye l'arn 'em with a lash."

"On children now our deputy whips," cried the German down the table. "Gott safe Lord North but the children put you in the stocks."

"Shet up, Mayer," Snook said. "I'm tired o' yourn runnin' mouth."

"Damn!" exclaimed the red man, and sneezed again.

"Noo that's preceesely what I say to ye, Dr. Connolly," said a small, middle-aged man seated next to Tom. "Damn! Ye've drunk a wee bit too much tonicht an' yer wits has addled. Dinna sneeze in my face, mon, while I say this. A wee pittance we get in the west here wi' no prospect o' more to come. Wha' representation ha' Philadelphia and Chester and Books Coonties in Assembly? Twenty-two, mon, by latest coont. An' wha' ha' we, the remainder six coonties, that air the bra' boon an' muscle an' sinew o' this Province? We ha' nine, mon, by latest coont. An'—"

"Damn!" said Dr. Connolly and sneezed again and again and again.

"Aye, damn, damn, damn!" cried the little Scotsman passionately, rising and knocking over his stool and slamming both fists on the board until the water bucket shook. "I'm removing mysel' from yonder fountain o' ignorance." He stalked away.

Mayer, the German, put down his knife and applauded loudly. "Speak you well, MacGregor," he cried after him.

MacGregor, seeing no vacant place at another table, returned to his stool with a dour expression.

"Evenin', Sheriff." Fergus, a hand wrapped around a quart mug of rum, hitched up a stool beside Philly and sat down.

Snook belched.

"This young feller's Micah Heath," Fergus said. "He's workin' fer me. He brung in these two young uns from over west to be bound out. Tell the dep'ty sheriff, Micah."

Reluctantly and slowly, Micah described what had happened from the moment when the party of Delawares appeared at the post. Everyone at the table listened intently, leaning forward and occasionally telling him to speak up; Dr. Connolly, staring at him vacantly, even failed to sneeze. When Micah had finished, MacGregor clapped his back and everyone except Snook and Dr. Connolly spoke at once, praising him and damning the Delawares.

Snook, staring at him fixedly, turned over his empty mug and held it out to Connolly. The doctor struggled to his feet and stumbled toward the bar with Snook's mug and his own. Then Snook spoke.

"Ye're Fogarty's bound boy, eh?"

"I *was*," Micah muttered.

"Whar's yer paper at?"

Taking off his cap, Micah removed the worn, greasy paper and handed it to Snook. The sheriff held it up and down, far off and close to his eyes before he made out Mr. Murdoch's scrupulous penmanship. Then his lips moved slowly as he read it. Connolly, sneezing again, staggered back with their drinks.

Snook took a long pull on his mug and said thickly, "Ye're bound fer sartain."

"He *were* bound," Fergus said, "but now I reckon the law finds him free. Fogarty's dead an' *him* is free. Dr. Connolly, ye've studied the law, ain't the boy free?"

Connolly's lips worked. "P–p–pos'tively," he said and sneezed.

"Ye're drunk, Connolly," said Snook. "This paper says he's a bound boy. Ain't he a bound boy?"

"P–p–pos'tively," Connolly said.

MacGregor, commenting obscenely on Connolly and the law, said that the boy was clearly free.

"The law." Snook drank again and smacked his lips. "Ye know nought o' law, ya Grassmarket haggis, MacGregor. Nor ye, Fergus, ya wool-headed woodsy." He hiccoughed. "Ye say, Fergus, the boy is your'n. He ain't. He's the law's. An' who's the law in Pittsburgh?" He prodded his belly with a dirty thumb. "Me."

"Election!" the German cried. "Let us now an election hold, Gott damn, and see who now the deputy sheriff of Pitt Township is."

"How'd they view it at the Inns o' Court?" demanded Snook. "They'd 'zamine the case—uh—mighty keerful. They'd ask, first off, what ev'dence the boy didn't murder Fogarty an' the Twillows too in tryin' to escape—"

His words were drowned in a roar of anger. Micah, a piece of meat on the point of his knife, scarcely heard the voices as he glared at Snook. The knife, he thought, would drive to the hilt softly in Snook's belly.

MacGregor, catching his look, gripped his arm and said, "Easy, lad, easy, yonder mon is daft drunk."

His impulse to lunge his knife suddenly chilled him. He just might have done it and ended on a gibbet. Remember that, he told himself, and rest calm. I'm lighting out of here. They can lock me in, but I'll fight out and run free. There's no justice here. There's only legality that takes no account of justice.

There came to mind a vivid picture of Red Deer waiting across the river in the dark, peaceful woods that stretched as wide as time. Then, looking down at Philly, he saw that she was crying. Tears rolled down her cheeks and she suddenly pushed back her trencher and buried her face in her arms. Tom, seeing her, began to wail too. Putting an arm around each, he told them to hush, that things would turn out all right. But it won't be right for them, he thought miserably, if I run away.

Snook banged his mug on the boards for silence and continued in a thick voice, "I ain't sayin' as I look at it that a way. I'm a sayin' the law looks at it that a way. I ain't 'vestigatin' the boy's tale. I'm takin' his word. But it's clear by this paper"—he pointed to it on the table—"the boy's gotta serve his time."

Reaching out, Micah picked up the paper and put it in his cap.

"Gi' us that," said Snook.

"Come and get it," Micah replied quietly.

"Wot's 'at?"

"I say come and get it, Deputy Sheriff."

They stared at each other until Snook's gaze shifted and he smiled vaguely. "In time I will, young coon, I will." He drank and said, "They's fi'-pound fine fer helpin' a bound sarvint escape, Fergus. An' ten shillin' a day fer every day ye harbor him."

Surprisingly, Fergus smiled at him. "'Course I ain't goin' agin the law, Sam." He raised his mug. "Drink up, Sam, an' I'll buy ye onc. Er kain't ye hold hit?"

"I holds it second t'none," Snook replied. "Now"—he swayed forward, looking down the table—"what'm I bid fer the sarvices o' this young coon? He's strong an' frisky, as ye kin see. Twenty pound anybody?"

No one answered him. They lowered their heads or looked away.

"How 'bout the young uns?" Snook called. "Single er pair. Three pound single er fi' pound fer the pair. They's plenty o' work in 'em in time."

Swearing, the German got to his feet and walked away. One by one others rose and left the table until only MacGregor, Connolly and Fergus remained.

"Git off to the jail," Snook said to Micah, "an' take them young uns with ye. I'll find bidders t'morrow."

Micah did not stir.

Fergus got to his feet, swaying slightly, and cried, "Drink up, Sam. The price o' the boy says ye kain't drain yer mug wi'out breath."

Snook actually smiled. "Eighteen, Fergus, if ye drink off yers an' still stand. Twenty-two if ye fall."

"On," said Fergus.

"The puir fool," MacGregor whispered to Micah. "Fergus canna hold more'n a drop wi'out fallin' blind."

"On'y ye stand too, Sam," Fergus said. "If'n ye fall an' I stand, the boy's mine clear an' outright."

Snook hesitated only a moment. He heaved himself to his feet. As they stood, hands resting on the boards, staring at each other across their quart mugs, word of their bet spread and the din of voices subsided. Somewhere a man offered heavy odds on Snook.

Dowelson quit his bar and came to the table. Smiling over his great leather apron, he said, "Gentlemen, your mugs." He poured a little rum from Fergus's into Snook's. To the silent room he called, "The gentlemen's mugs are both two-thirds full." Looking from Snook to Fergus, he said, "Take up your mugs." They lifted them. "When I clap my hands, drink to the bottom."

He stepped back and clapped his hands together sharply.

Throwing back their heads, they drank. In a moment Micah heard Fergus begin to gurgle for breath. He spread his feet and continued to drink, gasping and choking, while no sound came from Snook. It seemed that Snook's huge belly was visibly swelling as he drank, his head far back. Now the dark rum was running down Fergus's chin and he sounded as if he were choking to death. Still Snook drank silently. With a strange little scream, Fergus let the mug fall from his fist and toppled backwards on the earthen floor.

A groan rose from the watching men. Micah thought dully that there went his first chance to escape.

Snook held up his empty mug, bottom to the ceiling, to show all that he had drained it. A few men cheered feebly. Through the haze of smoke Snook's face appeared to be a greenish-purple. He opened his mouth, gasping for breath, his eyes glazed, his thick body swaying. In the sudden silence Dr. Connolly sneezed loudly. Snook fell sideways, as a tree falls, and crashed to the floor.

A great howl of glee rose and men pounded the boards and slapped one another's backs.

Through the roar, MacGregor shouted in Micah's ear, "Whist, lad, be on your way wi' the young bairns. Go east to freedom and ne'er come back to this Gomorrah."

IV

EACH day as they walked east, Micah thought of the west. I'll come back some day, he told himself, and live and die over yonder.

It seemed that he'd had to go east. He simply could not leave the young ones in Pittsburgh with Snook and his wife. They would have died; and he, constantly wondering about them as he traveled west with Red Deer, would have died a little each day with them.

MacGregor had realized it. So had Mayer, the German trader. They were willing to buy up Micah's time, but they could not do anything for the children in their bachelor quarters.

Philly had settled it. Looking up at them, she said, "I reckon we mought have kinfolk back Bedford way as 'd take us in." They snatched at that straw. Bedford was a hundred miles east by Forbes Road, but the country was at peace now. The trip, they reckoned, offered few hazards to a handy boy who had brought the young ones over the forty miles of woods trace from the Ohio.

Micah did not remind Philly that she'd said all their kin were dead. She was a smart young one. She knew that they had to get out of Pittsburgh and it was in her heart now to go east, as it was in his to go west. So east they would go, he dared not think where or how far, but simply east by the road General Forbes' men had cut through the wilderness years ago. Somewhere to the east he'd find a woman whose arms and heart would go out to the young ones; he'd get them a home somehow. And then he'd follow the sun again.

Mayer and others pressed money on Micah. MacGregor invited them to sleep in his store and awakened them long before dawn with a hot breakfast. He gave them a bag of meal and two extra blankets and walked with them to the foot of Grant's Hill.

But a bag of meal and a little money would not support them very long. Forever was a long time, yet it seemed to Micah that it would take them forever to reach some place they could call a destination.

The fear that Snook would pursue them seldom left his mind. The growing cold, their supply of food, the condition of their feet, the sharp questioning of travelers and settlers, troubled him constantly. But his greatest source of anxiety was Angus.

The big ox, grown gaunt and weak from lack of forage and rest, became a drag. Tom could walk now; they would make better time without Angus, Micah knew. If it were left to him, he told himself, he'd kill the ox and hasten on. But the young ones' love for Angus paralyzed his will to act. They were forever lagging behind, walking beside Angus and talking to him and patting his rhythmically nodding white head.

As they passed through the little settlements of the Bill Pens and Bushy Run, people demanded, "Who mought ye young uns be? Where at did ye git that 'ere ox?"

They were the Smith young ones, going to visit kin at Ligonier, Micah invariably replied. And always he thought of people discussing them after they'd passed east, two young ones and a half-grown boy walking with an ox. The word eventually would reach Snook, who could make a handsome profit by coming after them and seizing them and binding them out.

"Git!" He'd whack Angus.

But the ox crept more slowly each day.

Around noon of the fifth—or possibly it was the sixth—day out of Pittsburgh, the wind lowered and died. A gray sky pressed down and the earth breathed coldly on their feet. Road puddles darkened with the promise of ice sheen. It grew still, so still that you could hear squirrels and chipmunks rustling the dead leaves of distant thickets. The sky was preparing and earth awaiting the first fall of snow.

It came, a few fluttering flakes that made the children cry out in joy, as the road climbed steeply. Then snow enveloped them and there was no sound except Angus's labored, snuffling breathing.

After a while Micah heard the distant tinkle of a bell. It rose to a rhythmic jangle. A whip cracked like a pistol shot. From the snow ahead emerged a figure on a belled horse followed by a long train of horses, haltered nose to tail. Packers, going west to Pittsburgh, wicker panniers bulging with salt and dry goods and heavy hardware. A red-haired boy riding the lead belled horse breathed on his hands and grinned down at them. "Cold!" he cried. "Ye're on the Chestnut Ridge!"

Then he was gone and the file of horses passed slowly, heads low, whickering their disgust and fatigue. A long whip cracked over their backs and the driver bringing up the rear chanted, "Ap, ap, ap!" The driver, a bearded man wearing a snow-encrusted flat beaver hat, peered down at them in wordless astonishment as he passed. Then he, too, was gone and the bell tinkled slowly away.

As it faded, Angus uttered a strange whinnying sound and his knees buckled. He rolled onto his right side, moaning, and Philly dropped beside him, crying, "Angus!"

Her arms wrapped around his neck, tears streaming down her face, she looked up at Micah.

He breathed deeply. "All right, Philly. Get up and you and Tom go ahead."

"No!" she cried fiercely.

"I *told* you." He gripped her by a thin arm and lifted her. *"Git!* The both of you!"

For a moment her tear-stained face was raised to his in an expression of horror, and then she yanked her arm free and ran ahead into the snow.

"Git!" Micah told Tom.

As Tom raced after Philly, Angus made a frantic, floundering effort to rise. Then he was still, his eyes rolled back toward Micah. Like a human, he thought numbly. He could not bear to do it. Yet he could not leave the poor beast to be torn alive by wolves.

He stepped back slowly, his hands fumbling with his rifle. Angus lifted his head, raising it higher and higher to look around at him.

He caught up with Philly and Tom below the crest of the Chestnut Ridge. The snow had stopped, as suddenly as it began. Wind, backing to the southwest, blew a steadily advancing front of blue sky above the white world. Thaw, and then a late burst of autumn, but winter was coming fast.

Philly and Tom walked along with lowered heads. They did not speak, and he did not try to speak to them until, near sundown, they came to the crest. Then he said, "Ligonier yonder. Too far a piece for us tonight."

Behind them the Loyalhanna jaggedly gashed the snow-streaked wilderness. Ahead, where snow had not fallen, the red and golden forest stretched into the blue haze of approaching night. Away east, so dim that it might be smoke, the eye shaped mountains. That would be the Laurel Hill. This Chestnut Ridge was only the beginning of the mountains and the Laurel Hill was nowhere near their ending.

He hitched his pack. "We'll camp below the crest."

But Philly did not stir. "East," she murmured. "Hit gives a mortal strength jest to look east an' think o' the country whar they've cut down the trees."

She did not speak again while Micah built a fire and they ate fire-cake and rabbit meat. After a while she got up and walked away. When she'd been gone some time, Micah called to her. She returned, and he saw that she'd been crying.

"You try to forget Angus," he told her slowly. "He just couldn't go as far as we've got to."

She sat down and did not look at him for a long time. At last, gazing at him levelly, her gray eyes shining in the firelight, she said, "I know hit. But they's so few things for a body to love in this world—an' Angus was one of 'em. I—" She looked away and then at him again. "Micah, was you alus a bound boy?"

"No." He sounded angry. "Not to begin with."

"When did you git to be un?"

"I don't rightly remember."

She plied him with questions about his past, but he answered in grunts. The future was so cloudy, however, that it was easier to think of times past.

Sometimes he believed that he remembered a certain misty morning on a quay where gulls mewed. Again, he remembered standing beside his mother on a canting deck above a sun-dazzled sea while a bagpipe wailed and men lowered a weighted canvas overside. Yes, the pipes had wailed and his mother had clutched him to her. Surely he remembered, too, a clear summer evening on the Delaware, with the noise of Philadelphia close by and the ship's sails furled aloft. He and his mother stood with many others while strangers passed among them, questioning them, examining their teeth, feeling the muscles of men. Somewhere in the twilight someone cried, "Redemptioners!"

Once, when he mentioned these things to his mother, she had told him that he could not possibly remember Port of Glasgow and his father's death at sea and their arrival in Philadelphia. He'd been too young, she said emphatically; he'd only heard her speak of it.

But he believed that he remembered.

Positively one of his first memories was of Murdoch, small and dark, with large, dark, luminous eyes that seemed to reach into you and find whatever was there. As far back, too, was his first impression of Martha Tout, smiling at him and saying, "First you must eat something." He did not recall anyone else speaking as Mrs. Tout did until he learned the difference between gentlefolk and his own kind of folk. Although she was a farmer's wife and so not a gentlewoman, she spoke like one.

She had been a mother to him after his own mother died in the same wave of fever that took Murdoch's wife. He never could forget the bitter tears Martha Tout had shed after Murdoch told him firmly that he'd not heeded the warning given him and that he must go.

John Tout, standing stoop-shouldered in the kitchen and staring perplexedly from his wife to Micah, had said, "The trouble is he learned to ride. Sometimes I think the horses themselves learned him just because they love him so." He looked at Micah. "I warned you and Mr. Murdoch warned you there wasn't to be no jumpin'. I warned you horses are to *work* for the likes of you and me, not to *ride*. Mind my tellin' you about that Philadelphia tailor as was fined fifty pound for racing a horse?

A tailor ain't allowed to race a horse 'cause he ain't a *gentle*man. Who do you think you might be, you who ain't even a tailor?"

Sitting miserably, hands clasped between his knees, he'd known that he was *nothing*. The trouble was that a devil in him had prompted him to a hellish pride before Kathy.

Now, listening to the wind keening over the ridge, he imagined that he could see her clearly.

Kathy Murdoch was six months younger than he. For as long as he could remember she had passed the summers at the farm. When they were very young they played together as if they were brother and sister, alternately friends and enemies, quarreling and making up, united against all the world and divided against each other over a red apple, a top, a game of jackstraws. But he did not really *see* her in those days.

The time came when they no longer played together. Although she still was there, he was unaware of her. He was caught up in the farm and the changing seasons, in both the necessity and the desire of a boy to work like a man. The land claimed him. . . .

"Micah," Philly was saying now, "what's a real farm like? It was a *real* farm you come from back Chester County way, weren't hit?"

He stared at her reflectively. "On a real farm one thing always leads to another, Philly. It ain't any use to be a good axman 'less you know how to hone a blade. You're always learning something. Burn stumps, but don't try to plant a crop on new land till July of the second year. Sow buckwheat then, but it'll all go to straw. New land's too eager for much else. Cut it down and in the fall sow rye. Turn it under again before you try wheat. Time passes on rich new land before you've a good yield of wheat."

"Yes." Tom slept with his head in her lap while her eyes shone with pleasure. "I'm rememberin' what you say. Go on. Oh, Micah, tell me some more."

"Nothing's worthless," he said slowly. "Save the big rye straw for barn thatching. Hickory's the best cure for hams, so don't waste it on fences. Dig a root cellar mighty deep. Fill it with potatoes, beans, turnips, cabbages and corn." He smiled faintly. "Remember a woman likes flowers planted amongst her vegetables. Tulips and pinks, sunflowers, hollyhocks, snowballs, morning glories."

"Yes." Philly rocked, smiling. "Hit's good to hear you *talk*."

" 'Member how a woman feels about flowers so as she'll serve you in flax. That's her crop. She pulls it and dresses and hatchels and spins it. But save it all. Remember and always save everything. There can't be a farm without a woman. It's hard to figure if more women make a bigger farm or a big farm makes for more women."

But Kathy never had been numbered among the women at the farm. Thinking of her, he paid no mind to Philly's questions. He'd talked too much already.

Kathy's grandfather had cleared the land and built the fieldstone house. He was a farmer. Kathy's father had left the farm for the city, but the farm had not completely left him, for he returned to it when he could. Still, he was considered a city man, a merchant. And, no matter how much time Kathy spent at the farm, she never was considered a part of it. Kathy was going to be a lady.

No one ever heard her say so. But everyone knew it. No one about the farm spoiled her. That was not necessary, John Tout remarked once in an unguarded moment, because her father already had tended to it.

As time passed, Kathy's manner toward Micah had become patronizing. Occasionally he'd resented it. But most of the time he didn't care. He knew that she was practicing on him in her study of becoming a lady, a career that had nothing to do with his own.

Everything might have turned out differently (he had believed at the time) if it had not been for Kathy's little mare, Flyswat. She had learned to ride a pony, and then she announced that she detested horses after a governess insisted that ladies did not ride horseback. When she learned, however, that it was currently the rage among several advanced young ladies of the County to ride to hounds, she demanded and received Flyswat. Although she was only a child, she charmed several young men of the neighborhood—including the estimable young Mr. Anthony Wayne —into teaching her to ride. When she returned to the farm after a winter in Madame Torceau's "school for genteel young ladies" she seemed to have changed totally. She puzzled Micah until he realized what had happened. Kathy had become a lady.

Then he *saw* her for the first time and thus he remembered her. Slender and surprisingly tall in a mauve riding habit. Skin as fair as a pale tea rose. Hair piled in coils like gleaming golden bullion. Her eyes transfixed him when she finally deigned to look at him: large and curiously russet-colored eyes, long-lashed, with tiny yellow flecks. Her eyes and her smile mocked him.

He felt himself flushing. Shame at himself, a great awkward country lout, mingled with resentment of her, a girl who had simply happened to be born the daughter of Timothy Murdoch. Her mocking smile stirred something else in him, too: a sudden fierce desire to *be* something that he was not.

Strange things brought the feeling on him. When he saw gentlemen riding to hounds in their scarlet coats and buff breeches, anger flared in him. The faint cry of "View halloo!" when the fox was raised could pierce him like a knife. He knew that he rode as well as any of them.

No one could manage the stallion, Black Bruce, except himself. There was no fence too high for him to clear on Black Bruce. John Tout, horrified the first time he'd caught him jumping, had strictly forbidden him to jump any of the horses again. He still rode and jumped, however, when out of John's sight.

On the May morning when he first *saw* Kathy after she returned to the farm, he muttered gruffly and turned away.

"Micah," she called after him, "saddle Flyswat for me. I'm going for a ride."

He kept his gaze on the ground. "She's a mite frisky."

Her tone mocked him. "I presume you've found time to keep her exercised."

He went to the stable and saddled Flyswat and led her out. She paused, staring around at him as he tightened the girth. He saw Kathy on the mounting block beside the house, tapping her crop in a hand. She called to him impatiently.

The next he knew he'd vaulted astride Kathy's sidesaddle. His legs clamped the mare and she dashed. It was a hundred yards to the mounting block, but he swung the mare in a galloping turn with the pressure of one knee, off across the lower meadow, his muscles a part of Flyswat's flowing speed. She pounded around the meadow and he headed her for the stone wall beside the block where Kathy stood, staring at him. His legs gripped Flyswat tightly and he murmured to her as they neared the wall. She sailed—up and over and down. He glimpsed Kathy's furious expression, and he laughed at her as he passed. Slowing Flyswat, he turned her and trotted back to Kathy.

Swinging off, he bowed low and said mockingly, "Your horse, *Mistress* Murdoch."

"You—" She raised her crop, her face pale with anger. "You—bound boy! Never touch my horse again."

That afternoon Murdoch summoned him to the dining room where he and Kathy were eating dinner and lectured him severely for jumping Flyswat. He warned that if he did it again he would have to leave the farm, and he told him that he had strictly forbidden Kathy to jump.

Murdoch returned to Philadelphia the next morning, and after he had gone Kathy came to the stable in search of Micah. He heard her calling him. Now it was "Micah!" in a gentle voice. He hated her. He wanted to hide from her.

She found him behind the stable. "Micah." Her tone was humble, her eyes downcast. "I'm sorry I was angry." Looking up, she smiled at him uncertainly. And suddenly he did not hate her at all.

"Please, Micah, ride with me." It was not an order but a request.

He rode off with her gladly. When they were out of sight of the house she said that he must teach her to jump. She scoffed at his reluctance. "Don't be a timid mouse. I won't tell Papa." It seemed that she could make him do anything she wished.

Below the lip of the hill in the lower pasture he set a light bough on stones a foot off the ground. She galloped Flyswat at it unhesitatingly, and when the mare cleared the low bar, she cried out excitedly. Her eyes shone, her face was flushed with pleasure. "I'll be the highest jumper in the world!" Always higher; build up the stones and raise the bar. What a fool he'd been that day to raise the bar. And yet what a pleasure he'd found in being with her.

He forgot, in the excitement of riding and jumping with her, that she was a young lady with all the unfathomable pride and strange fears and angers that probably possessed all young ladies everywhere.

The next day they rode and jumped again. As they returned home, they saw Murdoch's chariot approaching from Philadelphia.

"I'll show Papa," she cried. "I'll take the wall."

Micah shouted warningly and pressed the stallion after Flyswat. When he overtook the mare and reached for her bridle, Kathy screamed at him and struck his hand with her whip. They were close to the wall then, and he swerved Black Bruce and pulled him up.

Flyswat gathered for the leap as Murdoch's chariot turned into the lane. Micah saw him standing up beside Billy, his driver, hands raised and face contorted. Flyswat was over the wall. But Kathy was off balance and teetering uncertainly in the sidesaddle. Then she fell and rolled on the ground, her slim legs thrashing in a welter of petticoats.

Micah knelt beside her. Her eyes blinked off the daze of her fall and her fingers found a small cut on her chin. "I've marred my face!" She glowered up at Micah. "Why did you try to stop me? It's your fault I fell. It's *all* your fault."

Murdoch stood there, cursing loudly. And after he found that she was not hurt, he spent his fear in wrath. She would be confined to the house, she would go nowhere and see no one until she'd learned to obey.

Kathy began to sob. "It's *his* fault!" she cried. "It's *all* his fault."

In a way that was true, he realized, as he knelt beside her and stared up at Murdoch.

Kathy suddenly stopped sobbing. She said, "Get rid of him, Papa."

So he had become the property of John Fogarty. . . .

These two years and a half later, sitting by the fire on the Chestnut

Ridge, Philly suddenly clutched his arm and asked, "Micah, but what mought it be *like* back east?"

After a while he replied, "It's hard to say, there's so much to it."

V

SNOW, which began falling three days before Christmas that year, lay deep on Chester County by the morning of December twenty-fourth when the sun climbed in a blue sky.

Undaunted by drifts and a cold northwest wind, the musicians Timothy Murdoch had hired to entertain guests at his farm on Christmas Eve rode out from Philadelphia in a sleigh driven by Billy, Murdoch's Negro slave. They were three French horns, a bassoon and three fiddles, heads wrapped in scarves and chins tucked under bearskin robes. Frequent stops at inns for warming mugs of rum had so imbued the musicians with the spirit of Christmas that by noon, when the sleigh lunged over the rise east of the farm, they were enthusiastically playing "Old Sol." Assailed by the sobering wind on the crest, the French horns suddenly broke into the melancholy notes of "Past Caring and Past Faring" while the fiddlers plucked its hidden lilt from their strings and Billy sang.

Kathy Murdoch heard the music. Pulling aside the chintz curtain at the front window of her bedroom, she gazed down at the strong horses tugging the sleigh up the lane. Smiling and tapping a foot, she sang, "Oh, I'm past caring and past faring . . ." She danced from the window and around the big walnut four-poster until she remembered that the guests soon would begin arriving.

Running out of the room and along the hall to the back stairs, she called, "Ida!" The clatter of pans answered her. Flying down the stairs, she flung open the kitchen door and cried, "Ida! Ida Mae, come up at once!"

Ida Mae Neiswander, the harelipped bound girl, stared at her stupidly from the cavernous fireplace where she was basting a turkey hung from a smokejack. Her cleft lip worked in her broad, fire-reddened face, but she did not speak.

"Now, Kathy." Mrs. Tout scowled at her across the wide, low-ceilinged kitchen. "With twenty guests coming we've much to do. Ida Mae is—"

"Dress me!" Kathy cried at Ida, and when the bound girl remained staring at melted butter dripping from a big wooden spoon in her right hand over the golden-brown turkey, Kathy slapped her behind. Ida yelped, dropped the spoon into the basting pan on the hearth, and trotted heavily to the back stairs. Kathy followed, whacking her a few times to keep her moving.

Shoving Ida ahead of her into the bedroom and slamming the door, she faced her problem. What would she wear? There was not actually a problem, for she knew exactly what she would wear this afternoon and what gown she would choose for the dancing this evening. But it was fun to pretend that she couldn't decide which to select. Her wardrobe, hung on three long lines stretched from the eaves, was surely the finest in the County. There were scores of petticoats and dozens of frocks, more gay than somber, made of silk and satin and velvet, of bombazine and Holland linen, of groset, moreen, millinet and French tabby.

Now what, she asked herself, would *he* like to see me wearing? But who was *he*? Tench Howe, presumably. She sighed. Tench was such a bore. Because she had flirted with him a few times he took it for granted, the popinjay, that he had made a conquest and that she wished he was her beau. She'd make him suffer for his conceit, but who was the *he* to make Tench jealous? Not Dick Wister, the shyling who stared at her with the moist brown eyes of a worshipful hound and blushed whenever she smiled at him. And not Harry Potter, a big baby only sixteen years old.

The jingle of sleigh bells drew her to the window and she saw old Mr. Pilch, the rich Quaker who had recently begun doing business with Papa in Philadelphia. Up the lane behind him rode a solitary horseman, his head lowered against the wind. Tony Wayne!

"*Mister* Wayne is arriving," she whispered to Ida. "*Alone!* Mrs. Wayne failed to come with him again."

Now there, she thought, might be a *he* to make Tench jealous. Although he was not handsome and did not cultivate charming manners, the impetuous Squire of Waynesboro had an air about him that Kathy found irresistible. Perhaps she was most attracted by his magnificent temper, seeming to be always barely controlled, that was apparent in his jutting jaw, his reddish hair, his hazel eyes. Even more attractive to her, however, was the faint reputation of scandal that had followed him since that really delicious brawl under the big buttonwood at Howell's Tavern last September. It was said that Mrs. Wayne hadn't spoken to him for a week afterwards. Well, it served him right for marrying such a mouse as Polly Penrose.

Looking down at him from the window as he dismounted and Billy took his horse, Kathy observed critically that his legs really were too thick and his feet enormous. If a man did not have a finely turned leg, she had recently decided, he was not worthy of her close attention. Tony Wayne was growing quite old, too; on New Year's Day he would be—twenty-seven. Old, heavy-legged, married to a mouse, and the father of a baby daughter. . . . She sighed. *He* was not the one to make Tench jealous.

"M—Mis' Kathy?" Ida looked at her questioningly and thrust her square hands toward one of the lines of gowns.

"Don't *hasten* me," Kathy snapped. Her elation at the prospect of the party suddenly evaporated and she felt desolate. Turning from the window, she flung herself on the bright calamanco counterpane which covered the bed. "I may not go downstairs at *all* today."

Ida's harelip worked painfully. "M—Miss Kathy." She moved toward the door.

"Stand there!" Kathy clenched her hands and scowled fiercely at the ceiling. Why wasn't there someone to be gay with, someone who— She heard sleigh bells again. "Who's coming now?" she demanded.

Ida looked out the window. "W—Wisters."

"Dear God, the Wisters. Mr. and Mrs. Wister and *Rich*-ard and Mary and Louise. Oh dear God, I can't stir from this room today."

The sisters, Mary and Louise, hated her. And she hated them. She knew that they hated her because she was beautiful. And she hated them because—because they were almost her age and so gangling and awkward that it made everyone think no girl of seventeen, not even herself, could be treated as a lady. To pretend throughout this day that she did not hate them would be more than she could endure.

Ida was making wordless sounds at the window again.

"Who?"

"Mmmm—"

"You stupid Ida." She swung off the bed and looked out the window. Widow March, swathed in scarves and a huge cape, was riding her big bay. Behind her rode a man on a prancing stallion. Now she saw him clearly. "Oh dear God," she whispered and dropped to her knees, staring. She had completely forgotten that Papa had said Alex March was coming too. She hadn't thought of him in— Why, she'd never really thought of him at all. He had just returned after four years spent in London and traveling on the Continent; how could he possibly have grown so handsome in that time? But then she had not been able to judge any man four years ago. Now he was—yes, twenty-one years old.

"Look at him," she whispered to Ida.

Under his beaver hat his lean face was set in a grave, abstracted expression. When his stout, red-faced mother hawked and spat, he frowned—and then he smiled. His smile was warm rather than disdainful, as if he actually found amusement in his mother's bad manners.

"Bil—ly!" shouted Mrs. March in a voice that surely could be heard in Germantown. "Where is that blackamoor?"

Alex leaped to the ground with a quick gracefulness and swung Mrs. March down from her sidesaddle. The wind, blowing back his blue cape, revealed his strong, well-shaped legs. He said something to his mother, then smiled and spoke to John Tout as John took the horses.

"Quick!" Kathy leaped to her feet. "Unbutton me, Ida. Don't stand there, you gnat-wit."

When she stepped from her dress and the voluminous pile of petticoats, she shivered. The room was cold, but she turned to the mirror leisurely and found the one place in the wavery glass where she had a perfect reflection of herself. Closing her eyes, she whispered, "I am a beautiful woman, a beautiful woman am I." Opening her eyes, she saw that she was. A young woman, to be sure. Just seventeen years young. A woman, nevertheless, who would grow more beautiful each year and who never would become old and coarse and dumpy.

Where, she wondered, must my beauty reside to make me the loveliest of all? In the face itself, silly; in legs and arms and breasts and hips; in the very bones themselves. You have them, and they cannot be denied. See? Leaning closer to the mirror, she saw. She saw her eyes, too. "Old cat-eyes," she said aloud, and suddenly she giggled.

Half an hour later she descended the front stairs. She wore a blue bombazine frock and her golden hair was piled high in the mode. She did not seem to walk, but floated (as Madame Torceau had taught her) on invisible, tiny, high-heeled slippers which hurt her feet painfully.

Definitely it was an entrance. The babble of voices died away. Mrs. March, holding up her skirts while she warmed her backside at the fire, gaped at her. Mary and Louise Wister, their hair hanging in ringlets, scowled at her. Mrs. Wister smiled at her uncertainly. The men stared, unmoving.

She simulated a pretty dismay. Her eyes widened, a hand fluttered to her throat. "La, Papa," she exclaimed, "I didn't realize so many of the guests had arrived."

The men leaped to their feet then. At least Tony Wayne and all younger than he leaped. The older men merely stood up.

Surely Alex March had been the first on his feet. She pretended not to notice him as she stepped to her father, but she took him in. He was above medium height and slender, and he was even more handsome than she had believed when she saw him from the window. His eyes were dark, his nose delicately arched under a high, wide forehead. There was nothing *County* about him, for he was more in the mode than any of the men —even than Papa, who took great pains with his clothing. His dark hair was dusted with powder and combed straight back and tied in a black silk ribbon. He wore plush breeches and clocked blue silk stockings and shoes of the finest leather. His stock was plaited, the ruffles at his throat and wrists were as white as snow, and the skirts of his gaily embroidered blue coat were stiffened with buckram.

It seemed impossible that he could be the son of that huge red-faced woman by the fire who suddenly bellowed, "Well, Kathy, you're quite turned out!"

Placing one foot precisely twelve inches behind the other, she dropped a stately and prolonged curtsy to Mrs. March.

"And I'm quite put out." Alex March spoke quickly in a low voice as he bowed to her. "If I'd known you had grown into such a beautiful young lady, Miss Kathy, I wouldn't have lingered so long in Europe."

Her heart raced as she curtsied to him and tried desperately to think of a reply.

Tony Wayne gave her time. "Gad, Alex," he said in his deep, gruff voice, "you must have studied more than law in London." He grinned at Kathy appreciatively. "Good afternoon, Miss Kathy."

"*Mister* Tony." She looked at Alex. "Precisely what did you study in London besides the law, Mr. Alex?"

"Ha!" exclaimed Wayne. "Don't answer that question, Alex, don't answer it."

Alex said, "But I must."

"Pray do," said Kathy.

"I shall, Miss Kathy." Did his smile mock her? "I became something of an authority on feminine beauty."

"Hear, hear!" said Wayne. "There appears to be something to be said for traveling abroad. A pity I never got farther from home than Nova Scotia."

"How goes thy Nova Scotian land company, Friend Wayne?" asked Mr. Pilch.

Kathy wanted to rip the horn buttons off the Quaker's flapping waistcoat and fling them in his long white face for spoiling this delightful moment.

"It goeth not at all, Friend Pilch," Wayne said glumly. "Rather, it goes backwards. I've retired to my sabine field and chimney corner and now await the curfew knell of life. I do not even have the expectations of Alex here"—his hazel eyes gleamed mischievously—"in the law, that is, in the law."

"Thy expectations are indeed auspicious," Pilch said to Alex, "for I hear that Mr. Joseph Reed hath found a place for thee in his office."

"A very small place, sir," Alex replied.

"From small acorns, Friend March." The Quaker looked him up and down blandly. "Yet thee appears already decked out for Court—though not a court of law."

The sarcastic old gander!

Alex, smiling, said, "It never was a straight path to the law courts, Mr. Pilch. You must know that if you've been to court—and I understand that you have."

"Kathy." Timothy Murdoch stood beside her, a small, dark, handsome man in his fine black smallclothes, staring at her with an odd perplexity. As if, she thought, I were some kind of business problem he had to solve. But she knew what she must do. She must tear herself away from Alex and go about being charming to all these people she detested. Perhaps it was as well, for she must not fling herself at him. She must, rather, so deport herself that he would fling himself at her.

"Kathy, good afternoon." Tench Howe, tall and blond, smiled down at her. His smile lacked its customary confidence, for she had not even noticed him when she entered the parlor.

"Good afternoon, *Mister* Tench," she said coldly and passed on, leaving him to rack his brain over how he had managed to offend her.

She took a glass of Madeira from the tray passed by Mulvaney, the butler at their town house on Arch Street whom her father had brought to the farm for the holidays. Sipping the wine, she smiled and spoke cordially to Dick Wister who blushed, as if his thoughts were not altogether pure when he looked at her. She made the round of guests as they continued to arrive. She made sure she spoke pleasantly to everyone, but her mind was not on a word she said. Without once looking at Alex March, she concentrated on willing his attention toward her: Alex, Alex, think of me; Alex, Alex, look at me.

At last she glanced at him and saw, happily, that *willing* had worked again. For he was watching her and smiling abstractedly. Then he was at her side.

"County society must seem very dull to you now, Mr. Alex, after London and the Grand Tour. You *did* make the Grand Tour, didn't you?"

"I made a tour on the Continent, Miss Kathy. It was quite grand to me. But now it's grander to be home again."

"Tosh," she said, touching his arm very lightly, "don't be courteous with me. Tell me, please, where you went and what you saw."

"I went to Paris and then to the upper Rhine by way of Strasbourg. I crossed the Alps in September and I came down into the most wonderful land in the world, Italy. It's a land of warmth and music and gaiety . . ." It was difficult for her to concentrate on what he said, for he was not concentrating on her. He was drawn quite out of himself and this raw and frozen country as he described a city whose name she hadn't caught in her concern at his distraction. His dark eyes seemed to be seeing something that she could not glimpse. It was—annoying.

Then, quickly, he was *back,* bringing the full warmth of his smile and his attention to her. "You've been attending Madame Torceau's classes, I hear. What do you study there?"

"Oh, la! Silly feminine things. Penmanship and grammar and syntax. A little French and reading and pronunciation and—"

"What do you read?"

She raised her chin proudly. "I think Mr. Pope is very witty and Gray is—is very elegiac."

"Yes, that's an apt description of Gray. He is—uh—very elegiac." She was not sure that she liked his tone. "Do you enjoy music?"

She loved to dance, both the minuet and the lively *contredanse.* She loved music that made your feet tap. But she could not read a note or carry a tune and she detested those lugubrious trios that played interminably nearly everywhere you went. Palma sounded like Pepusch to her and she detected no difference between Giardini and Geminiani. She rattled their names to him.

"I see the musicians have been refreshed out there." He nodded toward the long dining room. "I believe they await your orders to play. What would you have them begin with, Kathy?"

In panic she tried vainly to think of a single number. A name flashed into her mind. "Oh, something by Purcell."

His brows rose. Then he took her by an arm and they went into the dining room where the first violinist bowed deeply.

"Miss Murdoch desires something by Purcell," Alex said.

"P–P–Purcell!" the violinist exclaimed.

"What number by Purcell would you like, Kathy?" She did not like the way his eyes gleamed.

"You select it," she said uneasily. "I *insist* that you select it, Mr. Alex."

"But I insist that you do, Kathy." He was smiling faintly now and she hated him. He *knew* now that she was totally ignorant of music. She had done something terrible and stood exposed in all her childish ignorance.

He laughed suddenly, and she bit her lip. "Kathy, you are an extraordinary wit. You stun the orchestra with your suggestion of Purcell and hoped to stun your guests." He waggled a finger at her. "An *ode* before dinner, one of the St. Cecilias, you presumed. Can't you hear Tony Wayne when that assailed his ears? Even more, I vow, you hoped that in their consternation they'd break into 'Fly, Bold Rebellion!' Considering the times, which are indeed so sadly out of joint, it is most apt. But it would have been devastating, my dear, in there—" He pointed toward the parlor. "Most devastating. You must learn to keep a button on the point of your wit."

Her mouth fallen open, she stared at him.

"Play us 'The Partridge Song,'" he said to the first violinist and took her by the arm.

No one talked of politics and violence that Christmas Eve of 1771 at the farm. A hiatus had come to the years of disobedience. The mob seemed to be tired. And those gentlemen who found themselves to be the instruments of Parliament in America seemed tired of the struggle too. There in the County that winter, politics was of little consequence. For those gathered at Timothy Murdoch's house prided themselves on being civilized; they believed, therefore, in compromise. So they danced and laughed and talked about everything that was unimportant, thus avoiding any mention of politics or religion or intimate relationships between the sexes.

They assembled in the dining room at three o'clock. A full keg of fresh oysters, shipped from the Chesapeake, had been fried in butter and corn meal. There were roast turkeys and geese and ducks stuffed with oysters and chestnuts. Smoked hams, both hot and cold, nudged a great joint of beef. Steaming corn puddings and bowls of squash and turnips and sugared mashed potatoes were flanked by jellies and pickled cabbage and a dozen other kinds of sweet and tart preserves. Hot breads, white, yellow and dark, were mounded under napkins.

Murdoch proposed a toast to the King and then to "the well-being of our fair Province which has been so favored by divine Providence," a toast that could not offend anyone. Without drawing further attention to their Anglican God, though with a brief and polite silence for Mr. Pilch's Quaker God to whom he bowed his head in thanks, they sat down and ate unrestrainedly, washing down the savory food with bottles of claret and Madeira.

After the servants cleared the table and brought in a dozen kinds of pie and a half-dozen plates of tarts and bowls of cream cheese and whipped cream and an enormous steamed pudding, the guests guardedly loosened belts and stays and continued to eat while the musicians played. Even this was not the end, for the table was cleared again and baskets of apples and pears and bowls of hickory nuts and English walnuts were placed on it. At last, when Murdoch nodded to Kathy, the women retired to the parlor and the men and boys sank back in their chairs to doze and smoke and discuss a superb apricot brandy which Murdoch had imported from the Canary Islands.

As nearly always, Kathy wished she could stay with the gentlemen instead of going off with the ladies. It was impossible, of course. For almost a year now Papa had been giving her to understand that she was the lady of the house. It would have been easier for her if Mrs. Tout could have been invited into the parlor with the ladies, but that was as impossible as for Kathy to remain with the gentlemen. Martha Tout was good and kind and wise, her language finer than the Widow March's. But Mrs. March had been married to a gentleman while Mrs. Tout was married to John, the farmer who managed the place for Papa. So she was not a lady and could not be asked into the parlor.

After exactly one hour by the Venus clock on the mantel, Kathy invited the women upstairs to refresh themselves and change their gowns for dancing if they wished. When she descended the stairs in her new purple silk ball gown, the dining room table had been removed and the musicians struck up "Bobbing Joan." The young men rushed toward her. Alex was first, and they went down the middle together to clapping hands and tapping feet.

Her head thrown back, laughing at Alex, she was certain that she never had been so happy.

"Let's kick away care!" he cried.

"I can dance forever, Alex."

Tony Wayne, moderately drunk, shouted, "Widow March, my lovely, come have this dance with me."

"Aye, Tony," cried Mrs. March, "and mind your toes when I come down off yonder ceiling."

Everyone danced except Mr. Pilch, who snored in the parlor.

"This frolic shall not end tonight!" roared Wayne.

And it seemed that it would not. Occasionally the musicians played a minuet to please the aging and rest the young. But they favored the *contredanse* and, fortified with bottles of wine, they showed a pleasing disposition to play as long as anyone would take to the floor.

Kathy danced with every man and boy, but none equaled Alex as a dancer. When they danced together, it seemed to her that she floated on a vast velvet floor. He makes me more beautiful than I've ever been, she thought. I love him.

The words, forming clearly in her mind, startled her at first. She never had thought that of any man except Papa. Then, her first surprise abated, she asked herself, But does he love me? He *had* to love her. There must not be any uncertainty to spoil the perfect certainty of this endless evening.

She recalled later she was thinking those very words, *perfect certainty,* when the dreadful moment came.

As the musicians paused and the dancers gasped for breath, an excited shouting rose in the kitchen.

"It sounds like a mutiny out there," Alex said to her. "I've always wanted to see a mutiny."

He opened the door to the kitchen and they paused, staring.

Mrs. Tout, wailing incoherently, had her arms around a tall, dark-faced youth in dirty buckskin. John Tout was slapping him on the back and shouting at the top of his voice while the servants, both men and women, swung this way and that, babbling excitedly.

Then Kathy saw two children in ragged clothes, a tangle-haired girl holding a small boy by the hand while they stared around with wide, bright eyes.

"Mrs. Tout!" she called.

"Oh, bless God," wailed Mrs. Tout, "he's come back! And on his birthday too—his eighteenth birthday."

The tall youth turned and looked at Kathy, his thick tawny hair falling over his dark forehead. His sharp blue eyes startled her. The bound boy, Micah Heath!

He tried to bow, but he did not know how. "Miss Kathy," he said, "it's pleasing to see you again."

Her mouth opened, but she could not think of anything to say.

"He's come back!" Mrs. Tout cried again.

"Come back?" Murdoch stepped past Kathy and Alex. "What's happened?"

"Here's my paper, sir." Micah held out a dirty scrap.

Murdoch halted, his jaw slack, staring incredulously.

"Trader Fogarty drownded in the Ohio last October, sir," Micah said. "I reckon I belong to you again. These young ones, their folks drownded in the Ohio along with Fogarty. I couldn't find no home for 'em anywhere, so I brung 'em along with me. This here's Philadelphia Twillow. We call her Philly." The girl bobbed her head and shrank behind Micah. "This here's her young brother, Tom Twillow." The little boy ducked behind his sister. "I reckoned Mrs. Tout"—Micah lowered his head and swallowed—"I reckoned . . ."

"I reckon I do have a place for them," Martha Tout said. She reached out, smiling, and hugged Philly to her.

"But you came back," Murdoch said dully.

"All the way from the Ohio," Alex exclaimed. "I think that's wonderful—admirable. But how did you do it?"

"Mostly we walked, sir," Micah said slowly. "Sometimes we got rides."

" 'Twas Micah got us hyar." Philly's face seemed to glow as she looked up at him. "He took keer of us all the way. The Sheriff o' Pittsburgh come all the way this side o' Ligonier a'ter us an' we hid in the woods. He aimed to sell us out an' make a profit. Around Carlisle Tom wuz took powerful sick from the cold an' wuz like to ha' died if'n a good woman hadn't took us in. We stayed thar till Tom wuz better an' then we come on by wagon. We got to thank the Lord."

"And thank Micah Heath too," Alex said. He extended his hand and Micah took it slowly.

Kathy was shocked that Alex would shake hands with a bound boy. The musicians were playing again and she wanted to dance. But he seemed oblivious to her.

"Let me sit down with you while you eat," he said to Micah. "I'd like to hear about the Ohio country and the way east."

Whirling angrily, Kathy strode out of the kitchen.

VI

TOWARD noon one day in the following March, as Micah was turning over straw on the south side of the barn, a soft breeze touched him. He looked up, listening to the trickle of water and feeling that he was waiting for something to happen. He hadn't long to wait, he knew. Spring would burst soon.

He found himself walking up the muddy lane, leaping puddles, and then he trotted toward the woods on the height of land. Far behind, John Tout shouted to him. He ran, then, like a hound on the scent.

When the woods closed around him, he paused and breathed deeply through winter-starved nostrils. For some time the trees had known what he had just discovered. Pines and maples and balsams raised sap to the warming sun in the first authentic smell of spring. Tearing off a handful of balsam needles, he rubbed them between his hands and sniffed his palms. A red-winged blackbird sang two notes, and he saw it flash above a stand of birch. Far off a killdeer raised his wild spring cry: *Kill-dee, kill-dee, kill-dee-dee-dee!* All about him water flushed from the warming earth and spilled down the slope in noisy streams.

When he reached the crest, he stared west. A yellow haze lay on the Land of Goshen. In imagination he leaped beyond the rich farm country to the land that swelled toward the mountains, and across chain after dark blue chain of mountains to the Ohio. Had Red Deer gone down the river alone?

Now, as never before, he yearned to go west. What was there to stop him? The young ones had a good home. Mrs. Tout loved them and they loved her. Philly was blossoming like a gentian in the spring. Mrs. Tout, who was teaching her to read and write, called her the smartest child she ever had known. Yes, Philly and Tom were safe now. And I, thought Micah, can run away west.

As the days passed, he realized, however, that he dreaded to leave Philly and Tom and the Touts. And if he ran away wouldn't he betray Murdoch, who had given Philly and Tom a home? On the other hand, Murdoch was a shrewd businessman. In return for giving the young ones a home, he had bound them to him until they would be twenty-one, thereby making certain that in time the farm would have two strong young laborers.

At the end of April the problem was resolved for him when Murdoch, who had been living at his town house with Kathy since the New Year, stopped at the farm on his way to Lancaster. With him came a dark, burly man who wore a black patch over his left eye and walked with a slight limp. His name was Captain Jonas Bilby. He was, John told Micah, a Yankee who had been the captain of Murdoch's ship, the *Goodspeed,* until it burned on the Delaware in February.

As Micah led in a team from plowing, he found them seated on a stone wall abutting one of the whitewashed pillars which supported the barn.

"Micah," Murdoch called to him, "hand the team to Billy and come here." His dark eyes narrowed as Micah approached, and then he smiled cordially. "You're growing tall, boy, and filling out. John says you're the best man he's got. Do you like the farm work?"

"No, sir," Micah muttered, "not like I once did, though John's fair and good to me."

Murdoch nodded. "This is Captain Bilby, formerly of my employ, and now in—uh—business for himself."

The Yankee was a remarkably ugly man, with a shapeless nose like an old potato and a broad face pitted with pockmarks. Yet when he smiled and his single blue eye gleamed, he conveyed a remarkable warmth. He wore a leather waistcoat and breeches and blue yarn stockings protected by deerskin leggings which extended over his buckled shoes.

"Good day to ye, lad," he said in a deep voice. For fully a minute he studied Micah thoughtfully. Then he turned to Murdoch.

"He'll do," he said.

As Micah crossed the Schuylkill in the dawn of a warm May day and pressed Flyswat toward Philadelphia, he believed that a great change awaited him. Yet what it would be he did not know, for Murdoch merely had told him to bring Kathy's mare to his house on Arch Street this morning.

From the army barracks at Camptown in the Northern Liberties came the thump of the sunrise gun. And then the sun was over the rim of earth, as if in response to the gun's bidding. In the growing flood of morning light, the Market Way was crowded with farmers and their wives hurrying toward the city. Gabbling and shouting to one another in German and English, they bumped along in two-wheeled carts and on jogging horses. They were going to market, wooden carts and wicker panniers laden with vegetables and butter and eggs, with unplucked fowls and quarters of beef and heads of cheese. Although the road through the dogwood was officially named High Street, the farmers insisted on calling it Market Way or Market Street.

Micah, wearing his foxtail cap and carrying his long rifle across the saddle, told himself that he never would be like these farmers whom he cantered past proudly. He would not be a dull clod who haggled over the price of eggs and butter. He would be . . . What?

The houses grew more numerous on High Street, and soon he was at Eighth Street. Before him High was paved, with brick footpaths on either side. There was such a din that he barely heard the State House clock strike six. Through the clatter of hoofs and squeal of wheels and clamor of voices came a steady crunch as servants and slaves cleaned the paths with bricks dipped in water. Sure, he thought, there were ten times as many servants as there were citizens in Philadelphia. They hurried to and fro everywhere, lining up with buckets at each white public pump in every block, bearing the citizens' brightly painted and intricately scrolled chamber pots to back-yard privies, setting the citizens' breakfast tables on many front porches.

"Woodsy!" a towheaded boy yelled at Micah.

He wanted to laugh, but personal honor demanded that he scowl fiercely and shift his rifle menacingly. The boy ducked behind a wagon and fled.

Following the directions John Tout had given him, he came at last to the big brick house on Arch Street where Murdoch, a napkin tucked under his chin, was eating breakfast on the front porch. Kathy had not yet appeared, he saw with disappointment.

As he dismounted, Murdoch called, "Take the mare around to the stable and mind that black bastard Jimmy rubs her down and gives her a full measure of oats. Mulvaney will set a plate of breakfast at the back door for you. When you've finished, come around here."

Handing Flyswat to the Negro stable slave, he watched the boy rub her down and feed her. After he'd fingered his own breakfast off the plate which the butler left at the back door, he went to the front of the house.

Kathy sat across the table from her father. She wore a brightly colored wrapper and her hair was bound in a silk kerchief. Her skin glowed like the early morning sky, Micah thought, as he took off his cap.

"Morning, Miss Kathy," he muttered.

"Good morning, Micah." He was uncertain whether she was going to smile or yawn; then, to his surprise, she managed both.

"He brought Flyswat for you, Kathy." Murdoch sounded irritated. "But you'll not be riding her through the streets."

"You know I wouldn't think of it, Papa." She sounded as if she thought her father a fool. "I only want her next week when Sally and I visit the Raphaelsons. She said—"

"I don't know what's gotten into Henry Raphaelson," Murdoch grumbled.

"Money," Kathy replied. "A rich wife. It changes one, I hear."

"That's quite concise of you considering the hour, my dear. Considering, too, that you feign sleepiness. But things are not—" He waved his fork and then looked at Micah. "All right, boy, mind what I say now. You know where my office is on Front Street?"

"Yes, sir."

"Go there and ask for Captain Bilby. You are to put yourself under his instructions. You will do as he says. You do not know me. I do not know you."

"Sir?" Micah blinked at him.

"Did you not hear me? Did—"

"Papa, how intriguing," Kathy said. "You know him, but you know him not. He knows you, but—"

"You have not heard this conversation," Murdoch said to her.

"I have heard this conversation, but I have heard it not. It's deliciously droll." She smiled at Micah. "You will cease to be while still being."

He nodded, baffled, and tried to smile.

"Now go along and remember what I told you," Murdoch said.

"Yes, sir."

Kathy said, "If I pass you in the street, Micah, and do not speak, it will be because you are not."

"Yes, Miss Kathy."

"Go," Murdoch told him.

As he went, Murdoch said to Kathy, "I would prefer that you not have heard this."

"Don't be a silly." Her tone changed. "You know that you can trust me."

It was a mystery, he thought as he walked along the street, trailing his rifle. In time it would be solved, of course, yet he felt a vague uneasiness. He found himself thinking of the farm. And then he was thinking of Kathy, of how she looked and of what she had said. He wondered if it were true, as Mrs. Tout had surmised, that Kathy had set her cap for that pleasant young man, Alex March, and would eventually snare him. "Snare," at least, was the way Mrs. Tout put it. Yet why should Kathy have to *snare* anyone? The question was whether Alex March was worthy of her.

As Micah approached Chestnut Street he heard a rising din that reminded him of a strong gale in the western forests. Winnowing the noise, he distinguished whistles and jeering voices. He paused at the corner and stared at a great crowd flooding up Chestnut from the waterfront. Ahead of the mob walked two bareheaded, shirt-sleeved men tied to the tail gate of a cart which was pulled by a bony horse. A burly constable strolling behind them rolled his bullwhip and lashed the back of one of the prisoners. The man's piercing scream was drowned in the mob's roar of pleasure. Rolling his bullwhip again, the constable cracked it on the back of the other prisoner. The man did not cry out. Jeering, the mob pelted him with refuse hurled over the head of the constable. Both prisoners were so plastered with filth that the color of their hair and the expressions of their faces were almost indistinguishable.

"Introduce ye to the Philadelphia mob, boy," a fat, aging man said to Micah. He rattled his stick angrily on the pavement. "Look at 'em! That mad James Otis said it better 'n he knew. 'When the pot boils, the scum'll rise.' "

"What have those prisoners done, sir?"

"Petty criminals," the man said contemptuously. "Of the mob yesterday and of it again tomorrow after they've been pilloried and egged outside the prison. Waste no sorrow on *them,* boy."

But Micah did sympathize with the prisoners, especially the man who refused to cry under the whip. He stared at the approaching mob curiously. Who were they and where did they come from? There did not appear to be any respectable citizens among them. A few in the front ranks must have been flushed from reeking alleys, for they were thin and ragged and dirty. There was a pock-marked, barefooted woman dangling a baby who sucked frantically at her withered breast, and there a club-footed man in rags hobbled along with a dazed expression as if unmindful of where he was going. Yet there were few like them, Micah observed; there must not be many hungry people in Philadelphia. Most of the mob was made up of sailors and waterfront roustabouts who rolled along in varying stages of drunkenness. There were many young apprentices wearing leather aprons, who shouted raucously but without rancor as they tagged after the others.

For all its noise, he thought, this was not a purposeful or angry or organized mob. It was, rather, a group of the idle out for a lark, going in the same direction because they had companionship, pelting two prisoners for no more reason than boys stone cats.

A ferret-faced girl standing near him began to jig on her wooden clogs and utter a whinnying sound as the mob came on. Apparently she was a bound servant from a house nearby, for she held a pink china jordan by its wooden handle. As the cart came abreast, she suddenly dashed into the street and dumped the contents of the chamber pot over the head of the prisoner who refused to cry when whipped. The man closed his eyes and the mob roared delightedly.

Shrieking with laughter and swinging the empty jordan, the girl ran from the path of the mob. As she passed Micah, he dropped the butt of his rifle and tripped her. She fell, sprawling, and the china jordan smashed on the brick pavement. Screaming obscenities, she staggered to her feet and lunged at him. He raised his rifle butt and fended her off as the passing mob began to howl. Holding off the girl, he glanced quickly toward the street, prepared to run. At first he could not believe that the mob was howling derisively at the girl who so wished to be a part of it. Yet it was howling at her and calling her obscene names. A rotten potato struck her forehead. Turning, she ran.

"Come along wi' us, boy!" a man shouted.

He was a young man, wearing a dusty three-cornered hat cocked over one eye and the remnants of filthy linen ruffles at his throat, but he walked like an old man in quick, mincing steps. His lips and chin and nose were covered with sores. Micah looked away quickly.

After the mob had passed he stood, unmoving, wondering why it had turned against the girl instead of himself. Then someone clapped him on the back, and he faced Captain Bilby.

"So ye didn't care to join the mob, boy." Bilby grinned at him. "I seen you from over the street, tripping up servant girls and ready to defy the mob, I wager, not knowing their nature."

"I was set to run, Captain Bilby. And I was thinking that a mob is a bad thing."

"Sounds like a Quaker speaking."

"I'm nothing, I'm afraid."

"Then beware you don't join the mob. Come and we'll go down to Front Street together while I tell you about mobs. I'm an authority on 'em, for I've been in 'em and I've led 'em and I've been chased by 'em. The only predictable thing about a mob is that it's unpredictable. Including the Boston mob, which is a body o' Puritan saints led by Almighty God."

Micah glanced at him as they walked toward the Delaware. "You're a Boston man?"

"I'm a Boston man, Micah." He winked his single eye. "I'm one o' the saints, as they like to call us sarcastically down here in this city of brotherly love. I'm a Son of Liberty in good standing, but I'll be a son of a bitch if I really like a mob. I don't trust 'em—not in Boston nor New York nor Phil-i-del-phi-ay. A mob is for whatever is strongest, meaning usually itself. It's for English sojers when it thinks they're stronger than it and against 'em when it thinks it's stronger 'n them. It was for you back yonder 'cause you was stronger 'n the servant girl. If she'd tripped up you, it'd have been for her. A wise man shuns a mob and a very wise man uses it."

Bilby paused at the corner of King Street and pointed to a tavern close to Chestnut. In dull paint on its hanging sign was the likeness of a stick of wood. "The Crooked Billet Tavern, boy. Ye'll bed in the stable and eat in the kitchen whilst you work for me. When you're not elsewise employed I'll expect to find you there."

So this would be the result of all his expectations of adventure. Some menial tasks and a stable bed. His disappointment deepened into a dull resentment. "Tell me," he demanded, "what is it that I'll be doing for you?"

Bilby grinned at him. "Ye'll learn any hour now. First I must convince myself of your loyalty and next you must convince yourself of your reward."

"Reward?"

"Natcherly. I said I was a Boston man and any man from Boston knows that nobody does anything for nothing. Murdoch—Mr. Murdoch—is a mite behind us Yankees in his Philadelphia way of thinking and Charleston is further still. D'you like being a bound boy?"

"No, sir."

"Natcherly. Neither do I like you being one."

Micah stared at him.

"I don't like bound people working for me and I can't abide slaves. They ain't trustworthy. There's no reason why they should be—'less they're fools, and then I certainly can't abide 'em. I've run slaves in my time. Shipped 'em, that is. I didn't like it, but I like profits more 'n I dislike shipping slaves. That's my point. Everybody works for a profit. And Murdoch—Mr. Murdoch—agrees that you'll have yours after you've worked for me a spell."

"Thank you," Micah said impulsively.

Bilby rubbed his nose and shook his head. "You've got to sharpen up, boy. You thank me when you don't know what you're thankin' for. I said for 'a spell.' How d'you know how long that spell might be?"

"I don't. But I trust—"

"Trust no man, boy. Me any more 'n the next. And why are you so shy of asking what the reward might be? Pay no mind, I'll tell you. After a year working for me you're free."

Micah halted and his eyes widened. "Free!"

"Aye, free. Murdoch agrees to it." Bilby looked at him quizzically. "Hell's teeth, don't stare at me that way, boy. It sets ill to be giving you what God has already given every man. It's—it's—damn it, it's only business."

In a year I'll be free! The realization swelled in him until he felt like a child's soap bubble blown enormously large and floating up over the city and drifting high across the wide land.

"Free!" he cried.

"Oh, togwaddle," Bilby muttered, scowling fiercely and rubbing his nose.

"I'll be—" Micah's voice was drowned in the sudden clang of ships' bells. They had come to Front Street, but he had not seen it on his high bubble ride. Grounded now, eyes opened wide, he saw a forest of ships' masts and riggings rising from the wharves beyond the noisy street.

"Eight bells," said Bilby. "Come along, boy."

But Micah stood rooted, staring up and down the street and the river beyond it. He felt that he almost vibrated to the squeal of winches, the rumble of carts on cobbles, the shouts of swarming men. Through the brackish smell of the river he sniffed tar and fish and sun-dried lumber. There was the good familiar smell of horses as a dray passed, and then a wave of something strange, something sweet, perhaps spice. It threatened to waft him out of himself again and carry him away up yonder to that crow's-nest where a youth, surely the only idler on the river, curled catlike in the warm sun.

"Come along!" Bilby shouted, seizing him by an arm. "Ye can't sniff the day away like a young foxhound."

But he could have sniffed and gaped and listened the day away there on Front Street. For the world came to that street and the great wharves it thrust into the river. Conestoga wagons, those land-borne ships, came from west and south and north to exchange their burdens for sea-borne cargoes which came under vaster clouds of canvas. The sound of Front Street's commerce, Micah thought, was like the rumbling of a huge belly still unsatisfied from gulping a glut of tea, rum, wine, indigo, flour, hammers, window glass, cheese, cloth, fish, pork, hides, furs, buttons. Here, among the warehouses, offices, ropewalks, anchor forges, smithies, sail lofts and cooperages were the bright brass doorknobs and leaded windows of many famous merchants' houses. There apparently was the residence of one, a Mr. Robert Morris, according to the brass name plate beside the door.

"A merchant?" Micah asked, pointing.

"Aye," Bilby said, "a merchant prince."

"He *lives* here in this noise?"

"Aye. Reminds him who he is, no doubt. I vow that princes built the Tower of Babel."

They came, finally, to a gilt-lettered sign overhanging the pavement.

TIMOTHY MURDOCH, ESQ.

MERCHANT

Imports

Exports

Raising himself on his toes, Micah peered through a wide, leaded window into a long room where two rows of clerks sat on high stools behind high desks. The head of each clerk was inclined attentively over his work. At the end of the room, behind a desk set on a raised dais, Murdoch's tall, thin assistant, Barnaby Falco, was talking to a visitor. It would go hard to pass your life in that office cell, Micah thought.

"Come along." Bilby led him through an alley into the cobbled courtyard of Murdoch's warehouse.

Three young men sat on a loading platform swinging their legs to a tune one played on a jew's-harp.

"This here's Micah Heath," Bilby said. Pointing to the man with the jew's-harp, he said, "Bill Young." He pointed to the man on the left. "Otto Zeiman." And to the man on the right. "Si Poletski."

Their hair was closely cropped and they wore heavy boots and loose sailor pants and jackets. Zeiman was blond and florid, Poletski dark and swarthy, while Young was heavily tanned to the roots of his sun-bleached hair.

"Mornin', woodsy," Young said, swinging off the platform and strolling toward him. The others followed.

"Mornin'," Micah muttered.

Bilby vaulted onto the platform and went into the warehouse.

The three closed around Micah, staring at him. He kept his gaze fixed between Young's eyes. Poletski's right hand flashed and Micah ducked. Poletski, grinning, held his cap by its foxtail.

Backing slowly to the warehouse wall, he rested his rifle there and then walked toward Poletski. "Give me my cap," he said.

"Get it," Poletski replied, still grinning.

Micah rushed, dodged Poletski's upthrust knee, and spun him. He could not throw him, however, and they grappled, muscles straining until Poletski suddenly shook himself, like a dog coming out of water. A sharp pain stabbed Micah's face, the bright morning turned dark. He was stretched on the cobbles, blinking back the sunlight, while Poletski stood over him, laughing, his right fist still balled.

A wave of anger broke over him at the realization that they fought free style with no regard for fall rules. He rolled fast from Poletski and bounded to his feet, knife drawn in his right hand. His wrist numbed and the knife clattered to the cobbles. Young, sprung from nowhere, held his wrist and roared in his face, "A knife ain't a fist, woodsy!" He swung his left into Young's chin, rocking him back several steps, and rushed him, fists flailing, furiously determined to destroy that fixed smile. Twice he landed blows on the face before Young lowered his head and drove in. Grappling with him, then, Micah threw him. He flung himself on him, thumbs ready to gouge in his great rage.

A sudden pain racked his back and the morning grew dark again. Zeiman was shouting and laughing in his ear. Then he found himself pinioned prone on the cobbles, with the faces of Young, Poletski and Zeiman pressed close around him. He writhed and then grew still as Zeiman jabbed his thumbs deeper into his spine and Poletski twisted his arm harder.

"Shear the lamb afore ya skin him," Young cried.

Tears of rage sprang to his eyes.

Somewhere Bilby called in a cheerful tone, "Come about, gentlemen, come about."

"We daren't, Cap'n," Young replied. "Our hooks is full o' this young squid."

"Micah"—Bilby stood there, upside down, his hands on his knees—"what will ye do if these gentlemen friends of mine let you up?"

"Kill 'em!" he cried.

"Vas iss he?" Zeiman asked.

"Irish, I reckon," said Young.

"Scot," Bilby said.

"Same t'ing," Poletski said.

"Iss not." Zeiman patted Micah's back affectionately. "Iss vorse, like Cherman. Big, big hate to death in Scotch and Cherman."

"Micah," said Bilby, "what will you do if I command you to get up and not lay a hand on these friends of mine?"

He closed his eyes, thinking that some day, somehow, he'd even this unfair score. But Bilby said "command," and he was Bilby's to command. He opened his eyes.

"Come about," Bilby said and the men released him and got to their feet. He rose slowly, staring at Bilby.

The captain gazed at him shrewdly with his single eye. "Listen to me, boy. I talked of profit. Then profit from this if you will. Ye're a cocky young one, like all the young. You honestly think there's no man or thing as you couldn't best, don't ye?"

Micah lowered his head. He never had thought of it before. Probably it was true. Not probably, for it was true that in his mind, if not always in deed, he believed that he could conquer anything—horse or man or all the western never lands.

"Don't you?"

He nodded slowly and said indistinctly, "Yes, sir."

"And you see you can't. There's things a boy ain't equal to, such as three grown men. And there's things nobody's equal to, such as unfair advantages. That's what business is full of—unfair advantages. And business, which is life, is a thing you can study with profit—if you will. I asked these men to take unfair advantage of you for your profit—if you will. Note that they fight well without hating. Learn that, you must learn that, if you work for me." He clapped his hands on his belly. "Now, ye've a choice. You can walk out yonder alley and go back to Murdoch's farm. Or you can come along with us. What will it be?"

Micah looked slowly from face to face. There was no cause to hate them. He believed, dimly, that he was about to begin understanding something that would forever elude him if he turned back to the farm. Freedom, he thought, was a far more complicated matter than a slip of paper.

"I'll go along with you," he said to Bilby.

"Gut poy!" Zeiman slapped his back. "Iss a gut poy!"

He shook hands with each. They handed him his knife and cap and rifle. They dusted him off, and Young said, "Come have a spot o' somethin' warmin', Mike."

"I'd welcome a dish of tea," Micah replied.

"Tea!" exclaimed Young. "Tea! . . . Tea!"

The three roared with laughter until Bilby, smiling at Micah, said in a low voice, "There ain't a thing wrong with tea, boy. They's only right with it. Bless these thirteen colonies that they're so sot on their tea. It's the beverage of liberty. To drink tea is the right of every mortal who can afford it. To put a thruppence tax on it is the wrong of a government far across the sea that *we* never elected. So there's little of that government's East Inja Company taxed tea drunk these days. *We* drink tax-free Dutch tea."

"I've heard John Tout tell how they bribe customs collectors to let in the Dutch tea," Micah said.

"Bribe!" Bilby raised his eye with a pious expression. "Never mention that word, boy. It ain't ever used in business. Business understands as how every man has a natural right to exchange his property with whomever he pleases and where he can make the most advantage of it. It happens that the Philadelphia customs has lately raised the rate of exchange so high that there ain't advantage in it. You understand?"

"No, sir."

"Between us, then, the customs has got too greedy and aim to take a merchant's profit out of the beverage o' liberty. So how must we get our tea?"

"Smuggle it, I reckon," Micah said.

"Shhh!" Bilby winked at him. "*Never* mention that word. It's only a kind of business." He leaned toward him. "The business you're in with us now."

VII

ONCE, in July, as Kathy waited for her father outside his office, she saw Micah driving a covered wagon up Front Street. She started to call to him and then checked herself, recalling that she had said she would not recognize him. He remembered, for he did not speak or smile. There was something annoying about the way he stared at her, she thought, as she sat in the chaise.

Their gazes locked and hers demanded that he lower his. But he did not, and she would not, and so they stared combatively until she grew angry. What right had he to stare so at her? He looked—different. He looked older and he sat with a kind of careless grace, as if he were a gentleman of leisure and capacity driving a chaise instead of a bound boy driving a creaking old wagon. As he turned the wagon into the warehouse alley, she craned around despite her determination not to watch him. From the tail board of the wagon a rough-looking man wearing sailor's garb grinned at her insolently.

When her father climbed into the chaise, she said in a low voice, "I saw Micah Heath, Papa. What is he doing?"

"I know no Micah Heath." He smiled. "Nor do you, Kathy. I've heard of a Micah Heath in the employ of an acquaintance of mine, a Captain Bilby. He's said to be a good worker."

She saw Micah again one afternoon the following October. She was riding up High Street with Sally Mifflin and Sally's maiden aunt, Miss Mirabelle Conyngsby, who was a perfect chaperone because she was near-sighted and almost stone-deaf.

"Look," Sally whispered. "No, don't look now, but there's the most handsome boy staring at you."

Kathy looked out of the Mifflin chariot at Micah.

"Don't stare, don't stare," Sally whispered, and giggled. "You minx, Kathy, you stare so boldly. How do you have the nerve? Do you know him?"

"I never saw him before," Kathy said distinctly. And she thought, as she stared at him, that she never really had seen him thus before. He had grown taller and his hair and skin had darkened. He looked strong and quick and— She could not think of an exact word that described him.

"Kathy!" Sally almost writhed in an ecstasy of amusement and embarrassment. "If anybody sees you they'll think you a—a hoyden. I wonder who he is. He's not a gentleman."

"He certainly is not."

"And he can't be apprenticed in trade because he wears no apron."

"Rabble," Kathy said. "Just one of the rabble."

"But you stared at him so. S–suppose he—he'd— Well!"

"Attacked us?" Kathy asked in a tone she carefully made innocent-sounding.

"*Kathy!*" Sally held her handkerchief to her eyes. Like all the Mifflins, she was a Quaker, and Quakers presumably never thought of such things.

"Deport yourselves as ladies," said Miss Mirabelle Conyngsby in the flat tone of the deaf. "Deport yourselves. Compose yourselves. We're passing up High Street." She blinked about owlishly. "Ain't we?"

Kathy had a pretty good notion of what happened when a man attacked a woman. She had often speculated on it, but she never could decide how a woman must feel about it. Frightened, of course. Terrified. Swooning. But apart from that, how would you *feel*?

"Good deportment," said Miss Mirabelle, "the fruit of pure thoughts, gentle manners, a becoming modesty."

Sally whispered, "I never even thought of such a thing as you just mentioned."

What a lie, Kathy thought. But Sally need never worry about a man attacking her. She was too plain. She was thin and bony, her nose was rather long, and her short upper lip never quite closed over her prominent front teeth. Yet she was a good-natured, intelligent, warmhearted girl. Everyone liked her, though it was doubtful that any man ever would like her enough to attack her physically. Certainly Kathy liked her. More important to Kathy, however, was the fact that Sally, a Mifflin, actually adored her. A Mifflin definitely was somebody in society, while a Murdoch was practically nobody. Perhaps the Mifflins were not as important as the Hamiltons, Allens and Shippens, the Galloways, Tilghmans and Chews. But—

"Sally, I *know* you never thought of such a thing as I just mentioned. Neither have I."

Sally smiled at her. "Yes, you have. And so have I. Not with fear, which I just assumed in fun, but with an utter hopelessness."

Linking arms, they rocked with laughter.

"Girls, girls," said Miss Mirabelle, "do deport yourselves like ladies."

Micah was far behind them now, and Kathy forgot him in the anticipation of this afternoon's garden party at Clifton Hall, the home of the mysterious, rich Scot, Captain Charles Cruikshank. The horses' hoofs clopped faster as they left the pavement behind them. The city dwindled in the warm, golden glow of Indian Summer that radiated from the pale blue sky and was reflected by flaming ash and beech and maple where the land dipped toward the Schuylkill.

"A garden party in October," Kathy said. "There never was such a thing. It might have rained or come on frost."

"Then we should have stayed inside," said Sally. "But it didn't and Uncle Tom says that Captain Cruikshank knew it wouldn't because he spends half his time studying the weather."

"Will your Uncle Thomas be there?"

Sally nodded. "Everybody will be there—those who have been invited before so as they can see it again and those who've not so as they can say they have."

It did not seem possible to Kathy that Clifton Hall could be more elegant than Fort Hill, Thomas Mifflin's great house above the Falls of the Schuylkill, which she'd visited with Sally on several occasions. Recalling his gallery filled with paintings and antiquities and the elaborate gardens which were so extensive that Mr. Mifflin said he must raise a special windmill to pump water to them, she wondered if she ever would live in such a house.

"I wonder *why* Captain Cruikshank is inviting so many for tea."

"I think because he wants to be a peacemaker," Sally said. "The world has quieted this year and he wants it to stay so. I listened to Uncle Tom talking about it. He says that nobody is really divided over the fact that the Parliament is legislating against *us*. We're only divided over how far we'll go in resisting the Parliament. Uncle Tom says that the Proprietary Party doesn't really want to resist Parliament much at all. Next to them the liberal members of the Quaker Party—the men like Mr. Dickinson who will soon control the Assembly, Uncle Tom says—*they* favor more resistance than the Proprietaries. But Uncle Tom believes that in time *his* group—men like Mr. Reed and Charles Thomson—*they'll* take over the Whig leadership and *then* they'll make the Parliament see the light."

"Fola-dora-dola." Kathy had scarcely listened to her. "Why do you bother your head about it, Sally?"

"Because I think it's *interesting*." Sally frowned at her. "And surely you must too. Your father certainly concerns himself in it the way he stands with Uncle Tom and his group."

It was astonishing to learn so casually from Sally where Papa stood in the maze of politics. She tried to listen to him, but his remarks about politics usually baffled her. And then, with instinctive insight, she thought, What Papa *says* is not where Papa always *stands*. He always stands where the *money* is. Bless him, he'll buy us a Clifton Hall or a Fort Hill some day.

"That's why Captain Cruikshank has invited the important from all groups to Clifton Hall today," Sally said. "He wants peace so that nothing ever disturbs him in studying the weather and raising his peacocks and collecting his antiquities."

So she and Papa had been invited to Clifton Hall because Papa bore some weight in politics. What a ninny she was. She had believed they were invited because—well, because she was beautiful and popular. Now she was glad that Papa was absent on business in New York and she was able to go without him.

"The only people who won't be there today are the *radicals*." Sally lowered her voice. "They're no account, of course. Men like Timothy Matlack and David Rittenhouse. Presbyterians, westerners and such. And do you know what I've heard tell, Kathy? All the *Jews* are radicals. They're all really *Levellers*."

Kathy dimly remembered hearing that there had been a revolution in England long ago when, for a time, Levellers had deposed the King. It was a rather shocking thought, though not as shocking to her as it seemed to Sally. "Fola-dora-dola," she said vaguely.

She wondered again if Alex had been invited to Clifton Hall. She hoped that he would be there, for today she would dismiss him with a cold nod. She had seen him quite frequently since he went to work in Mr. Reed's law office last January. He often appeared in the homes she and Papa visited and they had invited him to their house. Each time she saw him her heart rose and lay down on its other side. And each time he saw her he came to her, smiling and surely studying her overturned heart. He engaged her, he fluttered her, and then, as inevitably as he was drawn to her, he was drawn away. Suddenly he would be gone and she was left feeling as alone as she had once at the farm when she ran through the empty house seeking someone to cling to in a summer evening thunderstorm. It was maddening.

Did he think she was too young? Oh, she could tell him a thing or two if ever in this life she could talk forthrightly to anyone, which it seemed that she could not. She was eighteen. She had long been a woman. She sometimes had strange dreams in which he did strange things that brought her awake, wondering, but never afraid. What was there about her, then, that he instinctively feared?

A hundred times since Christmas she had vowed to banish him from her mind. When banished, however, he invariably returned unsummoned. Then she would tell herself that he was not such a great catch. Handsome, yes, but so were numerous others. A gentleman, yes, but not as fine a gentleman as a hundred she could name. He was not as remarkable in the city as he was in the country. For what was he, really? A lawyer in the office of Mr. Joseph Reed; the son of a big, noisy, red-faced countrywoman who loved horses above everything else and frankly declared she knew not how she had served as dam to such a colt. True, his father had been a Philadelphia lawyer. True, Alex had graduated from the college at Princeton when he was fifteen and had studied law at the Middle Temple and made the Grand Tour. Nevertheless, he was without position and without fortune. Then why did so many people listen attentively to what he said?

As the Mifflin chariot rolled up the west bank of the Schuylkill, Kathy told herself that she positively would snub him if he appeared today.

They climbed a gravel drive between high rows of boxwood and suddenly emerged before Clifton Hall. The great house, which seemed to shine in the warm afternoon sun, made Kathy catch her breath.

"Kathy!" Sally dug her with an elbow.

She accepted the upthrust hand of a liveried footman and stepped lightly from the chariot. As she touched the ground she thought, I *am* a queen. For a moment Clifton Hall seemed remote and she was aware only of herself, as if she were an enormous loving eye scrutinizing slim satin slippers and flowered silk petticoats and hoopskirt and tightly laced stomacher ornamented with gold braid. She knew that her golden hair, pyramided high over a wire network in the mode, gleamed in the sun. She blinked her eyes wide and arched in her back as she lowered her silk shawl exactly two inches off her left shoulder. Quickly licking her lips, she opened them slightly and held them so, her smile fixed. There! Might she live through eternity looking exactly this way.

"Kathy," said Sally, "you look devastating this afternoon."

Aware of the world, now that she knew the world was aware of her, she turned slowly as a servant bearing a tipstaff bowed deeply and said, "Mesdames, your host, Captain Cruikshank, attends on your presence in the summerhouse." He gestured grandly toward a gravel path which crossed a wide, closely cropped lawn, where peacocks strutted, to a large and curiously cupolaed pavilion.

Numerous guests moved leisurely out there, and the sound of music rose on the still, warm air. Liveried servants darted everywhere.

"Isn't it exciting?" whispered Sally.

It was exciting, Kathy thought. But she said in a low voice, "Foladora. I'm a *radical!*"

Sally giggled. "Some day, Kathy, you'll turn the world upside down with the way you carry on."

It was a strange thing for Sally to say, Kathy thought, for it was exactly what she would like to do. "The World Turned Upside Down" was the haunting tune the Scottish soldier pipers played. The world as she would turn it upside down would find her forever here on its upside, on such a high, bright greensward, among such gay, bright people.

Captain Cruikshank was vastly disappointing, for he looked old and haggard and nervous, but he was "charmed" to meet her and she must see his peacocks and his statues of Fame and Mercury and walk the vistas and peer through the spyglass at the city. Fola-dora! A few moments ago it had seemed probable to her that every bachelor was conquerable, but now she thought that some bachelors—even rich, famous bachelors—were not worth the effort of conquest.

With Sally trailing in her wake, she was carried away on a wave of young men whom she knew. As was their wont, they quickly formed their court about her, their current queen—a self-appointed fool bouncing jests off a self-appointed chamberlain, a couple of self-effacing young ladies in waiting, a guard of honor, and every man would be the king. But she, encouraging all, encouraged none, and so maintained the balance of her power. It was a game, elaborate and formal in design, beneath the seemingly careless battledore and shuttle of their talk. They called it conversation, but it was not; none except she was permitted to speak at length, though she was too wise to expose her ignorance about nearly every subject in the world except the one dearest to her heart: how to draw and hold the rapt attention of a number of young men.

Servants passed glasses of wine and silver platters of tiny sweet cakes. The hum of conversation rose louder and the musicians outside the summerhouse played faster. Even as she felt that she could effortlessly maintain her court thus forever, she began to feel a vague boredom. She found herself looking about for Alex. She did not want to see him, she told herself, but she would like *him* to see *her* surrounded by so many beaux.

Eventually she came upon him unexpectedly as she toured the gardens with her court. They were gaping up at Captain Cruikshank's obelisk while Tench Howe, the court chamberlain of the day, lectured tediously about it. She started on.

Alex stood alone on the other side, fists planted on his waist, scowling up at the obelisk.

"Kathy, good afternoon." He did not bow; he did not even look at her. "Tench," he called, "I've been listening to your lecture. You've told us everything except what an obelisk is *for*."

Tench smiled. "Candidly, Alex, I haven't a notion."

"Then I'll tell you. It's a symbol of power. Roman emperors adored 'em and transported 'em to Rome from any place they could find 'em. I say that I've heard of emperors transporting obelisks to Rome, but never before"—he raised a hand toward Captain Cruikshank's obelisk—"have I heard of an emperor transporting one from Rome to troubled Galilee."

His metaphor dawned on her slowly. When she understood, she was disturbed that he had spoken critically of the conservative Cruikshank. But Tench laughed and applauded as did the others, except for one of the Hamilton boys who turned and stalked away.

"I understand there's a figure of Apollo hereabouts," Alex said. "Kathy, would you and Sally like to examine it?"

"Alex!" Tench spoke quickly. "It's in that—uh—labyrinth, but I understand it—"

"Then you've seen it, Tench, and presumably you and the other gentlemen of the—er—retinue do not care to join us."

There was a forcefulness about him that could leave her breathless, she thought as they walked between the labyrinthine hedges shaped from dwarf poplar and spruce. At last they emerged into a small square. There, in marble, stood a large figure of Apollo beside a marble tree trunk. My God, she thought, he's *naked!*

"Fascinating," Alex said. "It's a very decent replica of the Apollo Sauroctonus that—"

"*Mister* March!" Sally cried, and fled.

He blinked after her dazedly.

Kathy pressed her handkerchief to her mouth to stifle a scream of laughter. She knew that she should follow Sally as fast as she could.

Each second she lingered here with Alex in the presence of the nude Apollo her reputation for modesty and delicacy would decline in the estimation of those waiting outside. Run, she told herself. But she could not move. She stared hypnotically from Alex to the strong and graceful Apollo, whose right arm curved out and whose left arm curled up, perhaps to kill, perhaps to love.

"The Apollo," she said unsteadily, "he—he has no fig leaf."

He looked uncomprehendingly from her to the marble figure. "But it's the same as the bronze figure in the Villa Albani in Rome. It's youth, it's grace. See, he's about to strike the lizard climbing up the tree."

Unmindful of the lizard, she gazed curiously at Apollo, thinking, He's beautiful.

"My God!" Alex cried suddenly and struck his forehead. "I never should have gone away from here. I stayed away too long. I'd forgotten —I—" His tone became bitter. "How can I ever live out my life here?" Taking her firmly by an arm, he led her back through the labyrinth. "I'll apologize to all assembled, explaining that I did not realize—that—"

"Alex." She halted, gazing at him. "Don't apologize."

"But your reputation—"

"*Damn* my reputation!" she cried. "Don't apologize!"

He gripped her arms tightly, his gaze searching her face. Slowly his eyes widened, as if he found something new in her expression.

"You didn't run away when Sally did," he said with wonder.

Arms crossed on her breast, she napped on her bed at the farm that afternoon of the New Year until sleigh bells awakened her. Her eyes blinked and then she closed her hands on either arm as she remembered Alex's grip. He would be among the guests this afternoon. But, she wondered despondently, would anything really come of it?

There was a tap at the door. "Come in," she said.

Philadelphia Twillow entered on tiptoe and closed the door quietly behind her. "It's time to dress, Miss Kathy, and Mrs. Tout says I might help you. I ironed your dress myself."

Kathy turned her head and smiled. "Did you, Philly?"

What a delightful child, and born to serve. Kathy had observed her closely during this week at the farm. She was quick and quiet and seemingly concerned only for the welfare of others. She did not look like the child who had come out of the western wilderness a year ago. Her chestnut hair shone, her small, pretty face glowed healthfully, and she had grown considerably taller. Boys would notice her.

"The brush is on the dresser, Philly." She turned on her side and swept her long, loosened hair over the pillow. When Philly began gently running the brush through it, she closed her eyes. The child knew the stroke, full and soothing.

"Are you going to put it up on the wire mesh, Miss Kathy?"

"Not today. I'll wear it in a bag, quite out of mode, because I'm going sleigh-riding on the hill."

"I know. John Tout has made new sleighs and greased the runners."

She opened her eyes. "Philly, where do you want to live when you grow up?"

Philly stroked the brush silently for a long time. At last she said, "I don't rightly know, as long as it ain't over west. I reckon I'd like to stay right here."

"How would you like to live in the city?"

"That would be fine, Miss Kathy. Mr. and Mrs. Tout took me and Tom in one summer day and it was powerful exciting."

"Maybe some day you'd like to live in the city and work for me."

The brush hesitated and then resumed. "Yes'm," Philly said in a low voice.

She was almost dozing when Philly said, "That's two hundred strokes, Miss Kathy. You want I should go on?"

"Go on, Philly."

In a moment Philly said, "Miss Kathy?"

"Yes."

"D'you ever see or hear tell of Micah?"

She opened her eyes. "No."

"Oh, me," Philly said. "I'd sure enough like to see him again. He's such a good boy, Miss Kathy. The way he brung Tom and me clean from the Ohio sure was a fine thing."

Kathy yawned. "It must have been an interesting journey."

"It sure was, Miss Kathy. It sure enough was. If'n you ever see him, you tell him I was asking after him, would you, please?"

Kathy smiled. "Yes, Philly. Now, that's enough brushing. Go over to the petticoat line there and I'll tell you what I want to wear. . . ."

Late in the afternoon, when the crusted snow of the western slopes was as dark blue as the eastern sky, they went to the upper pasture hill. Laughing and shouting, they dragged tiny wooden sleighs behind them.

Alex capered beside Kathy in the van of a dozen young people who had welcomed the chance to leave the elders by the fire. She never had seen him thus before. He was like a boy, drunk on snow and cold winter air, plunging over his leggin' tops in the drifts and hurling snowballs at those who followed.

At the head of the pasture, against the wall of dark woods, he gestured to the slope below and said, "A virgin hill, Kathy, and yours to invade."

"You go first, Alex. I'll follow."

"Then we'll engage in the Swiss style."

Picking up his sleigh and holding it before him, he ran a few steps down the slope and flung himself prone upon it. She watched him as he gained speed. With the sleigh hidden beneath him, he seemed to be flying, down and down and then out over the snow field.

If only she were not a lady, she'd try his style. Sitting down on her sleigh and tucking her skirt and cape about her legs, she pushed off. Her lips compressed until, gaining speed and seized by its excitement, she opened her mouth and shrieked. The world dropped from under her and then, too soon, it caught her up giddily. Now, surely, it would throw her. Her mittened hands gripped the sleigh and first her left heel and then her right steered a twisting course on the hissing snow. She was slowing to a halt just when she wanted to go on forever.

He stood beside her laughing, a stocking cap over one eye, his face red from the wind. They were crying something to each other, but their words did not matter. He caught her hand and they trudged up the hill as others shot down, whooping and shrieking.

He was tireless. "Once more!" he'd cry. And she, as tireless, would reply, "Once more!"

The blue light of afternoon deepened into gray that yellowed as the moon rose in the east. The others drifted back to the house. They were left together at the top of the slope.

This time she said, "Just once more."

"Just once," he said.

"Let's try—" She paused. "Let's try to ride down on the same sleigh."

"Hang on," he said.

He sat behind her, holding her firmly. Her heart raced as she pressed against him and the world dropped from under them. She gripped his legs more tightly and moved her head against his face. They were flying. They tilted and settled, then tilted again and suddenly rose. They were whirling in snow.

They lay, unmoving, his arms still about her. He was saying something; his lips were at her ear, but his voice seemed distant. She would never stir again. But her legs stirred, certainly not of her volition, and tightened around his legs in the snow. Then her whole body stirred, certainly not of her volition, and moved upward against his. In her desire never to stir again she began to tremble.

He was trembling too as he whispered, "My God, Kathy."

She was still, her body's volition in truce with her desire never to move from him. She moved, then, quickly. Rising, she brushed snow off her cape.

He got to his feet slowly and stretched a hand toward her. But he did not try to touch her.

At last she stepped back and said calmly, "It's time we went home."

VIII

ALEX knew why he ran from her. Although extraordinarily beautiful, she was a vain, selfish, demanding girl who would bind a man to her like a slave. She was ignorant, too, and not inclined to try to overcome it. He would have forgiven her ignorance, however, had she not possessed such knowledge of her attractiveness to men.

Bind yourself to the mast, Odysseus, he sometimes told himself wryly. Blind your eyes and wax the ears of all your impulses. For inevitably she would destroy you in her vanity and selfishness and ignorance.

So he fled. After that New Year's Day of 1773 when they fell from the sleigh, however, he was more hotly pursued. Not by her; he tried in vain to detect her active pursuit. Worse, after that evening he was pursued by his own sure knowledge of her passion and how much he desired her.

But he would not be snared in his own trap, that dream of passion consummated with her. Like Odysseus, he told himself, you have a mast, a ship, a destination. He prided himself on being a man of reason, and it was not reasonable for him to expect that marriage to a vain, selfish, demanding girl would result in anything but fleeting physical pleasure. Marriage must involve the exchange of thought and emotion as well as the passion of animal coupling. Yes indeed, sir!

For one thing, Kathy did not try to understand the times. He, on the other hand, believed that he did. In the early spring of 1772, for example, he had believed it possible to reconcile the differences with England. A year later he was certain that reconciliation was impossible.

The calm of 1772 had been shattered in June when eight boatloads of men from Providence burned the customs schooner *Gaspée* in Narragansett Bay. The sparks had leaped to Massachusetts when it was announced that Governor Hutchinson and the Massachusetts judges thenceforth would receive their salaries from the Crown, thereby making both the executive and the judiciary independent of the people's power of the purse. In November a Boston town meeting, summoned by Sam Adams, created a committee to communicate Boston's aggrieved position to the world. In March 1773 the sparks ignited the Virginia House of Burgesses, which proposed that all the colonies appoint Committees of Correspondence to resist the policy of Parliament.

Alex, having no doubt as to where he stood, was stirred by each colonial act, however ill-conceived or willful, that sought to redress the unquestionably ill-conceived and willful acts of the British government toward the colonies. If he had possessed the means, he sometimes thought, he would rather have lived in London than in Philadelphia. Yet when he had sat in the visitors' gallery of Commons listening to the debates, he had known that he never could consider himself an Englishman. He was a Pennsylvanian, or, as his fellow students at the Middle Temple at first somewhat contemptuously referred to him—an American. The description came to delight him, for it had a bold outlander ring, like Chinese or Indian or Russian.

Once, when he jestingly called Kathy an American, she replied coldly, "Pray don't speak in riddles, Alex. What is an American? I am a Philadelphian."

Not a Pennsylvanian, mind you. But a Philadelphian.

"While posing riddles, Kathy, what is a Philadelphian?"

"A Philadelphian," she said slowly, "is a person of superior breeding with superior opportunities."

"Superior opportunities to attain what end?" he asked.

"Oh, Alex, you can be so worrisome." And she had spoken of something else, something trivial.

It pleased him, as it did M. Voltaire, to think of himself as a citizen of the world. Yet Voltaire was a Frenchman first, which gave him a leg up on being a world citizen. But to be an American was not like being a Frenchman, for all the world knew what it meant to be a Frenchman while no two persons had yet quite agreed on what it meant to be an American.

"History must work on the word for a spell," he said to Kathy.

"What?" She stared at him blankly.

"On the meaning of the word American."

"Oh, Alex!" She raised a hand in despair.

Perhaps she was wise to question nothing and simply think of herself as a Philadelphian. He knew what she meant. A Philadelphian was one of a few hundred ladies and gentlemen in a city of thirty-five thousand souls. A Philadelphian was a person with English ancestors who adequately disguised the trade whereby he had attained sufficient means to live in a manner acceptable to similarly disguised and yet sufficiently recognizable Philadelphians.

I am a Philadelphian, Alex thought, and I hope some day to be something greater. But to Kathy being a Philadelphian was the ultimate end.

He knew what he was and where he stood in his times. He was for "liberty" as opposed to "tyranny." Yet what did "liberty" mean, for instance, to a man like Timothy Murdoch? It meant freedom to pursue his goal of accumulating wealth without the tax and trade restrictions of established government. This was the "liberty" bandied by merchants, planters, land speculators and manufacturers. Opposed to it was the "liberty" conceived by English merchants, speculators and manufacturers to pursue their goal of wealth without restrictions from the selfish, tyrannical colonists.

"It's a *mercantile* situation," he said once to Joseph Reed.

Reed, fingering his high brow and staring at him gravely, replied, "These are *mercantile* times, Alex. And I, for one, am glad. Business ameliorates everything. Business, as opposed to the mob, is conservative and brings about change slowly. Without it there is no stability. The Greeks would have been happier if business had been a strong force in their time. They overthrew their tyrants and then, much worse, enthroned the mob of the ecclesia. The Romans, lacking the influence of business, abandoned a republic for a military dictatorship that eventually led to a terrible rule of personal despotism. And think how rashly our ancestors acted in a religious fervor that might better have been directed into the less sanguinary channels of trade and commerce. They decapitated a Stuart and enthroned a Long Parliament so immeasurably more despotic that they were forced to revolt again. The head of a Cromwell for the head of a Stuart—and then another Stuart to the throne."

Perhaps business did ameliorate everything. Nevertheless, there was widespread abasement of "freedom" here. The word should not be so widely bandied in a time when you could buy a Negro slave for thirty pounds on Front Street, when for twenty pounds you could buy the services of a hapless white child until he reached his majority. And was there any philosophically defensible justice in the fact that ninety per cent of the taxable population of Philadelphia was disenfranchised by a suffrage qualification of fifty pounds personalty or a fifty-acre freehold? Those peoples' notions of "liberty" were quite different from that of Timothy Murdoch.

Such thoughts could not be expressed in most of the homes Alex visited or he would have been socially ostracized for what he actually was: a radical. Few knew that he and Reed were ardent Sons of Liberty. If it were widely known in this conservative city, their practice would dwindle instead of growing. Business again, he'd tell himself wryly when he felt hypocritical because he disguised his radicalism.

In March, after word was posted north that the Virginia House of Burgesses had proposed the formation of Committees of Correspondence in all the colonies, Alex and a dozen other leading Sons of Liberty conferred for half a night at Reed's home, making plans on how to arouse Philadelphia from its apathy. It was agreed that a torchlight procession should be held the following night, a Saturday—a delicate way of saying, "Stir up the mob, such as it is," Alex thought.

He left his office at two o'clock that afternoon and ate lightly at the Bull's Head on Third Street, where he lived. A friend who ate with him, James May, left to visit a pretty seamstress on Walnut Street with whom he was having an affair. He carried a copy of *Pamela* under an arm.

"I read to her for an hour, Alex." He winked. "The most glowing passages. It puts her in the mood. She's totally illiterate, but she adores *Pamela*. Farewell all until tomorrow."

Watching him go, Alex rather envied him. He was reminded of his own affair in Rome with the Contessa di Falcari, who had been both literate and articulate. How could one possibly have an enduring liaison with a woman who could not read? The trouble with the literate and articulate women he knew in Philadelphia was that they were either ugly, conclusively married or inconclusively involved with other men.

Then he found himself thinking of Kathy. A brief affair would cool their blood. It was, of course, impossible. Unlike many men, he had no desire to indoctrinate young virgins into the mysteries of love. Dr. Franklin, always sagacious, had put it very well in London when he told him that a mature, experienced woman was the best companion for a man both in the drawing room and the bedroom. Even had he been inclined to attempt an affair with Kathy (and you are inclined or you would not dwell on it so, he told himself), they lacked both the time and the place to make it possible. She, like every esteemed young lady in the city, was as jealously watched as ever the Capulets had guarded their Juliet. And that was another trouble with Philadelphia.

Timothy Murdoch had invited him and others to his home this evening. He would not go. But he would go. The truth is, he thought, I can scarcely wait to see her, damn my eyes.

He'd enjoy wandering the streets this afternoon and dropping in at the Library Tavern and John Winter's print shop, but he had to work for the cause. The Committee had assigned him the task of writing a dozen leaders in the counties concerning the proposal of the House of Burgesses.

It was dusk when he finished his letters and went out for a stroll. As he walked down Chestnut Street he heard, through the clatter of horses' hoofs on the pavement, the sweet notes of a German flute issuing from the Sign of the Hogarth's Head. The flutist was the old Welshman, William Williams, he realized.

Stepping inside, he saw Williams seated in a corner, peering at his music sheet which was illuminated by a single candle. About him, listening attentively, sat a dozen young men and women who were his students or admirers. Alex recognized the music as the Hallelujah Chorus at the end of the first act of Handel's *Athalia,* sung by Jews who expressed courage under grinding tyranny. After finishing the chorus, Williams wiped his eyes with a huge handkerchief.

"Give us drums and trumpets as well as oboes," he said in his rolling Welsh accent, "and ye'll clearly hear the triumph of liberty." He peered at Alex. "Mr. March, good evening, sir. The pleasure of your company. Pray be seated and—" He paused, head cocked, listening.

Alex heard the sound, a muted rumble like distant thunder.

"The mob," said Williams. "Its tone is D-flat, ladies and gentlemen. Hark." He blew the note on his flute.

It was true; at a distance the mob bore the note of D-flat. As it approached, its tone dropped lower and then was split by shrill pipings. Williams imitated the tones on his flute. Alex went to a leaded window and stared through the wavery glass at the imperfect figures of people running ahead of the mob. He went to the door and opened it.

"Mr. March," called Williams. "I wouldn't step out there, sir."

It was irritating, he thought, that a Philadelphian should fear other Philadelphians. He was tempted to reply that he sympathized with the mob, but he silently stepped outside and closed the door behind him.

They marched in the glare of torchlights, a thundering wave of men and women and children, hoarsely chanting, "Li—berty! . . . Li—berty! . . . Li—berty from ty—ranny!" Alex's neck chilled as he watched them come in the flickering light of torches held aloft.

These people were not like the gin-soaked, starving wretches who rushed from windowless warrens to form the savage mobs of London. Although there were rousters and idlers among them, they were in the main decently clothed and fed. Many wore the red leather aprons of workingmen and apprentices, of clerks and shopkeepers' helpers. A committee's decision was not their reason for marching. What was this spirit abroad in the land that gave so many a notion of liberty?

Somewhere in the front ranks a man roared, "Huzzah, Virginia!" There were ear-piercing whistles and a woman screamed, "The Pennsylvania Assembly is coward!" Now they were jeering the Assembly, and then they began chanting again, "Li—berty! . . . Li—berty!"

Someone cried, "A fribble!" And then something black arched against the glare of torchlights. There was a sharp pain in his head. A man's hairy face loomed enormously large and then faded. He was sinking, his legs powerless to support him, down and down into darkness. . . .

He was being lifted up and then he was inside the inn again, brushing blood from his eyes and staring up from the chair where he sprawled at a strong young face.

"Micah Heath," he said and smiled. "You were with the mob?"

"Yes, Mr. March. Whoever threw that stone at you—"

"Called me a fribble." Alex winced. "That word meaning neither man nor woman, part fop, part poppinjay, part rake, and utterly worthless when it comes to the basic matters of fighting and *doing*. I—"

"Don't talk so much, Mr. March. You—"

"I always talk, Micah. I—"

Then the young ladies and gentlemen were fluttering about him and Micah was gone. A plague on them! They thought that he was *against* the mob instead of *for* it. The irony of it would have made him laugh if his head had not pained him so.

He left the Sign of the Hogarth's Head as soon as he could free himself of those flutterers and returned to the Bull's Head. He would not go to the Murdochs' tonight. But he *had* to go, for word would get about that he had been stoned and no one must think that pain or fear kept him indoors. He would powder his cut forehead and go, bearing this badge of irony that many would think a badge of honor. Such was the nature of society.

Word of what had happened preceded him to the Murdochs', and his arrival caused a flutter that was agonizing to him. Kathy reached him first. If only he were not so overpoweringly aware of her beauty.

"Alex, we hear you were magnificent! They say you stood at the door of Hogarth's and defied them to come on."

"Oh, dear God!" he said.

Her eyes widened. "You're in pain. Sit down over here and elevate your feet. It was wonderful of you to come after such a brave tumult. And you were unarmed, I hear."

"A brave tumult." His smile, he knew, was twisted. "Kathy, don't believe much that you hear and never inflate it. You'd be interested to know I was carried into Hogarth's Head by Micah Heath."

She stepped back. "Who?"

"Micah Heath. Presumably he was in the front rank of the mob. You know him. He—"

"I know no Micah Heath."

He stared at her, baffled. "But—"

"Papa." Murdoch stood there, nodding to Alex. "Do we know a Micah Heath?"

"No," he replied. "Alex, a pleasant evening to you."

"Good evening, sir. But, sir, the Micah Heath I mentioned is your bound boy, the one who displayed such magnificent resourcefulness in bringing those children from the Ohio."

"Oh." Murdoch fingered his chin softly. "Oh, yes, I recall him now. He passed from my—uh—services a year ago into the employ of someone else— What is this about your confronting the mob, Alex? We hear . . ."

They make me ill, Alex thought. He left as quickly as he could.

The spring worked both lethargy and restlessness in him. The land turned green and trees burst forth in clouds of white and pink and olive-gray. But he, it seemed, turned to nothing but the law and burst forth with nothing but his usual confounded rhetoric.

Go, man, and get yourself a wench, he told himself. Get drunk, bay at the moon, and suffer a sunrise remorse or two. Then return to your books, don wig, and plead another case in real estate before the Court of Nisi Prius. The trouble was that his sensibilities were ill-constructed for wenching. Rather, the wench he fancied believed she was a lady. Hearty wenching demanded a hearty, indiscriminate appetite that he apparently lacked; a hearty appetite was never squeamish, but flicked the dead fly from the cooked meat without disgust and ignored the wart on the willing maiden's nose. In wine, too, his taste was moderate, its warm glow never distorting his recognition of an impending aching head. He was left with nisi prius, which was not at all priapic, even in the spring.

He remembered that the life of reason is the life without offense, either given or taken. Thus Aristotle. *Honeste vivere, alterum non laedere.* And reasonable man, knowing that offense is inevitable, although quite unreasonable, must readily accept or tender reasonable amends. Thus, too, Aristotle and the life of reason he identified with the basic nature of the law. But not always thus Alex March.

The law had petrified, he often thought that spring, and he was petrifying with it. For centuries the law had been the command of a sovereign; for centuries that legal sovereignty, with its power over the rules applied in English courts, had been held by king and lords and commons. Now, questioning the capacity for reason in king or lords or commons, Alex questioned sovereignty. And, questioning sovereignty, he questioned the law itself.

He weighed his doubts as he rode forth from Philadelphia early one Sunday morning in May. Reed had sent him out on circuit to plead two defenses in Chester and bring a suit in West Chester. They were dull litigations, involving land again. Usually he rode on circuit with the judges, a politic custom since it never hurt to test the prejudices of a judge and please him if you could. And when the sheriff and justices of the peace met the judge outside the sessions town, as was their custom, it was helpful to be seen in his company. If no one else cared, your client did.

But this time he had decided suddenly, on waking early to a bright, warm Sunday, to visit his mother at the farm and ride on down to Chester sessions tomorrow. He seldom went to the farm which, at the age of twenty-one, he had inherited by primogeniture from his father. Although his name was on the deed, he always felt that his mother owned the farm and the farm owned her.

As he rode up the lane toward the stone house, she yelled to him and strode from the stable, sleeves rolled and skirts kilted to her knees.

"A quaint costume for the Sabbath, Mother." His voice was muffled as she hugged him to her.

Holding him at arm's length, she said, "You're thin and pale from too much penmanship, lamb. Come inside and I'll feed ye."

He grinned at her. "I'm not hungry and I wish you wouldn't refer to me as 'lamb.' It makes me sound prone to fleecing."

She grinned too. "Your wit's your father's, God rest his soul. What brings you here?"

"My genuine affection for you, Mother. The spring too, I presume."

She rested a hand on his arm as they entered the kitchen. "In spite of your glib tongue, Alex, I know the love. And I believe the spring." She sniffed deeply. "*Smell* it!"

When he sat down at the table, she said, "That bold hussy Kathy Murdoch rode over here yesterday."

"She *did?* I didn't know she'd come out to the County."

"Yes, she came to visit me, God knows why, for she hates me like a possum does skunk. Very polite she was. Just a friendly call, she pretending to take interest in the horses. I reckon she's set her cap for you."

"I don't reckon she has, Mother."

Mrs. March turned from the fireplace, arms akimbo. "I'm going to have my say and forever after hold my tongue, Alex. She ain't the right girl for you."

"Why?"

"She just ain't. She's a selfish heart, I vaw. And that's all I'll say. Now hitch up your chair and eat."

It occurred to him in early afternoon that he might easily become a countryman. He was sprawled in a comfortable chair on the porch with his mother after eating a hearty dinner. Legs out, mind slack, he was unaware of much except the hum of May flies and the quiet, rolling land. A calf bawled somewhere and he smiled and closed his eyes.

Yes, he could leave the city forever and become a landsman slow to think beyond the boundaries of his county. It was peaceful here . . .

He dozed and dreamed. He was in a fabulous land. Order, order everywhere, in fields and hedgerows and curving roads. Numbers were written in the sky and people came and went, smiling. He opened his eyes, trying to remember the numbers he had seen in the fleeting dream.

"You smiled." His mother looked at him. "It must've been a good dream."

"It was, but vague."

Mrs. March sighed and resumed sewing. "You know what store I set in dreams. My own have been troubled lately, as before your father died. I smell trouble brewing."

"Trouble is always brewing, Mother, but it doesn't always boil."

She looked at him. "Do you think this will?"

"This? You mean . . ."

"You know I mean the times," she said. "I'm not as buried off here as you would think. I've sharp eyes and ears and I know there's more discontent than ever in my time before. Those that ain't got wants to get, and those who has wants more. It's in the air. Parliament ain't alone to blame. Parliament's just the spout that lets the steam escape the boilin' kettle."

He leaned toward her alertly. "I haven't heard it expressed exactly so, but what you say is true. Perhaps that's what my dream was about. Every man a freeholder. Every man—"

"That's radical talk." She smiled dourly. "Do you speak so among your fine-feathered Philadelphia friends?"

"No."

"Then don't—yet. Just let me speak such pieces. 'Cause it's the way I feel. I've a mind there's going to need some *doing* to set things straight, come late or soon. You bide your time and when it's right, you *do* what's right—for the most people, I mean, not just your Philadelphia friends."

He stared at her, amazed. "To whom have you been talking?"

"Mostly to myself. I'm not much at thinking, as you know, but still I think and, as best I can, I think that a good horse deserves good oats and fair time in pasture. I mean that men and women deserve it too." She leaned toward Alex and lowered her voice. "D'you ever think the times might come to fighting?"

"I doubt it, Mother."

"Hmmm." She looked at him shrewdly. "Well, I wouldn't doubt it, but I'm no thinker. Still, the thought has come to me that worth-while things ain't never won without a struggle."

He closed his eyes, to think but not to sleep. She had told him something very important. Vague dreams never could become reality without courage. Did he have it? He had better have it, if the times required it, or he would live out his days in a turmoil of shame. He could not, after all, become a countryman and live contentedly with himself.

"Heavenly host!" exclaimed Mrs. March. He opened his eyes quickly. "If that ain't boldness for ye." She pointed down the lane to the road.

Kathy, riding Flyswat at a trot, was passing the lane. He found himself on his feet, muttering, "She's not coming in."

"'Course not. The minx don't want you to think she's chasin' you. She wants you to chase her."

He whistled shrilly and waved. Kathy turned her head and raised an arm, but she did not pull up Flyswat.

"I rather think I'll go for a ride," he said indistinctly.

"Oh, God," groaned Mrs. March. "Well, so be it. If ye're bound to go, take Dan. He's fleeter than your mare."

When he reached the road, he pressed Dan into a gallop. As he leaned forward in the saddle, the land flowing under him, he thought, Pursuing now, there's no question of it. The hell with consequences, I've spent too much time thinking of them.

He saw her far ahead as he came over a crest. She looked back and halted Flyswat as he slowed Dan. She wore a mauve habit and a brimless hat that fit her head like a helmet.

Smiling as he drew up beside her, she said, "I had no notion you were in the country, Alex."

"Pray who did you think was whistling and waving to you from my porch?"

She laughed. "A stranger. A forward stranger. No, I recognized you there, but I realized it would seem forward of me to ride to *your* house to call on *you*. I'm just out for a ride on this beautiful afternoon."

"And I. Where are you riding?"

"A circuit, around Willow Brook and home." She touched Flyswat into a walk and smiled over a shoulder. "Will you come?"

"With alacrity. Celerity too."

When they turned onto the narrow wood lane that followed the brook north to the Lancaster Road, she said, "We heard Mr. Reed remarking on the excellence of your work last week at Dr. Rush's house. He said he expects you to become one of the noted lawyers of the Province. It made me proud that I know you. You must enjoy your work very much. What is it like? I mean what do you really do?"

"That's a good question, Kathy. I often wonder myself. The truth is that sometimes I like the work not a bit. It's simply a business, and I don't really like business very much. When I started to study law I expected it would engage me in man's passions, but—"

"Passions?"

"Yes. Hatred, love, murder, lust, greed. Well, I dabble in greed constantly. Law, I've found, is chiefly concerned with the acquisitive passion, the passion for wealth. Law is the instrument by which men seek to seize and hold and increase their personal wealth."

"That is bad?"

He shrugged. "It's human. Everyone—well, nearly everyone—wants to be rich and, fortunately for my profession, a good many feel that a shrewd lawyer can help them attain their goal. Usually he can, too."

"But you feel there are more interesting passions than the passion for wealth?"

"Definitely."

She looked at him levelly. "What are they?"

His heart was beating faster, he realized, as he said, "The passion of a man for a woman which the woman reciprocates."

Her gaze did not falter from his. "I would imagine so. Have you ever been in love, Alex?"

He looked at the brown stream beside them which trailed the green tips of willow branches. Somewhere a robin piped of rain tomorrow. "I have."

"When and with whom?"

Now, he thought. Now, now, now or absolutely never. He reined in and dismounted. Pulling up Flyswat, she looked down at him curiously.

"Let me hand you down and I shall tell you, Kathy."

He lifted his arms and her hands rested on his shoulders. She swung down lightly and his arms passed around her. He saw her eyes closing and her lips parting as her hands gripped the back of his head. When he kissed her, it was as if they were swaying in a strong wind.

"My heart," she whispered, "it's bursting. Here." She moved her left hand and touched her breast.

"Here?" He covered her hand with his.

"Yes." She gripped his hand and drew it fiercely to her breast. "Oh, sweet God!" She pressed herself against him. Her eyes still closed, she ran her tongue along his lips.

Turning his head, he said unsteadily, "How can I wait?"

She opened her eyes. "And how can I?"

Still clinging to her, he said, "I love you, Kathy."

"And I love you and always shall," she whispered. "What are we going to do?"

He hesitated for only a moment. "Learn to wait a while longer, I guess. I'll speak to your father this afternoon."

Why, he wondered, on such a beautiful day did the confounded robin up there keep crying of rain tomorrow?

Timothy Murdoch listened impassively, then rose and paced to the parlor fireplace. He turned, hands clasped behind him, and stared at Alex.

"She is very young," he said. "She will not be nineteen for two months yet."

"I believe, sir, she is old enough to know her own mind."

"She has always known her own mind, Alex." Murdoch did not smile. "And you, presumably, know yours?"

Alex felt himself flushing. It would be easy to hate this man Murdoch whom he never had liked much.

"Under the circumstances, I think it would be wise to wait a time."

"Wait, sir? Am I to assume that you are taking my request under consideration and that you will inform me of your decision at a later date?"

Unclasping his hands, Murdoch spread them in a little gesture. "You don't understand, my boy." He glanced toward the closed parlor door and lowered his voice. "My decision has little to do with it. It is *her* decision, and she will give me no peace until I concur with her." His lips twisted in the effort of a smile. "It was most proper of you to come and speak to me, but you could as well have left it to her. I will tell you candidly that I like you and hear only good reports of you."

"Thank you, sir. But I detect a reservation."

"Since I am being candid, yes. Your prospects are bright, but what of your present circumstances?"

Damn you, Murdoch, he thought. But he said calmly, "I own a farm and am employed at a moderate salary. I am free of debt. Presumably my income will increase if I apply myself to Mr. Reed's practice or possibly launch my own."

"Yes." Murdoch nodded. "The future, as I say, is bright. But we are speaking of the present which so—uh—urgently confronts you now. Naturally a modest dowery goes with Kathy's hand. But I doubt that it would long keep her in the style of living to which she is accustomed."

Alex breathed deeply. "If I follow your line of argument, Mr. Murdoch, you will not flatly say no, but you seek in every possible way to dissuade me. Since you say that you like me, what is your fundamental purpose in this?"

Murdoch, eyelids narrowing as he watched him, actually smiled.

"Joseph Reed estimates you accurately, my boy. Would you be interested in entering business with me?"

"No, sir."

"Then, sir, let me say that I know many capable men of means who *do* seek Kathy's hand in marriage and *are* interested in joining enterprises with me."

"But does Kathy care anything about any of them?"

Murdoch sighed. "We argue full circle, Mr. March. We return to the point that Kathy is only eighteen, which is scarcely a proper age for a child to decide with whom she would live for the rest of her life."

Alex stood up. "I understand, then, that you decline to give your consent. I shall so inform Kathy."

"Please!" Murdoch raised a hand. "I have not declined my consent. I have merely said let us wait a year or so."

"Very well. I shall inform Kathy that you will render a decision in a year or so."

"Mr. March!" Murdoch's voice rose. "I am quite capable of discussing this matter with Kathy. You burst in here on a Sunday afternoon as if—"

"I did not *burst* in, sir! I rode to the door with your daughter and was admitted by one of your servants."

"I beg your pardon, sir, in my choice of language. I—"

"And I beg yours, sir, if my construal was hasty. I do not wish to agitate you further. I shall withdraw, if you will see me to your door, and not seek out Kathy until you have had the opportunity to discuss with her your—"

There was a tap at the door. They stood, motionless, staring at each other. Then Murdoch cleared his throat and said, "Who's there?"

The door opened and Kathy entered, smiling. "Papa! You've heard our good news?" She took Alex's hand. "Isn't it wonderful?"

Murdoch lowered his head and his shoulders slumped. "Kathy," he muttered, "I . . ."

"Yes, Papa?"

"I feel that you're very young for such a momentous decision."

"Fola-dora-dola!" She waved a hand at him.

"I feel," Murdoch continued doggedly, not looking directly at her, "that Alex is a fine young man, but the world is filled with excellent men who—"

"La de da de da! I've seen all the men in the world and I've only ever loved Alex." She gripped his hand tightly and then released it. Going to her father, she kissed him lightly on the forehead. "There, I wager you've said all the things that good papas are supposed to say, how we're too young and poor as church mice and all the rest. Now that you've said it and learned that our minds are made up, we'll begin tomorrow to talk of a wedding."

IX

"FINISHED," growled Captain Bilby one evening the following October. "Heave me keel cut and fire and scrub and pay my bottom! The Sons of Liberty hate tea."

He slammed his tankard on the oak table in the small back room of the Crooked Billet Tavern and scowled at the four who had been waiting more than an hour for him.

"There's nought for me but sea again," he said. "Weevil biscuit and sour beef. Sleet and fog and the Admiralty. A man who says he likes the sea's an ass, but now it's short shrift ashore. First it's Lord North and the goddamn East Inja Company underselling our twenty shillin' a pound tea at ten shillin'. And then it's the Sons of Liberty refusing to drink any kind of tea."

Bilby was an ardent Son of Liberty, Micah knew. An ardent Son of Liberty himself, he nevertheless understood the captain's irritation. Business was business, and for a year and a half it had been Bilby's to smuggle Dutch tea, at a profit, for Murdoch, who sold it at a larger profit. Everybody, down to the remote tea drinker, profited in the complicated transaction—except the Crown and the East India Company. Besides being profitable, it was patriotic to the cause of liberty.

Lord North's Tea Act, which retained the threepence tax first imposed by Charles Townshend, had disturbed this happy harmony of profit and patriotism. Smugglers, Sons of Liberty all, could not compete with the flood of cheap East India Company tea released by North to save the Company—or, more accurately, the Government's equity in the Company. Even merchants who did not deal in smuggled goods had become alarmed; give the Company a colonial monopoly in tea, they argued, and there would follow monopoly of wine and silk and—everything! Then where would the profits be? The only recourse, said the Sons of Liberty, was to proscribe the drinking of all tea, both taxed and smuggled.

"Finished," Bilby growled again, sinking onto a stool and staring at his tankard of ale. "Friends have become enemies. They close-hauled me on Front Street an hour ago and warned me the jig is up. 'Go straight,'

Charles Thomson told me. Go straight where? To sea, I reckon. God-damnation!"

They were men whom Micah scarcely knew. The hard core of the Sons of Liberty was a well-organized group—and shifty too; it did not march with the mob. "Let the mob march," they'd say to Bilby and a dozen others. And Bilby would say to Micah and Young and Zeiman and Poletski, "Saturday night, boys. The Boston Committee needs sympathy."

Now Micah knew how a mob was formed and why it was instigated. Its purpose was worthy, he believed, for it served to remind the powerful how much injustice there was in the world.

Someone knocked at the door.

"What?" shouted Bilby.

Barnaby Falco, Murdoch's tall, thin chief clerk, opened the door and thrust his long face into the room. "Captain Bilby, a word with you, sir."

Muttering to himself, Bilby got to his feet and followed Falco out.

"It's sea for me," Young said. "You, Mike?"

Micah shook his head. He had a better plan, one he had harbored for almost a year and a half now while waiting to be legally free. He was lighting out west. Bilby had paid him some small wages, even though he was a bound servant. He'd saved almost five pounds. He would not wait longer to be declared legally free; he'd free himself by running away.

Still, he'd miss Bilby and Young and Zeiman and Poletski. Once you'd learned to work with others, it was not quite as easy to go your way alone. He'd also miss the savor of living just beyond the limits of the law. They had a clearly defined enemy: the King's customs officers.

Until two years ago Murdoch and nearly all other Philadelphia merchants had dealt in smuggled goods as easily as the New York merchants, whose luck still held. They had simply bribed the customs and landed their goods unmolested. Then the Crown had named a new customs officer to the port of Philadelphia, a Scot named McGill who was appallingly incorruptible. He actually believed that it was his duty to uphold the law and collect its prescribed taxes. He and his staff, who were incorruptible only because McGill watched them closely, roamed the waterfront like inquisitive terriers. In their customs sloop they bobbed far down the river, nosing up inlets, boarding ships, harassing captains, irritating owners, and generally creating a public nuisance in the private path of free enterprise.

Bilby and his men had outwitted McGill with comparative ease. But they had enjoyed enough narrow escapes from the indefatigable customs officers to give zest to their work. They had to remain alert and uncommunicative about their business and employ a variety of disguises. They knew, however, that they could not have succeeded without the tacit support of their fellow Sons of Liberty, whom they repaid in numerous ways —carrying messages and supplying information and helping to turn out the mob. Now, without the organization's support, their days of smuggling were ended.

Sitting there in the back room of the Crooked Billet Tavern, waiting for Bilby to return from his conference with Falco, Micah thought how much he'd miss this life. No longer would they drive out singly in wagons long before dawn to meet in a prearranged place down-river. No more expeditions to the Head of Elk and the lonely bays where ships stood off awaiting their fire signals before unlading contraband by small boat. He'd come to love the smell of salt water and the hot pine barrens of Jersey and Delaware in summer. Rivers, sand, marshes, gulls, ships, the sudden dazzling blue of sun-drenched sea beyond the capes when you climbed a dune. . . . He'd miss it all, though never as keenly as he had missed treading the endless, silent, blue-black roll of the western country.

The door opened and Bilby walked in slowly. He stood for a moment, rubbing his big pock-marked nose thoughtfully before he came to the table. "Who's for one more go?" he asked in a low voice.

"Go?" Young stared at him. "Go where, Cap'n?"

"Never you mind," Bilby replied. "It's Murdoch's notion and he vows it's safe. They's fi'e pounds for every man in it."

Five more pounds would make a heap of difference in outfitting himself to go west, Micah thought. He did not hesitate. "On," he said.

Bilby winked his single eye at him. "I'll remember that, lad."

"Ja," said Zeiman. "I go."

Poletski and Young nodded.

"Then take your wagon-loads of hay and go," Bilby said. "The usual two-hour intervals. Heath first at ten o'clock. Then Zeiman. Poletski next. And then you, Young. I'll meet you on horseback tomorrow at the Harp and Crown this side of Bristol Ferry."

"Bristol!" Young exclaimed. "That's *up*-river."

"Aye," said Bilby, "I see ye know where Bristol is."

"But—"

"But no buts, Young. You're on?"

"On?" Young got to his feet, grinning. "It's crime to take the money."

Toward dawn, after driving eighteen miles through drizzling rain, Micah turned in at the Harp and Crown. A large inn, on a knoll close to the Delaware, it was astir with sleepy teamsters shouting for breakfast and going noisily to the stable.

After glancing at the confusion of the common rooms, he unhitched his horses and led them to the stable where he rubbed them down and fed them oats from his own supply. Then he burrowed into his wagon hay and instantly fell asleep.

A man shouting awakened him. Thrusting his head out of the covered wagon, he saw that it was about noon of a dazzling bright day. Zeiman's and Poletski's unhitched wagons stood nearby. Young was rubbing down his horses in the stable.

"You, there!" The fattest man he had ever seen pointed up at him. "You come to my wedding breakfast!"

Micah blinked at him. An aging man, wearing a bagwig and faded blue woolen, he supported his enormous weight on tiny feet and a heavy gnarled stick. His fat seemed to descend from his cheeks in huge coils; chin after chin eventually swelled into a balloonlike belly.

"You!" He struck the ground with his stick. "Come to the wedding breakfast of Peter Clipton of Crosswicks in the Jerseys. That's who I be. And who be ye?"

"Micah Heath of—Lancaster."

"Come down, Micah Heath of Lancaster. All night and morning me and my bride has journeyed from Crosswicks to have a fittin' oyster breakfast at the Harp and Crown in Bristol Town. And what's here? Oysters a-plenty, but ary guest has fled. How can there be a wedding breakfast with nary guest?"

Micah swung down. "I'm hungry enough, Mr. Clipton, and glad to join you. Let me see if there's other wagoners would care to swell your party."

"Aye, aye, aye," said Clipton. "I've had the table set on the sunny side the inn under an oak. Come meet Mistress Fanny Clipton, the pearl of Burlington County, and Monmouth and Middlesex too."

Micah awakened Poletski and Zeiman and hailed Young. As was their custom when they met on a mission, they pretended not to know one another.

They went around the Harp and Crown to the side yard where Young suddenly halted and muttered, "I vaw!" Seated beside Clipton at the table the landlord had set under an oak was a dark-haired young woman, pretty and well-formed. Staring at her, Young whistled softly.

"Set down, set down," cried Clipton. "This is Mistress Clipton, lads, the pearl of Burlington County. Yonder tall one's Micah Heath of Lancaster, Fanny."

She stared at Micah expressionlessly and then nodded.

"Good day," he said to the ground, annoyed by his sudden shyness.

"Who be ye three?" asked Clipton. "Welcome to Peter Clipton's wedding breakfast, but who be ye?"

"The musicians, Mr. Clipton." Young winked at him and smiled broadly at Fanny Clipton as he took his jew's-harp from a pocket. "Hark, now." He played four sweet notes. "The mating call o' the lark."

Clapping his fat hands together, Clipton cried, "Music we'll have! But first a toss of flip. Mary! Where's that damn wench? Mary, bring the loggerhead!"

A buxom servant girl ran from the kitchen with a red-hot poker as Clipton poured a pan of molasses into a huge jug of stale beer. "Give us it, give us it!" He snatched the poker from her. The brew hissed and sent off a pungent odor as he stirred with his left hand while pouring in a bottle of rum with his right. "The loggerhead must do its work at the same time as the rum elset it's flat." He stopped stirring. "Mugs all around. Fanny!" When he'd filled everyone's mug, he held up his own and said, "The bride," and drank deeply. "Wedded we are, but still unbreakfasted and still unbedded."

Micah observed that Mrs. Clipton did not blush, even though Young and Zeiman guffawed loudly. She merely stared expressionlessly at her husband and sipped her flip.

"Where's your home at, Mrs. Clipton?" he asked with an effort.

She fixed her dark eyes on him broodingly. At last she said, "Crosswicks." But that was all she said.

The flip glowed warmly in Micah as they sang "The Foggy Foggy Dew." The sun shafted through the yellowing oak leaves above their heads and pressed warmly on the land. In the radiance of autumn afternoon the Delaware glistened like a mirror and the Jersey shore seemed so close that you could touch it. The sun, great life-giver, poured its strength on earth; no wonder that Peter Clipton, old countryman, had his wedding breakfast out of doors. If I'm ever taken from the sun, Micah thought, I'll die.

Fanny Clipton was looking at him curiously.

"Iss not drunk," Zeiman said to her, elbowing Micah. "Iss never drunk. Iss happy."

"I'm drunk," Micah said, raising his face to the sky and closing his eyes. "I'm drunk on sun."

"Be drunk on oysters," Clipton said to him. "They's nought better to be drunk upon." He raised his voice. "Mary! The oysters—and beer all around!"

"Yonder," Fanny Clipton said. "A gentleman's arrived, Mr. Clipton."

Looking around quickly, Micah saw Alex March dismount and give his horse to a stable boy. Startled, he elaborately scratched his right ear in their customary signal that one would be recognized and the others must take care.

"Ho, there!" Clipton roared to Alex. "You, sir! Come to my wedding breakfast!"

Alex strolled toward them, smiling. Seeing Micah, he paused in surprise. Then he came on quickly, his hand extended.

"Micah, a pleasant surprise."

"The same, sir. I'm just freighting through."

"And I'm on a title search up Morrisville way. I haven't seen you since last March to thank you for dragging me into the Hogarth's Head."

Micah did not know how to reply. He had seen him several times since that evening, but Alex had never noticed him.

"Set down! Set down!" cried Clipton. "Here come the oysters."

The servant girl trotted to the table bearing a great wooden tray of steaming baked oysters. Seizing an oyster, Clipton fingered it off the shell into his mouth. "Good," he said, and grabbed another.

Baked with bread crumbs, butter and onions, seasoned with pepper and vinegar, the oysters were succulent. After they had washed down several trays with cool beer, the girl brought a heaping platter of baked bass.

"The gentleman ain't sung yet for his breakfast," Clipton said to Alex.

"Very well." He rose, smiling, and began singing "Barbara Allen." Everyone joined him. As the song ended, Fanny Clipton suddenly smiled at Micah.

In the rising babble of voices Poletski whispered to him, "Conkest."

Poletski was mistaken, Micah thought. He had not made a conquest because he was not out to conquer. Women troubled him, both in the flesh and in strangely disturbing dreams. There was nothing wrong with him, he believed, but there was something wrong with every woman. They giggled or were stupid or were unaware of you—like Kathy Murdoch.

As they sang the ballad of adultery, "Lord Orland's Wife," a deep baying voice joined theirs. Glancing around, Micah saw Bilby.

"Welcome, sir, to Peter—" Clipton hiccoughed loudly. "Oh, hell, set down, whoever ye be."

"The name is Jonas Bilby, thankee kindly. I—" His voice died and his single eye widened as he stared at Alex. "I see I'm amongst strangers save for this lad of my employ." He pointed at Micah. "A word with ye."

Micah followed him from the table.

"What's all this roistering?"

"All's in order, Cap'n."

"In order?" Bilby swore. "D'you know ye're settin' at table with one o' the leading Sons of Liberty in Philadelphia?"

"Who's that?"

"Mr. Alex March, that's who. He don't know me, but I know him."

Micah stared around at Alex with sudden new respect. "I trust him," he said slowly.

"I trust nobody," Bilby said, "but we're on course and can't broach now."

"Come set down!" Clipton shouted to them.

"There's one thing more, Micah. I've news for you." Bilby fumbled in a pocket. "Ye're free."

Micah stared at him incredulously.

"Here." Bilby unfolded and held out a paper. "I finally got Murdoch to do it."

"Free?" His voice sounded distant. The written words blurred as tears filled his eyes.

"Aye, free! I didn't mean it should take so long, but I couldn't shake Murdoch till now on this last go, damn his hide."

Free! It was impossible to believe. Now no man could bid him come or go or wait. He was as free as air or clouds or water. No bonds, no fear, no lengthy tether. *I feel*, he thought, *like the King of America.*

"Tell it to anyone." Bilby grinned at him. "Tell it to the world, boy. Ye're free!"

He leaped suddenly and released an Indian whoop such as he had not raised since the Ohio days. Before him was another big river, the Delaware. If he spread his arms he felt that he could fly from river to river in an instant. The people at the table stared at him stupefiedly. He did not care. He ran toward them, waving his arms, and then, because he felt like it, he somersaulted without touching the ground.

Peter Clipton, his fat hands fluttering helplessly, blanched and gagged.

"I'm free!" Micah shouted at him.

"Mad!" wheezed Clipton.

"No, free!" cried Alex, leaping to his feet.

Young and Poletski and Zeiman were pounding his back and Alex was wringing his hand while Fanny Clipton waved to him and her husband tried ineffectually to rise from his chair.

"Wine!" Alex shouted. "You, girl, a pipe of your best Fayall Madeira!"

The girl brought wine and Alex rose, holding up his glass. "I drink to Micah Heath, freeman, American."

They drank and Bilby said, "A good toast, sir. The best."

"And I," Micah said, rising, "drink to the man who did it. Captain Bilby."

"Wish I could drink to the man I got to do it," Bilby said. "But I can't."

"Meaning?" Alex said.

"Timothy Murdoch."

"May I see the document?" Alex said to Micah.

Studying it, he frowned. "This has been notarized, and it dates your freedom as of May fifteenth, 1772. Today is October twenty-fifth, 1773."

Bilby snatched the paper from him and peered at it. "That it does," he said slowly. "I ain't read it before."

Did it mean, Micah wondered, that he'd been free all this time he'd worked for Bilby? Why hadn't Murdoch told him when he left the farm a year ago last May?

Bilby's eye stared at him levelly. "I reckon you wonder if I knew this all along and held out on you. I swear I didn't, Micah. 'Trust no man,' I'm always saying to you, but now I'm asking you to trust me."

"I do, Cap'n Bilby." He trusted him above all men. "What matters is I'm free now."

"True," Alex said, "but every man has a purpose when he signs a document and this . . ."

Micah suddenly understood Murdoch's purpose. If I'd been caught smuggling, he thought grimly, old Murdoch could have produced this paper to prove he'd freed me and didn't know what I was doing. And all the time I worked for him for practically nothing.

"I'm especially sorry about this," Alex said heavily, handing the document back to Micah, "because I— In a fortnight I'm marrying Mr. Murdoch's daughter."

"Kathy?" Micah stared at him incredulously. He had not believed that Kathy would marry him. He was too—gentle. And she was—cruel? No, she was impetuous. Like me, he thought. And I believed—I hoped, but what could I have hoped?

"My good wishes," he said indistinctly. "Miss Kathy and I played together as young ones."

"Yes?" Alex looked at him pensively.

"Yes, I reckon—I know it'll be a happy marriage."

Alex smiled faintly. "Thank you." He paused, as if waiting for Micah to continue, but Micah did not know what to say.

"Congratulations, sir," Bilby said. "All goes well. The lad's free. You've a wedding coming and here we've—"

"Mary!" Clipton shouted. "Bring the chickens!"

They ate chickens stuffed with oysters and chestnuts. They ate coxcombs minced with sheep kidneys and pig livers. They ate pork pie and roast beef with horseradish sauce. They ate sillabub and lemon cheesecake. The landlord joined all his servants to watch them eat and drain away his best Madeira. The babble of their voices rose and fell like ocean waves and was succeeded by the long lull of satiety.

Then Peter Clipton decided he was hungry again and started anew with a plate of smoked shad, several links of fried sausage, and an entire heart with pickled cabbage rampant on it. The sun was going down, but they did not feel the chill of evening. In the gathering darkness they leaned forward to watch Clipton chomping. When he had finished the last sliver of ox heart, Clipton belched, fell back with his eyes closed, and began to snore. Fanny Clipton covered her eyes with both hands and burst into tears.

"Come about, come about, Mistress Clipton," Bilby said vaguely as she ran into the inn. He heaved himself to his feet and groaned. "We'll carry our host to his chamber."

It seemed to take all six of them to extricate Clipton from his chair. As they carried him, still snoring, they began to laugh hysterically. Laying him on the ground until they'd recovered their strength, they lifted him again. Straining, pushing, hauling, and weak from laughter, they finally got him up the back stairs and into the chamber which was lighted by two candles. Fanny Clipton sat in a corner of the room in nightgown and wrapper, crying quietly.

Clipton seemed to fill the wide bed. They took off his boots and pulled him as close to one side of the bed as they could before covering him with a quilt. Then, with swift glances at his weeping bride, they tiptoed out.

As they closed the door behind them, Bilby whispered, "The bride needs comforting. We'll tend the matter as gentlemen. We'll draw lots."

"I pass," Alex said.

"Sir, you cannot pass."

"But I can, sir. I'm shortly to have a bride of my own."

"More's the reason." Bilby's voice rose plaintively. "Good God, sir, this may be your last chance to comfort another female."

They had reached the head of the stairs when they heard Fanny Clipton cry out. Stumbling over one another in their haste, they clattered back to the bedroom door.

Bilby tapped lightly on the door and said, "Mistress Clipton?"

"Go away!" she shrieked. "Where's Micah Heath?"

Bilby jabbed him with an elbow. "Your duty, lad."

His mouth felt dry and he wanted to run. "Cap'n Bilby, sir, I—"

"Under *way*," commanded Bilby.

Hands opened the door and shoved him into the room and closed the door behind him. Clipton's enormous bulk seemed to fill the four-poster. Then his bride slowly sat up beyond him.

Micah stepped back, prepared to flee. But she smiled and said, "He fills this bed like a sow fallen in the trough. Don't you marvel that I married him?"

"Well," Micah said, "yes, I do."

She continued to smile. "A pretty young thing like me. Ain't it a marvel?"

"Yes, ma'am," he muttered.

"Money," she said. "That's why I did it. He's nigh the richest man in Burlington County. And I like to take my pleasures. So now you know. Haul him over so as I can get my breath."

He walked slowly to the bed and tugged ineffectually at Peter Clipton.

"Dear God, what ails you?" Flinging back the covers, she planted her feet against her husband's side, gripped the bedpost, and shoved. Micah glimpsed her bare legs before he closed his eyes and tugged at Clipton.

Clipton rolled suddenly, like a barrel, and fell to the floor with a crash that seemed to shake the inn. Fanny Clipton swung to her knees on the bed, staring down at him. Clapping her hands to her mouth, she screamed with laughter. As Micah bent to try to lift him, Clipton stirred, smacked his lips, and resumed snoring.

The men in the hall shouted with laughter and pounded on the door. "Heath!" cried Bilby. "Micah, lad, are you all right?"

"It's Mr. Clipton," Micah called. "He's fallen out of bed, but he's still snoring."

There was a stunned silence and then a shout of laughter. Someone tried the door.

"Go away with you!" shrieked Fanny Clipton. "The lot of you go!"

"Mistress Clipton," Bilby said unsteadily, "will you give us up our Micah Heath?"

"Go away!" she shrieked. "He's tending Mr. Clipton. Go!"

They went, muttering and laughing.

"I don't rightly know as I can lift him up alone," Micah said. "Maybe . . ."

"Let him be." She glanced at her husband contemptuously, and then she smiled at Micah. "I said I like to take my pleasure, but now I know they's some pleasures money don't buy." Her lips pouted as she walked around the bed and climbed into it. "Come around here." She smiled at him. "You're shy, ain't you? You've lots to learn and I'm the one to learn you the first lesson of what a pleasure a bed can be. They's no harm or wrong in it, but just a mortal pleasure."

Toward midnight two weeks later Micah led his team down the Old

York Road through a cold rain that poured on the Northern Liberties. The horses were dead beat, and he was beat himself.

"Scatter," Bilby had told them five miles east of the Bordentown Ferry. "Go easy. I'll meet you night after tomorrow at Chester Newman's stall in the Callowhill Market House."

He was wet to the skin, his eyes burned, his arms ached from hours of tugging at the horses as they dragged the heavily laden wagon through sucking mud.

It had been the longest, finest trip he'd ever made with Bilby—clear to Sandy Hook and back. He had traveled as a freeman and it was a mortal pleasure. At the recollection of those words of Fanny Clipton's he grinned in the darkness. It had been a powerful mortal pleasure he'd said when Bilby asked him about it as they crossed Jersey.

"Aye." Bilby had glanced at him shrewdly. "A great joy it is. Remember that, lad. Th'eternal itch satisfied, eh? But it ain't. Just don't let it plague ye. Remember it's a great joy and not a great sin, as the saints make it out to be. They say it leads to hell. And I say if that was so heaven'd be empty as yonder sky. There's so much rabbit in every mortal. Don't deny it, as Fanny Clipton didn't. I envy ye."

Was it possible, he wondered now, that you had a revelation of truth when you shared a bed with an undenying woman? In any event, he'd thought of Kathy as he lay with Fanny Clipton and he'd realized something that he'd long hidden from himself: Kathy, too, would find it a mortal pleasure. He knew it instinctively, as Bilby instinctively knew the nature of Fanny Clipton. And, as Bilby envied him, so did he envy Alex. Was the itch, as Bilby called it, never satisfied?

What was freedom anyway? He'd meditated on it as the wagons creaked across Jersey and he observed men who called themselves free while they remained the prisoner of a sandy farm, a span of oxen, a wife and swarm of young ones. What was their aim? As much wealth as they could acquire. It was the talk in every country tavern, as it was the talk all the way west to the limits of the country at Pittsburgh. The yield of crops, the state of barter, the shortage of hard money, the oppressive acts of the Parliament which were aimed at preventing the one thing a man reckoned to give him real freedom: a share of wealth.

You look to yourself and stop your dreaming, he told himself. If he were rich instead of poor and wore silk instead of linsey-woolsey and rode his own horses instead of driving another man's, then he would be— What? Perhaps the husband of Kathy Murdoch. But that was past, it was impossible and past. So he'd look to the future.

There wasn't much that he couldn't do with his hands and muscles. But only one thing was likely to give him a reasonable share in this wealth the world was seeking: fur trapping. No matter that he'd never known a wealthy trapper. He'd be shrewd and hard and driving out there and some day, if he felt like it, he'd come back east a wealthy man.

At the Cross Keys Tavern on the Highlands west of Sandy Hook they'd joined a tough gang of New York smugglers led by a pious-acting Quaker. The next dawn found them in a caravan of twenty wagons following several riders along the white sea-beaten beach of the Hook. Above the thud and wash of the surf on their right the Atlantic breathed a pungent salt air. As the sun rose higher over the empty sea, they left the beach and plodded over the low dunes. Beyond, they glimpsed the great bay, calm and slate-gray, where swarms of mewing gulls circled. They climbed over the crest of another dune and saw a large three-masted black Dutch ship at anchor. High in its rigging a lookout gave a shrill, wordless cry. Instantly a small boat shot toward the shore, sun gleaming on its stroking oars.

As the day wore on, the Quaker stood calmly in the center of confusion, checking off his long list while boats plied between ship and shore and the smugglers argued and loaded their wagons. Chests of tea, bolts of Holland linen and Lowland duck, tea, tea, Barcelona silk and handkerchiefs, tuns of Madeira wine, tea, kegs of gunpowder, tea, tea. It was almost dark before Bilby was satisfied that his four wagons had their proper loads of tea and linen and duck, lashed down and carefully covered with light bags of legitimate Lisbon salt.

We've done it again, Micah thought now, as he saw the lantern at the lower end of the Callowhill Market flickering through the rain. The horses, feeling cobbles underfoot, took sudden heart in the knowledge they were near journey's end.

Turning up the line of darkened market stalls, Micah saw a lantern flash and then swing toward him. He halted the horses and his right hand gripped the handle of the knife in his belt. The lantern rose high and in its glow he made out Bilby grinning at him. They did not speak. Bilby turned and he followed, leading the horses.

A double door creaked open and the light of four lanterns on a warehouse floor seemed blinding after the darkness.

"You're first in, lad," Bilby said.

Somewhere in the shadows a man spoke. "Jonas Bilby!"

Bilby whirled.

"Yon's the mon," another voice said. "Arrest him!"

Bilby flung his lantern in the direction of the voice. A flame split the darkness beyond as a pistol cracked.

"Run!" Bilby cried, dashing past Micah.

He ran beside Bilby, urging him on, resisting the temptation to pass him. Behind them rose shouts and the clatter of iron-cleated boots on the cobbles.

"Go on!" Bilby gasped.

Swerving, he shrank against a stall entrance. As the first pursuer passed, he tripped him and the man crashed headlong. He had not realized another followed so closely. There was a triumphant cry and thick arms sought to smother him. He dropped and then drove both fists into the man's belly. Two or three more were coming. He dashed on, overtaking Bilby again near the end of the market. Bilby, gasping for breath, waddled like a water bug stranded on land.

"Hide," Micah told him. "I'll lead 'em."

He halted and yelled wordlessly at two, three dim figures pounding toward him. Then he ran on. Bilby had disappeared. Looking back, he made out the three figures still following him. He ran faster, around the end of the market.

A figure loomed in front of him. He swerved and slipped in mud as a heavy man flung himself upon him. They rolled and Micah kneed his way on top. Then hands closed around his throat from behind and a man growled, "Got him!"

Bright morning sunlight filtered through a high barred window into the small room. Out there the world went its usual way. The din of carts and voices rose on Front Street; sailors chanted as they worked a capstan on the river.

By tilting back his head he could almost see a bit of the sky through the barred window above him. He stood, his bare back to the room, his arms stretched out with wrists in handcuffs riveted to the wall.

The door closed. He didn't turn his head. That would be the big Englishman returning. The whip tickled his back.

"Any change of 'eart?"

He didn't reply. Once, at Head of Elk, he'd met a Virginia wagoner who claimed to have walked away after two hundred lashes ordered by an English colonel whom he had somehow annoyed. He'd showed his scars. Proudly, too.

"I'm to ask once more," the big man said. "Who was with ye?"

He licked his dry lips and blinked at the sweat that poured down his forehead and stung his eyes. Once, in Chester, he'd met a deserter from a British man-of-war who told of one hundred and ninety-nine lashes for upsetting a bucket on his lieutenant's clean boots. He'd showed his scars. And proudly, too.

"Eighty-nine," the man said. "To begin with."

He clamped his teeth. Eighty-nine wasn't bad. Eighty-nine was only—

The blow jolted him from head to buttocks and stabbed through his back to his chest like a knife. Somebody's breath whistled sharply, and he realized it was his own. It was not simply a sharp sting, as he had expected. It was— The knife pierced lower this time and he groaned. He would not do that again. Three! He did not groan. Three from eighty-nine was— Pain had no limit, as he had expected. Pain grew and grew. Retching might relieve it, but he would not retch. He lost count at fifty-eight. His head hung limply. With a supreme effort he looked up and almost, but not quite, made out the sky through the barred window.

The buzzing in his ears became the sound of voices. It was ended, but the pain grew. They were fumbling at the handcuffs. He swayed and spread his feet. He would not support himself against the wall. But he had to support himself, and he pressed his hands and face against the cool wall. At last he turned slowly, refusing to touch the wall.

The little man stood beside the big Englishman. He said, "Now young mon—"

"You're no Scot," Micah shouted hoarsely, "you English-loving . . ." He called him every obscene name he could think of.

"Ayety-nine more?" the Englishman asked.

The little man pursed his lips and shook his head. " 'Twould na help. Take him off. He'll ken better after five years."

As he was led out, the bell of Christ Church began pealing.

Book Two

PROCLAIM LIBERTY

X

THE bell of Christ Church stopped pealing as Timothy Murdoch walked slowly toward the altar with Kathy on his arm that bright November noon.

He felt that he had reached an estimable place in society. Seldom had Christ Church held a more impressive assemblage. Coming down the aisle, he observed that there were representatives of the Shippens and Chews and Whartons. There was Robert Morris, his round, red face beaming above his small, brown-eyed wife, Mary. There was Morris's partner and Murdoch's close friend Thomas Willing, tall and straight, his thin lips relaxed in a faint smile. In the next pew Thomas Mifflin turned his handsome, florid face, his blue eyes shining. There were Dr. Benjamin Rush and Dr. Sharp Delany, Tony Wayne and his brother-in-law, Thomas Penrose, Hetty Griffits, Sally Robinson, the Misses Biddle, John Moland, Tench Francis, Tench Howe.

I have arrived at a certain station, Murdoch thought, turning his fixed smile toward the altar where Alex waited beside lanky Joseph Reed. He was handsome standing there in black silk and gleaming white ruffles. Handsome, but what else? Not enough, Murdoch thought bitterly. Not really worthy of this remarkably beautiful daughter swathed in white lace and satin who stirred a faint murmur of admiration from the crowd as she stepped gracefully beside him.

Before the altar he turned aside, glancing at Sally Mifflin, the maid of honor, who looked so plain compared to Kathy. How had it happened that Kathy was so beautiful? Her beauty had not come from him and scarcely from her mother, Margaret.

"Who giveth this woman?" said the rector, the Reverend Jacob Duché.

I do, he thought, but most reluctantly and only because she wills it.

He glimpsed Mrs. March in the front pew. Her lips were clamped tightly and she was frowning. So she did not like this either. At least she was faring better than he, for she shortly would be linked to the Murdochs by marriage while he would be linked to a land-poor country-woman.

He paid no attention to the rise and fall of Duché's voice as he asked himself, Why did this have to be? Why could it not have been a grand alliance, with important connections, that abetted the strengths of two families? Consider the Shippens. Consider the happy lot of Chief Justice William Allen. Even the Jews, especially the Jews, knew that marriage was the most valuable contract if you would increase a business into a great establishment.

Goddamn it, he thought, I need more capital.

"And now," said the Reverend Duché, "I pronounce you man and wife."

It was done. Alex and Kathy kissed and then she pecked his cheek. He was following them up the aisle, fighting back tears of self-pity. Suppose that never again so many prominent Philadelphians turned out to pay him their respect? They were strangers, all of them, names only. None of the old ones who knew the beginnings were here. Margaret dead; her father, Martin Bancroft, dead . . . There were many others, but he had invited few of them here today. They had not kept pace with him and now he was rising among strangers.

Looking up, he saw Thomas Willing staring at him thoughtfully. Willing knew! The times were bad and growing worse, the economy as soft as rain water, the struggle to keep your head above it exhausting. Yes, Willing knew and thought how far Timothy Murdoch had come and wondered where all of them were going. And Barnaby Falco's sharp eyes there in the back pew saw and almost knew, for Falco knew too much about some things and not enough about others.

Plunging outside into the blinding glare of midday sun, he heard the bell pealing above him and saw the line of chaises and coach wagons which he had hired to transport guests to John Biddle's Indian King for the reception. He'd hired the Indian King too, and if Biddle had been unwilling to rent the space Kathy probably would have expected him to buy the tavern. It seemed that he had bought or hired most of Philadelphia to consummate this contract of hers which promised to bring him no return.

Kathy and Alex rode away in the first coach, followed by two coach wagons filled with shouting, laughing members of the wedding party. He and Mrs. March were left to enter the third big coach wagon. They sat stiffly, staring at each other as the driver whipped up the horses. He wondered what she would reply if he said to her, "Of my positive knowledge there are presently nine coaches and thirty coach wagons in Philadelphia and I have hired four of them to ride five streets from a place I did not want to be to a place I do not want to go." Then he was glad that he had not spoken as she closed her eyes tightly and two large tears rolled down her weather-reddened cheeks. There should be something he could say to her, but he could not think of a word. Besides, he would have had to shout to be heard above the infernal racket from the bells and wooden clappers which the yelling members of the wedding party rang and rattled out the windows of the coach wagons ahead.

At Market Street their noisy procession was held up. Leaning out, he saw a mob flooding up Market Street jeering a prisoner tied to the constable's cart. He glimpsed the prisoner's bare back, bloodied from a lashing, and winced.

"Some fellow to the prison," he shouted to Mrs. March. "I don't like to see these whippings."

She nodded absently and looked out the opposite door at red leaves falling from a maple. "The fall's been early," she said. "A hard winter coming."

Conversation with her was impossible, he decided.

Most of the mob, finding a wedding of more interest than the prisoner, swirled around their procession. They jostled a way for the coach and eddied alongside, ogling Kathy and shouting good-naturedly. Murdoch, waving and smiling and listening carefully to the tone of the voices, was tempted to have John Biddle roll out a couple of kegs of beer when the procession reached the Indian King. But he decided to save himself the expense and slipped inside and asked the barman to pour him a quick tot of rum to calm his nerves.

Were all wedding receptions as chaotic as this? Musicians played and everyone ignored them, people shouted and could not be heard, good wine was spilled in broken glasses, good food wolfed by those who could not possibly be hungry. There were many toasts, much kissing, a few tears, and endless laughter.

Kathy, her eyes shining, seemed never to stop laughing. She looked, as everyone told him, beautiful. Moving about with a fixed smile, taking care to speak to everyone, he told himself that her happiness was at least a slight return for this abominable contract.

"Congratulations, Mr. Murdoch, on acquiring such an excellent son-in-law." Tench Francis studied him reflectively.

"Thank you, sir." He bowed and lied, "I believe so too."

Tench Francis was an unquestioned leader of the bar, but what did he know of the endless struggle to rise to a better station? Sitting in his fine law library, he never had tried to compute a barter profit on London dry goods in return for Greenwich cheese, or brass buttons for Chester Mills flour, or attempted to fathom the mysteries involved in the value of shoes and lime traded for flaxseed from Amwell and Woodston.

"A grand occasion, Timothy," said Thomas Willing. "It reminds of a decade ago."

Now here was one who understood. Murdoch seized his hand warmly and drew him aside. If he had gone to work as a clerk for Thomas's father, Charles, back in '42, instead of indenturing himself to Michael Phalen for three years, he and Thomas might be partners today. As it was, that strangely visionary gambler and sharp trader Robert Morris, whom Murdoch did not trust, controlled Thomas Willing's business now.

Willing either knew or accurately guessed nearly every important thing that Timothy Murdoch had done. Willing knew, for example, that in '42, at the age of fifteen he had left his father's farm, walked barefoot into the city with his shoes tied around his neck and apprenticed himself as a clerk. Willing knew that he had not loved Margaret Bancroft but had married her to gain control of her father's failing business. And he knew that he had made the business prosper by underpricing other bidders in contracts to supply Bouquet's western army. If some of that pork had been rancid, he was kind enough to believe it had not been Timothy Murdoch's fault.

Willing raised his glass. "Good fortune, Timothy."

Good fortune? He had been born to his, he floated at his natural station, and so risk was alien to him. After all, Murdoch thought, Willing understood only so far. He simply did not realize that unless you took great risk and had good fortune in it you would forever remain a glorified shopkeeper, trading glass beads in Goshen for firkins of butter.

Willing, talking at length about the present troubles, said reflectively, "At times, Timothy, it's difficult to decide exactly who is our enemy."

It would be interesting to see Willing's reaction if he replied, "A wise merchant has no enemies except other wise merchants." For it was true, he believed. The only enemy of the people in this crowded room was not an oppressive Parliament, but the wise English merchants who prevailed on that Parliament to oppress their competitors across the sea. Governments, bah! They were necessary institutions which wise men either manipulated or circumvented. Those who argued that it was fair for government to levy such huge taxes on the colonies were hoodwinked. Even though the government's debt had doubled to about one hundred and thirty million pounds after the war, George Grenville would not have demanded such high levies from the colonies without the prompting of the English merchants. He wished that he dared say to Willing, "Another war would help the economy, Thomas. Another war would give us an enemy with whom to trade."

Many of the fortunes represented here at the Indian King today would not be so large if there had not been a war and an enemy with whom to trade. His own fortune, such as it was, would not even exist if he hadn't traded with the French through neutral ports. If he were at the office now, instead of in this noisy milling crowd, he'd pull out the old record of that thousand-per-cent voyage to San Domingo. Casks of molasses and barrels of sugar for some hemp and flour and a few hundred quintals of refuse cod that would have made even a Yankee hold his nose.

Willing was speaking again. "Miss Kathy, or I should say young Mrs. March, is trying to attract your attention over there, Timothy. I believe the bride and bridegroom desire to leave."

He plunged through the crowd toward Kathy, cursing himself for having stayed away from her and feeling oddly panic-stricken. She's all I have, he thought, and she's going away. It must not be for long.

Darkness had fallen when Alex turned the chaise up the lane toward the Murdoch farmhouse where light glowed in the windows. Kathy, seated close beside him, pressed her hand on his knee.

She said, "The house will be ours. The servants won't come beyond the kitchen."

He said, "Very well."

Coming to the farm for a few days immediately after the reception had been her notion. It had rather surprised him, for she had led him to believe that she did not like the farm. He approved, for surely a woman who wished to return to her childhood home on her wedding trip bore happy memories that she wished to increase in marriage.

She said, "The Touts and the others sleep beyond the kitchen or in outbuildings. The house will be ours."

She had made her point, so why did she belabor it? Doubtless her nerves were on edge, as was said to be true of all brides.

She said, "As long as you approve of coming here and are happy."

"Of course I'm happy." He smiled at her and would have kissed her if John Tout had not suddenly stood beside the chaise with a lantern held aloft.

While someone led the chaise away, John carried their luggage to the door where Mrs. Tout greeted them warmly. "Your orders are followed exactly, Kathy," she said. "A cold supper is set on the table and—"

"We wish to change our clothing before we eat," Kathy said.

"Yes, Kathy." She stepped back, gazing at the floor. "The fire's lit in your room. Mind the hot stone in the warm-water bucket. Your supper is out whenever you want it. Ring if you wish ought. Good night." She was gone, without once looking at either of them closely. She was, Alex thought, a rather remarkable woman whose talent for tactfulness was wasted here in the country.

At the door of the bedroom where John had left their luggage Kathy passed a hand across her forehead and said, "I grow old if stairs trouble me so. I feel downright swoony."

His own heart was beating extraordinarily fast as he drew her to him. "My very aged Kathy." He tried to kiss her, but she turned her cheek and pushed him away.

"Downright swoony," she said. "Be a dear heart and fetch a bottle of wine from the dining room."

He went downstairs, light-footed with a greater tenderness for her than he had ever felt. She was only a child, of course, and in all her posturings as a woman of the world she merely sought to disguise her fears and uncertainties.

She sat on the edge of the high double bed, feet dangling, hands clutching her elbows. Her posture was that of a little girl and her face expressed a certain misery at the prospect of womanhood. There's no haste, he thought, smiling at her and setting glasses and the bottle on the dresser. They would drink, they would dine, they would talk. There was no haste.

Her hand shook when she took her glass. She did not look at him as he raised his and said, "To the great years, Kathy."

Drinking quickly, she said, "It was a fine wedding, wasn't it? It was the most wonderful wedding I've ever seen, don't you think?" She did not give him a chance to reply, but chattered on, mentioning nearly everyone who had been present, describing what they wore, citing various gaucheries, relishing the flattery that had been showered on her.

She talked as if he were a stranger to whom she was describing her wedding, he thought morosely. Her eyes shone, her voice rose high in animation. Of course, it had been her wedding. And, of course, she was very young. But was it possible that she would always babble so when she found herself enclosed in a room with him? Since she obviously did not expect him to speak, what was he supposed to do? His fixed, attentive smile was becoming fatiguing and his tight, new shoes had begun to hurt his feet. There was a chair in the corner, an uncomfortable looking split-cane chair. Going to it, he sat down and stifled a sigh.

Instantly she was silent. Then, not looking at him, she said, "I see you don't want to talk. Go down and eat, then. I'm not hungry."

"Nor I." He rose quickly. "But talk, yes. I've been listening to you with interest and I do not talk because I agree with everything you say—substantially. Would you agree with me when I say that we must not be hasty?"

"Hasty?" She frowned. "Hasty over what?"

"Over—anything." He strolled to a window and pulled back the curtain and looked out. "Did you observe as we drove from the city how the night took no haste in falling? The sun declined and leisurely disappeared, but its glow still lit up half the heavens. It's still there, of course, and we have merely turned from it for a spell. Venus appeared—most appropriately tonight." He turned and smiled at her. "Do you understand, Kathy?"

She shook her head, staring at him. "Not a word."

As I, he thought in despair, did not really understand a single word of your recent nervous babble, except that it told me you were both nervous and hasty in your judgments.

"Then I'll be more explicit, Kathy. I speak of the act of love, as inevitable and anticipated by both of us as the fall of night."

She raised her hands to her eyes and said, "You should not *talk* so!"

He smiled, observing that if she really thought he should not *talk* so she would have covered her ears instead of her eyes.

"I apologize if I've offended you, but I don't see how I could."

"Talk," she said unsteadily, as if suppressing either tears or laughter. Her empty glass rolled on the counterpane as she pushed her hands ineffectually at the bed. "I suppose we should eat something. Help me to the floor."

He went to her, smiling at the helpless childlike flutter of her small feet and slim ankles. As he grasped her waist, prepared to swing her to the floor, her back arched and she would have fallen backward on the bed if he had not held her firmly.

Poor child, was she fainting? And then her restlessly arching back told him, Poor child indeed!

"Talk," she said, looking up at him through half-closed eyes and clasping her hands around his neck. "Talk, talk, talk. I know what's in your mind. You think that I'm a child. Is this a child you hold?" She pulled his head to her breast and held him.

No haste, he thought dimly. But there was now, his own as much as hers. He did not wish it so, this quick and frantic grappling, like two animals in a hedgerow. Yet her wish, the stronger of the two, destroyed his own. Her desire, heaven knew, was no greater than his. So abandon everything—wish, idea, ideal—in this trembling, turning, tearing headlong rush to meet a desire too long delayed. Observe the image of desire, her smooth white flesh. But observe not too closely her aptitude, her panting desire for consummation. . . .

He was holding her tightly, staring at the flickering shadows of candlelight on the ceiling, when she said, "You so took me by surprise."

XI

ONCE upon a time, Philly told herself, there was a princess who lived in a big castle beside a roaring river and early in the morning she would make gold. First she'd bring live coals on a small iron shovel from a distant place and kindle a fire under a huge iron kettle which she filled with buckets of water from the river. In rain or snow or cold she'd build her fire in the castle. But in good weather, on a golden November morning like this, she always built her fire beside the roaring river.

Watching the water begin to boil in the kettle, she thought that she was getting pretty big to be play-acting. For the roaring river was only the little babbling creek, and the huge castle was only the small washhouse in the maple thicket, and the princess was only herself, a fifteen-year-old bound girl named Philadelphia Twillow.

Taking a knife and a big chunk of yellow lye soap from the basket, she scraped chips into the boiling water.

"Gold," she chanted. "Old gold. Be new and true bold gold." Then, holding the paring knife aloft, she danced three times around the fire, singing, "No one can see me and no one can hear me when I make new, true gold." Taking coarse sheets from the basket, she put them in the kettle and stirred them slowly with a wooden paddle.

The sky was blue this morning, the earth powdered with frost. A calf bawled in the lower pasture and somewhere up the creek a hairy woodpecker drilled a dead log. How could anyone sleep on such a morning? Surely Miss Kathy and Mr. Alex would come out today after failing to show themselves last night. Oh, do come out, she thought, and walk in the yard a little while so that all of us can see how grand and beautiful you are.

Lifting the sheets from the kettle one at a time she put them in the pounding barrel. After refilling the kettle with dirty clothing, she began to thump the sheets with the wooden pounder, singing, "This is the way we pound the gold, pound the gold, pound the gold. . . . This is the way we pound the gold so early in the morning."

She liked to wash. It was a pity that Mrs. Tout would not let her do the big washing but only a little washing once a week. I can wash, she thought, and I can iron. I can cook and sew and dust and clean and tidy anything. I can churn and spin and weave. I can read and write and figure and my thumbs are green as May grass. I reckon if they'd let me I could hitch a horse and plow a straight furrow.

Taking a sheet from the pounder, she carried it to the creek and dipped it in. Wringing it out in her hard, chapped hands, she put it in the basket.

A fat red squirrel galloped along a maple bough, chattering.

"Cha," she said to him, working the pounder. "Cha, cha, cha!"

He stopped and looked at her.

"You want some gold, old Mr. Bushytail?" she asked him. "You take some home for Mrs. Bushytail 'cause she, sweet thing, has lined your nest with the fur off'n her breast."

The squirrel chattered again. He was trying to tell her something. She stopped pounding. There was no sound except the gulping of the creek and the rustling of a red-backed mouse in dead leaves. She began to pound, and then she stopped. Somebody was watching her. She turned slowly and her heart bolted in fright.

A man leaned against a maple behind her, square in the path. He was a fierce-looking man, his clothing all muddied and flecked with straw, and over his left eye he wore a black patch.

"Morning, young miss." His lips parted in a grin.

By his nasal speech she knew he was a Yankee. Pulling the pounder from the barrel, she held it before her. She'd give him his servings if he came at her, as she had Jared Olsen when he'd tried to put his hands on her breast in the stable.

"Who are you?" She swung the pounder slowly before her.

"I ain't as sure who I am as who I was," the man said. "The name was Bilby, but this morning I don't feel like anybody much."

"Well, Mr. Bilby, just what do you aim to be doing here?"

He grinned. "I come to buy some gold off'n you."

So he had seen and heard her foolish play-acting. She felt herself flushing. "You get smart with me, Mr. Bilby, I'll stun you good and skin your hide."

"I reckon you could and I wouldn't lift a finger, young Miss Philly Twillow."

"How d'you know my name?"

"From a mutual friend. He's spoke of you a couple of times. Most respectful."

"Who is he?"

"Young fella name of Micah Heath."

Her heart leaped and the pounder fell. "Where is he, Mr. Bilby? Is he faring well?"

Bilby rubbed his jaw. "He's in Philadelphia. But he ain't faring well a-tall. He's in jail, accused of smuggling."

Tears sprang to her eyes as she hurried toward Bilby.

"We'll get him out the pokey, Mr. Bilby. I'll fetch things. What you need? A saw and chisel and hammer?"

"Oh sweet Lord of the heavenly host." Bilby sank on the ground, staring up at her.

"You mind your language in front of me," she said. "I'm Presbyterian and I ain't took with swearing."

"Yes'm," said Bilby.

"Now what you need?"

"What I need—and let me pay my respects to ye, Miss Twillow, as a young lady after my own heart—what I need is a powerful friend. And I need something to eat. I ain't et in I don't know when. I daren't show my face in Philadelphia and they're watching the roads north for me. They want to make an *example* of me and I don't aim to be an *example*. Last night I hooked a ride on a Lancaster wagon and flopped off near here with the notion somebody might help Micah. Is Murdoch about?"

Philly shook her head.

"*He* wouldn't be any help anyways," Bilby growled. "I guess my head ain't too clear, but I hoped—"

"You set right there," Philly said, "and I'll fetch you something to eat. Then we'll figure a way to set Micah free."

She ran over the knoll and past the stables to the kitchen. Slipping into the pantry unobserved, she filled a napkin with bread and cold pork. As she left the house, an idea of how to help Micah occurred to her and she broke into a run.

"Here." She thrust the napkin into Bilby's outstretched hands. "I got a notion what we'll do. Don't you reckon a lawyer could set Micah free?"

Bilby, cheeks bulging with the bread and meat he crammed into his mouth, raised his single eyebrow.

"I reckon he could," Philly said, "and we've got one right in the house now. Mr. Alex. Mr. Alex March who's said to be about the finest in Philadelphia. He married Miss Kathy yesterday and they come out here last night and it's time they was up this morning. I'll go up there and—"

Bilby, swallowing, was seized with such a fit of coughing that he seemed to be choking to death. She pounded his back hard.

At last he gasped, "Come about, come about, Miss Twillow. Thankee for this food which bids to save whatever's left of my life. So Alex March is here, eh?" He tore off another chunk of meat and chewed thoughtfully. "I liked him, but can I trust him? As you grow older, you'll learn life never is simple. But when a lawyer gets to muddling with it there ain't nobody can figure it. Still, you stand more chance of bustin' out of jail with a lawyer than with a saw and chisel—I think. On t'other hand, Miss Twillow, I don't reckon a lawyer'd want to take a case the morning after he's married. I don't reckon he'd want to be disturbed 'less for a hundred-pound fee."

"Why not?" asked Philly.

Bilby swallowed. "It's just the custom, Miss Twillow, just the custom."

"But Micah's in jail," she said, "and he's innocent. Ain't—isn't he innocent, Mr. Bilby?"

"Well." Bilby scratched an ear.

"Isn't he?"

"Well, not exactly."

"You shouldn't have let him do it if you're his friend," Philly said. "You're older'n him and you shouldn't have let him." Her eyes filled with tears. "He's a good, honest boy and—"

"Come about, come about," Bilby said hastily. "Some of our most prominent citizens are—or were—smugglers. It's—it's kind of like a game, see? But I'll tell you what. I'll set the day out in this wood if ye think nobody'll disturb me. You finish your washing so they don't come looking for you. Then, if you can badger Mr. March down here, I'll have a word with him."

While she finished washing she plied Bilby with questions about Micah. His answers didn't satisfy her, however, and she thought that she never would be content until she saw Micah again.

She left Bilby asleep in a bed of leaves when she carried the laundry to the house. He was a good man, she'd decided, though somehow he must have run afoul of the law since he dared not show his face in Philadelphia. The law certainly was a strange, perplexing thing which continued to plague people like Micah and Mr. Bilby just as it had tormented Micah and Tom and her in the west.

After hanging up the laundry, she went into the kitchen, wondering how she'd find a way to speak to Alex. Mrs. Tout had strictly forbidden all of them to go beyond the kitchen; kindly though she was, she never would tolerate disobedience. Ida Mae Neiswander whispered that Mrs. Tout was serving breakfast to Miss Kathy and Mr. Alex at this very moment in there; she pointed dramatically toward the closed door.

Opening the door a little way, she boldly thrust her head into the dining room. Mrs. Tout frowned at her as darkly as a thunder cloud coming over South Valley Mountain. But Kathy and Alex smiled.

"Good morning, Miss Kathy," she said quickly. "Good morning, Mr. Alex. I ain't allowed inside."

"Of course you are," Kathy replied. "Come in here, Philly."

How lovely she was, wearing a white dressing gown and her hair a-tumble. Remembering how much she enjoyed being told she was beautiful, Philly said, "Miss Kathy, you look beautiful this morning, like rose petals in a golden bowl of cream."

Kathy's head arched back with pleasure at the remark. She was too prone to flattery and so committed the sin of vanity, Philly thought as she stepped into the room. But the Lord would say, Philly you shouldn't tempt her so with flattery. And she would reply, I need her friendship for Micah's sake, Lord. Besides, she really is beautiful, ain't she?

"Rose petals in a golden bowl of cream." Alex stared at her so hard that she blushed.

"Now that you're in here," Mrs. Tout said to her, "carry that tray to the kitchen."

"Yes'm." She forced herself to look up at Alex. "If'n—if you come outside today, Mr. Alex, there's somewhat I'd like to show you." She picked up the tray, bobbed her head to both, and fled.

In the kitchen Mrs. Tout frowned at her, puzzled. "There's something at work in that head of yours. Will you tell me what it is?"

Philly looked at her innocently. "What do you mean?"

"Lord save us." Mrs. Tout raised her eyes and hands to heaven. "Now you've learned guile."

Philly went out and sat on the horse block. Closing her eyes and clasping her hands, she willed Alex to come outside. In about half an hour she heard him call and she leaped to her feet.

"A beautiful morning." He breathed deeply and stretched. "What have you to show me, Philly?"

"Would you walk to the creek with me, Mr. Alex?"

"Of course."

As they approached the washhouse she asked him if he'd seen Micah recently.

"Yes." He looked at her reflectively. "I saw him about a fortnight ago up Bristol way. He—uh—seemed well and happy."

"You haven't seen or heard of him since, Mr. Alex?"

"No."

"He's such a good boy, Mr. Alex. He wouldn't do anybody an injustice, so why should anybody do an injustice to him?"

He smiled and paused. "What are you trying to tell me, Philly?"

"I can't tell you much," she replied, "but there's someone here who can. Mr. Bilby!"

He sat up slowly in his bed of leaves, blinking his eye at Alex, and then got wearily to his feet.

"Captain Bilby!"

"A captain without a ship or crew or port," Bilby said, taking Alex's outstretched hand. "I regret troubling you at such a time—and felicitations, sir, felicitations. But I'm driven hull down and spars gone before the wind. I am, as they say, *persona non grata* in Philadelphia. In fact, I daren't show my face there under pain of imprisonment."

"But why?"

"It's a long story, sir. But in two words, caught smuggling. Or almost caught. I got away and warned three in my employ thanks to Micah Heath."

Tears flooded Philly's eyes and she wondered that Alex could stare at Bilby so impassively.

"Mr. March." Bilby took him by an arm. "Let's take a turn along the brook for a little discussion. If you'll excuse us, Miss Twillow."

She was left alone, thinking of Micah in that jailhouse, while they paced up and down, talking quietly. At last they returned and shook hands.

"Ye'll do what you can?" Bilby asked.

Alex nodded gravely.

"Then I'll be on my way. Miss Twillow, thankee for what you've done. I'll repay everybody some day, both the good and the evil. Some year I'll be back. Good day and thankee both." Turning abruptly, he hobbled down the creek toward the road.

Philly touched Alex on an arm. "You'll set him free, Mr. Alex?"

"I'll do all that I can, Philly, but I'm not yet certain what all I can do."

Something was troubling him, Kathy knew. She offered him a penny for his thoughts and he replied that they were worth a pound. Then a pound, she said, and he replied that his thoughts were not for sale. At last he said, "What I'm thinking has nothing to do with you and me." He paused. "Apparently." Strolling to the window, he looked out. "You remember Micah Heath?"

How strange. She had thought of him—recently, it didn't matter when.

"Yes." She made her tone vague, but she watched Alex alertly.

"He's in prison in Philadelphia."

How fascinating. What had he done? But she said indifferently, "Oh?"

"When I went out with Philly I happened into a man who told me about Micah. A Captain Bilby. Do you know him?"

Bilby used to work for Papa. "I don't know him," she said. "But what has Micah done?"

Alex faced her. "He worked for Bilby, who in turn was working for your father. Their job was smuggling."

"Oh?" She smiled. "From what I've heard, we'd all be poor if it weren't for the smugglers. So Micah was caught. What will they do to him?"

"That depends on the judge who sentences him after his conviction.

But he was caught when he might have run free because he helped Bilby escape."

"How foolish of him not to escape."

"I think not," Alex replied sharply. "I would say, rather, how brave, how honorable."

She shrugged. "Micah didn't have to be a smuggler."

"It's not that simple. Micah, you remember, was your father's bound boy. Your father introduced him to Bilby. He was a smuggler while in servitude to your father. He—"

"But Papa wouldn't— He couldn't—"

"True, *Papa* couldn't force Micah to be a smuggler," Alex said wryly. "But there was a subtle suasion involved—which, admittedly, the law takes no cognizance of. Your father most definitely is involved in this affair, Kathy."

"He can't be," she said in alarm. "He *must* not be. It would be most embarrassing if—"

"Embarrassing?" His tone was sarcastic. "Not as embarrassing as it is to Micah to be confined in that filthy hole for a few years and bear the stigma of a criminal. Your father should have thought of his embarrassment some time ago when he sought illegal labor at the cheapest possible price."

"How can you turn all this on Papa?" she demanded heatedly. "Think what he's done for us. Think—"

"I've been thinking, Kathy. Your father is an exceedingly shrewd man. Knowing the *embarrassment* he faced if Micah were caught, he had a document drawn that set him free when he began working for Bilby. But he took care not to inform either Bilby or Micah, thereby saving himself paying Micah wages such as Bilby drew on him for the other members of his gang."

"But how do you know all this?"

"Bilby told me."

"Bilby! You take the word of a—a criminal who— What was he doing here? Running away, wasn't he? Gone already, hasn't he?"

"Yes, Kathy. But I believe him. I tell you that boy has been done a great injustice. Don't you see that?"

She did see. The truth was that it *sounded* like the way Papa would do business. And it *was* unfair to Micah. There was an air about that boy, a boldness hidden beneath his shyness that had fascinated her long ago. If he had been a gentleman instead of a bound boy . . . She nodded slowly and lowered her head.

"When he comes to trial," Alex said, "he'd be wise to throw himself on the clemency of the court, plead guilty, and tell everything he knows. His sentence would be lighter."

Alarmed again, she said, "Tell everything? Tell about—Papa?"

"Why shouldn't he, Kathy? Why should he try to shield a man who's treated him unjustly?" His lips twisted. "But I'll tell you the sad, the ironic, element. It would be his word against your father's, for Bilby will not testify in court unless he comes as a prisoner. And the court would accept your father's word that he had freed Micah more than a year ago and knew nothing of what had happened to him since."

She stifled a sigh of relief.

"Yet there is one other witness acceptable to the court who could testify that Micah did not know he was free."

"Who?"

"Myself."

She leaned toward him tensely. "Alex, you *wouldn't!*"

He smiled slowly. "But I would, Kathy. I have no love for your father. And I have even less for injustice."

"Alex, you wouldn't for *my* sake, because I asked you not to."

"No, I won't testify," he muttered. "My testimony would not be admissible because I intend to serve as his counsel. I'll go into town to see him tomorrow."

Although all else had displeased her today, she found pleasure in Philly gently brushing her hair as she lay on the parlor couch.

Opening her eyes, she saw it was not yet four o'clock. Alex must have started back to the farm, but the heavy rain would delay him.

"Philly," she said, "what do you think of a husband who deserts his wife on the third day of their marriage and goes off to the city on business?"

"I reckon that depends what the business is, Miss Kathy."

That was the most aggravating thing about his going off, she thought. He hadn't left on big, important business, but only to talk with a bound boy in prison. She had managed to control her anger at him, however.

He must not think her a child. He must understand that she was a *woman* who would help him to become a respected, rich man of whom it was said, "He would not have risen so high without his wife." She would manage a fine household. She would steer their course wisely in society, drawing to herself and so to him the finest, richest, most powerful people. How would she accomplish it? I have my beauty, she told herself. And?

They should have a grander beginning than the small house he'd rented on Fourth Street. It was time, too, that he broke free of Joseph

Reed and started his own practice. Reed was beginning to show dangerous radical tendencies, it was said. Meanwhile, the truth was that she
dreaded to try to start managing a house with its hundred annoying details. And the truth was that she had innumerable acquaintances but not
a single close friend, not even Sally Mifflin. If only she could possess a
friend who would aid her in her gradual possession of Alex and the
great, gay, comfortable world in which they'd live.

"You'd be interested in Mr. Alex's business today, Philly," she said
slowly. "Micah Heath is in prison in Philadelphia for smuggling and he's
gone to see what he can do about it."

The brush hesitated and stopped. "I know, Miss Kathy."

"You *know?*"

"Yes'm. I was up before daylight and he told me when he rode away."
She ran the brush through her hair again and said, "Miss Kathy, may I
speak free to you?"

"Of course. Just don't stop brushing."

"Please don't be put out with Mr. Alex for going to the city today.
It was me put him up to it."

What on earth did the little minx mean?

"Yesterday morning this man, this Captain Bilby, came on me whilst
I was washing at the creek and told me Micah was in the pokey. It tore
me, Miss Kathy, to think of Micah, that fine, brave boy . . ."

The child's voice was filled with tears.

"So I got Mr. Alex outside and took him to Captain Bilby and they
talked and— You see, Miss Kathy, it's my fault he went away today."

"Philly, step around here where I can see you."

Gazing at her pensively, Kathy thought, Child indeed! This was a
woman beginning. Straight legs, brown skin that reddened under her gaze,
gray eyes that did not falter in fear. But eyes filled with tears now. Good
heavens, she loved that boy!

"Philly, don't you think I should be very angry with you?"

"No'm." Philly looked at her steadily. "You're good, Miss Kathy, and
you wouldn't do a mean thing. You shouldn't get so vexed with yourself
sometimes, because you're good."

She raised herself, thinking that she had not heard her correctly. No
one ever had called her good. They called her beautiful Kathy and bold
Kathy and bad Kathy, but never *good*. It was not true. If she was anything, she was more bad than good. Yet Philly had said . . .

A bubble seemed to burst in her and tears filled her eyes. Swinging to
her feet, she hugged Philly fiercely. A friend, she thought. I've so wanted
one and now I have her. I'll never let her go.

But what did you say? How did you find the words to express your happiness?

"Listen to me, Philly." She gripped her shoulders. "In another week we'll return to our house in town. Will you come and live there?"

"To work for you, Miss Kathy?"

She hesitated, wondering how to say it. But there was only one way. "Yes. And to be my *friend,* Philly."

Why didn't she answer? If she refused to go, there was no hope of ever winning a friend.

"I'll go, Miss Kathy, and do the best I can."

XII

PHILLY loved the house on Fourth Street from the moment she saw its bright brick face tucked between two similar houses. Kathy called it a small house, but she thought it large and grand.

On the November afternoon when John Tout drove her into the city she was so excited by the crowds that she almost forgot to look for the jail where Micah was held. Philadelphia sounded like rocks being shaken in a thousand iron kettles; you had to shout to be heard above the clatter of hoofs and wheels on the wide, tree-lined, cobbled streets.

When they arrived, a stout, middle-aged woman opened the back door and asked, "You the bound girl?"

"Maybe she is and maybe she ain't," John replied. "She ain't bound to stay, that's sure."

The woman scowled at him. "I vaw, the bumpkins get tarter all the time. I'm Mrs. Munger, a widow woman, and cooking's all I'm here to do." She studied Philly. "If ye're the child they took to clean and serve, you ain't half the size for it."

"Then I reckon I'll have to grow into it," Philly said, stepping into the kitchen and looking around. Mrs. Munger kept it clean, that much was sure.

"Philly!" Kathy, smiling, strode into the kitchen and hugged her. "I'm glad you're here."

She felt suddenly as if she had come from the cold to a warm fire. Why did Mrs. Tout and John doubt Kathy? They felt the fire in her, but believed it intended to burn instead of warm. It was foolish of them. Although she had been surprised when Kathy had said she wanted to be her friend, she had not doubted her sincerity. Like me and everybody, she thought, I reckon she *needs* a friend.

After John had left, Kathy took her to the third floor. Her room under the eaves was small and furnished only with a narrow bed and washstand, but it was her own, the first room she did not have to share, and it had a window of real glass which overlooked the back yard.

Looking out the window at the muddy yard hemmed by walls and slanting roofs, she said, "Come spring, Miss Kathy, we ought to set some things to growing there." Then she remembered that come spring she might possibly return to the farm. Or would she? For she saw Kathy looking at her oddly, as if she wanted to say, "Don't leave me ever, Philly."

Instead, she said, "Come spring, Philly, I hope we have lots of money and Alex buys us a fine place over toward the Schuylkill. Now I'll show you through this little place. It needs lots of doing, but you mustn't try to do it all. I'm going to get a girl to help you."

The house certainly did need cleaning, Philly saw. There was dust everywhere; webs hung in corners and from the small chandelier in the front parlor; the mirror set in the handsome chimney piece was streaked with soot. It made her ashamed to think visitors had seen it thus. Poor Kathy didn't seem to know what to do about it. Yet that was understandable, for she was a lady, and a lady did not clean her own house.

Philly went to work with broom and duster, with scrub bucket, sand and polish. She made the house shine. She lavished a kind of love on the furniture rented with the house from Mr. Powel as she discovered beauty in a cabriole leg, a fretwork leg, a claw-and-ball foot. The light openwork design of a chair back and the delicate carving of the escritoire seemed exquisite to her. And there was an inexpressible pleasure in simply looking at the strong, simple columns and graceful cornices of the chimney piece.

"Don't work too hard," Kathy kept telling her. "I'm going to get a girl to help you." But somehow she never found another girl. Philly was glad that she didn't, for there was a boundless pleasure in doing all of it herself, in feeling that the house was her own handiwork.

Alex observed her efforts and admired everything she did. Thoughtful though he was, he failed in the first few days to perform the greatest kindness of telling her what had happened to Micah. She did not question him. She was determined not to pester him, for she believed that he would do everything he could. Gradually, however, a feeling of despair over Micah grew in her.

The day after she arrived she went to the prison at Third and Market streets when Mrs. Munger sent her on an errand. It took all Philly's courage to enter the passageway connecting the two gray double-storied buildings. When she asked a rough, dirty man if she could see Micah Heath, he laughed at her and then spoke obscenely. She fled.

For days she felt a despair that only hard work alleviated. Basically, she admitted to herself, she had come to Philadelphia to be near Micah and try to help him. There were times when she thought she'd give up and return to the farm and Tom and the Touts. Mrs. Tout had cried when she'd left and made her promise to come back whenever she wished. But now she was ashamed to give up so easily and go back.

Eventually, one afternoon in December as she was serving dinner, Alex told her that Micah would come to trial in a couple of weeks. He would plead guilty, Alex said.

"I know only one way to try to help the situation." He frowned. "I'm requesting a conference in chambers in which I'll say that Micah's shielding some *important* Philadelphians whose implication would embarrass the Crown. It's the sort of vile trick that sometimes tips the scales of what is called justice. I'll use nuance. You see Polk, who will be the judge, has a brother who's an *important* merchant."

Kathy clapped her hands together. "Alex, how clever!"

He scowled at her. "How low, you mean. But I've not been able to find another way. If he pleads innocent, I must find a party of witnesses who will testify as to exactly what he's been doing this past year and a half. And what has he been doing? He's been living in shadows, without an identity. Better I should commit a small perjury in chambers than to try to place a dozen perjured witnesses in the chair."

He came across the Common as the State House clock struck eight on the morning of December twenty-second. Light snow had fallen during the night and the Common was as untracked as a mountain meadow; across its dazzling whiteness the file of men ground a dark, straight path. First came a short, stout man wearing a blue greatcoat and carrying a curled bullwhip. He came next.

Although he'd grown taller, she would have recognized him anywhere by the way he walked with his head up and gaze traveling restlessly, as if searching for something. Then she realized that he walked without his familiar free swing; there was a catch in his stride, almost a limp. His right leg, she saw, was chained to the leg of the man marching behind him.

She exclaimed sharply, and Kathy, standing beside her, told her to hush.

His head had been shaved. Although it was a very cold morning, he lacked a coat; his tattered linsey shirt was tucked into loose duck trousers and the iron was clamped to a bare leg above his boot top. Surely he saw her as they left the Common and came straight across Chestnut Street, for he kept turning his head, studying everything.

Unable to contain herself, she cried, "Micah!"

He frowned at her and then his eyes widened. He tried to smile. His right arm rose slightly and fell.

She started toward him, but Kathy seized her arm.

As the file passed within a dozen yards, he stared at them searchingly, then suddenly turned his head. Two raggedly dressed men marched in chains behind him and a thin man carrying a musket brought up the rear. On the three steps up to the double doors of the State House the last man stumbled and almost fell. Micah and the second prisoner halted and looked around at him.

"Git!" the guard shouted, hitting the man with his musket butt.

"I'd *kill* that guard," Philly said, jerking her arm from Kathy's grip. "I'm going in there."

"Philly—"

"Miss Kathy!" She wished she could see Kathy's expression behind her veil. "I'm going in there and I reckon you nor nobody else can stop me." Turning, she strode toward the State House steps.

Kathy had declared that she would not go to the court today; she'd run on at length about it not being a fit place for a woman to appear. Next she'd forbidden Philly to go. But Philly plainly told her that she was going and would not be stopped. At the last moment, Kathy had pulled on cloak, hat and veil and silently come with her.

Now, at the double doors of the State House, Philly turned and saw Kathy trailing behind her.

The State House was a man's world, Philly thought when they stepped inside. Its corridor, crowded with noisy, jostling men, smelled of woodsmoke and tobacco and sweat. The door to the Assembly room on the left was closed, but people eddied in and out of the room on the right which currently served as a court. She pushed through the crowd and struggled into a large, square room of many windows.

Behind a raised desk on the farther side of the room sat the judge, a big, red-faced man wearing a black robe and a curious long wig. He pounded a gavel while he stared out a window with an absent expression. On the floor below him an old man in black smallclothes was reading something that Philly couldn't hear while a bailiff walked about thumping a long staff and shouting "Order!"

She pushed on through the crowd with Kathy's hand on her shoulder until she reached a wooden rail. Forcing herself between two men, she clutched the rail and stared at Micah, who sat with the other prisoners on a low bench facing the judge, his back to her. Alex, wearing a wig and robe, sat at a small writing table behind the prisoners' bench. Paying no attention to the old man reading, he talked to another man in robe and wig at a table next to his.

". . . Micah Heath . . ." Catching the name read by the old man, Philly wanted to scream at the crowd to be quiet. And it didn't seem right that Alex went on talking so casually when he was supposed to be here to defend Micah.

The old man stopped reading. The judge turned his head and scowled at the courtroom. Slowly the babble of voices died and the room grew quiet.

"The prisoner, Micah Heath, will rise," the judge said.

As Micah got to his feet, the fat man who had led the prisoners to court took a key from a pocket and leaned down. He seemed to take an endless time before there was a click and Micah stepped free of his leg iron. He stood, swinging his head in a swift, searching glance at the windows. Philly sensed him gathering strength to spring. *Go,* she thought. *Run!* He could do it. He could throw himself through yonder window and land on the ground running and there was no one who ever could catch him.

Perhaps the judge sensed it too, for he leaned forward, peering at him curiously as he said, "The prisoner has heard the charge read. How does he plead?"

Micah did not answer. He turned slowly, as if the judge did not exist. Alex was on his feet. But Micah was not looking at Alex. He was searching the crowd for someone, his sharp gaze probing here and there until it lighted and fixed. On *me,* Philly thought, her heart racing. Kathy's hand tightened on her shoulder, gripping so hard that she almost cried out. She thinks he's looking at *her,* Philly thought, but he's looking at *me,* surely he's looking at me.

The judge rapped his gavel. "The prisoner pleads?" he said.

Alex said, "Your honor, my client—"

"I plead guilty," Micah said in a firm, deep voice that Philly would not have recognized as his.

"Before the court passes sentence on the plea of guilty," the judge said hesitantly, "does the prisoner wish to say anything?"

Again Micah turned slowly and stared. But not at *me,* Philly thought as Kathy's hand tightened on her shoulder again. At *her.* What was wrong? He was not looking at her with hatred or any other emotion. He was simply staring, as if waiting for her to speak. *I* could say so much for him, Philly thought sadly, but he wouldn't want me to if I could. He wants *her* to say something. But what in heaven's name would or could she say that he should stare at her so strangely?

Others were turning and staring now. Alex turned quickly and saw them. He faced the bench. "If it pleases the court," he said, "I should like to speak a few words concerning the accused—"

"Give the lad and us a true oration, Mr. March," a man called.

"Order!" shouted the judge, rapping his gavel.

"Order!" shouted the bailiff, rapping his tipstaff.

"It does not please the court, Mr. March," said the judge. "Save thy oratory for another day. The prisoner will come before the bench."

Micah stepped forward.

Frowning at him, the judge said, "Upon the prisoner's plea of guilty to the charges read, the court hereby sentences him to two and one-half years in the Philadelphia City Prison by order of the authority invested by His Most Gracious Majesty . . ."

Run, Philly thought. The bailiff was so slow in coming toward him. There was still time. *Run! Run! Run!* Through that window and away. But he did not stir. And then it was too late as the bailiff's hand closed on his arm.

She saw him indistinctly through tears as he went out a side door ahead of the man with a musket. Two and a half years! She had not known what to expect, but two and a half years was too long for him to endure that prison. She had hoped, she had believed, that somehow something at the last moment would set him free. She had prayed for his freedom. But what good was prayer?

Kathy was pushing her through the noisy crowd, a hand still fiercely digging her shoulder.

Outside, Kathy clutched the iron railing. "I'm ill," she murmured and tore back her veil. Her face was pale, her lips tightly compressed.

"You shouldn't have come, Miss Kathy." Philly took her by an arm.

"I wanted to come," Kathy said.

"You *wanted* to?"

"And I didn't want to, Philly."

"I don't understand."

"Nor I." She began pulling on her gloves and paused, staring beyond Chestnut Street at the Common.

Out there Micah walked ahead of his guard toward the prison. This time, Philly saw, they were not treading a straight path in the wide field of snow. Their path veered crookedly as Micah kept looking back at them.

XIII

"You go downhill quickly at first," said Israel Dorfenberg. "Then you go level, or not at all. If you stop going, you die. If you die, they carry you out or you bury yourself in these four walls."

Micah was not sure that he understood completely; although Dorfenberg spoke English without a trace of accent, it was difficult to understand the things he said. He was, to be sure, a Jew—and so suspect. He was the first to greet Micah when the guard pushed him into a stone-walled chamber after the judge had sentenced him.

Three men sprawling on straw looked up at Micah as the guard slammed and bolted the iron-studded oak door. He paid them no mind. First he paced the width of the cell—four steps, and then its length—six, to the high, iron-barred aperture which admitted faint winter sunlight and a blast of icy air. The cold fresh air failed, however, to purge the cell of its stench. This second-floor cell was, he saw, identical to that in which he'd been locked before his sentencing.

Grasping the iron bars above his head, he sprang up and, resting his weight on his elbows, stared at Third Street. Down there people went their ways in freedom. One bar seemed loose. He shook it hard.

"That route is impossible," said Dorfenberg and introduced himself.

Micah dropped to the floor and faced a young man of medium height, stocky and swarthy. His eyes were dark and very large, his nose thick and boldly hooked.

"Christ-killer," growled one of the men on the floor.

"A Jew," Dorfenberg said imperturbably, "though innocent of that particular crime. Innocent, in fact, of any crime except bankruptcy." He cocked his head at Micah, his hand still extended. "Of what crime are you innocent?"

"Smuggling," Micah muttered. He took Dorfenberg's soft hand reluctantly, thinking that you could trust a Jew least of all the untrustworthy creatures in this world.

"Tell him nought," said the man on the floor. "He's set to spy on us, the dirty Christ-killer." He was a scrawny little man with a wry neck that made him seem to be constantly looking over his right shoulder as if pursued. "If you're in debt," he said to Dorfenberg, "why ain't you over in the debtors' building 'stead of here with us?"

"You ask me that a dozen times a day, Smith. And a dozen times I tell you the debtors' prison is full and so they house me here. That, at least, is what they tell me, and I'm in no position to argue with 'em. Why is any one of us so important that they'd send a spy? To learn what? To learn that you, Smith, are innocent of rape? And Potter there"—Dorfenberg pointed to the white-haired, cadaverous man lying beside Smith—"is innocent of stealing a farmer's purse?"

Potter coughed rackingly and muttered, "Let us hear from the Thirty-fifth Psalm. *Plead thou my cause, O Lord, with them that strive with me, and fight thou—*"

Smith kicked Potter and got to his feet, wailing, "Locked in with a Christer and a Christ-killer!" He spun around, beating his fists on the door and shrieking, "I ain't gonna stick it another day!" Faint cries from other cells mocked him and, curiously, seemed to reassure him, for when he turned he was grinning. "What's your name, lad, and how long did you get?"

"Micah Heath. Two and a half years."

"Two and a half years! They got me thirty." He cursed *them* at length. "And I never done it. The dirty slut as said I—" Turning his body from Micah so that he could look directly at him, he whispered, "I ain't aimin' to stay."

"Nor me." Micah smiled suddenly and pointed at Smith's wry neck. "I reckon you didn't aim to do it. I reckon you must've been looking at another woman when you did it to the one accused you."

Dorfenberg laughed, and Smith laughed too. "Capital!" Dorfenberg cried. "You have imagination and you haven't lost your humor. We must pick each other's brains."

But he didn't want to pick Dorfenberg's brain, and he didn't want Dorfenberg picking his. He was suspicious of him. Although he'd never met a Jew before, everyone said that all were cheats and cowards, liars and tricksters.

He didn't want to talk to anyone. He only wanted to escape and run west. Failing that, he'd rather lie here and hate Murdoch—and Kathy. What she had to do with his being here he didn't know, but for some reason there was a pleasure in hating her now. Although he knew that Murdoch had not caused his arrest at the Callowhill Market, Murdoch was the cause of all his troubles. *He began betraying me long ago and never stopped.*

After a while, as he began to tire of imagining he was slowly strangling Murdoch, he heard Dorfenberg talking.

"When my father believes that I've been sufficiently educated by my sojourn here, he'll pay my debt and I'll be freed."

"You tell your father," said Smith, "that there ain't nothin' edjicatin' about the pokey."

"But there is," Dorfenberg said. "It's as edifying as any of the colleges at Oxford or Cambridge. The principle is the same. You are brought into contact with new ideas and persons and your movements are greatly restricted. For instance, I may gain some priceless information from Micah here that will serve me well for the rest of my life." He looked at Micah closely. "I'm sure that you know something about firearms. Do you realize that I never have held a pistol or musket in my life? I would like to know how to shoot. Some day I might want to shoot something. Can you describe to me how it is done, Micah?"

"You never even held a gun?" Micah asked incredulously.

Dorfenberg nodded and sighed. "My education has been sadly neglected. It's almost useless in this new country. I can read Greek, Latin and Hebrew. I speak and read German, French and Spanish. The mysteries of mathematics are fairly clear to me. But I cannot fire a musket and I would like to learn. Instruct me."

"You can't really learn unless we had a musket," Micah said.

"I can learn," Dorfenberg said firmly. "Some day when we are freed from here I'll go into the woods and shoot a bear and have my picture painted with one foot on its head. I'll send it to my father in London and he'll pass it on to our relatives in Antwerp and Rotterdam and Genoa and Paris and they'll say *Ja, Si, Oui,* that Israel is now *frekh,* which is the Yiddish word for bold. And whilst I and all my relatives know that I never was *frekh,* but an arrant *feiglink,* a coward, they will see the evidence that I have changed. They'll remember that I'm the first one of the family to come to America where I've had numerous adventures, including the terrible scandal of bankruptcy, and I've changed from *feiglink* to *frekh.* Now, Micah, let us imagine that these bits of straw which I lay here on this clear place are a musket. Instruct me."

And Micah did.

As prisoners, the inmates of the Philadelphia City Prison naturally were obsessed by the idea of freedom. They were, as Israel was fond of pointing out, dry tinder for the flame of liberty—not only liberty from these walls, but liberty to move freely across the land, to take, to hold, to enjoy. "License, really, is what most want," he'd say, shaking his head. "But where does liberty end and license begin?"

By means never clear, news from the outer world reached the prison as soon as it did the majority of Philadelphia residents and was passed quickly from cell to cell. On Christmas Eve, for example, while they were unmelodically singing "Kiss Me Quick My Mother's Coming" in the cold darkness to celebrate Micah's twentieth birthday, they heard a shrill whistle.

"A word!" Smith got to his feet and groped in the darkness for the wooden shutter which a jailer had handed in yesterday to cover the barred aperture. The shutter clattered down and Smith cursed. "H'ist up, Micah, you're spryer."

Micah gripped the bars and sprang up. Above the whine of wind he heard a man shouting through the bars of the adjoining cell, "Hear this and pass the word. D'you hear?"

"Aye," Micah cried. "I hear."

"Post from Boston to the London Coffee House tonight. D'you hear?"

"Aye, the London Coffee House." He had a sudden vivid image of the tavern at the southwest corner of Front and Market streets and he longed to be close to that roaring fire where an ox haunch always turned on a spit.

"In Boston," the invisible prisoner shouted, "a week ago Thursday eve, the sixteenth, we boarded three tea ships and dumped three and a half hundred chests of their blasted tea in the harbor. Up liberty! Pass the word!"

"Up liberty!" Micah shouted joyfully. He whistled shrilly and Israel and Smith pressed close below him in the darkness to listen. "Hear this and pass the word," he cried against the wind.

"I hear ye," a voice called faintly from the cell window on the other side.

"In Boston," he cried, "a week ago Thursday eve, the sixteenth, we boarded three tea ships and dumped three and a half hundred chests of their blasted tea in the harbor. Up liberty! Pass the word!"

"Up liberty!" the voice cried.

Smith and Israel were shouting excitedly in the darkness, and then Israel, plucking at him, demanded, "Tell me, tell me this, Micah. You said *we* boarded the ships and dumped *their* tea. Is that what the fellow in the next cell said? Did he say *we?*"

"Of course."

"Oi! Oi! Oi!" Israel stumbled about excitedly in the darkness. "A stranger says 'we' and you say 'we, of course.' Those London idiots, those *Narren,* that do not understand *we!*" He tripped over Potter and grasped Micah's shoulder. "Don't you see? *We* here are the—the dispossessed, we're *nothing.* And *they* over there in England don't understand. They think tonight, this Christmas Eve, as they sit by their warm fires— You do not understand unless you have seen them, those sots, those *nouveaux riches* and opportunists brought to power by a stupid king. *They* think that *we* are only a handful of discontented merchants and planters and a few small mobs that the merchants pay to riot now and then. They do not understand us. But it will be much worse if *we* fail to understand that *they* mean to grind us under heel as they've ground their unfortunate, passive fellow Englishmen."

Israel knew how to make imprisonment endurable, Micah soon realized. He simply reached into the resources of his mind for sustenance, as a hungry man reached into a larder. Their food was scant and very bad; twice a day, at morning and evening, a jailer unbarred the door and thrust in two loaves of moldy bread, a pitcher of water, and a pot of watery, lukewarm soup, with a plate of fat meat scraps and a few cold potatoes added twice a week. Micah feared that he would weaken and sicken on the diet. Yet Israel seemed to thrive on it. Worse than unappeased hunger, however, was the constant cold of the unheated cell. During the day they endured it by pacing and exerting themselves, but at night, when the four of them huddled together under two threadbare blankets, it was almost unendurable. Potter was slowly dying of the cold, Micah believed, and Smith developed a racking cough. But Israel seemed warmed by some internal fire.

While Israel sustained himself by reflection and monologue and conversation, Micah sought a way to escape. Above all, he decided, he needed an ally outside the prison. And on the New Year, 1774, after only nine days of imprisonment, he was certain that he'd found one.

In midmorning a jailer opened the door and led him to a room on the ground floor.

"Micah, it's pleasant to see you." Alex March stepped toward him, hand outstretched.

Micah gripped his hand, and then he saw a woman—a girl wearing a cape and cap. "Philly!"

She came toward him slowly, one hand in a little raccoon muff, her gray eyes staring up at his and filming with tears. What a pretty thing she'd become. But what was she doing? Her arms passed around him in a strong hug. He felt her young breasts straining against him, and he started back in embarrassment and a kind of alarm. This wasn't the woods trace; it was years later and he was different and she— Then he felt the weight of something she dropped from her muff into his right pocket. He knew the weight.

"Here now," the jailer said roughly, "none o' your—"

"But he's my brother," Philly exclaimed indignantly, stepping back and swirling her cape as she faced the jailer.

Alex stared at her, his jaw slack. So he did not understand her purpose! The jailer said, "That don't mean, young miss—"

Now she was charming him, smiling and explaining that this was a basket of food they'd brought to her *brother,* Micah, and because he looked like such a kindly jailer, who must have children of his own, she'd brought him a hot pie and a cold pie too which she'd baked herself. Wasn't it a shame that a man had to work on New Year's? Now the jailer was her prisoner, for he was grinning and saying that it wasn't to regulations for food to be brought a prisoner.

"And this isn't to regulations either," Alex said, pressing coins into his hand. "But if the world always ran to regulations it sometimes wouldn't run at all. Would it?"

"No, sir. Thankee kindly, Mr. March, sir."

"Thank *you*," Alex said. "And I'll see you again after Miss—Heath has paid further visits to her *brother*."

"Micah"—Philly stared at him searchingly—"I want you to know I'm very happy living with Miss Kathy and Mr. Alex. They have the nicest house on *Fourth* Street just *eight* doors south of Walnut on the *left* side. I have my own room at the top with a window, a real windowpane, looks out on the back yard. How's it faring with you?"

"All right." There were many things he wished to say to her, but he could not. Nor was it the presence of the jailer and Alex that prevented him; even had they been alone beyond the Ohio he doubted that he could have found the words.

When the cell door slammed shut behind him, he dropped the basket of food on the floor and plunged his right hand into his pocket. Gripping the knife Philly had put there, he whooped and leaped straight up. Then he leaped forward, spun on the balls of his feet, and faced the three, his knife drawn. They gaped at him.

"You can't beat a woodsy!" he cried. "I'll take even a little girl woodsy to the best man in town." He gestured grandly to the basket of food. "Help yourselves, share and share alike."

"Chicken!" Potter muttered hoarsely. "Pie!"

"But the knife," Israel whispered. "How did you get it and what are you going to—"

"My woodsy girl dropped it in my pocket." Micah laughed silently. "With this knife I'll cut my way out of this prison."

"Oi! Oi! Oi!" Israel held his hands to his head. "I believe you would. I believe you could."

"And why not?" Micah demanded, surprised. "We'll *all* go free with this." He spun the knife and caught it. "I've figured the way—the only way." He thrust a thumb over a shoulder at the window. "I'll carve out a bar, working nights. It's thirty feet to the ground, I figure. The last night, the night we leave, we'll cut these blankets and weave us a rope that'll—"

"Oooo!" Israel rocked, clutching his head as if in pain. "Loosen the bar, make the rope, swing to the ground, escape from the castle—and away!" He looked up at Micah. "Where do you think you are? The four-teenth century and you a Crusader? Away where—and to what?"

"I'll tell you," Micah said fiercely. "Away west, that's where. Beyond the mountains and down the Ohio where—"

"Oi! An escaped prisoner, always pursued by the law—"

"Where I'm going there ain't no law but the law I make."

Israel shook his head. "Every day since I landed I've seen what a romantic people live on this continent. So today I see it too."

"You don't got to come with us, Dorfenberg," Smith said. "I always heard how Jews was coward."

"I wish," Israel said sharply, "that every time we disagree you were not so sure that you were right and I wrong simply because I'm a Jew. In the first place, it's impossible for me to squirm through that window with only one bar removed. I'm too fat. And I'd judge that your shoulders won't squeeze through either unless you remove both bars, Micah."

Micah, pausing as he cut the fresh loaf of bread into four equal portions, looked at him searchingly. He liked Israel. Now that he felt he'd escape soon, he realized how much he'd miss him. "Israel," he said, "I'll h'ist you up there and if you can't get through I'll take out both bars 'stead of one."

To his amazement, Israel's dark eyes clouded with tears. "That's the greatest kindness offered me since I came to America," he said. "Maybe it's the greatest kindness of all my life. You may hoist me up and then I'll hoist you and you'll see that you must remove both bars to escape yourself. It may take a week or more, however, for you to understand why I decline the honor, the very great honor, of escaping from this prison with you."

In time he came to understand not only Israel's reason for refusing to try to escape, but many other things. He had a great deal of time, for working at the bars was a slow and painful task. Smith was too frail to support Micah's weight for any length of time, but Israel proved to be as solid as a rock despite his apparent softness. While Micah stood on his shoulders and worked at the bars, he would sit on the floor and talk end-lessly about his youth in England, his travels on the Continent, his family who ran a large international banking establishment.

"You must be mighty rich," Micah muttered to him one night as he stood on his shoulders and chipped at the mortar.

"Obviously," Israel said drily. "You can see that from my present cir-cumstances. Please move your left foot a fraction to the right. Thank you. Presumably my father is rich, but I shan't be unless I increase my acumen. Since I was a young boy I kept saying to him, 'Papa, I want to go to America,' and one day, almost three years ago when I was twenty-one years old, he called me in and said, 'Go to America, Israel, and try to collect these debts.' So I came and my father's debtor in Boston was an imprisoned bankrupt and my father's debtor in New York had disappeared without a trace. But I fell in love with the country and I wrote my father that it was a land of opportunity and that I wished to stay. So he replied with a draft of two thousand pounds, saying, 'See what opportunity you can make of this, Israel.' I met the most enchanting man who took me into the York forests—magnificent country—and I invested in fine rich land. My friend and I planned that settlers would move in and buy from us and develop the land, but they did not. I wrote my father that it was a great land of opportunity and that I could use more capital, so this time he advanced me one thousand pounds and wrote, 'View opportunity with care, Israel.' I came to Philadelphia, a delightful city where I hope eventually to establish myself and bring my second cousin's sister from Dusseldorf and marry her. Her name is Esther and she is beautiful—but that is another story. I found an excellent opportunity to invest in a flour mill on the Schuylkill, though in order to do so it was necessary for me to try to recover some of my investment in land, but for complicated reasons the value of the land had declined and so— Do I bore you, Micah?"

"A mite, Israel. I don't ken business."

"Nor do I as well as I should, it seems, despite all my father's careful training. However, believe me, the flour mill will prosper in time, for we have devised a scheme— But it has not yet. We had bad luck. A ship sank. The insurer was insolvent. Blow after blow of outrageous fortune. Suddenly I found myself owing more than five thousand pounds in addition to the three thousand I owed my father. I won't try to explain to you how this can happen, but believe me that it can. A creditor hounded me . . ."

It fairly made Micah's head swim to hear of the baffling, terrible things that could happen when a man entered business, even in this land of opportunity.

He tried to describe Israel to Philly when she made her weekly visits to the prison, but she was more interested in learning how he was faring. There wasn't much he could tell her in front of the jailer. He was able to make her understand, however, that he was progressing with his escape plan, and that he would go to the March house where she apparently had some means of helping him on his way.

Despite his persistent nightly efforts, it was March and his knife was worn to a stub before he exultantly announced one morning that in three or four more nights the second bar would be loosened.

He had made careful plans. Smith and he would swing down the rope and go separate ways; Israel then would haul up the rope and replace the bars. The jailers were so unobservant when they flung in food that it might be a day or two before they realized that two had fled. He had feared that the jailers might deal hard with Israel after they discovered the escape. But Israel assured him he would have no trouble; his father would pay his debts and free him any day now. If it weren't for the fact that his credit would be forever ruined, he would escape with them, he said. Potter did not concern Micah, for the old man seemed out of his head most of the time. He was dying, they knew. As Israel put it, Potter already had buried himself in these four walls.

The morning after Micah said they would escape in a few nights, he was surprised upon awakening to see Potter staggering about the cell, muttering to himself. When the jailer swung open the door and put their rations on the floor, Potter suddenly gripped him by an arm and mumbled to him. The jailer tried to shove him off. But Potter, tears streaming down his cheeks, clung to him and begged to speak to him in the corridor.

"He's mad!" Israel shouted. "Pay no mind to him."

Micah, springing to his feet, swung a fist at Potter's head to stun him. The blow glanced off Potter's head and struck the jailer, who roared for help while Potter screamed and the others shouted incoherently. The jailer, with Potter clutching him, stumbled into the corridor and slammed the door shut.

Guards manacled them together at musket point and searched the cell. They found the worn knife and loosened bars. Israel, tears streaming down his cheeks, said it was his knife and that he had loosened the bars.

But Potter, standing at a distance, shrieked, "The Jew's innocent and I'm innocent, praise the Lord!" He pointed. "It's the wild and godless young one there as did it. Micah Heath!"

"Six months in solitary will tame him," a jailer said.

XIV

FAR into the spring Philly continued to hope that any night she would hear a pebble tossed against her window and know that Micah had escaped. Even after Israel Dorfenberg called on her late in April and told her there was no hope of his escaping from solitary she believed he somehow would win his freedom.

She liked Israel and rejoiced with him that his father had paid his debts and he was now able to launch a new career in this land of opportunity.

Israel was such a sympathetic young man that it had been on the tip of her tongue to tell him her darkest secret. She wanted to go with Micah. She *would* go, as far west as he wished. *I love him.* She was sixteen years old now, she was a woman. And she was willing, she wanted to be *his* woman. Lord help me, she often thought. It was sin. But it was true. *I love him.* But supposing he didn't love her?

For weeks she was in torment. And then, one evening as she was planting a back-yard garden, she told herself, You've been having mighty nonsensical thoughts. You'd best put him from your mind. She never quite succeeded in forgetting him. But she tried. And in trying she found pleasure in other things.

For one thing, there was her garden which she hoped would eventually—some year, though not this—turn the drab back yard into a pleasant riot of flowers and herbs and vegetables. She planted sunflowers and honeysuckle at its bottom to cover the unsightly fence and then set out gooseberry and currant bushes. In the fields beyond Tenth Street she found boneset and pennyroyal which she transplanted. She grew vegetables, of course, to justify the garden's existence. But squash and peas and runner beans were pale satisfaction compared to hollyhocks against a wall and sweetbrier trailing over a path, to say nothing of squills and yellow day lilies and peonies and syringa.

A garden, as she planned it, was all future. She would grow sage and anise and mint and balm. There would be roses to make rosewater, and sweet-smelling lavender to place between the sheets in the linen chest, and rosemary to pick and carry to church where she would sniff a sprig when the sermon grew intolerably long. If it were really her own garden, a place where she would *stay,* she would have quince and apple trees and trellised peaches and apricots. All this sweet confusion she would enclose in a boxwood hedge, and in the exact center of the garden would be a summerhouse where she would sit, in early morning and late evening, enjoying her small private world while she did needlework or read a book in which she'd mark her place with a blade of striped grass picked at her feet.

Although her garden was small and incomplete, she liked to sit there on a bench. She'd do the mending or, when she had time, read books which Alex recommended to her, spelling out on a little slate words she did not understand and later asking him their meaning. Occasionally, however, she simply sat, her eyes half-closed, letting her strong body enjoy a sense of languid weakness while her thoughts flitted like random butterflies.

Another pleasure was going to the big stalls on Market Street with Kathy each Wednesday morning. Philly bought much of their food from street vendors on other days. But on Wednesday, "big market day," Kathy insisted on going herself, not because she enjoyed it (she detested it), but because every real Philadelphia lady went to market on Wednesday. Only the infirm and the ignorant *nouveaux* rode in fair weather; the real ladies walked, as Philadelphia ladies had walked to market for a century. The ladies of the Allens and Shippens, the Willings, Francises, McCalls and Hopkinsons, the Logans, Norrises, Mifflins, Pembertons and Powels walked. And so Kathy walked.

She brought a dash to the ceremonial chore that delighted Philly. Each week she wore a different hat, either a wide, flat skimmer or a great scooped horsehair bonnet which hid her face tantalizingly and made every man who passed her want to peer into it. On a bright day she'd protect her fair skin from the sun with a green mask which she held in place with a little bar between her teeth. Finding it impossible to talk without removing the mask, and learning it was considered very French and daring to shade herself with an *umbrilloe,* she eventually discarded the mask in favor of a red silk parasol which her father ordered for her from Paris.

Philly, carrying a basket, always walked three paces behind her, as was the custom of each lady's maidservant on market day. Unlike most ladies, however, Kathy was forever chattering over her shoulder. "Alex tells me I've got to be more economical," she'd say. "What did I pay for beef last week, Philly?" "Sixpence a pound, Miss Kathy, and it ran heavy to fat." "It did that, Philly, and I'll have a round with Longstrom himself at his stall today."

But she never did. In fact, she seldom entered one of the fabulous hundred-foot stalls and wandered its length, pricing and comparing and demanding the best cuts. Instead, she was forever meeting ladies outside and gossiping and laughing interminably until, glancing over a shoulder, she'd call, "Philly, be a dear heart and pick up those things." And Philly would dive into the crowd that eddied through a stall, shrewdly pricing and comparing and demanding the best available.

When she lugged her laden basket from the stalls, she'd find Kathy talking and laughing somewhere. Kathy's beauty, her quick tongue and laughter invariably somehow refreshed her, just as it seemed to refresh the fascinated ladies with whom Kathy talked.

Eventually, when they were homeward bound, Kathy would say over a shoulder, "You're a gem, Philly, an absolute gem. I don't know what I'd do without you. Hold your head high, dear, and take small steps. Show those trim ankles to the three sailors coming."

Philly, flushing with pleasure and holding her head high despite the weight of the basket, tried to ignore all pigtailed sailors who forever swaggered through the streets with their glazed black hats cocked jauntily.

Almost invariably, however, they'd cluck or whistle softly to her as they passed.

Sailors and shopmen and laborers in striped ticken breeches never stared or smiled at Kathy, for she obviously was a lady. And gentlemen, who tipped their hats and bowed to Kathy, never stared at Philly, for she obviously was a maidservant. These manners had nothing to do with the nature of men, Philly came to realize. They were, rather, the nature of society.

Although she did not seek closer friends than Kathy and Alex and Mrs. Munger, she discovered through other servant girls whom she met at the public water pumps and the Sixth Street Presbyterian Church that "society" was not confined to ladies and gentlemen. No one lived in total isolation; everyone *belonged* somewhere. The society of servants in the homes of esteemed citizens was eagerly sought by laborers and their families—who usually were rejected. Craftsmen, or "mechanics" as they were called, generally looked down on servants but respected shopkeepers, while shopkeepers usually were respectful to responsible servants and skeptical of most mechanics.

Yet no group conformed rigidly to prescribed social rules, Philly learned in time. If living in the city was like being a raisin in a huge mound of dough, it was at least a yeasty loaf. People moved—up and down and sideways. There existed, everywhere, the expectation of change for the better. A youth's greatest expectations lay in trade, a girl's in making a shrewd match with a shrewd youth. Although the butler of a prominent household stood at the pinnacle of servant society, a wise servant girl knew that an energetic shopkeeper's assistant might some day own his own shop and eventually become a powerful merchant who would hire a butler for his prominent household. Besides, shopkeepers' assistants almost invariably were younger, handsomer and gayer than butlers.

Although living in an age of great ambitions, Philly did not seek to be more than a good servant to Kathy and Alex. In a time of inveterate matchmaking, she had set her heart on making a match with a prisoner in the city jail who probably seldom thought of her. She was not in a hurry; time, she believed, was on her side.

But Kathy, she constantly observed, was in a great hurry. She could not understand why. At the age of nineteen Kathy surely was envied by ninety-nine of every hundred women in Philadelphia.

Nevertheless, on a warm afternoon in May, Philly came upon her crying quietly in the back parlor. As she started to tiptoe from the room, Kathy said, "A terrible thing has happened, Philly."

She whirled, her heart knocking. "Is Mr. Alex—"

"Oh, he's all right." Kathy dabbed at her eyes. "He's *not* all right, but nothing has happened to him in the way you mean."

"He's *not* all right, Miss Kathy?"

"It's *his* fault," Kathy said angrily.

Her tears always evaporated so quickly. Perhaps her anger concerned a matter that sometimes worried Philly. It was time, she believed, that Kathy showed signs of bearing a child.

"It's all his fault"—Kathy's angry flush deepened—"that we aren't invited to the Allens' tomorrow."

Philly stared at her in amazement.

"I've just learned from Sally that *everybody* will be there—except us and the Reeds. And I've concluded Joseph Reed isn't really *anybody*."

Why in the mortal world should she be so upset?

"Alex has been acting like an ass."

"Miss Kathy!"

"He *has*," Kathy said heatedly. "Do you know what he's become? He's a *radical!* He and Joseph Reed. It's terrible. We'll be ruined socially. Papa is greatly upset about it. But I didn't realize it was so widely known until the Allens didn't invite us to their garden party tomorrow."

Philly knew that Alex was a radical in politics. And, although she'd never discussed the subject with Micah, she reckoned he must be one too. After all, a radical was simply a person who wanted more people to have the right to vote and had harsh notions about the way the Parliament was treating the colonies. If you were a man, what could you be except a radical? What a pity that a woman was no account in politics.

She finally interrupted Kathy's tirade. "I allow you might as well know, Miss Kathy, that I'm radical bent too."

"Get out of here!" Kathy cried, her eyes flashing.

She went into the kitchen where Mrs. Munger asked, "What's the Queen of Fourth Street yelling about?"

"You shouldn't talk so about her. She's just upset."

"She's upset half the time nowadays," Mrs. Munger said. "But what's she upset about *now?*"

"I told her I was radical bent."

Mrs. Munger grunted. "Till now I wasn't sure I was anything. But if she's agin' radicals, that's what I am." She sniffed scornfully. "There's two things that girl needs. First, a man as'll give her a good beating, and second, a healthy baby. But she's got the barren look."

Philly, horrified, thought that it sounded like a curse. "What d'you mean?" she whispered.

"She's got the barren look," Mrs. Munger repeated. "She's got the hips for bearing, but the barren look is on her face and it don't ever deceive me."

"Philly!"

Hearing Kathy's voice at the kitchen door, Mrs. Munger began noisily rattling a spoon in a pot. Philly opened the door quickly and faced Kathy.

"She's got the barren look!"

For days Kathy pondered Mrs. Munger's remark which she'd overheard. She was not angry. To the contrary, she hoped that Mrs. Munger was right. What pleasure was there in children? A child in the womb caused a mother pain and deformity; a child in the cradle confined a mother in her prime; a child grown left a mother old before her time. It would be wonderful to enjoy love's passion without ever suffering love's pain. The judgment of Mrs. Munger, a wise woman, surely was right. It was time she raised Mrs. Munger's salary.

She wished some similar chance remark would relieve her anxiety over Alex. In some respects he was a good husband. Six days a week he walked to and from his office with his lawyer's green bag over a shoulder and worked diligently. More important, he loved her ardently.

But socially he had become impossible. His notion of a good time was to bring home odd strangers—westerners and Yankees and southerners—and discuss all manner of obscure matters until she could have screamed with boredom. He turned his back on the influential people who could help him rise. And he could not afford to do that. For, no matter how hard he worked, they remained quite poor.

Then, after the events of the nineteenth of May and the succeeding days were explained to her, she was angry with him. *He* never explained those events satisfactorily. Fortunately, Papa did.

On Thursday evening, the nineteenth of May, a boy ran to the house panting that Alex was wanted immediately at the City Tavern. Some man named Paul Revere had ridden in with important dispatches from Boston. Alex dashed out of the house so quickly he forgot his hat.

On Friday morning when she awakened she discovered that he was not lying beside her, that he had not slept in their bed. Thoroughly alarmed, she sent Philly flying to the City Tavern in search of him. Before Philly returned, he appeared. At first she thought he was drunk, for his eyes were bloodshot and his hair disheveled and he was singing some wild ditty as he marched into the house.

"You've been drinking all night long," she wailed, "while I—"

"Not a drop of liquor, my darling!" he cried, hugging her and kissing her hard on the lips. True, she noticed, his breath did not smell of spirits. "But I *am* drunk, Kathy, drunk on the cup of liberty!"

Such wild talk! As best she could make out from listening to him while he ate a huge breakfast, there was the devil to pay in Boston. As a result of those hotheads throwing the tea in the harbor last December, the port was closed, commerce suspended, and a tough military man, General Thomas Gage, had arrived as the new Governor of the Colony of Massachusetts Bay. Now the Boston Committee of Correspondence had sent Revere south with letters to Committees in other colonies, seeking advice and aid. But what was a Committee of Correspondence?

He grinned as he dipped a piece of bread in a fried egg. "My dear Kathy, you obviously never listen to a thing I say. You sleep with a member of the Philadelphia Committee of Correspondence. He's your *husband*. A Committee of Correspondence is a group of men dedicated to the idea that our rightful liberties in these colonies are endangered by a foolish, callous government. A Committee knows it is rather like a log: quite useless by itself, but when joined with many others it offers a stout bulwark."

All right, she told him. Forget his fanciful flights of speech. Where had he been all night?

Discussing strategy with Thomson and Reed and Thomas Mifflin and a few others, he told her, and then helping Thomson compose letters to people in Boston she'd never heard of—a John Hancock and a Thomas Cushing and a Samuel Adams (Oh, yes, she'd heard Papa speak of *him*, the wild Boston radical).

But what did he mean by "strategy"?

He frowned. "To try the almost impossible, Kathy. To try to goad this old Quaker woman of a province, this smug, timid place called Pennsylvania, into awareness of its proper role in the affairs of these colonies. We need strength and vitality here of the sort that Massachusetts and Virginia possess. We have it in the western counties, but Philadelphia suppresses it."

"You ought to be ashamed of yourself," she snapped, "standing up for those pigheaded Yankees over your own people."

"I've never been in Massachusetts," he replied, "but I've met and corresponded with many men from there, and I feel that they are my own people. Much more than the Government's placemen and timeservers here, opportunists like Joseph Galloway and the whole Allen tribe . . ."

She did not really listen to him after such blasphemy. He was tired, she decided; he needed rest.

But he could not sleep. After an hour of tossing, he was up and off somewhere—certainly not to attend his practice, she knew. At three o'clock he appeared again, bringing to dinner none other than that mere *messenger* from Boston, Revere. Increasingly Alex displayed absolutely no discrimination in his associations, she thought. Revere was a plain, ruddy-faced, middle-aged man, with a wide mouth and dark warm eyes somewhat like Alex's, but by his own statement at the table he was a mere silversmith, a *mechanic*. Noting his blunt, strong hands, Kathy thought that he must not perform very delicate work. Yet Alex, to her annoyance, plied him with questions about his craft as if it were as important as the law.

They left together after dinner and she did not see Alex again until almost dawn on Saturday morning when he stumbled exhaustedly into bed and immediately fell asleep. When he awakened around noon, he told her something about a mass meeting at the City Tavern. He had been appointed to a committee to frame a reply to Boston. And then he left again.

The watch carried him home long after midnight. She never had seen him drunk before. He was courteous, but when he bowed deeply to her he fell down. Then he sat on the floor and cursed some of the most respected gentlemen in Philadelphia as cowards because they refused to give full support to Boston.

She forgave him on Sunday morning, however, when he made ardent love to her. The city was quiet, iron chains barring the streets to wheeled traffic while the hundred bells of Philadelphia rang out for Christian worship. Pagans worshiped too, she thought drowsily, in the warm, real flesh. If only every day could be a wonderful pagan Sunday.

But Monday, unfortunately, was not like Sunday. A few minutes after Alex went off to his office Papa called and commanded her to *listen* to him.

"Unless you shake Alex out of his *radicalism,* he won't have an important friend left in Philadelphia," he said as he paced the front parlor, hands clasped behind him. "He and the other radicals argue that we should join with Boston in halting trade with England until they give us back some of the liberties they've taken away."

Although Papa admitted that sounded logical, he asked her what would happen if the British closed *all* the colonial ports? And supposing Philadelphia merchants lived up to the agreement while merchants in other cities continued to trade surreptitiously? Philadelphians would be ruined. No one knew this better than John Dickinson, the most esteemed and brilliant gentleman in Pennsylvania. Why, demanded Papa, did Alex go out of his way to antagonize this moderate gentleman who was the coming leader of the Province? No wonder that ladies were cutting Kathy and that they were invited no place of consequence. One could not attack John Dickinson and survive socially in Philadelphia.

"The worst thing about radicals," Papa said, "is that they don't confine themselves to the important facts of trade and business. They have all sorts of half-cocked notions that can lead to dangerous social changes. They want to—unify and tamper with the—structure of the *classes*. What would you think, Kathy, if one of these street vendors had a vote that was as good as mine?"

It was unthinkable, she agreed. She promised that she would *talk* to Alex.

She tried, but it was futile to argue with him. He twisted things about so persuasively that he almost had her believing he was right and *she* in the wrong.

There was only one recourse, she decided. She would not let him make love to her until he changed his reckless political course that threatened to ruin them both. It was her one formidable weapon against him. Her mind never could gain mastery over his. But her body, his desire for her body, could. His strength as a lover she could and she would turn into his fatal weakness.

She considered going to the farm, but finally rejected the idea. Social ostracism in town was preferable to the deadly monotony of the country. Instead of moving to the country she'd simply move into a separate bedroom.

For days he acted baffled. Once he remonstrated with her over "this frostiness in June." Soon now he'd see the light of reason, she thought.

She was totally unprepared for his reaction when he returned home one day and exclaimed, "Kathy, I'm such a fool! It's just occurred to me. Is it—is it possible that you think you—we might be going to have a child?"

Laughter seemed to explode in her. "No!" she gasped. "No, I'm not going to have a child."

He glared at her. "Is that cause for humor?"

"It is," she said sharply. "So you think *that's* why we have separate rooms. The conceit of the man! The happiness of the woman who tells him no! What greater source of humor?"

"The *happiness* of the woman!" he cried. "Do you mean—"

"I mean"—her tone was calm—"that I don't want a child, that I won't have a child."

"So that's why—"

"No, that's not why we have separate rooms. I won't have a child because I'm barren."

"Barren?" He raised his brows. "How do you know?"

"Never mind. I *know*."

"But—"

"I said I *know*. It has nothing to do with our separate rooms, which are caused by quite another reason. Don't you know what it is?"

He shook his head wonderingly.

Carefully controlling her tone, she said, "Because you're failing me—us, as a husband. You are *not* trying to make us prosper. You're wasting your time and energy in a hopeless cause in politics. You have antagonized everybody who *is* anybody in Philadelphia, leaving me friendless and with no social position whatsoever."

"You are a wench, Kathy," he said slowly. "You're quite a wench. Let me make sure I understand you. You want me to withdraw from politics, snuggle up to the Front Street royalty, go into practice for myself where the *money* lies, and try to be the most popular man in town. Is that right?"

She nodded.

"And *then* you will resume being my wife?"

"Yes."

"You like to drive bargains, Kathy. You must have been talking to your father."

"That's unfair to me," she said hotly. "And you should show him more respect."

"And he should show me more respect. But no matter." He stared at her, his expression inscrutable. "Leaving *Papa* out of this, it's interesting to ponder what I should do besides what you tell me I must do. I could, of course, take a belt to you and then, just for the hell of it, rape you too."

"You wouldn't *dare!*"

"Of course I *dare,* Kathy. And I would, if I thought it would do any good. But I don't believe it improves a woman's character to beat her. When you choose to be a wife again you know where your husband is."

He strode from the house.

So she had not won, she thought numbly. She never could win against him. Going to her room and flinging herself on the bed, she cried. Not quiet tears, but wail after wail of desperate anguish until Philly, hearing her, came running and tried to calm her. But she would not be calmed until she was exhausted.

Bathing her flushed face and swollen eyelids with cool rosewater, Philly murmured, "There now, Miss Kathy, you'll be all right. Everything will be all right."

Nothing was right for many days, however. She and Alex were like strangers. She knew that Philly realized something was wrong. Several times she started to explain the trouble, but Philly always changed the subject. Gradually she came to realize that Philly knew what the trouble was and failed to sympathize with her. At first it made her angry. Then she told herself that she must learn to keep her own counsel.

She realized the strength to be found in this course when her father called late in June. She used to tell Papa everything while he told her nothing; as a result, he was stronger than she. Now she told him nothing, not a word about her quarrel with Alex or her chagrin at social failure. As a result, she felt stronger than Papa.

Perplexed by her reticence, he talked more than usual. She listened alertly, remembering that what Papa said was not always what Papa meant. He was, she realized, subtly shifting his stand of a few weeks ago. It meant, inevitably, that he was shifting with the prevailing powerful opinion of Philadelphia.

The fact was, he said, that in August gentlemen of the first fortune throughout the colonies would begin gathering in Philadelphia to confer on the troubled times. There would be much socializing. Philadelphia must put its best foot forward. Philadelphians must close their political ranks and present to all the colonies a solid, sane phalanx. . . .

Now she was beginning to understand. For the first time she savored this boiling pot called politics. What was said seldom was meant, and what was meant seldom was said. It was—intrigue, wherein the strong kept secret counsel. It struck her fancy, it fit the mold in which she was determined to shape her future.

Mulling for hours her father's remarks, she came to a conclusion that surprised her. It mattered less that Alex be on the winning side than that *she* be. If she remained friendly in the camp of his enemies, then he would have to follow her after his defeat. It was the way to possess him—and much more than him. She knew from what Papa had said that Philadelphia had come to a decision about Alex and those of his persuasion. Since it could not silence them with ice, it would smother them in a warm social embrace.

A couple of days later a liveried servant delivered a letter at the door just before dinner. When Philly handed it to Kathy in the parlor, Alex glanced at her inscrutably over the paper he was reading.

As she broke the seal and read it, her hands trembled.

MY DEAR MRS. MARCH:

Mr. Dickinson and Mother and I request the pleasure of the company of yourself and Mr. March at Supper on Wednesday next, 6th July. Of late we have seen too little of such widely esteemed friends as yourselves. We do Pray that both of you, especially amongst others invited, may be free to join us in these times that cry for the gaiety and warmth of Friendship.

Your Devoted Friend,
MARY NORRIS DICKINSON

FAIRHILL
1ST JULY 1774

Your devoted friend! Mary Dickinson scarcely knew her. Invited by the great John Dickinson and his wife to Fairhill where even Papa never had set foot! More than a formal invitation, this was the extended hand of friendship and equality.

She marveled at her calm tone as she said, "It's an invitation to supper at Fairhill Wednesday next."

Alex smiled wryly. "There should be something in the Bible about loving to death an enemy you cannot destroy. Would you care to go?"

She swallowed. Would she care! Was there anyone in the Province who would not care? *Keep your own counsel!* Surrender, it seemed, was the most complicated and difficult act. He who accepted, gave; he who gave, accepted. In surrendering, one could encompass and eventually defeat one's victor. She swallowed again.

"I think," she said in a low tone, "it's important to know what you wish to do."

He stared at her, his brows rising. "That's most thoughtful of you, Kathy. It sounds pleasant to me. But let us be guided by what you wish to do."

Oh, joy, she thought, this is his capitulation!

"Since it sounds pleasant to you," she said, "let's go."

She wondered if she had time to move her things back into their room before Philly served dinner.

XV

THE road north from Philadelphia to the crossings of the Delaware curved under a huge black oak a half-mile outside the village of Frankford. It was a place Alex always remembered.

He rode out from the city with more than a score of men that August twenty-ninth of 1774 and waited in the shade of the oak to greet the Massachusetts delegates to the First Continental Congress.

Thomas Mifflin, who led the party from the city, had invited Alex because he had corresponded with one of the Massachusetts delegates, John Adams. Mifflin, wearing a richly embroidered plum-colored suit, was the only member of the Pennsylvania delegation to the Congress who went to Frankford. He certainly had not acted like a Quaker for some time now, for he affected a martial air and wore vivid colors and talked as militantly as a Yankee. Yet Joseph Galloway, firmly controlling the Pennsylvania political machine, considered him so ineffectual that he let the Assembly name him a delegate in the otherwise solid bloc of conservatives.

Thomas McKean, the delegate from Delaware, stood by his horse's head under the oak, his thin, hawk-nosed face turned to the road into the village. John Sullivan, the heavy, florid New Hampshire delegate, talked loudly with Edward Rutledge, the younger of the aristocratic brothers in the South Carolina delegation, whom Alex had marked as impetuous and militant. The others, like Alex, were "mere patriotic observers and followers," as one of them, Dr. Benjamin Rush, put it.

"They're coming," called McKean, pointing.

Out of the village lurched a large, dust-covered coach pulled by four chestnut geldings and flanked by two armed horsemen. A groom sat beside the driver. Behind rode two liveried footmen who were barely recognizable as Negroes under a coating of white dust.

"Let no one say Massachusetts lacks style," said Rush.

"No one here does," growled McKean, raising his lace-fringed hat and waving it. "But I hear the coach and servants were loaned to the delegates by John Hancock, the first fortune of Massachusetts."

The driver began pulling in his horses with rigid arms, the groom slowly eased back the brake handle. Above the jangle of harness chains the brakes squealed as the heavy-bodied coach rocked to a halt under the oak and the footmen simultaneously leaped to the ground like released jack-in-the-boxes. The waiting men broke into a spontaneous cheer.

Alex glimpsed a large white hand pushing aside a dusty red silk curtain, and then he saw a pale, weary, heavy-browed face that shook slightly as if with a constitutional palsy.

"Gentlemen," the man said in a high, nasal voice of little force, "good afternoon. Permit me to introduce myself as Samuel Adams of Boston."

Surely this could not be the one they called The Man, the one they knew to be the force, the very spirit of liberty. Then Alex observed the pale blue eyes which, like Dr. Franklin's, were patient rather than probing.

Mifflin stepped forward as the footmen opened the door and dropped the step. Sam Adams descended first, carrying his wig in a trembling hand, as if it were a Parliamentary scalp, while his other hand plucked ineffectually at his dirty linen and untidy clothing. Two other men descended stiffly, men of undistinguished appearance who would have been passed unnoticed in any crowd. Adams introduced them: Thomas Cushing and Robert Paine.

"Brother John?" Sam Adams called into the coach.

"Coming, Brother Sam," replied a dry voice, "as soon as I've untwisted myself."

"My cousin, Mr. John Adams," said Sam with an inflection of pride.

John Adams was not a tall man, not more than five feet six, nor a large man, nor did he give off any of the magnetism one associated with a great man. Rather, he was a compact man, plump and yet muscular, who moved quickly and surely. A balanced man, Alex judged from his well-shaped head. His complexion was ruddy, his eyes bright blue and penetrating, as his Cousin Sam's were not.

Could these be the vaunted lions of the north? The Virginia delegates would be surprised when they met them; Joseph Galloway and his friends would secretly smile. Sam Adams, impoverished tax collector and professional agitator; John Adams, Thomas Cushing, Robert Paine, Boston lawyers. Sam and John and Tom and Bob they called one another.

McKean rubbed his jaw thoughtfully.

Suddenly Rutledge, the aristocrat, smiling warmly as he was introduced to Sam Adams, rested a hand on the agitator's shoulder and said loudly in his slurring accent, "The pleasure of a lifetime, sir. I wish you to know, Mr. Adams, that I, among many in my province, have great affection for Massachusetts—and put not a feather of trust in the word of King George the Third."

Voices died in a startled silence. The Massachusetts delegates stared at one another.

And then John Adams, smiling, said, "I didn't know, Sam, that we had cousins south of Connecticut Valley. . . ."

Alex waited near the oak again on the morning of May tenth, 1775. Again the purpose was to welcome the delegates from Massachusetts, accompanied by some from Connecticut and New York, to a new and momentous Congress, the Second. But the scene was quite different from the preceding August.

This time he wore a small sword and a light green uniform with a white leather belt crossed over his chest and a green jockey cap plumed with a red cockade. The uniform was that of the Silk Stocking Company, though he now was Captain Alex March of the Philadelphia Associators. A captain, to be sure, by virtue of politics rather than training, he thought. A captain of only a few days with a commission hastily scribbled soon after a beat rider thundered down this road bearing word that the Yankees had fought pitched battles with British soldiers in a couple of obscure towns named Lexington and Concord. Yet an enthusiastic captain, eager to learn and to fight.

He sat his horse in a ragged line with other mounted officers of the city: Major Thomas Mifflin of the Quaker Blues, who had been read out of Meeting; Captain John Cadwalader of the Silk Stocking Company;

Major Joseph Reed; and Captains John Shee and Robert Magaw of the Associators . . . The roll of Philadelphia officers was long; longer, it seemed, than the roll of privates. Surely everybody was an officer. Even— or especially—John Dickinson, *Colonel* John Dickinson, who sought to command every situation. Including this situation under the oak.

Alex, studying Dickinson's thin, intelligent face as he tried to hold his slender, frail body erect in the saddle, wondered what history would make of him. Or would history, he wondered, allow more than a footnote to all their passions, dismissing them as a mild, confused revolt of colonial bumpkins quickly put down?

He instinctively liked Dickinson, as he knew Dickinson instinctively liked him. But he instinctively mistrusted Dickinson's caution and dread of change, as Dickinson instinctively mistrusted his boldness and desire for change. If he would disavow radicalism, Dickinson would welcome him into his conservative camp. Joseph Galloway had exiled himself now to his country place, Trevose, all prestige lost; "Tory" he and his followers were called after the First Congress defeated their purposes.

Now it was the turn of Dickinson, who seemed conservative to John Adams but was a wild radical to Galloway. Alex knew that Dickinson respected his intelligence, his ability in writing and speaking. If he would desert Reed, Dickinson would make sure of his election to the Assembly and perhaps, eventually, grant his greatest desire by seeing that he was appointed to the Congress. For Dickinson controlled the Assembly and so controlled the Pennsylvania delegation which was the pivotal power of Congress. Sitting on horseback under the Frankford oak, John Dickinson probably was the most powerful man in America.

Here came one who knew it, Alex thought, as the driver of the first in a train of carriages from Philadelphia turned off the road and drew up his chariot in the green field across the road from the line of waiting officers. Mrs. Alex March, Kathy, rode in it with Mrs. John Dickinson, Mary, and Mrs. Edward Peacock, Hettie. Tilting her green silk parasol, Kathy smiled and waved to him.

It would be unmilitary, he presumed, to wave to her from a formation.

"Go ahead and wave, Alex," said Magaw, "she looks so pretty over there."

"You look pretty too, Bob," he replied. "She's probably waving to you."

Shee guffawed and waved his cap, crying, "Good morning, Kathy."

"Gentlemen!" Dickinson called sternly. Then, to make it clear his reprimand did not include the ladies, he rose in the stirrups and doffed his hat to them.

Carriage after carriage filled with ladies and gentlemen wearing bright spring colors lined the edge of the field which glistened with morning dew. There were no outright Tories and few forthright radicals among them, Alex noted, because outright Tories had no use for this Congress and few forthright radicals had a carriage or the time to ride up the Old York Road on a bright spring morning. Most of these people represented the opinions between Tory and radical. But, eventually, what would they become? Eventually, could you be anything except either an outright Tory or a forthright radical?

The growing crowd was irresistible to Dickinson. The politician in him overcame the soldier and he left the formation and rode along the line of carriages, speaking to everyone. When Kathy made some smiling quip to him, he beamed and actually laughed.

She was a shrewd one, Alex thought, and this closemouthed shrewdness often troubled him. He knew that she held his friend John Adams in contempt, although she never had spoken a word against him. Now here she was welcoming John Adams to the city. She did so because Mrs. Dickinson did so. Because she charmed everyone, the Dickinsons apparently had forgotten that she also had charmed Dickinson's enemy, Galloway. During the hectic social life that attended the opening of the First Congress and cut across party lines, as everyone sought to charm everyone else, she had seen to it that she caught the fancy of Galloway, who could not resist the flattery of a beautiful woman. The truth was that scarcely a man living could. Not even rough and hearty John Shee, a fighting radical who hated Galloway and all his ilk. "Kathy," John called her, quite unaware that she tolerated him only because he was a friend of her husband.

Everybody liked her these days because everybody believed that she liked them. With time and careful cultivation of her talent for charm, she could become the most popular woman in Philadelphia. Men would rise and men would fall, but Kathy would go on forever. It was rather terrifying. And he never would be able to make her understand why. She simply refused to try to comprehend the importance of causes, the moral necessity of believing in a principle and hewing to it.

Now a horseman galloped up the road from Frankford, waving an arm and shouting, "They're coming!"

Dickinson reassumed his military role at the head of the line of officers and cried, "Pre—sent!"

Their swords winked raggedly in the morning sun. Mifflin's horse plunged and he almost dropped his sword; his face red with mortification, he clung desperately to the saddle.

The northern delegates rode quietly under the oak. Seeing John Adams' grave expression, Alex remembered him saying the previous October that he believed he was leaving Philadelphia forever. What optimists they'd been at the close of that First Congress. With the Association for Nonimportation agreed upon, the Declaration to the People of Great Britain approved, and the Petition to the King signed, they had believed peace would magically descend, like snow in burning August.

But now they were plunging violently, though reluctantly, into a strange rebellion. . . .

Six weeks later, on the morning of June twenty-third, Alex rode out of Philadelphia to the Frankford oak a third time. He was one of a large company traveling that far with the new Commander in Chief, General Washington, and his party on their way to Cambridge. He did not join in the group's gaiety; never in his life, he believed, had he felt so low.

Joseph Reed, knowing how he felt, drew him out of the formation of militia officers to ride with him behind the generals. Reed, flushed with excitement, could well afford to be gracious to his junior partner in law and politics, Alex thought glumly. For he was Colonel Reed now, secretary to George Washington at the General's invitation. There, too, rode Major Mifflin, aide-de-camp to the General. They were off on a great adventure, while he stayed behind. Had he somehow failed to meet the approval of the tall, silent, fox-hunting gentleman from Virginia? That was not so, he knew, telling himself to stop wallowing in self-pity. It was Reed's doing that he was staying in Philadelphia.

A few days ago, after Congress appointed Washington to command at the instigation of John Adams, Alex had drawn the General aside following dinner at Reed's house.

"General Washington, sir, I wish to place myself at your service in any capacity you desire. I mean, sir, preferably in the field."

The General's cold blue eyes studied him penetratingly, his expression impassive. His thin, wide lips worked for a moment over his bad teeth. "Or at my headquarters, Captain March?"

"I am certain, sir, that your headquarters always will be in the field."

The General's blue eyes lighted, the strong muscles of his broad, pockmarked face tightened against the impulse to smile. He turned. "Colonel Reed."

Reed moved quickly to them.

The General said, "I believe, Colonel Reed, that our cause could make good use of Captain March with us at Cambridge. You've commended him to me before."

"Indeed I have, sir," Reed replied, "and I do again. He has great capabilities, not the least of them being to inspire the confidence of all manner of men." Reed looked at Alex. "But—"

"I'm a good horseman, sir," Alex said quickly. "I'm adept in the use of arms. My health is excellent. I've been studying Saxe and Puységur and drilling my company."

"All of us have need to learn, Captain March. We—myself foremost— are but imperfect soldiers."

The General actually had doubts of his own capabilities, Alex realized with surprise. The modesty he'd seen him display on numerous occasions must stem from deep self-doubt.

Looking at Reed, the General said, "You were remarking?"

"I was remarking with deep regret, sir, that while Alex—Captain March—would ably serve our cause in Cambridge, he can better serve it here."

"Do you mean, Colonel Reed"—again the General almost smiled—"the cause of your law practice?"

"No, sir." Reed tried to distort an expression of annoyance into a smile, and Alex wondered how long he would work cordially with the General. Would the Virginian's ice quench Reed's fire, or would Reed's quick warmth thaw some of the cold barrier behind which lay—what? Another as yet unknown military genius, a Scipio Africanus or a Charles XII of Sweden?

Reed, considering the General's remark sarcastic, was striving desperately to control his quick temper, Alex saw. The General saw it too; his mouth worked, as if he wished to sink a rotted tooth in his thin under-lip, but dreaded to show both his teeth and his regret at his remark. He was said to struggle constantly to control a violent temper—"A hell of a temper when roused," Richard Henry Lee of Virginia had described it to Alex. So he understood Reed's struggle. He understood a lot about men because he had tried to understand a lot about himself: the impulses to anger and overweening pride. His trouble was that he lacked a grace with words, those most precious instruments of facility in human relationships.

"Our practice, sir"—Reed, firmly in control of his temper now, mustered a smile—"has fallen away to almost nothing. We subsist, like Elijah, on what a few ravens bring us . . ."

They were not quite as hard put as Reed made them sound. The trouble was, as Kathy frequently remarked to Alex, he and Reed spent far more time working at politics than at the law.

"My purpose in wishing Alex to remain in Philadelphia," Reed said, "is that he's so highly useful to the cause of liberty here. Of course you know the condition of Pennsylvania, sir."

The General nodded.

So he would not ride off on the northern road to military glory, Alex knew despondently as Reed talked. True, the Pennsylvania Assembly did not represent the opinion of the majority of people in the militant cause of liberty. True, the colonies could not present the essential united front to redress the wrongs of King and Parliament unless the attitude of the Pennsylvania delegates to Congress was changed. True, therefore, that the radicals must gain control of the Assembly in order to change the Pennsylvania delegates to Congress. But was it therefore essential that he remain here to continue in that political struggle while the final cause was resolved on northern battlefields?

He thought not. He was known as Reed's man and Reed wanted to be remembered here while absent in the north. Reed was ambitious, for Joseph Reed as well as for the cause of liberty. I'm Reed's man, he thought bitterly. And I'm Kathy's man. Nearly everybody wants me while all I wish to be is my *own* man.

There was no hope in the face of the arguments Reed carefully marshaled for the General. The General might be an aristocrat, but he was a radical to the tips of his large, bony fingers. If history bothered to observe him, it might easily ignore that fact, failing to remember what radical meant. A radical believed in meeting threats with force. A radical believed in the necessity of presenting a united front to a common enemy. A radical like the General did not yet believe in anything so rash as independence, but that was only because he was a man who approached new and revolutionary ideas slowly and cautiously. Ideas, as such, held little appeal for the General unless they were practical; when, therefore, the General believed it practical to enlarge the struggle to one for independence, he would seize on the idea enthusiastically and prosecute it forcefully. For he was a radical. He had proved it when he offered to raise a thousand Virginians at his own expense and march to the defense of Boston, as John Dickinson had proved he was not a radical by forbidding the Pennsylvania Associator companies to drill until news came of Lexington and Concord.

"Captain March," the General said, "I'm—grateful. I'll remember your offer."

"Thank you, sir," Alex muttered.

Then, to his astonishment, the General rested a large hand on his shoulder, and the blue-gray eyes tried to express something his working lips could not. Perhaps, because he looked at all men through his own experience, he remembered some earlier time when his own desire for service had been thwarted. You could not be sure, you never would know because of his hesitation over words. With sudden insight, Alex thought, He doesn't *dare* speak for fear some warm spontaneous sentiment would rush from his lips that would embarrass him because it would mark a flaw in his overwhelming passion for self-control. The General's hand fell heavily to his side and he turned away.

Riding beside Reed now toward the Frankford oak on this bright spring morning, Alex paid little attention to his suggestions and directions as to how he should conduct himself in the political struggle. Yes, he would continue his voluminous correspondence, he would continue to speak and confer and write for the newspapers under the pseudonym of Ajax. Yes, yes, yes, Joe—pardon, Colonel Reed, sir. But he had no stomach for politics this morning.

He watched the General riding ahead, his tall, thick body sitting his big roan stallion with unconscious grace. All self-consciousness gone now, taking with it all his awkwardness, the General was at ease. This was his element, astride a strong horse, passing through green fields at the head of a goodly company of warm friends and admirers. He wore black riding boots and buff breeches and a beautifully tailored blue coat with swallowtails buttoned up and gold epaulets lying low on his sloping shoulders. His dark brown hair, powdered, was tied in a queue, and on his head he wore a plain low-crowned, wide-brimmed civilian hat stitched to the crown in back and at both sides near the temples. A black cockade in his hat, the epaulets, and a small sword at his side were the only distinguishing marks of the soldier. Otherwise, he might have been ready to spur after the fox at the cry of "View, halloo!"

Alex did not hold the General in awe, but he had insatiable curiosity about him. What was the General thinking as he rode at the head of this bright cavalcade while the drums rolled and the fifes squealed "Hot Stuff" back there among the neophyte soldiers and fledgling politicians? Did he realize they were not the hot stuff that British soldiers knew themselves to be when they marched to that lilting music?

Could the General detach himself from this winding column, as Alex did, and view it from the impersonal viewpoint? If he could, did he see how small and somehow pathetic they were crawling across the infinite sweep of water-coursed land? Had he any sense of history, of that personal sense of destiny that might be the very bones of history? Probably not. Unquestionably not, if you recalled his watchful withdrawal into himself whenever ideas were being discussed.

Probably he did not know, for example, that this cavalcade followed a tradition ages old, that since the days of the Achaemenian Empire it had been the custom of politicians to go a little distance from the city gates with their military heroes. It was quite possible that the General never had heard of the Achaemenian Empire. It did not matter. He had heard of the British Empire. If he fancied himself a mere Virginia fox hunter rather than an Alexander come to Gaugamela, it was far better for their great experiment in liberty.

Close to the General rode one who had a sense of history and personal destiny. Major General Charles Lee, the eccentric former British Army major, had sought in vain the position of Commander in Chief. He seemed never to cease talking and the General seemed never to cease listening to him. Perhaps the General believed he was learning something from Lee; perhaps he was merely being politic.

It troubled Alex that the fox hunter was a political general, with no military experience except some inconclusive brushes on the frontier years ago. Actually, however, all the generals were political appointments.

Take Major General Philip Schuyler riding behind the General. He was a sallow, waspish man, clearly without force. But New York must be represented in this brain child of Congress called the Army. And so they'd agreed on Schuyler, a man of wealth and social position with no military experience. Yet by what means other than politics could generals be raised?

"What are you smiling at?" Reed demanded sharply.

"I was just thinking what a fine general I'd make, Joseph. If I dwell on it long enough I'll prove conclusively to myself that I'd be an excellent commander in chief."

Reed's expression struggled between a smile and a frown. "Guard your tongue, Alex," he said in a low voice. "Keep your balance."

Yes, sir, Colonel Reed, sir, Alex thought drily.

Balance. That was a word. It resolved his wandering reflections. Balance was the quality of the fox hunter. Imbalance was the characteristic of Major General Charles Lee. This civil war required men of perfect balance. If the fox hunter preserved his, he would indeed be perfect as the General.

Alex said good-by to Reed under the Frankford oak where the military escort and the chattering Congressmen halted. The fifes shrilled and the drums beat and the General rode on with his party. When he'd gone a little way he reined his roan stallion around and courteously lifted his plain flat hat to them. More significant, to Alex, was the sincere humility with which he bowed his head.

Alex heard a low, whistling sound. Looking around, he saw John Adams seated on an old pad he'd hired from some livery. The sound, he realized, had been Adams exhaling through his pensively bared teeth. The pendulant tip of his nose seemed to droop lower and he suddenly looked old.

"I feel low," he said to Alex. "When shall I see Abigail and my children and Braintree again?" He gestured toward the General's party. "They go. We stay. There's pain for all of us, but far more glory on that road north than for us who turn back south."

He sawed his nag around and kicked her toward the city. But he glanced back north, as Alex did. The General had touched his stallion into a canter and was leaning forward in the saddle, as if he were a part of his flowing-muscled horse.

Adams pursed his lips. He opened his mouth and then closed it firmly and turned his face toward Philadelphia. Alex knew that he wondered exactly what he had wrought when he created the General.

XVI

HE WALKED out slowly into bright morning sunlight as the deep, resonant clang of church bells rolled about him. *Free,* they told him. *You-are-free-free-free!*

His gaze swept the cloudless blue sky from west to east until he stared the sun straight in its glaring eye. Blinded, fighting tears he blamed on the sun, he lowered his head and blinked around. Everywhere small suns blazed in the quiet, deserted streets of Philadelphia. A young woman walked toward him out of a fiery sunball.

"Micah."

"Hello, Philly." Her small hand gripped his strongly. "I've been looking old sun straight in the eye." Now he saw that her gray eyes were filled with tears. "Reckon you must have been sun-staring too. It's Sunday, ain't it?"

"Yes," she said, "it's Sunday, the twenty-third of June."

"In '76."

"In '76, Micah."

He breathed deeply and grinned. "Well, hello old summer Sunday on the twenty-third of June in '76."

"Micah—" She hesitated. "Are you feeling—tol'able?"

"Tol'able?" He threw back his head and laughed silently. "Philly, you just watch how tol'able I am." The earth seemed to push its strength up through the cobbles as he ran a few steps. Somersaulting without touching his hands to the pavement, he whirled and grinned at her expression of amazement. "That's how tol'able I am."

"What—what d'you reckon you'd like to do today, Micah?"

"Be a deer," he cried, "and race to the top o' the Tuscarora. At the cliff there I'll change me to a hawk and spread my wings and fly all over the world."

Here now, he told himself, you simmer down. You're twenty-two years old and away past play-acting time, but Philly clearly enjoyed his spirits, for she was smiling like the summer sky.

"You're free!" she said.

Free—and strong, he thought. He'd kept himself in shape these two and a half years while trying to escape and forever being caught. After he and the other prisoners had been transferred to the new city jail at Walnut and Sixth streets in January he'd found a close friend in another prisoner who wanted to escape, Macaroni Jack Maloney. A muscular, middle-aged man with a broad face scarred from temple to chin, Macaroni Jack had been a sergeant major who deserted the British Army.

"Have you seen Macaroni Jack since he was let free last month?" he asked Philly.

"Alex made him the company sergeant," she said. "He's been drilling and drilling the men. And when he's not at the Common he's mostly in our kitchen."

"Listen here, Philly," he said, alarmed, "don't you let Jack loiter 'round your kitchen. He's a good soldier, but he talks rough and—"

"He does *not*," she said. "He's as polite and good-spoken a man as you ever saw. I think he's took with Mrs. Munger, she's the cook and a widow, and I know Mrs. Munger is took with him. First time Macaroni Jack came in with Israel, she saw he had warts on his left hand. The moon was right and we had new potatoes, so she charmed his warts and the next morning they were gone. She more than charmed his warts, I reckon, because ever since then he's been sitting around the kitchen eating everything in sight and staring at her like he's moonstruck. He chops our wood and hauls our water too."

"That don't sound like Macaroni Jack to me." He caught the basket from her hand. "I hanker to get off these pavements a while and breathe some fresh air. You've vittles in this basket?"

"Yes, Micah. Fresh bread, jam, sweet watermelon pickle, pressed beef tongue. And lemon tarts—I recollect how you like 'em."

When they reached Market Street, he turned left. In a moment he said, "I see I've still got the bird-homing instinct. I turned west without thought."

She looked up at him intently. "You still aim to go west, Micah?"

"In time," he said. "In time. I'm *en*-listed first. I reckon you heard how Alex—Captain March enlisted me along with Macaroni Jack whilst we was still in jail. When we've cleaned out the British, *then* I'm going west."

"And get yourself some land and build yourself a cabin?"

"Well"—he rubbed his shaved head—"not right away. You can have yourself a heap of land, Philly, just traveling over it and hunting and trapping it. There's no need to plant yourself on a little of it like you was an oak."

"But you need a place to go from and to," she said. "You need yourself a place."

"In time," he said. "In time. I reckon you'll never go down west again."

"I reckon I will if I get the chance," she replied quickly.

He looked her up and down and smiled. "You've gotten mighty citified for going west. That's a pretty blue thing you're wearing."

"Thank you, Micah." She tossed her head and smiled up at him, fluttering her long eyelashes.

He frowned. "No cause to thank me. I just said it was pretty. And don't you start those eye-fluttering ways. It ain't—well, it ain't becoming to you."

She flushed. "I don't know what you mean. But—well—" She suddenly doubled her arm and held it out to him. "You think I'm not strong enough for living west, you just feel this muscle."

"And don't *ever* do that." His frown deepened. "A man'd think— Well, it's different with you and me." She looked so troubled that he said quickly, "Let's see that arm," and touched her muscle delicately between thumb and forefinger. "Hard as iron." It was, too. It was harder than a girl's should be.

She works her too hard, he thought. But he didn't want to mention Kathy. "You work too hard, Philly. You need fun when you're young."

"I'm not so young," she said quickly, "and I have fun. I'm having fun this morning and I—" She pointed to a frame building at the corner of Ninth and Market streets. "One day a week I have fun there. That's the Committee of Safety building. We go there and pick lint and spin and weave flax and wool they bring in from the farms. We're making shirts for the army."

"We? You mean you and Kathy?"

She shook her head and looked away. "But we don't serve lamb at home. You remember that now you're free. Don't eat any lamb since you're for nonimportation. The lambs must grow so we'll have wool."

He checked himself from patting her bare head. There was no question where *she* stood.

"This city's pushing out," he said. "It's no time since it was country here."

"There's country just beyond," she said.

He sniffed it soon, the almost forgotten warm summer smell of sun on land. He walked faster, breathing deeply, as the houses fell away. There were fields of wheat, rippling in a breeze, and woods beyond. The land dipped, the Schuylkill glinted in the sun.

He vaulted a snake fence. "I'll hand you through, Philly." But she, silly girl, grasped the top rail and vaulted too. She sprang gracefully, but her foot tripped on the high rail. He dropped the basket and caught her.

She was light enough, but his sense of surprise jolted him like a heavy blow. She was soft as a kitten and she smelled sweetly of something that grew in the woods, verbena or sweet fern. He saw her wide eyes close to his. He did not want to let her go. Then, remembering how good she was and disgusted by his sudden desire, he set her on her feet.

"Don't," he said and picked up the basket and walked ahead.

"Don't what?"

"Don't vault rail fences. It ain't ladylike."

"But I'm not a lady."

He took care not to look around at her as she followed him through the wheat field. "Just try to act like one and maybe you will be some day. You—you remember you're growing up, Philly."

"All right," she said meekly.

A girl of her age needed a father to look out for her, he thought. "When boys are around," he said, "you—you just keep a halter on your spirits."

"All right, Micah. I will."

Swallows skimming the wheat made him want to skim the earth and he suddenly cried, "I'll run you to the trees."

She dashed past him, running like a boy, her skirt pulled high on flashing, white-stockinged legs. He bounded after her and they ran side by side until they reached a stand of pines.

"There," she gasped, "I reckon you'll say I should have haltered my spirits."

"It's different with me, Philly. I'm like your older brother."

She groaned.

"What's wrong?"

"Nothing," she said. "I'm trying to get my breath."

He sniffed deeply of resin as they passed through the pines. There was the twang of a nuthatch, he told her. Look at that red squirrel leaping. Smell the sphagnum, he said as they skirted a bog. Hear the chickadees.

They came, at last, to the Schuylkill and sat down in the shade of a beech. Chewing on a blade of grass, he gazed across the river at the fields rolling beyond and tried to calculate the distance to the deep woods.

Philly said, "You'll never rest easy, Micah, till you've gone back there."

He looked at her sharply. "I reckon not."

"Then why don't you go?" She sounded almost angry. "Why do you want to fight in this war? You haven't asked me once this morning anything about what's been happening. I could tell you lots. But you don't care. So why do you want to fight?"

"I know enough," he said. "I know there's British in this country where they don't belong. I know that the likes of me never will be anything till we're rid of 'em."

She rested her chin in the palm of a hand and stared at him. "Tomorrow you'll begin drilling with the company. And any day now you'll all march away. Nobody *told* me that. But I know it. I can tell from the way Alex and Kathy are acting."

"How's she acting?"

Philly looked across the river. "Upset. Why shouldn't she be? She *loves* him. She don't agree with him, though she's not a Tory. But she loves him and she can't bear the thought of him going away Lord knows where."

"What about old Murdoch?"

She shrugged. "You know *him*. He's always all things to all men. I know he's making money selling supplies to our army."

Micah cursed him silently.

"Have you heard Jack say what sort of a captain Alex is?"

"He says he's the most decent officer he's ever known. He's inclined to be too kind to the men, Sergeant Jack says, but he reckons with experience Alex will be a fine officer. He says he's better than Colonel Magaw, who's the colonel of your regiment. *I* know why Magaw's the colonel instead of Alex. Everybody knows. They—the Associators—made Alex stick with politics where they figured he's ablest and they made Mr. Magaw and Mr. Shee the colonels of the two regiments. Now the old Assembly is dead and Alex says his job is done. He's ready to go."

"And so am I," Micah said.

"Kathy knew I was going to see you today, Micah. She wouldn't ever mention this to you. But she said to me, 'If the company really goes, I hope that Micah will watch out for Alex.' I know she wanted me to say that to you and I know that you will watch out for Mr. Alex."

Micah took the blade of grass from his teeth and studied it. So Kathy thought he was stronger than her husband.

" 'Course I'll watch out for him," he said slowly. "But I reckon he can watch out for himself. Alex is a good strong man, Philly, and don't you ever forget it. He did everything he could for me, coming to visit me often in prison and all the time knowing there's not much I can ever do for him."

Both he and Macaroni Jack probably would still be in prison if Alex had not come to their aid, he knew. It had helped, too, that the new jailer was a patriot and Associator.

One day in May, after Israel had returned from his unsuccessful venture in the Indies and joined Alex's company, he and Alex had come to the prison. The jailer certainly respected Alex, for he'd let them come into solitary where no visitors were allowed. When they'd entered the dim corridor, Micah and Jack, in adjoining solitary cells, were drilling. That is, they stood at the bars of their cells and shouted military orders to an imaginary company. Some would call it play-acting, they knew, but it helped to pass the time.

Although Micah longed to go west as much as ever, he reckoned that he'd join the army for a spell when he got out of prison—if he ever got out. He'd heard that the British had turned out the Indians and that they were burning and massacreeing and running wild clear to the old Shawnee Hunting Grounds near Bedford. Then go out there and kill Indians when you're free, he told himself. The trouble was that he hadn't much stomach for killing Indians. But both he and Macaroni Jack had a mighty yen to kill British and the hired Hessian mercenaries who were said to be on their way to America. When they learned, at the end of March, that the British had evacuated Boston and General Washington's army had taken the city, they were alarmed. This civil war might end before they had a chance to fight in it.

He and Macaroni Jack were keeping the war going the day the jailer brought Alex and Israel to solitary. They were shouting out the orders! "Measure loads! . . . Measure out your loads! . . . Dry your powder pans and keep 'em dry!"

"Silence!" a voice cried. "I'm the jailer, Noah Tatum!"

"Lie down, old Tatum," replied Macaroni Jack. "You're in our field of fire."

"Micah!" Israel called. "It's me, Israel, and Captain March. We—"

"Captain of what?" demanded Macaroni Jack. "A raft or a clothes press or—"

"A company of soldiers." Alex's voice rang clearly. "A company that could use you if you fought as well as you talk a fight."

In the sudden silence water dripped somewhere. Then Micah said quietly, "Mr. Alex—Captain March, we fight better than we talk. But all we can do here is talk. Yonder's Sergeant Major Macaroni Jack Maloney, lately of the British Army, who's ready. And I'm ready. When can we get out o' here and fight?"

"God help us every one," said Tatum, "if *them* was what stood between us and the Hessians."

"God help us if they don't," Alex replied. "I found a good soldier yesterday in Private Israel Dorfenberg. And I've found two more today in Private Micah Heath and Sergeant Macaroni Jack Maloney. . . ."

Now, staring at the Schuylkill glittering in the sun, Micah said, "Alex got the jailer to admit Jack's time was long since up. He was in Lord knows how long for stealing a Quaker's watch, though he has no recollection of it. He was drunk at the time, and they kept stretching out his sentence 'cause he kept trying to escape like me. Alex got him out, and he made 'em let me out when my time was up today, no matter though I did keep trying to escape."

Philly rested a hand on his knee. "I've been thinking the soldiers will need women along to wash and cook for 'em. I'd like to go along if the company goes and cook and wash and do for you and Mr. Alex and Israel and—"

"No!" He swung to his feet, staring down at her, aghast. "You put such notions out o' your head and don't you ever even *think* anything like that again. Women that'd do that are—are—" He raised his hands. "No!"

She did not speak, but her expression pleaded with him.

"No! Sometimes, Philly, I think you're out o' your senses." He backed away. "Now I'm going to dip in the river and try to rid some prison dirt. You set out those rations and we'll have a feast when I come back."

He took off his shirt and boots and waded into the river. He had not intended to swim, but the water was so refreshingly cool that he dived. Surfacing, he swam out leisurely to the middle of the river and floated there, staring at the sky.

There was strength in water, as there was in earth, he thought vaguely. You could feel it. Away up north on the frozen cap of the world some strange power surely sent down mighty currents that old Dr. Franklin never would catch in his lightning jar. And away west some other power sent mighty currents eastward. Together they wove the strength of the land and the water. A man who lived on their net always would be strong; they supported him, as the wind supported the hawk floating on motionless wings up there. Nobody understood this truth except those who lived close to it. But the currents remembered who knew them; the currents flowed with you and kept you free.

He swam upstream and then turned toward the beech tree. Philly, he saw, had taken off her shoes and stockings and waded out a little way.

Treading water, he shouted, "Philly, you stay near that shore!"

XVII

"SHORTLY now." Colonel Robert Magaw wiped his broad, sunburned face with a red handkerchief and leaned over in the saddle. "Wednesday next, Alex, the third of July."

Alex stared across the Common where the companies of Magaw's 5th Pennsylvania Regiment and Colonel John Shee's 3d Pennsylvania Regiment drilled to the tap of drums under the hot sun. It was Saturday, the twenty-ninth of June.

"Company!" bawled Sergeant Macaroni Jack Maloney. The company drummer, a freckled fourteen-year-old boy named Saemus O'Reilly, gave a final roll and silenced his drumhead with crossed sticks as Maloney shouted "Halt!" Facing about, Maloney saluted Lieutenant Adoniram Vanderpeyster, a pink-cheeked boy of twenty who had been read out of Friends Meeting and disinherited by his father when he joined the 5th. Vanderpeyster returned the salute by tipping the hilt of his sword to his chin. Men smiled at the high shriek of his voice: "Com—pany—left—face!"

"A fine company, Alex," Magaw said. "General Mifflin says our brigade, the 5th and the 3d, is the flower of the army."

If that were true, Alex thought, it was a dry season for growing soldiers. The company table of organization called for ninety-six men and four officers. It mustered seventy-seven men and three officers. And it would not have mustered that many if it had not been for the unceasing recruiting efforts of Macaroni Jack, who had persuaded a number of waterfront roustabouts and young boys that glorious adventure awaited them at six and two-thirds dollars a month. The organization said that each soldier was to be equipped with a ten-pound smoothbore musket and an eighteen-inch bayonet, with a blanket and haversack, a cartridge box, a bullet mold and a bag of extra flints. Nineteen men who lacked muskets had armed themselves with shovels and picks which the quartermaster had been collecting for weeks. Only six had bayonets. Thirteen had haversacks. Blankets disappeared so rapidly that it was impossible to estimate the shortage.

They did not have uniforms. Alex had wrangled butternut shirts from the Committee of Safety, but already several men had sold or lost them. If there was any uniform it was a bit of brown bucktail which each man had fastened to his hat. Otherwise, the company had no uniformity except youth. There were two aging rum-pots whom Alex expected to disappear after the next payday and there was Hezekiah Scapple, a thirty-five-year-old barber with a clubfoot. The rest were boys or very young men. One or two were nearly as tall as Micah, but the majority were short and wiry. Only a few were as plump as Israel, who dazzled everyone by drilling in a plum-colored suit of broadcloth. Few could read and write, for they were apprentices and shopkeepers' assistants, wagoners and longshoremen; two were sailors, one a smith; three came from ropewalks, and one was a patriotic miller who had closed his mill and enlisted. Less than a dozen were American-born; they were Irish and Scotch and German and Dutch and English. One with an unpronounceable name came from Poland. And an aged patriot named Reeser had sent his Negro slave, Moab, with the promise of granting him freedom when the war was over.

The flower of the army, Alex thought. If they were to become the flower, it would be thanks to the diligent cultivation of Sergeant Macaroni Jack Maloney. *He* had mysteriously acquired a uniform patterned after the Delaware Regiment's: a handsome blue coat faced and lined with red, a white waistcoat, buckskin breeches, white woolen stockings and black gaiters. Upon his round head he wore a small, round, black-jacked leather cap with a peaked front. Alex suspected that it *was* a Delaware uniform. He had a well-oiled musket and a brightly polished bayonet, a short-sword and spontoon. He also had two well-filled haversacks and three blankets which Private Moab carried for him.

Thief, rogue, convict—and superb soldier. Macaroni Jack had fought and drunk and whored his way with the British Army since he was thirteen years old. He told chilling tales of death and disease and discipline. "The System," he called it, the obscene, obscene System. He cursed it, but he could cry over it. In '63 at Gibraltar, when the System got too much for all of them, they'd mutinied. He had been one of the leaders, he said proudly. After their officers had promised to improve their lot, they'd laid down their arms—and the officers had hung a score of them. He didn't know how he himself had escaped. But after that he knew he was a marked man to the System. It had broken him to private, but you couldn't keep a natural sergeant major down. He'd climbed again, rung by painful rung. But the System watched him. He believed it was about to destroy him, in the person of a cruel young captain, when he sailed on a troopship to the Indies in '71. The ship had been blown off course and made harbor at Newport for repairs. Macaroni Jack had deserted the British Army there. And nothing had gone well with him since.

"The flower of the army," Alex said reflectively.

Magaw grinned. "But lest the flower wilt away, we shan't say ought of Wednesday, the third, to the men. We'll lay on our arms here on the Common Tuesday night. We're bound for New York. Word is that General Washington has made great progress with fortifications since he brought the army down from Boston. We're strong now, Alex, and there should be glorious service with the General . . ."

We are *not* strong, Alex thought grimly. And he had heard from Joseph Reed that service under the General was not glorious. Reed in fact had told him despondently that he doubted the General was capable of his command. Courageous and honest, yes. But his task of trying to form an army from an undisciplined rabble of bumptious Yankees would have staggered Caesar. For one as painstaking with detail and as slow to grasp any large idea as the General, the task was fantastic—and pathetic.

Reed had come to Philadelphia last November on the plea, only partially true, that he must help reorganize the Provincial government. The truth was, he admitted to Alex, that he simply couldn't bear another day of service at headquarters. Mifflin felt the same, as would any man of quick intelligence. Endless, wearying detail was one's lot in the headquarters of the cold, humorless General. He must really believe that the pen was mightier than the sword, for he seized on the pen with the desperation of a drowning man grasping at a straw. It was pathetic, Reed said. When the General clutched a pen in his big fingers he struggled with the language. Yet he would not abandon the struggle to express himself. It was exhausting, Reed said, exhausting and pathetic. Alex had read many of the letters the General wrote Reed from Cambridge. Some revealed a man in torment. All revealed a man who respected Reed, a man who obviously wished he could emulate Reed's facility with the language, his forcefulness in expressing ideas. The letters made Alex ashamed, not of General Washington, but of Colonel Joseph Reed.

As the State House clock began to strike noon, he strode to Macaroni Jack, returned his salute, and faced the company.

"Com—pany! . . ." A clamor rose on the Common behind him. "Dismissed until Tuesday morning at seven." The men broke ranks and he heard his mother crying, "Lamb! Alex, lamb!" He turned and gaped.

Feet firmly planted, she wrestled the head of a recalcitrant steer. There was a shout of laughter from the men as he ran toward her. Jerry Ewell, her recently hired hand, struggled with another steer tied to the tailboard of their wagon.

A dozen men grasped the steer and Mrs. March kissed Alex loudly.

"Mother, what in heaven's name—"

"Fresh meat on the hoof for your company."

Macaroni Jack, hearing her, ordered three huzzahs for the good lady.

"And I've brought something else in the wagon," she said to Alex. "I've been making breeches for nigh a year, big, small and middle-sized. Soldiers need extra breeches, I vaw, and there's sixty pair in that wagon."

"Another cheer for this good lady," cried Macaroni Jack.

"And one more thing," she said. "I brung you another soldier boy." She turned and pointed at Jerry Ewell, who backed away, looking about furtively.

"Seize that man!" cried Macaroni Jack.

He was seized.

"I don't need him," Mrs. March said. "It's a shame for a big fellow like him skulking around in the country when them lobsterbacks—"

Her voice was drowned in a roar of laughter.

As Alex took her by an arm and led her aside, she said, "At your livery stable you'll find Heartbreak, a fine stallion. He's yours."

"Mother, it's most kind of you to—"

"Kind in a blind mare's eye," she said. "It's smart, that's what it is. If we all gave all we had I reckon we'd be shut of the King and all his toadies in a month." She stepped back and looked at him admiringly. "How grand you look, lamb." Her eyes suddenly clouded with tears. "An honest-to-God captain. I reckon you'll all be going away soon."

"Very soon, Mother. Come along and we'll go home and—"

"No." She shook her head firmly. "You've got your wife and you'll soon be missing her and her you. And I've the farm that needs me."

On the way home he stopped at his office, discharged the clerk, and locked the door. The law was dead. Reed had left Philadelphia three weeks ago to rejoin the General's staff as Adjutant General. Their cause, the radical cause, finally had triumphed and a new, radical Assembly was struggling to be born. Alex, as a delegate to the Provincial convention that had met five days ago, had helped frame the resolution declaring Pennsylvania's readiness "to concur in a vote of the Congress declaring the United Colonies free and independent states."

He knew that he could be elected to the new Assembly and probably be appointed a delegate to Congress. At times the idea had appealed to him; he'd find great pleasure in working with bold, brilliant men like John Adams, old Dr. Franklin and Thomas Jefferson, the freckled, rawboned delegate from Virginia with whom he'd developed a stimulating friendship. Now, however, he wanted to fight rather than talk. Yet he wished that he could be a delegate during these crucial few days while Congress debated the question of independence.

That weekend his thoughts hovered over the State House like a restless swallow. He had to force himself to stay at home with Kathy on Sunday and listen to her fret about his going away. Oh, he loved her and he did not want to leave her. Nevertheless, he struggled against the desire to slip away to the anxious conclaves at the City Tavern or Mrs. Yard's, where many of the New England delegates lived. Surely there was something he could *do* to help the cause. If nothing more, he'd carry beer and sharpen quills for Tom Jefferson, who was working on the draft of a declaration in his second-floor rooms at Mr. Graaf's on Market Street.

I love you, he kept telling Kathy. But his thoughts wandered to the taverns and boardinghouses where men were trying to persuade others that independence was essential if the cause was to attain unity and strength and ultimate victory.

On Monday he ate a late breakfast on the front porch with Kathy while Philly waved away the swarming flies. Philadelphia raised its morning clamor into a hot white haze. Above the din of voices and clattering hoofs and wheels, starlings quarreled among the limp, dust-yellowed leaves of the plane trees. "Lavender!" sang a girl at the corner of Locust Street. "Rally up and buy, buy sweet, sweet lavender!" At the corner of Walnut a huckster chanted, "Peasecods! Peasecods! Please-please-please-please buy my peasecods!" Answering him, a fishmonger called, "Fresh fish, fresh fish, fresh from the bay this mar—nin'l"

The world went its way, oblivious to the momentous struggle in the State House.

At last, unable to contain his restlessness longer, he rose and muttered that he had to settle a few last affairs at the office. Kathy called after him urgently as he hurried down the street.

Taking the path through the State House yard between Walnut and Chestnut streets, he paused under an open window of the Congress chamber. A hum of voices drifted out. Then someone was speaking. The voice, he believed, was John Dickinson's. He heard the impassioned tones, but he could not catch the words.

He lingered under the window, however. Two old men gossiped in the shade of a chestnut tree and a little boy whirled a spool on a string. In the past he had been only vaguely aware of idlers while he forever hurried purposefully, trying to nudge the world on its way. But now he felt he had no place to go; he was suspended in sympathetic fraternity with all idlers everywhere. A foot touched a bit of wood, and he picked it up. Taking out his pocket knife, he began to whittle. He didn't know how to shape anything with his knife, but he whittled anyway as he slowly paced the yard.

Thunder rumbled and he looked up at mountainous, flesh-colored clouds churning in the west. Soon heavy drops of rain spattered down. As the old men and the little boy moved leisurely into the corridor of the State House, he followed them. The old men stood in the doorway, staring out at the pouring rain.

"He give it to her good," one said, "and I don't blame him. Told her she had a tongue like a knife and . . ."

Alex strolled along the corridor, whittling at the bit of wood.

The door of the chamber opened and Dr. Franklin stepped out. "Good morning, Alex." He peered at him over his spectacles and smiled.

"Good morning, sir. Is the session ending?"

"Far from it. The call of nature takes temporary precedence over the call of country. John Dickinson"—his tone went dry—"your friend and mine, if not the friend of the people, has had his say. He was in best form against independence. It seems that no people in history have done what we would attempt. Therefore, never being in favor of something that has not succeeded before, Dickinson says it's folly to try and impossible to achieve. What an old wife he is."

"Then it won't carry?" Alex asked.

"Not today. Not the Pennsylvania delegation. I'm for it, of course, and I think I'll carry Jim Wilson with me. But not the others—Dickinson, Robert Morris, Thomas Willing, John Morton, Charles Humphreys."

Alex snapped the piece of whittled wood between his fingers and scowled.

"I've answered a question of yours," Franklin said, "and now you answer one of mine, Alex. Why is a young man like yourself, with so much time before him, so impatient? And why does an old man like me, with so little time before him, dwell patiently and hopefully on tomorrow?"

Then he was gone, his cane tapping lightly along the corridor.

Alex learned the outcome that afternoon at the City Tavern, where he went after the rain stopped. Independence had failed to carry by the desired unanimous vote. For it were New Hampshire, Massachusetts, Rhode Island, Connecticut, New Jersey, Maryland, Virginia, North Carolina and Georgia. New York could not vote because its delegates lacked instructions. Delaware's two delegates were split, with the third delegate, Caesar Rodney, who favored independence, ill in Dover. South Carolina was opposed. So was Pennsylvania, by the five to two vote of delegates that Franklin had predicted.

"Defeated," Alex muttered glumly to Dr. Benjamin Rush.

"Linger a while, Alex, and we'll catch later news," Rush said. "There's a fermentation at work in this bottle that can't be corked by Dickinson, Willing and Morris."

They lingered and heard hopeful news. Edward Rutledge of South Carolina finally had listened carefully to John Adams when he rose and eloquently defended independence against Dickinson's attack. He had proposed a postponement of the question until tomorrow in the hope that they might then attain a unanimous vote. And McKean of the Delaware delegation, who favored independence, had sent a post rider down the Dover Road to bring Rodney, who favored independence and could break the tied Delaware vote. But the most exciting rumor was that Dickinson was preparing to capitulate to the growing strength of independence. He and Morris were said to be closeted now, trying to find a way to retreat gracefully.

When Alex returned home in the evening and tried to explain what had happened, Kathy cut him short. She said she did not want to talk of politics, tonight of all times. She did not even want to hear how John Dickinson had turned his back on history and prepared his own political grave.

Alex arrived at the Common early the next morning in a pouring rain. The men, slow to muster, grumbled that it was not a fit day for soldiering. During a morning of confusion and trying arguments over equipment and supplies, he glanced frequently toward the State House.

Magaw, as interested as he in what was happening over there, passed along rumors. Rodney had arrived, galloping up from Dover on a spent horse, his cancer-ridden face masked by a green silk handkerchief. Dickinson and Morris had absented themselves from the voting. South Carolina had swung its vote to independence. And Pennsylvania— what of Pennsylvania?

Toward noon Magaw strode to him, grinning. "Franklin and Wilson were for it, Alex. Humphreys and Willing opposed."

"And Morton?" Alex demanded. "What did Morton do?"

"He saw the light." Magaw slapped his back. "They say it nearly blinded him, but he saw and voted *aye*. Independence has carried, Alex!"

"Say it once more," she whispered.

"I love you, Kathy, and I always will."

"And I love you, Alex, and I always will."

Then he was gone. She imagined she still felt his lips on hers and his arms clasping her tightly. But he was gone. The front door closed quietly as the clock struck four. Clapping both hands over her mouth, she tried to stifle her sobs.

"Four o'clock of July third," the watch called at the corner. "Four o'clock of a fair morning. Four o'clock and all's well!"

"I can't ever bear it," she whispered, sinking down in a chair.

Dimly she heard voices in the kitchen. Philly opened the door into the hall, holding a candle above her head.

"Miss Kathy," she said in an even tone, "you coming with us?"

Kathy turned her head away. "Where?"

"To see 'em off. Mrs. Munger and I are going."

"Yes," she cried, leaping to her feet. "Yes! Let's hurry!"

"Oh, Lord!" Mrs. Munger moaned in the kitchen. "Oh, Lord!"

"You just hush, Mrs. Munger," Philly said sharply.

"It ain't in my stars," groaned Mrs. Munger. "It ain't anywhere in my stars to be so took with a man at my age. And him a soldier! They's ten thousand men in this city getting up and going about their business and I have to be took with a soldier."

"You just hush," Philly said, "and try to act your years."

"Stop your chattering, the both of you." Kathy dried her eyes. "What hat'll I wear? Philly, run fetch my gloves."

"*Kathy!*" Philly put down the candle. "I don't give a hoot what hat you wear or if you don't wear none at all. I'm walking out that door now and anybody wants to come with me can."

Kathy and Mrs. Munger followed her, silent and bareheaded.

Gray light grew in the silent streets as yellow dawn crept up the eastern sky.

Philly touched Kathy's arm and pointed to the State House tower against the sky. "It looks like a clenched fist, don't it? It's like liberty itself stove its arm up through the roof there yesterday when they finally did it."

"Did what?"

"You didn't hear? Didn't Alex tell you?"

Foolish Philly, Kathy thought. A man going to war had more important things to tell his wife.

"They voted it," Philly said. "Independence, I mean. They'll sign it soon, I hear. But they voted it, Pennsylvania too."

"Independence?" Kathy asked dully. "Whose independence?"

"Ours," Philly replied.

A din rose from the Common. Men shouted, whips cracked, wagon wheels squealed. A drum began to beat somewhere, then other drums joined it until the air seemed to quiver.

"Where's Captain March's company?" Kathy cried to a man stamping out a fire. He pointed vaguely and did not answer.

"Over here," Philly called.

They followed Philly through a mass of grumbling soldiers as the drums suddenly were stilled.

"Com—pany!"

Alex sat Heartbreak between Lieutenant Vanderpeyster and Ensign Roe facing the company which stood at attention in double column. The drums crashed. The shouts of sergeants cracked above their roll. The soldiers were turning and moving, turning and moving, and then the chaos of a few moments ago dissolved into order. Now Alex rode at the head of the company and the faces that had been indistinguishable were burnished by the flood of morning sunlight.

"Alex!"

He glanced at Kathy in amazement, then he smiled and lifted his hat to her.

She and Philly and Mrs. Munger and a dozen other women trotted beside the company, calling to the men.

"Hey, Philly!" shouted Micah. His teeth gleamed in a wide grin. "You be a good girl, Philly, and I'll bring you an English scalp."

Philly, darting to him, leaped up and kissed him on the cheek while men whistled and groaned.

"Kathy." Micah raised his hat and smiled at her as he passed. And then he looked back at her quickly.

"Eyes front!" bawled Sergeant Macaroni Jack Maloney. "Silence!" Then, smiling and tipping his cap, "Good morning, ladies. Mrs. Munger, I'll miss the pleasure of your company."

Mrs. Munger uttered a wordless wail.

"But we'll be back soon," he shouted.

"Good-by, Philly," called Israel Dorfenberg. "Good-by!"

But the company had not passed, Kathy realized. She and Philly ran beside it. She didn't care that she was running bareheaded through the streets of Philadelphia. She had to reach Alex once more.

As she came to the head of the column and grasped Alex's stirrup, the drums crashed again and fifes shrilled. It was a strange, lilting tune, a tune she had not heard before. Alex, leaning down and catching her hand, said something she could not hear above the roar of singing voices.

"Yankee-Doodle went to Boston,
  Riding on a pony,
Gave all hell to old man Howe,
  Called it macaroni!
Yankee-Doodle keep it up,
  Keep the lobsters running,
Let the bastard redcoats know
  That Yankee-Doodle's coming!

Yankee-Doodle went to hell,
  Claimed it was right chilly,
Spend a month in Philly-town

And hell is willy-nilly!
Yankee-Doodle keep it up,
Yankee-Doodle dandy . . ."

She and Philly stood now at the edge of the street, panting for breath and trying to sing. The soldiers were passing. They were going, but she believed that they never would be gone from her for the rest of her life.

Book Three

LONG RETREAT

XVIII

THEY went north, as a snake goes, wriggling, twisting, pausing. They did not march. They simply trudged along, with drums silenced, as each man hit his own stride in a single file strung over two miles.

"Magnificent," Israel Dorfenberg said as they wound through Bristol and took the road to Morrisville and Trenton.

"Magnificent?" Macaroni Jack swore.

He had pleaded in vain that the company march in a column of fours. "Closed up in fours we cover a quarter the distance at twice the pace," he'd told Alex. "Are we soldiers or ain't we? Sir?"

"We're soldiers, Sergeant Maloney," Alex replied, frowning back through the dust at the straggling column. "Brigadier General Mifflin has ordered us to march in single file. It's the route march of the army. To those who see us we appear more numerous this way than we really are."

"If I seen us," Jack growled later to Micah, "I'd puke. If I was that fat farmer settin' there on that fence I'd laugh myself silly. The flower o' the army!" He spat. "We're virgin all right and ripe for the grenadiers to deflower us."

Micah did not share Jack's annoyance. Their pace was slow, but he did not see why marching in fours would make them better at killing English and Hessian soldiers when they reached New York—or wherever they were going.

He never had been happier. He was free and he did not wish to become the prisoner of regulations thought up by his recent fellow prisoner. What had gotten into Macaroni Jack since he got out of jail? He should be enjoying this new freedom instead of forging new chains.

Philadelphia lay behind them, a place to be forgotten, while ahead strange roads led to new places. Above, the enormous blue summer sky pressed on the fertile land, crushing its ripeness into creeks and rivers. Once, when he went far off the road and drank deeply from a cold spring hidden in sweet fern, he thought that it was like tasting the juice of the land. He lay by the spring for a while, bemusedly watching a spider spin a web, and as he rose he felt stronger.

But when he caught up with the company, Macaroni Jack cried, "You stop that straggling."

Micah grinned at him. "I had some business back there."

He had a lot of business with this land that was not the business of the army, he thought. He had a hundred fields of clover to sniff, a thousand woodlands to ramble. He straggled so often that Israel as well as Jack despaired of him.

Israel was too intent on being a soldier, Micah thought. He seemed trying to prove something when there was nothing to prove. Why did he act as if the outcome of the war depended on his forever plodding obediently along the dusty road? You'd think he was an officer himself the way he helped Jack and the officers worry stragglers out of wayside taverns. Yet his generosity and good nature made him as popular with the men as he obviously was with Alex March.

"Damn it!" Israel cried once beyond Trenton when Micah caught up with the company after eating dinner with a friendly Dutch farmer and his family. "Try to act like a soldier, Micah."

"I am one." Micah smiled at him. "I'm *here,* ain't I? And I'll be *there* when I'm supposed to be. My musket's clean and so's my bayonet. D'you reckon, Israel, you'll remember to twist your bayonet when you drive it in an Englishman's belly?"

"Please!" Israel grimaced, and then he said firmly, "Yes, I will remember."

"I brought you some cold beef from that Dutchman's back there, Israel. Help yourself. Tell Jack there's some for him too when he simmers down enough to speak civil to me."

Israel smiled suddenly as he took the bread and meat Micah had carried from the farmer's house in his haversack. "They *are* a friendly people here, Micah."

They seemed a very friendly people. You would have thought there was not a Tory in New Jersey as people turned out to cheer the long column trailing through the dust of the old King's Highway which wound from Trenton to Brunswick. At nearly every farmhouse women offered mugs of beer and buttermilk and cider and gave bread, meat, cheese and eggs for the asking. It was a well-fed column of men and thus it was a good-natured column, whistling and calling to the laughing girls who leaned over fences to watch the soldiers pass.

"Up liberty!" the girls would cry. "Kill the Hessians, boys!"

And the boys, who thought of themselves as men, would whistle and shout while a few paused to chat with the girls and investigate just how far their notions of liberty extended. Invariably, however, there was a father or older brother lurking nearby who discouraged the boys and sent them on their way faster than their officers could make them move.

Beyond Princeton the land began to swell and the plains fell away south in the heat haze. Here in Somerset County Dutch and Germans had worked some of the land lovingly and skillfully for half a century. And the land had made them prosperous and content.

Wherever Micah fell out to drink a mug of cider and chat for a while, he studied the farms carefully. Many of the houses were as permanent— and as complicated—as the huge German locks with mechanisms exposed on the double Dutch doors. It would take a man years to finish such long sloping roofs and rough stone gables surfaced with lime and pebbles. If you ever built one, you never would leave it. You'd stay here forever, looking up and down the road and wondering what lay beyond its distant turnings.

He'd hurry on his way with no envy for the stolid farmer and his family who remained forever. And when he caught up with the company, Macaroni Jack would curse him and growl, "Why can't you keep going?"

Well, he was going, and he could have gone much faster while seeming to go slower if he weren't entangled with this long, dusty column that halted, bunched up, crept on, strung out. Nevertheless, they were going, east now more than north. Dim, low hills began to shoulder the northern haze. At Van Tilburgh's Inn in Kingston Micah would have liked to follow the Millstone Valley north into the hills, but the King's Highway went east—and so did the column.

They passed through Brunswick in a thunderstorm while people cheered them from the porches of brick houses which had curious long gables descending nearly to the ground. They crossed the Raritan and trudged on to Piscataway, an old village with a long main street lined with tall trees. In Piscataway it required the efforts of General Mifflin himself to clear Hull's Tavern of thirsty stragglers.

Beyond the village the column turned north on a narrow road that led through Woodbridge and Elizabethtown to Newark. The land stretched, flat and hot, in a white haze from which there eventually emerged low, green, wooded hills curving west and north. Micah said the hills would make a cool place to lie up for a spell, but Israel said they'd form a stout bastion.

"Well, General Dorfenberg, it looks to me you aim for us to run and hide from whatever's over there." Micah jerked a thumb east toward New York. "I reckon we'll take the English as easy on the plain as holed up in the hills."

"I hope so," Israel said. "I do hope our legs refuse to run."

They camped outside Newark and then went east, across the Passaic and the Hackensack, following a corduroy road through vast swamps, where mosquitoes swarmed. Toward nightfall of the eighth day after they left Philadelphia they trailed into the village of Paulus Hook.

Beyond the wide, gray Hudson opening toward the sea, the white church spires of New York shone in the setting sun.

"New York Island," Israel said. "Manhattan. Look at that beautiful country north of the city and see—"

"You look, Israel." Micah gripped him by an arm and pointed south.

In the harbor narrows off Staten Island and Long Island lay nearly two hundred British ships.

Israel caught his breath. Everywhere men stood motionless, staring south at the dark hulls and forests of masts. In the fading light, pennants winked brightly from the network of yardarms. Ships of the line with three tiers of frowning guns and high forecastles rode near graceful frigates and unwieldy transports. Clustered about them, like hounds straining at the leash, were the tenders and galleys which would land thousands of troops.

"Must be the biggest army the British ever sent anywhere," a voice muttered.

"Fall out, fall out, you blubbers who never fell in," Macaroni Jack bawled cheerfully. "London town's out there, come to see you." He whistled shrilly. "Fall out, I say!"

But the column of men shifted feet uneasily and continued to stare at the great waiting fleet.

"Lookee!" shouted a Yankee militiaman, pointing at the company. "Southerners! Damn nigger-owners!"

"They got a nigger with 'em," another shouted, pointing at Moab.

"Com—pany!" cried Macaroni Jack. " 'Ten—shun!"

"Com—pany!" mimicked a Yankee. "Fall out!"

The company, tired of waiting in the heat for the regiment to form, muttered angrily. They had been idling here for almost two hours after being ferried across the Hudson. This was New York, said to be the most sinful city on the continent, but Sergeant Maloney held them on its river-bank in an annoying state of grace.

Alex finally rode up and sat his handsome stallion before the company, gazing abstractedly over their heads at the great fleet in the sparkling bay.

"Boys," he said quietly, and then he smiled. "Gentlemen. It's been tedious for you waiting here, but Colonel Magaw and I had to find our bivouac ground. There are two things you must be warned against. The water—"

"We'll stick to rum, Captain March," someone called.

"Silence!" roared Macaroni Jack.

"Three things," Alex said. "The rum and the water and the women. There's a well of pure water in the yard of a white-shingled cottage next our bivouac. Drink none other. The women, most of them who want your pay, have the French disease. There is one thing I urge you to remember. We're Pennsylvanians—and proud to be."

A couple started to cheer for Pennsylvania only to be shouted into silence by Macaroni Jack.

"But first, before we're Pennsylvanians, we're Americans. Independence has been voted and we're now one nation. Some from other parts of the country will rile you at times. But if you act like you know an American should, you'll shame them into acting like Americans too. Remember, you're soldiers in the *American* Army, not a Pennsylvania army. You belong to the 5th Pennsylvania Regiment of the *American* Army. And the 5th belongs to General Mifflin's brigade of the *American* Army. And the brigade belongs to the Second Division of the *American* Army, and is commanded by General William Heath, an *American* from Massachusetts."

Macaroni Jack ordered three cheers for Captain March and three cheers for American independence and three cheers for the American Army. Macaroni Jack was not a fool, Micah thought. The louder you cheered, the better you felt—even about such a matter as belonging to the same army as a parcel of rummy Yankees.

Drums began to tap and they marched at last, around the fort where small cannon peeped at the huge British fleet, and up the street called Broadway. New York, Micah saw quickly, was a different city than Philadelphia. Though not as large, it seemed bigger. It was noisier and everyone moved faster; even sedan chairmen trotted instead of walking. There were more drunkards, both men and women, staggering and yelling in the crowded streets, and whores solicited trade openly. There was more poverty, too. Thin, ragged beggars stumbled through the crowds and dirty children ran beside the marching column crying, "Penny, penny, penny, for a poor, poor soul!"

Yet it was a joyful city. People seemed happier than they did in Philadelphia. Fiddles scraped in taverns although it was broad daylight, and even the music which blind or crippled beggars fluted on nearly every corner was lilting rather than plaintive. Hucksters sang their wares more loudly and the shop signs were bigger than the signs in Philadelphia. Nobody seemed to mind the stench of accumulated filth in streets and alleys; the city had abandoned order in the cause of happy confusion. A rabble who called themselves the soldiers of an army had poured into

New York, and New York was peddling, hawking, cudgeling, and thimble-rigging with a bustling abandon such as these visitors normally enjoyed only on rare country Fair Days. Now every day was Fair Day in New York.

It wrapped itself around you, picked you up and carried you along, as if taking you to something that you could not possibly imagine. It made you forget the vast British fleet waiting out there. Let the fleet pounce, New York seemed to say, and our streets will hide you from the enemy.

When the regiment reached its bivouac area in the West Ward beside the Hudson, however, Micah saw that not all of the army had passed all of its time roistering in the teeming streets. Earthworks had been raised along the riverbanks; wharves had been demolished and their timbers scattered in flimsy redoubts which, said Alex, were as likely to confuse the defenders of the city as to confound its attackers.

This army obviously had a great passion for digging. It was left with little time for drill and musket and bayonet practice as it dug in Manhattan and Long Island and Governor's Island. Men more accustomed to the spade than the musket dug steadily and with curious enthusiasm. Not content with digging at trenches and earthworks all day, many dug into the bivouac area and roofed the holes with scrap timber and canvas. Like moles, Micah thought, they wanted holes to hide in when trouble came.

He was soon bored with so much digging, and like many others, he stole away when Macaroni Jack and the officers weren't watching. He drifted through the city, as if searching for something. But if he sought, he did not find. He drank some sour flip that made him vomit. With several Carolinians he became involved in a fight with a gang of Connecticut militia. At evening he wandered to the "holy ground" near Trinity Church and then hurried away when he saw that the whores who lived and worked in the ramshackle houses were as fierce and dangerous as panthers. Going toward Broadway through the churchyard in twilight he stumbled over the bodies of other whores who called out and clutched at him as they lay among the headstones plying their trade with soldiers. He watched a gang of drunken patriots ride a screaming Tory on a rail. Although he thought he hated Tories, he would have freed the man if he could.

He did not wander in the city again. He was glad to resume digging, pointless though digging seemed when he had enlisted only to fight. New York was not the joyful place it had appeared to be at first, he decided. It was fit only to be burned and abandoned, as Alex March and some of the other officers proposed, so that they could fight the enemy in a better place.

Early on the morning of July nineteenth Micah was elated when the regiment was ordered to break camp and march away. Macaroni Jack and the officers would not say where they were going, but as they crossed the city toward the East River everyone was certain they were headed for Long Island. Then, suddenly, they swung north into the country. They were on the Bloomingdale Road, someone said.

From a rise Micah looked back at the city on the island finger which pointed at the anchored British fleet.

"General Dorfenberg," he said, "why are we leaving?"

"I don't know." Israel smiled. "But if I were General Howe instead of General Dorfenberg, I'd do what Captain March says he'd do. Sail up the rivers and cut us off on these islands from above."

"Do you reckon General Washington ain't thought of that?"

"I reckon he's thought of everything, including some things we haven't. At least I *hope* he has."

Manhattan was an island of rolling low hills coursed by ravines. Among the wooded crests were scattered prosperous farms and large, isolated mansions. Where the Post Road forked to the right from the Bloomingdale Road, the regiment halted and Colonel Magaw held a long conference with the officers.

"They don't even know where they're going," Micah said disgustedly.

"They know where," Macaroni Jack replied. "They just ain't certain how to get there."

"What a stupid, puny army this is."

"I ain't seen you trying to improve it," said Macaroni Jack.

The officers decided they would stay on the Bloomingdale Road. They discovered their error in early afternoon when the road ended at the house of a farmer named Hoadlandt. So the wagons were sent back to find their way to the Post Road and the companies went on north through woods and fields. It began to rain as they stumbled down a draw into a valley. A farmer told them they were in the Hollow Way. They found a road in the valley, turned east on it and eventually came to the Post Road.

Darkness fell as they marched north in the rain, tired and wet, hungry and grumbling. A couple of hours later they scrambled up a rocky road and were told to fall out. A few smoky fires sputtered in the darkness, and men clustering around them turned out to be members of the 3d Pennsylvania.

Early the next morning Micah saw that they were on a hill about a mile long at the northernmost part of Manhattan. To the west the land pitched down sharply to the Hudson, while to the east the hill dropped into a deep valley. Beyond the valley and a further steep hill was the

Harlem River. Their job, Alex told them, was to help finish Fort Washington, which the 3d had begun building several days ago. Micah stared west across the Hudson at the brown cliffs of the Jersey shore a mile distant and wondered if he could swim the river and scale the cliffs. He had enlisted to fight, not to dig on a rocky island.

Alex saw to it, however, that all of them dug from dawn to dark. He stood over them through rain and suffocating heat, directing and pushing them ruthlessly. And he refused to be satisfied with their efforts. The trouble was that he fancied himself an expert on fortifications, Micah thought. Even though Colonel Magaw was satisfied by the end of the first week in August that they'd built a fine fort on this rocky ridge, Alex wanted to continue working.

Micah observed one day as he listened to them argue that Alex's attitude aggravated Magaw.

"It's simply not finished, Bob," Alex said. "It's only begun."

Magaw, his face reddening, insisted that it was finished as he studied the pentagonal earthwork with five bastions covering about four acres of ground.

"It's just an open earthwork with surrounding abatis," Alex said. "That ditch isn't worthy of the name. Where's our fuel to come from? Where's our water supply except two hundred and thirty feet down there?" He pointed to the Hudson. "We have no outworks and no obstacles. Our magazine is that wooden shack there and where are the barracks? Where—"

"Goddamn it, Alex," cried Magaw, "Colonel Rufus Putnam laid out this place and Colonel Robert Magaw says it's done. Our regiment alone could stand off all of Howe's army from this hill." He stalked away.

Everyone on the bare, rocky hill was disgusted. The food was scant and bad. The bits of canvas which they scrounged offered little protection from the driving August rains. It seemed that they always were wet, with sweat when not with rain. The company was disgusted with Captain March and Sergeant Maloney, who, in turn, were disgusted with the company and the fortification it had helped to build.

When the company finally received sufficient powder and shot to permit a little actual musket practice, Micah became enraged with his fourteen-pound musket. Loading was an involved process. You bit off the end of a cylindrical paper cartridge containing powder and ball, shook a little powder into the pan, closed its lid, dropped the butt on the ground and poured the rest of the powder into the barrel, shaking the musket to jar some powder into the touchhole. Then you rammed in the ball with a heavy steel ramrod. But the balls were too large or the barrel too small, for he had to use a rock to pound down the ramrod. Firing was as aggravating a process as loading, for all too often when you pressed the trigger, nothing happened. You had to pull it hard and hope that the flint of the cock showered sparks when it hit the steel frizzen—and hope that the sparks ignited the powder in the pan—and hope that the flame passed through the touchhole into the charge. Then, if all went well, you were jolted and there was a resounding crash. There was no point in trying to take careful aim, for the musket lacked a rear sight. Furthermore, the musket bores were untrue—or, at least, *his* was untrue. The first shot he managed to get off went wide of the easy wooden target seventy-five yards away and he actually saw the ball bound along the ground fifty yards beyond the target.

"I want me a *rifle!*" he cried angrily and then became embroiled in a shouting argument with Macaroni Jack over the relative merits of the musket and the rifle. Jack said you could get off two or three shots a minute with a musket, which was faster than the rifle. Micah replied that was the *notion,* but it was only true if the ball fit the barrel. Jack said the musket ball was heavier and knocked a man down. Micah said the rifle ball had a longer range and a true sight that enabled you to deal a mortal wound.

"Look at Israel," he said. "He ain't got off a shot yet and he ain't done a thing wrong."

"It's the damnable touchhole that keeps plugging," Israel said. He pulled his trigger again. There was a spurt of flame, his musket leaped convulsively, and he was rocked backwards. "It fired!" he exclaimed dazedly.

"It fired," Micah said, "but what did it hit?"

"God help the lot of you," groaned Macaroni Jack.

God help the lot of *them,* Micah thought that evening as he took a swim in the river. I'm going to steal me a rifle.

He swam farther out than he ever had before. Gradually he realized that he was testing the current, trying to see whether this big river was stronger than he. It wasn't, he found. He could swim it—though not with a rifle.

"This waiting dulls my edge," he told Israel that night. "It's hard to keep hating the British and Hessians while they just sit out there in the bay."

"It's almost impossible," Israel said. "I hate my musket and shovel and wet blanket and aching feet and this canvas called a tent. But I can barely remember the time when I rested comfortably in Philadelphia and hated the British. Will the time never come when we can fight?"

The time came.

On the morning of August twenty-second, after a night of heavy winds and rain, Micah thought he heard the sound of guns. The next day, a Friday, the regiment was paraded and Colonel Magaw announced that the enemy had landed yesterday on Long Island.

They waited restlessly.

On Monday they listened to rumors brought by teamsters who said the enemy had been defeated in a great battle on Long Island. Micah, despairing of ever fighting, told Israel that they'd been cheated.

About sundown a messenger galloped into Fort Washington on a lathered horse. A few minutes later the drums began to beat them into formation. They were issued three days' rations and told to lay on their arms.

Long before dawn the drums beat them to their feet and they marched south toward the city.

XIX

HANDING Heartbreak to the horse boy outside the Black Horse Tavern on the Bowery Road late that afternoon, Alex went inside and ordered a mug of ale, and paper, pen and ink brought to his table. He sipped his ale and wrote,

My Darling—

The pen poised in his fingers, he stared out the open door at afternoon sunlight. The American camp on Brooklyn Heights across the river was quiet now. Ominously quiet, he thought, after a day of heavy cannonading. But New York was ominously noisy. It seemed that the entire population was milling in the streets, flowing after every purposeful horseman with shouted questions and ebbing into taverns like the Black Horse to exchange rumors about what had happened across the river this morning.

My Darling—

What would he tell her? The regiment had just reached the city from Fort Washington and he didn't know exactly what had happened on Long Island. He was inclined, however, to believe the rumors of defeat. Yet he must not tell her how desperate he feared the situation was.

Your cause now is mine with all my heart, darling, she had written in the one letter he'd received from her since he left Philadelphia. Heaven keep her feeling so, he thought.

He sipped his ale and watched a very young man wearing a major's red cockade on his hat dismount outside and enter the tavern at the slow, stiff pace of one long in the saddle. He was covered with dust and his luminous dark eyes were shadowed with fatigue. Seeing no vacant table and noticing the buff captain's plume on Alex's hat, he came toward him slowly. Actually he was a boy, slender and handsome.

"May I sit at your table for one drink, Captain?" he asked hoarsely.

"Certainly." He'd met him somewhere before, Alex thought as he rose. "I believe—"

"Yes." The young man's gaze focused on him and his red, bowed lips rose over gleaming white teeth in a wide smile. "We have met. In Philadelphia two years ago. At Dr. Rush's. You are— March, Alex March. Pardon me, *Captain* Alex March." He extended his hand. "My name is Burr. Aaron Burr."

Alex signaled a barmaid. "Pray be seated, Major Burr." Now he remembered him, the son of the Reverend Aaron Burr, second president of the College at Princeton, and a grandson of Jonathan Edwards. "As I recall, you had been reading theology at Princeton when we met at Benjamin Rush's."

"There's a great similarity between theology and military tactics," Burr said. "Both are deeply concerned with logic. And I've come to be skeptical of American authorities in both fields— How is your lovely wife? I remember her well at Dr. Rush's. I never forget a beautiful woman."

"*And* her husband," Alex said, smiling.

Burr laughed and ordered a mug of ale from the barmaid. "What are you doing in this army?"

"I'm with the 5th Pennsylvania. Magaw's regiment."

Burr grimaced. "You poor fellow. I've just come from over there"— he nodded toward Brooklyn Heights—"and finally found Mifflin over here. The message I brought orders you people to join us over *there*."

"That's bad?"

Burr shrugged. "How is your wife?"

"Missing me, I trust. I was about to write her, but I can't think of a thing to tell her except that I love her and Major Aaron Burr wishes to be remembered to her."

"That's enough to tell her. Under no circumstances tell her the truth about the situation in New York."

"What is the situation, Major Burr?"

Burr hitched his chair closer as the barmaid slammed down his mug of ale. "This city is infested with Tories," he muttered. Then, looking at Alex closely, "What is your opinion of our strategy in New York, Captain March?"

"Abominable. How can we hope to hold Long Island and Manhatten Island without a single ship against a fleet of five hundred?"

Burr nodded. "Having finally met an intelligent man, let me unburden

myself. We can't. We haven't. We won't. The worst has happened over
there—" He gestured vaguely toward Brooklyn Heights. "We've lost
nearly half the army and the *General*—Washington, I mean—is bringing
the rest of it into disaster. It's my duty, my unfortunate duty, to be an aide
to a brave, warmhearted, stupid old fool of a general named Israel Putnam. *He* may have lost the war for us over there today. He claims, of
course, that *he* didn't do it, but Sullivan did. And Sullivan, who's been
captured, will claim if he ever gets free that Old Put did it. While they're
walking around dazedly over there trying to figure out what happened,
they shouldn't forget to blame *the* General. Washington, I mean."

"What did happen?" Alex asked.

"If Greene hadn't been taken sick with a fever everything might have
been different. You can trust *him*. First Washington put Sullivan in to
take his place and then changed his mind and superseded Sullivan with
Old Put. 'Aaron,' Old Put says to me"—Burr made helpless little motions
with his hands—"'Aaron . . .' and then he goes off somewhere and I
have to follow him and try to read his mind to understand what he wants
me to do. Well, Put, with the agreement of Washington, moved forces
out from our strong position on the Heights to cover the passes through
a further line of hills. Stirling was out there and he and his men fought
well. The trouble was that our left was dangling in the air. I thought—
oh, God, I'm not a general, but only an aide to Old Put—but *I* thought
that *he* had the Jamaica Pass on the extreme left covered, and he claims
that *he* thought Sullivan had it covered and I don't know who Sullivan,
the pompous ass, is blaming in his British prison this afternoon. At any
rate, the British came through Jamaica Pass with ten thousand men and
caught us in a pincers. We were crushed, like a walnut in a cracker."

Burr's eyes suddenly filled with tears. "I saw some terrible things over
there today. Forgive my emotion, but I've scarcely slept in nearly forty-
eight hours. However, the worst thing I saw was poor Old Put, brave Old
Put, making no effort to recall Stirling when he heard the British were
advancing on Bedford. 'General Putnam,' I kept yelling at him, 'have
you any word for General Lord Stirling?' And Old Put would walk up
and down, fluttering his hands, and muttering, 'Aaron . . . Aaron.' Poor
old man, I say, but what about two or three thousand officers and men—
including Stirling—who were captured or killed? And while we're blaming
Old Put, let's not forget that the *General* was there. Washington, I mean.
He was within the camp all day today. Why did he let Put destroy us?
Why did he refuse to *command*? Why did he let our obviously weaker
force strung out over six miles of that ridge stay there and be destroyed
piece by piece?"

"I don't know," Alex muttered. "And now he proposes—"

"To bring *you* over," Burr said. "He's already brought Hugh Mercer over and more of Mercer's men are coming. And he's bringing Mifflin. You'll be there in the camp tomorrow. The only sensible thing to do is get *out* of Long Island. What is the General trying to do? Put the whole army in a hopeless position and surrender it at once?"

"I don't know," Alex said. "I—"

"One bit of advice, Captain March." Burr got to his feet and drained his mug. "I've got to get back over *there*. When you come, don't bring your horse. Leave it here. You'll never get it off Long Island. If you get off yourself, you may need it. Good day, sir."

Turning abruptly, he walked away.

Alex stared at the sheet of paper before him on the table. *My Darling*— Crumpling it slowly, he tossed it on the floor.

They crossed over the misty East River in the gray light of the next dawn. No one spoke as they stood in the flat-bottomed boats, listening to the splash of oars and creak of oarlocks. When the boats grounded, they waded ashore and formed in columns of fours near the small ferryhouse.

The drums rolled and they marched up a silent street of deserted houses, the sergeants bawling the step cheerfully on the flanks and the 5th's red and gold banner floating ahead on a rising breeze. They must look very strong, Alex thought, to two officers sitting their horses beside the road on the Height. One, he saw, was Mifflin. As they approached, Mifflin saluted the regimental and then turned to the other officer and extended an arm toward the marching column with a proud gesture, as if saying, "The flower of the army." How could he possibly believe it?

Now the other officer was saluting them and a faint cheer rose from the company ahead. Alex recognized the General. New lines were drawn in his tired face; he looked a decade older than Alex remembered him a year before in Philadelphia. His lips were twisting in a smile, but his expression remained grave as he watched them closely. Did he wonder whether he was presiding over a debacle?

Suddenly touching a heel to his big bay, he rode out to them and beside them, saying, "Lads . . . We've work for you today, lads . . ." His voice was drowned by their cheering. Forgetting his growing mistrust of this big Virginia farmer's capacity to lead them, Alex cheered too. Whatever his military capability, the General radiated confidence on the 5th. You almost could believe that the regiment was the flower of the army when he rode beside it.

Alex wondered if the rest of the company felt the same vague fear that he did. Was he afraid to die or afraid that he might die badly? He did not know.

Somewhere a man began screaming, a man who was not dying well, a man to whom patriotism now was an illusion in the reality of pain. The sudden stench of flesh was nauseating. They were passing an improvised hospital, a surgeon's butcher shop of a few tents and a couple of wagons where wounded men lay on the ground staring at them vacantly.

They marched through Brooklyn, a cluster of houses at the crossing of roads, and passed many soldiers lying on the ground. Some slept in exhaustion, but others turned their heads and stared at them as vacantly as had the wounded. They bore, Alex thought, the invisible but mortal wounds of men convinced they were defeated. The atmosphere of defeat smelled more strongly on this neck of land than the stench of its hospitals' blood buckets and severed limbs.

Beyond Brooklyn they came to the line of works which had been dug for a distance of about a mile and a half from Wallabout Bay to Gowanus Cove. Several redoubts, mounting cannon, were connected by earthworks which were ditched and fraised with sharpened stakes pointing outward breast-high.

The 5th went into line behind a stretch of earthworks near a redoubt grandiosely called Fort Greene. In a few minutes the 2d Rhode Island, badly mauled yesterday, crawled out of the works. They were unshaven, hollow-eyed men who stumbled with fatigue. They did not march toward the rear, but simply walked away with lowered heads. The 5th moved into the trenches and stared over the breastworks at a jungle abatis of felled trees with sharpened limbs. Beyond, out of sight somewhere, were the British lines. It was inconceivable that they had not attacked today, Alex thought; they could have swept aside these frail defenses and ended the war by noon. They still could.

Magaw summoned the company commanders after he conferred with Mifflin. He delivered quite an oration on courage. Then, rubbing his jaw, he allowed that the best idea was to call for volunteers to go skirmishing.

"Colonel Magaw." Alex realized that the dry voice was his own. He swallowed. "My company volunteers for that duty."

Magaw nodded, and somebody laughed nervously and said, "Take the cockade off your hat before you go, Alex."

He returned to the company, his mouth dry and palms sweating. A brave man would have shaken off his fear the moment he volunteered, Alex believed.

"We're going over there for a little musket practice," he said to Macaroni Jack, nodding beyond the works. "I volunteered us."

"Very good, sir." Macaroni Jack grinned broadly.

"Good for you, sir." Somebody slapped him on the back and he faced Micah.

The boy's face was alight with his eagerness to fight. Why was he so eager? Society had treated him ill. Perhaps that was why he was unafraid. And Alex wondered if he personally was afraid because he'd had only the best of life and so dreaded to leave it.

"Where did you get that rifle, Micah?" he asked.

"*Found* it, Captain." Micah grinned. "Just picked it up with this here powder horn and pouch after we came ashore. You stick along with me out there, sir, and we'll have us a dance."

"*Private* Heath," growled Macaroni Jack.

"All right, Sergeant Maloney," Alex said, "come along the line with me."

He was feeling better. He still was afraid, of course, but not as afraid as he had been now that he'd found two who were eager. And here was Israel Dorfenberg, a man who would have been his intimate friend had they met under other circumstances. Dorfenberg was afraid, as he was, but Dorfenberg was smiling and eager to end his fear. Passing down the line, talking with each man, Alex thoughtfully studied the frightened and the brave. However each felt, all were going.

At the prearranged signal of the blast of cannon from the redoubt on the left they climbed over the breastwork and threaded the felled trees. Beyond the abatis, Alex turned his back to the invisible enemy and formed the company in a double skirmish line.

He could not bring himself to give the order to advance, however, when he remembered how he always had burlesqued the pretentious statements of military glory. "Charge!" he used to say to himself sometimes when Kathy swept upon a social gathering. "Forward, grenadiers!" he'd think when social allies cornered a parlor enemy.

Sheathing his sword, he said quietly to Macaroni Jack, "Let's go." And twisting his hat to make sure his captain's cockade was obvious to the enemy, he turned and walked ahead toward a line of trees. Macaroni Jack, who loved military glory, roared, "For—ard!" Lieutenant Vanderpeyster and Ensign Roe, leading the second line of skirmishers, echoed him.

Soon Alex saw a movement in the trees a hundred yards ahead. Muskets blazed and something plopped into the earth near him. The fire was so light that it could come only from a picket line. Drawing his sword, he shouted, "At the double!" and ran toward the trees.

Micah was bounding beside him and he ran faster, determined that he should lead. But Micah continued to run beside him. He saw the crossed white belts of a British soldier standing under a tree, his musket raised. Micah halted, fired, and the soldier dropped his musket and fell slowly. Other soldiers were running away.

"We pushed in their picket line," Macaroni Jack called as they approached the trees. "Not too fast, sir, not too fast! You're 'way out in front of us."

Now, Alex realized, he was not afraid. He had been shot at, but it had not occurred to him to turn and run. Now his recent fear was like something he'd heard described long ago.

The English soldier lay on his back, legs twisted grotesquely, blood oozing darkly from the hole in his chest and spreading across his red coat and the fresh pipe-clay paste with which he'd whitened his trousers and straps and belts this morning. He was only a boy, his mouth fallen open as if in sleep. As Alex stared at him, the hands twitched and then were still.

Micah, Alex observed, took care not to glance at the body of the soldier he had killed. But Israel stared, his face pale, and then wrenched his gaze away.

They halted at the edge of a meadow about three hundred yards wide. From another woodland beyond it rose the din of a large camp.

"Far enough, sir," said Macaroni Jack. "By the noise I'd say that's Mr. Howe's main army yonder."

Alex dispersed the company in two lines within the cover of the trees and they waited. The sun crept up the sky slowly. Around noon two British officers walked into the meadow and studied them through telescopes.

In midafternoon, drums rolled and red-coated soldiers emerged and formed in the shade of the trees. Alex counted a company wearing the tall miter headpieces of grenadiers.

"Those hats are empty, boys," he called. "Let's make 'em pay for these trees. Hold your fire until I give the word."

"Here they come," said Macaroni Jack. "They ain't even bothered to shell us. Look at the mad bastards marching closed up." Unaccountably his eyes filled with tears as the British drums beat louder. "Aim low, boys!" he roared. "Aim at their officers!"

They came on with their double line dressed, swinging in cadence to their beating drums, their bayonets winking in the afternoon sunlight. Although not numerous in the wide meadow, they were awesome.

"Steady!" Alex shouted. They were a hundred yards distant and doubtless expecting a few scattered shots before the bumpkins ran away through the woods. "Steady! Hold it, boys. Steady!" Seventy-five yards. Fifty.

"Fire!"

The first line fired and moved back to reload as the second line stepped forward.

"Fire!"

Beyond the eddying smoke the grenadiers had halted. Men were down out there. They were closing up and dressing their lines as the shrill voices of officers lashed at them.

Alex's own voice was shrill when he changed his firing line again. There was a sound like the sudden patter of rain on the trees and he realized the grenadiers had fired.

"Hold your fire! Hold it!"

Now the grenadiers ran at them, shouting hoarsely, bayonets held low.

"Fire!"

The grenadiers slowed but did not halt under the close fire. The company's first line fell back through the second.

"Fire!"

Alex glimpsed Israel's powder-blackened face as he loaded methodically behind a tree. He was grinning, no longer afraid. Macaroni Jack parried a grenadier's lunge and drove his own bayonet into him.

They fell back slowly through the trees until Alex established a line of about twenty men with loaded muskets. Then they went forward, firing carefully, while Vanderpeyster formed the rest of the company behind them. The grenadiers faded before them, picking up their wounded as they went. Beyond musket range in the meadow an officer re-formed them and they marched away in cadence to their drums.

"We beat them!" Israel cried. "We broke a company of grenadiers!"

Alex passed among the grinning men, praising them. One, a man named Davis, was bleeding badly from a bayonet thrust through an arm. Someone found Ensign Roe bayoneted to death under a tree.

After Alex had counted eleven British dead and sent a report back to Magaw, he realized with surprise that the death of Roe, a gentle boy, did not grieve him deeply. Now that he knew he was not a coward, nothing else seemed to matter.

Toward sundown they were recalled to the lines.

Rain drove out of the northeast the next morning, trampling their backs, drenching their muskets and powder. They leaned in the shallow, muddy trenches, glaring at one another and listening to the unceasing scrape and thud of the British digging approach trenches beyond the abatis. It was impossible to build a fire in the rushing rain; they ate their pickled pork raw with sodden biscuits. By late afternoon some were standing waist-deep in water in the trenches.

Tension grew in Alex as he slithered through the mud, trying to speak cheerfully to every man. It didn't seem worth the effort. They heard the

British digging closer out there, and they knew that the company had only seven bayonets and not an ounce of dry powder. At any time—in an hour, in five minutes, now—the British could march over the earthworks with fixed bayonets and the war would be ended.

What would you do when the enemy came over the earthworks with bayonets? Run? Throw down your wet musket and raise your arms in surrender?

Everyone was asking himself the question, Alex knew. He saw it in their expressions when they stared at him, as if to read the answer on his face. Wherever he turned, he could not escape their eyes watching him. They felt they had been betrayed. He did not blame them. A Virginia farmer had led them out to an island to stand in the rain until they died or were captured.

"Goddamn *him*," a man muttered. And Alex knew he meant the General.

Darkness, falling early, brought relief from their searching eyes. But it also brought the certainty that the British would leap upon them at dawn.

"Captain," someone wailed, "we stayin' here all *night?*"

He did not know what to answer.

Toward midnight a messenger summoned him to Magaw's headquarters in a small, abandoned stable. Magaw, his face haggard, peered at his officers across a single candle flickering on a barrelhead.

"You'll not inform the men," he said hoarsely. The officers pressed closer, their wet clothing steaming in the humid warmth of the stable. "The army's evacuating Long Island. The General has assembled boats and the evacuation's already begun."

"When do we leave, Bob?" someone asked.

Magaw scowled. "We don't. Not yet." He struggled to lift his head, as if it bore a heavy weight. "We hold a post honor. We and the 3d and the Delawares and what's left of Smallwood's Marylanders and Chester's Connecticut battalion. We're holding the works."

Someone remarked obscenely on a post of honor. An officer next to Alex shivered suddenly.

"We'll get off," Magaw said. "But we'll get off last. No word to the boys, mind you. Nobody moves out till I give the word myself. That's all."

A couple of hours later Alex heard Magaw shouting his name.

"Here, Bob. Over here."

Magaw gripped him by an arm. "Form on the road," he muttered. "And be quiet about it."

"There must be a mistake, Bob. There hasn't been time—"

"I know, I know, goddamn it to hell. It's what I said when Mifflin told me and it's what Mifflin said when he got the word from the General's aide, Major Scammell. But that's the order."

Alex called in the sentries and formed the company on the muddy lane. The men moved quickly and quietly, stifling murmurs of relief.

The regiment walked through the rain, stumbling in the darkness, slipping in the mud, and the sound of the British digging faded beyond the deserted works. They had almost reached Brooklyn when the head of the column halted suddenly. In the darkness men behind collided with those ahead and the entire column began milling and cursing.

Alex hurried ahead to learn what was wrong. An officer on horseback held a lantern aloft. In its faint light two men leaned toward each other in their saddles. One was Mifflin; Alex recognized his voice, shrill and angry. He could not hear the voice of the other, but he glimpsed the taut, thin-lipped face of the General thrust into the lantern light toward Mifflin.

Then Magaw slogged through the mud, cursing. "A mistake," he growled. "A mistake on a mistake on a mistake. Face the goddamn regiment about. We've got to go back there."

They went back, frightened and angry, and resumed their places in the works. The rain stopped and there was no sound except the scrape of shovels and thud of picks as the British dug closer to them.

Just before dawn Magaw ordered them out of the works again and they formed in the lane. But they did not march. They shifted from foot to foot restlessly, listening to the squeal of wagon wheels and slosh of hurrying feet. When Alex began to believe that some of them surely would break ranks and flee, the column moved, slowly at first and then faster.

The first gray, greenish light of dawn found them hurrying through Brooklyn. There were men hurrying ahead of them, but they could see none behind. The road led down into a white wall of mist that rolled upward from the river. They halted, staring behind them. The light grew and they moved again, down into a white world of milling shadows.

As they shuffled onto the ferry landing and waited to take their places in the boats manned by Glover's weary Marblehead regiment, the General rode out of the mist. He leaned toward them, trying to smile or perhaps to speak to them. Then, turning his horse abruptly, he rode in the direction from which they had come and the mist swallowed him.

A gray-haired, broad-shouldered officer wearing the black cockade of a general started after him, then reined in his horse.

"Well doon, lads," he shouted in a broad Scot accent. "Well doon, Colonel Magaw and a' your men."

"Thank you, General Mercer," Magaw replied.

"Dinna thank me," said Mercer. " 'Tis the General's sentiment that he's na the time t'express. Yon's a harried mon, Magaw, but he's snatched us from the jaws o' the bloody lion. Hoot!" His lined, aging face widened in a grin. "I'd gi' mooch t'see Mr. Howe when he l'arns we've left the field wi' a' our baggage. A bra battle, Magaw. Let's na be doon-hearted."

He urged his horse into the mist after the General and then called back, "Save me a hearty breakfast in Noo York, Magaw. I'll be aboord the last boat wi' the General."

"How can he be so cheerful in retreat?" Alex asked.

"He's a Scot and a fighter and so he's accustomed to defeat," Magaw replied. "A stubborn man who enjoys a fight and never has been a winner, from Culloden in the old country through all the French wars on the frontier. And he knows the General should have told us, 'Well done.' " Magaw looked around and lowered his voice. "I wonder, Alex, whether good generalship or good luck and Howe's slothfulness got us free of this island alive. And I wonder if there's spirit left in enough of us ever to win."

XX

"WIN or lose," Timothy Murdoch often said to Kathy that summer, *"we've* got to win."

By *we* he meant, of course, himself—and her.

"Yes, Papa," she'd reply, smiling, "we must *forestall* defeat."

He thought it a capital joke that she understood so well the nature of his business. For he had become deeply involved in what was called "forestalling." That is, he bought up at the lowest possible price the available supply of items which the army would need later in order to sell at a great profit.

Kathy was amazed to learn that a few radicals thought the practice wrong. Unfair to whom or what? One must look out for oneself and be shrewd if one would rise in life—and there was nothing more desirable for anyone than to rise. It made her indignant to hear oafs like Timothy Matlack criticize merchants like Papa and Mr. Morris and Mr. Willing who were only seeking a fair profit for their considerable risks.

Business was fascinating, she had decided. It involved even more intrigue than politics and society—and was far more profitable in its results. She was greatly pleased that she was able to draw Papa out on the subject of his business and to understand much about it readily.

In the process called "forestalling," he pointed out to her, you asked yourself what an army needed. Cannon, muskets, powder, blankets, shoes, tents, pork, flour . . . Obvious, my dear Kathy, but no wise merchant was going to try to do business in cannon or start the manufacture of muskets. Think again, remembering that there was large profit in small things. A big musket was useless without a tiny—flint! America depended principally on Europe for its flints. Now at St. Eustatius in the Indies there was a Dutchman named VanGross who had received from Rotterdam a large shipment of flints consigned for the Spanish Empire. But— VanGross could turn a handsomer profit with Pennsylvania flour than Mexican teak (the Spaniards were not spending gold for flints at present). So—you took the flints now before Thomas Willing or some other shrewd fellow heard about them and you held them until the inevitable time when the army cried desperately for flints. Then you sold them to the army for almost whatever price you asked.

"Papa," she'd say, "how *engrossing*."

He chuckled and slapped his thigh the first time she made the pun, realizing delightedly that she was learning rapidly. For, like every "forestaller," he desired above all to make the ultimate step and become an "engrosser." For, if you could engross and so control the market in anything, you could command exorbitant rather than merely handsome profits with your commodity. Robert Morris had engrossed the Philadelphia flour market for a time years ago. A Quebec merchant—d'Agincourt, or something of the sort—had engrossed the beaver market for a spell. You never knew when the opportunity would strike, but you had always to be prepared for it by remaining informed, respected, secretive.

In one of their long conversations about his business Kathy remarked wishfully one day in September that it would be fine if you could engross the market in something everybody used or ate—oh, say, pork.

He looked at her sharply. "What have you heard?"

She clapped her hands and laughed. "Papa, you haven't engrossed the market in *pigs!*"

He shook his head, watching her narrowly. "But what is essential to pork?"

"Fodder— Oh, you mean to preserve it. Brine—salt! Papa, how clever of you! Seizing the thing everybody is fighting and haggling for and the army needs to preserve its pork and nobody can get enough of because of the blockade."

He leaned toward her. "Kathy, you're *sure* you've heard no word?"

"Of course not. Don't you *trust* me to bring you every morsel of gossip I hear or can worm from anybody?"

"Yes." He smiled. "You're being most helpful, my dear. That was a very important word Dick Peters of the War Board let drop to you last week about shoes. You're my right arm." He squeezed her right arm. "Now I'll tell you *our* secret. By considerable expenditure and luck and daring I've run in a shiplade of salt from Lisbon. It arrived at Wilmington on Monday. I sent Barnaby Falco there to handle the matter personally."

"Then you're rich!" she exclaimed. "A whole shiplade of salt with the price at—"

"Not as rich as I will be, Kathy. The price of salt can only go up, and ninety per cent of that shiplade will wait the day when salt is at its highest."

"If Philadelphia knew, there'd be a riot."

"Philadelphia will not know—until the day I'm prepared to sell *some* of my salt." He frowned suddenly and his voice rose plaintively, as if defending himself. "Think how much it cost me. Think of the daring it took for me to run the blockade."

He had not personally made the hazardous voyage, of course. Nevertheless— "Papa, you're wonderful. Why, now you can afford to buy a Fair Oaks."

"Not yet," he said hesitantly. "But soon. Just wait, Kathy. The day's coming when you'll be able to snap up some of those large estates for a song."

"Then you think we'll win?"

"We?" He looked at her curiously. "*We* are bound to win."

She knew that he meant he—and she—would emerge prosperously from this civil war. But she had meant by *we* the colonial cause. Sometimes she had to remind herself that it was her cause now. Alex belonged to it, and didn't Papa profess it as his cause? He *seemed* to, though to a loyalist like Mr. Shippen he might *seem* to have strong loyalist leanings. Whatever his true political beliefs, he urged her to be—or at least to appear—strongly militant for the cause of liberty.

"It gets you about, my dear," he'd say.

It did, though the places she went and the people she met were not as gay and interesting as in the old days when the moderates and loyalists were ascendant. Unfortunately, these militant patriots were a little dull, a little common.

She was vastly disappointed, for instance, on meeting General Washington's wife at Mrs. Reed's house. Lady Washington, they quaintly called her, in a laughable effort to lend some social stature to a quite commonplace woman. Though rich and a tidewater Virginian, she impressed Kathy as a plain, stout, rather closemouthed woman with no dash. She was staying then at the City Tavern where she recently had recovered from the effects of a smallpox inoculation which the General had insisted she take. In Esther Reed's parlor she sat silently and knitted a sock. It really was shocking to find the wife of the Commander in Chief knitting a sock at a Philadelphia social gathering, as if she were a farmer's wife from the far back country. She did not charm easily, Kathy realized with consternation, until the conversation sank to commonplace things like food and servants and smallpox inoculations. Then she became voluble.

"I never was more disappointed in all my life," Kathy told her father that evening.

"But you must remember that she's a very rich woman," he replied. "The very rich can afford eccentricities, Kathy."

Sometimes, when he made such remarks, he irritated her greatly. When, oh when, she'd ask herself, is he going to admit that he's rich and not just trying to become so? With all his talk of enterprise and gains where, indeed, was the money? Did he keep a great horde of gold locked in a chest some place? She tried to find out and became utterly bored by his vague talk of credit. And when she finally asked him about his *money,* he decried monotonously the woefully weak status of the continental currency: too much paper being printed and inflation rising rapidly.

In general, however, she found her father a more interesting companion than ever before. Late in July she closed the Fourth Street house and went to live with him on Arch Street. It happened by coincidence and she did not intend to stay permanently.

John Tout had driven to the city one day in mid-July and begged her to let Philly come to the farm for a spell; Martha Tout was gravely ill with a fever and he reckoned only Philly could pull her through. She had let Philly go reluctantly and only because Philly insisted that she must. She decided not to go to the farm herself that summer for fear of catching the fever that was sweeping the county. With Philly gone, she missed Alex more than she had since he went away. After a few days of boredom and loneliness, she told Mrs. Munger to take a holiday and moved her clothing to her father's house on Arch Street.

Although it was not a socially gay summer in Philadelphia, Papa was eager to entertain people whom he considered influential in his business. Congressmen and officers and merchants came frequently to dinner or supper with their ladies, and she was invited almost everywhere with Papa. It was rather like the old days before her marriage, except that she lacked the pleasant excitement of beaux and flirtation.

As time passed, she thought of Alex less frequently. When word came that the army was retreating, she began to believe it would be defeated. Secretly she hoped it would. Then Alex would come home and she would *live* again after this meaningless war had ended.

Only such things as Papa's importation of a shiplade of salt interested her. She wished that she were a man so that she could ride down to Wilmington, as Barnaby Falco had, and direct the careful, secretive shipment of the salt by wagons to warehouses in Philadelphia and an abandoned old log stable at the farm. (How clever of Papa to think of hiding half of the salt at the farm.) There was a reality about business that pleased her. It would be perfect if at the heart of a business there were a great chest of solid gold pieces. She was beginning to doubt, however, that there really was such a chest in Papa's business. But if there were, she thought abstractedly, she would draw and draw from it and buy—a great house, a fine coach and four. She'd buy—people to do her bidding. A man to bow and a great strong man to go through the street and push back the mob in front of her, and a man . . . How utterly ridiculous, she told herself, to be daydreaming like a child.

Then, one evening toward the end of September, she was shocked by her father's sense of business as they ate a late supper together at home.

"John Tout came to the office today with a curious request," he said. "He offered to buy up your Philly's time and set her free."

She stiffened. "What did you tell him?"

"Well, I thought I should consult you, my dear, since you've been so fond of her. But John put forward a surprisingly strong case." Murdoch smiled faintly. "Hard money. None of your worthless continental paper. Portuguese johannes. He held a fistful under my nose." His expression became abstracted. "I wonder where he got them. I—"

"Papa!" Her voice rose in anguish. "You wouldn't—you *couldn't*—"

"No," he said quickly. "Of course not, Kathy, if you don't wish to lose Philly . . ."

She raged at herself for her selfishness of the past weeks. Because her father's servants did everything here, she had let Philly linger on at the farm after Mrs. Tout recovered from the fever. Lose Philly? It was unthinkable. But to *force* her to continue being her friend, her servant, *was* to lose her.

"You must admit," Murdoch was saying, "that in these times hard money—gold—is mighty tempting. It might be said too that I—uh—have pressed legality in binding some of my servants for—uh—extensive periods. The—"

"Papa!" She hated him suddenly. "Papa!"

"Now then, Kathy," he said querulously. "Now then, everything has been so pleasant between us, let's not permit some minor—"

"Minor!" She swung to her feet, thinking dimly that it was good to be fully alive again. "John Tout has awakened me to something terribly wrong with *us*. We're selfish!"

"Now Kathy, pray don't . . ."

His voice died as she swept from the room. What an idiot he was. But so was she to have let him beguile her for so many weeks with his talk of money, money, money. And where was the money? In the hands of a hard-working farmer with the decency to see that Philly should be free.

Whirling in the parlor, she returned to the dining room doorway and said to him, "I'm going to the farm tomorrow. I want you to prepare a document freeing Philly to take with me."

"But Kathy!" His hands fluttered upward in distress and she knew what he was thinking: John Tout's gold gone and Philly gone and Kathy gone out of her senses. She bit her lip to restrain herself from saying that she loathed him. "Kathy!" And then the nervous flutter, flutter of his hands. "You said yourself you wanted to *keep* Philly. If—"

"If I can't keep her as a free servant at wages, then I can't keep her as a *friend*. You have that document prepared for me, Father!"

He did.

He watched unhappily as she rode off in the chaise driven by Billy. She did not wave good-by to him.

It seemed to take an interminable time to reach the farm. When the chaise finally pulled up, she leaped out and almost ran to the house, fighting the impulse to call Philly's name.

Mrs. Tout looked at her in surprise and said nothing.

"It's good to see you've quite recovered," Kathy told her. "Is Philly about?"

"She's staying a spell with Mrs. March who's had a touch of the fever too."

"Oh?" Something was wrong, she thought. Mrs. Tout never had acted so coldly. "Well, tell 'em to saddle up Flyswat and I'll ride over there. I'll have a bite before I go. And have one of the girls bring up warm water while I change to a habit."

"The *girls* are having their rest hour," Mrs. Tout said heavily. "And the men are up at the old stable fixing the roof to keep that *salt* of your father's dry. It's none of my business, but I don't like that salt and John don't like it either. There's people can't cure their pork for lack of salt and some haven't even got it for the table. It's not right."

Kathy flushed. "It's true, Mrs. Tout, that it's none of our business. This *is* my father's place, you know." Turning, she went upstairs.

Mrs. Tout did not speak when she brought warm water to her room and she had little to say when serving her in the dining room. It was annoying. She acted as if this were the Tout farm rather than the Murdoch farm. While Kathy was eating she heard John's voice in the kitchen and she waited in vain for him to come and greet her, as was his custom. They were angry, she thought, because her father had not agreed yesterday to let them buy up Philly's time. It was none of their business, but— She rang the table bell.

When Mrs. Tout appeared, Kathy said, "Would you and John step in here a moment—please."

John came in reluctantly. He nodded but did not look directly at her when she greeted him.

"You're both vexed with me," she said, "because you think I don't want Philly freed. You're wrong. I've the paper here that declares her indenture ended and I've come to give it to her."

As they stared at her, tears came to Mrs. Tout's eyes. "Free, Kathy? You mean she'll be free to do as she pleases?"

"Of course."

"You mean you don't want her to stay on working for you?" John asked.

"Of course I do. But it's for her to decide if she wants to—as a free girl at wages."

John rubbed his chin. "Martha and me aimed to do it ourselves, Miss Kathy—"

"And make her feel duty *bound* to stay here," Kathy snapped.

"I reckon," John said, "that now she'll feel duty *bound* to stay with you since you want her. I—"

"John." Mrs. Tout touched his arm. "The point is that Philly's free to do as she pleases." She looked at Kathy. "Thank you for doing it."

Now, Kathy thought, everything would be all right. She would feel again that she was in control and at ease.

But John would not let her feel so.

"I'm bound to speak to you about the salt, Miss Kathy, as I done to your father. This here's a *farm*. It ain't a place to hide and horde a thing my neighbors need. That fellow Falco's mighty highhanded, bringing in wagons after dark and ordering around my two men and the boy, Tom, like . . ."

She rose abruptly and left the table. As she passed through the kitchen, she thought that the bound girls were barely civil. Outside she spoke kindly to Tom and commented on how he'd grown when he led up Flyswat, but he looked at her with downright hostility. He reminded her of the first time years ago when Micah had looked at her thus in this same yard; she could not understand why Tom acted so now any better than she'd understood why Micah had then.

As she cantered down the lane she felt vaguely alarmed by the change in everyone. But it would pass, she told herself. Here was the road and the familiar land curling into a golden September haze. This was *her* country. The Pilch place there and beyond it the Harrisons' and away yonder the Wisters'. She would have stopped and chatted with Ned Pilch, but he merely nodded to her and hurried past with gaze averted. She waved to Mrs. Wister in her yard and Mrs. Wister disappeared into the house. What was wrong? Something more than a fever had swept the county this season. There was an unrest and suspicion in people such as you found in Philadelphia parlors when the company was uncertain of one another's political loyalties. No one here was sure of where she stood, as she was not positive who was patriot and who loyalist. They failed to understand that it did not matter to her *what* anyone was.

She had forgotten the vast ringing silence of the country. Now it pressed a sense of loneliness on her and she thought of Alex. Where was he in this golden afternoon? Did he ever wish to be with her as intensely as she wanted to be with him at this moment?

As she rode up the lane, Mrs. March thrust her head out an upper window and cried, "Kathy! Land sakes, girl, it's good to see you."

For the first time in her life Kathy thought that she was glad to see Mrs. March.

"Any word of Alex?"

Kathy leaped from Flyswat. "No news is good news, Mother March."

Philly hurried from the house, smiling and calling to her.

Kathy hugged her and kissed her on a sun-browned cheek. "I've good news, Philly."

Philly's eyes widened. "Let me guess. We've had a great victory in the north."

"No."

"Then Mr. Alex and the company are coming home."

"No. It concerns you."

"Me?" Philly looked puzzled as they walked arm in arm to the house. "How can there be good news about me?"

"What do you want most in all the world?"

"Oh, Lord save us, Kathy, I—" She flushed and Kathy laughed. "I don't know." Mrs. March appeared wearing an old dressing gown. "Ma'am," Philly said to her, "you shouldn't be out of that bed yet."

"I never knew a better time to be up," snapped Mrs. March and kissed Kathy's forehead resoundingly.

"I've set Philly a guessing game," said Kathy. "What does she want most in all the world, Mother March?"

Mrs. March stared at Philly thoughtfully. "What she wants would be something she never says. Can't be a beau, for every boy and man the county over is willing. Now let me think—"

"Oh, here," Kathy said impatiently, taking the paper from a pocket. "If you can't guess, I'll have to tell you. You're free, Philly."

Her lips moved, and then she whispered, "Free?"

"Yes, your indenture's ended. This notarized document from my father proves it. Here, read it and see—"

"Free." Her eyes filled with tears. "Kathy, thank you—"

"It's long overdue," Kathy said brusquely. "I'm a selfish-minded ninny that it's not been done before."

"Kathy, do you mean you don't want me with you any longer?"

"Heaven help us, no. I just don't want you to *have* to be. I want you to *want* to be."

"I do want to." Philly smiled and whirled suddenly in two fast dancing steps. "I've loved the country and now I feel the city busting in me. I dare say the house is a fright, Kathy. It's time I got back and cleaned it so it's proper for the new year when the war's won and Mr. Alex and the company come home."

"Yes," Kathy said slowly. "*Yes*. It's time I went home too. We'll go together, Philly, and wait the end of the war."

XXI

THE war would end soon in the crushing of all their great hopes, Alex believed. For days and weeks he fought the drag of deep depression, which was aggravated by a heavy cold and persistent fever. The entire army seemed to share his despair.

After Glover's Marbleheaders and the Salem men of the 27th Massachusetts performed the magnificent, exhausting feat of taking ninety-five hundred men and their supplies and equipment off Long Island in a single night, the army collapsed in New York. It lay uncoiled, stunned, in the soggy morass of its tents and baggage. And then, after a day or two, desertions began to sap its remaining strength.

Men faded into the reeking alleys of the city. You saw them hurrying north on the Post Road at nightfall and skulking through fields and woods. Small groups wandered the waterfront, avoiding the patrols as they sought boats. Sometimes the patrols themselves disappeared.

Everyone wanted to get off the island. It was rumored that the General himself wanted to withdraw north but that the Congress had ordered the army to stay. Pulled this way and that, slowly draining away, the army stretched its ebbing strength in thin lines about the island.

In its stretching the 5th was sent north to Harlem Heights, and there its companies were dispersed widely. Alex's company set up camp in a clearing below the Point of Rocks, about midway of the Heights. Here they waited, with no discernible duty except to patrol a section of the Heights and to continue struggling to survive. They made shelters, they scrounged for food, and they waited for the British to strike again.

There was an eagle's view from the summit of the Point of Rocks where Alex passed much of his time after the days turned bright and warm. He'd lie, coughing, on a sun-warm stone slab and gaze south through half-closed eyes. Often he'd see the island as a great ship, deck slightly canted from west to east, plunging south between its blue rivers under a white canvas of wind-bellied clouds.

Then on September fifteenth the bright, hot morning silence was shattered by the rumble of guns. Alex scrambled up to the lookout. When he reached the summit, panting and coughing, Macaroni Jack pointed south to the East River. Orange gun flashes punctured a roiling cloud of smoke as British frigates pounded the Kip's Bay defenses.

He descended to the camp, paraded the company and awaited orders. But none came. In midafternoon Micah uttered a plaintive, chilling cry from the lookout and Alex climbed up to him.

Micah wailed, "Look, sir. Retreat again!" He pointed southeast toward the Post Road which unraveled in a yellow thread of summer dust from dark green woodland and disappeared north beyond a shoulder of the Heights. Along it scurried tiny antlike figures. They were men, running north in disorder. "Ours!" Micah cursed. "Running away again!"

The last tiny figures straggled out of sight and the road was empty. A jay squawled somewhere in a thicket below. There was no other sound. Manhattan rolled south in a pellucid afternoon. It appeared to have been deserted by every living thing except the jay that squawled, squawled, squawled.

"Watch the hawks," Micah said.

Alex saw two, three and then a dozen rising slowly from the woods that stretched south in a green tangle two miles wide between the Post Road on the east and the Bloomingdale Road on the west. The hawks circled upward on slowly beating wings.

"*They* know. Listen!"

Alex heard nothing.

"Here they come," Micah said.

Abruptly the yellow thread of the Post Road was stained red where it emerged from the woods. The dark red stain crept steadily forward, sending a white stream of dust over the fields beyond it. Sunlight glittered on brass, and then, faintly, Alex heard a tuneless piping and the throb of drums.

"Look!" Micah pointed toward the Bloomingdale Road to the west.

A cloud of dust rose from the road, and out of the dust poured a ragged stream of men loping north.

"Ours. Look at 'em run."

"They must be Putnam's men escaping from the city," Alex said. "They don't know the British are paralleling 'em. And the British don't know it either or they'd cross over and—"

As he watched tensely, the British column halted and scouts flanked westward, tiny red specks in a vast brown bowl. When the red specks reached the summit of the low gray ridge which twisted out of the woods, they would see the fleeing American column. And then, Alex thought, another part of the American army would be destroyed. The specks edged on, hesitated, edged on—and turned back. The Americans continued to pour north.

The dark stream flowed on the Post Road again, even as the last Americans plunged into the Hollow Way and disappeared from view.

"We'll soon know what happened," Alex said. "We'll fight soon."

But days passed before they heard how the Americans broke and ran at Kip's Bay while the General cursed and lashed them with his sword, and how Aaron Burr led Putnam's forces to safety just before the British closed their trap on the city. They saw nothing, except the fiery glow in the sky when much of the city was destroyed in the great fire. They heard how others fought, at Harlem Heights and Throg's Neck and Pelham and White Plains in the army's long retreat northward. But the 5th and 3d did not join in battle or retreat. They were withdrawn to Fort Washington, the place Alex detested and believed untenable, while the war swept around them.

Summer died. The nights grew cold. Frost whitened the ground and maples and ash flamed along the Palisades. They were the only element of the American army left on Manhattan, but they were a powerless element, Alex knew. On this high ridge they were prisoners whom the British could take at leisure.

For a long time he was certain that the post would be abandoned and they'd be ferried north to join the main army. Instead of being relieved, however, they were slowly strengthened by a trickle of men and supplies and equipment brought from Fort Lee across the river in New Jersey. He and several officers continued to hope that someone in the high command would see the hopelessness of their position and withdraw them before it was too late. Eventually their hope ended in despair.

Alex quarreled heatedly with Magaw over the matter for Magaw, as frustrated as Alex by the long inaction, had convinced himself that he would fight at Fort Washington—and hold it against any force.

Magaw told everyone of high rank that his men could hold the fort. And everyone believed him simply because it was a pleasant notion to believe. Putnam believed him, and it did not matter to Magaw that Putnam was an incompetent general. It seemed unlikely that Greene would agree with Putnam on anything of much tactical or strategic importance, for Greene, in the opinion of many, was the most intelligent general officer in the army. And then Alex lost faith in him when Greene agreed that Fort Washington should and could be held. What did Lee think? Lee did not choose to give an opinion, Alex heard, and he knew that Lee would issue the *right* opinion *after* the fort had been held or lost. Their fate was left to the General, who should have made the decision in the first place and ignored the desire of the militarily inept Congress to hold a small, useless parcel of land on Manhattan for propaganda purposes.

"If I believed in prayer," Alex said to Vanderpeyster, "I would pray to that vague Providence the General is forever invoking. I'd ask Providence to whisper a little wisdom in the General's ear. It's not too late for him to stop his eternal hesitating and blundering."

But the General did not act. Even after November seventh, when the passage of three British ships up the river between Fort Washington and Fort Lee demonstrated that both forts were useless, the General continued to say he would defer to the opinion of his staff. By the morning of November fifteenth it was too late for him to act.

A white flag fluttered in the valley that morning, a solitary drum tapped, and up the hill toward Fort Washington strode a British officer followed by a standard bearer and drummer. Magaw came down to the picket line where the British officer, introducing himself as Lieutenant Colonel Patterson, said that the American position was untenable and demanded the surrender of the post. Magaw delivered a short oration on his determination to hold it. Patterson replied that the entire garrison might be put to the sword if Magaw persisted in his folly. Magaw orated again on his strength. Patterson turned and strode away.

"We will hold to the last extremity," Magaw thundered at a meeting of his officers. Although it was a cold morning, his red face shone with sweat. "We will . . ."

He was in an orating mood, Alex thought grimly as he rode Heartbreak back to his post. But oration could not disguise the fact that Magaw had dedicated himself to a hopeless and idiotic task. He had about three thousand men with whom he proposed to defend a perimeter of four or five miles against Howe's army. Worse, his men were disposed in small, disconnected units. Colonel Moses Rawlings was posted in a small redoubt a half mile north of the fort with his regiment of Maryland and Virginia riflemen and a battery of three guns. Colonel John Baxter's Bucks County militiamen occupied flèches on Laurel Hill near the Harlem River. The 5th, the 3d, a party of Rangers and a detachment of Colonel Samuel Miles' Pennsylvania riflemen, composing the largest group of about eight hundred men under the command of Lieutenant Colonel Lambert Cadwalader, were a couple of miles south of Fort Washington in the old Harlem Heights entrenchments. Other small groups were scattered about on high ground, while Magaw himself remained in his beloved fort with two companies.

"The game will begin tomorrow morning," Alex said to Macaroni Jack when he returned to the company from Fort Washington.

"We're too far out, sir." Macaroni Jack's broad face was knit in lines of worry.

"Try to tell that to Colonel Magaw."

Macaroni Jack fingered his tight collar. "He don't know the feel of a rope about his neck, sir. I deserted *them* and if they was to capture me—"

"They capture Sergeant John Monroney, freeman of Lancaster County. I revised the company roll a couple of weeks ago and entered you so. You'd have seen if you'd bothered to check it. I've told Vanderpeyster and Micah and Dorfenberg and they've passed the word around. Remember your name. No one would betray you."

Macaroni Jack blinked quickly. "Thank you, sir. Then you expect—"

"The worst," Alex said.

But what the worst might be he did not know. Defeat here on the Heights, surely. But death for some of them before defeat. For those who lived there waited—what? Prison? The gallows? In recent weeks his confoundedly vivid imagination had rioted through every eventuality until his fear was numbed by despair. Quick death, he now believed, was preferable to this slow rotting. He had lived beyond the point of compromise. There seemed no worse fate than to return to Philadelphia some day as a man old and embittered while still young in years. He— all of them—always would feel that they had not been defeated by the enemy as much as they had been betrayed by the stupidity of their leaders.

That night, as they waited in the front lines of the crumbling old entrenchments, he tried to think of Kathy. In imagination he saw her, but she did not touch him and he did not want to touch her. It was strange. His desire for her seemed as dead as the spring of some year long past. The little things that loomed so large to her were smaller to him now than ever. War revealed the fatuity of one's place in society. Only the strong inherited the earth. Their marriage, lacking strength, had been a strange mixture of pride and passion. *Had been?* Remorse tugged him, as if he had been unfaithful to her. And then he knew the trouble: he wondered whether she had been faithful to him.

Yet he felt almost cheerful in the chill gray dawn as he walked the company's line and hungrily munched a slab of half-cooked pickled pork and a chunk of hard bread. At exactly seven o'clock, as the sun rose over the rim of frosted earth, the British batteries opened fire from the eastern bank of the Harlem and from a frigate in the Hudson. The company huddled lower in the shallow trenches and stared south across the Hollow Way.

Shortly before ten o'clock the gray and brown autumn woodland south of the valley was flecked with red and blue and yellow. The colors massed, extended, and flowed forward in two gaudy columns that descended into the Hollow Way. White puffs of smoke rose from fieldpieces, and a howitzer crumped. An outpost of the 3d turned and trotted back to the lines.

In a few minutes the van of one column came over the crest north of the Hollow Way, marching closed up, arms swinging in cadence to the clear, sweet music of massed fifes.

"The Light Infantry Song," growled Macaroni Jack. "The bastards!" He blinked quickly and turned his head from Alex.

As the Americans' single six-pounder opened fire, the head of the second column came over the crest. Its band of drums and horns and hautboys drowned the British fifes with a harsh, disturbing marching song.

"Hessians," Alex said and lifted the telescope which Macaroni Jack claimed he had "found" a few days before.

He heard the men muttering, "Hessians . . . Hessians . . . Hessians . . ." as they leaned forward uneasily for their first glimpse of the troops whose fearful reputation had preceded them.

Out from the Hessian column fanned a company of green-coated Jägers. They ran lightly with rifles at ready, ducking from rocks to trees, although they were far beyond the range of the American line. They were like tumblers, warming themselves for their act, Alex thought. Behind them the blue-coated grenadiers lumbered heavily forward to the thumping blare of their band.

Alex focused Macaroni Jack's glass on a grenadier. Somewhere under that heavy equipment, said to weigh almost a hundred pounds, there was a man. To cumbersome white belts were attached a heavy cartridge

box, an enormous sword, a gallon canteen, a hatchet, knapsack, haversack, rolled blanket and folded section of tenting. Beneath the blue-
skirted coat Alex made out a yellow waistcoat and yellow breeches
extending into black gaiters. But where was the man, the master of this
equipage? There was the brass-fronted high cap—and now, as the strange
creature turned at some word of command, he saw the long queue of
blond hair, braided in a thick paste of flour and tallow, swinging over
his waist. But where was the face? The heavy musket, tipped by a sharp
and shining bayonet, hid it. Then, suddenly, he saw it clearly: white,
expressionless, a mask. If that really was a man marching out there, he
was thoroughly disguised.

Lowering the glass, he said to no one in particular, "I don't like
their music. Their brass is flat."

Israel laughed, loudly and nervously. A couple of men started and
frowned at him.

"Captain March doesn't like their music," Israel said. "It's flat, he
says."

The remark did not strike them as funny, but it amused Alex when
he heard it repeated.

"It's a moral victory for us," he said, grinning at Israel. "Their music
is imperfect."

As the British light grenadiers and the Hessian heavy grenadiers came
on, a brightly uniformed officer on a lean horse galloped between the
marching brigades and out ahead of them.

Macaroni Jack, studying him through the telescope, exclaimed, "It's
Earl Percy! I mind him at the Battle of Minden. Son and heir of the
Duke of Northumberland he is and a damn good man." He swore
softly as Earl Percy, followed by an aide, continued to gallop straight
toward the lines. "Captain March, you look like him—I mean, sir, he
looks like you. Take a look." He handed Alex the glass.

Alex focused on the slender, smiling face of Hugh, Brigadier General
Earl Percy. Their similarity of appearance was superficial, he thought
wryly. For Percy clearly was unafraid, while his own mouth was dry with
the dread of what must come.

"He's nigh inside my range," Micah said, training his rifle on the
galloping figure. "Seventy-five yards more and he'll never be the Duke
of whatever."

"Take your aim off him, Micah," Alex said.

"But sir—"

"*Off* him!" Alex snapped.

Micah looked around at him, scowling.

"It's murder," Alex said.

But so, of course, was war. What made him wish to spare Percy's life? Was it more valuable than the life of a faceless Hessian? He displayed a sentimentality that ill befit a determined rebel, he thought glumly. Micah's reason for wanting to kill him was clear and simple: as the commander of those two advancing brigades, Percy slain was more important than a hundred grenadiers slain.

"*Not* shoot him?" Micah demanded fiercely.

Macaroni Jack roared, "You heard Captain March's order!"

"But you, yourself, say shoot their officers, Jack. You—"

"You goddamn fool, that ain't just an officer! That's *Earl* Percy of the 5th Fusiliers. What d'you know of the house of Percy and the Earls of Northumberland, you wool-headed woodsy? You ain't ever even *seen* Alnwick Castle."

"I *seen* this much," Micah cried. "I seen the inside o' your hide just now when it comes to fighting this here war. Your head's still full of dukes and such, Macaroni Jack, and your heart's gone with your head—"

"If you'd watch the *enemy,*" Israel said, stepping in front of Micah as Macaroni Jack swung toward him, "you'd see the target has passed from range. The argument, like most arguments, is hypothetical."

Percy had turned back, Alex saw. The brigades were marching obliquely to the left and disappearing behind a large wood.

But, Alex thought, the argument had not been as hypothetical as Israel maintained. The noble sentiments about freedom expressed by a John Adams would remain only sentiments unless a Micah Heath committed murder after murder.

During a lull in the British cannonading they heard the patter of small-arms fire to the north. It was like a game of chess between master and novice, Alex thought. Percy's troops held them here while their fate was arranged on another part of the board.

Late in the morning the British and Hessian brigades emerged from the cover of the woods, extended the length of the American works, and flowed from column into line. As they advanced measuredly, Alex felt a strange sense of relief.

"Hold your fire! Hold it! Hold!" His voice rang confidently as he stared down the hill. In the glare of sunlight the enemy line seemed to glow and flow forward like quicksilver. Before it ran the green-coated Jägers with their rifles.

Something snapped the right sleeve of Alex's coat and he wondered vaguely what could have torn it.

"Down!" shouted Macaroni Jack. "Get down, sir!"

Martin McDermott screamed suddenly and clutched at his throat. His scream died in a bubbling moan and he pitched forward. Abruptly Alex

vividly remembered the smithy near the Arch Street viaduct where he had
recruited McDermott; he tried in vain to rid himself of the memory,
but he seemed to be standing in that Philadelphia smithy, saying . . .

"Hold it!" His voice was lost in a ragged crash of muskets as the
company failed to wait. Men stood up and shot blindly and ducked
down.

Beyond the smoke rose a roar, like the sound of a river in flood, and
then he saw a massed blue wall of Hessian grenadiers flowing toward
him from the smoke. He raised his musket, fired and glanced around.
He was alone.

His voice rose piercingly above the roaring voices of the charging Hessians, cursing the vanished company. Then a hand was dragging him backwards and another hand seized him. Micah. Israel. And then Macaroni
Jack, crouching low, his bayoneted musket clamped against a hip, swung
in front of them.

A Hessian leaped the trench, roaring, "Yonkee! Yonkee!" and lunged
at Macaroni Jack. Macaroni Jack's musket butt flashed, knocking the
Hessian's bayoneted musket from his hands. The grenadier stumbled forward on the momentum of his lunge, sinking to his knees, his big hands
groping emptily, his bright blue doll's eyes raised bewilderedly. His eyes
widened and an inhuman scream was torn from his throat as Macaroni
Jack's bayonet sank into his broad chest.

"Yonkee! . . . Yonkee!"

Two more Hessians rushed at Macaroni Jack as he tried to yank his
bayonet from the wriggling, screaming grenadier on the ground. Israel
and Micah sprang forward. Alex plunged between them, jabbing his bayonet at one of the Hessians.

His hands suddenly were numbed, empty, and he glimpsed a white
grinning face, a bayonet flashing back to drive through him.

There was a sickening crunch as Micah clubbed the Hessian with his
rifle butt. The Hessian's bayoneted musket wavered and fell. The grinning face became a porridge of blood and brains and yellow hair that
tottered silently, blindly, tilted on jerking legs, and then fell backward.

Alex ran. The direction did not matter as long as he escaped the sight
of the broken head that moved on jerking legs. Aware, finally, that Micah
and Israel and Macaroni Jack ran with him, he halted and turned. But
they grasped him and dragged him on. Then the earth opened before
them and they fell into a trench.

Men were staring at him, their eyes asking, What next? The Hessians
and British had halted in the first line of entrenchments a hundred yards
away, although they must know that they could sweep easily to the fort.
But maneuver was more important in their practiced art of war than

brute force. They were extending their lines, east toward the Harlem and west toward the Hudson, while they waited for their plan to develop elsewhere.

"They got us soon as they want us," someone muttered.

"No," Alex said firmly. "We'll hold them here."

What a cheerful liar, he thought as he passed along the line, spreading out the men and linking up with the company on the right. There was no one on the left; open ground marked one of several holes in the line. Their position was hopeless, but he continued to hear himself saying cheerfully, "We'll hold them here."

The broken ground stretched under the bright noon sun. Surely the sun should be farther down west. It seemed to hang, unmoving, above the clots and lines of motionless men. They waited, and the sun waited with them. Heavy musket and rifle fire along the Harlem had ended abruptly some time ago. Now, in the oppressive silence, no one stirred.

A man coughed somewhere. A gust of wind soughed through a stand of pines. And then, faintly, a wail of bagpipes rose in the rear of the American lines.

The earth shook suddenly to the crash of cannon. Jerry Ewell, leaping from the trench, raced to Heartbreak. Scrambling onto the stallion's back, he galloped toward the fort. As the men cursed him, there was a roll of drums in the Hessian works and the grenadiers flushed out in blue and scarlet lines.

The company on the right fired wildly and broke from their trenches. Alex glimpsed Lambert Cadwalader trotting backward, gesticulating wildly, trying to rally the fleeing men, his long, pale face bearing an expression of pained concentration. He looked, Alex thought irrelevantly, as he had once years ago awkwardly trying to execute a minuet at the Philadelphia Assembly.

The panic was infectious. Now his own men were firing blindly and clambering out of the trenches. In vain he and Vanderpeyster shrieked at them to hold.

"They *can't* hold!" Macaroni Jack shouted. "Keep with 'em and they'll re-form."

Micah thrust his face close. "Cut loose and fight down to the river. We can do it!"

"And drown in the Hudson?"

"We can *swum* it!" Micah shouted. "You and me and Israel. I'll—"

"Stop them by the knoll!" Alex sprang out of the trench with Micah and raced after the running men.

Cut loose, he thought bitterly. Even if he had the strength to swim the river, he could not attempt it unless there was a way across for every member of the company. He was their commander, goaded to lead and doomed to stay, a prisoner of his men and his pride. Although he had ceased to believe in the organization, he could not cut himself loose from its wreckage.

Beside the knoll he and Vanderpeyster, with Micah, Israel and Macaroni Jack, rallied a score of men. A dozen from the broken company on the right joined them. They fired a careful round at the advancing Hessians and retreated slowly north toward the fort. As they fell back on a larger force commanded by Cadwalader, Alex began to hope that they might finally hold on the last crest south of the fort.

Spreading out in a pine grove below the crest, they waited until the Hessians were fifty yards distant before loosing a concentrated volley. The grenadiers halted and slowly recoiled despite the raving and sword-beating of their officers. Somewhere an American whooped joyfully. But his cry was lost in a furious roar of voices at the eastern limits of the pines. Through the roaring voices pierced the keening and wailing of bagpipes playing "When All the Blue Bonnets Came Over the Border."

"The 42d!" yelled Macaroni Jack. "The Black Watch! They've come over the Harlem."

The tall men of the 42d, Royal Highland Regiment of Foot, shouting in Erse, trotted into the eastern limits of the wood with their pipers. In the shafts of sunlight their kilts and bonnets and short scarlet coats leaped like racing flames. Their flowing dark tartans and white goatskin sporrans flickered among the pines as they fanned in search of Americans. One twirled a broadsword above his head; a man screamed and the sword flashed behind a tree.

The Americans ran.

Alex glimpsed Israel's startled, powder-blackened face as a Highlander, a dirk between his teeth, raced at him. Alex took careful aim at the charging Highlander, but his musket misfired. Israel dropped to a knee, bayonet raised. As Alex ran toward him, the Highlander fell and his bayoneted musket arced from him. He did not rise. Beyond Israel, Micah was swiftly reloading his smoking rifle.

Micah did not have time to finish. A half-dozen Highlanders converged on them while the sobbing of the pipes grew louder. *When all the blue bonnets . . .*

"Cut to the river!" Micah shouted. "The river!"

"I can't swim!" wailed Macaroni Jack. "Run!"

As they ran after the others toward the fort, Micah grasped Alex by an arm and tried to turn him west toward the Hudson. "The river! Stay with me. I'll get you across!"

Alex shook his arm loose. "No!"

A musket flashed to their right and Israel stumbled and would have fallen if Micah had not grasped him. Touching his left hand to his right shoulder, Israel stared with astonishment at blood on his fingers.

"It doesn't hurt," he panted. "It—"

"Git!" Micah swung to the right, reloading his rifle, while Alex gripped Israel around the waist and hurried after Macaroni Jack.

"Cut west to the river," Micah called after them.

They paused at the crest and looked back.

"Cut west!" he shouted.

"No!" Alex's lips worked. "We *can't.*"

"If you can, sir," Israel said, "go with Micah."

"I said I *can't.*"

He pulled Israel along and they did not see Micah again.

They pressed through panicked men who milled in and about Magaw's beloved fort. Nearly twenty-five hundred men were trying to jam themselves into works which could not hold a thousand.

Finding a place for Israel against one low wall, Alex examined his slight wound caused by a musket ball grazing his shoulder.

"Pay it no mind," Israel said. "There's more fighting to be done."

Alex shook his head slowly. "No. It's over."

A few minutes later Magaw, tears streaming down his cheeks, surrendered Fort Washington to Colonel Johann Gottlieb Rall.

The word was passed around. Stack your arms. Form by companies behind your colors. Alex took Heartbreak from Jerry Ewell, who was crying, and led him out of the little fort at the head of the company. Their drums silenced, they walked with lowered heads between two regiments of Hessians who watched them curiously.

They halted and waited while Magaw handed his sword to Lieutenant General Wilhelm von Knyphausen at the end of the Hessian lines. Knyphausen, scowling grimly, did not speak to Magaw; he glanced contemptuously at the stacked colors of the American units and turned to a small group of British officers standing beside the road. He said something and spread his hands, palms down, in a gesture of disdain. The British officers did not answer him as they watched the column shuffle on and Hessian officers step forward and take the horses of Magaw, Rawlings and other American officers.

When a swarthy Hessian officer tried to take Heartbreak's bridle from Alex's hand, a British officer said, "A handsome stallion, your lordship." Then Alex saw Earl Percy.

Gripping the bridle, he led Heartbreak to Percy and bowed slightly. "He's yours, sir," he said and turned away.

"Sir!" Percy stepped forward, gazing at him thoughtfully. "My thanks. I'd appreciate the name of the donor."

"Captain Alex March, your lordship."

"Mister March—"

"*Captain* March, sir."

Percy smiled. "*Captain* March, my thanks." He ran a hand along Heartbreak's neck. "And you call the stallion?"

"Heartbreak, sir." Alex nodded to him and returned to the column that shuffled down the road toward New York.

XXII

"YONKEE!"

At the hoarse cry Micah flattened himself against a boulder. There was a flash among the rocks above him and a bullet ricocheted, whining, off the boulder. Three, four green-coated Jägers clambered down toward him. Resting his rifle on the rock, he fired at one and missed.

"Yonkee!"

Sliding, slipping, clutching at loose shale which slid with him, he plunged the remainder of the way to the Hudson. River, be my friend, he thought. Its small waves answered him with a smacking sound, like a toothless old man drinking a dish of tea. Glancing over a shoulder, he saw a Jäger above carefully aiming his rifle.

He leaped to the left and ran, weaving, into the river. He stumbled on a rock and rose and ran again until the river suddenly grasped him in an icy fist and he sank over his head. Only then did it occur to him to let go his rifle. He came up, gasping, and glimpsed the Jägers close to the shore. Breathing deeply, he dived and swam underwater until he felt he was strangling. But he managed to turn on his back and raise only his face above the surface. Something lashed the river near him and he saw the Jägers firing from the shore fifty yards away. Diving, he swam again.

When he came to the surface he doubted that he could swim the mile through the icy water to the Jersey shore. His arms and legs were leaden weights. Yet they moved, and he moved, farther from the New York shore, though not noticeably closer to the brown Jersey cliffs. He tore off his pouch and powder horn and worked out of his boots and leather jacket. For a few minutes he felt lighter, then the numb heaviness dragged at him again. Perhaps he'd feel better if he pretended this was the Ohio.

O-hi-o. He swam to the rhythm of the word, wishing he could make up a song as Philly used to do. *I-am-swim-ming-the-O-hi-o-like-I-use-ter-long-ago. . . . Though-they-call-hit-Hud-son's-Ri-ver-hit's-O-hi-o-this-I-know.* His cold lips ached when he grinned. *I'm-a-po-et-an'-ne-ver-knowed-hit.* He was going west, out of this river and up the cliffs yonder and by road and trail across the Allegheny and away down the Ohio till he found an Indian away west somewhere who spoke the Delaware tongue. He'd say to the Indian, "Brother, do you know Captain Alex March and Sergeant Macaroni Jack Maloney and Colonel John Magaw? Do you know Kathy Murdoch and her father, Timothy the tyrant? Brother, have you heard of King George or General Washington or a Tory or Son of Liberty or British or Hessian soldier or what the white men call smuggling or a white man's jail or a white man's war?" And the Indian would reply, "No, brother." He would ask the Indian one more question: "Do you hear any talk of freedom in these deep woods?" The Indian would reply, "No, brother, for we are free here and do not need to speak of it." Then he would say, "Brother, I've come to live out my days with you, to build me a shelter and hunt with you and take me a squaw to love. I aim for your ways to be my ways forever because, believe me, brother, there ain't nothing back yonder where the sun rises that's near as good as this life where it sets."

His arms and legs still moved in the icy water and he moved slowly west. The mighty current dragged him toward the sea and his heart shriveled in the numbing cold. Yet his heart still beat and his arms and legs beat against the seaward-dragging current. He was going far down-river, but he was going across too.

He never did remember reaching the western shore. At one moment it seemed he was somewhere far out in the river and the next he was lying face down on a flat rock, gasping for breath and shaking with cold. He rolled over. The sun had fallen behind the cliffs which jutted darkly toward a blue sky.

At last, still trembling with a deep chill, he rose and crept north along the rocky shore on bare feet. Seeing a few dry sticks of driftwood, he thought vaguely that he should build a fire. But he had lost his flint and steel and his hands were shaking so badly that he doubted he could have ignited tinder. At least his knife had remained in its sheath during the long swim.

"Knife," he said aloud. "Sheath. Belt. Trousers. Shirt." Thinking of his remaining possessions cheered him somewhat. He knew his wits were dull. "Be sharp," he said. But he knew that he wouldn't be until he somehow warmed himself. At least he had reached the Jersey shore. But freedom was less important now than warmth.

The current had carried him far down-river. The heights of Fort Washington were dim in the distance. The woods and fields of Manhattan were silent, the river deserted. He seemed to be the only living thing left on earth as he stumbled along the base of the cliffs.

Then swallows darted from the cliffs and swept, crying, over the shadowed river. High above him somewhere a cock crowed faintly. A small boat was moored between two rocks, and a path climbed steeply. He stumbled up its switchbacks, his teeth chattering.

The red glare of the setting sun struck him in flat trajectory. He turned his head, blinking, and saw a small house. An aging fat woman sat on its doorstep, puffing on a short pipe and staring at him.

Taking the pipe from her mouth, she spoke over a shoulder into the house. "Amos. 'Nother deserter."

A man appeared behind her, holding a musket. "Git," he said and jerked his head. "Git on yer way, ye scurvy scum."

Micah stumbled on along a rutted lane. Deserter? He repeated the word dully to himself. He'd just been looking out for himself, hadn't he? Was there a bird or beast or man anywhere who wouldn't use all his skill to avoid capture?

He stopped and looked back. The man, still standing in the doorway, raised his musket menacingly. He walked on, shivering. Running might warm him, but he was too tired to run. He was too tired even to be angry with that snailmonger back there.

The lane wound through fallow brown fields and around a low wooded knoll. In the failing light he saw a house and outbuildings ahead and he tried to walk faster. As he approached the house, a woman called sharply, "Deserter!"

He made her out, leaning over a fence.

"I ain't no deserter!" His voice was hoarse.

"Then what air ya?"

She did not retreat as he walked toward her slowly, but he saw her raise a heavy stick in a strong hand and tap the top rail of the fence.

"A soldier. They took Fort Washington today. I escaped and swum the river."

"Ya *swummed* it?"

"Yes."

"Come here."

She was tall, the top of her head coming well above his chin, and her shoulders were wide against the silver western glow. A big hand felt his shirt roughly.

"Ya must've swummed it," she said. "Ya're wet and shakin' cold."

"I got to get warm," he said. "Can I go in the house yonder and get warm—please?"

"No," she said. "It ain't my house or I'd let ya in. It's a Tory lives there, an old man name o' Tilburg and his wife. He's decent enough in his way, considerin' he's Tory, but he'd not take ya in 'less ya said ya was desertin', and ya says ya ain't."

He shivered. "I'd say I was just to get *warm*."

"You come wi' me." She slipped through the fence and he followed her. "What's yer name?"

"Heath. Micah Heath of the 5th Pennsylvania before it was captured."

"My name's Minna Clark. My pa was killed in the battle at Long Island and the sheriff at Bergen bound out all us young uns. Though Pa was a patriot, old Tilburg took me 'cause I'm strong."

"Bound out? Ain't you getting on to be bound out?"

"I'm eighteen— Mind the choppin' block there and pay no mind that hound— In here."

A door creaked and he felt warmth and sniffed good familiar stable smells: manure, leather, straw. A horse whickered and clomped a hoof somewhere.

The girl said, "Set down where you air. I'll be back in a whisker wi' somethin' warmin'. Nobody'll mind you're here. Old Tilburg's laid up with the gout an' his wife's the sciaticay. They's deaf as posts anyways an' the hired men's gone now that winter's nigh. I'm tendin' the place myself, the stock too."

The door creaked shut and he sat on the floor, shivering and thinking that his luck was running good no matter how bad he felt. A deserter? He'd try to make the girl understand the war was over.

She returned soon, carrying a bull's-eye candle lantern and two blankets and a basket which she put on the earth floor. She removed the lantern shutter and he saw her distinctly for the first time. For some reason he'd believed she was pretty. She wasn't. Her nose was long and her face broad. In the dim light her eyes glittered yellowly as she looked at him. When she smiled at him suddenly, her thin lips rose on broken, darkened teeth. She closed her mouth, knowing how bad her teeth looked, but still she tried to smile.

"You're too big for a pair o' Tilburg's wool drawers I brung out," she said. "Wrap yourself in these here blankets."

She crouched on one heel, like a man, though half-turned from him, with the modesty of a decent woman. "Take a pull on this." She handed him an earthen jug of rum as he wound the blankets around himself.

He drank, feeling the rum light a fire in his belly and slowly radiate its warmth. "Thanks," he said.

"They's fresh-killed pork an' bread I baked today. Tarts too."

He drank again, staring at her over the jug. With her face turned from his she was not bad to look at. Her breasts were large and firm, her hips and legs strong and rounded.

"I reckon you know the war's about over," he said.

"No, it ain't." She looked at him sharply. "They took Fort Washington, you say, but we still got Fort Lee."

"Fort Lee ain't worth a bottle without Fort Washington. Besides, forts don't mean a thing without *men,* and nearly all the men ran over there today." He watched her put chunks of pork on a thick slice of bread. "I reckon you're thinking I ran too. There were some good men over there today but finally all of us *had* to run. I know three I wish could have swum with me. Reckon they're in prison now. My druthers was to drown in that river over prison. I been in prison before." He frowned, thinking that the rum had warmed his tongue as well as the rest of his body.

"What for?"

"Smuggling."

"Set down that rum and eat this," she said, handing him the bread and meat.

He ate, slowly at first and then ravenously, while she watched him. At last she said, "Where you from?"

"West of Philadelphia."

"Ya got folks?"

He shook his head. "I was bound out young too," he mumbled through his full mouth. "Time past I've been far west as the Ohio and I aim to go back there."

"You *air* desertin', ain't ya?"

Why did everybody insist he was deserting just because he'd risked his life rather than go back to prison? Probably it was impossible to make her understand that the army had deserted him rather than he had deserted it.

"I told you the war's all but over."

"It *ain't.*" She stood up. "It ain't never goin' to be over till we win. After you're rested up you're goin' to Fort Lee if'n I got to take ya there myself."

He grinned at her. "You ain't big enough." He got to his feet and his grin faded. He felt weak, dizzy; the lantern on the floor seemed to swing slowly. Perhaps he would have fallen if she had not grasped him as the lantern swung higher . . .

He dreamed of Jägers and Highlanders who pursued him faster than he could run and surrounded him with jabbing bayonets. His cry of terror brought him wide awake. He lay on straw in sweat-soaked blankets.

A shadow moved against dim light and the girl, whatever her name was, rested a cool hand on his hot forehead.

"Ain't nought to be afeared of," she said gently. "You sleep."

He tried to sit up and fell back weakly. An icy chill swept up from his knees and he began to shake.

The girl knelt beside him silently. She rolled him out of the wet blankets, wrapped him in dry ones and made him drink a bitter, fiery liquid. But he could not stop shaking. Then something warm pressed heavily on him from feet to chin, and he knew dimly that she was lying on him, gripping him tightly, as if her strength could still his shaking. Gradually he grew warmer and slept.

When the crowing of a cock awakened him, chill and fever had passed. He still felt weak, but it was a pleasant weakness of the body rather than the head. Like a feather on fresh grass in the sun, he thought as the morning light grew. Sparrows chittered. The horse whickered and a calf bawled somewhere.

When the door squeaked open and he saw the girl, he smiled at her. "That's powerful medicine to cure me so quick."

"God A'mighty." She gazed down at him, hands resting on her strong hips. "You been out o' your head." She smiled suddenly without drawing down her lips to try to disguise her bad teeth. "I'll say for ya you're a strong man when ya set to fight the wollydockers o' your nightmares." She blew out her breath. "Whooks, I'm tuckered a'ter most all a night o' keepin' you down."

"I don't remember none of it."

"It's November seventeen morning," she said, "an' luck for you ya don't rec'lect your dreams an' ravin's. I took your clothes an' washed an' mended 'em. You got no drawers." She sounded indignant. "What ails the army they don't give their soldiers drawers? I pieced out a pair an' here's two pair o' wool socks. I've scoured everywheres for boots, but there ain't none big enough to fit ya. Air ya hongry?"

Now he remembered her name. "Starved, Minna."

It seemed that she could not bring enough food to fill him. He sat in the straw and ate slowly and drank quantities of cold water for half the morning. As his strength returned, restlessness grew in him. He bathed himself in a bucket and currycombed the horse and made friends with the hound, a black mongrel named Jonah who pressed his wet, flat nose against him.

It was time he moved on, he knew. He'd go tonight if he could find something to cover his feet.

Toward nightfall, Minna came on him wrapping and tying pieces of burlaping around his feet. "So you aim to git back to the army," she said. "Tonight?"

He nodded, not looking at her, not knowing how to tell her that there was no army worth the trouble to go back to.

"That burlap ain't fit, Micah. Here." She held out a pair of moccasins. "I been workin' at 'em most the day. They ain't proper 'cause I ain't had time to work the hide. But I reckon the stitchin'll hold till the hide cracks. An' last night I fixed you a kind o' jacket out o' this old blanket. Here."

He rose slowly, staring at her, thinking that now he *had* to go up to Fort Lee, even for a short spell, because of her faith in him.

"Minna—" He took the moccasins and rested a hand on her shoulder. She took one step toward him, gazing at him gravely in the fading light. Something stirred in him, his heart beat faster. He dropped the moccasins and drew her to him. They did not kiss; she lay her head against the stubble of his lean face and they gripped each other tightly. Suddenly she dropped her arms and he let her go.

"I got to feed the old folks," she said indistinctly, turning away. "I'll be back with supper for ya."

After darkness fell he started out the door a half-dozen times, telling himself he should go now and not wait longer. Each time he turned back, however. She had saved his life, and he could not simply walk away without thanking her and saying good-by decently. Still, her warm, strong, pliable body, the clean smell of her when he'd instinctively pulled her to him, lingered in his memory and troubled him. It was neither the time nor the place for him to have dallying notions. He'd go. But he could not bring himself to leave without saying good-by to her.

At last she appeared, carrying the lantern and a crock of steaming stew. "Eat hearty," she told him. "I've somethin' more to bring from the house for you soon as the old folks is asleep."

He ate his fill of the thick stew of beef and potatoes and turnips and onions while she watched him silently.

"You'd best tie the hound." He drank the remainder of the juice and sighed. "He's set on following me."

"Let him go with ya if he's the mind. He's a roamin' dog an' there's nought here for him."

She stepped close to him as he got to his feet.

"Minna—" Again his foolish arms opened instinctively to her and she leaned against him. Her breathing quickened as his hands moved down her flanks.

"I ain't much," she whispered, "but I ain't loose. I never had me a man 'cause till now I ain't found one strong enough to take me."

Holding her tightly, he leaned back so that she was lifted off the ground, the length of her body pressed against his. It seemed impossible that he had been weak so recently, for now he felt stronger than he ever had. Her strength had flowed into him, he thought dimly, and now he would return some of it to her.

They were lying on the blankets, the lantern extinguished, and her hands plucked at his shirt and then at the buttons of her woolen dress. "Here." She moved away quickly. "I reckon I hoped—" Her voice was muffled by her dress as she pulled it over her head. "I know I—" She pressed against him, naked, and he knew that she had come from the house wearing only the woolen dress, hoping—"Here!" Her hands tore at his shirt.

Outside a cold wind was rising, but here on the sweet crushed straw their bodies were locked in mortal warmth.

But when he tried to kiss her, she turned her head. "My mouth's bad and shames me so," she said. "But this ain't bad." She grasped his head in both her hands and drew it to her breasts and held it there.

Then he was talking to her, saying crazy things. He heard his voice, as at a distance, babbling about cold and warmth, ice and fire, roundness and softness. She whispered, fiercely and incoherently, begging something of him as her hands moved over him. A gold-red sun seemed to glow in the darkness, a winter sun that gleamed on the thick dark ice of a forest pool. This lonely winter place, he thought, and wished for words to describe it to her. But she would not have understood or even have heard him in the urgency of her hands and words to break the ice-locked solitude of the winter place. Then spring, he thought, the crashing of a pine into the ice.

She cried out, in exultation, at the breaking of the ice and coming of the spring and flowing of the river that bore them on its long passage to somewhere, and now back, and then on to somewhere. Her nails scratched his shoulders in her desire to stay with him on their long passage to somewhere. And then she found the rhythm of the passage and learned, perhaps, that all of God's creation, even she, lived by rhythm. The gold-red sun blazed hotly now and the passage to somewhere was an exultant leap into a trembling void where there was peace, darkness, whisperings that faded into silence, and, finally, sleep.

The whining of the hound outside the door awakened him. It was raining. Gray morning light filtered through chinks in the stable logs. She slept beside him in the blankets, curled in the curving of his arms and legs. So they'd slept the night through. He chuckled. It was a strange sound; he didn't remember sounding so before. But neither did he remember having been so drawn out of himself as she had drawn him last night. The strange excitement stirred in him again and he drew her to him.

She started awake, then pressed against him and laughed softly.

He said, "I ain't heard you laugh before, Minna."

"I ain't heard myself," she said.

They made love again and then she left him and went to the house. He slept, awakening when she brought him breakfast, and dozing once more to the drumming of the rain.

Late in the afternoon she came to the stable, frowning. "Old Man Tilburg's taken it in his head to git about agin soon as the rain's over," she said. "He mustn't find ya here."

"I'm going tonight, Minna, whether the rain stops or not."

"Goddamn my soul!" She snatched a bit of straw and bit it fiercely. "It's like there's a fire or somethin' burnin' in me I can't put out." Her yellow eyes flashed toward him and then away. "I told him I was cleanin' the stable, but if you've a mind, I can think o' other ways I druther pass half an hour."

Her passion seemed insatiable. He remembered Young saying once that every man reckoned he wanted a passionate woman until he had one, and then he didn't know what to do with her. But Minna's passion was pleasing to him rather than perplexing. He didn't want to leave her.

A couple of hours after dark she came to the stable. She wore a hooded cape and carried a basket and Tilburg's musket. "Here." She thrust the musket at him. "This is for ya to take. It's more business with a soldier 'n a Tory."

He took the musket and powder horn and pouch without hesitation, but he frowned at the basket. "What's that for?"

"Vittles. Blankets. I'm goin' with ya."

He shook his head. "You can't, Minna. I've no place to take you and you can't just tramp the roads with me."

"Oh can't I?" She scowled at him. "The roads is free an' if'n you won't let me walk *with* ya I'll just foller behind. I kin walk fast as you an' I'm goin'."

"But you—"

"I want to git shut o' this Tilburg place an' where I end up ain't none o' your affair if'n ya don't want to make it so. I said I'm goin' with ya, so let's git. Tilburg vaws he's gittin' out early in the mornin' an' I aim we'll be a far piece from here."

He knew that he should not let her come. It wouldn't be hard for him to bolt out the door and escape from her in the rainy darkness. But the truth was that he didn't really want to escape from her.

He did not speak as he pulled on the jacket she'd made him. They went out together and turned west on the winding road. The hound padded through the rain behind them.

XXIII

NOT long after morning light began to grow they heard a clamor of voices ahead. A drum started to roll and stopped.

"Fort Lee yonder," Minna said.

She slogged beside him untiringly. Around midnight they had turned in at a deserted cabin and slept for three or four hours. When they awakened, the rain had stopped and they walked on. A half-mile back the northward twisting muddy road had forked, the left descending northwest from the heights toward the Hackensack River. The right led to Fort Lee, Minna told him. He had not hesitated in turning toward the fort. His mind was made up. He'd go back and serve out his enlistment to the end of the year, partly because she expected him to, but chiefly because he didn't want to think of himself as a deserter for the rest of his life.

"The army starts the day early," Minna said.

He listened to the growing din curiously as they climbed toward a crest, thinking that Fort Lee had a disorderly garrison. Then suddenly a man shot over the crest and ran toward them. Another, three, four, a dozen came after him, running hard, their hands empty of weapons. Their faces were strained as they panted past with a heavy *slock-slock-slock* of feet in the muddy road.

"What ails ya?" Minna cried after them, but they did not reply or look back.

Another man, wearing only drawers and boots, raced down the hill toward them. His mouth, stretched wide in terror, looked as if it had been slashed by a bloody ax. "Run!" he shouted hoarsely as he passed. "Them's on us! Run!"

Micah swore. "Introduce you to the American army, Minna." He trotted up the road and Minna and the hound followed him.

He smelled the camp before he saw it. The northeast breeze, morning sweet in the hollow, was fouled by the stench of the open latrines as he approached the crest. In the past three days he'd forgotten the bad smell of a camp. He slowed and almost halted, dreading to return to the army. But curiosity about the cause of the panic carried him on to the crest.

In the wide clearing surrounding the low-walled fort stood hundreds of tents and scores of kettles steaming over the morning fires. A few men still scuttled among the tents, snatching up blankets, muskets, knapsacks. One man struggled to strike a tent; it suddenly collapsed on him and he fought free of its folds with a wail of anguish and ran. Here and there an officer with drawn sword shouted at the men, not trying to form them, but urging them to flee down a woods road that dipped west off the plateau.

A popping of musket fire rose north of the fort and bagpipes shrilled. "When All the Blue Bonnets Came Over the Border."

"The Black Watch!" someone shouted.

A soldier tottering under a load of plunder dropped all of it and raced an officer toward the crowded woods road.

"Come on." Micah snatched Minna's basket and hurried her along.

"Ain't we fightin' 'em?" she cried.

"Not by ourselves."

She smiled crookedly at him and he slapped her buttocks good-naturedly and said, "If you be in this army, girl, you got to learn to *run*."

A mob, not an army, flowed down the woods road. It was as dirty and disorganized a mob as any ever seen in Philadelphia, Micah thought. It had not acquired courage or discipline, although it had agreed to call itself an army. But it had acquired many other things. Fear, visible in its strained faces and running feet. Lice and scrofula, visible on the neck of the man in front of him. Disease, there in the man who hobbled along, coughing rackingly. Plunder, too. Kettles, muskets, blankets, a toma-hawk, and there some ribbons and bows, cast aside as the mob ran in panic down the woods road. It also had acquired a large number of girls and women who ran with their men, shrieking like barn swallows before a hawk. Most of them were unkempt country girls, good for nothing but the one thing girls were supposed to be good for.

He hated this mob. And then, glancing at Minna, he hated himself for being no better than any member of it.

A man toting a small sack and musket shoved Minna aside and she would have fallen if Micah hadn't caught her. As the man trotted past, Micah tripped him. He sprawled; his sack split on the ground and spilled white crystals.

"Salt!" Minna flung herself on the ground and snatched a handful.

"Salt! Salt!" a woman shrieked, rushing at the split sack and ignoring the blows of the man who had risen to his knees.

Micah kicked him hard, and the man staggered to his feet and ran on. Staring at Minna and the woman fighting for the sack of precious salt, Micah wondered dully who was not a thief. Who, indeed, was decent?

A sutler's wagon careened down the road, the driver lashing his team and roaring obscenities at those in the way. Micah dragged the fighting women off the road just in time, but the bag slipped from their clutching hands and the wagon wheels ground salt into the mud while the women screamed piercingly at the driver. A moment later a wheel of the wagon crashed against a stump and the singletree broke. The horses ran free and the driver pitched forward as the wagon teetered and overturned, spilling kettles and pans and barrels.

"A kittle!" Minna yelled, forgetting the salt and running toward the overturned wagon. "We needs a kittle!"

Micah dropped her basket and walked to the sutler who lay motionless on the ground. His neck was broken. Two soldiers had stopped his horses and were riding away while a half-dozen women had joined Minna in plundering his wares.

Micah walked on. He'd had enough of running. He believed that he'd had enough of Minna. But after a while, when he heard her calling to him, he stopped and looked back.

"Got us'ns a kittle," she crowed, holding it up as she trotted toward him. "Got salt an' tea an' a ton o' flour in the basket."

He stared at her expressionlessly.

"Ain't we runnin' no more?" she asked.

"No more."

"Ain't ya pleased wi' what I got us?"

"Yes."

"I'm a good providin' woman," she said proudly.

"That sutler back there broke his neck. He's dead."

"Sarved him right," she said, "runnin' folks down wi' his wagon."

He wanted to say something to her, but he wasn't sure what it was.

"Air ya put out wi' me, Micah?"

He shook his head and walked on. Jonah padded at his heels. She followed the hound, lugging the heavy basket.

The woods thinned out and the road slanted down steeply to where the Hackensack looped out of the morning mist, shone briefly like silver, and faded into the vast brown marshes. Far ahead the army poured toward the bridge across the river, but here on the slope few ran now.

A horseman pounded up the road and someone shouted, "It's Gin'ral Greene." He passed at a gallop, a compact man leaning forward in the saddle, pale and frowning. "Must want to git hisself shot goin' back *thar*," someone said. "Hit's hisn's fort," another said. "He was so took with hit let'm be *took* with hit."

"Why did everybody run?" Micah asked.

"Brother, I mought ask you-all same," a man said. "Why did *you* run? 'Cause'n *I* run, an' I runned 'cause'n *you* run. An' we-all run 'cause'n the colonel run. Part'n the colonel bein' yaller, he run 'cause'n Gin'ral Greene says git out o' thar an' head fer Hackensack, the British has took us by s'prise agin with us'ns in our drawers. An' so thar's Greene goin' back to the fort. Thar ain't no sense to this hyar war. I'm goin' *home*."

True, Micah thought, there wasn't much sense to it. He wished he could feel again the way he had that day he was released from prison and knew he was going to be a soldier and knew the land would be a better place when everyone was free. Now nearly every one of them running down this muddy road was going to free himself. But would any of them ever really be *free*? It was too big a problem for him to worry at it so.

Ahead, where the road planed into the marshes, men were shouting. One voice bellowed above the others: "Come about, come about, goddamn ye, and form up!" A heavy man wearing a blue coat hopped about the road, brandishing a pair of pistols, while men flowed around him toward the bridge.

Micah broke into a run. "Cap'n Bilby!"

Bilby's single eye widened in amazement and then he roared with pleasure, flung his arms around Micah and pounded his back. Letting him go, he cried, "Where've ye been, boy? At war I see, but what regiment?"

"The 5th."

"It was captured at Fort Washington."

"But I escaped and swum the river and—"

"Escaped?" Bilby grinned widely. "Escape ye did, God bless your mighty heart, but— Never mind now. Saul, Saul," he shouted to a thin, dour-faced man in a glazed sailor's hat. "Here's one for us and man enough for six he is."

"Sailors." Micah looked at a score of armed men wearing jackets and dirty canvas pantaloons who were trying to stop those fleeing toward the bridge. "But not at sea, Cap'n Bilby?"

"At sea I be, lad. At sea in a bloody swamp. What a tale of woe I've to tell ye. But there's woe enough here. And a cap'n I be after fortune stove me end-to and keel-hauled my bottom. But a cap'n on land that ain't dry enough. A cap'n in Johnny Glover's Marblehead regiment, God save my soul."

The man named Saul said, "Th'Almighty's small use for your soul, Jonas, after hearing your everlasting blasphemy."

"This is Private Saul Judson, Micah." Bilby grinned. "A good man in a fight though a codfish Christer. It's a *democratic* army we have from Massachusetts Bay, ye see, where a private takes his cap'n's language to task."

"A cap'n we 'lected," Saul Judson said calmly. "We can hold another 'lection."

"Ye've held three," Bilby said, "an' I'm proud to say that Marbleheaders persist in electing a Boston man their cap'n. Hullo"—he snapped his eyepatch at Minna who stood behind Micah—"your business, young woman?"

"I'm wi' him." She nodded at Micah.

"Hmmm?" Bilby looked up at him quizzically.

"I reckon she saved my life after I swum the river, Cap'n Bilby. She 'lowed she'd leave the Tory she was bound out to and trail 'long. Her name's Minna Clark. This here's an old friend, Cap'n Bilby, Minna."

She ducked her head to him and Bilby bowed and said, "Hmmm." Then, smiling at Micah, "Ye might as well be a Massachusetts man a while, lad. We're set out here by Johnny Glover at the command of General Washington himself to check any lobsterbacks coming this way."

"Don't you reckon the war's about over?" Micah said.

"Over?" Bilby looked surprised. "It ain't half begun."

The chaos that day around the village of Hackensack on the western bank of the river made Bilby seem a poor prophet. As in New York after the retreat from Long Island, the army uncoiled torpidly like a snake emerged from its winter den. Drums beat and no one heeded them. Men wandered aimlessly. Two full companies of Jersey militia marched off home and no one bothered to jeer them. The two taverns in town did a thriving business with those who had money, while several of those who lacked it stole eggs and chickens and a keg of rum. Sensible people barred their doors and decided not to venture outside until the British arrived and re-established law and order. Many of the rebel rabble that called itself an army were not decently clad after having been routed from their blankets at Fort Lee early that morning. Many were unarmed. A few officers talked of digging carthworks until someone remembered that all of the entrenching tools had been left at Fort Lee.

A big man on a roan stallion rode here and there with an aide beside him. One and all treated him respectfully, but it was difficult to determine exactly what he was doing.

"That's General Washington," Micah told Minna.

"*Eeee,*" she murmured, staring at him with awe.

They walked to the village from the bridge in lemon afternoon sunlight after the Marblehead pickets were recalled from the eastern shore. Bilby wanted Micah to stay with the company, and Micah said he would return once he'd found a Pennsylvania regiment that would record his name and certify he had not deserted.

Eventually he found a man who belonged to a Pennsylvania militia regiment. The regimental adjutant was in the Swan Tavern, the man told him. In the crowded, noisy tavern someone pointed out the adjutant, who sat very drunk singing a ribald song about a girl who danced on a table whene'er she was able, which was only paaa-art the time. Micah walked out of the tavern without speaking to the adjutant.

Minna sat patiently on a log, Jonah and her basket and kettle at her feet. To the west a low line of wooded hills shouldered a smoky haze. High above the village a skein of geese flowed south behind the melancholy honking of their leader.

"I'm pushing on." He stared up at the geese and took care not to glance at Minna.

"Ya leavin' me here?"

She would be a weight dragging at him. And yet he did not want to leave her.

"Come along if you've a mind," he said.

She shook her head. "Only if you've the mind to have me come."

"I've the mind," he said slowly.

She got to her feet and gathered up the kettle and basket. "Where we goin', Micah?"

"Over west somewhere till we're shut of this army."

"Then ya *air* desertin'."

He looked at her hard. "This army ain't a fit place for you."

"It's a *place,*" she said firmly. "I like it. But I like you more'n it an' I'll go wi' ya if you're bound to go. But if ya stay your time I'll take care o' myself an' you too."

As they walked along the muddy street of the village, he suddenly cried, "The trouble is there ain't anybody gives a damn about nothing."

She said, "That Cap'n Bilby . . ."

"Thanks to him I landed in jail once." He halted and turned to her. "Why can't I ever do anything *legal?* There's no justice in it. You understand?"

"No," she said.

He clapped a hand to his head in despair. And then he said, "I've got no hat." And finally, amusement struggling with his despair, he gave a wild shout of laughter.

A man said, "I understand."

A smooth round face looked out a hole that served as the window of an old log hut. Beside its doorless entrance a pennant on a stick had been thrust in the muddy ground. The limp pennant had no significance to Micah. This army had innumerable pennants; even a New Hampshire baker had proudly borne his own on a pole about Manhattan.

"You understand *what?*" Micah demanded.

The man said, "I understand how unjust it is when a just man has difficulty in doing justice legally. What troubles you, lad?"

"This army does."

"This army troubles nearly everyone but its enemy." The man came to the cabin entrance. He was plainly dressed and of undistinguished size and features. "You're thinking of leaving it. Why?"

"Because it don't know I exist and don't care," Micah said. "I was in the 5th Pennsylvania at Long Island and Manhattan. After the battle at Fort Washington I escaped and swum the river and aimed to join up again to prove I wasn't deserting. But I can't find anybody who'll make a record of me."

The man rubbed his nose and nodded. "A record is important. You want a *doc*ument and you've come to the right place. This is General Greene's Headquarters. I'm serving him as a voluntary aide. Not an officer, mind you, but nevertheless an aide, and I'm a great hand at documents. Come in. Come in."

Micah walked to the hut hesitantly. Stooping low, he stepped inside. On a barrelhead were a quill and bottle of ink and several sheets of brown paper.

"I was sitting here of a mind to write something," the man said, hitching a stool up to the barrel, "and now you've given me something to write. Your name, lad?"

"Heath. Private Micah Heath."

The man inclined his head over the barrelhead and his pen scratched swiftly. In a moment he looked up and said, "I'll read it to you.

"Hereby is certification that Private Micah Heath of the 5th Pennsylvania Regiment did escape at the surrender of Fort Washington, sixteenth November, and swam the North River to New Jersey where he rejoined the army at Fort Lee."

It sounded mighty fine.

"What unit of the army do you now propose to serve with?" the man asked.

"Colonel Glover's Marbleheaders," Micah said. "I got a friend there who—"

The man wrote again and then read to him, "In Hackensack, the Jerseys, on twentieth November, he did voluntarily enter the Massachusetts Regiment of Colonel John Glover there to serve out his enlistment or until such time as he be transferred to another unit of the army."

Micah grinned with pleasure.

"I've affixed my name as an aide at General Greene's Headquarters and the date," the man said, handing him the sheet of brown paper. "You keep this, lad."

"Thank you, sir, I'm mighty grateful." He folded it carefully. "May I ask your name, sir?"

"Paine. Tom Paine."

"Thank you, Mr. Paine." They shook hands. "I knew a family name of Paine out Lancaster way a long time back. You any relation?"

"No." Paine smiled faintly. "No relations that way I know of. Good luck, lad."

Outside he told Minna, "I got a document. We're going back to Cap'n Bilby's company and I'll serve out my time. It's *legal* now. That was luck the fellow there happened to hear me."

"It was to be," Minna said.

"There ain't nothing was to be," he replied scornfully. "You knock that notion out of your head, Minna. There's luck but never no 'was to be.' If it was to be, why wasn't that militia adjutant sober enough to record me proper instead of me having to bother some fellow at General Greene's Headquarters? You understand?"

She started to say no, and then she nodded slowly.

The men of the Marblehead regiment were pretty good fellows even though they were Yankees, Micah decided. The fact that they talked through their noses did not prevent them from speaking their opinions plainly. Some of them were all-fired religious and given to quoting Scripture, and all of them were forever talking about money. But most of them were good soldiers because they had been good sailors. Although they thought and acted independently, they depended trustfully one on another.

He envied them their pride, a matter which their chaplain was constantly carping against as a mortal sin. It was puzzling, for the chaplain seemed to be the proudest man in the regiment. He shared the men's pride in Marblehead first, Massachusetts second, and New England third, in Yankee fish and thrift and know-how and ships, in the fact that they had sailed on Yankee ships and the fact that they were *not* sailing them now when there were fortunes to be made in privateering. The chaplain was as proud as any of them over what the regiment had done on Long Island and in getting the army off the island and in holding off General Howe's army at Pell's Point and—now—in being selected to serve as the rear guard at Hackensack. But, above all, the chaplain seemed proudest of being on more intimate terms with God than anyone else in the regiment. All this pride, which he preached and prayed against strenuously, was a source of considerable strength to him. It made him courageous in battle and calm in retreat and so righteous that Micah, greatly awed, told him Minna was his wife.

Seated beside a fire that evening, Bilby recounted his adventures after he escaped from Philadelphia and made his way to New York and became a smuggler there. Young, Zeiman and Poletski had disappeared, he said, and he had not heard of them since. He told Micah he'd tried in vain to find a way to help him escape from prison.

Fortune was the word Bilby bandied. There was a fortune to be made just beyond the limits of the law if only *fortune* would smile. It had smiled on him as a New York smuggler. He'd bought an interest in a privateer and put to sea as skipper of the ship. Becalmed off Trinidad, the ship was taken by a British man-of-war and the crew transferred to a small transport bound for Halifax. Then luck once more when the transport was separated from her escort in a storm and driven hull-down into the blessed sands of Nantucket where the prisoners became the captors. After he set foot on Massachusetts soil, Bilby vowed he'd never go to sea again. With a half-dozen Marbleheaders who'd been members of his crew, he joined John Glover's regiment where "by force of character" he became a captain even though he was a Boston man.

It's been land now for a long time, lad." He stared into the fire. "But some nights I smell the sea and when my time is up—" He shrugged and his shoulders slumped. "There's a fortune to be made, Micah."

But his voice rang hollow, Micah thought. The truth was that Captain Bilby was tired and growing old. His faith that he would make his fortune was not as firm as it once had been; there must be times when he secretly believed he would die a failure.

Was it foolish for a man to believe that he could win a fortune and so become something greater than he now was? If foolish, then what could he believe in?

There was the pleasure of his strength, he thought that night as he lay in the blankets with Minna beside the Hackensack. There was the earth and water and the wide sky, filled with bright stars that anticipated bright morning. There was cold, held at a distance by the warmth of their joined bodies. And there was, finally, sleep.

Awakening later, he asked himself, But what is there for a man to believe in? He lay here now, strong and young, beside a strong and young woman. Now he could believe in *them,* but what could he believe when he grew old and tired, like Bilby? Perhaps if he loved Minna, as he sometime had dreamed that he loved Kathy, he would feel differently. But he did not love her; he did not even feel a tenderness toward her, as he'd sometimes felt toward Philly. Minna merely was warmth and strength and passion, a reluctantly accepted companion in his wandering.

You go to sleep, he told himself, and find something tomorrow to believe in.

XXIV

WITH each tomorrow of those weeks he sought and winnowed what he found. Like a farmer selecting seed, he rejected and accepted what came to hand. Eventually, when he harvested that early winter crop of his experience, he began to understand its seedtime.

He believed, first of all, that his luck was good. Most would have reckoned it bad to be in the rear guard of a retreat. But he and the Marbleheaders considered it an honor when they formed at the bridge the next morning with two other skeletal Massachusetts regiments, numbering scarcely three hundred men in all, while the rest of the army staggered to its feet and walked off west across the flatlands. He watched them go contemptuously, those tatterdemalions who called themselves soldiers, disappearing into the misty marshes with banners furled and drums silenced.

That mob, he thought, did not belong to anything. He, on the other hand, belonged to the Marbleheaders now as firmly as if he had lived all his life in their town, for they understood and reminded him of a simple fact: Nothing came easily, least of all liberty. He was lucky to belong to them. And he was lucky that Minna belonged to him. For he quickly realized that in a bad time such as this it was good both to belong to others and to have someone who belonged to you.

As the General rode out of Hackensack behind his retreating men, the rear guard began to tear up the planks and wreck the pilings of the bridge. A force of British dragoons approached, but the Yankees drove them off with musket fire and finished destroying the bridge before a long column of grenadiers streamed down from the heights in early afternoon. Only then did the Marbleheaders ask one another, with shaking of heads, why the bridge hadn't been destroyed yesterday.

Minna, who had baked bread and fetched water and refused to go on west with the rest of the women when Micah told her to leave, sat patiently beside the road with Jonah and did not stir as the British column across the river opened fire with a six-pounder. When the regiments formed and marched west, she gathered up her plunder and fell into step beside Micah. Although they did not halt until long after dark, she never lagged or complained.

The next morning they came to another bridge across another river. The Passaic, someone said, and the village beyond it was Aquackanock. This time they did not bother to wait for orders before they began tearing

up the bridge. When a committee of citizens came out from Aquackanock and protested the destruction of their bridge, the Yankees curtly told
them to get out of the way. The citizens went home and barred themselves
in their houses while the Yankees allowed that Jersey was a spineless
colony scarcely worth fighting for.

In the afternoon, they marched south on a road which meandered
along the west bank of the Passaic. Toward noon of the next day they
trailed into Newark through a heavy rain and found the remainder of
the army lying about dejectedly.

"They's a sight worse than at Hackensack," Bilby said, "and a sight
fewer. It ain't even an army now. But wait till we join up with Stirling's
brigade at Brunswick. Virginians and Haslet's Delawares is among 'em.
Then, by glory, we'll turn and *fight*."

The fact that the Marbleheaders were not issued rations during their
first two days in Newark did not prevent the company from eating
adequately. Bilby found a loose plank in the locked store of a man he
alleged was a Tory, and after nightfall they obtained a quantity of pork
and flour and dried peas. They lacked tents, but they built large fires to
keep themselves warm.

Not content merely with subsisting, Bilby engaged in a good deal of
socializing. "There's nothing like a retreat to draw men together and get
'em learning from one another," he said. "In victory, they get to putting
on airs, but in retreat they're mighty friendly."

More than once Micah saw him talking with Colonel Henry Knox,
the big fat artilleryman whom Bilby had known as a Boston bookseller
and still addressed as Harry. Even Colonel Reed, the adjutant general
and a cold-mannered man, was drawn into conversation with Bilby.
Micah reckoned that he must be on speaking terms with just about
everybody in the army except the General, and if the retreat lasted long
enough probably the General would be speaking to him too.

"You mind my word," he said to Micah, "it's the men with brains
and without fear as will see us through. Your Captain March is the same
stripe. Have ye writ that he's alive and captured?"

Micah shook his head, feeling ashamed. He'd promised Philly to look
out for Alex March. But I didn't desert, he thought. I'm *here* and he
could be too if he'd stayed with me.

"I've nought to write on and no way to send it," he muttered.

"There's always a way for everything if ye've the mind." Bilby looked
at him thoughtfully. "I know a young miss name of Philadelphia
Twillow would like to hear you're safe."

Micah frowned. "I reckon she's took up with other things. She's just
a child."

"Be that as it may, Grandfather, I've seen that word's been sent about Captain March and I even squeezed in a word as how you escaped. Matter of fact, it's the way I brought myself to Colonel Reed's attention. Mighty distressed to hear about Mr. March he was and glad to enclose my note to Mrs. March in his correspondence to Philadelphia." Bilby frowned. "Heard something interesting today. Bought one of the headquarters officers rum at the tavern and he told me of hearing a conversation between Reed and the General. The General asked Reed if he thought the Pennsylvania back country would support us if we was forced to retreat there."

"It will!" Micah exclaimed. "Out Ligonier way—"

"That ain't what Reed told the General. He said that if eastern Pennsylvania gives in, the west will follow."

"It won't! Reed ain't been on the frontier. He don't know the west."

"I'm just telling you what he told the General," Bilby said. "And you know what the General said? He crossed his hand over his throat and says to Reed, 'My neck don't feel made for a halter.' The General says to Reed that we can pull back to Augusta County in Virginia and fight there and if driven out we can cross over the Allegheny and—"

"Yes!" Micah gripped Bilby by an arm, wishing for the power to describe the land beyond the Allegheny. "It's a big land yonder and—" He lacked the words, but he could see it in his mind; the General must have seen it too in his youth and know—"Let 'em take all this *east* if'n they want it and we'll take and hold the big land yonder and grow us a country that's free and better'n all your east."

"Well, now"—Bilby looked at him strangely—"I'm a Boston man myself and I've no hankering to be an Injun. If Boston ain't free there's no freedom on this continent."

"But the General," Micah said, "*he* knows. I've heard tell he loves his plantation, but he's been west and he knows how big the country is, bigger than anything that can come against it. You go into it and if anybody comes after you the country will take care of you. See?"

"No, I don't see." Bilby smiled. "But then I'm a Boston man and getting of an age when I'm content to make my fortune and settle down on Sudbury Street."

It was a pity Bilby could not understand, Micah thought. But it was fine that the General knew the nature of the land. He might not be the greatest general ever, as many claimed he was not. But since he knew the land so well, the land surely would bring him victory in time, drawing him into its distances, curving its rivers between him and his enemies, sheltering him in the mighty shoulders of its hills.

He felt heartened. Remembering his old intention beside the Ohio to

go on a long hunt, he thought that now he was on his greatest, longest
hunt, and when or where it would end he did not know. Perhaps
never. If the General went beyond the Allegheny, some must go with
him, and he would be among them. He wished for words to describe
to someone—Bilby, Minna, anyone—exactly how he felt.

And then, on the night of November twenty-seventh, Bilby told him
that Mr. Paine was across the common reading aloud something that
he had begun to write. Micah hurried across the common and found
many gathered around a large fire where Paine sat beside a drum. As
Micah approached, a cheer rose and someone yelled, "Read hit agin,
Tom. Read hit good and loud."

Mr. Paine, smiling faintly, said, "I'll have no time to write on if I'm
forever reading it because it's nowhere near finished."

"*Read* hit, Tom."

Mr. Paine lifted a sheet of brown paper from the drumhead and
turned it toward the firelight.

"These are the times that try men's souls," he read in a high, clear
voice. "The summer soldier and the sunshine patriot will, in this crisis,
shrink from the service of their country; but he that stands it *now*
deserves the love and thanks of man and woman. Tyranny, like hell, is
not easily conquered; yet we have this consolation with us, that the
harder the conflict, the more glorious the triumph. What we obtain too
cheap, we esteem too lightly; it is dearness only that gives every thing
its value . . ."

He heard himself cheering with others after Mr. Paine had finished.
These were the words that expressed exactly how he felt. Here was an
eloquence that had been denied him.

The General (Bilby said) passed his time in Newark writing as busily
as Tom Paine, though not half as eloquently. He wrote to General Lee,
politely suggesting that he bring the rest of the army over the Hudson and
join them. He wrote the Governor of New Jersey, asking him to send
all the militia. He wrote the Congress, asking it to send anything and
everything in the way of troops. But General Lee declined the honor of
joining in the retreat, fresh Jersey militia simply failed to appear, and
Congress said that all it had was the remnant of the Philadelphia
Associators—who would take a while to get there.

Actually, many disappeared from Newark but no one appeared—
except the van of Lord Cornwallis's troops marching down the west bank
of the Passaic with colors flying, drums rolling and fifes whistling the
Light Infantry Song on the morning of November twenty-eighth.

The army had only two hours' warning of their approach. It picked up what it could carry on foot and hurried west toward the low line of the Watchung Hills. As the rear guard walked out of Newark, it watched over shoulders the winking brass and dull crimson of the British van.

Micah walked in the rear with a score of men. They were armed with rifles and each carried an ax and blanket. Pioneers they were called, and they were commanded by a big, slow, angry Virginia sergeant named Hezekiah Horton who profanely complained that he had been retreating for what seemed years through a series of incredible misadventures all the way from the gates of Quebec. He had been given up for dead three times; he'd lost his teeth from scurvy and half of his left ear to an Algonquin tomahawk and all of his bowels in forty-eight outrageous assaults of the bloody flux; he had lost about everything that a man could lose except his legs and arms, and he allowed that he'd be goddamned glad to lose them if just once he could go forward instead of backward.

Weak, confused and cowardly though this army was, it always managed to do some things pretty well. Somehow, Micah observed, it always quickly found enough good men to form a strong rear guard, without discernible planning or management but by a kind of chaotic luck. One minute men shouted that the British were across the Passaic in force, and a minute later, in the alarmed rattle of drums and scampering of fear, a rear guard was forming. "Pioneers!" a voice roared, and a case of axes, magically produced, was broken open on the hard November ground. I'm a strong axman, Micah thought, and Bilby, as if reading his thought, nodded and said, "You're right for it, lad. Minna'll stay with us and have no fears for her. Gi' us that musket, I've a long horn for ye." As magically as the axes had appeared, Bilby thrust a rifle and pouch and powder horn into his hands.

Minna allowed she'd stay with him, but he ordered her to go with the Marbleheaders, and she was pushed, propelled and finally whirled away, crying out plaintively and finally disappearing in the current of the retreat. The pioneers did not form; they simply were tossed up by some erupting force in the deep rumble of confusion. They stood, armed with rifles, apparently as magically as Bilby had armed Micah, and hefted axes and eyed one another shrewdly—not all of them woodsmen; indeed, several of them little city men and one a barefoot boy with a strange accent that no one understood. Hezekiah Horton growled that he was a sergeant and that some obscene officer, he neither knew nor cared who, had told him he was in command, and did anybody want to make anything of it? Nobody did.

So they were organized, had instinctive faith each in the others as completely as a long experienced and tightly knit battalion of the King's own guards, and if somebody—anybody with the slightest authority—had told them to advance on the advancing British, they unquestionably would have. But nobody told them to do that or anything else. And so they simply waited until the army had scampered like mice west from Newark and until they heard the shrill, triumphant whistling of the British. Then they walked slowly west after the walking rear guard of Connecticut Continentals, talking profanely and observing silently that the brass of the British column swinging into the northern end of town shone brightly even though it was a cloudy day.

They instinctively liked and respected Hezekiah Horton because, in a sense, he chanted an eloquent lament over this long retreat to nowhere. His slow, drawling, endless talk was a kind of music to which they walked, up the gradually slanting land through fields and impinging woods, and down for a brief spell to a brawling creek crossed by a wooden bridge. Hezekiah, still talking, let his ax bite the bridge with a singlehanded downward sweep. Then he rested his rifle and stopped talking and went to work with his ax. The others joined him, working swiftly and efficiently and wordlessly, and at a distance the strokes of their axes sounded like heavy rain. The little bridge was gone in a few minutes. Hezekiah walked fifty yards up the narrow road and paused at a large maple. When he began to chop, a man joined him, and then two men began chopping on the other side of the big tree, strokes falling in turn, chips flying. Micah, judging the angle of fall of another maple across the road, went to work on it. Three men joined him, and others slashed brush. Hezekiah's tree crashed down across the road, and a minute later Micah's fell upon it. Even as the men dragged brushwood into the tangle, two red-coated horsemen appeared beyond the creek. Someone squeezed off a shot and one of the horses screamed and reared and fell. The men walked on. Half an hour later, hearing the thud of a six-pounder far behind them, they grinned at the thought of the cautious British shelling an undefended treefell.

Their speculation over whether the General aimed to hole up in the hills ahead or continue running was answered when the road swung south and wound through a patchwork of woods and cleared farmlands where houses were shuttered and barred. Keeping the hills on its right, the army streamed south and then southwest. It was far ahead of its rear guard, and the rear guard was well ahead of the pioneers who clogged the road at intervals with trees and brush, and once, in a mutual, spontaneous burst of energy and artistry, moved a stone wall across the road—just for the hell of it, as someone said.

Shortly after noon the sky cleared, not slowly, but with a furious suddenness. Somewhere over west, Micah thought, that old Delaware wind god Shamokatan, whom he hadn't thought of in years, must have inflated himself and given a mighty blow. The bare trees knocked their limbs together as if it were February and the gray clouds went tumbling and swirling east before a swiftly advancing front of icy blue sky. Frost tonight with roads hardening, and then two bright, cold days before the west wind relented and a southward sigh rolled in a multitude of white puff clouds. He'd seen it happen often in November, but now it amused him to wonder if that old devil Shamokatan was on the side of Britain and hard roads for turning wheels.

He liked this weather, even though it favored the enemy. He liked a hard blue arrowhead sky and a steady wind that cooled the heat of axwork. The sun pleased him too on its southerning orbit, shining steadily without any coyness at cloud curtains, giving off a steady glare of heatless light that pushed a purple band to the limits of the far northern darkness. By late afternoon they had worked around the southwest-turning hills straight into the sun's red eye.

When Hezekiah muttered, "I wonder where they all be at," Micah said, "I'll take a look."

He was glad to go back along the road, to be alone in the afternoon and hear no sound but the wind. He trotted a way so that his muscles would not stiffen after the sweat of the last treefell. And then he walked, thinking about his moccasins which had cracked and worn thin and would last—who knew?—two days longer at most. The hills turned on his left, and he turned with them, leaving the sun behind. Suddenly, as if he had stepped through a door, it was evening in the place where he found himself. He had come back three or four miles without seeing a sign of life or hearing a sound and now he hunkered down on his heels below a crest. Before him the road dipped through a wide clearing that broadened into a large swale on his right.

It was an ideal place to bag a deer coming down from the hills to feed just before dark, he thought. A fat gray squirrel played foolishly in a naked oak behind him. Something moved in the clearing. It was a red fox, tail and belly to the ground, sneaking among the brush. Perhaps he was mousing, perhaps he was sneaking simply because a red fox enjoyed sneaking; nobody ever would figure out the mind of a red fox. The fox faded into the brush as an eight-point buck paused at the edge of the clearing. He took two, three steps into it, then wheeled and disappeared up the hill with white flag bouncing. Something had alarmed him. Something stirred on the other side of the clearing.

A man carrying a rifle moved quietly along its edge. He must be an American, Micah thought, for he moved like a woodsman, pausing, watching, testing the wind, and going on. He must have seen the buck and now he froze as he watched the red fox in the brush. He came on, following the edge of the clearing all the way around.

Checking his flint, Micah muscled behind a stump and rested his rifle barrel on it. The man would pass—there, a dozen yards in front of him. In the twilight he appeared to be dressed in black. Then, straining his eyes, Micah saw that he wore a dark green hunting shirt and breeches and a dark, flat beaver hat.

"Stop right there!" he called sharply.

The man froze.

"Drop your rifle."

The man hesitated.

"Drop it!" He rose. The man saw his leveled rifle and dropped his own.

"Who are you?" Micah asked.

"The name is Renshaw." His accent was English or high-falutin' New York Tory.

"Where you from?"

The man sighed audibly and a trifle impatiently. "Northumberland."

"What're you doing sneaking 'round this clearing?"

The man turned his head and his teeth gleamed in a smile. "You sound like a gamekeeper accosting a poacher. I was scouting, or trying to, and obviously doing a bad job of it."

"You weren't doing bad." For some reason he took kindly to this Englishman; he wasn't sure what he'd do about him, but he knew he wouldn't kill him. Sensing the man relax, he said, "It's a pity you came in my sights and now I got to shoot you."

"*Got* to?" Renshaw asked.

Micah controlled a grin. "It's what it's about, ain't it? The war, I mean."

"God help us if we must stand here discussing the causes of the current difficulties," Renshaw said coolly. "It *is* possible to take prisoners, you know. I'd make a charming, co-operative prisoner."

"You know the trouble with you, Renshaw?"

"God help me, I've been told of innumerable things."

"Nobody's told you the *present* trouble," Micah said. "You came out this evening to play a *game,* and I'm playing for keeps."

"That's a damned astute remark," Renshaw said. "Who are you?"

"It don't matter."

"But it does. If I knew, I could arrange a fitting reward to you for not shooting me."

"Don't act so high and mighty, Renshaw. You mean you've got money and I ain't and you aim to *buy* me. It fries my ass the way you English think you can buy off everybody."

"That's a neatly descriptive phrase I haven't heard before," Renshaw said. "Frying one's ass, that is. If I'm fortunate enough to return alive to England, I'll repeat it everywhere. In fact, dozens of people will find this conversation priceless."

"If you were alive to repeat it."

"Oh, don't be so bloody *menacing,*" Renshaw snapped. "If you're going to shoot me, go ahead before it's too dark to see me."

Micah did not try to control his grin; he certainly shined to this Englishman. "You an officer?" he asked.

"Yes. But I prefer not to give my rank or regiment."

"And you just came out by yourself for a little scouting lark?"

"Well, yes," Renshaw said. "At home, when in the country, I enjoy stalking, and so, knowing you fellows were up ahead of us—"

"Did you see a deer here in the clearing?"

"Yes. As I moved along yonder a six-point stag—"

"An *eight*-point, Renshaw."

"My dear fellow, I was closer and I distinctly— Very well, *you* are holding the rifle and if you insist that it— But really it—"

"See anything else here?"

"A red fox."

"What was he doing?"

"He may have been hunting field mice. Or he may have just been creeping about. They love to creep about, you know. I say 'you know,' but actually nobody ever has fathomed the mind of a red fox. I remember—"

His voice was drowned in Micah's delighted yell of laughter.

"Damn it all," Renshaw cried, "you're one of my lads having a joke on me. I've a mind to—" As he stooped to pick up his rifle, Micah leaped on him and lifted him, struggling, from the ground. He was a light, almost frail, young man.

Setting him down, Micah thrust his face close. "You see I'm *not* one of yours, Renshaw. *Look* at me. You see I'm not and never will be. I laughed because I thought the same thing about a red fox whilst I watched the one there. We ain't at all alike and never will be, but we *thought*—"

"Damn it!" Renshaw straightened his hat. "There's not a person in St. James's Square will believe a word of this conversation. You really should be with us—what *is* your name?"

"Micah Heath." He grinned down at him. "You tell 'em in London town that you had a brush with the toughest fighter in America, Micah Heath. You tell it everywhere."

"I certainly shall, though I wish I had some sort of affidavit. I—"

"Go on back now and tell Cornwallis himself." Micah pushed him roughly.

"I shall, I shall. Just let me pick up my rifle."

"I'll keep that."

"God deuce us both, Heath, don't spoil it all. Don't you *trust* me?"

" 'Course I do, 'specially 'cause I'll have my rifle aimed at your head till you're out of sight."

"Heath, Heath, my dear fellow." Renshaw's voice rose plaintively. "Can't you understand? The fellows scoffed me frightfully for coming out scouting like a red Indian. If I go back there *without* my rifle, they'll— It'll be frightfully *humiliating*. Be a good fellow, Heath, and let me take my rifle."

Micah stared at him thoughtfully. "All right," he said slowly.

"One other thing would conclude this perfectly," Renshaw said as he picked up his rifle. "Let's both simply turn about and go our separate ways in trust without looking back."

"Oh, no."

"Really, Heath, it's the proper ending. To show we *trust—*"

"*No.*"

"Very well." He extended his hand.

Micah shook his head. "I'm not shaking hands. I told you, Renshaw, you fry my ass. You think it's all a *game*. If I meet you head-on tomorrow I'll shoot you dead."

The Englishman smiled bleakly. "I believe you would," he said. "Good hunting, Heath." He turned on his heel and walked north across the clearing.

As Micah walked back to the pioneers, he wished there was someone to whom he could describe his encounter with Renshaw. And then, suddenly, he wished that he had not met him.

"How far back air the varmints?" Hezekiah Horton asked him.

"Four, five miles."

"Ain't they scouts out?"

"Saw one."

"Git him?"

"He run off," Micah said.

On the afternoon of November thirtieth they crossed the bridge over the Raritan into a seething turmoil of men in Brunswick. They walked slowly, exhaustedly, and when an officer wearing a pink cockade in his hat waved an arm and ordered them to begin tearing up the bridge, they stared at him dully. Hezekiah profanely told the officer that they had not had anything to eat in twenty-four hours and to tear it up himself.

"Not yet, not yet," squealed a plump young officer wearing a green cockade. "We've got to get across."

"You goin' back *there?*" someone asked.

"We're going to our homes," the young man cried. "Our time's expired. It's the thirtieth of November and our time is up."

Hezekiah cursed him and all the Jersey militia while the officer wearing the pink cockade wailed that he was under orders to destroy the bridge and the militia officer shrieked at his men to hurry east across it. A score of men following the militia officer seemed to break a dam in Brunswick, for a hundred ran behind them. The rattle of their feet on the planking drowned the jeers of a gang of dirty, bearded men who wore the tattered remnants of the once bright Delaware uniform.

The pioneers dissolved their organization simply by easing themselves into the crowd and disappearing. No one knew where the Marbleheaders were. No one knew anything, Micah thought dully, except that the army had reached the end of its road. In Brunswick it had ceased to be. Two thousand time-expired men, the Maryland and New Jersey militia brigades of General Reazin Beall and General Nathaniel Heard, were scampering out of town in every direction like squirrels in the twelve-year madness. With them, infected by their determination to get home, went company after company of Pennsylvania militia whose time had not expired.

Here and there an officer harangued them futilely. A man with flushed face wearing a handsome blue uniform and the black cockade of a general angrily rode his horse into a knot of departing militia, cursing them. They spilled around his horse and ran as he roared curses after them.

"That's Stirling," someone said. "They say he's been towering mad at the militia ever since he was captured and traded, but I never seen him madder than he be today."

A dog barked and Jonah leaped up at Micah. In a moment he heard Minna shrieking his name. She hugged him to her, crying, "Ya air a sight for certain, all duff and dirt—and barefoot too. Where's them moc'sins at I made ya?"

"I threw 'em away, Minna. They were plumb wore out."

"Like yourself, I reckon. Never ya mind. I've made ya 'nother pair, only I ain't had time agin to work the leather and they won't last. Ya *air* a sight for certain. Ya need a bath an' shave an'— Hongry too, I reckon. I've a chicken saved for ya as flew dab into me yesterday yonder side of town whilst I was foragin'."

The Marbleheaders, encamped near the river, had raised a lean-to shelter for Minna. She hustled him into it as if he were a child, and brought him warm water and took his clothes and started the chicken roasting on a spit. After bathing and wrapping himself in his blanket, he honed his knife and scraped his whiskers and tied back his annoyingly thick shock of hair with a bit of string.

As he started to wolf the chicken and bread, he paused and silently held out half of the chicken to Minna. She shook her head. "You eat," he said. "You don't look so perky yourself."

"I ain't hongry," she said.

"Eat!" He grasped her wrist roughly and thrust the half chicken into her hand. She ate, slowly at first, and then ravenously. "You're a good woman," he said to her.

Her eyes gleamed. "I told ya I'd take care of ya."

He wondered why. Neither ever had mentioned the word love to the other. He did not love her; he scarcely had thought of her on the way from Newark. And surely she could not love him, for he had not done anything for her—only *to* her, taking her virginity and then taking her away from shelter and comfort to tramp the roads and live out in the weather and starve.

"Anything I can get for you?" he asked.

She smiled with pleasure again. "I'd dearly love a speck of salt. Ours is gone and there ain't none anywheres. If'n ya find any, take it."

He'd like some salt himself. The chicken was flat, and, when he came to think about it, he'd rather have a taste of salt now than a huge chunk of the flat bread.

Bilby limped up while they were eating, talking to himself and waving his arms angrily. His single eye was blackened.

"Cap'n." Micah grinned at him. "Did the British do it to you?"

Bilby flopped on the ground and cursed the militia. He had been trying, it seemed, to stop their flow homeward.

"It was in my mind we'd fight in Brunswick, but now there ain't tit nor tattle to fight with. They's a small passel of us Yankees and Stirling's Virginians and Delawares, but they's as dead beat as us. Worse, we've no wagons. All as was left has gone on west with the powder and most of the artillery. And you answer me this: what's that son of a bitchin' Lee doing holding five thousand men up on the Hudson? Why don't he join us and *fight*? Howe ain't going anywheres north with winter coming on, except maybe Newport, and who gives a witch's whisker if the British spend the rest of their lives in Newport? There ain't nowheres to go from Newport except to sea again. Howe's going to Philadelphia. The General knows it. They talk against the General, but leastways he knows the difference between a channel and a reef. We're all there is in Howe's channel to Philadelphia, but Lee—"

"Don't get so upset," Micah told him calmly. "Just because they take

Philadelphia, they won't win the war. We'll fight 'em in the country. We'll fight 'em at Lancaster and York and Ligonier and anywhere they want to go. They can't hold the country, only the city—"

"But who controls the city controls the country," Bilby said.

"The hell they do. The country feeds the city and there's some of us just might spend the rest of our lives picking off wagons bound for feeding the British in the city." He stretched and yawned, and then he smiled. "You just listen to old General Heath and stop your frettin', Cap'n. I'm tuckered. It's dark enough now to sleep."

He was awakened later by Minna pressing against him and he thought it natural and not surprising that their desire was stronger than fatigue.

At some time in the night she whispered, "You asked to git me something. You *have*. Never ya mind about salt. I ain't leavin' ya agin—never."

But she would, he thought sleepily.

She did.

They were awakened in the morning by a long roll of drums. No one needed to say that the British were approaching, for everyone knew it. If the army had grown a sight weaker, it also had grown a sight smarter, Micah told Minna.

There was not the frightened din that he had heard at Fort Lee and Hackensack and Newark. Men moved more slowly and knowledgeably. The bridge across the Raritan had been destroyed, and although the river was low and there were a half-dozen fords nearby, everyone knew by this time that British soldiers would rather build a bridge than wet their feet. The sight of smoke and flames rising from the encampment where the Delawares were burning their tents dismayed no one, for everyone knew that the army had not a single wagon left to carry tents or any other thing. It was totally a walking army now.

Yet it was an army. Small, to be sure, infinitesimally small, and short on everything that was supposed to be essential to an army. Yet it waited here on the west bank of the Raritan, not stunned and reeling as in times past, but stripped and calm, like a light hamlet fighter ready to throw for a fall with a heavy county champion.

Men leisurely collected whatever equipment they had. The regiments formed in the King's Highway of Brunswick: Massachusetts, Connecticut, Rhode Island, Virginia, Delaware. The soft fat of the middle colonies had been cut away, someone said—and good riddance. Then a few cheered at sight of one company of Jersey militia, come from nowhere and grinning proudly. A post rider, stripped to his short jacket, came out of the General's headquarters, sprang into the saddle, and galloped for one of the northern fords. Everyone knew his destination: Lee, that son of a bitch. A few minutes later another post rider came out and pounded away west. Philadelphia-bound, they remarked, but you couldn't count on those bastards in the Congress offering any help. Nevertheless, it was heartening to know that the General was in the house there, still writing letters. Some day, if he kept on writing, one of his letters might set fire to somebody some place.

There was no cry for pioneers this time. Micah, carrying his rifle and ax, went to the site of the destroyed bridge; it did not occur to him to go elsewhere. The same instinct brought all of the pioneers, reinforced by a dozen new volunteers, to the same place. When he'd told Minna to remain with the Marbleheaders, she had not protested, despite her whispered determination last night to stay with him. She, too, knew now what she must do.

Two six-pounders were unlimbered near the end of the wrecked bridge. The bony gun teams stomped and whickered in the rear. A gunner tossed his sponge from hand to hand and listened to Captain Alexander Hamilton talking earnestly with Major Aaron Burr. As Burr nodded in agreement with Hamilton, the gunner nodded too.

After a night and early morning of heavy rain the day had turned bright and cold, the sort of day when it seemed improbable that anything bad could happen. It was a likely Fair Day or Militia Day, with everyone possibly awaiting the arrival of a judge or the governor himself before festivities began.

Noon passed while the army sat and stretched out in the King's Highway. Shortly afterwards Micah heard a whispering in the east, like a light breeze in buffalo grass. Hezekiah Horton and a couple of others heard it too. They glanced at one another and then they smiled at the sight of those city boys, Aaron Burr and Alexander Hamilton, who heard nothing except their own voices as they agreed, agreed, agreed. The whispering grew into the patter of drums and shrilling of fifes. Soon the inevitable scarlet threaded out of the inevitably wooded horizon and Burr stalked away majestically to his duties while Hamilton began to shout orders unnecessarily soon, as if the fate of the army depended on him.

Knox rode up on a scrawny little mare that seemed to wince under his huge bulk. He raised his telescope and then he raised his voice, the loudest in the army: "Artillery ready!" His bull bellow surely carried the length of Brunswick.

Hezekiah Horton uttered a single, short obscenity. "Play-actin'!" he growled. "They *do* like their play-actin'."

Drums rolled, the regiments formed in line. But they did not march off west. To Micah's delight they faced about and marched east to the river and paraded back and forth, with drums crashing and banners whipping in the breeze, while the gunners stood beside their pieces with fuses burning.

On the opposite bank the British paraded too. They unlimbered a couple of guns and fired several wild rounds. Captain Hamilton's six-pounders replied without discernible effect. After a while, as if tired of wasting energy in its senseless parading, a regiment swung onto the King's Highway and others followed. Captain Hamilton harnessed in his guns and they lumbered off west. The Delawares were the last to go. The pioneers followed them, walking leisurely and watching the citizens of Brunswick opening their houses to greet the British.

In that early December the people of New Jersey treated them as if they were hostile invaders. Farmhouses and barns were barred to them, stock driven away and hidden. It did not seem to be the same land Micah had passed through five months before. But neither was he the same person, he knew.

He vaguely remembered feeling that he was on a gay lark when he came north in July. Now, however, he was angry much of the time. He thought that he hated these fat, prosperous, turncoat farmers as much as he hated the British. He was hungry and they would not give him food, cold and they would not shelter him—not because he had done anything to them, but simply because he was on the losing side.

All of them hated the people of Jersey. They took what they could find, though they did not force their way into houses or burn barns. Much as they hated Jersey, they maintained a stubborn pride in trying to be good soldiers and trying to believe that these Jerseyites were their own people.

The pioneers, destroying bridges and raising roadblocks behind the Delaware regiment's rear guard, fared as well as any in the army. Only one day's ration was issued to them in the retreat from Brunswick to Princeton. But each day Hezekiah detached two men to forage the back country for hidden stock, and each evening and morning they ate heartily of beef or mutton which the foragers drove in and butchered.

They reached Princeton on the night of December fifth and rolled in blankets close to fires in the college yard and complained one to another that they'd had enough of being pioneers. The General had gone on to Trenton with a part of the army, leaving Stirling with his brigade of Virginians and Delawares in Princeton. It didn't make any sense splitting what little was left of an army, Hezekiah declared. Micah agreed with him. Tired, cold, hungry, he remembered his resolution and confidence in Newark and Brunswick through a haze of exhaustion. It's like I was drunk then, and now I've sobered up, he thought. If I could get a bellyful of hot salted food and a night's warm sleep, I reckon I might turn drunk again.

They lounged about Princeton for another day and night, hungry, cold and complaining. Before dawn of the following morning a rider galloped into town, yelling that Cornwallis was three miles away and coming fast. The brigade formed quickly and marched for Trenton. The pioneers followed, destroying a bridge south of town and slashing angrily at trees which did not fall as easily as the trees outside Newark had fallen to their axes. A detachment of thirty Delawares kept about five hundred yards in advance of them, ready to come back and fight.

Toward noon, as they finished another roadblock, Hezekiah's jaw fell open and, for once, no words came. He gestured limply and the others stared as a solitary horseman cantered toward them. It was the General.

Reining in his big bay stallion, he said, "Good day, soldiers."

They saluted and the barefoot boy whom no one understood tugged his forelock of mouse-colored hair. They shifted from foot to foot and stared and finally one said, "Good day, General."

"Where is your officer?" the General asked.

"Ginral," Hezekiah said, "sir, your honor, we been fellin' trees an' tearin' up bridges since Newark, the most of us, and we's yet to see hide nor hair of ary officer. I reckon, Ginral, sir, I'm in charge here 'cause I'm a sergeant, Sergeant Hezekiah Horton of Morgan's Virginia Rifles, sir, an' I—"

"And a well-done job it's been, Sergeant, by you and all your men." The General looked too tired ever to smile again, Micah thought. "Continue with your work."

He pressed the stallion with a knee and rode around the roadblock toward Princeton.

"God save the hull bloody pack of us, he's goin' back thar alone," Hezekiah muttered. Then, cupping his lips, he cried, "Holt up, Ginral, an' some o' the boys'll go with ye."

The General rode on, ignoring him.

Micah said, "You can't yell at the *General* like that, Hezekiah."

Hezekiah allowed that the General was, after all, a valuable man. Then, beaming, he began to orate on what a *great* man he was. And, finally, "He come back here to be with *us'ns*. I vaw to Christ I'll foller that man to hell."

The General returned from scouting while they were working on another roadblock. They expected him to ride back to the army, but he did not go. He stayed near them all afternoon, silent except for occasional suggestions. Under his shrewd gaze they forgot their disgust and fatigue and worked with proud show-off of skill and strength.

As it grew dark and they were close to Trenton, the General rode along a muddy embankment after scouting the rear again. Then both hind legs of his stallion suddenly slipped in the mud and the horse started to fall. Dropping the reins, the General grasped the mane in both big hands and rose in the stirrups. The stallion did not seem to recover balance of his own accord but to be lifted, supported, and thrust on by the strength and skill of his rider.

That's not just good horsemanship, Micah thought. It's the way the General is with us when our backs are to the wall. But I reckon it wouldn't mean much if I told it some day when I'm old to a bunch of very young ones.

XXV

ONE'S young years were the happiest, Philly had heard it said. But after the bad news came, on November twenty-ninth, she thought she never would smile again.

Esther Reed brought Captain Bilby's message that afternoon. And after she had gone, Kathy called Philly into the parlor and silently handed her Bilby's note. Micah had escaped, but Alex had not. Her eyes filled with tears when she looked at Kathy.

There were no tears in Kathy's eyes. She looked—angry.

"I know," Philly said, "that Micah promised—"

"But he escaped," Kathy snapped.

"I don't reckon it was because he was a coward, Kathy."

"Who said he was? I know he's not. But he went free and Alex could have too if he'd had the—the courage."

Philly stared at her in amazement. "You can't mistrust his *courage,* Kathy. It must be a wide river up yonder and in the cold of November—"

"I'd trust Micah to get him across," Kathy said in a low voice, "or die in the trying." She turned to a window, her back to Philly. "But I know Alex. He'd think of his *honor* as an officer. He'd think he had to stay and surrender with his company."

"He *did* have to," Philly said. "And Micah should have stayed too."

Kathy turned quickly and her gaze locked with Philly's. I'm defending Alex and accusing Micah, Philly thought numbly, while she . . .

"No, Micah should not have stayed." Kathy's tone was weary as she walked slowly to the escritoire. "He knows what prison is and Alex—I sometimes wonder what Alex knows or thinks. But we'll get him out."

She picked up a pen and scowled at it. "I'll write Colonel Reed a properly tearful letter and his wife is writing him, too, after the little fit of hysterics I displayed for her benefit. I'll get Dick Peters to work on it and— Where is *Colonel* Tony Wayne now? I remember. That place in the north he calls Golgatha, what's its name? Ticonderoga. He can't help. Now let me see. Mr. Adams spoke to me most civilly a week ago. He's a power. But if the British knew that John Adams wanted Alex exchanged I reckon he never would be. There's—Papa!" She turned. "Philly, be a dear heart and run down to his office and tell him I've the hysterics and fainted dead away because Alex has been captured."

Philly was uncertain whether Kathy fascinated or horrified her. Apparently she was angry rather than grieved that Alex had been captured, but she was willing to—

"Oh, I shouldn't order you about so. Send Mrs. Munger." She flung the quill on the escritoire. "Damn men anyway! It's dull without 'em and impossible with 'em the way they run around at war as earnest as little boys playing games. Sometimes I don't blame the British for being so mightily peeved at the way our *men* have upset everything by—"

"Kathy!"

"Don't you turn on me too," Kathy cried. "I'm trying to be calm and—"

"All right," Philly said quickly. "All right now. I'll run to your father's office and fetch him."

Although Kathy damned men, Philly personally would take them to women. She did not run to Timothy Murdoch's office; she walked slowly in the gathering darkness, thinking that she never had felt so low. Why hadn't Micah written that he had escaped and Alex and the rest had been captured?

Oh, Micah, she thought. Then, remembering stories she'd heard Macaroni Jack tell of British army prisons, she thought, Poor Alex and Jack and Israel and all the others.

"Poor!" a woman had just said sharply to another as she passed them. "That's what we all are now except some of *them*."

It was the worst time she remembered, with prices rising and the poor growing poorer and the army defeated and the cause facing disaster. The army must not give up. Wherever it was up there in the Jerseys it must fight and fight to save all their hopes.

Micah was with the army, she told herself, and where Micah was hope always abided. *But why didn't he write?* Nevertheless, he was there, under this same cold glassy sky that slanted east into darkness. If she could be with him now instead of tied here uselessly with a parcel of hysterical women, she would cook and do for him and try to give him the heart to keep fighting. She'd try to give the whole army heart. What was the name of the French maid Alex had told her about once? She had been just a simple girl who disguised herself as a man and rode forth and rallied the French army and . . .

When she turned onto Front Street she scarcely saw it. She was in the north, wearing buff breeches and blue coat as she rode astride a handsome charger, and on her left rode General Washington and on her right rode Micah, and behind them marched the army, singing, with banners flying, and Micah was the only one in all the army who knew that she was Philly Twillow. So General Washington, whom she'd advised wisely and for whom she'd led many fearless charges, General Washington called her—Phil Twillow. "Phil," said the General, "after thinking it over I reckon we *can* retake New York. Now Phil . . ."

"*Philly!* Mistress Twillow."

She looked up and found herself in Timothy Murdoch's counting room at the foot of the aisle of high desks where four, six, eight young men sat on high stools with pens going *scratch-scratch-scratch* like mice in a loft. The scratching stopped and four, six, eight pairs of eyes gleamed at her, each pair raised over the glow of a single candle on a desk. At the head of the aisle Barnaby Falco had risen on his dais and spoken her name in a sepulchral tone.

"Philly. Good afternoon."

She hated him. She had hated him when he brought the wagonloads of salt to the farm and tried to be friendly to her, forever staring at her with his tongue curling over his yellow teeth and forever trying to get close to her and put a long thin hand on her. Now she hated him more for looking at her with that expression while the clerks stared and smiled.

"Afternoon," she said. "Miss Kathy has sent me to fetch Mr. Murdoch."

She knew it would happen. His vulture talon was on her arm and he leaned close to her. She hated the smell of his stale clerkly sweat and the breath of the disguising clove he bore constantly in his mouth.

"Mr. Murdoch is closeted with Mr. Pilch," he whispered. "Is anything wrong?"

She hesitated. "Yes. Miss Kathy has just learned that Captain March was captured at Fort Washington and—"

"Come." She found herself pressed into a tallow-smelling cubicle with him. "I am grieved to hear it, Philly. And I'm glad you spoke to me first." His voice sank to a whisper. "Now you and I can share a little secret, Philly. *I* can help more than all your soldiers and politicians. It will be *me* Mr. Murdoch turns to when Miss Kathy—uh—beseeches him for help. Mr. Murdoch trusts me, and well he might, for I have *contacts* in New

York, I have *ways,* Philly." He raised a long finger to his lips. "Our little secret . . ."

Somehow she got out of the cubicle and almost ran up the aisle between the staring clerks. Slamming the door behind her, she gasped deeply of the cold wind.

What did he want? Don't be coy, she told herself. He wants you. You're nobody, but you're pert and full of ginger. He was nobody, but he's bound and set to become somebody, and he's on his way. She had seen it happen a score of times in Philadelphia with a score of chief clerks who wanted to rise above their raising but not marry above it. But never, she thought, had she known such a loathsome chief clerk.

In the following days a turmoil grew in Philadelphia as rider after rider galloped into the city from the north. The army was retreating. No, it was not retreating; it was fleeing across the Jerseys and the British were dashing after it. The army had ceased to exist. The British were at Brunswick, Princeton, Trenton. The British would march into Philadelphia in two days—tomorrow. Patriots flee for your lives. Fathers send your daughters to the country to preserve their virginity. Householders bury your silver.

General Mifflin and Colonel Reed rode into the city and delivered patriotic orations to all who would listen. The remaining Associators marched north, fifteen hundred strong, to join the remnants of the army. Shops were closed and all day and half the night the streets echoed to the noisy, desperate haste of people loading everything they could into wagons, closing their houses and seeking refuge in the country. Word came that the British had captured General Lee in New Jersey.

And now, at last, Congress turned over to the General full powers to conduct a war that everyone knew was lost—and fled for Baltimore. Patriots cursed their Congressmen. Tories jeered them. The Tories were bold. Joseph Galloway, John and Andrew and William Allen, and many others announced their loyalty to the King and joined the British at Trenton. John Dickinson retired to his farm in Kent County, Delaware, and spoke querulously of peace.

On the first day of panic Kathy announced, "I'm *not* going to the farm. I'm staying here."

Timothy Murdoch, who had come panting into the house a moment before and ordered her to pack and leave immediately, faced her. "You are *not* staying here, Kathy."

"If I must be raped," she snapped, "I prefer to have it done in town rather than the country."

"Oh, God!" cried Murdoch, clapping his hands to his head. "Why must I have a daughter who *talks* so!"

She smiled at him. "It's what was in your mind, isn't it, Papa?"

"Yes—no! It doesn't matter. You shouldn't *talk* so. You shouldn't utter such a word." He turned to Philly. "Reason with her, Philly. I can't. *You* are going to the country and *she* will want to be with you."

"I'm not going to the country unless Kathy wants to, Mr. Murdoch." Philly smiled faintly. "I've got me a good sharp knife and so has Kathy. We'll account for any two Britishers or Hessians as try to rape us."

Kathy laughed shrilly and Murdoch stalked to the parlor door and opened it. He paused, scowling back at them.

"Are you leaving for the country, Papa?" Kathy asked.

He shook his head. "I have business interests to watch over here."

Business with the British, Philly thought. The only difference between him and Barnaby Falco was that he was short and plump while Barnaby was tall and thin.

He said, "May I once more entreat, Kathy, that—"

"No!"

"Then may I request you, as a favor to your father, that you come and stay at my house again until—things have quieted down."

Kathy slowly kicked a foot back and forth and frowned at it. "Very well," she said at last. "Provided Philly comes with me. And Mrs. Munger too. She's a better cook than your Lucy and they can spat in the kitchen and let Mrs. Munger get her mind off her troubles."

Murdoch nodded abruptly. "Yes, Mrs. Munger too. I might as well enjoy her services since I'm paying her wages." He hurried out before Kathy could reply to his parting dart.

Philly knew why Kathy wished to stay in Philadelphia. The excitement of the panic appealed to her. She dashed about the city in those days like a hungry wrenny bird flown into a Mennonite picnic, returning home with eyes shining to relish every morsel of gossip and rumor and fact about the tilt and slide and overturn of Philadelphians' fortunes in the crisis. All revolution in human affairs appealed to her as long as her own affairs remained stable. She did not really care who won, Philly thought sadly, as long as she was present to see the effects of conflict. Agony eluded her because she was not at all interested in a loser; but how a victor fared amused her vastly.

Besides, she was infatuated with the idea of danger. It was she who thought up the notion of their carrying little encased knives, and she went to Harrow's with Philly to purchase them. The place to carry their knives, she decided, was in the cleft of their breasts. When she gaily said, "Isn't it fine we both have bosoms capable of hiding knives," Philly agreed. But she was shocked when Kathy indulged in a little play-acting.

"Observe, Philly, the British colonel— Remember we're ladies and not to be assaulted by less than a colonel—comes toward you—" Clapping her right hand to her breast and extending her left—" 'Unhand me, sir,' you say, but the British tell us they're invincible in the advance and—" Arching her back and crying, "No! No!— Are you watching, Philly?— His arms wrap around you and— Now watch—" The knife flashed from her breast in her right hand and she groaned and started to fall. Then, herself again, she clapped her left hand over her eyes and let the knife fall and cried, "The beast! But I *did* defend my honor." Her expression grew pensive. "I wonder what they do to you for stabbing a British officer? Nothing, I reckon, if you act in self-defense. They're said to be just. Let 'em come."

But the British did not come. Sir William Howe pulled up at the Delaware, paused, hesitated, and finally decided to send his army into winter quarters. He'd take Philadelphia in the spring.

Kathy, who had been so amused by the flight of Congress to Baltimore, now was delighted by the plight of the Philadelphia Tories. They who had been going about with arms boldly flung wide to welcome Sir William suddenly found themselves deep in a country of angry enemies.

"Now," Philly said, "it's time the army hit back at Howe."

"Now," Kathy said, "I don't suppose we'll have to stay much longer in the 'fort.' "

For so she had begun calling her father's house on Arch Street. To their annoyance, Murdoch had made them feel they were living in a state of siege. He would not let them go out after nightfall because there had been some looting of empty houses and assaults on several respected citizens. Worse, he was trying to conserve fuel, which was in low supply throughout the city, so that everyone was cooped in the small back parlor until it was time to scuttle to a cold bedroom. Worst of all, he had brought Barnaby Falco into the house to eat supper with them each night and sleep in the lower front hall with a musket beside him.

"I hate that creature," Philly said on Christmas night after they'd crept into the bed they shared for warmth.

"I know you do," Kathy replied. "He *is* struck with you and he *is* a bore. He nigh spoiled our Christmas, such as it was, with his yes-yes-yessing Papa and snerking up to you. He's loathsome. Are you going to marry him, Philly?"

"Kathy!"

She laughed and snuggled against Philly. "Listen to that wind and there's ice in the river so early in the season. What a terrible winter this is."

"I wish," Philly said distantly, "I was out in the winter. I wish I was with the army."

Kathy shivered. "At least Alex is under shelter. At least a prison has a roof."

"And the army doesn't," Philly said. "But I wish I was out there with it."

Kathy gripped her arm. "Because *he's* with it. Forget about him, Philly, because I know—bad as it may seem to you—that nothing ever will come of how you feel."

"How do you know?"

"I just do."

"Yesterday was his birthday," Philly said. "He was twenty-three this Christmas Eve."

"I know."

Philly turned over. "You *know?*"

"Yes. I remember— It doesn't matter. We were children together and I—I was bad to him, Philly. I sent him away west because—because—I don't know why. Can you ever forgive me?"

"I reckon I can. I reckon because you did you put in his heart the thing he loves the most—the west. And if he hadn't gone out yonder I'd never have known him. Tom and me would have been eaten by panthers or took off by Indians. You did a greater good in sending him west than I did in bringing him east. That's on my mind often. He'd never have come back if it hadn't been for Tom and me. I—I *made* him do it, young and ignorant as I was. Come back here to all the things he didn't rightly want."

They were still, clinging to each other and listening to the rising wind.

XXVI

WIND rising since noon, was blowing a northeast gale by four o'clock dusk of Christmas Day when the Virginia Continentals came to the river.

"A forlorn hope if'n ever I seen hit," Hezekiah Horton said to Micah. "But we *air* goin' for'rds 'stead o' backwards."

As in times past, this feeble excuse for an army had raised a forlorn hope. There was a plan; nobody in the ranks knew what it was or who had thought it up, but there was a plan. Like all plans, it required men—not necessarily volunteers, but men who judged themselves and were judged by their officers to be capable of a final effort. They gathered in the shallow valley back of McKonkey's Ferry on the Delaware at noon of

Christmas Day and were judged and judged themselves. Many remained shivering in formation and the others crept back to the shacks, lean-tos and holes which they had raised and slashed and clawed in the brushwood.

It was, when you came to think of it, surprising what this army could do. For it still found something where apparently there was nothing. It was supposed to be out of wagons and rations, yet wagons rattled into the valley and each shivering man in the formations was issued a three days' supply of hard bread and pickled pork. It was supposed to be out of blankets, yet after search, parley, indignation and acceptance, each man in the formation had a blanket. Everyone knew that the army had lost all of its muskets, bayonets and ammunition a dozen times, yet after brief confusion each man except the members of the rifle regiments found himself possessing a musket with bayonet and forty rounds.

So they knew that the plan entailed their fighting and they knew that whoever had thought up the plan was smart enough to realize it probably would be too wet or windy for firelocks and the work would have to be done with the bayonet. On this basis alone they figured that the planner was shrewd and an able scrounger, so he must have a pretty good plan. There had been so much talk in the past couple of days about their going down the river and working over the Hessians at Trenton that they figured Trenton must be the last place in the world they would go. Not Trenton now if the planner was as smart as they began to suspect.

The one thing this planner had not been able to do was to dig up warm clothing or shoes, which meant simply that they didn't exist. The men took care of the lack as best they could, swapping rags and tattered, greasy bits of old blanket ends. It was agreed that barefoot men, of whom there were many, were not fit for the job, whatever it was. But many men who were barefoot judged themselves fit if they could only find something to cover the dirty veined marble of their callused, chilblained feet and shanks. There was an outpouring of sympathy and rags for these men, most of whom were boys. (Actually the forlorn hope gathered in the valley was made up almost entirely of boys, if anyone wanted to get technical about it, which no one did, because everyone thought of himself and the others as men.) Next to shoes, and ignoring such luxuries as coats and gloves and hats, the greatest lack was in the seats of breeches, which covered the most frequently used section of a soldier's anatomy except his feet. Quite apart from the fact that it was damnably cold to try to fight a war without a seat in your breeches, it was damnably demoralizing. A man suffering from that lack was unable to think of anything else or to do much except wander around trying to clutch tatters of breeches over his bare behind. Fortunately, a quantity of red flannel had appeared magically that morning and the camp women, of whom only a score remained, had been busily sewing red woolen seats into breeches with needles and thread which had appeared from some other magic source. In general, everyone began to see, the situation was improving.

There was a plan and there were the men to carry it out, better equipped and supplied than they had been in several weeks now. There also was an organization, if you could call it that. Some said there were twenty-six hundred men gathered in the valley, others said twenty-four hundred; there must have been almost two thousand anyway. They formed a division, though no one could figure out its order of battle until about one o'clock when the drummers tightened their drumheads and gave the long roll and the division began to parade.

The parading fooled no one. At first its purpose appeared to be the usual reason for parading in December: to keep the division warm, or at least less frozen than the wind-whipped, congealing mass it had become. No one kept step in the parading; it was, rather, a stumbling, skittering dance in the wind as the men tried to draw blood to feet as numb as turnips. Gradually, however, any observant man who had been with the army any length of time could see order growing in the milling mass. The General was not present, but the men he trusted were there. The brigadiers sat their horses in a little knot around Greene: Lord Stirling and Hugh Mercer and Adam Stephen and the Frenchman, Roche de Fermoy. At a little distance Sullivan stamped his feet and walked his horse with the lank Pennsylvanian, Arthur St. Clair.

Stephen rode suddenly toward his Virginia Continentals and orders were shouted. They halted, faced about, and marched toward the road leading out of the valley. Behind them Mercer bellowed something, and out of the parading flowed unit after unit from Connecticut and Massachusetts and Maryland, falling in behind Stephen's men and following them out of the valley.

"Us'ns of Virginia 'll lead the van," Hezekiah crowed to Micah.

Although Stephen's men were composed of skeletal Virginia Continental regiments, not all of them were Virginians. Micah had chosen to stay with Hezekiah and join the Virginians after the army crossed the river from Trenton three weeks before and began living in dead leaves and icy rain, for the Marbleheaders had scattered up and down the river, collecting boats, by the time he crossed and found Minna on the Pennsylvania shore. When the pioneers evaporated and Hezekiah urged him and a few others to come along to one of Stephen's regiments, he had agreed.

Now that he found himself in the van, he was glad that he had joined the Virginians. Many were Virginians by designation only, however. Among the men from tidewater Virginia, who spoke softly, and the men from back country Virginia, who spoke harshly, were several who claimed they could not understand a word the Virginians said. There were men from New Jersey named Hendrack Probasco and Reyneir Veghte; there was a Martinis Neyvus from York and a Jost Kesciu from the Mohawk Valley; a Dick Jones from Worcester bore a curious, impassioned hatred of Massachusetts; there were several Carolinians, who claimed that they detested Virginia. There were a half-dozen Negro slaves who had been sent to fight in their masters' places with vague promises of freedom and who had been used mostly as servants to hew wood and tote and fetch; but on Christmas Day in the valley they were judged so cheerful and durable and so willing to join in this last mad venture of the white man's army that they shuffled along now with the others.

Minna, standing near a fire with several camp women, waved and seized Jonah by the scruff to prevent him from following Micah as the column passed.

"Damn good woman," Hezekiah said to him.

She was, Micah thought. Even here in the last extremity of the army she had not failed him but had endured as stoically as a squaw. He had taught her the Indian way of living, the most comfortable and healthful under the circumstances of the bleak December country. He'd dug a pit, about the size of a bury hole, well below frost line, and roofed it with boughs and leaves. Searching out trots, he set horsehair tie-ups and they regularly ate their fill of rabbit roasted over the small smokeless fire which they kept burning perpetually at the foot of the hole. That hole had been as warm as a Philadelphia kitchen. It was the way the entire army could live healthfully if lazy men only could learn to nourish a fire perpetually and never foul a dugout no matter how bad the weather. Now, leaning into the wind, he remembered the hole and the unsalted rabbit meat with longing. A rabbity life, he thought, and smiled down at the roughly sewn rabbit skins which encased his feet.

It was not yet dark when they reached the river and saw, with consternation, that it was ice-clotted. Ice had begun to break up in the northern creeks around noon and now was swirling down-river in wide, broken sheets with a sound like dried beans shaken in a hundred young ones' gourd play-rattles. Around the ferry landing the horses of the Philadelphia Light Troop danced in the cold, kicking and shying and snorting white smoke. Knox, stamping his feet on the landing, shouted, "Cannoneers!" in a voice that surely would have carried to Princeton if the wind hadn't been in his teeth. The General rode a chestnut sorrel past the Virginians, chin tucked into his cape, his nose a bright red.

As darkness closed suddenly, first on the Jersey shore and then on the river, there rose above the churning of the floating ice a *bang-bang-bang-*

bang, growing louder and mingling with the shouting of men. A voice roared, "Ye goddamn scupperhead, Maitland, ye broached again!"

The voice was Bilby's, lost on the wind, and Hezekiah said that the Marbleheaders were bringing down Durham boats from an island hiding place up-river. The banging of ice on the thin hulls grew louder, and then two, three boats reeled out of the darkness and boat hooks bit the landing.

"Christ Almighty you're late!" Knox bellowed.

"Christ all Harry Knox," roared Bilby, "we're due at dark and dark it just be!"

The waiting infantrymen danced from foot to foot, teeth chattering, hugging and beating themselves, while the cannoneers groaned and cursed and heaved their pieces into the canting boats. A boat shot away into the darkness and someone wailed that only two cannon were off and there were sixteen yet to go.

The General had hired Knox to curse for him that night, someone said. If he had, it must have cost him a pretty penny. Yet despite Knox's fluent cursing at full voice, the embarkation proceeded with nerve-racking slowness. It began to rain. The wind backed east of northeast, having its way with the rain and hardening it into sleet that lashed backs and heads and crusted the metal of muskets and bayonets. The boats came empty and went again, bearing cannon and the stolid artillery horses and then the nervous, mincing horses of the Light Troop.

About eleven o'clock, as the sleet changed to snow, the Virginians started to creep to the landing. Then they almost ran as Knox roared at them. Micah glimpsed the General by the faint light of a lantern, hands gripped tightly together, as if he feared he might wring them, his lips a thin line, his nose almost scarlet from the cold, his eyes glittering like icicles. He found himself in a boat with others, crouching low in the deafening crash of ice against the thin shell.

Surprisingly soon he stumbled ashore and Hezekiah said, "Jersey under foot agin."

No one ever did tell them that they were going to Trenton. By midnight, however, everyone knew that Trenton was their destination because it was the only place held by the enemy that they might remotely hope to reach. Now they reckoned the plan was the General's and they picked flaws in it: they had moved too slowly; the Hessians would be waiting for them rather than being taken by surprise; their powder and pans were wet and useless; why in hell bring all that artillery over the river? Yet they had to go somewhere or cease to be an army, and Trenton was the only place they could hope to reach. It wasn't much of a plan after all, and it wasn't working well. They should be in Trenton soon after midnight, yet they stood here, freezing, seven miles away.

At some unknown hour of the morning the General was among them again as they stood, stamping their feet, backs to the wind. Knox was there too, his broad beam flitting with surprising gracefulness among his beloved artillery, his big hands fondling the frosted cannon as if they were living creatures. A story spread that made men grin. When Knox flung his big bulk into the General's boat on the Pennsylvania shore, he had nearly capsized it. "Knox," the General had snapped, "shift your ass and trim the boat."

It was three o'clock, someone muttered, and all of the army still was not over the river. Then it was said to be over, but they did not move out. Lieutenant James Monroe was shouting an order he had memorized. But the wind took his voice away and Micah caught only snatches of it. ". . . silence to be enjoined . . . no man to quit his ranks . . . pain of death." A password was repeated from man to man. "Victory or death." And still they did not move.

It was after four o'clock when the order finally was shouted. "Shoulder firelocks!"

As Micah and Hezekiah swung out fast in the van of Stephen's men, Hezekiah muttered, "We kin do hit, we kin do hit." But the toothless grin he turned on Micah was not convincing.

In their hearts they and all the others doubted now that they could do it, Micah knew. He was beginning not to care, much as he wanted to care. The cold seemed to be inside him rather than without, a belly of ice that crept through his veins as he walked lightheadedly onward.

Yet they were walking, on and on, past a crossroads, past a darkened tavern where a sign of a bear's head creaked in the wind. No one spoke. There was no sound except the wind and the slashing of sleet. Once, when the wind gave one of its strange leaps from earth into upper darkness, there was a stunning silence. Then the silence was filled by the *shner-shnook-shner-shnook* of their hurrying feet. And then the wind returned to earth from its wild upward spiral and they no longer could hear the slogging of their feet.

Occasionally the General dropped back from the point of the column, leaning far over in the saddle so that they could hear his weak voice in the wind. "Soldiers, keep with your officers . . . Soldiers, keep with your officers . . ." I reckon he wants to believe in somebody, Micah thought, and it's mighty hard for him to believe in *us*.

It seemed that many of them could not go on, but they were going, faster surely, though not as fast as they must. A crossroads hamlet sprang out of the white darkness and they halted. Birmingham, someone said. Some dropped in the road and instantly were asleep while others broke out the rations of hard bread and sour pork. The whiteness grew and houses and a frozen orchard took shape. It was dawn and they were too late to take Trenton.

A man trotted from a house and lifted a mug of rum to the General. He nodded, took the mug in a gloved hand, and drank. They watched him, licking their lips and shivering. He returned the empty mug to the man and wiped the back of a hand across his mouth. Since they were too late, they might go back now, across the river to a warm fire where they could think of another chance, another crossing later. The General said something to Stephen.

"Shoulder firelocks!"

They kicked awake the men asleep in the slush and went on.

Beyond the frozen orchard Micah made out a column slanting off to the right by another road. So the plan still was working. Their force divided, some by one road and others by another. But darkness had been essential to the plan, and light was growing. Ahead, the General rode with his gaze continually turning eastward and once he raised his left hand and let it fall helplessly, as if he would have drawn a curtain on the dawn.

A man asked the time and the question was passed far back until it reached an officer who had a watch. Past seven o'clock the answer eventually came back.

Men moved in a white field far to the left. A squad of the Light Troop galloped out and brought them in. Hezekiah recognized them: a patrol of Stephen's Virginians who had been sent scouting yesterday. The General was gesticulating angrily to Stephen. The word of what had happened spread back, alarming them. The patrol had fired on a Hessian picket, not knowing of the attack. Now the Hessians would not be taken by surprise. Now their hope was less than forlorn.

They went on.

A farmer stood bareheaded in his yard, an ax poised above his chopping block, his jaw fallen open at sight of the ghostly column winding out of the sleet. The General galloped to him, reined in, asked a question. The man let his ax fall and pointed up the road toward a house.

As he pointed, blue-coated Hessians ran from the house. Two muskets crashed. The Light Troop spurred forward and the Hessian pickets turned and ran toward Trenton village.

"At the double!"

They were running, lightly and easily, even though it had been painful to walk a moment before. A cannon boomed somewhere and an officer shouted, "It's Sullivan! He's t'other side of town by t'other road ahead of us."

Trenton, so long distant, was suddenly upon them. They could see the tiny figures of Hessians milling around the meetinghouse as drums rolled and bugles blared above the howling of the American officers who were trying to make their column do something. Then Micah understood. "Left! Left!"

Stumbling and slithering in the slush, they slanted to the left, off the road and across the fields that rolled to the edge of town. Behind them Mercer and his officers were shouting their men to the right while Captain Forrest and Captain Hamilton unlimbered their artillery and trained the guns south down King and Queen streets, which forked into town. It was all that Micah could see of the plan, but it was enough. He understood it now. Two hands about the Hessian throat of Trenton—and squeeze.

They crossed the Princeton road and finally halted, bunched up, and then stringing out of their own volition as they began to understand their job. To the right now and forward into town through yards and side streets. But what was wrong with the crazy officers? They were running up and down, waving their swords and shouting them back, back. Hezekiah roared curses at Captain Granger. Micah heard himself howling with rage at being brought to the edge of Trenton and ordered to stand there, in a naked field, against no visible enemy. Cannon crashed, a Hessian band began to play somewhere, and still they stood there angrily.

"Yonder!" Hezekiah yelled, pointing.

Around a house ran three, four, five blue-coated grenadiers, their starched black pigtails flying as stiffly as the handles of frying pans. They slithered to a halt at sight of the Americans. Micah raised his musket and pulled the trigger. The hammer clicked emptily and he cursed the musket and heard others cursing theirs. The Hessians raised their wet muskets and tried in vain to fire. Wheeling, they ran back into town.

Micah and Hezekiah ran after them. The entire company and part of the regiment was running too, and now the officers stopped shouting and ran with their men. Forward at last instead of backward, Micah thought. But his musket was useless in this sleet despite the grease rag he'd kept wrapped around pan and lock. "Dry 'em out!" he cried to Hezekiah.

There was a house, a door. They thrust their shoulders against it together. It swung open and they staggered into a suffocatingly hot room. A woman screamed and cowered behind a large chair in a corner.

Hezekiah grinned toothlessly at her. "Hit ain't the times, ma'am," he shouted, "hit's the goddamn firelocks as tries men's souls. If'n ye please, ma'am, whar's yer pincushion at?"

The woman screamed again and slid out of sight behind the chair.

"Pore soul," Hezekiah said. "She fainted plumb dead away at the sight o' liberty."

"Here." Micah knocked over a spinning wheel as he reached for a pincushion on a table. Snatching pins from the cushion, they picked out the touchholes of their muskets. A half-dozen men crowded into the room, cleaning touchholes with pins, drying flints and priming pans with bits of cloth they found in a sewing basket. They loaded their muskets, glanced out windows, and dashed outside.

The sleet pressed an acrid fog of gunpowder on the town as artillery crashed incessantly and wild firing spread everywhere after men found means of drying their muskets.

But, as Hezekiah obscenely demanded, where was the obscene enemy?

At last they found one, a big blond boy who ran toward them crying, with a white handkerchief held aloft on a spontoon. They captured him. Another shot at them from a window. Martinis Neyvus called to him in German and, when he thrust his head out the window, shot him.

The officers kept trying to lead them south toward Assunpink Creek, which must have been a part of the grand plan. But now they were intent on their own grand plan: to hunt and find, to kill or capture. They worked their way west to Queen Street and broke into houses. Drying their muskets again, they fired from windows into the seething, shouting mass of a Lossberg regiment which stubbornly tried to form in the street after each round from Forrest's four fieldpieces at the head of the street. The Hessians suddenly broke and ran.

They followed, flitting from house to house, firing carefully, whooping with the delight of at last being the hounds instead of the rabbits. Out of the wild confusion, Micah thought, there would surely grow some clearly defined action when they would charge with bayonets. But at Third Street Captain Granger, cursing them as if they were the enemy, turned them east and drove rather than led them back to the edge of town.

There, to Micah's surprise, they found themselves swept again into the General's plan, for they ran into the main body of Stephen's and Fermoy's men, drawn in a tight ring around a small orchard where the Hessians were forming. Finding a place in the ring, they waited. The Hessian drums rolled, their officers shrieked an order, and the grenadiers advanced. Two cannon stitched the advancing thin lines, but the American musket fire was weak. Micah's own musket again failed to fire. Now, he thought, the bayonet and sweet revenge for the long retreat from Long Island.

But the grenadiers had halted. An officer roared at them, but they did not stir. There was no sound except the lashing sleet. Then a Hessian officer raised his hat on his sword and the grenadiers began to throw down their muskets.

"They's surrendering to *us*'ns," someone muttered.

"I don't reckon," Micah said to Hezekiah, "that you and me got to the right place in this town today to do much good."

"We *got* here," Hezekiah said, "and it was the *gittin'* as counted."

Book Four

THE LION'S MOUTH

XXVII

HISTORY is a chronicle of destruction, Alex thought. After you had seen everything and remembered everything, you realized that there was no reason in the witless, bumbling, accidental course of human affairs called history. There was only destruction.

In the course of his own destruction he was struck once by a sense of wisdom as pure as the filthy matter of wisdom ever could be. He was not certain of anything except that it was winter and that he was between decks of the prison ship *Grosvenor*.

He lay dying, but there was a preternatural clarity in his eyes that saw far in the darkness, as far as a foot from his twisted head, to the yellowed, almost transparent face of Cook, Cooke, Coke, whatever was the name of the boy from Connecticut who had been cuckolded by something called patriotism. Now history had almost completed its process on the boy; at any moment the lids would shoot open and the eyes fix sightlessly.

As Alex watched, with the cunning of the destroyed, a brown maggot crawled from the boy's ear and crept across his beardless, yellow cheek. It paused uncertainly. In some previous incarnation, before he understood the process of destruction, he would have reached out and knocked the maggot off the boy. But now he could not stir; he had been destroyed; he was dead, and his only remaining hope was that no fantastic process existed in the cosmos whereby the dead could live again—and so be destroyed again.

He watched, with a sudden glow of wisdom, the brown oily glow of the maggot on the cheek. An expert now, long experienced in the customs of maggots, lice, weevils, rats and all the nameless vermin that were the agents of history, he knew why the maggot had crawled from the ear and waited on the cheek.

Now! There was a slight spasm of the face, which must seem an earthquake to the wise, wise maggot that clung to its world with mucous pads. *Now!* Oh, what a wise maggot. It resumed its course toward its historical destiny in the nutritious human interior: across the cheek, around the scallop of the nose. For a moment it paused, and then probed ahead and disappeared from view.

The eyelids of the face shot upward. With what an exquisite sense of timing history had endowed a maggot.

The world shook suddenly. The boy's eyes, refusing to fix within their open lids, rolled to the twisting of his face. You fool to want to come back, Alex tried to shout at him. Submit now and never be destroyed again. But his dead lips could not utter a sound. And then, with wonder, he realized that his dead ears heard.

"Hell!"

The boy, who had lain lifeless long by the current measurement of time (was it days and months still, or only hours?), writhed. His dirty, curled, yellowed hand plucked at his nostrils. Then his fingers dragged the squirming maggot from his nose and he uttered a weak cry of triumph as he held it between trembling thumb and forefinger. Indignant now, with the outrage of the mortal fool who refused to understand his immortal role in the destructive process, he crushed the maggot and wiped the remnants of history's agent on the deck.

Tears sprang to Alex's eyes at the predicament of this boy who refused to understand. Yet the sound that bubbled at his lips was like laughter, a low *"B-b-beee."*

There were voices somewhere in the darkness.

"Coke 'pears bounden to live."

"March's done fer. Out'n his head."

They were right that he was done for. But reason had not abandoned him. He had abandoned it after having acted most reasonably. When he tried to remember, however, he could not recall the sequence of his reasonable acts.

Eventually, after he had died three of four times and had been resuscitated each time for further destruction, he stood Accused, with a capital A. The charge was that he had acted unreasonably.

Weak, sick, confused, he offered in his defense a bit of doggerel he had made up, a riddle of sorts:

> *"The maggot agent moves in season,*
> *His destiny entwined with man's,*
> *And though man seeks a state of reason,*
> *The maggot completes history's plans."*

That frightened the accusers and caused them to add insanity to the bill of particulars against him.

Only one, a girl, tried to understand. Because she tried, he smilingly called her "counselor" and made wry suggestions for his defense as she cared for him in the cell to which he had been assigned.

"Those frightened by doggerel would be thrown into a state of terror by poetry," he said one bright, warm day as he sat by the window. "There's so much truth in it. A pity I lack real poetry, Philly."

For the girl was Philadelphia Twillow and the place was the house on Fourth Street and the time was June in 1777. He had not died after all—not yet, though he felt that he had merely been resuscitated in order to undergo final destruction.

"Poetry is the way man expresses his integrity," he said, studying her thoughtfully. "Why prose is incapable, I can't determine—Philly, do you think I'm mad?"

She looked up from the sock she was knitting and he marveled at the fine-boned lovely young face that had eluded the agents of history. "I don't think you're mad, Alex. You've been close to death and you're angry for some reason. I wish you wouldn't be angry with those who are trying to help you."

"Counselor"—he smiled bleakly—"I am not angry with thee. I'm simply annoyed with the Accusers, who are annoyed with me: Kathy, Murdoch, that Falco fellow who takes credit for rescuing me, as he puts it, and seems to know more about my life as a prisoner in New York than I do myself." He smiled again. "Persevere, Philly, and teach me tolerance. You are the exception to all the rules. You express your integrity in prose, for example. Do you have any poetry for me this morning—or a few lines of doggerel?"

"I learned a new hymn at the Committee of Safety meeting yesterday. But you would only scoff at it."

"I will not scoff, counselor. Sing it for me."

"I won't sing it. But I'll recite a stanza. It's called 'The American Soldier's Hymn':

> " 'Tis God that girds our armor on,
> And all our just designs fulfills;
> Through Him our feet can swiftly run,
> And nimbly climb the steepest hills . . ."

Her face glowed, reflecting her faith in the verse she had recited. Her interpretation of these times was vastly different from his own, he thought. She believed in God and His divine guidance of this curious cause. All acts of civil disobedience required the justification of divine leadership in order to achieve their ends. It would do for her, though not for him.

Mortals were forever calling God into their schemes. If He existed, perhaps He heard; and if He heard, perhaps He sometimes answered.

"I don't scoff," he said to Philly. "I commend any interpretation of the course of human events—even the interpretation of divine right. But I do suspect that some of our British enemies feel that God is on their side and sing hymns of divine leadership to Him. Has that occurred to you?"

"Of course," she replied. "But I reckon He knows that right is on the side of freedom, or why did He have us born with the wish to be free?"

"Your Presbyterianism has been considerably leavened by Tom Paine, Philly. But let me recite another bit of doggerel, a riddle of a kind:

> "Then came the Fire, and burnt the Staff,
> That beat the Dog,
> That bit the Cat,
> That ate the Kid,
> That my Father bought,
> For Two pieces of money.
> A Kid! A Kid!"

"I somehow like its sound," she said. "But I don't understand a word of it."

"Israel told it to me in prison before he—"

"Passed away," she said quickly. "Yes, tell me—"

"Israel did not pass away, Philly. Israel died, slowly and needlessly and in great agony." He frowned. "Pray stop trying to spare my feelings, as if I had been party to a social gaucherie. I would rather remember my imprisonment than forget it. I passed some profitable time trying to solve the riddle Israel posed in that doggerel. It's an old Jewish saying, he told me. Jews somehow understand it instinctively, for it recounts the history of the world."

"I never could guess its meaning, Alex."

"Then listen and you won't have to read Plutarch. The Fire was Alexander the Great. He destroyed the Achaemenian Empire whose Staff ruled the world after having beaten the Assyrian Dog. That is the Dog that bit the wise Babylonian Cat. And that is the Cat that ate the tender Kid, the chosen tribe that God bought from Moses. It is history, as the Jews so well understand it: an endless process of destruction."

"But Alexander lived a long time ago," she said. "It doesn't tell what's happened to the world since then."

"It doesn't need to. The historical processes that preceded Alexander have succeeded him. In all history a Fire has a way of burning out quickly, and from its ashes there always rises a tender Kid. The Kid of Alexander's

Empire was eaten by a wise Cat that was bitten by a savage Dog that was beaten by a Staff that was burned by a later Fire. The process of destruction and consumption goes on endlessly and there is no new thing in history. Unlikely though it seems, we might happen to win this civil war. If we did, we might be remembered a long time hence as a Fire. And if we are so remembered, it will be by a tender Kid of a people that—" He shrugged.

Philly grimaced. "If what you say is true, and I don't know that it is, but if it is—I'd rather live now in the time of Fire."

The time of Fire, he often thought in those days. If he wished to record its heat and glow for a posterity that lived in an age of the tender Kid, what would he say?

Gentlemen, we did not recognize it as a time of Fire after the first sparks were struck. We lived in cold and darkness. The truth of the times was expressed more accurately in the New York prisons than at Lexington or Bunker Hill or the early meetings of the Congress . . .

Words would fail him and memory blur. He remembered irrelevant things.

John Martin, a private of the 5th Pennsylvania from Chester, kept a small notebook and pen after he was captured at Fort Washington. By skillful chicanery he obtained ink and almost every day wrote in a cramped hand a record of events that concerned him vitally—and would give posterity an inadequate notion of his suffering. Perhaps, however, the diary served its purpose by sustaining Martin. "I got a record on it!" he'd cry proudly in a hoarse voice. "I got a record, Captain March!" Now Alex did not know what had happened to Martin, but he could remember passages from his diary.

New York, Munday, the 18th day Novembere, A.D. 1776. This day I, John Martin, was marched to New York under guard with several hundred others four deep from Harlem. Along the way we was much frowned on by all we saw. We was called Rebbels a-going to the Gallows. Arrived at York at 9 o'clock we was counted off and marched to North Church and here confined under guard. No provisions. Wet and windy. . . .

Accurate, John, but inadequate. You failed to mention the burned-out desolation of a city nearly destroyed by fire and the ferocious, torchlit faces of citizens who screamed and hurled refuse at us and would have swarmed upon us with clubs had it not been for the protection of our Hessian guard. Who was the enemy? Not the Hessian with whom Israel talked in German and who gave him a clean bandage for the shoulder wound that would not heal.

> *Saturday, 23rd. All joys gone, sorrows increase. We much derided & filthy as hogs. Drawedd 6 oz of pork per man which we eat alone and raw. Verry cold. Some making up to the Enemy . . .*

Naturally, John. The will to survive is strong. Vanity is strong too. It was understandable that Moab was pleased by the curious British officers and soldiers who came to look at him, the first blackamoor they had seen. His black skin, previously a source of shame, became a source of distinction. And what is the difference between distinction and honor? Why should he not leave a filthy, crowded prison to don bright livery as the distinctive, well-fed servant of a king's colonel? When he left, grinning happily, while the patriots cursed him as a black bastard, he expressed the ancient wisdom of the African jungle and the eternal slave:

"When you stick your head in the lion's mouth, you got to pat his head a little."

Extraordinary wisdom, said Israel, watching Moab with feverish eyes. In North Church he and Alex passed much time discussing the varieties of wisdom. It had been the wisdom of Micah to run the peril of death and escape. It had been the wisdom of Moab to trade masters. And it was the ancient Jewish wisdom of Israel, seeing life as a process of destruction and seeing imprisonment as the natural state of man, to endure.

"Wisdom, wisdom," he muttered once as his wound suppurated and fever grew in him. "In every generation of my family someone has died in prison—simply because he was a Jew. Why can't I be wise enough to accept my fate?"

On reflection, it could be argued that everyone acted in his own infinite wisdom and with the utmost reason—those who went over to the enemy and those who refused, those who endured and those who inflicted. It was reasonable to men like Israel and John Martin to prefer death to submission. And it was reasonable to their guards to steal from them and inflict the cruelties that gave a sense of power.

Even such a feared and hated man as the lank, hawk-nosed Tory jailer, Devore, unquestionably believed that he was acting reasonably in behalf of the most important person in the world: himself. Devore was a friend of Joshua Loring, the Commissary General of Prisoners, whose wife was General Howe's mistress. Devore was all-powerful and knew all. It must have been he who informed Barnaby Falco of most of the counts in the indictment later raised against Alex.

For Devore himself one day called out the name of Alex March in North Church and personally led the guard that conducted him to the enormous, gray, stockaded Liberty Street Sugar House. There he turned him over to a captain who simply requested his word of honor not to try to escape. They walked silently to a house on Wall Street where the captain ushered him into a large, warm room and closed the door.

Earl Percy looked up expressionlessly from a chair near a window. "Mr. March." He smiled faintly. *"Captain* March. Sit down." He nodded to a chair opposite him.

Alex sat down slowly. "I trust your lordship will forgive my appearance. The facilities of North Church leave a bit to be desired."

Percy frowned. "I know. That is, I hear." He gazed at Alex thoughtfully. "A couple of my officers remarked on a similarity of appearance between us. It's less marked now. I was going to ask if you're English-born, but it reminds of a dead old joke. I could inquire if your father passed his youth in England and you might riposte by asking if my mother had spent a while in America." He did not smile. "Your stallion, Heartbreak, is enjoying excellent health."

"Pardon, *your* stallion, if you recall."

Then Percy did smile. "Don't you ever feel you're on the wrong side in this unpleasantness?"

"No. Do you?"

"Not any more. I was highly sympathetic to America before I came. And then the damned Yankees irritated me greatly. I don't know if you heard, but I conducted the relief column out from Boston to Lexington last year when the bloody mess began. Most unpleasant experience of my life with those damned farmers. However, the jig is nearly up for you people, March." He frowned. "If we showed more initiative it would be over now. If I— It doesn't matter. Where are you from, March, and what do you do?"

"I was a lawyer in Philadelphia."

"Did *we* teach you the law?"

Alex smiled. "I passed some time at Lincoln's Green—and enjoyed London thoroughly."

"Whiled away at White's and Will's, did you?"

"Indeed."

"We might have met, you know." Percy frowned. "However, my purpose in—er—inviting you here today is this. I marked you well after that stupid little engagement up the island last month. It was not my intention that you should languish in this filthy predicament so long, but I was called away to Jersey chasing Mr. Washington's phantoms. I wish to inform you now that you're free to return to your home and resume your normal life. I must ask, in return, your word that you won't bear arms against us again—a parole, we call it."

A cart rattled over the cobbles past the house. He closed his eyes and believed that he was home again in Philadelphia. He opened his eyes and said, "Lord Percy, I deeply appreciate your kindness. But I'm unable to take advantage of it."

Percy scowled at him. "Unable?"

"That's right."

"Why not?"

"I couldn't give my word not to bear arms again."

"Damnation, March, you're difficult. Perhaps I put it badly." Percy hesitated. "Let me put it this way, and I wish you'd not bruit it about. I've resigned and I'm going home. The rebellion is not being prosecuted as vigorously as I believe it should be. On my word, I don't hate many of you people personally. But you have raised a—a contretemps, and there's nought to do with a contretemps but step on it and walk on and forget it. However, we aren't doing this, March. There's nothing between us and Philadelphia now except some wind-blown fields. But it has been decided that we'll go into winter quarters—and so I have decided that I'm going home. Now—I'd feel rather good if I could do a decent thing before I go. You and I can rather cancel each other out, March. You one less for *them,* and myself one less for *us.* What d'you say?"

"Thank you, but—"

"And take your stallion, March, take him. He's good and knows a firm, wise hand. Take him and ride out of this pesthole and go home and forget your folly."

Alex rose. "Thank you, but— No."

"You're being unreasonable!" Percy cried angrily.

He had not been able to convince Percy that the unreasonable course would have been for him to desert his men, who found some solace in the fact that he shared captivity with them. He had requested, since his lordship wished to do something decent, that Israel and three other men he named receive medical attention.

Devore, knowing he had rejected Percy's offer, cursed him for a dirty rebel all the way from the Sugar House to North Church. At the entrance to the church Alex stumbled on the steps and fell. Still cursing, Devore turned and kicked him. As he got to his feet, Devore seized him and shook him angrily. After he was thrust into the jammed, stinking room, he found that his watch was missing.

Furious then, he beat his fists on the door and yelled for Devore until the sergeant of the guard pushed in and told him to pipe his noise. Devore was a thief, he cried, and the sergeant knocked him down and left. That night he was taken to the guard room where two soldiers beat him for five minutes as timed by Devore, who sat holding the gold watch which Alex's father had given him on his sixteenth birthday.

"You mind, Captain," John Martin whispered later, as Alex lay in his allotted space on the crowded floor, his head and body throbbing with pain. "I'll put in my record what they done to you."

> *Sunday, 22nd. We drawed ¾ lb of pork, 1 gil of peas. Such hardness and sickness prevail. Snow today. Sunday gone and no comfort. Deaths multiply . . .*

"Shut the Jew up!" someone had cried.

But Israel could not be silenced in his long delirium of that Sunday. If Percy had ordered a surgeon to North Church, as Alex believed, something had prevented his coming. The bullet sting, as simple as a thorn scratch, had festered. They'd treated it as best they knew, and for days it seemed that it would heal. The arm stiffened slowly. The pain increased steadily. There was a morning when it swelled and an evening when it receded. Then it began to swell enormously while Israel watched it patiently, as if it did not belong to him. Finally, on that Sunday morning, he became delirious. A Jew from Lancaster among the captives said that he talked in Yiddish and that he seemed to think he was at home with his family. Around dusk he grew still. Alex, sitting beside him, heard his harsh breathing stop a couple of hours later. In the morning Alex and Macaroni Jack carried out his body under guard and dropped it in the open lime pit behind the church where all the dead were thrown.

> *Thursday, Decr. 26th. Terrible storm as ever I seen. I feel poorly. Drawed bisd. More gone to the prison ships today. Another listed in the King's service . . .*

"I *got* to, Captain March," Macaroni Jack had whispered. "It ain't to stay, I swear to Christ. It's only till I can escape and join up with *us* again. Somebody must've talked."

Alex stared at him impassively. "Nobody has talked, Sergeant *Monroney.*"

"They *must*'ve." Macaroni Jack's hollowed eyes glittered with fear. "That Devore knows something. I can tell the way he looks at me. And today that captain who come in and looked at me with Devore, *he* knows me. He's Ganston of the 47th. He knows me well. Say you understand why I *got* to do it, sir."

You might have said that you understood he believed he was acting reasonably, Alex told himself later. But at the time he could not think or say anything except "Traitor!"

And then Sergeant Macaroni Jack Maloney was gone.

Saturday, 28th. Several more broke out with the pox. Drawed bisd. High winds & verry cold. The officers granted parole of the city today . . .

Their purpose was obvious: Separate the officers from the men "from sun to sun" and then both groups would more easily see the light of royal reason.

He walked the wind-swept streets, wondering how he could obtain money to buy food for himself and as many of the men as possible. The prices were outrageous. Fresh meat a shilling a pound, cheese two shillings, butter three shillings, turnips and potatoes a shilling a half-peck, milk 15 coppers a quart.

On lower Broadway he saw a sign in a window CLERK SOUGHT. So he walked into the counting room of Thomas Ridgeway & Son, Merchants —and into the second count of the indictment.

Why, they demanded much later, didn't you introduce yourself as Timothy Murdoch's son-in-law? Ridgeway would have communicated instantly and your exchange would have been expedited.

They refused to understand the reasonableness with which he acted. Ridgeway was a Tory merchant, an enemy, who was willing enough to hire a qualified rebel prisoner for the clerking job he needed to fill. And Alex was willing enough to work for an enemy in order to obtain the food and oddments of clothing which he took to his starving, shivering men in North Church each night.

Finally, being so intent on acting reasonably, he had committed in the minds of the Accusers the crowning folly.

Although constantly weak and cold and frequently lightheaded, he believed that he retained a legal sense. The terms of his parole were that he could go about the city in the daylight hours as long as he returned to the stinking warren of North Church at nightfall. And those were the only terms. When Devore recited them to the officers, he did not say that they were forbidden to communicate with their army.

Of course, when the terms were announced, everyone believed that the army had practically ceased to exist. And then, as he copied letters and bills of lading in Thomas Ridgeway's counting house that January, he learned with amazement that the army did indeed still exist. It not only existed; it had marched and struck at Trenton and again at Princeton; it had retaken all of Jersey, except Amboy and Brunswick, and now was wintered within the protective arms of the Morristown hills.

The army was there, waiting, only twenty-five miles away, while he sat here computing the money that Thomas Ridgeway was making in his dealings with the enemy. The army could do nothing for Alex, but he told himself that possibly he still could do something for it. He watched and he listened.

Item: The British had five thousand men around Brunswick and five thousand more at Amboy instead of the seven thousand they claimed at each place. *Item:* The British knew that inadequate American forces guarded the supplies and magazines at Peekskill. *Item:* Scarcity of forage in and around New York had reduced the enemy to a walking army for six months to come.

In retrospect he realized the pathetic nature of the intelligence he gleaned. Jersey was said to be such a vast camp of spies that the General and his staff must have possessed the information he painstakingly ferreted. But he was incapable of realizing it at the time. He was only capable of realizing that he must do something to vindicate his continued existence. Simply to obtain fresh meat and bread to swell the impossible rations was not enough.

Like every innocent who turned to spying, he believed that he was acting with extraordinary shrewdness. He desired a contact, someone who would communicate his information to the army. If he had not been so weak from hunger and cold, would he have acted so naïvely? He desired a contact, and behold, quite soon, he had one as magically as if his imagination had conjured him.

The fellow was vaguely familiar the first time he grinned and nodded when Alex passed him on Broadway. That afternoon he was lounging outside Ridgeway's as Alex left the office. He followed Alex, and then he was walking beside him.

"Afternoon, Mr. March," he muttered. "Don't pause. Just walk along. D'you remember me?"

Alex stared at him. "No."

"D'you remember the Harp and Crown nigh Bristol Ferry more'n three years ago? Remember the fat man and his bride and—"

"Yes!" Alex halted.

"Don't pause, Mr. March, don't pause. Let's turn in at the tavern yonder and I'll buy us a tot of rum."

"I recall the incident," Alex said, "but your name eludes me."

"The name is Young, Mr. March, but don't repeat it."

Young ordered rum in the tavern and whispered that he knew he could trust Alex. Indeed he could, Alex told him. Young said that he'd been sent over from Jersey to collect information; did Alex have any word to send anyone?

Not a word, he replied, vastly pleased with his shrewdness. Young seemed disappointed. Information was hard to come by, he said. It must be, Alex agreed, and asked what he'd been doing. Young described service on a privateer and at the forts on the lower Delaware.

"And now?" Alex asked with an innocent expression.

Young looked about furtively, then drew a tiny paper cylinder from a boot top and slipped it under the table to Alex. The paper, signed by General Greene, described him as an agent of the cause of liberty.

"If'n I'm caught," said Young, "I just swaller the paper. I practiced it. You get any information, Mr. March, I'll be here at this tavern this hour for seven more days."

Each afternoon of the next four days, as he returned to North Church, Alex glanced into the tavern. Young was always there, always alone. Studying him with what he felt was a newly developed shrewdness, Alex began to trust him.

On the fifth day, a Saturday, Alex walked into the tavern, sat down opposite Young, and whispered his information. Didn't he, Young asked in a disappointed tone, have a document? Of course not, Alex growled; the information was a simple matter for him to remember. He wished Young good luck and walked back to North Church.

An hour after dark the guard called out his name and marched him to the foul-smelling room in the adjoining house which Devore called his office. Devore, drunk, roared that he was a spy. He denied it. William Young, his gaze wavering, stepped from the shadows and repeated the information that Alex had given him. He was stripped and given fifty lashes by the sergeant of the guard before he fainted.

Later he was marched to the Liberty Street Sugar House and thrown into a tiny dark cell where he lay without food or water until Monday morning. Rats ran over him while he lay there and he was afraid to fall asleep. Methodically he lived through past days, as Israel had taught him. When his memory arrived exhaustedly at the first days of his capture, he remembered seeing Young talking with British soldiers. He cursed the wishful thinking that had made him fail to remember the informer.

After a summary trial conducted by a British major on Monday, Alex heard his sentence dimly:

"The court finds the prisoner guilty as charged. The court sentences the prisoner to be hanged by the neck until dead at eight o'clock tomorrow morning, and may God have mercy on his soul."

In imagination he died that night as he lay sleeplessly in a cell. At dawn imagination resuscitated him with the reasonable argument that it soon would be over and he would not have to endure destruction again.

He was led out to the Sugar House gallows in the cold, gray morning. The usual throng had gathered for the excitement of an execution. The major stepped forward and asked the prisoner if he had any last words. The age expected oratory of its condemned, he knew. But he was suddenly tired of his—or any—age; now, by the slightest effort of the imagination, he welcomed his destruction.

He shook his head and started on. The major placed a detaining hand on his arm and they stared each at the other. The major's gaze faltered and he looked beyond Alex toward the oblong tunnel entrance to the Sugar House.

Then Alex knew what would happen, even though the emissary had not yet appeared. He would be reprieved—not as a result of justice, but as a result of reasonableness. As it had seemed reasonable to him not to give Young a document, so it seemed reasonable to the major that he would have, had he actually been guilty. The major, knowing how men acted in his age, had waited to hear him speak the truth on the gallows. The major respected truth. But the only truth was that he had spied and he had lied and, by persisting in his lie to the very end, he had caused the major to believe that he'd finally found out the truth.

A sudden sense of guilt made him open his mouth. But he could not utter even a whisper of truth as an officer strode from the Sugar House waving a rolled paper.

He had died once from fear of the gallows as he waited in a dark Sugar House cell. He had died next of guilt over his lie at the foot of the gallows. Again, he had died of an ordinary human disease in the black hole of the prison ship *Grosvenor* in Turtle Bay when the smallpox blackened and pitted his face and body.

In each renascence he was more familiar with death. Yet he was not stronger as a result, he thought during that warm Philadelphia spring. The familiarity that allegedly bred contempt did not apply to familiarity with death. Rather, intimate knowledge of it weakened one's will and slacked the desire to participate in the febrile human vanities of ambition, growth and change. Death was a positive case of ignorance being bliss.

One morning, meditating on Philly's blissful ignorance, he said to her, "I'm sorry about everything that has happened since I was—oh, nineteen years old."

"Well, world a-wonder!" she exclaimed. "You certainly make a body look forward to growing old." She flung back the window curtains. "What a beautiful morning. It's good just to be alive."

Yes, that much was true, he thought. He had not really wanted to be destroyed after all.

She turned from the window, arms akimbo. "Isn't it?"

He nodded slowly.

"Then *say* it!" she cried.

"Yes," he said, and grinned at her.

XXVIII

ON THE afternoon in May when they had expected Alex to arrive, Mrs. Munger had voluntarily assumed a lookout post at a front second-floor window. Kathy twisted her fingers and stared at the clock. Philly knitted at a stocking. Timothy Murdoch slowly paced the parlor.

At ten minutes after three he said, "I've missed my dinner."

"For heaven's sake, Papa!" Kathy clenched her hands and lowered her voice. "It isn't necessary for you to wait."

"Of course it is," he said stoically. "I'm deeply concerned about his welfare—and deeply involved in the whole matter, you must admit. The post from Barnaby in Elizabethtown could have been misleading. But I *have* sent the coach to Bristol to meet them, and from yesterday's post we know that this afternoon . . ."

No matter what the subject under discussion for the past month, he invariably dragged in the fact that he now owned a *coach*. Since he let her ride in it, however, Kathy forgave him his pride. After all, he had succeeded in arranging Alex's release after everyone else had failed. When Alex took her in his arms, she would have to give credit to Papa for working the miracle of his return.

She believed that she had lain awake all last night thinking about Alex. The letter to Murdoch from Barnaby Falco, reporting the successful accomplishment of his mission, had said that Alex was "not in the best of health" after his imprisonment. But that was to be expected, she thought. Once he had returned, she would *love* him back to the best of health. She realized that there had been times in the past winter when she had not expected him ever to return. Now, unable to put the thought from her mind, she felt guilty that she could have dismissed his passing so casually. Now, she carefully told herself, she must overcome the notion that she was expected to love a stranger. Alex was the one returning. Alex, Alex, Alex, she repeated to herself.

Upstairs Mrs. Munger suddenly shrieked, "It's him!"

Kathy leaped toward the hall door. Although she moved quickly, Philly was ahead of her; and then Philly stepped aside and let her pass.

She stood on the porch staring at her father's coach approaching along

Fourth Street. Billy sat on the box, his new livery covered with dust; beside him rode Sammy, the matching Negro slave Murdoch had bought to serve as footman in his new equipage. Barnaby Falco thrust his long pale face out a window and failed to smile as the coach halted before the house and Billy and Sammy leaped down.

She felt Philly's hand urging her down the path to the coach, but she seemed unable to move. Sammy opened the door. She heard Mrs. Munger breathing hoarsely in the hall. Then Barnaby backed out of the coach, supporting something, and Sammy reached inside to help him.

She dimly heard her low exclamation of horror as Barnaby and Sammy lifted a scarecrow in loose rags to the ground. It could not be—

"Alex!" Philly ran down the path toward him.

He turned, and she thought that it could not possibly be he. With growing horror she saw that his emaciated, lined face was pitted with pockmarks.

"Great God in heaven," murmured Timothy Murdoch.

Tears sprang to her eyes as Kathy went down the path to the coach.

The stranger's lips curled back on yellowed teeth in an attempted smile. "Philly, good afternoon."

"Alex!" Closing her eyes so that she would not have to see his face, Kathy clutched him to her, thinking, It isn't he, it's something of skin and bones that never belonged to me. He even smelled badly, like something left long in an enclosed place. "My darling," she said, hoping that if she said it she would believe it.

"Kathy, love." Something touched her cheek and she realized that he had kissed her.

She opened her eyes, but she could not bring herself to look directly at his face. "It's so good to have you back, darling."

"Why, yes." The voice was not too weak to express his old sense of irony. "It's good to return a victorious hero." He looked beyond her. "Mr. Murdoch, sir, good afternoon. And thanks are in order to you and Barnaby, he's given me to understand. Thanks that I'm here at all, that is, if this really be I and—"

"Alex." Murdoch extended his right hand and tears filled his eyes.

Kathy understood his tears. He pitied Alex, but he pitied her and himself more. It was awful. He had a new coach, one of the finest in Philadelphia, with matching grays and matching liveried slaves, that came now at his bidding and deposited on her doorstep a—a scarred and monstrous gray spider—

"Oh, Alex!" Ashamed of herself, ashamed of her father, she dashed a hand across her eyes.

He was looking at her strangely. Philly flashed her a dark glance and said, "It's really home you are, Alex, and we all thank God."

Then Mrs. Munger rushed to him, babbling his name and asking news of Macaroni Jack.

"I presume he's in the best of health, Mrs. Munger." His tone was weary. "He joined the enemy several months ago."

Mrs. Munger stared at him, stunned. Her mouth worked and at last she said, "But he's *alive.*"

"And with the enemy." Alex started up the path and Philly caught his arm to support him.

Murdoch and Barnaby looked at one another and then at Kathy.

"Billy," Murdoch said, "drive and fetch Dr. Rush here. Tell him Mr. Murdoch requests him to attend Mr. March. Sammy, assist Mr. March to his room." He scowled at a passing small boy who had paused and was staring with wide eyes at the strange scarecrow being helped into the house. "Scat!" he said fiercely and the boy ran.

In the hall Kathy said, "Dear heart, you'd best lie down in your room and . . ." Her voice trailed off. *Dear heart!* The words rang hollowly to her, and they must to him, for he gripped the newel post and stared at her oddly.

"And we'll bring you what you'd like to eat," Philly said quickly. "You say what you'd like and—"

"I'd like to stroll through my house and look at the rooms." His lips curled back again. "A sentimental notion—"

"It's been a grueling journey for you," Murdoch said, "though I trust the *coach* was comfortable. My poor fellow, you'd best lie down. Sammy will assist you."

Alex looked at Kathy, then turned silently and started up the stairs with Sammy supporting him. When he had climbed three steps he looked back and said, "The coach was most comfortable, sir. It's a handsome coach. Thank you for sending it to Bristol for me."

Kathy turned into the parlor. The room seemed to swing wildly. She wondered vaguely if she were going to faint, and then she knew that she wasn't. She was simply walking about the room swiftly, as if looking for something. When her father and Barnaby stepped in, she swung out through the back parlor and found herself in the kitchen where Mrs. Munger sat crying while Philly busily fixed a tray.

She said something inane and Philly looked at her sternly. "I'm surprised to find you here, Kathy. You should be upstairs helping *him* get to bed."

"Sammy can undress him and put him—"

"By all means let the *slave* do it, Kathy. By all means don't attend your *man.*"

The unexpected sarcasm, in a tone she never had heard Philly use before, made her recoil. She flung out of the kitchen and through the hall. When she strode into the parlor, Barnaby and Murdoch stopped talking. She could not bear their looking at her so. Turning, she slowly climbed the stairs. The door to *their* room, as she had thought of it last night, was closed. Now it was *his* room, and that left her—where? She wandered from room to room, picking up things and putting them down, until there was nowhere to go except to the closed door of *his* room.

When she finally tapped on the door, his voice sounded surprisingly cheerful. "Kathy?"

She opened the door and caught her breath. He sat on the edge of the bed, his back to her, while Sammy gathered up his rags. In a shaft of sunlight from a window the skin stretched tightly over his bones appeared a mottled blue. She closed her eyes and opened them quickly and saw that his back was a mass of sores and scars. She leaned against the door, clutching the knob with both hands.

"Good boy, Sammy," he said, not looking around at her. "Now pray bring me barrels of hot water and soap. I *stink*. And burn that clothing, Sammy. Burn it."

Sammy grinned and hurried out with the rags and old boots as she took a step into the room.

"Poor Kathy," he said.

She took another step toward him. "Why do you say that?" she asked in a remote voice.

"I looked at myself in the mirror. The first time I'd seen myself in—a long time. And, lo, I was not myself but someone else. I remind me of a maggot, Kathy. And while I have tremendous respect for maggots, I know that you do not."

"Oh, Alex!" Raising her hands to her eyes, she dropped down on the opposite side of the bed from him and sobbed uncontrollably.

After a while she heard him moving, and then he stroked her hair with a hard, dry, clawlike hand. She dimly saw him standing beside her, clutching a blanket with which he tried to cover his foul-smelling, unsightly body. But the blanket could not hide his pock-scarred face and filthy feet and scabrous, wasted legs.

"I'm sorry, Alex." She closed her eyes.

"It's *I* who's sorry, Kathy, to expose you so to—to me. There should be a place where one could go and either die or get well without—without tormenting others."

Angry suddenly—at him, at herself, at the whole pointless chaos of the times that created such unnecessary horror—she cried, *"Why* did this happen to you? Why? Why?"

"Kathy." He swayed and supported himself against the bed. "It's not a time for asking why. It's a time for a man like Sammy who never thinks of asking why but simply totes rags and fetches hot water and allows that with luck—and never asking *why*—we'll all endure. Now go downstairs, Kathy, and see me sparingly until some day when I'm—"

"But—"

"Go, Kathy. Please."

She went downstairs quickly, seeking a target for her burning anger. She believed she found it in the kitchen where Philly was heating water and a beef stew on the stove while trying to help Sammy lift the big bathing tub from the storage closet.

"He's got to bathe before he eats," Kathy snapped, "and so you needn't be so hasty with that—"

"And you"—Philly whirled on her—"needn't be so hasty in venting your rage on the first one comes to hand."

"Get out of my kitchen!" Kathy cried.

"I'd gladly get out of your kitchen, Mistress March, if'n I thought you could git anything out of hit yourself for your *man* up thar." Philly advanced on her, eyes blazing. "There've been times I've knowed—knew —known you needed a good whacking, but never such a time as this."

Kathy fled along the hall and into the parlor where her father and Barnaby sat, holding glasses of brandy and talking in low tones.

"Why," she cried at Barnaby, "didn't you see that he had a place to bathe and change along the way after he was released. Why—"

"Kathy!" Murdoch shouted. "Sit down!"

She sank into a chair, thinking numbly that Papa never had shouted at her so before. Barnaby had nervously spilled brandy on his dusty waistcoat and entangled his long legs while trying both to rise and remain seated at the same time.

"Here." Murdoch poured brandy into a glass and thrust it at her. "Drink it."

She sipped the brandy and grimaced.

"Drink it! God knows we all could stand a bottle of brandy."

She drank again and decided that she was tired of bursting into tears. But she could not be ordered into silence like a child.

"How could the British be so cruel as to do to anyone what they did to him?"

Murdoch poured himself more brandy, then went to the door and called Philly.

She stepped into the parlor, face flushed and sleeves rolled up, as if for battle. Barnaby leaped to his feet and smiled at her.

"Pray close the door, Philly," Murdoch said, "and be seated. Since I know you'll want to help Kathy with our—problem, I want you to hear this too. It will help you understand the—er, obstinacy of—what we're confronted with."

Philly closed the door, folded her arms, and said, "I'll stand, thank you. There's things on the fire and Mrs. Munger ain't a mite of use today."

"Alex arrived in this condition," Murdoch said, "because there was no room at any inn along the way."

"In Brunswick," Barnaby said, "we were let sleep on the floor of an inn. He was deathly ill when released near Elizabethtown and he hasn't been able to hold much on his stomach. No one would give facilities for decent—excuse the word—bathing because they thought he had some bad disease, I reckon. That's why he arrived in this condition, Miss Kathy. I did my best and I hope you'll excuse my own condition. But travel in these times—"

"Yes." Murdoch sniffed his brandy. "Barnaby has done very well." He looked at Kathy and Philly. "I got him the proper exchange papers and pass—after no little trouble, I confess. But *he* made the journey and returned with Alex." He sipped his brandy and frowned. "The point I wish to make is that it wasn't *necessary* for Alex to be a prisoner so long or to suffer what he did."

"Not necessary?" Kathy asked.

"Tell 'em, Barnaby."

Barnaby crossed his legs and folded his arms. "Honored by Mr. Murdoch's confidence and as an aid to him in his transactions, I have established solid contacts in New York—for business purposes of Mr. Murdoch only, you understand." He sighed. "From these valuable contacts I learned that Mr. Alex behaved with—uh—if I may say so, unpardonable folly when a prisoner."

Philly frowned at him. "What did he do, Mr. Barnaby? Please out with it, I don't want the stew to burn."

"First of all," Barnaby said gravely, "I was informed by his jailer, Mr. Devore, he was offered his freedom to return home last December if he would not bear arms against the Crown again."

Kathy's glass trembled in her hand. She heard Barnaby say that Alex had refused this magnanimous offer made by no less a personage than Earl Percy himself. He didn't want to come back to me, she thought dully.

"In the general parole of officers soon afterward he went to the firm of Thomas Ridgeway. He found employment there and he *never* mentioned that he was Mr. Murdoch's son-in-law. Can you imagine? Ridgeway, one of our most esteemed merchants, respecting Mr. Murdoch so greatly, would have . . ."

Papa was talking again, but she didn't want to listen to him.

". . . using his money to spend on food for other prisoners," Barnaby was saying. "But that was not *all*." He leaned forward and lowered his voice. "He also took to spying. Apprehended, he was taken to the very foot of the gallows, and there given amnesty because of the magnanimity of the British. He was taken to the prison ship *Grosvenor* and continued to be—if you will excuse me—*truculent* against authority . . ."

His voice, running on and on, was like a buzzing in Kathy's ears. None of the rest of it mattered now. All that mattered had been said, she thought. He did not want to return to me when he had the chance.

After she had curbed her anger at him and subdued the feeling that he no longer loved her, she'd sit with him for a couple of hours a day and chat about the places she went and people she met with Papa. It was not particularly pleasant, for he talked little and did not seem much interested in what she said, but it made her feel that she was being a good wife. Sometimes she thought that if he would stay in his room long enough, lying in bed or sitting by the window, the stranger in him would leave and gay, exuberant Alex return.

She had to admit that Philly found ways to stimulate his appetite and get him to eat more than he ever had. He gained in weight; an ointment Dr. Rush prescribed and Philly applied did wonders for his sores. They would go in time, she knew, though he would bear his pockmarks to the grave. But although Dr. Rush insisted that his health was improving steadily, his spirits remained apathetic.

Nothing seemed to interest him much except the dull, old books in which he buried his nose. On the other hand, she was delighted to observe that he did not appear interested in the progress of the war or what Congress was doing. Surely, she thought, he was finished with the army and politics. Some day he would resume practicing law and concentrate on making money. And then, surely, life would be better than it ever had been for them.

Yet he might have stayed in his room forever if Philly had not coaxed and teased and goaded him into coming downstairs and, eventually, going out to her little back-yard garden to sit in the sun. Visitors came at the urging of Philly and Dr. Rush. Alex treated them politely, but he answered all questions about his imprisonment evasively and he seemed to tire of conversation quickly. For reasons Kathy could not understand his visitors irritated her. His mother was too loud, John and Martha Tout too dull, and Tom too inquisitive about the army. Joseph Reed, who had been promoted to Brigadier General in May and had absented himself from the army again, was too immersed in politics. Dick Peters, General Mifflin, Sally Mifflin, Papa himself . . . As she watched and listened to the stream of visitors who came and went, she began to think that all were too intent on *something*.

"What's wrong with people?" she asked him one day early in July as she sat in the garden with him after John Adams had visited briefly.

Alex looked at her, his eyes suddenly alive—as they used to be, she thought. He smiled; his teeth were white again, she observed, and he no longer resembled a death's head when he smiled.

"That's an interesting question, Kathy. Next to 'what's wrong with myself?' it's the most interesting question I know. Were you thinking of John Adams?"

"Of him and nearly everybody who comes to call. They're all so—intent on something."

"You surprise and delight me, Kathy. It's life they're so intent on. Getting and begetting. I'm surprised that you, of all people, don't recognize and enjoy it. Have I infected you with my malady that you no longer recognize and enjoy?"

"Your malady?" She frowned at him. "You never speak plainly any more. What is your malady?"

"Perhaps it is that I don't speak plainly to you." He smiled again. "Actually, Kathy, my malady is that while I still recognize life, I just can't seem to savor it any more. I'm as sated and glutted with it as Catiline, even though I have not found an Aurelia Orestilla."

"Speak plainly," she said sharply. "I never heard of Aurelia Orestilla."

"She was a celebrated whore of Rome such as we—fortunately or unfortunately—lack in Philadelphia at the present time. Sallust remarked severely of her that 'No good man, at any time of her life, commended anything but her beauty.' "

Kathy eyed him searchingly, wondering what he meant.

"But I'm in antiquity again," he said drily. "My beguiling escape from where I find myself. We just found ourselves with John Adams. I thought that you liked him better than you used to."

"I do."

"Fortunate Kathy. You don't suffer from my malady after all. For I like John Adams less than I once did. He did not perceive the change in me because his perceptions are not as keen as they used to be, I noted. But I also noted that he still is extremely observant of himself. Before long he will observe that he likes me less than he once did. He won't call again. There's nothing for him to gain in talking with me."

"You mystify me," she said.

"I mystify myself. And John Adams mystifies me even more. Once I thought he was the heart and soul of the Revolution. But . . ."

"Revolution?" She frowned. "I don't like that word. If you mean this rebellion—"

"But rebellion no longer describes it, Kathy. The British scarcely are important now to what's happening here. It's a Revolution—nearly everywhere in nearly everyone, and essentially it hasn't much to do with firelocks and parades. There's a *revulsion* with things as they are and a murky *evolving* toward something different. People seem to breathe it in the air and to some it's as debilitating as it is invigorating to others. I saw an example of it only this morning. An old street sweeper in ticken breeches sweeping the gutter with his twig broom. I've glimpsed him a hundred times in years past, an old man, nameless, as gray as the dust he sweeps, another cipher in time's ledger. The foreman, that Methodist fellow— Mirkin I believe his name was when last I knew the politics of this ward— came along and expostulated with him over something. I don't know what it was about. Perhaps a bit of unswept manure. Perhaps the nature of the cosmos. Bang!" Alex clapped his hands together.

"This nameless, old, gray cipher who has accepted expostulation and correction all his days, docilely and submissively, whacked down his broom on the cobbles. Split it clean in two and walked off the job. The Methodist foreman—Mirkin—gaped after him, dumfounded, as if the world had split open at his feet and the cipher had multiplied into a thousand numerals. As, indeed, it had. It couldn't have happened five or even two years ago. It can only happen now. That is the Revolution. I got the window open as fast as I could and leaned out and shouted after the old man, 'Bravo! Bravo!' He was too angry and the foreman too stunned to hear me. Such is the lot of an observer."

He didn't make any sense, she thought wearily. He must be insane to open the window and shout like that. If the Sorrels across the street or the Wickershams next door had seen him, they'd know that he was mad.

"I chatter on today," he said, smiling at her. "Our subject was John Adams, wasn't it? Once he was the heart of the Revolution, I said. But today I observed that his heart is not very large. It's quite a small heart, capable of little more than supplying blood to a large and well-equipped brain. You heard our discussion of the *democratic* spirit."

"I wasn't paying close attention." She looked away, wondering how to still his talking after having tried so often to make him talk.

He pursed his lips at her and then he smiled. "I heard with astonishment that he is opposed to it—actually opposed. John Adams' petulant lips and pendant nose told me this afternoon that he's on his way to becoming an autocrat. Power, power, man's perpetual-motion machine. Give him a sword and he'd fancy himself a general. You heard that he fancies himself a more experienced soldier than I." He grimaced. "And while casting the mote out of John's eye may I not forget the beam of jealousy in my own. I really know only this: Some day, if both of us live long enough, I shall cast a vote against John Adams—provided he has not disenfranchised me of my right to vote."

It occurred to her suddenly that he was talking in the way he used to. She did not exactly understand him, but then she never had. Could it be that he had not changed so vastly in his absence while she somehow had changed and so had failed to recognize him when he came home?

"Alex," she said in a low voice, "you've never told me about your imprisonment and how you felt and what you did."

He looked at her gravely. "But you have told me all about it, Kathy, and objected strenuously to how I felt and what I did."

She lowered her head and plucked at the hem of a sleeve. "I'm sorry."

"And I am sorry that I acted in a way you couldn't understand."

"But can't you see?" she cried. "Don't you understand how I felt to hear that you refused to come back to me when you could have?"

"I didn't think the terms were honorable, Kathy. Though I think I knew more about honor then than I do now. For I went on to spy, to lie, to die a thousand times—and still to exist."

"At the gallows"—her voice was almost inaudible—"what did you think?"

"That I did not want to die."

"And you thought of me?"

"Of course."

"And how you'd miss me?"

"Yes."

Her eyes dimmed with tears. She blinked them away and saw him looking at her dry-eyed. "Dear Alex." Why didn't he reach out and touch her? "Alex, what—what are you going to do now that you're getting better?"

"Do?" He rubbed his chin. "I hadn't thought much about *doing*. I've mainly thought about *being*. I've asked myself, What shall I be? And I've thought that I'd prefer to be an observer. Some day, if I ever summon the energy, which I'm sure I won't, I might write a history of my times. *Follies and Vanities of the Revolution* by a Philadelphia Observer. But if we win, no one would print it because everyone will be very pious about our little war. Nearly everyone will decide it was an Act of God abetted by God-directed men. You've probably noticed, or maybe you haven't, that as a people we're forever falling back on piety because it saves us the necessity of *thinking*."

"You mean"—she leaned toward him intently—"you aren't going back to the army?"

"I rather think not. I think the army can bumble along without me."

Thank God, she thought, clapping her hands together. "And politics?"

"I rather think not. It's impossible to remain long in politics and observe much except one's own increasing sense of vanity."

Gripping his arms, she kissed him on the cheek. The fact that it was pock-marked really didn't matter. "Thank God."

"Beware of piety." He smiled. "Remember, *think*."

"Please—"

"I'm sorry, Kathy. You are a beautiful thing."

"And you love me?"

"And I love you."

"And I love you," she whispered. "We've been apart too long. May I come back to *our* room tonight?"

"Of course." He looked at her quizzically until she blushed.

"*You* should ask *me*." She added quickly, "But you've been ill and—and now you're all better and everything is turning out happily. Everything will be better than it ever has been."

But it was not.

He lacked his old ardor in making love to her. She lay awake for hours afterward, unsatisfied, telling herself that he really loved her, that soon everything would be better than it ever had been.

XXIX

ALEX agreed with Dr. Rush that his health was restored. He did not complain or ail. But neither did he *do* anything except read and stroll about the city.

He troubled Philly greatly. She realized that Kathy had hurt him by her refusal to understand his bravery and patriotism in prison and by her revulsion at his physical condition when he returned home. Moreover, Kathy refused to understand why he disliked Timothy Murdoch and the social life she continued to lead. When, in time, Kathy tried to make amends in little ways, Alex rebuffed her. Then Philly was almost as annoyed with him as she had been with Kathy.

Once, as she sat in the garden while he read aloud to her, two pigeons lighted on the grass nearby. The male, cooing, strutted toward the female.

She turned from him, without coyness, her yellow eyes angry. He strolled away and fed indifferently on the grass.

Alex stopped reading and watched the pigeons. At last he said, "Yesterday I saw them fall in love. Today they are falling out of love. It's easy to do something about falling in love. But what do you do about falling out of love, Philly?"

"There's a difference between pigeons and mortals," she replied, vaguely alarmed by what he'd said. "Mortals have brains that let them reason and act sensibly."

"Some mortals do," he said and resumed reading.

It was incredible to her that Kathy could not constantly love him tenderly, devotedly, passionately. Sometimes, before she cut short wild fancies, she could imagine herself falling in love with him if they had met in some idyllic past when he was single and she— What nonsense! She must never forget who she was: born a woodsy, growing a bound girl, free now, but forever a servant to the high and the mighty. Lord, always let them be worthy of their station, she'd think. As he is. Yes, and as Kathy is too, despite her attitudes sometimes.

It also was incredible to her that he could not love Kathy tenderly, devotedly, passionately. She was so beautiful. There was so much good in her that only needed to be sorted out and put in order once in a while, like the beautiful, useful objects in the escritoire drawer. If only he would take more pains and show more patience with her, she would prove to be a tender, devoted, loving wife.

But what could a third mortal do about two others falling out of love?

They did not really need her now that he was well again, she believed. Curiously, however, both seemed to depend on her more than ever. Often they communicated through her, as if she were the only interpreter who understood their different languages. It was a strain.

In mid-July they decided to go to the country for relief from the humid heat. After a good deal of arguing they finally agreed to spend two weeks at the Murdoch farm and two weeks at the March farm. And they insisted that Philly come with them.

They rode out from Philadelphia on a bright, hot morning, crowding themselves with valises and boxes into a two-horse chaise which Alex had hired. Philly closed her eyes and listened to the whir of wheels, the creak of shafts and leather, the spanking of hoofs on the dusty road. Cicadas rasped and the land smelled sweetly of warm grass and clover under the burning sun. Opening her eyes slightly, she imagined that she saw the army moving far off in the summer haze.

Although she was constantly preoccupied with Alex and Kathy, she was forever thinking of the army. It held a fascination for her that she could not exactly understand. Perhaps it began when Micah marched away to join it. These days she thought of Micah less as the person she had known than of him as a part of the army. In reason she knew that the army was composed of many individuals in many units scattered in many places. But she did not like to think of it so. She chose, rather, to visualize it as one great, strong, indivisible force, a benign and powerful serpent curling over rivers and curving around hills—striking, lashing, recoiling, always resilient and never breaking as it sought to destroy *them,* the cruel and remorseless enemy of *us.*

As best she could, she'd talked to Alex about the army in the past weeks. She'd bought a little map of the northern colonies at Marshall's and on it she traced the news and rumors she read in the papers and sidewalk bulletins. Her map lacked roads, but on its surface she saw the tracks of the strong, benign serpent.

Occasionally she came close to quarreling with Alex over news about the progress of the war. He confused her. When the *Pennsylvania Packet* reported that the army had gone *there,* he'd study her map and ask (pointing) why didn't it go *here?* And then, when she was prepared to follow his logic, he'd say it couldn't have because it probably didn't know what was happening *yonder* (pointing to some other place she hadn't thought of). Taking heart in the belief that Alex must agree the General was a great and wise man, she'd extol his wisdom in having led the army *there,* as reported. But invariably Alex would make her despair by shaking his head glumly. The General did the very best he knew how with what he had, Alex would say; but he was not an inspired general, he was only a tenacious general.

At the Murdoch farm she finally lost her temper with him.

The farm was a disappointment to her that summer. Her notion that she would spend some time with Tom and "be a sister" to him turned out to be foolish. He neither needed nor wanted a sister; he was thirteen years old now and big and strong for his age. Such a person as David Reppelthwaite was far more important and interesting to him than a nineteen-year-old sister who came from the city for a couple of weeks.

Reppelthwaite, a new hand John Tout had hired through the fall harvest, was always willing to describe how he'd served with the militia for eight weeks following the Battle of Trenton. To Philly it was a thrilling story she never tired of hearing.

One day when Alex and Kathy were playing draughts in the summerhouse and Reppelthwaite and Tom were scything grass nearby, Philly thought it might interest Alex to hear about the Battle of Princeton from one who had fought in it. Perhaps it might even help inspire him to return to the army.

Reppelthwaite was glad to stop work and tell of his days of military glory. How he'd joined the army after it crossed the Delaware again following its victory at Trenton. How the General led them over the river once more and they found themselves penned between Assunpink Creek and the Delaware at Trenton on the night of January second.

Cornwallis and his army waited across the Creek to destroy them in the morning. But someone had discovered a road that led *around* the enemy and north to Princeton, and, leaving their fires lighted, they stole away in the cold night. Dawn found them outside Princeton where they clashed with a body of British troops who made them break and run at first. Reppelthwaite saw Mercer, the commander of his brigade, bayoneted to death. And then the General galloped up and rallied them and led them straight at the enemy.

It was a glorious victory. But they dared not linger in Princeton, for Cornwallis was coming up fast behind them. So they took the road north, with the British pursuing. They hoped to reach Brunswick, but they were too exhausted. At Kingston they took the Rocky Hill Road down the Millstone Valley and eventually reached safety in the hills around Morristown.

When Reppelthwaite had finished his story, he ducked his head to them and walked back to his scythe. Tom followed, waving his arms and killing British soldiers.

A cicada shrilled in the silence. It was hot summer, but Philly imagined that she had been enduring the cold of the past winter for a few minutes.

"What a wonderful thing the army did," she said.

Alex and Kathy looked at her expressionlessly, and then he said, "Yes."

"What a wonderful General he is."

Alex looked down at the draught board and up at her.

"That will long be argued," he said. "Certainly he's a brave general, his moral and physical courage unquestioned and often inspiring to others. But is he really wise? Certainly he's slow to learn. Although he seems to be patient in every other way, he often seems impatient of trying to learn. One could forgive him the mistakes of Long Island if he had profited by them and immediately got the army off Manhattan Island and kept it together instead of splitting it up and—"

"He *had* to stay in New York," Philly cried, "because the Congress told him to. I read that myself in—"

"The Congress!" Alex said contemptuously. "That body is in decline. It isn't what it was. It's more concerned these days with haggling with itself than prosecuting the war. When will the General learn that he can turn over in bed without consulting Congress by letter?"

"I say it's a *wonderful* thing he did." Her voice rose indignantly. "Going back over the Delaware—"

"And boxing his army in between the creek and the river on his second return to Trenton," he said.

"He *had* to go back over the river, Alex. If he didn't . . ."

"He had to go back because of the mistakes he began making on Long Island. But he didn't have to put his weak, largely green army in jeopardy by returning to Trenton. Joe Reed told me about it. He was there. He went scouting with a few light horse that night and found Assunpink Creek fordable a mile upstream. If Cornwallis had crossed there he'd have smashed the army into the Delaware and ended the war. The General left his flank dangling again, as so often before. 'Gloomy' is the way Reed described his mood when he found himself in a box again. Only luck—and the British—saved him once more. There's a military maxim that the stronger army shouldn't attack toward nightfall. The British army adores maxims and sound literary battles."

"But—"

"Please." He looked at her severely. "I respect your patriotism but look askance at your blind worship of the General as an infallible god of some kind. Provided he *had* to cross the river again and provided he *had* to be penned in as a result of unfortunate circumstances, it wasn't he who saw the way out of the trap."

"Then who was it?" Philly demanded.

"Reed says he honestly doesn't remember. He's racked his brains since and sometimes wondered if it were himself. It might well have been and he and all the others were too distraught to note it at the time. They met that night, Reed says, in St. Clair's headquarters at the house of a man named Douglass. They were desperate men, you must understand, who realized their predicament and didn't know how to get out of it. There was only one candle flickering on a table and they sat in the shadows, hacking and coughing and scratching themselves. They were exhausted, dirty, unshaven, Reed says. I can see it. I know how it was.

"Reed isn't even certain who all was there with the General. Greene, of course, and Knox and Mercer and St. Clair and Cadwalader and General Dickinson of New Jersey. He remembers them. The General didn't say much, as is his way, according to Reed. Someone would start to say something and then stop. Reed said he had to get a grip on himself to keep from dozing. Then several of them talked at once, arguing whether to stay where they were and fight in the morning or retreat down-river and try to cross over somewhere near Philadelphia. And then suddenly someone said, 'Let's take the new road through the woods to the enemy's rear,' and somebody chimed in, 'And get to Princeton and even on to

Brunswick.' And then someone said no, it was folly by all the maxims of warfare, and someone else said that by all the maxims of warfare they were dead geese so the *hell* with maxims. And there was a great babble, as always in these conferences born of desperation, from which there suddenly emerged a desperate unanimity. Of course the General was for it. The desperate unorthodox quality of the maneuver would appeal to him. And he executed it. They *did* it. That's what counts.

"Only afterwards, when people began to look on it as a stroke of genius, did anybody try to take credit for it. St. Clair claims it as *his* idea, but Reed gives him credit for no ideas except the glorification of St. Clair. Reed thinks it might have been Mercer, who was an unorthodox fighter. But Mercer died at Princeton and so can neither lay claim to the idea nor deny it. No one really is certain who said it except that it wasn't the General."

Kathy yawned and stretched.

"Well," Philly said, staring at him, "well—the General led them on their way."

"Of course." He frowned. "But let's not *deify*."

Her growing annoyance with him flared suddenly. "You try me, Alex," she cried, "with your eternal *picking* at things!"

Kathy, lowering her arms, laughed shrilly.

Important events that interested her were far from the County that summer. She read about them and heard them discussed and tried to follow them on her map.

Away in the north General Burgoyne was advancing from Canada by way of Lake Champlain and Lake George with the intention of cutting New England from the other colonies. Closer at hand the General with his main army was matching wits with the powerful army of Sir William Howe. In the Jersey high country the General marched and counter-marched, from the highlands of the Hudson to the Delaware.

It appeared logical that Sir William would go north to meet Burgoyne, Alex said. Instead, Sir William's forces marched west from Amboy in June, apparently bound for the Delaware and Philadelphia. The General hung on their flank, watching them but refusing to be drawn down from the high country into a full engagement. Apparently discouraged, the enemy turned back to Amboy, burning and pillaging as it went. The re-treat deluded the General and drew him out of the hills. Turning, the enemy struck, only to have the General withdraw his army safely into the hills.

Word came that Howe was embarking his troops at New York. And then came shocking word that St. Clair had abandoned Ticonderoga without firing a shot in its defense and that the way to Albany was open to Burgoyne. The General swung north and his army stood athwart the highlands of the Hudson, convinced now that Howe would advance up the river to join Burgoyne. Instead, Howe's great fleet weighed anchor and disappeared into the Atlantic.

Seeing that he had guessed wrong again and certain that Howe's destination was Philadelphia by way of Delaware Bay, the General rushed his army pell-mell across Jersey. But on the eastern banks of the Delaware, he became bemused by the notion that Howe had put to sea merely as a ruse to draw him from the Hudson. He waited, hesitating, his army dispersed all the way from Morristown down to Trenton and Coryell's Ferry and Howell's Ferry.

Then word was posted north that the enemy fleet had been sighted off the Delaware Capes, and the General quickly put his main army over the river.

Now the war, so long remote, came to the County.

On a bright morning early in August Philly heard at the March farm that the army was encamped at the Falls of the Schuylkill near Germantown.

"Mrs. March," she cried, "please lend me a horse. I want to ride to the Falls and see the army—and Micah."

"You'll have a horse," said Mrs. March, "but you must have company too. It ain't nowise safe for the likes of you to go riding into an army camp with your skirts all kilted up and showing those lovely limbs to them rude men. Alex had best go with you."

"I asked him, but he doesn't want to go. He said there's nothing beguiling to him about an encampment of the army."

Mrs. March scowled and muttered, "Beguile, beguile, beguile, by God! I think it's time he—" She tightened her lips and then winked at Philly. "I'll ride with you."

They cantered over the dusty roads to Germantown, their saddle panniers filled with sausage and bacon and cheese for the army. Around a curve of the Schuylkill they came to a hillside scorched by dead fires and scarred by open-trench latrines. The latrines stank in the heat; flies swarmed over refuse scattered on hard, rutted ground. An old man poked at rubbish with a stick.

"Where's the army?" Philly called to him.

"It went today." He spat. "And good riddance." Raising his stick slowly, he pointed it northeast. "Yonder."

Beyond the farthest line of hills there rose a cloud of yellow dust.

Mrs. March wrinkled her nose and said this was a dirty place. But Philly, unaccountably, felt close to tears.

As they rode home, Mrs. March broke a long silence. "Alex should get back to the army, Philly. It's the place for a man to be these days, dirty and poor though it be. I've had a mind to tell him so this long time, but I can't bring myself to say it. It ain't the place of a mother to speak so to a son who's been through what he has."

"I've been of the same mind, Mother March," Philly said.

Mrs. March looked at her. "You *speak* to him, Philly. Watching him these days and wondering what ails him, I know just one thing: You're the only one he'll listen to."

She tried to speak to him.

She had ample opportunity. The day after she and Mrs. March returned from the deserted camp on the Schuylkill, Timothy Murdoch sent word that he was at his farm for a few days and invited Kathy and Alex to join him. Alex, displaying a new interest in working the March farm, refused to leave. Kathy, bored and irritable, announced that she was going and asked Philly to come with her. But Mrs. March, complaining suddenly of an aching back that almost incapacitated her, begged Kathy to let Philly stay and help her. Kathy went alone, crossly, and her chaise was scarcely out of sight when Mrs. March lost all symptoms of a backache.

That afternoon Philly carried a bucket of cool barley water to the men scything buckwheat. Alex, sunburned and sweating, thanked her and drank in the shade of a locust tree. He looked happy, as he used to long ago.

"We'll finish the job by nightfall," he said.

"I'll pitch in too, if you'll let me, Alex. I can swing a scythe as good as a man."

He shook his head and grinned at her.

"You've not enough good men," she said. "There's never enough." If she did not tell him now, she thought, the time never would be right again. "I reckon the army knows that these days."

His grin faded and he studied her thoughtfully.

"By good," he said, "you mean strong, able, willing—"

"And *believing* in what they're doing," Philly said. "Like you believe it's important to finish this field by nightfall."

"Enough good men," he said slowly. "I vaguely recall Edmund Burke using that phrase once in a speech to Parliament. Something about the forces of evil winning in the world if enough good men do nothing."

"I never heard tell of Burke saying that, Alex. I just . . ."

"Thanks for bringing us water, Philly." He turned away and picked up his scythe.

Philly walked back to the house disconsolately.

"Have you spoke to him yet?" asked Mrs. March.

"I tried," Philly said. "I started to, but it only reminded him of something he'd read instead of listening to me. Something that Burke said once in a speech to the Parliament—"

"Burke bah! Speeches, words, words! The trouble with him is that he's set on using his head and forgetting he has a heart."

But Mrs. March was wrong.

After supper Philly strolled around the yard and garden, examining the flowers until all their colors became deep blue in the gathering darkness. As colors faded, scents seemed to grow more fragrant. She breathed deeply of roses, honeysuckle, sweetpeas, verbena. Rubbing a nasturtium petal in her fingers, she thought that thus the world must smell a mile deep underground. A warm breeze rose from the south, as if the night had yawned, and bore to her the sweetness of clover and grass. The jangle of insects increased until their throbbing made her want to dance.

When she came to the stile, she climbed it and sat on its top bar, staring into the field where sheep grazed. She smelled them and listened to their delicate munching, and, in time, she made out their shapes moving slowly. Far in the east heat lightning flashed in the sky. Thunder muttered, waited, and muttered again, and then all the eastern sky flamed with lightning.

The army, she thought, and the thought did not excite her now. Let it stay over yonder, go far away, and never come near the peaceful valleys of sheep and insects and flowers and clover.

Someone walked quietly along the fence. She knew it was Alex, but she did not turn her head until he spoke.

"A celestial army marching for you over there, Philly."

Her spine chilled, as if she were afraid. Perhaps it was his tone, the words he spoke; perhaps it was his sudden presence as he rested his arms on the fence rail beside her.

"The heavenly artillery," he said, "launching an attack on firmament. Did the crickets pause and listen just then, or do they really care?"

"They stopped and listened." Her voice was unsteady. "They always do to thunder. But they know it won't rain here tonight."

"How do they know?"

"They just always *know*. And when it rains they molasses up their backs and sleep the rain away until it's time to sing again."

"I never heard that before," he said drily.

She stifled an impulse to laugh shrilly. "Neither did I. I just made it up."

He made no sound, but she knew that he was smiling in the darkness. It was time she went inside, she thought. A deep chill grew in her, although the night was warm. Gripping the bar tightly with one hand, she rose and stepped over it uncertainly. He caught her hand.

She did not know whether she slipped or he lifted her. But she knew that her feet would not touch the ground. He was holding her. She felt that she was whirling dizzily, ecstatically, as not long ago she had on a summer evening. To steady herself, she drew her arms around him tightly. They kissed. *I love you.* She did not know if she or he or both of them said it, or even if they spoke. There was a low sob, whether from him or herself or both of them she did not know. She knew only that she must let go of him and that she never wanted to let him go.

Then she was running toward the house, gasping for breath, tears burning her eyes. She raced up the stairs and into her room, wishing she were dead.

Toward dawn she finally fell asleep, and it was late when she awakened. Sleep had failed to solve anything. She could not stay here. She could not go to Kathy. She could not return to Philadelphia. Finally, she forced herself to dress and go downstairs. The house was strangely quiet. Hurrying to the kitchen, she found Mrs. March crying quietly.

"What's wrong?" she demanded.

"Nought." Mrs. March rubbed her eyes with a handkerchief. "Only good. He rode off before daybreak. I gave him my last good stallion, Wanderer. He told me he'd go by the Murdoch place to say good-by to Kathy. He asked me to say good-by to you. I'd have wakened you, but he wouldn't let me. He's bound for the city first to learn where the army might be and then he'll seek and find it. I don't know what you said to him, but . . ."

She found herself in a chair, crying. She could not stop. Then Mrs. March was kneeling on the floor, holding her close, stroking her hair.

At last they looked at each other, faces close, Mrs. March's eyes dry. Philly took a deep breath. "I—"

"I know."

"But I must tell you. I love him."

"I told you, Philly, I *know.*" Mrs. March got heavily to her feet.

"But what am I going to do? I can't go back to Kathy."

Mrs. March scowled. "That's nonsense. 'Course I'd like you to stay with me. But that's worse nonsense. You go on back to Kathy, and if you can't stand it you come back to me. But I vaw you'll stand it 'cause that's what you've *got* to do."

"And—and *tell* her that I—"

"You'll tell that baggage nought. You'll just go on as if nothing's happened. You'll stand it all right and learn what it means to be a woman."

XXX

"CLOSE the churches an' hesh the bells!" shouted a one-armed man, dancing excitedly. "Damn the sabbath, damn the Quakers! 'Cause *they's* comin' down the Old York Road. Neshaminy night afore last. Germantown last night. Death to the British tomorrow! You hear me?"

The crowd in Front Street pretended to ignore him.

"You *hear* me?" He wiggled his arm stump. "I give this up in the Short Hills. I . . ."

"That man is drunk," said Timothy Murdoch. "He should be arrested."

But he did not speak loudly, for the man was a veteran of the army that would appear at any moment.

Although it was a Sunday, Murdoch had opened his office and invited —in fact, commanded—Kathy, Philly, Mrs. Munger, Barnaby and all his clerks to come and see the army pass. "We must make a brave show for our brave boys and all the patriots to see," he'd said.

He sat now at the open window of his office with Kathy beside him, her expression sulky at having been routed up at such an early hour of a Sunday morning. Philly stood beside her and Barnaby beside Murdoch; the servants and clerks were clustered on the sidewalk below them in the crowd that thronged Front Street.

They were arranged as if for an artist's sketch, Philly thought. She did not want to be with them; she wished she were off in the crowd where she could privately thrill to the army passing on its way to meet Howe's army, which was reported far up Chesapeake Bay. But Murdoch had commanded her to be present and bring Kathy.

Glancing down guardedly at Kathy, Philly could not believe that she had wanted to stay in bed and not even look at the army. For Alex surely would be with it. Since he'd left and they'd returned to Philadelphia, Kathy had mentioned him only twice—each time angrily. She was perpetually restless and angry these days, turned in upon herself and aware of little about her. Nevertheless, Philly refused to believe that she actually hated Alex and did not want to see him again.

It had rained in early morning, but the sun was burning through a white mist and promised a hot, humid day. As ships' bells clanged six along the waterfront, Murdoch took out his large gold watch and frowned at it. "They're late," he said. "Seven o'clock was the promised hour and—" High in the rigging of a ship moored at Carpenter's Wharf a lookout uttered a shrill, ebullient cry.

There came, far up Front Street, a whispering sound. The crowd murmured and swayed forward as the sound grew into the rattle of drums and whistling fifes. Philly, unable to contain herself, swung to the door and leaned out.

"The new flag's leading 'em!" she cried.

The flag approved by Congress in June was borne by a tall soldier marching alone at the head of the column: thirteen alternate red and white stripes, thirteen white stars circled on a blue field.

Behind him marched a massed band, twelve abreast, of fifes and snare drums. Now the fifes were silent and the drummers flammed—a light tap with the left stick and a hard one with the right, sticks falling in perfect unison, drumheads swaying rhythmically against each drummer's left leg. Suddenly, unanimously, the sticks rolled and fifes were raised. Above the crashing of the drums the fifes shrilled into the high, sweet notes of "The Old Continental March."

It seemed to Philly that the music was in her as well as all about her and she wanted to tap, tap, tap, tap and go, go, go with this band that was, surprisingly, made up mostly of boys. Kathy felt the music too; she stood at the window now, leaning forward, her lips parted. Murdoch leaned out beside her (to be seen rather than see, Philly thought), clapping his hands and saying, "Applause, everyone, applause."

But the polite clapping was drowned in a roar that rolled through the crowd down Front Street.

The General, riding a big bay, turned his head from left to right and smiled gravely in response to the cheers. Beside him rode a tall, thin, very young man.

"That's the Frenchman Lafayette," someone shouted.

Behind them rode a body of horsemen. "Hey, Tench!" roared a man in the crowd. "Tench Tilghman!" "Greene, there—on the left." "That's Sullivan!" "No, it ain't, that's . . ."

"All honor to our great leaders!" yelled Timothy Murdoch, leaning so far out the window he might have fallen if Barnaby had not grasped him.

Now the street echoed to the clash and clatter of hoofs on the cobbles. "Moylan's troopers," someone said. "The General's guard." Color flowed in the street: blue coats, red waistcoats, buckskin breeches, the glint of sabers above the arching necks and bobbing heads of horses. Young men all, Philly saw. The finest gentlemen in all the land, graceful, sure, proud and smiling. They're invincible, she thought.

Horsemen still filled the street. "Bland's 1st Dragoons . . . There's Allen McLane."

"Alex!"

She clapped her hands over her mouth, certain that her cry had risen above the shouting of the crowd. Perhaps he heard her, for he was looking directly at her. And then he rose gracefully in Wanderer's stirrups and raised his hat and bowed from the waist. To *me,* she thought and shrank back from the doorway, crying uncontrollably.

Through her tears she dimly saw Kathy leaning out the window, a hand raised to him. He bowed to her, Philly thought. He must have. And then Kathy looked around at her with a strange expression. Did she know? She must not. There must never be anything for her to know. There must be—nothing. When he rode past just now he rode away from me forever—but not from her.

"Dear God," Murdoch said over a shoulder to Barnaby, "he's wearing the green cockade of a *lieutenant.* He's let himself be *demoted.*"

Kathy, eyes dry, continued to stare at her strangely. Unable to meet her gaze, Philly stepped outside into the pressing crowd and found herself beside Mrs. Munger.

A company of pioneers marched past, axes over shoulders. There was another band of fifes and drums playing a strange, quick tune she never had heard before, and behind them a regiment of infantry. "From Muhlenberg's brigade," a man said. She saw the men dimly, for it seemed to her that she had gone on down Front Street and turned up Chestnut with Alex. She must stop thinking of him.

Clenching her hands, she stared hard at field guns and caissons rumbling past behind straining horses. Infantry followed the artillery. This was the army as she had imagined it, a benign serpent, curling through Philadelphia on this hot morning of August twenty-fourth as it marched to great and final victory.

"Weedon's brigade . . . Woodford's . . . Scott's . . . Lincoln's . . . They ain't in step."

"They are *too!*" Philly said to the man who seemed to know so much.

Yet she saw that many were not in step and few wore any pretense of a uniform. Most were dressed in shabby linsey-woolsey or old fringed hunting shirts and leather breeches. Among those who had hats, many failed to cock them, and everyone appeared to wear his at a different angle. They didn't toe out in the approved military fashion and their lines were uneven; many walked with heads lowered while others looked around, grinning, and called to the crowds. Yet they marched along, with sergeants bawling the step on the flanks, and no man fell out—perhaps, as rumor had it, because the General had ordered thirty-nine lashes for any who did. If they lacked uniforms and military bearing, all at least were marching through Philadelphia wearing green sprigs in hats or hair as the emblem of eternal hope. No matter what their critics said, Philly thought, they *were* an army.

She paid no attention to the officers riding on horseback as she searched the ranks for Micah. She repeated his name to herself, determined to think no more of Alex.

At the window above, Kathy cried, "Tony! *General* Wayne!"

He rode at the head of his Pennsylvania brigade, wearing a handsome uniform and smiling happily. He saluted her as the crowd yelled its approval of him and the Pennsylvania Line.

"Look at the sergeant coming," said the man who knew everything. "Where did they get him?"

Standing on tiptoe, Philly saw a sergeant more splendidly uniformed in blue and buff and red than General Wayne himself. Wearing a sword and bearing both spontoon and musket, he seemed to dance rather than march to the beat of the drums. Roaring the cadence, rotating up and down the flank in time, he seemingly kept his company in perfect step and line by an extraordinary personal will. The crowds along the street lapsed into awed silence and then applauded as the magnificent sergeant and his perfect company approached.

Mrs. Munger suddenly shrieked, *"Macaroni Jack!"*

He could not possibly be Macaroni Jack, yet he was, Philly saw. He almost, but not quite, lost step as Mrs. Munger again shrieked his name and struggled through the crowd toward the passing company with Philly after her. "I got to follow him," panted Mrs. Munger. "I got to get *to* him!" But the crowd was too dense and the company passed on toward Chestnut Street while Mrs. Munger wailed in anguish and people laughed.

Philly heard a familiar voice counting cadence as another company approached. He must be a sergeant now, she thought dully. Then she saw him, marching on the company flank, and she wished that her heart raced as it would have not so long ago.

"Micah!" she called.

He seemed a stranger. The boy she had known was dead and in his place there walked a man, leaner even than the boy, skin darkened by wind and sun, eyes darkened as if from brooding.

"Micah!"

His gaze was flat, hard. And then he looked stunned, so that she thought perhaps the girl she had been was dead too. His lips smiled uncertainly, but his gaze remained hard, calculating, as it swept over her and up to the window where Kathy stood. Then he had passed, and he did not look back.

Watching him go at his old effortless stride, remembering times past, she believed that her heart did beat faster. After all, she had always believed that he was bound to become a hard man and she had always believed that she was bound to love him forever. He had become what she expected. And she?

"I'm goin' after Jack to the place where the army camp's at," muttered Mrs. Munger.

"I'll go with you," Philly said slowly.

Philadelphia never had known such a Sunday. The army took three hours to pass, and a growing crowd formed a turbulent wake behind it, down Front Street, up Chestnut, across the Common, and then west to Middle Ferry where a great throng cheered as the army crossed the Schuylkill. Church bells rang late, but few attended services. Patriots roamed the streets, boasting of their mighty army, while Tories stayed in their houses. Several windows were broken. There was an extraordinary amount of drinking after the constables mysteriously disappeared. The few Quakers who ventured out bore the aggrieved expressions of saints in hell.

Philly and Mrs. Munger were swept along in the noisy, milling crowd that followed the last unit down Front Street. At Chestnut they struggled free of the crowd and walked home by quieter streets.

"It was *him* all right," Mrs. Munger said indignantly, "and that was Micah too, both of 'em struttin' along like they didn't know us. I vaw that Jack's all dandied up to catch him some poor girl. But he ain't runnin' from me after being so close to beggin' my hand in marriage."

"It's folly, Mrs. Munger."

"You think I don't know what folly is?" Her voice rose. "Forty-eight years I've lived and watched all folly. High time I tried a mite of it myself instead of always watchin'. You don't got to come."

You should not go, Philly told herself. She would not. She was utterly confused. She had loved Micah and she had loved Alex, but what was the sense in going to find one just because she dared not go to the other?

"I reckon," she said, "I'd best put a cold wet cloth on my forehead and cool off."

"I'd do that, Philly," Mrs. Munger said sarcastically. "I'd bury me in a kitchen forever and avoid all folly—and never *live*. Land o' *Goshen!* How many years I've seen you moonin' over that Micah Heath and then you see him and he sees you. I watched it. I seen the look on him that's different than he ever was before. He's a man now, Philly, and he sees that you're a woman. He's a—a—well, if you don't see what he is now you're the only blind woman in Philadelphia. He ain't for the likes o' me, Lord knows, but if'n I had your years an' bounce I'd— Lord, what am I sayin'?"

They were at the back door then and Philly paused, staring at her garden that lay still and lifeless under the burning sun. She knew perfectly well what Mrs. Munger was saying. The garden, the house, were dead. But over west through the city rolled a tide of joy and passion. The army moved there, bearing its freight of hope and life.

Mrs. Munger clattered about the kitchen, collecting things in a basket, muttering, "I ain't goin' empty-handed. . . . Scissors . . . needles and thread . . . There's parsons in that army, by gum, and women too, I've heard tell, as go with their men. Should I take a pair o' blankets from Miss Kathy or do you reckon Jack will have . . . I ain't goin' empty-handed."

"I'll go," Philly said dully. "But I won't stay. I'll just walk out to the camp and take him some of those little cakes I baked yesterday and a half-ham and some of those candied elderflowers. And I'll come home tonight."

It was time she did *something,* she told herself. And this was the only possible thing that she could do. Go out there and find him and say, "I brought you some vittles," and he would thank her and they would talk and possibly—certainly, then, they would not feel that a year had passed. He was a hard man, but he would be tender to her when he remembered their strange, lost days since the Ohio. And she would love him again as she learned to forget her great folly of believing that she had loved Alex. She would stop dreaming of the impossible and do the possible: Go over the river with Mrs. Munger and visit the army. If he said it was possible that he loved her, she would say it was not impossible that she loved him. But she would not be his woman now. She would only be his wife.

"Runnin' away," groaned Mrs. Munger as they left the house. "Lord preserve me. I never was a wanderer, not even when a child, and here I am a-goin' wanderin' at forty-eight. Ain't even gone to my own room at Mrs. Pratt's house. Just runnin' away." Her face brightened. "But I might be back by nightfall."

The tide of excitement in the city lifted them and bore them along west. In the atmosphere of festival, they were scarcely aware of the oppressive heat. It was after noon by the time they had crossed the river and reached the triple forking of roads where a crowd of farmers and their families lingered after having watched the army pass.

"Where's the camp at?" Mrs. Munger asked a man.

"They went down the Darby road." The man pointed south toward a cloud of dust that hung over the rolling land. "Some says they aims to camp on Darby Heights tonight."

"Darby!" wailed Mrs. Munger. "There ain't a woman born as has walked from Philadelphia to Darby."

"They's some as does," a thin-lipped woman said disdainfully. "Tarts and trollops followin' after the army with the baggage train. Children too, poor little mites. The General dasn't let 'em be seen in Philadelphia today. They come down from Germantown this mornin' with the baggage an' sutlers an' pulled into Hiram Burger's big clover field around the bend yonder. Pastured their stock too. Never asked so much as a please of Hiram, who's ravin' mad an' vaws he'll go to Congress over them tramplin' down—"

"Come along." Mrs. Munger grasped Philly by an arm and started on. "I can't abide these tongue-waggin' country women as condemn every patriotic soul."

The road curved sharply around a woodland. They heard a din of shouting mingled with the crack of whips, the squeal of wheels and rumble of wagons. Then, around the bend, they halted and stared in astonishment.

Hiram Burger's big clover field seethed with activity. Wagoners, shouting and cursing and cracking their whips, jostled their teams into a line that moved out of the field and turned south toward Darby after the army. Women and children dashed here and there, shrieking and yelling, gathering up packs and bundles, trotting beside the wagons and begging to ride. A woman leaped for a tailboard, lost her grip, and fell; she sprang to her feet, and hands dragged her into the covered wagon.

They were dark, quick, noisy people, Philly thought, like the gypsies who had camped near the farm one summer. But there was a difference. The gypsies had worn bright colors, while these women were drab. Most were bareheaded, with hair falling around faces darkened by sun and smoke and dirt. Nearly all wore black. They reminded her of crows, cawing, flapping, predatory. And they were ugly, most of them, from excess or dearth: some drunk or fat, others gaunt or marred by sores or racked by coughing. Most of their children were ragged, dirty, and wild as hares, screaming, clawing, fighting, or simply rolling in the crushed sweet clover with shouts of delirious joy.

A sutler tried to force his cart into the line of wagons. A wagoner's bullwhip flashed and curled around and around the sutler's arm; the wagoner tugged his whip and dragged the sutler, howling, from his cart. Drovers, starting a large herd of army cattle toward the road, were cursed by the wagoners and cursed them in return. Many army stragglers and a few women who lingered, drinking, around sutlers' wagons parked in the field, yelled delightedly at the milling confusion of wagons and cattle.

A drunken straggler shouted obscenely at Philly and staggered toward them from a sutler's wagon.

"Lord save us," cried Mrs. Munger, "we've come to hell!"

They ran toward the line of supply wagons which had come to a halt among the bawling cattle. Mrs. Munger, panting and moaning, gasped to a driver, "In God's name give us a ride."

"Walk, y'old whore," he replied without heat. He winked at Philly and said, "Swing up, young one."

Mrs. Munger swayed and blinked dazedly. She seemed to swell and then to wither as Philly supported her.

"Then ride," the driver said calmly, "the both'n you. I see you ain't o' *them*." He gestured his whip toward a sutler's wagon where camp women squawled excitedly.

Suddenly a woman's agonized scream rose from the sutler's canvas-covered cart. Voices were stilled and the wagoner's expression grew abstracted. The scream rose again, high-pitched in agony.

Philly touched her tongue to her dry lips and murmured, "What is it?"

Mrs. Munger seemed to shake herself. "It's . . ."

"It ain't a mite o' use," wailed a pock-marked woman, thrusting her head out the back of the sutler's cart. "It—"

The woman screamed piercingly again in the cart and the women clustered outside it flinched, raised hands, and gabbled nervously.

"Christ in heaven," cried the pock-marked woman, dropping to the ground, "I've helped my share in my time, but I ain't no midwife."

"Well, I *am!*" exclaimed Mrs. Munger, squaring her shoulders and striding toward the cart.

"Her man went off a while back to git somebody," a woman said to Mrs. Munger. "Who're *you?*"

"I'm *Mistress* Martha Munger of Philadelphia on my way to j'in my—husband with the Pennsylvania Line. And the woman's yet to die whilst I'm seein' her through one o' *these*."

The women fell back, staring at her.

"She's been laborin' since last night, I swear," said the pock-marked woman. "I've knowed her since—I can't remember when, we've been goin' so long an' such far pieces in all seasons. Her man an' mine got us rides with a wagoner from Germantown this mornin', but an hour back he throwed her out an' drove off, he couldn't stand her moanin', an' we carried her into Dirty Danny's cart."

"Look hyar," whined a dirty-faced man who came around the cart. "That's him," said the pock-marked woman. "Dirty Danny."

"Look hyar, gals," he whined, "I got to git on the way an' she kain't—"

"Ladies," said Mrs. Munger, mounting the rear step of the cart, "dispatch yonder man."

They swarmed upon him, squawling, and he fled.

"Philly," Mrs. Munger called, "come in here."

The interior of the cart was stiflingly hot and glaringly bright under the thin canvas. In a narrow space between barrels and crates a sweating woman lay under a blanket, her eyes closed tightly. She writhed suddenly and uttered a gagging sound that died away in a moan.

"All right, love," Mrs. Munger said to her soothingly. "All right now. It's harder to get one o' these out than it was to put it in, but we'll do it. You got Martha Munger here now, the best midwife in Philadelphia."

She pulled off the blanket and Philly saw the woman's naked body, legs drawn up grotesquely, belly and breasts swollen enormously and coursed by distended blue veins. Sweat dripped from Philly's eyebrows; she closed her eyes and when she opened them, the woman looked no less grotesque. It was unbelievable that anyone could have loved this ugly, sweating, writhing creature who strained in vain to deliver the burden that struggled within her.

Mrs. Munger shook Philly by an arm. "Clear out this plunder, I said."

Later when she saw the crates and barrels she'd thrown out of the cart, her strength surprised her. After she had cleared space around the woman, Mrs. Munger thrust the blanket into her hands and commanded: "Cut it . . . knot it . . . lash it."

While she cut the blanket with a knife and knotted its strips together, Mrs. Munger, kneeling, moved her hands expertly over the woman. The woman, opening her eyes, stared at them glazedly and suddenly screamed piercingly.

"That's the love," said Mrs. Munger. "The more the pain the better the baby."

At her direction, Philly lashed the ends of the strong blanket cord to the sides of the cart.

"Love," Mrs. Munger said to the woman, gently wiping the sweat off her face and brushing back her lank, wet hair, "you hear me now?"

The woman nodded.

"Take this." She put the stout blanket cord in the woman's rough hands. "And hold this." She placed tightly rolled handkerchiefs in her mouth. "Bite down. And now—" She raised the woman's dirty, callused feet and planted them wide apart against the piled, heavy kegs and crates which Philly had not thrown out of the cart. "Now," said Mrs. Munger, kneeling, "when I say, you pull an' you push an' you bite an' you give me that baby elset I'll come an' take it." She glanced over a shoulder at Philly. "If those gabblin' hens out there ain't got water boilin' yet, you do it, an' get cloths if you got to rip up every one o' your petticoats."

Philly swung to the ground as Mrs. Munger cried, "*Now!*"

Water was boiling in a kettle, and none of the women had gone with the baggage train which was disappearing down the road in a cloud of dust. The herd of cattle followed. The sutlers and stragglers were going too, jeering Dirty Danny, who sat under a tree holding his head.

"*Now!*" cried Mrs. Munger inside the cart.

The women grew still, listening attentively. Their children, grouped in a curious ring around the cart, were silent.

The silence was unbearable, Philly thought. It was lasting too long.

Suddenly the woman screamed again and again and again. A heavy keg of rum toppled out of the cart and clattered to the ground. No one moved. Then there was a faint wail.

Dirty Danny raised his head and the women shrieked with delight as Mrs. Munger shouted from the cart, "Philly, I need that thread and scissors. Come here an' bring me wet cloths."

She leaped into the cart and took the baby from Mrs. Munger's hands.

"A boy!" cried the pock-marked woman as Philly stepped down carefully. "The biggest I ever seen."

After they had bathed him, Philly tore off one of her petticoats and wrapped him in it. She realized that she was laughing and chattering foolishly while tears filled her eyes.

When Mrs. Munger stepped out of the cart, the women cheered her. She washed her hands and said, "His ma wants to see him. I've cleaned her up an' packed her with cloths. She's dead beat, but she won't go to sleep."

Philly carried the baby into the cart and held him before the drawn, gray face of the woman who refused to close her eyes.

"Ma," Mrs. Munger said to her, "you got yourself a son. What're you goin' to call him?"

The woman stared at the bawling child. Her lips worked, but they could not hear what she said. They leaned closer.

"Liberty."

Mrs. Munger pursed her lips. "That's a nice sentiment," she said, "but it ain't much of a name. 'Specially for *this* big, strong boy."

"Liberty," the woman repeated.

"Well," said Mrs. Munger, "he's yours to name. Liberty what?"

"Liberty Heath."

"Heath?" Philly said dazedly. "Is your name *Heath?*"

The woman shook her head. "I'm Minna Clark. The father's name is Micah Heath."

After he crossed the river, he spoke to people in the crowd that still milled along the Market Way.

"There's a woman across the river needs a good midwife. Where'll I find one?"

Two or three said they didn't know. One woman gave him careful directions on how to find the house of a midwife on Second Street—and then remembered that she'd gone to Germantown yesterday. Disgusted, he cut south from the crowd and trotted again.

There was nothing for him to do now but fetch Mrs. Munger, he thought. The best midwife in Philadelphia she'd called herself more than a year ago. He'd glimpsed her this morning when he saw Philly and Kathy on Front Street as the column passed. What would he say to her? "There's a woman across the river needs help bad." That's what he'd tell her. And if she asked *who,* he'd say, "Wife of a friend of mine." He'd have to pay her later, for he had no money. Maybe he could borrow a chaise to get her there faster.

"Hurry," Mary Trotter had told him as the column passed the parked baggage train. Captain Newman gave him permission to fall out when he explained the trouble. The captain knew he'd be at Darby by tomorrow morning. Newman trusted him, remembering all he'd done these past months, Newman had to trust him. Passing his musket and pack to men in the company, he had trotted back, inquiring for a midwife along the way.

"Goddamn them," he said aloud when he thought of those country women across the river who wouldn't lift a finger to help an army woman in trouble.

It was high noon, he observed, as he reached the country end of Walnut Street and swung toward the city. He trotted faster, thinking grimly that a woman was a parcel of trouble. At least Minna had been a parcel of trouble ever since she'd refused to stay on as a servant at the Digges' house in Morristown. She'd have been comfortable and well fed there and when her time came Mrs. Digges would have seen her through it. But she had refused to stay and insisted on trudging along behind the army as it marched back and forth across Jersey, while she grew bigger and heavier with the child until it fairly made him sick to look at her.

A couple of times he'd been tempted to say he'd marry her if she would agree to go back to the Digges' place in Morristown and stay there until he returned or could send for her. But he couldn't bring himself to do it. He respected her as a good enough woman, strong and handy and willing, but he didn't love her. Certainly not enough to spend the rest of his life with her, though he'd provide for her and the child as long as he could. The truth was that he was tired of her and no longer wanted her—a big, heavy woman, old before her time, forever following him like a dark shadow. He did not have another woman on his mind. What he wanted, he thought, was a *lack* of women. If he could be shut of them for a year or two, it would suit him fine. And when he found a woman again she would be as unlike Minna as a mortal could possibly be.

He found himself thinking of Philly as he loped down Walnut Street. She had surprised him when he saw her this morning. For a moment, failing to recognize her, he'd thought, What a beauty. Then he'd realized, with amazement, who she was.

Seeing the prison, he trotted faster. Philly had waited for him there the day he was let out and they'd walked together to the river. Remembering suddenly how he'd warned her to behave more carefully around boys, he groaned aloud. Damn men *and* women, he thought. Goddamn me, anyway. What did you do about having a bastard child? How did you explain it to a proper girl like Philly? You couldn't. You just never mentioned it. But what did you say when the girl found out?

Near Fourth Street he stopped at a public pump to breathe himself and rinse his mouth and sweating, dusty face and hands. Then he walked around the corner to the back door of the house and knocked. There was no sound inside. He swore to himself and knocked again. When no one came, he tried the door. It swung open and he stepped into the kitchen.

"Philly?" he said. "Mrs. Munger?"

Footsteps approached in the hall, the door opened and Kathy stared at him. Her right hand moved slowly to her throat, but she did not speak. He felt his face flushing, and he thought, I ain't even been thinking of *her*.

Then she said in a high tense voice, "Micah!"

"Hello, Kathy." He tried to smile. "Didn't mean to give you a turn. I'm looking for Mrs. Munger."

"You gave me a turn all right." He wished that she wouldn't stare at him so. "What do you want Mrs. Munger for?"

"This woman, the wife of a friend of mine, is in a bad way across the river. She needs a midwife. I came for Mrs. Munger."

"She and Philly haven't returned from the parade yet. I just came back myself. She'll be along in a minute. Come in and sit down."

He looked down at his dusty boots and breeches. "I'm not fit for sitting in parlors, Kathy. There's a mortal dust on the roads today."

"Fola-dora-dola. Come on."

He followed her into the back parlor and took care not to sit down until she had. Then he perched himself on the edge of a chair and looked at his hands.

"Have a glass of wine."

"Thanks." He wished she'd offer him something to eat, but apparently it didn't occur to her that he was hungry. She poured two glasses of Burgundy and he drank his faster than he'd intended. She refilled his glass and said, "You're still *with* the army, aren't you?"

"Sure." He grinned at her then. "Least till the end of the year."

"Your company looked very fine today," she said.

"We're not much. But we're better than we was."

"So you like it, Micah?"

"*Like* it?" He frowned. "The army, you mean? No. But it's as good as there is to do now. It's the place for the likes of me."

"The likes of you." She smiled reflectively. "What *are* the likes of you?"

"I—I—I don't reckon I know what you mean." He felt himself flushing.

She said something with laughter in her voice and then she asked him how it felt to swim the Hudson River in November and, before he could answer, she asked him more questions about the army.

He heard himself talking in a low voice, as if he were afraid somebody would overhear him. He wasn't saying much, he knew; he was simply telling her where the army had been and what it had done. Yet she listened with such interest and asked such shrewd questions that he went on talking when he knew that he should stop.

Finally, the rattling of the front door knocker made him pause. He remembered, uneasily, why he had come here. "Could that be Mrs. Munger?" he asked.

Kathy raised a finger to her lips and shook her head. "Sunday callers," she whispered. "I don't want to see 'em."

The knocker rattled once more. In a moment the lid of the brass box squeaked as someone lifted it and dropped a card inside.

The silence lengthened as they stared at each other. If he could manage to speak now, everything would be all right, he thought vaguely. But what would he say? Glancing through the doorway into the front parlor, he saw a portrait which looked somewhat like Kathy's.

Getting to his feet quickly and going to the doorway, he pointed at the painting. "Is that you?"

"Of course." Her tone was petulant. "Mr. Charles Willson Peale finished it just two days ago. He's quite the rage. Everybody—well, nearly everybody is having him do their portrait or miniature. Don't you recognize me, Micah?"

He frowned at the painting. "It's you all right, Kathy. But then again it ain't you at all."

She rose and stood beside him in the doorway, gazing at the painting. "What do you mean?"

"The hair," he said, "it's not golden like yours. And the eyes aren't yours, Kathy. They—they don't have the—the flash and danger—" His voice trailed off as he found himself looking into Kathy's eyes instead of at the portrait. "I—I'd best go," he muttered, turning away.

She closed the door on the portrait. "Are you still afraid of me, Micah?"

"I never was afraid of you, Kathy."

"You're afraid of the *likes* of me. But do you know that you and I are alike?"

He nodded.

"I'm tired of monotony," she said evenly. "I'd like some danger. Can you give it to me?"

"I—I don't reckon I know what you—"

"Yes, you know. Right here in this room. Now. Are you afraid?"

He pulled her to him, uncertain whether he loved or hated her, knowing only that he wanted her.

"I'm not afraid of what you think," she whispered, thrusting her body against his, "because you've always known what I'm like."

He walked dazedly up Walnut Street in the dusk, thinking of her. Alex was dead to her, she'd said. *You,* she told him, are the only man I've ever known. It would not happen again. And then, yes, yes, it must happen again and again. *You* are the man I need and must have forever.

Finally, when she'd said for the last time that he must go, he'd helped himself to food in the kitchen while she went upstairs. He stood in the kitchen, wolfing food as voraciously as he'd wolfed love in the parlor, until he suddenly saw himself clearly as though he stood before a perfect mirror. Disgusted, he threw down the food and walked away.

It was dark by the time he reached the western bank of the river. He took the Darby road and walked faster. But when he came to the place where Minna had waited with the baggage train, he saw that the field was empty.

Picking up a stone against his foot, he walked on toward Darby. After he'd walked a little farther, he suddenly hurled the stone into the darkness. "That bitch!" he cried.

XXXI

CRICKETS in the garden cried, *A-like, a-like, a-like.* She closed the back door and went through the house, lighting all the candles, wondering why he had left without saying good-by.

Glancing at her portrait in the front parlor, she thought that she didn't like it much now. She stepped to the mirror and studied her flushed face, her shining eyes. A better portrait of me as I am, she thought; he'll come back as soon as he can. Smiling, she went to the back parlor and poured herself a glass of brandy.

Later, when the back door slammed, she was curled on the couch, stroking its nap, wondering when and how she would see him again.

"Kathy!"

The urgency in Philly's tone startled her; she had forgotten that Philly existed.

"Kathy!"

Reluctant to shed the pleasant glow of brandy and the memory of what had happened in this room, she did not stir as Philly hurried through the hall and opened the front door. Voices rose, a man's protesting, Philly's firm, and then there was a strange mewing sound. Rising slowly, she went into the hall.

Philly, holding a small bundle, was giving money to a dirty little man. A big, ugly, gray-faced woman sagged against the door.

"Philly," Kathy said sharply, "what is—"

"It's the price you agreed to for bringing us here, Dirty Danny," Philly said to the man. "Thank you and go along." She pushed him out, pulled the woman inside and shut the door. The woman staggered to the stairs and sank down, her head lowered, her hands curled in her lap.

"Philly!" Kathy cried.

Philly came toward her, holding out the bundle, her expression inscrutable. "Hold him," she said.

Kathy found herself holding the warm, wet, stirring bundle and looking down at a tiny, red, wrinkled face.

"What *is* it?"

"A baby," Philly snapped. "Born this afternoon. *Hold* him, I told you." Placing her hands under the woman's arms, she lifted her gently. "Minna," she said, "we've got to climb these stairs."

The woman nodded and gripped the rail. With her right arm over

Philly's shoulders, they crept slowly up the stairs while Kathy gaped after them.

"Bring the baby," Philly called from the top of the stairs.

"But—"

"Bring him up hyar! And bring a candle."

She found herself in the side bedroom, holding the baby and bewilderedly watching Philly slip off the woman's dirty dress and help her into bed. The woman said something as her eyes glittered yellowly at Kathy in the candlelight.

"Sure enough," Philly said, plumping up the bolster and smoothing the woman's hair, "and you'll stay. You've got to rest and do a mother's work, Minna. He's a hungry one. It's all that ails him." Turning, she took the child from Kathy's wooden arms and settled him at the woman's breast. "I'll be back with something for you to eat." She left the room without looking at Kathy.

The woman said something.

"What?" Kathy asked abstractedly.

"Thankee," the woman said.

Kathy nodded abruptly and followed Philly down the back stairs, angry now.

"You see here," she said in the kitchen. "And stop rattling those pots and turn around. What's the meaning of this? You bring a woman and child into my house as if— Turn around!"

There were tears in Philly's eyes when she faced her. "You listen, Kathy. Mrs. Munger and I went over the river today to see the army. We happened on this army woman in labor and Mrs. Munger saw her through it. She has no place to go, so I brought her here. Mrs. Munger went on with some other women to find Macaroni Jack. If she finds him, I doubt she'll be back."

"What right have you to bring that dirty woman here?"

Philly's eyelids closed; when they opened, her tears had vanished. "No right, Kathy, except the right to be decent. Do you know what that means?"

"You snot-nosed wench!" Kathy cried. "You've gotten 'way above yourself to lecture *me!* You take it on yourself to run too many other people's business. The woman must have a husband."

Philly shook her head. "She has no husband, Kathy."

"Why then she's a—a—" Philly rubbed her forehead distractedly. "She's just a—a— You bringing her here with her bastard child! Where's the man that fathered it?"

"I don't know," Philly said.

"Who is he?"

Philly's lips worked. "Micah."

"What?" She had misheard her. *"What?"*

"Micah."

Kathy's left hand groped out and struck the table. She moaned, as if the blow had hurt her mortally, and her hand clutched for the table, for the door, for something to grip tightly. The table seemed to tilt toward her, and then the door swung open, and she was walking uncertainly along the hall. She must not go in the back parlor; she must never go there again. Seeking a dark room somewhere in the house, she wondered dazedly why she had lighted so many candles.

The woman's name was Minna Clark, Philly told her. But she thought of her only as The Woman. The child was named Liberty, Philly said. But she thought of him only as The Child.

For three days after Philly brought them home Kathy could not bear to go near the side bedroom where they lay. The woman made no sound and the child did not cry after the first night, but their presence filled the house. They drove Kathy out of doors and scuttling aimlessly about the hot streets. The house no longer was hers; it belonged to the woman and the child whom Philly tended devotedly. Neither she nor Philly mentioned them; they had little to say to each other.

On the afternoon of the fourth day, as she crept quietly to her room to change clothing and sally forth somewhere, anywhere, she noticed that Philly had left the side bedroom door open. She did not want to look into the room, yet she was drawn irresistibly. Tiptoeing to the doorway, she looked in.

The woman lay on her back, asleep, her mouth open, her hands curled on the sheet. Kathy grimaced. She was such an ugly woman. *That* was the horror pursuing her everywhere these days: to realize that *he* had bedded brutishly with *that* and gotten it with child, *he* who had taken her so passionately that she had been convinced he'd wanted only her all his life. And so the loathsome creature had linked her with *that*.

The child suddenly uttered a low wail, and the woman's eyelids shot open. Her left hand swung instinctively to the child lying on the large pillow beside her, and he was quiet. She closed her mouth and drew down her lips in an expression intended as a smile.

"Afternoon," she said.

Kathy nodded and backed away.

"Mrs. March—" The woman's gaze was piercing. "I want t'ask ya somethin'. D'ya know my man, Micah?"

Trapped by the woman's piercing gaze and a sudden sense of fear, she nodded slowly.

"A good man," the woman said. "Reckon ya've contempt for him —an' me. Don't have, Mrs. March. He's got no love fer me, but he's mighty decent. We was a—a couple o' young uns sort o' lost an' alone. It seems a long time ago, though it ain't a year yet. I weren't much, but I weren't the sight then I am now. It jus' plumb wore me down, all that walkin' here, there an' yonder. But I'd do it agin if'n I had the choice. Ya understand?"

Kathy nodded. "Yes," she said indistinctly. "You go back to sleep." Turning, she fled from the room.

The woman knew something, she thought. As instinctively as she'd reached for her child on wakening, she knew that— But she could not possibly know what had happened. For an instant Kathy had almost pitied her. Yet there was no reason for pity. There was no reason to understand anything except that *he* had debased her by linking her with that coarse, ugly woman.

True, she had given him the opportunity by offering herself to him. What had happened to her? She never had heard of anyone in her social position being seized by such a fit of burning animal passion. But that was because no husband ever had turned coldly from a wife as beautiful and willing as she in the way that Alex had in recent months.

Tears filled her eyes as she sat in her bedroom. Alex was to blame for what had happened. She hated him. She hated Micah. If she could find the means, she'd go to some place far away. But where and how?

She could not go any place. She was trapped here. At least, however, no one ever would know what she had done, what had been done *to* her—except Micah, who was only an animal. Supposing he had got her with child?

Sweat started on her forehead. The notion had not occurred to her because she had believed, as Mrs. Munger had said, that she was barren. But she did not know positively that she was. Supposing . . . If she were, Alex would realize that he was not the father.

Swinging to her feet, she paced wildly around the room.

The fear grew in her. She counted days, but the days crept too slowly toward a date in September. She did not want to see anyone, least of all her father. Yet she could not simply sit and wait in this house dominated by the woman and child who reminded her of her own possible fate. They must go. Each day she sought and failed to find an excuse for sending them on their way.

Meanwhile, she flung herself into a feverish cleaning of the house that amazed Philly. The furniture had to be rearranged. The back parlor was changed completely and, over Philly's strenuous objections, that perfectly good and comfortable couch was given to a poor preacher in Logan's Alley.

The woman, Minna, insisted on getting out of bed and helping with the cleaning. Kathy, who could not bear to watch her, took to digging in the garden and transplanting flowers that, she knew, would die.

On a hot Monday morning, September eighth, as she started toward the garden, she heard a crash and turned back to the kitchen.

Minna and Philly stood transfixed, a piece of shattered china on the floor between them.

"What is it?" Kathy cried. Then, looking down, "My best teapot that Papa had shipped from—"

"I'm sorry, Kathy," Philly said. "It slipped from my hands while I—"

"No'm," Minna said, "it didn't. I did it an' I didn't mean to. I was—"

"You clumsy wench!" Kathy wailed. "You—you— It's time you packed and went from here!"

Minna lowered her head. "Yes'm," she said and walked slowly from the kitchen.

"Kathy." Philly looked at her levelly. "Do you really mean that?"

"I certainly do!"

Philly turned and went up the back stairs.

"Where are you going?" Kathy called after her.

"With 'em."

She did not believe that Philly actually would leave her. Yet in twenty minutes Philly was gone. She watched from a window as they walked up the street, Philly carrying her belongings in a basket and the woman carrying the child.

She was alone now. She did not know where they were going and she told herself she didn't care. She simply was glad that she was alone at last.

The stiflingly hot days did not seem to be terminated by the humid nights. Tuesday, Wednesday, Thursday extended into the longest week of her life. Although she could not bear to think of the future, it obsessed her as she continually asked herself what would become of her.

On Friday morning a din rose in the street before it was fully light. The State House bell began clamoring at five o'clock, summoning the members of Congress to an extraordinarily early session. Thrusting her head out her bedroom window, she called to a woman hurrying along the street and asked what had happened.

"Defeated!" the woman cried. "Down by the Brandywine yesterday. The army's scattered, they say, and Howe'll be on us any hour."

Defeat or victory, it didn't matter to her, she thought dully. Yet before she had finished dressing, Timothy Murdoch was hammering at the front door.

"Get your things together," he said when she let him in. "You're leaving for the farm. The British will be in the city by nightfall. Take Philly with you in the coach. That woman and babe Philly dragged here will have to fend for themselves."

"Philly's gone. The woman too. I didn't bother to tell you."

"Gone?" He frowned at her. "What happened?"

"We quarreled. I—I sent her packing."

His frown deepened. "Kathy, it's no time for you to be losing a good servant like Philly. What ails you? You look pale and—and not yourself. It don't matter now. You've got to hurry. The army was roundly beat at the Brandywine and what's left of it's at Chester. There's nought but twenty miles of open country betwixt us and the British."

Studying him thoughtfully, she began to smile. "But *you* aren't going, are you, Papa?"

He tugged nervously at his ruffles. "Well—no. At least not yet." His voice rose plaintively. "If I go, I'm ruined. They'll seize everything I possess. My credit will be gone. It's the end of this rebellion, Kathy. Now—"

"I'm not going anywhere, Papa."

"Kathy!"

"I'm *not* going." Before her unwavering gaze, his faltered and fell. "And you don't believe any more than I do that the British are going to pillage us. You merely think it would *look* better if I went to the country."

"Now Kathy—"

"You listen to me. I *know* you, Papa. You said yourself the rebellion's ended. The British want friends. They want to do *business*. I'll spend the night at your house if that makes you feel better. In time I may move in with you. I'll see. The times have finally changed. I'm right and you know it."

"Yes," he said uncertainly. He walked out to his coach, muttering, "Yes, yes, yes."

She found it amusing to walk the streets that Friday and observe the mounting panic. Patriots who had once talked and swaggered belligerently now scampered everywhere, sweating and yelling as they loaded their families and furniture into all kinds of vehicles. Almost everything that could be moved from Philadelphia was being loaded onto anything that had wheels. Some members of the Committee of Safety were even taking down church bells and trundling them away—to be melted down for bullets, they shouted. The fools didn't realize that the rebellion had ended, Kathy thought scornfully.

Strolling across the State House yard, she paused and watched two men load the Congress's little printing press into a wagon. A woman, gesturing toward the State House, demanded if *they* were running away again. The men said no, but the woman shook her head skeptically. If not today, it wouldn't be long before they ran again, Kathy knew.

As the day lengthened, wagons, carts, chaises and chariots formed steady streams pouring north and northwest. Those who lacked vehicles walked, carrying what they could. A shoemaker stumbled along behind a wheelbarrow on which he'd loaded his tools and last and leather. Few had any notion of where they were going, but talked incoherently about "the Jersey side" or "far north" or "reckon to make Lancaster."

"I didn't see a single coach except the Mifflins'," Kathy told her father at his house that evening. "Sally leaned out of it, shrieking at me to hurry. I laughed at her, the ugly old maid. What would the British do to *her?*"

"Please." Murdoch held up a hand. "I've much on my mind. Davis came to me this afternoon, *demanding* twenty-five barrels of horseshoes for the army, offering to pay anything. 'What army?' I asked him. It raised his bile—and his price. 'In what currency?' I asked him. The fools have rushed out so much paper money that it's not worth—"

"You'll hold on to everything," she said peremptorily. "And sell it to *them,* when they come, for solid money."

He looked at her curiously. "Suppose they take what they want and pay me nothing?"

"You've stored some things in the country, haven't you?"

"Of course. But suppose the rebels seize them?" He rubbed the top of his head. "It's risk, risk, risk. An honest man like me who wants no more than to do rightful business runs awful chances in a time like this. We've no security, no . . ."

He bored her with his perpetual fretting. If he were a woman, if he were she, he'd have something to worry about. For a time today she'd almost forgotten that this was the twelfth and tomorrow was the thirteenth and the next day was the fourteenth.

At his insistence she spent the night there, sleeping fitfully and awakening early in the hot morning. The thirteenth. She thought that she could not endure another day of wondering.

After her father left for his office, she idled on the porch, uncertain what to do with herself. At last she got to her feet and walked listlessly home. The empty house was hot, still. For the first time she missed Philly. Where had the foolish girl gone?

Toward noon, a boy ran down the street shouting, "They're comin'!" She dashed outside and heard a distant throb of drums. So they had come at last; now, perhaps, uncertainties would end and a new way of life begin or an old way resume. She hurried toward Chestnut Street with several women who babbled about the British.

The small crowds lining Chestnut Street were not cheering. A woman said, "It ain't the British." She sounded disappointed.

People stared silently as the army passed. The soldiers did not step out proudly as they had three weeks ago when they marched south through the city. They walked along with heads down, tired, sweating, dirty, their clothing ragged and many barefoot. It was a smaller army, a defeated army. But it still *was* an army.

She did not want to look at it. Turning away, she walked slowly home.

As she opened the front door she heard footsteps, and paused in alarm. Then the kitchen door opened and Alex appeared, his clothing and face so powdered with dust that she scarcely recognized him. In one hand he carried a belted brace of pistols and in the other a haversack. As he walked slowly toward her, his heavy saber clanked against his leg and his spurs clattered on the floor.

"Kathy." He was smiling faintly. "How are you?"

She had been certain that she hated him. But now—"Alex!" She raced to him, threw her arms around him and kissed him on the lips. "You're home to stay." She made it a positive statement.

"For almost an hour." He held her loosely, smiling at her. "I left Wanderer at Morgenstern's livery for a decent rubdown and some oats. And I'm as good as my horse. A change of this filthy linen and a bath are what I need. Are you here alone?"

"Yes. Mrs. Munger went off after the army to find Macaroni Jack. I thought that he had—"

"And so did I. He gave me a turn the first time I saw him on the Neshaminy a month ago. He came up, saluted, and apologized." Alex grinned. "Wanted me to know everything was in good order. After he deserted us and enlisted with the enemy, he proceeded to desert and enlist with us again and request a court-martial that promptly cleared his name. An irrepressible man Macaroni Jack— Where's Philly?"

"She left this week. I don't know where she went."

"You don't know where?" He looked at her sharply. "What went wrong?"

"We had a quarrel. That is, we didn't quarrel, but she was getting altogether too uppity for a servant and— Do you want something to eat?"

"I want a bath." He rested his haversack on the floor and laid his belt and pistols and saber on a chair. "So you don't know where she went. She just—"

"No, I don't. I'll get the tub."

"I'll get it."

He took the tub upstairs and then carried two wooden buckets out to the street pump while she searched the pantry for something he might eat. There wasn't much. It was time she found a new servant, she thought vaguely. She couldn't continue carrying water and trying to cook, and it certainly was unbecoming for him to be seen at the public pump. Following him upstairs, she leaned against the door of their room and watched him searching a drawer for fresh linen.

"So the army lost the battle." It was like speaking casually to a stranger, she thought.

"Of course." His tone was dry and he did not look at her as he searched the drawer. "Howe simply marched around Washington's flank again and took him by surprise—as if he'd never heard of such a maneuver before. There was much shooting and confusion and then we retired—in panic. If Howe weren't so lazy he could have marched into Philadelphia last night. But someone said the General knew Howe wouldn't push his troops in this heat. And we had to rest too. I suppose that's true. In any event, I've stopped planning the General's battles for him."

"So you're getting out of it for good? The army, I mean."

He glanced at her swiftly and passed from view behind the screen where he'd filled the tub. "No. I mean I'm simply going along doing what I'm told and exercising whatever sense I have. I reckon the lowliest dragoon of His Majesty's forces could cut me to ribbons, but I do have a good horse and I can ride. That's why Allen McLane tapped me for his troop. I didn't use to care much for McLane when I met him about town. Thought he was a fearful snob. I've changed my mind. He's a good man. We were over the Brandywine with Bland's men day before yesterday. We scouted to the Great Valley Road and detected Howe's flanking move around Trimble's Ford. We sent word of what was happening. It was confirmed by others, Joe Reed told me later— Pray pass me soap, Kathy."

Walking forward slowly, she picked up a chunk of yellow soap and put it in his hand above the screen.

"Reed has become a most eloquent critic of the General. He claims that the General totally misunderstood what Howe was doing. Took it as a terrible blunder on Howe's part to divide his forces at such a time and . . ."

She did not listen to him as he talked and sloshed in the tub. He was like a stranger pausing at an inn for an hour on his way some place. He did not love her any more, and she did not love him. He was merely using this house and it didn't matter to him that she was here. Well, he would serve her as she served him. He *had* to serve her now in order to save her—and, unwittingly, himself.

While he continued to talk, she undressed quickly, silently. She heard him get out of the tub as she stared at her nude reflection in the mirror. Then she stepped around the screen.

He sat on the low three-legged stool, toweling himself. Glancing up at her, his eyes widened and his hands were still. "Kathy, what—"

"You've *got* to, darling." She dropped to her knees beside him, pulling him to her.

She heard her own quick breathing, her sudden cry, and she let her nails rake his back with a savage joy in hurting him. He uttered no sound, and at last they were still. Then he was gone, around the screen somewhere, and she lay on the floor in a bright pool of hot sunlight. She began to sob uncontrollably.

He was standing over her, gazing down at her queerly. His lips moved and at last she made out what he was saying.

"Kathy, Kathy." Tenderly, as to a child. "What is it?" He knelt beside her stroking her hair. Tenderly, she thought, but not with love. Tenderly, as he would stroke a disturbed horse or whore who had served him well.

"I hate you!" she sobbed.

"Kathy, will you listen to what I say?"

"No!"

He left again. When she finally stopped crying, she rose and covered herself with the towel and moved around the screen. He was not in the room. Snatching up a robe, she put it on and went to the head of the stairs. He stood in the lower hall, buckling on his saber and looking up at her with the same strange expression.

"If nothing else," he said to her, "I want to speak of something practical. Before many days I think the city will be occupied. You're safer here than at the farm, but you shouldn't stay here. It was the reason I stopped off today. I want you to go to York or Lancaster or somewhere as far away. I'll make arrangements. Will you go?"

She felt herself beginning to smile. "No! I'm staying here."

He continued to look at her for several seconds. Then he picked up his haversack. "Good-by, Kathy."

XXXII

SHE was a courtesan who had not yet gone to court, Alex thought as he rode Wanderer toward Germantown that afternoon. She turned the troll instinctively and perfectly, but she had not yet turned trollop. You met and knew her at the very beginning of her career, he told himself, and he tried to smile.

What had made her act so? Lust, presumably. Yet a courtesan was not a wastrel; only those who loved were prodigal. A courtesan poured her natural lust into profitable channels, solving the insoluble equation: pleasure for profit and profit from pleasure. And what profit did she expect from giving him pleasure on this hot noon? She hated him, she'd said. Then what had been her motive?

There was something Rabelaisian about what had happened that Count Pulaski and the Comte de Fleury and the Baron de St. Ouary would appreciate. He never would mention what she had done, of course. But he wished he could discuss it with one of the Europeans he had met. Europeans might understand her. Americans, as yet, would either adore the wench or burn the witch at the stake.

He'd come to admire several of the Europeans with whom he'd become acquainted since returning to the army. The important thing about the best of them was that they valued an idea above all and put the lowest possible value on their lives in the pursuit of it. Their battle-rapture at the Brandywine had infected him and others. Pulaski, roaring in his fervor, *"Vorwärts, Brüdern, vorwärts!"* as he led the horse to check the crimson wave of infantry. Poor St. Ouary pressing so hard with his excited cries *"Pour liberté!"* that he found himself alone—and captured. The Marquis de Lafayette so enraptured with battle that he was unaware he had a bootful of blood. These men sought more than a fortune in the new world. They had been showered by the sparks of a startling new idea, liberty, that sprang from God knew where—perhaps the land itself. If the flame survived and burned brightly, it would be more thanks to some of the Europeans than to most of the Americans.

They helped him clarify an idea toward which he'd been groping recently. What eventually happened here was less likely to be resolved by passages of arms in rustic places like the Brandywine than by events in Europe. America was merely an extension of the Continent. Too weak as yet to determine its own destiny, its future was bound to the caprices and fortunes of the grand alliances, the traditional enmities. The Brandywine, that moiling confusion where he'd put the lowest possible value on his own life, was a mere skirmish in the endless struggle of empires.

Now he had a small plan of his own that he must execute quickly. Philly and his mother must get out of the County to a place of safety, for he was certain that the County would be fought over, plundered and despoiled.

He did not wish to think about Philly. What had happened at the farm last month was merely a midsummer night's dream such as might befall any man out of love with his wife and out of sorts with himself. Although a summer dream, it nevertheless haunted him these weeks later.

He did not know why she and Kathy had quarreled, but he was certain that Philly had had sufficient provocation and had returned either to the Murdoch farm or to his mother's. Of course, he had no authority to go to her and order her to flee somewhere. But neither had she authority to pursue his thoughts so hard.

When he reached the camp at the Falls above Germantown, he told McLane that he wanted to go to his farm and start his mother on the way to a safer place.

"Go ahead," said McLane. "But mind yourself in that country."

"It's my own country, Allen. I know it well."

McLane rubbed his lean jaw with a hairy hand. "It's no longer your country, Alex. It belongs to the Tories. And as was predictable, Howe is acting unpredictably."

"Isn't he moving against Philadelphia?"

McLane shook his head. "From what the scouts report he seems intent on moving north well to the west of the Schuylkill, feinting and weaving as he comes."

"And so cut us off from retreat west," Alex said, "and pen us between the Delaware and the Schuylkill."

"We won't let 'em do that. Tomorrow we're moving west to the vicinity of Warren Tavern beyond Paoli. We've got to try to keep between Howe and the stores and furnaces at Reading and thereabouts. Join us day after tomorrow at the Warren Tavern, Alex."

As he rode west from the Falls that afternoon, Alex pondered the almost insoluble problems facing the General. Civilians and many soldiers doubtless thought that all he had to do was to hold his still strong army between Philadelphia and the enemy. Howe would like that, for then he would amble up to Reading and destroy the army stores and ironworks before coming back leisurely to crush the army between the two rivers.

The General had learned something about supply after having been so short of it so long. Metal and powder were the bones of the army's flesh—and there never was enough of either. No wonder Harry Knox loved his artillery pieces as if they were his children. When you remembered the slow, painful task of forging a single cannon, the nine hundred pounds in a six-pounder seemed worth their weight in gold. If the General had the choice of preserving either Philadelphia or the source of the army's precious metal and powder, he must give up Philadelphia.

Each time he was critical of the General, Alex was annoyed with himself afterwards. With all his shortcomings, the General had long been aware of a necessity that he was just beginning to understand. The most important thing was to keep an army in being, no matter how small or weak it became. As long as a small hard core of the army refused to disintegrate, it would grow again to fight in a later season. Let the British occupy cities and sections of country; *space* did not matter. But the continued existence of the army preserved the Revolution.

It was dusk when he reached the farm. As he rode up the lane, the hounds bayed, as if he were a quarry. His mother shouted, "Who's there?" and moved from the shadows of the stable holding an ancient blunderbuss.

"For heaven's sake, Mother, put down that firelock before you hurt yourself." He swung off Wanderer.

"Lamb!" she cried. "What brings you here?"

"I've come to send you away."

"Whooks, you're lightheaded from nothin' to eat. Come in and I'll feed ye. Jack, come fetch Wanderer."

Alex shepherded her through the kitchen and into the parlor and shut the door.

"All right, Mother, I'll eat something in a moment. But I don't want to waste any time. Is Philly here?"

Mrs. March looked at him thoughtfully in the candlelight and shook her head. "She's with John and Martha Tout. She rode over to visit me yesterday and I told her she shouldn't be larrupin' about the country by herself in these times."

"Indeed she shouldn't. Then you know there's trouble coming. I want you to start loading a wagon tonight. Bedding, food, everything valuable you have. By dawn you're to be on your way to Lancaster. The Hethertons will welcome a visit from you. I'll fetch Philly to go with you. Take the hired help if they wish and drive whatever stock you value. You—"

"What's all this pother?" she cried. "Turnin' me out o' my home and off my land! Have you lost your senses?"

He argued vainly. This was *her* home and she would not budge from it. When he grew angry, she responded heatedly.

"What about your wife? Have you seen to her?"

"She won't leave the city."

"But you think you can send me packing!"

He sighed. "Mother, if you don't care what will happen when raiders from both armies come plundering—and they will and I know your temper— If you don't care about yourself, think of Philly. She's a young girl who—"

"All right," said Mrs. March. "All right, let's *talk* about Philly. What's she to you? Why are you, a married man, so all-fired upset about what happens to a servant?" She lowered her head and her voice fell. "I'm sorry, lamb. Forgive me. I understand about Philly. She should be got away from here. But it don't mean I've got to leave too." She looked up. "Don't act so wild distraught. I'll tell you what to do with her. Land sakes, for a lawyer you've less guile than a nesting hen. Send her back to Kathy in the city."

"But—"

"Take her there yourself—tomorrow. Tell her Kathy wants her. And I'll mind Kathy does want her even if she don't admit it. Philly told me yesterday they'd had words, but I could tell she bears Kathy no ill. Don't worry about me here. I'll keep a curb bit on my tongue, whatever happens. I reckon you're right that *they'll* occupy Philadelphia. And you're right a young woman's safer there than out here. For certain a young woman like Philly."

He wished that he could candidly tell her how he felt about Philly. But he scarcely dared discuss it with himself.

He had fled from Philly—back to the army, where she had convinced him that he belonged. Yes, she was wise. She had instinctively known a truth that he could not bear to face after his release from prison. Despair and doubt, such as imprisonment and the aftermath with Kathy in Philadelphia had instilled in him, could only be overcome by joining others who retained belief. Now he felt strong again. Now he believed more firmly in their joint cause than ever before.

Philly saw him riding up the lane early the next morning as she crossed the yard. She stared at him, her heart beating faster.

"Good morning, Philly." He swung to the ground, smiling.

"Alex." She wondered if he observed her face flushing. "I didn't know the army was so near."

"It will pass close today. I came to ask a favor." He seemed to be looking all around her instead of directly at her.

Anything he wished, she thought, but she did not speak.

His gaze finally met hers. "Would you go back to Philadelphia and stay with Kathy?"

She looked away. Of all the things he might have asked her to do, why did it have to be this?

"I know you quarreled," he said. "Would you tell me what went wrong?"

She would not tell him about Micah and Minna and their child. She regretted having told Kathy. It was not her story to tell anyone. After she and Minna walked to the farm with Liberty, she had introduced Minna to the Touts merely as a friend whose husband was in the army. Now Minna had insisted on going and taking Liberty with her. John

Tout had driven them to Germantown yesterday after she'd heard that the army was headed there.

"Have you seen Kathy?" she asked.

He nodded. "Yesterday. She—she's sorry that you left."

"Did she ask for me to come back?"

"She wants you to. You know Kathy. She—"

"Yes, Alex, I know Kathy. I reckon I was short with her. The day the army passed through Philadelphia toward Brandywine I trailed after it a ways with Mrs. Munger who was set on finding Macaroni Jack. We came on an army woman who'd come to her time with a child. I brought the woman and baby home because there was no place else for them to go. It got on Kathy's nerves, I reckon."

"I see." He scowled at the bridle in his hand. "I can imagine what happened. Nevertheless, I wish you'd go back there—and stay. Personally, I think the British will occupy the city before many days. I don't think we can check them. Even so, you'll be safer there than here. Kathy is staying in the city and you can help fend for each other. You're better off under British martial law than in the lawless country."

Was he concerned more for Kathy's safety or her own? It didn't matter. Looking at him, her heart beating quickly, she thought that she was a bad one. Being safe meant nothing to her; she wanted to go with him and the army. Why did the mind torment a body with evil so?

"You're worried about me?" she asked slowly.

"Yes." His face was flushing too.

"Everybody's worrying these days," she said quickly, almost gaily. "John wanted to pack off Mrs. Tout and Tom and me. He says he can't leave and she won't leave and I'm not going off somewhere by myself. That's foolish."

He took a deep breath. "But you *will* go to the city and stay. Because I ask you to."

"Yes," she said.

"Then get your things." He smiled at her. "I'll give you a ride there. While you're packing I'll speak to John and Mrs. Tout."

There were a hundred things she wanted to tell him as they trotted toward the city on that bright Sunday morning. Yet she could not bring herself to say much of anything. She wished, for one thing, that she could describe Micah's relationship with Minna, as Minna had described it to her.

Minna is a fine woman, she wanted to tell him. *And Micah is a good man. I loved him once and I thought I still did. Minna guessed it, I think. But I reckon I don't love him any more. Because after I got over the first shock of learning about him and Minna, I didn't feel the way a*

*girl in love should: not angry or jealous or badly hurt. What happened
to them just seemed natural and understandable, like it would if it happened to me. Isn't that terrible—of me, I mean? It's contrary to all the
preaching I've listened to, and I've listened to a heap in my time. What's
the matter with me, Alex?*

But it was not really necessary to say a word to him on such a quiet,
beautiful Sunday morning. She could ride thus forever. Probably it was
unmilitary for an officer to be riding alone with a girl behind him while
he clutched her big wicker basket in one hand. But if it was, he did not
seem to care.

They came, too quickly, to Philadelphia. In the somnolent, empty
streets of sun-drenched noon Wanderer's hoofs echoed noisily. A constable stepped into Market Street, shaking his staff at them.

"For shame, sir!" he cried. "Two a-horse and the lady's limbs exposed.
On a Sunday noon, sir!"

She leaped to the ground, blushing. Alex, laughing, dismounted. "I'll
take my basket," she said quickly. "Pray forgive me, Alex. I'd clean
forgot—"

"Forgive you what? And I'll carry the basket." Grinning at the constable, he said, "The proprietors smile on your alertness, Grandfather.
May archangels decorate your staff and Friends commend thee to
heaven."

The constable gaped after them as they walked down Market, Alex
leading Wanderer and carrying her basket. They walked so slowly that
Wanderer began to nudge Alex's shoulder with his nose. Alex frowned
thoughtfully in the dazzling sunlight, as if trying to decide how to say
something. But he did not speak until they came to the house on Fourth
Street.

"I'll leave you here, Philly."

She looked at him, surprised. "You aren't coming in?"

"No."

"Don't you want to see—"

"No." Extending his right hand, he gripped hers tightly. "Take care
of yourself, Philly."

For an instant she thought she was going to cry. But she tried to smile
and said unsteadily, "You take care of . . ."

"Yes." He sprang into the saddle, wheeled Wanderer, and cantered
away.

She watched until he was out of sight, but he did not look back and
wave to her.

Walking slowly to the back door, she pushed it open. The kitchen was a sore sight, she thought. It needed cleaning, and cleaning a kitchen was what she needed to do.

"Kathy," she called.

Kathy walked quickly along the hall and paused in the doorway, staring at her.

"I'm back," Philly said.

Kathy began to smile. "I'm glad you are, Philly."

XXXIII

THE first time he saw him he thought that he wasn't much.

It was Saturday at the old camp, near Germantown, which the 7th Pennsylvania reached in midafternoon after the long march from Chester.

They swung off the Manatawney Road onto the big slope where he halted the company and faced it from column into line and called the roll from memory: "Addams . . . Ardweiler . . . Bartlow . . ." After he finished the roll, holding in his mind the list of absent and quickly deciding who was likely to turn up again, he dismissed the company. Most of the men dropped down, spread-eagled in the dusty short grass, staring up vacantly at white clouds flowing before a freshening northwest wind. They were dead beat after their whipping at the Brandywine and the long march from it.

As he started off to find Captain Newman and report the absent, he saw Minna walking slowly toward him across the slope carrying something in an arm. She waved and called to him, but he pretended not to see her. Yet she wouldn't go away just because he pretended she wasn't there. Besides, he'd let her down badly on her laboring day, the last time he'd seen her. How badly it still wrenched him to remember.

Scowling, he strode to her.

"Afternoon," she said.

"You look perker," he told her. "Sorry I couldn't find you a midwife that day. But I hear from Mrs. Munger that she happened on you in time."

"Where's she at? I'd mighty much like to chat wi' her an'—"

"Riding the baggage train most like. Queen of the baggage train they call her now. Macaroni Jack's company was peeled off and ain't come up yet. Is that him?" He nodded at the bundle in her arm.

Her face lighted. "It's him all right." She thrust the bundle toward him. "Liberty Heath."

"Liberty? That's a hell of a name." *Liberty!* It was a mighty fine name, he thought, but he didn't care to let her know he thought so.

"Take him," she said.

He shook his head and fell back a step. Then he leaned forward cautiously. The child's large blue eyes stared at him gravely. There didn't seem to be much to him except the eyes in a round face.

"What color's his hair?"

Minna pulled back the hood of the gray blanket in which he was wrapped and Micah saw soft blond down on a round skull.

"He's not much." His tone was indignant. "You couldn't tell him from a girl."

"You for certain can." Minna sounded indignant too. "You just heft him. I vaw he weighs a stone already. A hearty mite. Hands'll grip your finger tight. Toes all straight an' fine like little periwinkle flowers. A great butter an' sucker at feedin' time. Never cries, 'ceptin' a warnin' wail when a stranger comes nigh. Reg'lar little watchdog he is. See, he knows ya ain't a stranger."

Micah rubbed his jaw. "Is that a fact?"

"It for certain is. Philly, who's a great hand with babies, says she ain't never seen—"

"Philly? You mean Philly Twillow?"

Minna nodded.

"Mrs. Munger never told me. She just said you'd got a boy and were all right and being taken care of somewhere in the city."

"Philly was with her," Minna said. "She took us home to that fine house she was workin' at—"

"You told *her?"*

Minna, staring at him expressionlessly, nodded again.

Oh, Christ, he thought. So Philly knew about—everything. "W–Was she put out?"

Minna shook her head slowly. "But that fine Mrs. March, she struck me as put out, don't ask me why."

"She knows about—about it too?"

Minna nodded.

Sweet Jesus Christ, he thought. "Listen," he demanded, "is there anybody you ain't told about—about—this?"

"We didn't tell 'em at the Tout farm where we walked to a'ter I busted one o' Mrs. March's chiner teapots an' we left. Philly said we'd best not speak about it any more. She didn't say, but I reckoned you must 'a been a wild young un an' she didn't want 'em sayin' they'd always knowed ya'd come to no good end. I'll tell ya somethin'. I never knowed a better girl 'n Philly, an' I reckon there was a time she was sweet on you."

Groaning, he walked away to report the absent to Captain Newman. There was a time, he thought. And now? He cursed himself and Minna too, wishing he'd never seen her and never would see her again.

But at evening, in that cool and purple time between the drumbeat of retreat and taptoo, he found that it wasn't bad to have her with him again. He had decided that he wouldn't take her any more, though her gaze followed him everywhere, begging. One little bastard was enough, he thought. Furthermore, he didn't *want* her. Like a Shawnee brave, he wished for a wilderness purge of women: a long hunt or warpath of months' duration when he would be renewed or die.

Nevertheless, he admitted to himself that evening by the Schuylkill that it wasn't bad to have her back. She made him comfortable, building a fire and cooking up a hearty meal of tasty vittles she'd brought from the farm. They shared their food with Mrs. Munger, who arrived toward nightfall in a Conestoga, and Macaroni Jack, whose company marched up a few minutes later. In return, Mrs. Munger presented them with a sheet of tenting.

Mrs. Munger was rapidly becoming a highly respected and powerful person among the ranks of the army. Now in September there was a harvest of infants sowed as wild oats in the cold of last December when men and women huddled together for warmth. Mrs. Munger reaped this harvest; as a midwife, she had not lost a mother and seldom an infant.

She was much sought after, too, as a fortuneteller and dispenser of medical advice. Her advice was interesting, the cures attributed to her extraordinary. Consumptives should breathe for fifteen minutes each morning from a hole cut in fresh turf. In the event of a violent nosebleed, place a slip of white paper under the tongue. For cancer of the breast apply goose dung externally and swallow an infusion of distilled horse's leg warts in a pint of warm ale. It was no wonder that Mrs. Munger, like the Queen of Sheba, was forever attended by a court of admirers.

That evening after supper, however, she and Minna retired into the tent she shared with Macaroni Jack where their voices could be heard babbling without pause. To all visitors who approached the tent asking for her she called, "I ain't to home this evenin'. I've a conference with a friend here." All departed respectfully except a Virginia wagoner who twisted his hat in red hands and wailed, "Mrs. Munger, Smith 'pears took wi' the apoplexy." She promptly replied, "Give him a pint o' salted warm water and make him sweat. Now go along, Jarvis."

Micah and Macaroni Jack sat by the fire, smoking short clay pipes and still talking about what had gone wrong at the Brandywine. Since Mrs. Munger caught up with him, Macaroni Jack was at times happier and at other times more despondent than he had been, Micah observed. Although he thoroughly enjoyed her company, he was thrown into profound gloom by her determination to lead him into marriage.

But that evening both felt content despite defeat and the drag of women and the slow deterioration of the army. There was something mighty pleasant about sitting here with Jack, Micah thought, while the women murmured and the sounds of the encampment died away in sleep. Although he was talking of the Brandywine, he found himself thinking of Liberty asleep there in the tent.

He was surprised when Jack leaned toward him and said in a low voice, "Let's us get that Liberty out here and look at him." Jack had glanced at the child so askance earlier that Micah believed he wasn't much taken with him. "You get him," Jack said. "I've no use for infants, but I'd like a closer look at this one."

Going to the tent, he told Minna to lend him the child for a minute. She placed Liberty in his arms and he carried him gingerly to the fire.

"He's awake," he said, peering down at the wide blue eyes, "but he don't cry except around strangers."

Macaroni Jack thrust his head close. "Look at that," he exclaimed. "I ain't a stranger to him. Look at the little bastard."

"Don't you ever call him that," Micah said.

"No, sir! I didn't mean it, Micah. I'll never call him that."

"I ain't had a good look at how he's built." Micah unwound the blanket and lifted Liberty. "She has him in a dress like he was a girl."

"He's wet his breeches," Jack said.

"It takes 'em a while to get house-broke." Micah began pulling off Liberty's dress. "Look at the little varmint squirm, but he don't cry." Stricken by a horrible thought, he said, "I've heard tell as infants that don't cry are sometimes deaf."

"Wait a minute." Jack crept behind Liberty's head and clapped his hands resoundingly. Liberty's eyes rolled upward and he wailed. "He ain't deef," Jack shouted delightedly. "The little b— varmint just ain't a cryin' baby. You're liable to catch him his death undressin' him in the night air."

"Not him," Micah said proudly. "He's *tough*."

He was such a young baby that you couldn't tell much about him. But you could tell something, Micah thought. His body was long and his shoulders square. Instead of crying, he worked his legs and arms in the cold wind.

"Goddamn," Micah said softly.

Although he didn't see much of Liberty in the following days, he thought of him often. On the worst days, when luck was against them, it cheered him to think of his son back yonder somewhere with the women.

Nearly all the days were bad in those weeks. Luck seemed to be forever against them. Many felt that their own officers and the weather conspired with the enemy to turn on them.

On Sunday, the day after they'd arrived at the old camp, they forded the river through waist-deep water and marched west in an unseasonably cold northwest wind that kept them shivering. The wind, blowing colder and harder, circled to the northeast on Monday when the fortunate spent their last night under tents in an encampment near the Warren Tavern beyond Paoli. The next morning the General ordered the baggage and women away to the east.

Watching Minna and Liberty ride off in a Conestoga with Mrs. Munger, Micah said to Macaroni Jack, "Now we're for it."

"Maybe." Jack looked gloomily up and down the lines of shivering men and spat. "But I don't smell much strong battle sweat on us."

They marched on to a little shallow valley where the White Horse Tavern lay. On a hill beyond stretched the crimson and green of Howe's main army in line of battle. Nevertheless, they marched on into the valley over soft ground as the wind increased. When orders were shouted to form from column into line with the soft ground in their rear and the enemy on the hill above them, Macaroni Jack howled wrathfully. It was certain destruction, Micah thought. What ailed the General that he didn't realize it?

But someone realized it, someone who had more influence with the General than sergeants had. They withdrew from the valley and, as they formed on the hill facing the British lines, rain suddenly blasted from the northeast in drenching sheets. Within minutes there was not a dry musket or flint or powder charge in the army. The earth melted into mud under them and many sank above their knees. The British and Hessians across the flooding morass of the shallow valley were no better off, they knew.

After a while orders drifted downwind and they slogged off through the rain along a muddy road. No one knew where they were going except that it was on west. No one much cared. To pull each foot from the sucking mud and push it ahead became a painful effort. But they pressed on, all through the day and far into the night.

They knew by the keening of the wind that they were on the brow of a hill when they were told to fall out. Pitching down, they fell asleep in a muddy field.

It was still raining the next morning when they got stiffly to their feet. Someone said they were at a place called Yellow Springs and that they'd come eleven miles yesterday. A little bread was issued and everyone agreed that there wasn't an ounce of dry powder left in the army.

They went on through the rain. Eventually they heard that their destination was Reading Furnace where they would draw a new supply of powder from the magazines. The roads were even worse than the day before and they had made only nine miles when the General must have seen that they couldn't move another rod. They slept without fires on the ground again. At three o'clock in the morning they kicked one another awake and crept on toward Reading Furnace, still twelve miles distant.

Late in the afternoon they staggered into the Furnace, too tired to care that powder awaited them. They ate hot food, their first in three days. Afterwards, men fell asleep as they cleaned their firelocks.

At three the next morning they were up and on the road back to Yellow Springs. No one could remember what day it was; no one cared. They swung along faster, for the mud had dried, though the creek fords still were high. About sundown they found themselves at a ford high up on the rain-swollen Schuylkill. Parker's Ford, someone said. They reckoned they'd camp the night there. But they didn't.

"Get up! Get up!" the officers roared. "We're crossing!"

It took all night for the army to cross. Men held muskets and pouches aloft in one hand above the neck-deep, swirling water and clutched at suspended ratlines with the other hand. The artillery and caissons were freighted across in frail boats while the horses swam and floundered behind.

Dawn found them on the east bank, and they walked again instead of sleeping. At first they thought they merely were hunting a decent campsite, but as the sun climbed and the day turned hot they knew that the General had no intention of letting them rest. They stumbled on, with the river on their right, past Swede's Ford, seven miles below Parker's. Eyes half closed, panting for breath in the stifling heat, too tired to curse, they came late in the afternoon to Richardson's Ford, ten miles below Swede's. There the column didn't so much wheel off the road onto a lane along Perkiomen Creek as simply slide onto it and pitch down and fall asleep along the bank.

The next morning, when the baggage train still had not appeared and no rations were issued, a number of men disappeared.

You couldn't blame them, Micah thought. As best he could figure out, they were just about where they'd been a week ago after marching nearly a hundred miles in bad weather over almost impassable roads. They had lost their powder and recovered it. But in the days of plodding strain they had lost their fighting edge, and they could not recover it as they had their powder.

Tempers were short. Men too tired to fight were not too tired to quarrel over whether or not the General was a fool. They and the Schuylkill again lay between the British and Philadelphia. But the British again lay between them and their stores at Reading Furnace. How could the General hope to protect both his stores and Philadelphia? Why didn't he make his choice and pick his ground and fight it out?

That day, as they stretched grumbling and cursing along Perkiomen Creek, Micah saw Alex. Covered with dust, his horse flecked with foam, he galloped up to headquarters from the south, apparently bearing a message. Micah turned away quickly when he saw him.

He had hoped that he would never have to confront Alex again. For Alex had been his friend and he had betrayed him in the vilest way that one man could another. He didn't want to be reminded of anything in the past. The only happiness left him seemed to be in thinking of Liberty Heath, that hearty little varmint.

Late in the afternoon word spread that Wayne and his Pennsylvanians had suffered a terrible defeat near Paoli. "A massacree," men called it. Wayne, heeling Howe's army, had holed up in a forest meadow near Paoli Tavern with the intent of ambushing the British rear. But the ambushers had been ambushed by Major General Sir Charles Grey and the Black Watch, who had done their bloody work at night with the bayonet. Hundreds were said to have been slain and hundreds of others to have thrown away their muskets and fled in panic.

"One thing's certain," Macaroni Jack said. "Now that Howe is free of Wayne at his heels, he'll stop mousing. He'll pounce."

And when they were routed up at three o'clock the next morning, they believed that Howe had finally pounced indeed. But instead of marching south toward Germantown and Philadelphia, they marched north along the east bank of the Schuylkill. After going ten miles, they halted for a long break. Men laid five to three odds they'd now march back south again. But they continued north five miles farther and camped near Pott's Grove where the baggage train finally caught up with them late that night.

Admirers of the General pointed out how smart he was. The British were said to be camped along the western bank of the river from Valley Forge to French Creek. Now, they said, the army's right was secure from a flanking movement and the British could not take the stores at Reading.

Then the next day word came that the British were not at Valley Forge. In a forced march they had darted away, crossed the Schuylkill at Fatland Ford twenty miles to the south, and now lay between the army and Philadelphia. Everyone knew the General would not go down and try to engage them. His men were too worn out.

As Macaroni Jack expressed it, "Mr. Washington said, 'Check,' and

Mr. Howe said, 'Mate,' because Mr. Washington moved to the place where Mr. Howe wanted him to be."

The twenty-sixth of that September was an interesting day in the history of Micah Heath as well as in the history of the war, he realized later. It was the day the British marched unopposed into Philadelphia. It also was the day Minna found a red rash on Liberty's chest. The interesting thing about his own reaction, Micah thought eventually, was that he no longer much cared that the British had taken Philadelphia, but he was greatly concerned by the fear of Liberty catching the smallpox.

They marched from Pott's Grove back to Perkiomen Creek that day and camped near Pennybacker's Mill. And Micah worried all the way about the rash Minna had discovered on Liberty that morning. When the wagons and women arrived at evening, Mrs. Munger tried to reassure him. Liberty didn't have the pox and she was curing his rash with a mercurial salve, she said. But he had no faith in her old wives' remedies. He sat up half the night watching Liberty.

The next day he knew that he should try to find himself new shoes, for his were almost worn out from the long marching and he didn't want to join the hundreds of barefoot men who lagged on the marches. But he didn't go scrounging for shoes that day. He simply sat and watched Liberty, feeling his forehead frequently for fever and pondering what would become of him when winter came.

The army moved again, five miles to the Skippack Road. Now that he knew Liberty didn't have the pox, he reckoned that he should be happier. But he felt tired and indifferent. Once, staring west at the golden October haze, he thought of lighting out over there with Liberty and Minna. Yet he realized that although he might be able to go it alone, he was too tired to fend for them.

Everyone was tired and many were sick. In the damp mornings the sound of coughing that rose from the encampment was like the croaking of ten thousand bullfrogs. Sleep did not relieve the bone-deep aching of their bodies. There never was enough to eat; although no one was starving, everyone was famished.

The army crept on again, three miles down the Skippack Road to Metuchen Hill, sixteen miles above Germantown. They did not know that the General had hatched out a new and elaborate plan.

At seven o'clock on the evening of October third they formed and marched off toward Germantown through a night as black as the inside of a wolf's mouth. Wayne led them. Sullivan's men were ahead of them, and Conway led the van.

When morning light cracked the eastern sky they were on Chestnut

Hill. Coming through Mount Airy in the growing light, Micah saw the Skippack Road reaching straight into a rising mist. The houses of Germantown strung along the road in their rail-fence enclosures seemed to stretch for a hundred miles. Now there was heavy firing ahead as they moved to the left off the road and formed from column into line and waited. The mist grew thicker, and then Wayne roared at them and they went ahead into the fog.

Forgetting their fatigue, they advanced like veterans, smashing fences before them to straighten their lines. Musket fire blazed blindingly from the mist. They replied and ran forward at the double in a bayonet charge, smashing into a body of yelling shadows. One lunged at Micah. He sprang aside, but he was heavy with fatigue. The bayonet stung his thigh. He thrust his own bayonet at the shadow and it fled, shrieking, into the mist.

Fingering his thigh, he thought that it was only a scratch and moved on with Newman, shouting at the men behind to keep their lines dressed. When it seemed that they had passed all the way through Germantown, they heard a growing din of firing behind them. "We're cut off!" someone shouted. "No!" Micah cried. "Steady on, steady on!"

In a moment a horseman loomed out of the roiling smoke and mist. Wayne thrust an excited face toward them. "About!" he shouted and Micah wondered dully, About what? Then he understood that they were to turn back. Sullivan's men, supposed to be on the other side of the road in the dense fog, must have run into trouble.

"Cut off!"

As they started back, with officers and sergeants crying steady, firing broke out behind them. But they did not panic. They groped on toward the rising crash of cannonading and musketry. Suddenly a mass of trotting troops loomed from the mist on their right, halted, and fired on them. They fired back and again someone shrieked, "Cut off!"

Instantly their lines broke into a howling pack of frightened men that spun Micah around as he roared at them to hold. Dimly he saw the men to the right who had fired on them breaking and fleeing too. An officer who stood waving his sword and trying vainly to halt them, shouted over a shoulder, "Stephen's Brigade!"

"Wayne's!" Micah cried to him. "We're Wayne's!"

Then Wayne himself was there, screaming curses into the fog after his disappearing men. Micah stood still, cursing steadily at this doltish army that had frightened itself out of victory by firing on itself.

He was getting out of it. He was finished with this log-headed, stumbling, fumbling, bumbling war.

He did not run. He walked along through the mist, around the sound of heavy firing. A tide of men swept him up and carried him along the road through the mist. Sweating, panting, yelling incoherently, they poured around him and around a body of horsemen stationed in the road. He glimpsed Alex March's powder-blackened face as he sat his horse, forlornly staring at the fleeing men. Lowering his head, Micah walked around him too.

The General rode among them, his hands raised imploringly, his weak voice lost in the patter of their hurrying feet and the thunderous firing behind them. Micah stared up at him defiantly, wishing the General would look at him. For if he would glare angrily at *him,* he'd halt and, arms akimbo, stare out of countenance this mighty General who forever fumbled and blundered and lost.

But the General rode back toward the firing without glancing at him.

He felt weak and lightheaded as he walked along. Then he realized that his left leg was wet and, looking down, he saw that his breeches were soaked with blood. Turning into a yard with a well sweep, he sat down and studied the oozing cut on his thigh. He ripped a strip off his shirt and bound the wound tightly. Then he lowered the well bucket and drank deeply, pouring the remainder of the bucket over his head and leg. He walked on.

Eventually he fell in with some men who said they were from Muhlenberg's brigade. They told of seeing General Stephen lying dead drunk in a fence corner, of courage and cowardice, of the feel of certain victory in their grasp, and then the sudden confused empty sense of loss.

At times he wondered if he possibly could reach the camp at Metuchen Hill before his weakness felled him. Lagging behind group after group of hurrying men, he came late in the afternoon to the scarred and fire-blackened campsite. It was deserted.

"Get along," a mounted officer called to him. "We camp tonight at Pennybacker's Mill."

Sinking to the ground, he lowered his throbbing head between his knees. In the past twenty-four hours he had walked thirty-two miles and fought in a battle and taken a bayonet wound and not had a bite to eat. Now *they* said he had to walk eight miles more. He did not think he could do it. Falling back, he slept.

Voices awakened him. It was dusk. He raised himself on an elbow and saw that a few men still moved up the road. A group of horsemen approached, riding their poor spent beasts at a walk. He watched them dully, envying them. The officer leading them leaned over in the saddle to stare at him and Micah saw that he was Alex March.

"Micah!" He turned off the road and dismounted. "Your leg, are you—"

"A scratch," Micah said thickly, wishing he could crawl away in the gathering darkness. With a great effort, he got to his feet.

"Swing up," Alex said. "You'll ride to Pennybacker's Mill."

"No!" He shook his head violently, unable to look at him. "Thanks, no!"

"But—"

"No!"

He walked on up the Skippack Road.

Around midnight he stumbled into the camp with queer, jerky steps. Someone led him to the regiment's bivouac.

Then he was lying on the ground beside a fire and Minna was kneeling beside him. He became aware of Mrs. Munger and Macaroni Jack as he swallowed something hot with the good strong body of meat in it.

"For certain you ain't going to die long as you stay away from the surgeons," Mrs. Munger said. "I'm fixin' you a fine poultice of toasted cheese for that cut."

"It'd set better in my belly." He tried to grin. "Where's Liberty?"

"Right here." Minna held him over Micah's head.

When he took his son he thought that he could feel strength returning to his arms. He said, "Look at the little varmint laughing at me."

XXXIV

LATE on a bleak December afternoon they came to a vast field at the foot of a densely wooded slope that climbed to a ridge about two miles long.

"This hit?" muttered Feuchtwiler.

"Yes," Micah said. "The village is beyond the ridge yonder."

They had crept up from Gulph Mills through oozing mud which had begun riming in a northwest wind. Stringing out and bunching up like freezing cattle, they had not marched or even seemed to walk. Rather, they had stumbled, slithered, crawled on north without an officer once raising his voice in command.

No one ordered them to halt now. They simply stopped in the road by a kind of unanimous consternation and stared at the snow-streaked brown land rising into gray trees that rattled their branches in the wind. Somewhere a man, an officer presumably, shouted incoherently. There was a squeak as a boy tightened his drumhead.

The sudden roll of a drum made Feuchtwiler start nervously. Another, and then a third, joined it.

"Here." Micah, who had carried Liberty all day, held him out to Minna. "Here." She had sunk beside the road, coughing. "Take him." She stared up at him dully, too tired to rise, and then she held out her arms and took Liberty.

"Com—pany!" Micah cried.

"For Christ sake," Feuchtwiler said, and the other eight remaining members of the company stared at Micah stupidly.

Ahead, Macaroni Jack cried to his company of twelve. And then they were in a double column and marching, not in step, but marching nevertheless in a kind of wild, skittering dance to the drums that rolled too fast. Off the road and around the edge of the vast field, as if they were celebrating something. Crows rose, cawing, from the woods and were echoed by the mocking cries of the marching column. Glancing back, Micah expected to see the column breaking. But shoeless, almost naked, men who had barely moved on the freezing roads danced along at a quick-step now, circling into the vast field. They shouted, jeered, brayed, cursed, laughed, wailed—at themselves and their luck and the fate that finally had brought them to this place called Valley Forge.

As they circled, leaderless except for the drummer boy who apparently led them wherever he wished, the officers shook themselves from their torpor and dashed here and there. They brought the crazy drummer boy to heel and, shouting conflicting orders, they brought chaos to the fairly orderly progress of the men around the field. The women and scrawny children flapped among the milling men, looking and sounding like the startled crows that had fled over the ridge.

"Hoooeee!" Micah cried disgustedly. He halted, coughing, and spat into a patch of dirty snow.

Turning, he stalked up the slope. When he reached the edge of the woods, he looked back and saw Feuchtwiler following him. Minna stumbled behind Feuchtwiler, clutching Liberty and her bundle and kettle. The four, six, seven, eight remaining men followed slowly.

"Up *here?*" Addams called angrily.

"Up here," Micah replied. "Out of the wind. Wood handy. Feuchtwiler, pack the kettles with snow in the woods yonder. Merton, start a fire. Schlossberg—"

"That new colonel," Schlossberg said, "whatever his name, he says we're to form down yonder—"

"Pope's his name," Micah said, "and Pope he is. He can tell it to the officers."

Several jeered. The company did not have an officer. At Whitemarsh, Captain Newman had talked himself free to go on recruiting duty.

Bounty-hunter, Micah thought contemptuously. If they ever saw Newman again it would be in the spring.

"Schlossberg, go find Major Gant. See what you can draw."

"The commissary!"

They jeered him *and* the commissary. The wagons had not come up. No one had seen them in almost two weeks since the British threatened them at Whitemarsh. After that most of the women had refused to stay with the baggage train and now walked with their men. Some said the wagons had been sent off to Trappe, but no one knew for certain.

"You go on, Schlossberg."

Schlossberg went, calling back, "Pope's down yonder wavin' his arms an' cussin' us."

Micah saw the strange young militia colonel railing at Macaroni Jack far down the slope. Macaroni Jack paid no attention to him as he led his dozen men up the slope. They, too, were without an officer. As Continentals, they would be damned if they'd pay any mind to this new militia menace from Lancaster who wanted them to camp down there in the wind. Micah saw Wayne hobbling toward Pope, calming him down, telling him that his boys would take care of themselves for tonight at least. Wayne's face was contorted as he clutched his strapped chest; he still suffered from the splintered breastbone that had not healed since Germantown when his horse was shot under him.

Everyone's face was contorted, Micah thought, looking around slowly. Minna's gaunt face was twisted in a fit of coughing as she sat on a rock holding Liberty. Leaning down, he pulled aside the blanket fold and stared at him. His eyes seemed enormous in a face that was wizened now rather than round.

Cursing to himself, he turned into the woods. Although he was bone-tired, he moved quickly and quietly, searching the snow patches for rabbit tracks in the fading light. When he finally found a trot, he tied horsehair twitch-ups and went on, searching for another trot. It was almost dark when he came to the ridge. To the north, beyond the ridge, the Schuylkill curved from west to east. Turning, he looked at the flares of innumerable fires around the vast field. West, where the ridge dropped away, Valley Creek flowed north into the river, he remembered.

They would winter here, in this elbow of creek and river. It could be made into a strongly defensible place, he knew. But once these trees were timbered out for huts and abatis and firewood, it would be desolate.

As he went down the slope through the brush, he doubted that he would winter here. In twelve days his enlistment would be up and it was desperately necessary that he do something about Liberty. Unless he quickly found him a warm home and decent food, the child certainly would die. And the only place he could take him was to the farm.

He swung a hand at a low branch, raging at Minna again. For weeks he'd raged at her for stubbornly insisting on tagging along with him, as if he were more important than Liberty's life. Something was wrong with her. A natural mother would think first of her child and of finding him a safe place. Though she took the best care of Liberty that she could, something was mighty wrong with her for refusing to admit that the child couldn't possibly survive this perpetual exposure and near starvation. She was wasting away with her racking cough; it appeared to him and to Mrs. Munger that she had the consumption. Nevertheless, she stumbled doggedly after him, clutching their weakening child and forever staring about with glazed eyes as if she didn't know where she was.

Refusing to yield to his raging or begging and return to the farm where Martha Tout surely would make a place for her and Liberty, she had persisted in following him through all the pointless marching after Germantown. The army had moved hither and yonder aimlessly in those weeks, as if restlessly looking for something and never finding it. There had been one good day, October eighteenth, when general orders reported the surrender of Burgoyne at a place called Saratoga in the north, and a double ration of rum was issued.

That stupendous victory had heartened Micah. He heard how the victorious southward march of Burgoyne's British and Hessians had slowed as men and boys flooded out from farms and hamlets to oppose it. Eventually the green American summer soldiers had outnumbered, outfought and surrounded the vaunted professionals. There had been nothing for Burgoyne to do but surrender to General Gates, whom Macaroni Jack called "an old woman lucky enough to have been married in a military way to General Benedict Arnold, the man who really fought 'em." Men alone had not defeated Burgoyne, Micah thought. The land had done it, swallowing his ponderous baggage trains in its vastness, turning its rivers against him, refusing to feed him as the Americans scorched the earth before him. Burgoyne had carefully taken into account all except one thing, the most important thing: the land that defeated every would-be conqueror who failed to understand its vast, harsh, unyielding nature. Tread me lightly, cautiously, swiftly, said the land. Linger, struggle against my tracks and hills and rivers, and you will die.

Except for the news of Burgoyne's defeat, the days of the depleted main army in Pennsylvania had crept by emptily and painfully. The surrender at Saratoga demonstrated that the British *could* be defeated— But how could a victory ever be won by the pointless marching the General forced on his exhausted men?

That stupid marching, Micah thought. From Perkiomen up to Towa-mencin, and then clean down to Metuchen Hill. From there they went to Whippany, no one knew why, and then to Whitemarsh, for reasons as pointless. Once, in the dull days at Whitemarsh, they'd started across the Schuylkill for an unknown destination, but a British force had caught them crossing Matson's Ford and they'd turned back to Whitemarsh again. By the time the General had decided that they'd winter at Valley Forge they were so worn down, hungry, sick and short of clothing that it took them almost a week to walk the thirteen miles from Whitemarsh to the Forge. During four of those days they'd huddled around fires at Gulph Mills, without shelter, because the ice-rutted roads were too rough for barefoot men to travel.

I want out, he thought angrily. And he would go. In twelve days now he'd take Liberty and Minna and walk to the farm. He'd leave them there and go on west to Lancaster or York when he felt strong enough to walk it. Somewhere out there he'd find work freighting or doing any mortal job that came to hand. Some day he might enlist for a term again. But not this winter. Not here in this miserable Valley Forge.

Everything went wrong. In his dazed and weakened state he had crazy notions that he couldn't shake from his mind. Sometimes the world seemed a great freezing icicle and he a drop of water that froze to it when he tried to roll free; congealed, packed in, his being lost in the vast freeze, he was powerless to move.

As the new year approached, however, he was surprised at what he had done. All of them were surprised at what they accomplished in their dazed state that was like a walking death. They chopped timber, rolled and carried logs, thawed frozen clay and raised cabins of the exact dimensions that someone—Pope, Gant, Wayne, perhaps the General him-self—ordered in voices they heard remotely, on the far horizon of awareness. Sixteen feet long by fourteen wide, with walls six and a half feet high, the cabins somehow rose in orderly spacings. Sapling ridge-poles, boughs lashed on, mud, straw, mud, mud. A fireplace and chimney of logs lined with eighteen inches of clay—at least eighteen inches, mind. Split oaken doors, with hinges painfully carved from oak. But it was not the end. There must be twelve bunks to a cabin, three in a corner one above another. It rained, and water streamed through the roof and choking smoke rolled from the fireplace. Nevertheless, they had done something.

They had built a cabin, yet everything went wrong.

Minna lay in a lower bunk of the cabin with Liberty. She had tottered there from the tent she'd shared with Mrs. Munger while the cabins were raised. Although Mrs. Munger had been Mrs. Maloney for more than a month and proudly referred to herself as Mrs. Munger-Maloney, everyone—even Macaroni Jack—still called her Mrs. Munger. She came each day from the adjoining cabin where she lived with Jack and his company and sat for hours with Minna. Why, Micah often wondered, should a big strong young woman like Minna have fallen so weak while Mrs. Munger, who was much older, remained so spry?

Minna troubled him so much that he couldn't stay in the cabin with her any length of time. Wherever he crouched in that dark, smoky hole, her eyes forever glittered at him. Sometimes, when he was far from the cabin, he thought that he still heard her coughing.

"She's goin'," Mrs. Munger said to him on the last day of the year.

"Going where?" he asked dully. One of the things that had gone wrong was the hopelessness of his plan to walk to the farm with Minna and Liberty on the first decent day of the new year; now Minna couldn't totter farther than the latrine.

"Goin' to heaven, I pray," Mrs. Munger said. "It's the consumption. She's spittin' blood now, and that's near the end. Why don't you let her die happy, Micah?"

"Ain't I doing everything I can?" he cried angrily. "I've worn out my shoes hunting food." He pointed to his feet wrapped in rags. "I've done without myself to—"

"She's past food," Mrs. Munger said. "It's love she needs. If you'd let her know you love her, she'd go content. Let me get the chaplain to—"

"No!" By God never, he thought. He had learned about this matter called living. It was a trap, an enormous deadfall set to hem you in forever. You leaped forward one day in your springtime onto bright green turf that suddenly crumbled under you, and far into the winter of your life you were trapped in a deep pit.

"No!" he shouted again at Mrs. Munger, who stared up at him, her eyes hard, her lips sunken stubbornly. He knew the trap too well now. If he let the chaplain mumble the marriage ceremony over Minna and him, the next he knew she'd be up and about, following him everywhere again. He'd be married to her forever.

"If I was to marry—" He was silent, his jaw slack. Not wanting to look at Mrs. Munger for fear she read his thoughts, he turned and walked away. If I was ever to marry, he thought, it'll be a girl like Philly, not a withering crow like Minna who forever caws around me.

He had done his best for Liberty and her in these last worst days of the year. In the two-day famine, when not an ounce of anything was issued to the brigade, Liberty and Minna had eaten. Tired though he was from raising the cabin, he'd worked rabbit trots evening and morning beyond the limits of the camp. When he came back through the frosty murk of dawn with a pair of rabbits, the men in the cabin hung about him like wolves, watching every move of his swift knife. In the stillness of morning, as the strong smell of roasting rabbit meat filled the cabin, their empty bellies rolled thunderously. He gave each the same share as himself, but they resented the larger shares he saved for Liberty and Minna.

Sometimes, waking in the night with hunger pains, he'd wonder how Liberty could survive another day—or had he died within the hour? Leaning over the edge of his bunk, he'd listen to his quick light breathing in Minna's bunk below. Through Minna's rattling breath and nightmare moaning Liberty sounded like a spent puppy. By every human measure he should be dead. Minna's failing breasts had dried the day after they came to the Forge and Mrs. Munger could not find a wet nurse anywhere. Now Liberty sucked through bits of straw a thin gruel of coarse flour and warm water, choking and nearly drowning himself until they learned to pinch the straw and slap his back. Micah, whose teeth remained strong, chewed meat for him and fingered pinches of it into his gaping, slobbering mouth. Somehow his tough little guts milled the strength to keep him alive.

The rabbits disappeared; one morning there was not a fresh track in the snow anywhere and he could not fathom where they had gone. He stole a sack of meal from a wagon in Learned's brigade one night in the dark of the moon, slipping past a dozing sentry, knowing that if he were caught he'd receive a hundred and ninety-nine lashes and be broken to private. He stalked crows, remembering dimly how he used to like those shrewd birds and how John Tout detested them; at last he cawed one curious old yellow-beak to his cover and winged him with a lucky shot. An officer chased him for firing his musket, but Micah outran him and doubled back to the cabin. They boiled the crow for three hours, stinking up the cabin, but it remained so tough and bitter that they vomited after eating it.

Although it was January and his time was up, he could not go. He could not even bring himself to walk to Pope's cabin and say that the regimental records would show his enlistment had ended on the first of the month. With growing horror he knew that he was waiting for Minna and Liberty to die.

Many who had the strength to flee were deserting. Two men of the company failed to return from sentry duty on the third of January and Addams disappeared the next night. Pope railed at him for letting three of his men escape, as if he were a jailer. Micah scarcely listened to him; he felt too indifferent even to tell him that his own time was up. Yet he didn't blame them. He couldn't blame any who escaped, not even Wayne, who worried a leave from the General and went off to the comfort of his home after having talked so loudly about sharing the discomforts of his men. On sentry duty one bitterly cold night he watched a man stumble off south through the snow and did not even bother to challenge him.

It was the night a man named Deacons or Dakkins or something of the sort died on the post east of Micah's. He was a tall, gaunt man, out of his senses with fever and talking to himself when they took over their posts at midnight. Minna, too, had been out of her head with fever when he left the cabin. The wind, rising from the northwest, bore the awful screaming of the famine-struck artillery horses. The sound, to him, was worse than the raving of the sentry. The whole world, even the horses, was going mad, he thought numbly as he stomped to the limit of his post.

When he returned, the sentry, whatever his name, sat in the snow, giggling and chanting, "Oh, sing a song of sixpence, a pocketful of rye, six and forty officers spat in my eye . . ." Micah shouted at him to get up and tried to drag him to his feet, but the sentry rolled away in the snow, laughing and chanting louder. He shouted for the captain of the guard. And when no one responded, he stumbled to the sentry on his right, who stood with his feet in his hat for warmth, and told him to pass word for the captain of the guard. But the man refused to move his rag-wrapped feet from his hat.

Cursing him, Micah left his post and went to the cabin of the brigade's officer of the day where the captain of the guard, a young lieutenant, was playing loo and drinking flip with two other officers. They roared at him to get back to his post immediately or take a hundred lashes, when he blurted that a sentry had gone out of his head. He stumbled back to his post, raging, and found the sentry asleep in the snow. He could not rouse him. Looking up, he saw a figure, fool or wise man, stumble south from the lines. There was no sense in challenging him since he was only one more victim of the mad, unchallenged world.

He stomped his post, listening to the screaming of the starving horses and going to the sleeping sentry on each return. At some hour of the morning, he believed that the sentry was dead. On his next return, he knew that he was. On the third, he observed that the sentry wore shoes. On the fourth, he tried on the sentry's shoes. They fit him comfortably.

When the guard was changed at four o'clock, he helped the sergeant of the guard drag away the body of Deacons or Dakkins or whatever his name was. The captain of the guard did not appear. He was still playing loo and losing steadily, thank God, the sergeant growled.

Micah walked back to the cabin, grinning down at his new shoes and feeling almost happy for the first time in weeks. When he opened the door, he saw that they'd let the fire nearly burn out again. Liberty wailed suddenly. Before leaving, he'd put him in his own bunk, carefully wrapped, for fear Minna would crush him in her tossing delirium. At least the young one still lived, he thought. A couple of men snored, but Minna made no sound.

He lifted a log onto the fire and sank back on his heels, holding his red, chapped hands to the warmth. As the flames leaped up, he glanced at Minna's bunk and caught his breath. He was looking at Feuchtwiler's face. As he stared incredulously in the growing firelight, Feuchtwiler's eyelids flickered open. For an instant his expression was as astonished as Micah's, and then he leaped to his feet, trailing a blanket. Minna lay in the bunk, asleep, her dress pulled high on her shrunken legs.

Micah sprang as Feuchtwiler leaped toward the door. Catching him by a wrist, he spun him, drove his balled left fist into his gaping mouth and felt teeth break. Feuchtwiler was on his knees, blood streaming from his mouth, his eyes raised whitely in terror. Micah hit him again and felt his nose spread softly. One of them somehow got the door open and they were outside in the snow, swinging wildly, sobbing for breath. Then he drove both fists at the dim, bleeding head in front of him, and Feuchtwiler fell and did not stir.

Staggering inside, he slammed the door and dropped the bar, only dimly aware of the frightened faces of the five men who crouched in their bunks staring at him. He walked numbly to Minna's bunk, pulled down her dress and covered her with the blanket.

Liberty wailed again. For a long time he stared down at the wizened little face. Then, with shaking hands, he heated water and made a flour gruel and found a couple of straws. Holding the child awkwardly in his lap, he fed him.

Toward dawn, as he sat on his heels before the fire, he realized that Minna was watching him.

When he looked at her, she smiled and whispered, "Come here."

He moved slowly to her.

Reaching up and placing her feverish hands on his temples, she whispered, "Reckon I'll die happy now. Reckon ya care a mite about me after all, comin' to me like ya did last night. I was most outa my senses, but I remember ya comin' to me. Thankee, Micah."

He feared that he would cry. But he blinked and nodded and patted her forehead roughly. "You get to sleep," he said. "The boy's been fed."

When the drums beat reveille he went outside. Feuchtwiler had dragged himself away. Hesitating only a moment, he walked to Macaroni Jack's cabin and told Mrs. Munger to fetch a chaplain because he was marrying Minna today.

Mrs. Munger did better than fetch a chaplain. From over the river she brought, toward nightfall, a jolly Presbyterian parson. He was an extraordinary man, less because he radiated a happy nature than because he brought a jug of fresh milk and a crock of baked pork and beans.

He married them after retreat. Everyone remaining in Micah's and Macaroni Jack's companies was present, except Feuchtwiler, who had disappeared. After the ceremony, they divided the pork and beans and watched Liberty drink milk. Lying in his bunk above Minna's after taptoo, Micah thought that the night-screaming of the starving horses did not trouble him as much now.

The next morning Minna seemed better. He sat on her bunk, talking with her for a while before he left on a work detail digging entrenchments.

Late in the afternoon Macaroni Jack came to him and led him away from the men. "Minna," he said, "she took a bad hemorrhage around noon."

Micah stared at him dully. "It's bad?"

Macaroni Jack nodded. "She's dead."

He had told himself to sleep five hours, and when he awakened he knew that it was about three o'clock. While he fed Liberty, he gulped cold firecake and hot water. Then he loaded his musket and wrapped Liberty in two blankets and went out into the darkness.

Carrying Liberty against his left shoulder and trailing his musket in his right hand, he walked due south, past the hollow where they'd buried Minna yesterday. The morning was still, cloudy, cold. There was no sound except the soft crunch of his feet in the snow. They'd killed the starving horses yesterday and today there would be rations of stringy horse meat, but he would not be here to gag on it. In his time he'd eaten nearly everything, but never horse meat. Perhaps some day he'd be hungry enough to eat it, but not yet, and certainly not at Valley Forge. For he'd never come back here.

Pausing behind a tree, he peered ahead toward the outer works. Liberty squirmed and murmured.

"You hush," he whispered, squeezing him. "You want a bullet in your bottom?"

He knew this post well. The sentry should be there, about twenty yards to the right. Staring hard, he thought that he made out a man hunkered down against a tree. Far to the south a wolf howled. The figure did not stir. Resting his musket and Liberty, he packed a snowball and threw it far to the sentry's right. A boy's voice quavered, "Who's there?" and then the figure moved uncertainly toward the sound on his right.

Snatching up Liberty and his musket, Micah ran southeast, bending so low that his trailing musket butt swished in the snow. When he reached a stand of pine, he halted, panting, and knew that he was free of Valley Forge.

Liberty uttered a low "Ahhhh." The little varmint was laughing. Micah squeezed him and whispered, "You like to run, eh? You and me'll be Injuns some day."

A wolf howled, closer this time, and killed his pleasure in the moment. There was something about a wolf howl that always chilled his neck. Fear, of course. Where was a lying fool who claimed no fear of wolves? They had been coming closer these nights; a sentry in Muhlenberg's brigade on the extreme left was said to have been attacked by one. No one knew why the wolves had come this winter, as no one knew why the rabbits had gone.

Because of the wolves he was sneaking out through the lines instead of walking out the south road between Woodford's and Scott's brigades. For he had a pass, a slip of paper signed by Pope that stated Sergeant Micah Heath of the 7th Pennsylvania had permission to go through the lines with his infant son on a three-day furlough. The trouble with leaving by the road was that the picket disarmed all men going on furlough, and he had no intention of traveling unarmed through a country of wolves.

He was rather pleased with his shrewdness, as he'd been rather surprised at Pope's acquiescence. Pope, it seemed, was green and inexperienced rather than cruel. He had agreed to the furlough on the condition that Micah re-enlist for another year. If he re-enlisted, he would retain his sergeancy. When Micah told him that he hadn't been paid in six months, Pope replied that the regimental records were missing. How did he know that Micah had not been paid? How did he even know that he'd served a year? Besides, no money was available for pay, though next month it was planned . . . Micah had heard that fanciful tale too often to believe it. Yet, since the records were so badly kept that no one knew for certain how long a soldier had served, he'd re-enlist. In an army where nearly everyone was forever coming and going, deserting and reappearing, he'd remain a sergeant. But a sergeant on a long furlough, he thought wryly. If he decided to serve again some day, he'd confound the record further with some fanciful tales of his own.

Moving faster now, he cut southwest toward the road. The slight breeze was from the south; he was still upwind of the wolves. When he reached the road well below the picket, he turned south and walked faster, wishing for dawn and listening to the wolves.

The varmints certainly were on the prowl this morning, to both west and east of him, and then circling downwind behind him. One, catching his scent, yiped higher, and he broke into a trot. Faint light was growing in the east, but it grew too slowly. He wanted glaring bright sunlight that pierced a wolf's black skull and sent him skulking into shadows.

They were quieter back there now. They'd caught his scent and he knew what they were about. They'd be snapping, snarling one at another, hating each other, hating the pack because they were wolves and loners, but drawn together now on the scent of man. Usually there was one or more that had the heart to attack a man if hunger was sharp enough, but always alone and never in pairs like man-trained dogs.

The sun was not with him today; his wind was beginning to fail him too. Liberty, crowing happily at all this running, seemed to weigh two stone. The road slanted up now, a sunken darkness in the dawning gray of woods and fields. There was something in the road ahead of him. A doe, a calf, a dog? His belly suddenly felt cold and he almost halted, as the wolf expected him to do. Then, gripping his musket more tightly, he ran straight on.

The wolf bounded ahead, grinning back at him. This would be the one with the heart to attack, he knew. A wise one, who had hunted and been hunted, for he seemed to know the range of a man's fire stick as shrewdly as a grenadier.

On the bank above the sunken road there was a small gnarled oak, a big stone, a bit of broken fence. He leaped up the bank and stood for an instant, gasping for breath and glancing around at the deserted country in the dawn. Then, standing on the stone, he lifted Liberty high above his head and placed him in the precarious cradle of three forked boughs he'd glimpsed from the road below. Leaping to the ground, he counted seven, eight, nine wolves fanning off the road.

But one came running straight at him, one with heart and hunger who lacked the shrewdness of the one ahead that he had not forgotten. Now he felt calm, remembering everything and glad that he always had remembered everything, especially the advice of the packer on the road west with Fogarty years ago: "Make a powder pill to fit the powder pan. It's your powder horn as loses you time in loading."

Aiming carefully at the wolf racing at him, he pulled the trigger. Not waiting to watch the varmint complete his death somersault, he whirled, cocked, bit off a cartridge, rammed it home, slipped a powder pill in the priming pan. He was none too soon. The wolf with heart and hunger, and wisdom too, flashed toward him up the bank, exactly as he had expected. He fired, and by the time the wolf had rolled down the embankment to the road he had almost reloaded again.

The others hung far back, as he had hoped they would. Then he was aware of Liberty in the tree above him, shrieking with fright at the crashing of the musket. Stepping onto the stone, he lifted him down and said, "You hush if you want to grow into an Injun boy."

By God, he *is* one, he thought, as Liberty grew still and blinked at him curiously.

"By God," he said, thrusting his face close to Liberty's, "I'll never call you a varmint again. Don't reckon I'll call a wolf a varmint neither. Not after meeting that one who timed the fire stick. Reckon there must be some wolf in me to think like him."

Liberty smiled at him.

"*You,*" Micah whispered fiercely, "are a sweet, hardy little bastard." And he kissed him for the first time.

He walked on and soon he heard the hungry ones back yonder squabbling over the carcasses of the two who had heart.

An air of desolation hung over the winter land like a dank mist. It was familiar country, but he barely recognized it. He passed burned barns, boarded-up houses. The fields were empty of stock. Picked clean by both us and them, he thought, so clean that even the winter crows had given up and flown away somewhere.

Toward midmorning, as he approached a crest, he heard the jangle of harness ahead. Leaping off the road, he sank into a thicket just before a horseman appeared on the crest. He studied him perplexedly, for he was dressed strangely in dirty white patched with all colors, like a costume worn by the French tumblers he'd seen years ago at an Annapolis Fair Day when he was smuggling with Bilby. Other horsemen sifted over the ridge behind him, several wearing the same dirty white. One even wore an old dressing gown and another clutched a blanket around him. All were heavily armed with sabers, pistols and muskets. Such tatterdemalions must be ours, he thought. Then he remembered hearing a few days before that Allen McLane had had uniforms made from his table linen for some of his almost naked troopers.

He started to rise and then sank back, holding Liberty tightly. Alex was one of McLane's men and he did not want to see him; twice at the Forge he'd narrowly missed confronting him.

A wagon followed the horsemen with two scrawny milch cows tied to its tailboard and more troopers riding behind. They were a rough-looking crew of gaunt scarecrows, he thought, and then realized that he must look even worse. At least they rode, while he walked. Grudgingly he had to admire them for keeping their thin horses better groomed than they were themselves. A wave of envy swept over him at the thought of riding instead of walking, of raiding to the edge of Philadelphia instead of crouching at the Forge, of *fighting* instead of always standing in the snow.

As they passed close, he glimpsed the thin, grim, pock-marked face of Alex March. Anyone who hadn't seen him in a couple of years wouldn't recognize him now, he thought, staring after him. And then he wondered, Would anybody recognize me?

Before leaving the thicket he tore his furlough pass into tiny pieces and scattered them. Where he was going, he thought, he might have to deny and curse the army he had served.

By early afternoon, when he was about a mile from the farm, his growing uneasiness made him forget his fatigue and break into a trot. The notion that something might have happened to Philly had been gnawing at him ever since he saw a burned-out farm and a scarecrow of a woman flitting away into a woods.

"The British bastards," he muttered. They'd worked the country over. The houses and barns which still stood obviously belonged to Tories. At the Wisters', those Tories, a few cattle actually nosed at straw in the barnyard. He thought of going to the door and begging some milk for Liberty, but they were certain to recognize him and possibly inform the British about him. He hurried faster, and by the time he reached the last crest before the farm, he was almost running.

Breathing hard, he halted and began to grin when he saw the house and stable and outbuildings. But no smoke rose from the chimneys. When he reached the lane, he was certain the farm was deserted.

Sudden panic made him run again. He heard himself shouting wordlessly and then he was pounding on the locked back door. Liberty began wailing. Cursing, he walked to the stable.

The stock was gone. There was no sound except the scampering of mice. Then he heard a faint clucking. As he walked toward the sound through the stable gloom, the clucking rose into the triumphant cry of a hen that surely had laid the finest egg on earth. When he found her in a corner of a stall, her victory cry squawked away into fear. Putting down Liberty and his musket, he sprang at the hen as she flapped from her precious egg. He wrung her neck and stooped to pick up the egg.

Something hard was thrust against his back and a voice said, "Holt right where y'are." He froze, and the voice said, "Who are ya?"

"Micah Heath."

"Micah!"

Swinging around quickly, he faced a boy holding an old fowling piece. The boy's face was indistinguishable in the gloom, but making a guess, he said, "Tom!"

"It's me sure enough. You went an' took the last hen."

"Where's everybody at? Where's Philly?"

"We had bad trouble, Micah. They came an'—"

"Where's Philly?" he demanded, seizing his shoulder roughly.

"She's in the city. She's been there this long while."

"She's safe?"

"If you say bein' in the city with the bloody lobsterbacks is safe, I reckon so. What's that 'er bundle?"

"A baby. My son."

"Eeee," Tom murmured. "How do ya be a soldier an' git a son too?"

"Is there a cow left on the place?"

"Nary one. Let's git outside so as I can see that 'ere son o' yours. I been layin' up in the loft these two days with my firelock, suckin' eggs an' watchin' for John Tout to come back."

As they stepped out of the stable, Micah saw that Tom had grown into a husky, towheaded boy whom he wouldn't have recognized.

"You look bloody awful," Tom said, staring up at him. "You got lice too." He pointed. "There's one goin' up—"

"I know it." Micah struck angrily behind his left ear. "You get so you don't mind 'em. What's happened here? Where's Mrs. Tout?"

Tom looked away, his eyes filling with tears. "Gone to heaven."

He caught his breath. "You mean—"

"Gone to heaven!" Tom wailed. "And them as sent her there'll go to hell. I'll *kill* 'em. I tell ya we had it bad here two days ago. Now John's gone off, most out o' his senses, but I keep thinkin' he'll come back rememberin' I'm still here. It was all 'cause o' the salt."

Micah gently rested a hand on Tom's head. "You simmer down and tell me what happened whilst I cook this chicken."

"*They* locked the house," Tom cried. "You can't git in without bustin' a winder an' you dassent do that. They's no fire, no—"

"Pick up that hen and egg, Tom. We'll bust a window. We'll *make* a fire and cook that hen. This is about where you and me began, ain't it? Scrounging some vittles and making a fire." He tried to smile. "We ain't come far."

"It ain't where I been that worries me," Tom said, following him. "It's where I'm goin'. What are you doin' here yourself, and where you goin'?"

"I'm not certain," Micah muttered.

But he was certain now. He'd have to get into the city somehow and find Philly and leave Liberty in her care.

XXXV

THE pebble tossed against the windowpane brought her awake instantly, her heart racing. At first she thought, He's free of prison at last. Then, remembering that it was January of 1778, she believed she had dreamed.

Another pebble tapped the pane and she leaped from bed, feet falling into her slippers, arms finding the sleeves of her robe. As she hurried down the back stairs, it did not occur to her that the person outside could be anyone but he. Touching a candle to a coal in the kitchen fireplace, she unbarred and opened the door. A gust of cold wind swept in.

"Micah?" she said quietly.

A tall figure loomed in the darkness and she stepped back. Staring at him above the flickering candle, she almost cried out in alarm. For the man who carried something in his arms was not he. Strange fierce eyes glittered at her in a thin, dark face. And then he grinned.

"Micah!" He lunged inside and she shut the door and leaned against it. "You've no hat." Her voice was shrill. "No overcoat. You—"

"You knew it was me," he said, still grinning. "How'd you know, Philly?"

"I—" She pointed at the bundle in his arms. "You've—"

"It's Liberty." Unmoving, he continued to stare at her across the flickering candle. "Minna's dead."

"Dead?"

"Two days ago at Valley Forge."

As she placed the candle in a table stick, she thought numbly that everything suddenly was different. Her life had changed since she went to sleep a couple of hours ago. Turning, she held out her arms, and he gave her Liberty.

"You alone?" he asked.

She nodded, gazing down at the small, pinched, dirty face wrapped in worn blankets.

"*She* is . . ." Her voice trailed off. "Out." What would she say to him? "Build up the fire."

He moved quickly and she put Liberty on the table. Cry, you poor mite, she wanted to say to him. Why don't you cry? But he simply gazed at her passively in the candlelight as she unwound the blankets. His emaciated body was as filthy as his dress and wet short pantaloons. Lice crawled in his hair and there were scabs and chafing sores on his chest and legs. She closed her eyes. What should she say to Micah?

As she worked quickly, she could not bear to look at him. She knew that he sat on his heels before the fire, watching her as she got a large pan, clean cloth, a bottle of witch hazel.

"Reckon he's hungry," he said when she began to bathe Liberty.

"First he's got to be *clean*. How did you get into the city?"

"Walked in. Told 'em some lies. Cussed the Continentals. That was tol'ably easy."

She tossed Liberty's filthy dress and pantaloons at his feet. "Burn them."

"But—"

"*Burn* 'em." Slowly he dropped the clothing on the fire. "I'll make him new. Is that milk warm?"

"Yes'm."

Drying Liberty and wrapping him in warm flannel, she picked him up and held a cup of warm milk to his lips. "Don't know," she said, "if he can take it this way."

"He can," Micah said.

She became absorbed in Liberty as he crowed and sucked at the rim of the cup. "So you brought him here to me," she said abstractedly.

He rose suddenly and she observed him closely for the first time. His clothing was tattered, his hair long and greasy. He exuded a musky odor that was vaguely familiar to her; then she remembered the smell of Indians long ago.

"I don't seem hospitable," she said gently. "Liberty took me up. Soon as he's fed I'll fix you something proper to eat."

He turned his back to her, staring into the fire, his red, chilblained hands clenched tightly.

"You tend *him,* Philly. I'm all right. There's something I'm bound to say to you. I reckon you've a low opinion of—of what I've done. It ain't any lower than my own of myself. But the day before Minna died, I married her and I reckon it made her die happier."

Blinking at sudden tears, she said, "I know it did, Micah. You mind I knew Minna. She was a fine woman."

He turned quickly. "She was a good woman for certain. But I—I didn't love her and—and I—"

"You just hush." Avoiding his gaze, she looked down at Liberty. "Don't talk any more about it. I understand what happened. I understand it all and don't you talk more about it."

In a moment he said, "I'll finish feeding him. There's something else I've got to tell you."

Shaking her head, she thought, Something bad. Something that he feared would make her drop or hurt Liberty. But no matter how bad it was, better that while she heard it she was holding Liberty and giving him life again.

"I walked by the farm from the Forge today."

She looked at him. "Is everything all right?"

"Tom's all right." He lowered his gaze. "Mrs. Tout's dead."

It was impossible, she thought numbly. The one abiding mortal in the world, the one who always stayed while others came and went. The cup trembled in her hand, but strangely she did not cry.

"What happened to her?" she asked unsteadily.

"It was the salt." His hands clenched and did not relax. "You knew about the salt that bastard Murdoch stored in the old barn?"

"Yes!" she said. "What happened?"

"Tom says Murdoch sold the salt to the British. He'd already sold 'em all his stock, every last horse, sheep, cow and suckling pig. Did you know that?"

"No, but what *happened?*"

"They came and took away the last of the stock a week ago, Tom says. It fair drove John out of his wits, Murdoch stripping his place for British money and leaving his people to starve. I know how he must've felt. There was only John and Mrs. Tout and Tom left then. The bound girls ran off after the stock began to go—with the Touts' blessing, Tom says.

"Anyway, John went off a-foot three days ago to try to find McLane's raiders or any responsible soul in the army. He was bound *we'd* get that salt of Murdoch's. Before Murdoch began to sell off his stock some of McLane's men stopped by a couple of times. They didn't plunder 'cause you know Alex March is one of 'em."

"Is—is he alive and well?"

"Alive and pekid like the rest of us. For certain he was this morning. I saw him riding back to the Forge with a troop."

At least thank God for that, she thought.

"Tom says John gave 'em a couple head of cattle each time, even though the cattle weren't his to give. The Widow March gave 'em all her stock, he says. Anyway, John waited too long to tell 'em about the salt. Two days ago, before he came back, British dragoons rode up. They must have been drinking all the way from the city by what Tom says. They were wild." He paused.

"You *tell* me!" she cried. She had put down Liberty and stood, hands locked.

"They demanded the salt and she said there wasn't any. They got rough and started spoiling around the house. Tom went at 'em and they knocked him down. I reckon he was a wildcat 'cause they finally tied him in a kitchen chair and gagged him. And then Mrs. Tout went at 'em. They—

they strung a halter 'round her feet and hung her heels up, head down, from a hook in a kitchen beam and went out, spoiling 'round the place."

Philly closed her eyes. "Go on," she whispered.

"Tom did his best to get free and cut her down, but he was tied too tight. It's no good to think of, Philly, but since you're bound to hear it all and true, it's best to know this. She never once screamed or cried out whilst she was hanging there, Tom says. It was like her to be so brave. And I don't reckon she suffered long. The blood blots the senses fast in a heel-hanging. Her face turned almost black and Tom reckoned she was gone. He heard wagons outside and then in comes Falco and an officer.

"Falco took one look and screamed like a woman, Tom says. The officer cut her down and said she was dead. He freed Tom, and Tom lit out straight for the barn where he'd hid an old fowling piece. He aimed to kill a trooper or two. Lucky for him the piece wouldn't fire. From the loft, where he kept trying to work his old firelock, he saw the officer round up the drunken troopers and cane 'em hard. I can see what happened. They were part of the wagon guard that came on ahead and they found some rum along the way.

"Tom watched Falco lead the wagons up to the old stable and load the salt. Some of the troopers dug a grave by the maple—you mind the one just below the mounting block—and they buried Mrs. Tout. When the wagons came back, Falco had the troopers board up the house, and then they all went back to the city.

"John came home late in the afternoon. Tom doesn't know if he ever got word of the salt to Valley Forge or what happened. 'Cause when Tom rushed to him, most like crying, John never said a word. He just sort of moaned, Tom says, and took out walking across the fields. The last he saw of John, he was going up over the height of land, and he ain't seen him since."

Philly brushed at tears. "Where's Tom now?"

"At the farm."

"Alone?" Her voice rose. "You left him there alone instead of bringing him here to—"

"He wouldn't come. I reckon it's as well, 'cause the first British soldier he saw he'd be liable to try to kill him. He's all right, Philly. Reminds me of how I used to be. Being *alone* never hurt me none."

"But what's to become of him? What—"

"I don't rightly know." He rubbed his jaw and then he looked at her. "But if you can fend for Liberty a spell, I reckon I'll fend for Tom."

"I'll fend for Liberty all right."

"What about *her?*" He nodded toward the closed door to the hall. "Philly, she, Murdoch, Falco—all of 'em are turncoats."

Kathy was a trial, Philly thought. Gone tonight to the Old Southwark Theater with Renshaw to see a play by Howe's Thespians; gone some place every night with Renshaw. Knowing so much about her father's affairs these days, she must have heard what had happened at the farm. Yet surely she did not know that Mrs. Tout had been hanged. She could not be so heartless that she would fail to grieve over the death of the woman who had been a mother to her and all of them.

"I can't stay here any longer," she cried suddenly. "Everybody out there"—she gestured vaguely—"is suffering and *doing* something for the cause and I just stay here, warm and comfortable—"

"You hush, Philly." He reached out to clasp her shoulder and then let his hand fall without touching her. "There's nothing out yonder but a plague of war and winter. The best you can do is stay here and care for Liberty—and yourself." He turned to the fire. "*I* want you to stay in the city just because I ask you to."

Staring at him, she realized that his words were almost the same as Alex's when he'd brought her here months ago. He cared for her, as Alex did. And I? she asked herself dully. She cared for him. But she cared for Alex too. She felt confused and frightened.

"Now here," she said, "I've not given you a bite to eat. Sit down at the table and—"

"Philly." He faced her again. "Suppose *she* won't let you keep Liberty here? What's to become of you—and him?"

"Humph." She tossed her head. "You'd think I was a helpless *lady*. You forget I'm a good worker. There's plenty of folks will hire me, Liberty and all. Only this week Mrs. Pemberton stopped me on the street and asked if I'd like to come work for her."

"You walk the streets?" he asked dubiously. "With all the redcoats about it don't seem—"

"They're harmless if you don't go out at night. The worst they do is speak rude and whistle. The greencoats, the Hessians I mean—they're no worse than the redcoats."

Returning from the pantry with bread and cold mutton and cheese, she was strangely shaken again when she looked at him. He stood instead of sitting, his shoulders slumping tiredly in his rags as he held Liberty and fed him warm milk.

"You *walked* from Valley Forge today, carrying him," she said in dismay. "I don't know what I've been thinking of not to— Sit down, Micah."

"And dirty up a chair?" He grinned at her. "I'm filthy and I stink. Least I know it."

"Sit down."

He sat and watched her as she sliced bread and carved meat.

"It's bad at the Forge, isn't it?"

"It ain't good."

"Will the army last it out?"

"Some of it will, I reckon."

"Eat," she said, taking Liberty from him. "Eat it all. I'm making tea and there's cold tarts. Eat every blessed thing you can and what you can't you'll take with you. Now let me think, what else do you need?"

He stuffed meat and bread into his mouth and mumbled, "What don't I?"

"Blankets," she said. "I'll fetch a pair. And an overcoat. There's a greatcoat belongs to Alex that—"

"I reckon he could use it himself he looked that pinched cold this morning."

"*Two* coats," she exclaimed. "I know there's two. One for you and one for him."

He ravenously bit another slice of mutton. "And tell him I got it from his *wife?*" He looked at her quizzically. "You 'pear to think I'm going back to Valley Forge."

Surprised, she asked, "Aren't you?"

Swallowing, he drew a long knife from under his tattered shirt and cut a chunk of cheese. "Valley Forge," he said, studying the cheese, "whooo! I didn't aim to go back there when I left."

"You—you're deserting, Micah?"

"No, I ain't deserting." He sounded angry. "My time's up. I aimed to go over west a piece. I told you I'd look after Tom, didn't I? What would you say if I took him over west a ways with me? I'll learn him a trade or two, like I was learned. I'll learn him to be shifty in a new country."

"Send him here to me."

Micah shook his head. "He'd go to hell fast in this garrison city. Besides, he won't come. Before I left he pestered me to take him back to Valley Forge. If I took him there he wouldn't need to go to hell 'cause he'd already be there."

What should she say to him? You never were alone, and how did you discern the proper sacrifice for others? Life, like the sea on which Jonah sailed, was wrought and tempestuous. But how did you ever know the proper one to fling away in order to calm its turbulence?

"Good cheese," he said. "Good mutton. Thanks." His tone became angry again. "Only a fool would go back to Valley Forge once he was shut of it."

"Then you *do* think you should go back," she said slowly. "And you wonder if you should take Tom."

"I don't wonder at all." He sounded very angry. "I *know* I shouldn't. There's boys younger than him there now and it's no place for 'em. The dirt and disease and starvation and monotony. It's like carting an innocent child into hell."

"You say he won't come to me. And we can't trust John to come back to the farm or look out for Tom if he does. And I can see you're not sure Tom can walk it west with you in winter or that you can fend for him out there." She paused, and then she said softly, "I know what troubles you. It's that you never have a choice. There's always somebody else in tow. It's always being a bound servant—to Murdoch or Fogarty or Bilby or the army. Once there was Tom and me in tow. And then there was Minna. And now there's Liberty—and Tom again. I reckon I know how you feel. You must wonder sometimes what's all this talk about the freedom you're fighting for."

He sat motionless, gazing at her.

"You've done enough, Micah. It's time you went free. You go. This time you've a choice. Fetch Tom here to me. There won't be any trouble. I'll see to it. And you go free for a change."

Looking at his knife, as if he never had seen a knife before, he shook his head.

"You're a good girl, Philly. The best I'll ever know. I did some hard thinking all the way here from the farm. I'm going back to the Forge—because I want to, though it's getting hard for me to tell *having* to from *wanting* to. I won't try to make you a fine speech. I just remember Martha Tout hanging in her kitchen. And I know that sort of thing has got to stop. So I'm going back for one last time. You want me to take Tom with me, as he wants, or bring him here to you, as he don't want to do?"

"Take him with you," she said quietly.

He speared a piece of meat with his knife and lifted it slowly to his mouth.

She turned away. "I'll fetch whatever things you need."

"Alex's greatcoat is all, Philly. I'll tell him you sent it. There's more than enough of everything at the farm for us to take. Warm heavy clothes for both of us, blankets, plenty of food Mrs. Tout stored by for winter." He tried to smile. "We'll be the finest turned-out soldiers at Valley Forge."

"How are you going to get out of the city? They stop everybody who doesn't have a pass."

"It's easy. The Schuylkill's frozen. I'll mind the patrols and slip across in the dark of the moon between five and six. Good luck, it's a cloudy night." He stretched and yawned. "I'm tired. Can I sleep here on the floor till it's time to go?"

"No. *She's* likely to find you here. They generally come in around three or four o'clock."

"They? Who's *he?*"

"His name is Lord Renshaw."

"For Christ sake!"

"You mind your tongue," she said sharply.

"Yes'm. I'm sorry, Philly."

"You've no right to judge."

"I'm the last to judge," he said.

Yet I judge her, she thought. Certainly Kathy had betrayed the cause. Probably she had betrayed Alex too. But she told herself that she did not want to know. She tried simply to live here, a dutiful servant to a former friend, a prisoner assigned to this comfortable dungeon by Alex March. But it was impossible to ignore the change in Kathy. Even at night, when she latched her bedroom door and buried her head under the pillow, she could not shut out the sounds of Kathy's changed way of life. The hearty voices of the officers, the shrill laughter of Kathy or Becky Franks, the crash of a breaking wine bottle which she would sweep up in the morning. There was the night that a small military band and a quartet of drunken officers serenaded "Be-you-ti-ful Kathy" in the street with a song composed by Captain André. There was the morning when she found Lord Renshaw and Lord Rawdon still engaged in a standing drinking bout at eight o'clock.

"You'd best take Liberty and get some sleep up in my room, Micah. I'll waken you at whatever hour you wish."

He shook his head. "I'll go now. You get to your room with Liberty and latch the door."

She realized that he understood her dread of those pawing, drunken officers. Yet he must have a few hours of sleep after his exhaustingly long day of walking.

"It isn't proper." She looked at him levelly. "But it's *rightful*. You'll sleep on the floor of my room and I'll take Liberty to bed with me."

As he stared at her, she believed that she knew what he was thinking. She trusted him and didn't fear him, he must know. Suddenly it was very important for him to realize that. For his own sake. He must understand that she thought he was only good, and never evil.

"All right." He rose slowly. "Get Alex's coat and I'll wrap myself in it and sleep."

He understood, she thought joyfully.

They did not speak after they entered her room and he latched the door. She wanted to say good night to him, as she used to want to say good night long ago in the innocent days of their long journey east. But now, as then, he was asleep instantly, breathing lightly.

Lying with Liberty pressed to her, she could not sleep. Her imagination raced out over the dark and silent country, back through the years to that time when Micah brought her to the farm and Mrs. Tout greeted her with love.

When the front door banged open, Micah awakened. She sensed him listening alertly to muffled voices, laughter, the tread of feet. After a while the front door closed and the clopping of hoofs faded down the street.

Micah whispered, "Philly."

"Yes."

"It's time I go."

Leaving Liberty asleep, she crept quietly down the back stairs with him. She lighted a candle and thrust bread and meat into the pockets of Alex's coat before he put it on.

He started toward the door and turned. "Thanks, Philly," he said.

Reaching up, she pulled down his head and kissed him on a cheek. Uttering a low, choking sound, he started to draw her to him. He stopped. Then his lips brushed her forehead, and he was gone.

XXXVI

THE throbbing of her head became the pounding of the front door knocker at some ghastly early hour of gray morning. Hearing Papa's voice, loud and demanding, she buried her head under the pillows. But his voice grew louder, rising above Philly's, and then he was hammering on her door.

"Kathy!" he called, "I'm coming in there!"

As he flung open the door, she sat up in bed and cried, "How *dare* you, Papa? By what right—"

"Because I pay the bills!" His red wattles quivered with anger like a turkey gobbler's. "Philly!" he shouted over a shoulder. "Come in here!"

Philly took her time, and when she appeared she looked at him with such contempt that Kathy could have kissed her.

"I want you to answer my questions." He folded his arms. "In front of Kathy, since *she* won't answer me anything. *What* is going on in this house? It's become a public scandal. Every Quaker in Philadelphia looks at me askance, and now this morning Friend Pilch and Pemberton have just paid a call, chiding me about the conduct of my daughter, a married woman running about with officers at all hours of the night, inviting them into her house, seen everywhere in public—"

"*Friend* Pilch!" Kathy leaped from bed, trembling with rage. "You call a man friend who—"

"It is impossible to do business in Philadelphia," he said calmly, "unless one gets along with the Quakers."

"Goddamn business!" she cried. "Goddamn the Quakers! Goddamn this dull little city!"

"Have your tantrum," he said, "and then listen to me. I admit that I was not displeased when you chose to be courteous to the—uh—some of the British leaders. I—"

"Not *displeased!*" She laughed hysterically. "It was you who urged me on to—"

"Have your tantrum," he said heavily, "but listen to me. You've gone too far. Has it occurred to you what would happen if the British left Philadelphia? *I* have begun to think about it a great deal. *I* am taking pains to keep in communication with associates in York and Lancaster, explaining that we're virtual prisoners here. It's time you . . ."

She had not thought about it. They were here and they would stay, Gordon said. If they ever leave, she thought now, I'll go with them, away from this dingy, gossiping little place into—what? And where and how?

"So I ask you *what* is going on here that there should be a public scandal?"

She did not reply. Staring beyond him vaguely, she hated him.

"Will you tell me what is going on here, Philly?"

"Mr. Murdoch, I have no notion." Philly, arms akimbo, gazed at him with an unchanged expression of contempt. "But if you don't think all is well here you might propose we go to the farm for a spell. We could help your *bound* girls. We could help tend your *stock*."

Her tone of sarcasm made him wince. How, Kathy wondered, had the minx learned that the bound girls had run away and that he'd sold all his stock for solid gold?

He said, "Now see here—"

"Maybe," Philly said, tears welling in her eyes, "we could help *Mrs. Tout*."

He stepped back, the color draining from his face.

"Papa," Kathy said sharply, "what's wrong with Mrs. Tout?"

"There was an accident," he muttered, "a tragic unfortunate accident—"

"Because of your salt!" Philly cried fiercely. "Because you're a turncoat jobber who—"

"What happened?" Kathy grasped Philly's arm tightly. "What happened to Mrs. Tout?"

"She was hanged." Philly continued to stare at Murdoch. "In her kitchen. By the British soldiers sent to bring in the salt *he* sold to 'em."

Mrs. Tout hanged in the kitchen, she thought numbly. She had a sudden vivid memory of Mrs. Tout smiling in the kitchen doorway years ago, lifting her up and hugging her tightly and saying, "I just *love* you, Kathy." Then she was crying uncontrollably.

Papa was babbling excitedly, his face pale. "The culprits will be punished . . . Not *our* fault . . . A tragic, regrettable accident . . ."

"Get out of here," she sobbed.

"But—"

"Get out!"

He started out and paused in the doorway, looking back at them. Something in their expressions made him hurry away.

Still crying, she clutched Philly to her. Then she was sitting on the edge of the bed and saying, "I've done nothing wrong, Philly."

"I'm sure you've not."

"Truly, I've done nothing wrong. Do you believe that, Philly?"

"Of course I do."

"I like a good time. But I've done nothing wrong. I'll send a note to Gordon—Lord Renshaw—this morning. I want the men who—who did that hanged. Every last one of them. He'll see to it. And then I never want to see him—any of 'em—again. How did you hear about it?"

Philly sighed. "From Micah. He came here last night."

"*Here?*" She started up and sank back, her fingers digging at the bed. "What—what did he want?"

"He left me Liberty to care for. Minna's dead. If you don't want Liberty here I'll find another place to work."

She shook her head, thinking, Did he expect to see *me?*

While she was trying to compose a note to Gordon at the escritoire, a corporal came to the door with a note from him. Telling the corporal to wait on the steps, she studied his almost illegible scrawl.

MY ESTEEMED KATHY:

I sit in my desolate quarters, almost *re*duced to idiocy by the plagued insomnia that only adoration *in*duces. Pray do me the honor of attending on your presence at a decent hour this afternoon. Then fly with me on silver runners, if the snow prevails,

to Germantown where we may discuss the merits of a small
supper in company with a few ladies and gentlemen.

> Devotedly & Eternally yr Humble Serv't,
> GORDON L.R.

On the bottom of his note she wrote quickly:

> It is impossible for me ever to see you again. A great wrong has
> been done. There must be justice.

K.M.

As she had expected, he arrived within the hour, rattling the knocker
loudly. In the back parlor, where she sat, she heard him say to Philly,
"Dear girl, my compliments to your mistress and may I pray see her at
once— Dear God, a baby!"

The minx had carried Liberty to the door with her.

"Well, sir," Philly said, "I was changing him and you're fair breaking
the door down. Miss Kathy says she's not at home to visitors."

"But a baby!" Renshaw cried. He was in the hall, closing the door behind him and driving Philly before him into the front parlor. "I *adore*
babies. Let me hold it. Whose is it?"

"You shan't touch him. His name is Liberty."

"Dear, dear God in heaven," he said.

"Lord Renshaw, your language is highly offensive."

"And you, dear little rebel heart, are highly *de*fensive. God doesn't
mind. He's already punished me by sending me to America. Where's
Kathy?"

"I told you that—"

"Then I'll sit down and wait until I learn what wrong has been done.
Hmmm, nothing to do with the baby, has it? Wait, Philly, don't flounce
out and leave a miserable sinner to contemplate his sins alone. What's
Liberty's last name?"

"Heath."

"Heath? Heath? What's his father's name?"

"Micah."

"Micah Heath? *Micah Heath!*" Kathy heard him leap to his feet. "It
cannot be, but by heaven it must be." Kathy was drawn to the parlor
doorway. "Hullo, Kathy, didn't know you were home to visitors." His dark
eyes, set deeply in his handsome young face, studied her shrewdly. "A
wrong has been done, you say. And you—"

"I'm grieving." She touched a wisp of handkerchief to her eyes.

"Pray grieve on, Kathy. It becomes you fetchingly. Grief brings a
heavenly alabaster to your skin that—"

"What have you to say of Micah Heath?" Philly demanded.

He grimaced. "There's a *democratizing* in this country that leaves one breathless. One calls on the mistress and feign must entertain the handmaiden." He grinned at Philly. "Before you run me through, fair rebel, I'll tell thee." His smiling gaze turned quickly to Kathy. "And thee, fair Kate, since there appears to be a magic in the name of Micah Heath that can cause the grieving heart to—"

"Oh, talk sense, Gordon," Kathy said impatiently.

"Very well, I shall." He laughed silently. "Though I thought I was running on rather well for such an abominably early hour. The subject, then, dear ladies, is Micah Heath, a name—et cetera. A long time ago in the Jerseys I set out one evening to stalk the phantom of *Miss* Twillow's army. I fancy myself a clever stalker, but I was outstalked by your Micah Heath. It was a humiliating experience, but I liked him. He disarmed me, and then he gave me back my rifle. But he refused to turn his back when I did and walk away."

"He was smart," Philly said. "You'd have shot him."

"Indeed I would not!" Renshaw looked at her aghast. "Shoot him in the back when he declined to shoot me in the front, God save my soul? Besides, it's an ancient English custom never to kill a legend."

Philly suddenly smiled at him.

He pointed at Liberty. "Who is the mother of this infant?"

"She's dead," Philly said. "She died at Valley Forge."

"Oh? Well—how did he get here?"

"Micah brought him here last night."

"Heath *here* last night? God deuce it, I wish you'd told me. We could have split a bottle and had a merry-oh. I'd have got him a pass and maybe a ride out of town." He peered at Liberty. "The baby looks puny."

"And well he might," Philly said. "He's been nigh starved to death and carried hither and yonder in all weather because *you* people—"

"Ah! Ah!" Renshaw waggled a finger at her. "Heavy, heavy, heavy. Don't grow heavy, Philly. I neither made this baby nor this war nor the deplorable condition of Mr. Washington's army. I'm here because it appeared to be my duty—et cetera. I grow heavy too." He looked at Kathy. "Is *this* what you meant by a great wrong having been done?"

"Something far different, Gordon." She briefly described Mrs. Tout's death. "Those men should be hanged."

"Indeed they should. Indeed they shall, the swine." Smiling, he took out his large gold watch and compared its time with that of the Seth Thomas clock. "I shall call for you at five, Kathy, and—"

"I can't go," she said indistinctly. "I'm in mourning and I'm not going into society for a long time."

He continued to smile at her. "Five o'clock, Kathy."
She would not go, she told herself. Yet she knew that she would.

Gordon Charles Renshaw, First Marquess, only son of Gordon, First Earl Renshaw, had been born in Northumberland on March eighteenth, 1750. After education at Eton and Magdalen College, Oxford, he'd taken up residence in London and established a pleasant reputation as a mild wit and knowledgeable gambler. When he succeeded to the earldom in 1774, he had discovered that his inheritance consisted of little besides a title and a barren stretch of the Northumberland hills. As a shrewd young man, he realized that he was a good catch and that his wisest recourse was to marry money.

Gordon, Second Earl Renshaw, was wise to the ways of the world and, he believed, to his own ways. But there was one thing he did not know about himself: he was extraordinarily affectionate, improbably romantic. Even when he set out to marry money, he felt that he must first love where there was money. Surprisingly, for one so affectionate, he failed. It was the way of the world, he believed, that all the single young ladies of means whom he met were too fat or too thin, too cold or too eager, too . . . It never occurred to him that it was his own way to find them so.

Like many romantic young men, he decided that the army offered an escape from his dilemma. The notion struck him suddenly, when he was out of debt and well ahead in a winning streak at cards. He bought a lieutenant colonel's commission in the 44th Royal Regiment of Foot and, more quickly than he really desired, found himself landing on Long Island in the army of General Howe. Nothing very pleasant happened to him from that time until a year from the following October, when he met Kathy at a supper given by Joseph Galloway, who had returned from exile riding beside Cornwallis.

Kathy heard some facts about Lord Renshaw and intuitively grasped others. She realized almost at once, for example, that he was extremely affectionate—a quality she greatly admired in men. But to her perpetual wonder and excitement, he was not simply a man; he was a creature from a distant glittering world that she could only breathlessly imagine, a nobleman, a *lord*. If he had been only a man, she would have felt more positive of her capacity to resist his siege.

For, true to his nature and her expectations, he immediately laid siege. He assumed the charming posture of aggressor and she the equally charming posture of one intent on retaining her virtue. Against his romantic approaches, she defended the strong fortress of her practicality.

From a practical standpoint she knew that she had everything to lose by capitulation to Renshaw. She was a married woman who never had been quite able to retain a stable social position in a small provincial city. He was a nobleman, handsome, young, who could expect his title to win him a vast fortune some day. She was fascinated by him, but she did not love him, as long ago she had loved Alex.

There were occasions that made her question the intensity of his design. At times he seemed merely to want to *talk,* when a little *doing* might have won him the ultimate favor he appeared to desire.

Riding home with him one cold morning from a party in Germantown, she felt strangely depressed despite a night of gay dancing and conversation. She closed her eyes as they passed through the Northern Liberties. North of the Callowhill the houses had been destroyed and orchards and fields laid waste by a jungle of abatis and redoubts. A stench of filth hung over the northern part of the city, even on a cold and windy morning.

"I used to be proud of this city," she said. "Now I detest it. I'd like to go away and never see it again."

He started talking about the unfortunate nature of the war. It was so unnecessary, he said. He talked all the way to her house and then came inside and continued talking. He was rather tipsy, she observed.

"Do you ever think of your husband on such a night?" he asked her. "Poor fellow up there on that drafty river . . ."

She could have slapped him. "I hate him," she said. "He thinks this all is *necessary*. He has no sense of how a woman feels about anything. I wish I'd never see him again, just as I wish I'd never see Philadelphia again."

"Oh?" Swaying slightly, he blinked at her. "To be sure. But—to be sure."

"I'm cold," she said, turning toward the stairs. "I'm going to bed and try to get warm." She glanced back at him.

To her amazement, there were tears in his eyes. "Why," he cried, "must we all suffer so as we brave the storm of passion? Like Virgil's shipwrecked sailors we are *rari nantes in surgite vasto*. We are . . ."

She stifled hysterical laughter. Even Alex, in his most trying days, never had spouted Latin or Greek or whatever it was at such a time as this. Suffering? She was not suffering, except from her eternal torment over how to make a difficult situation end happily.

At such times she almost wished that she had been attracted to someone like Lord Rawdon; although he was the ugliest man in the British Army, he always acted purposefully and knew exactly what he wanted. Even Major General Grey, whose coldly cynical eyes stared piercingly through her beneath his low monkey's forehead, might be preferable. Captain John André or Captain Oliver Delancy, flirting flibbertagibbits though they were, would not act so childishly.

In that gay winter, the gayest Kathy ever had known in Philadelphia, the excitement of the season mounted steadily in an increasing round of theatricals, dances, "routs" and "drums." There were handicap horse races on the Commons when Gordon and Delancy vied with reckless Banastre Tarleton for first honors. Skating parties on the Delaware were followed by sleighing parties to Germantown where she took care never to gaze beyond the outworks at the bleak country. It was exciting to attend dinners of fourteen courses at the Penn manor house, though it sometimes troubled her to think that the fine houses of patriots—Dickinson's Fairhill and Mifflin's Fort Hill, among others—had been destroyed.

Sometimes she thought that when she wasn't attending a party, she was dressing and preparing for one. To their gay occupation of the city the British brought a fascinating flow of goods that stimulated her sense of fashion as it stimulated Papa's sense of business. Styles changed. Gowns became deeply décolleté; the cork rump came into fashion; the hair was dressed higher than ever. The new style in hats was startling at first: flat and round and the size of a big japanned tea tray.

Kathy felt that she had never had as gay and interesting a friend as beautiful Becky Franks, the daughter of the rich Philadelphia Tory, David Franks. In the past Becky had snubbed her, but that winter they became close friends.

Becky could press a daring conversation farther than any woman she ever had known. She often wondered if Becky had retained her virtue until she realized that Becky wondered the same about her. It shocked her, and then it pleased her to be considered so bold. Becky slyly hinted that virtue no longer was in the mode. Kathy smilingly replied that modes changed, that yesterday's was tomorrow's and today's would be the fashion day after tomorrow.

They were talking thus on that frightening evening late in February.

Becky came late in the afternoon to tea and stayed on, waiting for Gordon and Major Platt to call and take them to the weekly assembly at the City Tavern. She had brought some delicious morsels of gossip with her. A pretty bound girl purchased by—well, she daren't say whom—had danced in the nude for a private party of officers at the Indian Queen last night. Afterwards—*well!* Becky rolled her dark eyes and laughed.

"Now who," she asked, "would be the father of such a girl's child?"

"Just name the regiment," Kathy replied, laughing, "and she could give such child a number instead of a name."

"On the other hand," Becky said, "if the wench was smart—which she doubtless wasn't—she needn't worry at all. Did you hear what Banastre Tarleton said to Oliver Delancy at the Galloways' last week when they both were drunk? Oliver mumbled something about eliminating the possibility of something or other and Banastre yelled, 'Why 'liminate it when you can *enemate* it?' "

Kathy laughed immoderately. She'd heard what Banastre had said, but the word never failed to amuse her. It recalled her own childish ignorance and needless worry of only a few months ago. She might still be living in naïve innocence over how to *eliminate* the worry of that certain problem if it hadn't been for the forthright remarks of that really horrid Beauchamp woman at the Christmas Eve dance.

"We'll have some more tea," she said, ringing for Philly, "and then—"

There was a crash of glass and something thudded softly on the carpet and rolled to the center of the parlor. Becky screamed and cold air gushed through the broken windowpane. Philly, entering the room, put down the tray and raced to the door.

A stone partially wrapped in brown paper lay on the floor, Kathy saw. She picked it up.

"Don't unwrap it!" Becky exclaimed. "It might be—"

"Nobody there." Philly slammed the front door and came from the hall.

Kathy slowly unwrapped the stone and smoothed the sheet of paper. A few words were scrawled on it.

> *Mrs. March—*
> > *We will remember.*
> > > *The Patriots*

She read it aloud in a dull tone. Looking wide-eyed from Philly to Becky, she cried, "Remember what? I haven't done anything. What is there for anybody to remember? I haven't done anything wrong."

"That filthy scum," Becky said. "Those—"

"Give it to me, Kathy." Philly held out a hand. "Please."

Kathy handed it to her and she studied it closely. "Let me keep it and see if I can—if anybody knows who did it." She poured their tea. "I'll get something to cover that window hole."

After she left the room, Becky whispered, "Kathy, you shouldn't trust her. She's one of *them* and—I'll tell you, Banastre Tarleton, among others, is right put out the way she hums 'Burgoyne's Surrender' and 'War and Washington,' and some of those tunes when she's serving your guests. Do you know how much of your food she sneaks off to the rebel prisoners? Only a couple of days ago Mrs.—"

"I know," Kathy said vaguely. "She tells me. She doesn't steal. Some of those prisoners are so hungry they've been tearing up the winter grass to eat the roots." She shivered suddenly. *"Who* would do such a horrid thing to me?" She touched the stone on the floor with a pointed slipper and shivered again.

I've got to go away from here, she thought. But where—and how?

As Philly was covering the broken windowpane with a board she said over a shoulder, "A visitor coming. Your father."

He hurried in, gasping for breath, calling, "Kathy!" Then, seeing Becky, he tugged off the beaver hat jammed low over his ears and bowed abruptly. "Miss Becky, a pleasure to see you. And how is your father?" Before she could answer, he went on, "Kathy, a dreadful thing has happened. Some rascal threw a stone through my front window. It was wrapped in a paper that said— Here—" He dug a piece of brown paper from an overcoat pocket. " 'Mr. Murdoch— We will remember. The Patriots.' " He crumpled the paper. "It's outrageous! I've not done anything wrong. I've just stayed here trying to maintain my rightful business . . ."

She laughed hysterically.

Becky said quickly, "Kathy's a mite unstrung, Mr. Murdoch. Somebody just threw a stone through *her* window with a note saying the same thing."

Papa gaped at her and then closed his mouth firmly. "I'm appealing to my patriot friends to desist from this nonsense," he said. "And I'm going to appeal to whatever forces are upholding law in Philadelphia to—"

"Here come some of the forces of law now," Philly said drily at the window. "I'll let 'em in."

Gordon and Major Platt came in, singing, *"And a tra-la-la-la-ing we will go-oh-oh, a tra-la—"* They stopped and looked at Papa in surprise.

"Lord Renshaw, greetings." He bowed grotesquely low. "Greetings, greetings."

It was disgusting, Kathy thought, the way he groveled to Gordon simply because he was a *lord*. Lord, lord, God or nobleman, take me away from here.

"And greetings to you, Mr. Murdoch. Greetings, greetings." Straight-faced, Gordon mocked him with a bow as low.

Then Papa was pouring out his fear, his anger, his demand for protection. It made her feel so mean and low that she could not bear to listen to him.

Gordon acted as promptly and directly as Rawdon or Tarleton would have under the circumstances. Stepping to the door, he whistled shrilly through his fingers. His corporal appeared as magically as in a play and Gordon directed him to see Mr. Murdoch to his home and place a guard on the house while another guard should be sent here. Then Papa left, bowing out backwards, and Gordon, smiling, resumed his singing.

But she did not share his tra-la-la-ing joy at the City Tavern assembly that night. It was, as Gordon said, a gallant gathering; even General Howe himself appeared with Mrs. Loring and sat torpidly for a spell, staring at the musicians with a bored expression while Mrs. Loring smiled and shook her fan at numerous friends. But there was little pleasure in the occasion for Kathy. She felt that invisible eyes were watching her. Even the obsequious waiters troubled her. How did one know whether they were friend or foe?

Saying she felt ill, she asked Gordon to take her home early, at one o'clock. He left reluctantly, irritably kicking awake the private who drove his chariot. He became happy again, however, when she let him hold her hand. The drive was short through the moon-bright morning, but she imagined that she saw someone lurking in every shadow. Even the soldier on guard before the house frightened her. He merely drew attention to the house, she thought. Everyone passing through the street would see him and think, Oh-ho, now Mrs. March has a guard.

"Send him away," she said to Gordon.

"But my dear Kathy, you—"

"Send him away." She shivered. "How do you know he wouldn't break in himself during the night?"

"God save us, Kathy, you're speaking of the British Army. One of my own best men. It's Higgins." He peered at the soldier, who presented arms and braced himself. "Hullo, Higgins, anything to report?"

"This is Arthwaite, sir," a boy's voice replied. "Nothing to report, sir."

"Arthwaite? Arthwaite? Damned if I know an Arthwaite. Dismissed, Arthwaite. On your way and send the chariot too. I'll stand the guard myself." The soldier and the carriage clattered away down the silent street as they stepped inside. "Raise the drawbridge," Gordon said. "Drop the portcullis. Renshaw will man the tower and fight to the death within the keep whilst you, fair Kathy, entwined in slumber's gentle embrace—"

"I'm *cold*," she said.

"It's a damn cold night. I'll kick up the fire and we'll have a spot of that brandy I sent you."

He was such a child, she thought, watching his thin, handsome face as he intently poured brandy into two glasses. But a beautiful child.

"Will the army leave forever some day, Gordon?"

"I"—he hesitated—"don't know."

"You do," she said in a low voice. "You will go. And I'll never see you again."

He looked at her quickly. "And would that pain you so?"

She nodded. "Terribly."

"Dear God." His hand trembled as he handed her a glass. "Then it shan't be the last you see of me." His expression was—stricken. "I've declared my love for you a thousand times. If you feel so, I swear by all that's holy and unholy I shall come back to you. If it's only to see you from a distance, to stand in some shadow and glimpse you as you pass. . . ."

Silly boy, she thought, controlling a smile. Silly, silly boy. Stepping closer to him, she rested a hand gently on his cheek and said, "Gordon."

His eyes widened, his hand shook so that brandy spilled from his glass. As she pressed against him, he gasped, "Sweet heaven," and dropped his glass.

"For heaven's sake, Gordon, take my arm. I think I'm swooning." She backed from him toward the hall door.

"Dear God!" He leaped to her side.

"Support me!" she whispered fiercely.

"Yes, yes, dear God, yes," he muttered as she led him up the stairs.

Philly had left a candle burning in her room, as she always requested. Falling on her bed, she said, "Don't stand there all a-twitter since you've brought me here. Shut the door, you naughty Gordon."

XXXVII

ABOUT three miles from the Germantown outworks McLane rode his horse close to the two-wheeled cart creaking along the Manatawny Road. Alex, slapping the rope reins on the back of the bony horse pulling the cart, did not turn his head for fully a minute. Then he looked at McLane and grinned.

McLane, smiling, said, "You'll do. You've learned the role well, I see. And you don't look at all like Alex March, Philadelphia gentleman."

His role was that of Joel Harris, a country lout wearing ticken breeches and a shapeless hat, who was carting four baskets of fresh shad from Bevin's Ford to market in Philadelphia. "Shad!" he bayed nasally at McLane. "Fresh shad!"

McLane laughed and turned back. Looking around, Alex saw Micah on Wanderer raise a hand to him and then wheel and ride away north with the patrol.

The password of his mission was *rum crew*. And what a rum crew we are, he thought, as he lumbered on through the May dawn.

A couple of weeks ago he'd nearly laughed aloud when Hamilton at Headquarters referred to the raiders as "our cavalry." They numbered, at present, a hundred and fifty men, including fifty Oneida Indians who could not ride and were frightened of horses. John Tout and Tom, who

proudly called themselves "horse masters of the troop," presently reported fresh mounts as numbering forty-eight. Not long ago, in the worst
days of winter, the troop had totaled only a score.

"Rum crew," he muttered and tried to smile.

A month hence, with the annual appearance of summer soldiers and
fresh horses, they should be a strong, well-drilled force. But they would
not be, he knew. They would slowly evaporate. This army never would
have a cavalry worthy of the name because the General—a fine horseman,
ironically—did not want one or comprehend how to train and use one.
Cavalry patrols might have saved his flank at Long Island. And although
he'd had several regiments of horse available at the Brandywine, he had
not used most of them and had failed to believe or comprehend the report
of Howe's flanking march which Alex's troop observed.

One trouble, Alex realized, was that the General had learned his first
lessons of war on the frontier, where cavalry was useless. The angry striv-
ings of Count Pulaski for a corps of cavalry were of slight avail against
the General's fixed notion of what his army should be. Men must march
with muskets. Horses were for the convenience of officers and the messen-
gers who forever dashed hither and yonder with letters, letters, letters.

Throughout the winter it had often been necessary for McLane and
Alex to *borrow* able horsemen and fighters like Micah when mounts were
available. Today, for instance, when Wanderer was free because Alex had
volunteered for this mission into Philadelphia, they had borrowed Micah
from his company. For the last time, his regimental commander declared.

The army was combing its ranks for *walking* soldiers. Next week John
Tout and Tom would leave the troop to join Micah's company. On a cattle
raid into Delaware a couple of months ago they'd captured a British drum
which Alex had brought Tom. Practicing on it happily, Tom could
scarcely wait now to abandon his job as horse boy and become a company drummer.

Although needlessly bereft of the eyes and ears of cavalry, it *was* an
army again, Alex thought. And thanks to the tireless efforts of Steuben
and his passion for drill, it was a better disciplined army. In the green
spring its strength rose like the sap of the maple groves as the rigors of
the past winter faded from men's memories.

Another season, he thought, and chirped to his horse. *Rum crew* was
not, after all, a fitting password for his mission. Perhaps *rum go* would
be more appropriate. For he felt it was rum luck that he should go into
Philadelphia today. There had been no alternative, however, if he would
continue living with himself.

It was foolhardy for McLane to go this time, because he had been
recognized and almost captured during a previous mission into the city.

So Alex had said, "I'm for it," and McLane had nodded, not knowing that he once had stood at the foot of a gallows in New York as a spy. It was an experience that cooled one's ardor for spying, but he never had mentioned it to anyone in the army.

Damn my memory, he thought, staring ahead at the British flag fluttering behind the Germantown works.

It sounded like a simple task, as explained by the General to McLane and Alex. For some time it had been known that Howe had resigned, having learned the bitter lesson that taking American cities would not quell the American Revolution. Dr. Franklin, knowing the truth of this, had expressed it aptly on his mission to the French Court, Lafayette delightedly reported at Valley Forge; informed in Paris that General Howe had taken Philadelphia, Franklin replied that, to the contrary, Philadelphia had taken General Howe. The war could not be won without reinforcements, Howe complained. But his government, faced with the prospect of a vaster war now that the French had signed an alliance with the Americans, would not send him the men he sought. It was known, too, that Sir Henry Clinton had arrived in Philadelphia two days ago, on the eighth of May, presumably to take over the command from Howe.

But the General did not know Clinton's military intentions. Would he take the field or withdraw by land or sea to his stronghold in New York? Intelligence had failed to disclose a clue. One of the most reliable sources in Philadelphia, who had not been heard from in some time, was a woman named Mary Brack, a servant in Dr. Franklin's house where General Charles Grey and his aide, Captain John André, were quartered. André knew a great deal and talked a great deal; Mary Brack listened carefully at closed doors. She knew that anyone who spoke to her on any pretext and mentioned something about a "rum crew" was from Valley Forge. So—

"Shad!" Alex drawled nasally as a sentry ordered him to halt. "Fresh shad for the city." His voice rose plaintively. "I vaw, can't a man do business in these times?"

A bribe of a half-basket of fish resulted in a pass for Joel Harris and a stern warning from the officer of the guard to be out by nightfall.

He drove on, his palms sweating.

It was simple, he told himself, very simple. He would hawk his fish to the door of Dr. Franklin's house and learn—something or nothing. There had been much ado about netting the shad and finding the cart and being escorted a few miles along the way. Perhaps it had been much ado about nothing. But that seemed to be the nature of this war: great efforts and fantastic involvements in the hope of slight, random gains.

When Micah heard he was entering the city in disguise, he'd asked if he could go in his place or at least accompany him. In refusing, Alex did not tell him the General had specified that an enlisted man must not be trusted with the mission.

"If you happen on Philly in the city," Micah said, "ask about Liberty and tell her Tom's all right." He frowned, as if trying to say something else he was unable to express, and then he turned away.

Micah's desire to see Philly was no stronger than his own, Alex thought. He'd like to stroll into her kitchen and see Liberty and tell her Tom was happy and healthy. She'd be interested, too, to learn he'd happened on John Tout stumbling through the snow toward Valley Forge last January and made a place for him caring for the horses in the camp.

He could tell her how Micah had ridden and raided with him when possible. In the fraternity of the partisan raiders, Micah had shed his puzzling coolness. Perhaps he'd felt guilty for deserting the company after the defeat at Fort Washington. It didn't matter; they were close friends now. If he wished, he could tell her, "Micah loves you, Philly." Although Micah had never said so, he knew it was true. But they were not rivals. For Micah was free and he was not.

If Philly still loves him, he often thought, there's nothing I can do about it. And if Philly loved me, there would be nothing I could do about that either. What is this freedom we seek—except a desire to become the captive of someone or something else?

He would not go to his house on Fourth Street and see Philly, however. The reason, like so many reasons in these times, was ironical. Kathy was there. And, irony upon irony, he did not trust his wife—not after McLane's guarded remarks when he returned from his mission into Philadelphia last month. Kathy, it seemed, was *socializing* with British officers. And Kathy's notions of *socializing*, he thought bitterly, doubtless extended farther than McLane realized.

As the cart crept through the Northern Liberties, he looked about sharply, observing that the British and Hessian billets were widely dispersed in the devastated area. There were no signs of concentrations of troops such as might indicate an impending sortie from the city. A long work detail of unarmed British soldiers filed south, braying at him and begging fish as they passed. He brayed back, saying he had fish only for men who were going to fight the damned rebels. A sergeant cursed and said they were on their way to fight *pavilions* for the great farewell pageant to General Howe. Alex tossed him a shad and asked when that would be. The eighteenth of May, the sergeant replied, sniffing the shad. Alex blessed Howe and tossed the sergeant another fish.

It was almost noon as he approached Chestnut Street, leading the horse. He'd stopped hawking, for servants and housewives were altogether too eager to buy. The disguise, which he'd believed so clever, had turned out to be foolish; fresh shad attracted too much attention. He'd seen several familiar faces this morning, though he was sure no one had recognized him.

Along Chestnut Street strolled Mr. Pilch, heavily lidded eyes seeing all. Cursing his luck, Alex ducked under the head of his horse and swerved to avoid a heavy wagon. Behind the wagon rolled an open phaeton driven by a British soldier. He glimpsed the handsome face of a young officer, and then he saw Kathy seated beside him.

She was twirling a parasol and her head was cocked attentively to hear what the officer was saying. Her red lips were wide in the familiar "Oh!" of pleasure and her back seemed to arch like a—a— He must not look at her, but he could not take his gaze away. The officer's expression proclaimed her *mine*.

Feeling the knife strapped under his shirt, he fought a wild impulse to draw it and leap into the carriage. To kill whom? Not himself. Whirling, he gripped the edge of his cart so tightly that a fingernail broke. The cart continued to roll slowly and he moved awkwardly with it, seeing Kathy's face in an empty fishbasket. He heard her laugh, and then the phaeton had passed while he clung weakly to his moving cart.

Beyond the cart he saw Pilch's face, staring after the phaeton and then staring at him with an inscrutable expression. Lowering his head and suppressing a groan of rage, he stumbled to the head of his horse and dragged the beast faster along Chestnut Street.

As he approached Franklin's house, he raised his head and bawled angrily, "Shad! Free-esh shad!" Proximity to a philosopher's house did not lend him any philosophy with which to accept his having been cuckolded, he thought grimly. "Shad!"

Two housemaids converged on his cart, but no one came from Franklin's house. Dropping fish into the pans they held out and making change carelessly, he walked boldly to the back door of the Franklin house and pounded on it.

A spare, dark woman opened the door and stared at him.

"I hear," he said, "that Mistress Mary Brack wants some fresh shad for a rum crew."

"Draw your cart into the yard," she said and closed the door.

In a moment she came out, carrying a basket and frowning. "How do I know this shad ain't stale?" she demanded shrilly. "Let's see it."

He tipped a basket toward her and she whispered, "You're a fool, Alex March. At least one person recognized you coming into the city this morning—and told me. A friend of ours luckily." She raised her voice plaintively over the state of the shad while he gazed at her, alarmed.

"They demand reinforcements for the Indies," she whispered. "There's nought for Clinton to do but withdraw to New York. Raise your voice about the shad, you fool."

He babbled inanely about the fish and she rattled a reply.

"I'll get word to the General when the time is certain. Don't you or that other foolish young gentleman, Allen McLane, come into the city this way again. They're all took up now with a farewell pageant to Howe the eighteenth." Raising her voice, "I'll take it then."

As he dropped the fish in her basket, she whispered, "Get out of the city at once. Don't go to your home."

"Who," he muttered, "who is the man who rides about with my wife? I—I—"

"Lord Renshaw of the 44th Foot. Forget it, Mr. March. Go!"

She hurried into the house and he slowly led his cart from the city.

She could not believe that she was the first woman Gordon had taken. Yet he acted as if she were. At first she was greatly flattered, but in time she became rather bored.

He was an anxious, hasty, not very satisfying lover, she had observed that first night in February. Worse, he suffered a profound remorse that made him pace the room, muttering that he was hell's foulest fiend to have seduced her. She feigned a few tears, to convince him that he had indeed.

As the days passed and she continued to put him off, she was delighted to see the hold she had on him. Somehow she must use her power for some practical purpose. But what it might be she could not decide. He talked of making her his wife, and the notion of being Lady Renshaw and living in London pleased her. But as a practical matter she already was a wife—and in her personal experience she did not know any woman who had rid herself of a husband except by merciful death.

Growing rumors that the British planned to evacuate Philadelphia alarmed her, for she knew that she was considered a Tory now.

Yet her alarm was mild compared to Papa's. Early in April he actually closed his office and sent notices to acquaintances and newspapers everywhere that he had ceased business. His alarm was far from alleviated when he read in a Lancaster paper that "A Philadelphia merchant, T. M., having harvested two fields, now sits on the fence waiting to see in which field the harvest next shall be. More apt, he sits on a chest of British gold."

There was, as he nervously complained, "an angry current running 'neath the placid surface." That spring both he and Kathy were painfully aware of the number of small tradesmen who had endured the occupation and now began to look at them askance. They were held in greater contempt than Tories who never had deviated from their beliefs, Kathy

knew. Turncoats was the way those common people described them behind their backs.

"Turncoat" was the word frequently chalked on her door at night as
the spring progressed. After Philly scrubbed the door clean, it regularly
was marked a few nights later with "We will remember."

The words made Kathy frantic. What was there to remember? What
did she herself have to remember except nights and days of gaiety and
pleasure? *And what was wrong with that?*

There was a spring madness in the air and in the very land. Reluctant
at first, the spring burst suddenly and riotously. South wind and gentle
night rain, warm sun and the return of songbirds made winter seem remote. Through the stench of unburied filth and refuse came the sweet
smell of flowers. As Philly said, "There's a mad budding and bursting like
I've never seen before."

The spring madness infected nearly everyone. Those who had endured
the occupation quietly became rude and noisy. Those who had danced
the winter away danced longer and faster as the spring ripened. There
seemed to be in nearly everyone a longing for something that had not
been and possibly never could be.

Certainly a longing for something pulled Kathy this way and that. She
decided that she loved Gordon and would be his mistress until she could
become his wife. She took him to bed three times. And then, vaguely
dissatisfied but still determined to marry him some day, she put him off
in the fear that if she satisfied him absolutely as a mistress she might
not have the opportunity to satisfy him as a wife.

The nameless spring longing found a direction for her and others in
what Gordon vowed would be the most splendid pageant ever seen in
the colonies to honor General Howe before his departure for England.

The gaudily colored tickets called it the Meshianza. Gordon said it was
an Italian word meaning medley, though no one else seemed to know
what it meant or even agreed on how it should be spelled. According to
the plan, fourteen officers dressed as knights would joust in an entertain-
ment symbolizing their seeking the favor of fourteen beautiful, socially
prominent Philadelphians dressed as Turkish maidens. The jousters were
divided into two teams. The Knights of the Blended Rose bore the device
of entwined roses and the motto WE DROOP WHEN SEPARATED. The
Knights of the Burning Mountain bore the device of a volcano and the
motto I BURN FOREVER.

General Grey grumbled that every officer and man in the army was
absorbed in this expensive folly. He complained that he even found himself taking orders from his aide, Captain André, "one of the chief
instigators of this crime." Certainly Gordon had no time for anything else.

As one of the Knights of the Burning Mountain, he spent long hours in Kathy's front parlor carefully designing and painting his individual crest on his shield. He developed the device of a large red heart showered by numerous golden arrows, but struck only by one. The motto he painstakingly lettered was ONLY ONE PIERCES ME.

To Kathy's unrestrained delight, she had been selected as one of the Turkish maidens despite the protest of some Tories that she was the wife of a rebel officer and not even a *maiden*. But Gordon arranged it. She dared not tell Papa, who acted frightened of his own shadow these days as he went about saying that the British surely were leaving Philadelphia. Let Papa hear about it afterwards. She didn't care. It was too great a social distinction to reject.

When Philly heard about it, she stared at her, arms akimbo. Then she said slowly, "I never saw you acting such a fool before, Kathy."

She tossed her head. "I didn't ask your opinion, Philly. I'm going."

She went, riding west in a brightly polished army carriage through the golden May afternoon with Becky Franks, another of the maidens. She never had felt so happy. Today she was a Lady of the Burning Mountain, one of the fourteen most prominent ladies in Philadelphia.

Her white silk mantua dress was in polonaise style, with long sleeves. A gauze turban, spangled with gold, covered her piled golden hair. It was a more beautiful turban than she ever had imagined, crested with a red feather, edged and spangled with gold and pearl on the left side, while from its right side a gold veil descended to her waist.

It appeared that the entire city was milling around Knight's Wharf and spilling along the riverbank. As liveried footmen conducted her from the carriage onto the wharf, her heart beat faster at the crowd's exclamations on her beauty. Friends and people she had not been certain were friends called to her from the train of decorated boats and barges and galleys moored at the wharf. As in some incredibly happy dream, everyone expressed approval of her and wonder at her beauty.

Gordon leaped from a barge and conducted her to the foremost galley of the train, murmuring incoherent words of admiration. As the train of boats moved slowly from the wharf, the cheering of the crowd drowned the sweet music of violins and flutes. They drifted slowly down the blue Schuylkill between the green spring banks where people cheered and waved. She heard herself chatting gaily, but her only thought was that this was the moment for which she'd lived all her years.

They came at last to Joseph Wharton's mansion, which had been confiscated the previous fall when Wharton went into exile with other rebels. Although the great house had been despoiled and plundered, it had been completely refurbished for the Meshianza and a large amphitheater and lavishly decorated pavilion a hundred and eighty feet long had been raised near it.

The massed bands of the army began playing a stirring martial tune as they disembarked and strolled slowly up a gentle slope, between lines of grenadiers standing at rigid attention, to a great wooden arch raised in honor of General Howe's brother, Admiral Lord Howe. They moved on through other arches to the amphitheater where heralds conducted the Turkish maidens up carpeted steps to sofas on a dais. While the music continued to soar and thunder, the amphitheater filled with guests. General Howe, walking heavily beside Mrs. Loring, was followed by his brother, the swarthy-faced admiral. There was Sir Henry Clinton and behind him Lord Cornwallis. Everybody who was *anybody* was here today, Kathy thought exultantly. And she sat on a dais, smiled on and smiling, with the most distinguished gathering in the history of the colonies.

The music played faster as into the amphitheater rode the Knights of the Blended Rose, an esquire walking before each knight, carrying his shield and pink and white lance. The music stopped as a herald appeared with three trumpeters. The trumpets blared and the herald cried that the Knights of the Blended Rose declared the superiority of the Ladies of the Blended Rose to any in all the world. Into the opposite end of the amphitheater rode the Knights of the Burning Mountain preceded by their esquires. Their trumpeters sounded and their herald proclaimed that they would refute with deeds the vainglorious presumption of the Knights of the Blended Rose, for the Ladies of the Burning Mountain surpassed all others in all the world.

Kathy leaned forward breathlessly. Never, she thought, had there been a play like this. It did not really seem to be a play. It was true, every word and deed of it.

Slowly the knights circled the field in time to the quick music of the bands. How well they sat, Kathy thought, and none rode better or looked more handsome than Gordon. Turning suddenly, he dashed with leveled lance at a Knight of the Blended Rose who came toward him at full gallop. Destroy him, Gordon! She almost cried the words. The lances shivered against the shields, but neither knight fell, and they rode on, firing pistols as they passed. She could have groaned in disappointment.

Then two more knights charged each other. But again neither fell, nor did any of the following combatants. It was beautiful, she told herself. Yet it lacked the passion that she'd felt when the trumpets sounded. For a moment she thought that she was going to be bored. Then she leaned forward as the knights rode toward each other with drawn swords. Now, she thought, there would be more exciting action. The knights circled each other with flashing swords, but they merely beat their swords together above their heads and did not attempt to strike. In a moment their playing was interrupted by the judges of the field who separated them and proclaimed a happy draw.

It was rather ridiculous, like the playing of little boys, she thought as she and the other Turkish maidens descended the dais and walked in a grave procession to their knights. And then she realized that it was rather ridiculous of her to want to take playing so seriously.

She smiled warmly at Gordon and told him he was the bravest and most handsome knight on the field. Placing her hand on his arm, he escorted her up carpeted steps into the Wharton mansion which glowed in the twilight. Mirror-lined walls reflected hundreds of candles and made them appear to number thousands. Liveried servants served tea and cool punch, and the musicians began to play a minuet and the knights led their Turkish maidens in to dance.

The clang of a huge gong halted the music at ten o'clock and the servants opened the windows.

"The most splendid yet," Gordon said, leading her to an open window. "The art of Captain Montrésor. Twenty exhibitions of—"

A series of red rockets burst in the sky. Green, orange and white light illumined their faces as Kathy and other women cried out delightedly. Wonder succeeded wonder, in the sky and in the gardens, until, at the climax, a triumphal arch burst into a leaping fountain of light. On its apex appeared the figure of Fame with trumpet outlined in red. Yet the art of Captain Montrésor had one more extraordinary expression. For, as they gaped, from Fame's trumpet there suddenly issued in letters of fire the words, *Tes Lauriers Sont Immortels.*

As the words and the triumphal arch faded into darkness, there was a stunned silence. Then everyone burst into wild applause and men shouted, "Bravo! Bravo!"

But their shouts died away and their hands were stilled as flames leaped into the northern sky toward Germantown.

"I didn't know there'd be more fireworks," Kathy said foolishly.

Behind her General Grey swore loudly and strode from the room, calling the names of officers as he went. "Barrow . . . Stevenson . . . Lorcliff . . . Not you, André, stay and play your game."

"What is it?" women asked. "What's happened? What—"

Faintly from the Northern Liberties came the roll of drums.

"Ladies, rest at ease." The voice was General Howe's, heavy and genial. "Merely some extra little fireworks for your diversion. Have the musicians play again and let us resume our dance."

"But what's happened?" Kathy clutched Gordon by an arm.

"Nothing, dear thing." He patted her hand. "Possibly a few wild rebels shooting at the sky again, as they do every other night. Let us dance."

XXXVIII

"DANCE, Britons!" Alex roared as the flames leaped upward.

"Dance, you British bastards!" McLane cried.

The figures of a few British soldiers rose above the glare of flames along the works, firing wildly. Rifles flashed from the darkness and the British fell.

"An American Meshianza," Alex shouted into the glow of the whale oil they had stealthily poured along the works and then ignited with flints.

"Tell 'em, Captain March," a voice drawled in the darkness. "Give 'em a true oration."

A cannon crashed somewhere and a distant bugle sounded.

"They're calling up the dragoons," McLane said calmly. "We'll save our oratory for another day." He swung onto his horse and called, "Mount!"

"What an opportunity was lost tonight," Alex cried as he galloped away beside him. "Half the British Army in tights and the other half *tight*."

"The General said no," McLane replied, "though he didn't object to our having a little fun."

The General always said no, Alex thought. When would he say yes?

They'd had a little fun again, like boys playing the game of war. But when would they leap at the lion's throat instead of forever nip at his heels?

"Another day, Alex," McLane said. "There'll come a dawn . . ."

". . . dawn on you for a single instant what you were doing? You've created a public scandal. You've ruined my name and your own reputation. Everybody in Philadelphia is talking about you and what you did, a married woman, going to that unholy affair as a . . ."

Of all Papa's angry and tiresome tirades, this was the angriest and most tiresome. But she had anticipated it and she had her answer ready. Turning from the parlor window and facing him, she said: "I don't care what Philadelphia thinks. Because I shan't be here to know. When the British leave, any day now, I'm going with Gordon."

His lips worked; the color drained from his face and he began to tremble.

"Oh, sit down," she said impatiently, "before you have a stroke."

"A drink," he said hoarsely.

She reached for a decanter of brandy.

"Water," he said. "I want a drink of water. I was raised a poor country boy who—who—I—I—" Raising his hands to his face, he began to sob.

It was awful. She ran from the room and along the hall to the kitchen, nearly tripping over Liberty, who snatched at the hem of her skirt and laughed as he crawled across the floor.

"Philly! Get Papa some *water*. He's having a crying fit in there."

"Crying?" Philly took a glass from the cupboard. "What's he *crying* about?"

"I told him I'm leaving. I'm going away with Gordon."

"Oh?" Philly filled the glass from the water bucket and started toward the parlor.

"Did you hear what I said?" Kathy cried. "I'm *leaving!*"

"I heard you." Philly did not pause.

Liberty rolled on the floor, chuckling, as at a joke. He looked like a large butter ball, Kathy thought distractedly. Then she followed Philly, dreading to enter the parlor, but drawn to the doorway to listen to Papa sobbing and babbling about his ruined life.

Philly watched him expressionlessly as he sipped the glass of water. Glancing at Kathy, she said, "You're not going."

"I *am*. And no one can stop me."

"No one will try. For certain not *me*. But you'll stop yourself. When the time comes, you won't be able to leave Philadelphia."

Papa began to babble again.

"Mr. Murdoch," Philly said sharply, "you'd best go out to your coach and take yourself a ride around the city." She marched from the room.

"Kathy," Papa said pleadingly. "Kathy—"

Whirling, she raced up the stairs and slammed her bedroom door. She was going, she told herself.

Gordon continued to beg her to leave as the days passed. She would have passage in a ship and he'd meet her in New York. Then he would resign his commission and they would sail to London. "A new life for both of us," he kept saying. "I'll have your marriage set aside and you will marry me." Lady Kathy Renshaw. But how was a marriage "set aside"? He could not explain.

Nevertheless, she was going. Everyone of consequence in Philadelphia was leaving. For the third time in nineteen months the streets of the city were heaped with household goods as families closed their houses and left. But this time the Tories were fleeing, dispirited and angry at what they considered British betrayal. Yet, as Gordon pointed out, the British, far from betraying them, offered every loyal citizen a passage to safety.

Early in June he brought her a ticket of passage and she went with him to see the accommodations on a transport moored at Carpenter's Wharf. The air was stifling between decks; the stench of bilge and crowded humans made her ill. She could not wait to get off this ship that swarmed with wailing children and dour-faced Tories. Ascending to the main deck, she breathed deeply of the sweet fresh air and gazed at the church towers of Philadelphia against the blue sky. Unaccountably, she wanted to cry.

She was going. But not by ship, she told Gordon. She would find another way across the Jerseys later and join him in New York. He grew distraught, and he made her distraught. His glowing description of what their life in London would be like weakened her desire to stay here a little longer. She learned, however, that Becky Franks was not leaving yet and that the Shippens and the Chew women were staying. Papa's horrified, tearful remonstrances made no difference to her. But the fact that such women were staying made her determined to linger too.

Yes, she promised Gordon, she would leave soon and join him. But not yet.

The evacuation moved steadily. The troopships laden with more than three thousand refugees slipped down the river. The army itself would march across Jersey. Redoubts were built at Cooper's Creek on the Jersey shore of the Delaware to protect the crossing, and horses and wagons were ferried across daily. On the night of June fifteenth the shipyards were burned. Two days later she and Gordon tearfully kissed good-by. She would see him soon in New York, she promised. He left, and after a while she heard the notes of "The World Turned Upside Down" fading through the streets.

Early on the morning of June eighteenth Becky called for her in a phaeton driven by a Negro slave. As Becky had requested, they took Philly with them.

"I suppose you know why I asked you to come along, Philly," Becky said drily.

"Yes'm." Philly smiled. "I've a mite better reputation with some folks here now than you have. And I'm happy to watch 'em leave." She shifted Liberty in her lap. "But why do you want to watch 'em go, Miss Franks?"

"I don't." Becky smiled too. "But I do adore to suffer."

When they reached Gloucester Point, they found a crowd of several hundred staring silently at the boats plying between the Point and Cooper's Creek. Sitting in the phaeton, they watched the British rear guard climb into the boats. No boats were returning from the Jersey shore now. As the last pushed off and its oars began to wink in the morning sun, a few people cheered. Others turned and started home with lowered heads.

There were tears in Becky's eyes and Kathy saw the receding boats dimly through her own. "There should be music," Becky said. "Perhaps 'The World Turned Upside Down.' And us on its down side." She told her driver to take them home.

As he gathered up the reins, he paused, his head cocked, listening. Then Kathy heard the clatter of galloping hoofs.

Along the road from the city galloped a rider. Behind him came two, a dozen, a score. They were lean, nondescript men riding lean horses. The crowd scattered before them as they thundered to the riverbank, yelling to one another.

Philly put Liberty in Kathy's lap and swung to the ground. She ran toward the riders, crying, "Alex!"

Alex, Kathy thought numbly. But where among those strange, coarse men? And how had Philly recognized him?

"Captain March," a rider shouted, laughing. "No British for you, but leastways a pretty girl."

She saw him then, recognizing him by his quick gracefulness as he swung from his horse. She held her breath, remembering suddenly that winter day long ago at the farm when she'd seen him from her window. He was holding Philly's hand, talking to her, and now he was looking toward the phaeton.

"What's gotten into the baggage?" Becky asked. "Is it her lover that—"

"That is my husband," Kathy said indistinctly.

"Sweet heavenly God, what a priceless situation!"

He walked toward them, talking animatedly to Philly and leading his big horse. His face was thin and dark, Kathy saw, and he walked with shoulders stooped instead of in his old erect manner.

When he looked up at her, his expression was grave.

"Alex." Her voice was shrill. "I— Well, it's not my baby I'm holding here." She laughed inanely.

"I know." He smiled. "I know about Liberty."

And what else did he know? she wondered.

"Miss Franks." He nodded to Becky. "Surely it's been years since I had the honor."

"La, Mr. March." She smiled at him. "Speak for yourself, for I've not been around that long."

He blinked. Once he would have made a witty reply, Kathy thought, but now he seemed indifferent—or was he contemptuous?

"I'm glad to see you're in good health, Kathy. I—I must get on. May I suggest that you and Philly and Liberty go to your father's house and stay there. Don't go out after nightfall." He took Philly's hand. "It may be a while before I see all of you again. Take care of yourselves. Good-by."

As he swung into the saddle, Becky called gaily, "But what about me, Mr. March? What's to become of me?"

He grinned at her. "Miss Franks, from what I hear, hanging's too good for you."

They had come full circle of a tremendous irony, Alex thought as he rode away from Gloucester Point. Kathy, who always had cared so much what society thought of her, now was condemned by it. And he, who never had cared much about the opinions of society, now was upheld by it. The new society emerging on the wreckage of the old was more ruthless than Kathy remotely realized.

The arbiters of the emerging new society had passed the winter in desolate, dreary places like Valley Forge while the old society comfortably danced itself into oblivion. A man like Joseph Reed, whom Alex marked as the coming arbiter of Philadelphia, made and amended lists of names. War had ground down whatever humanitarian instincts Reed once possessed. Ironically—and Alex had come to realize that revolution was primarily a story of irony—Reed was no more humanitarian than such powerful arbiters of the past as Joseph Galloway and John Dickinson. Perhaps he was even less humane. For he and others carefully marked those they believed to be the enemies of the coming new order. They cared only whether one had been a staunch patriot, and woe betide a turncoat. Ostracism, public ridicule, exile, imprisonment, perhaps a hanging or two—they weighed the punishment they would mete for the crimes, real or imagined, of those who had not shared their season of danger and deprivation.

McLane and the troopers never mentioned Kathy to Alex. He presumed that they discussed her among themselves and pitied him as the victim of a wanton wife. They might even tolerate her because he was one of *them*. Respected, trusted, he was a loyal veteran of the bad season. To some, he knew, he appeared a hero, all the more interesting because he had an untrustworthy wife.

Sometimes he felt hypocritical because he failed to declare to everyone that he did not love his wife and did not care what became of her. But such a declaration would be even more hypocritical. For, when he wished he were rid of Kathy, he knew it was because he wished he were free to marry Philly—if she would have him. Only by remaining silent did he feel that he retained integrity.

Yet he had been momentarily tempted to break his silence early in June when Reed spoke to him. Reed had one of his damned lists of names. "Enemies of the cause" he called them. His brow was furrowed, his expression dour. The subject he had to discuss was unpleasant, but discuss it he must. Presumably Alex had heard what Mrs. March had done.

At first Alex thought Reed meant his mother, whom he'd taken to the little Moravian community of Bethlehem in December after Hessian raiders burned the house and outbuildings. He wondered, What has Mother done now?

"I presumed," he said, "that she was still trying to be of some assistance in that abominable army general hospital at Bethlehem."

"Not your mother," Reed said quickly. "That good woman is offering outstanding service in—"

"Oh, you mean *Kathy*," Alex said. Reed always had called her Kathy.

But then Reed said heavily that *Mrs. March* had appeared in that sinful Meshianza pageant as a *Turkish maiden* with *thirteen prominent Tory young ladies*. Wearily Alex started to tell him that he knew all about it, but Reed was waxing wrathfully righteous. He was a good man, courageous and able and dedicated, Alex thought. But what had happened to his magnanimous spirit? He had become too enraptured lately with his lists and "informations."

Reed said it appeared that *Mrs. March* was a *turncoat*. Positively her father, Timothy Murdoch, was. He had here (holding up a letter) full "information" on Murdoch's transactions with the British from a patriot merchant in Lancaster. He had here (holding up another paper) a deposition by a citizen and soldier, one John Tout, declaring that Murdoch had sold *twelve ton* of salt to the British army at a time when there was scarcely a sack of salt in the Continental army. What was the proper punishment for such actions?

Hang him for all I care, Alex thought. Hang him by the feet until he's dead, as Mrs. Tout was hanged. And shave the golden hair from his daughter's beautiful head and drum her from the lines, as the woman convicted of informing the enemy was drummed from Valley Forge. I don't love her and I detest that greedy little man. So—

But he looked at Reed strangely and did not speak.

In Lancaster, said Reed, a soldier and a civilian convicted of trading with the enemy had been hanged. It was proper punishment, everyone agreed.

Alex continued to stare at him silently, remembering the day long ago when Reed had protested extreme violence and said that business ameliorated everything. Perhaps Reed remembered too, for his gaze fell and he shuffled his papers.

Now, cantering through the almost deserted streets of Philadelphia, he knew that he never could bring himself to speak against Kathy and her father. And he knew his silence was like a strong wall protecting them from the vengeance of the coming new order.

He found McLane at the City Tavern, where they had agreed to meet. McLane already had sent a messenger galloping to Valley Forge with word that the British had evacuated the city and crossed to Cooper's Point. General Benedict Arnold would arrive tomorrow as the military governor of Philadelphia, he said.

"And now we'll strike them as they cross Jersey," Alex said. He could scarcely contain a sense of exultation he had not felt since the days before the Brandywine when victory seemed imminent.

They were strong, eager and well trained. Even now the General must be putting his twelve thousand men on the road out of Valley Forge. At least two thousand more awaited him in Jersey besides the militia. If he acted skillfully and with daring, the General could strike Clinton's column on the march.

"Clinton has ten thousand men," Alex said, "and must move slowly with that tremendous baggage train of loot and Tory followers."

"Has he?" McLane looked at him thoughtfully. "Must he?"

Alex looked away, thinking that the admirable quality of McLane was his demand for proof in every situation. *Has he? Must he?* It was easy to dream of charging Clinton's column gloriously. But it was not pleasant to think of studying his army at close range. Yet someone should do it.

"I believe"—his mouth suddenly felt dry and he cleared his throat— "I'll cross over the river this evening and have a look at Mr. Clinton's army."

McLane grinned. "I had the same thought. We'll go together."

They rowed across the Delaware as darkness fell, and hid their boat. Carrying packs on their backs, they walked up the road toward Haddonfield.

Fires lighted the sky and from the camp rose a din of shouts, laughter, the clang of metal, the barking of dogs. It was like a city spread on the Haddonfield plain.

When a sentry accosted them at the edge of the camp, they identified themselves as Tories from Chester trying to escape the damned rebels and make their way to New York with friends who were somewhere in the camp. The sentry let them pass.

They did not speak to each other or anyone. Their job was to count and listen as they walked together through the sprawling camp. In the confusion it was impossible to count men and wagons accurately; one could only estimate—and listen.

The British were retreating in style. Tables were set with linen, silver and candles before the tents of officers. Amazingly, they even carried chairs with them. Women laughed and chatted with lovers and husbands while servants poured wine. The Empire moved leisurely and lived comfortably; Philadelphia yesterday and New York in its own good time. No one acted as if it were a retreat.

Lord Renshaw of the 44th Foot was hereabouts somewhere, Alex thought indifferently. He did not hate him. How could you hate a man you suspected of making love to a woman you did not love? Apparently time healed a cuckold, though time could not make a cuckold love the same wench again.

Passing behind a tent, he heard a man say loudly, "Five thousand men to the Indies and three thousand to Florida, heaven help us. What can we hope to hold except New York?"

Was it proof of British intentions or only rumor? The General needed better intelligence than conversations overheard in the enemy camp.

This wandering through the camp in disguise proved little that was not already well known. The British had looted a city and were moving strongly, confidently, ponderously, to another city. As always, they gave outlanders a grudging sense of awe.

Around midnight he and McLane slipped out of the camp and returned to their boat. There were well over a thousand and possibly fifteen hundred wagons in the baggage train, they agreed. Stacked arms indicated a force of possibly ten thousand men.

"They're strong," McLane said.

"But slow, Allen. Now is when we need a cavalry force to hit 'em on the march."

McLane rested on the oars and sighed. "That's what *might* have been, Alex. But what actually *is?* What would you do if you were the General?"

"Attack and attack and attack," Alex said. "Hit them forward and aft and in the middle. Wear 'em down and finally bring on a general engagement when they're exhausted. It's his one golden opportunity of the war."

"I agree," McLane said. "It's what I'd do. But neither of us is the General and so we're talking about what *might* have been. I ask what actually *is?*"

XXXIX

THERE was confusion and disagreement among the army's leaders over what to do about Clinton's leisurely progress toward New York, Alex learned with dismay.

The orders sent McLane were, as usual, vague. He was to put himself and his men at the disposal of General Maxwell and observe and report on the enemy's movements. Maxwell, with thirteen hundred Continentals, was moving ahead of Clinton's left flank, obstructing roads and destroying bridges.

The long British and Hessian columns, crawling northeast on parallel roads at the rate of about six miles a day, paid no attention to McLane's men as they rode close. Clinton, knowing that the Americans had no cavalry worthy of the name, had harnessed his dragoons into pulling wagons.

For once the elements were against the British. Stifling heat was broken by torrential rains which failed to cool the air. The sun burned through, drying up the sandy roads where men and wagons floundered in mud or dust. The sound that issued from the creeping columns was like a long groan of wheels and voices muted by the heat. The Hessians, green uniforms stained black with sweat and staggering under their nearly hundred pounds of equipment, sometimes collapsed by squads. Watching the serpentine crawl of the column in the burning heat, Alex often expected it to come to a final halt. But it always stirred, groaned and moved again.

The elements were equally against the main American army, he knew, as it poured over the Delaware and came east across Jersey through heat and rain. The two armies appeared, on the map, to be racing at a snail's pace toward the key town of Cranbury. Late on June twenty-third he believed exultantly that the Americans had won the race when he learned the General's forces had reached Hopewell. Maxwell ordered him to take a message to Headquarters informing the General that the British were at Allentown and could not reach Cranbury before him.

It was almost dark when he swung off Wanderer at the house in Hopewell which was serving as Headquarters and Tench Tilghman, of the General's staff, took the message and told him to wait outside. As he left the house, someone gripped him by an arm and said, "March."

In the gathering darkness he made out Alex Hamilton.

"Where are they now?" Hamilton asked.

"Allentown. I've just come from there."

Hamilton led him away from the house. "You've been scouting, I presume. What would you propose to do?"

"Attack, naturally. Aren't we merely waiting for the moment? Is there any other plan?"

"There's every other plan. *I'm* for attacking, but I'm not a general. Do you know the greatest influence in this army still? Charles Lee. *General* Charles Lee, as he calls himself. After all his fiddling and faddling, his getting captured and getting himself exchanged, he still holds the General under a spell. 'Build the British a golden bridge to New York,' he tells the General. 'Let 'em begone, sir,' he says, 'and good riddance. We'll hold the country *and* our army.' "

"But surely—"

"Sure as the devil in hell, they're listening to him and nodding." Hamilton looked around and lowered his voice. "I've got to talk to someone or I'll explode. And I trust you, March. Speaking of trust, Lee doesn't trust our army. And why should it trust *him?* He's nothing but a golden tongue with his talk of a golden bridge. He daren't say it outright in front of Lafayette, but everybody knows what he means. Don't commit us. Preserve the army. Wait till the French come and let them do it. Goddamn!"

To fail to strike now, Alex thought, was to default the very purpose of the army's existence.

Hamilton muttered, "If you repeat what I've said to anyone I shall be forced to deny every word of it." And then he was gone.

Trust? Not even Hamilton trusted him to be silent. Did anyone in this army trust another? But the most depressing lack of trust was that displayed by the leaders in failing to believe in the will and ability of their men to fight.

If I could, Alex thought, I'd walk away now and enlist as a private in the first company I found.

But he was committed to his present duty, even though he soon learned, with disgust, that it now consisted of being a Headquarters courier. As twice before, in the previous winter, Headquarters had snared him again. Tilghman was pleasant about it. "We need intelligent couriers, March." But he was firm. "You will remain here on call."

He watched the generals file in for another conference at nine o'clock the next morning. There was an eclipse of the sun at the time, and he thought glumly that it symbolized the eclipse of hope for a decisive victory.

When they straggled out of the house, Wayne saw him and strolled to him.

"How are you, Alex?"

"Unhappy, Tony. Pardon, General Wayne. I thought we would fight."

"We will," Wayne said. "But not a general action, Alex. It's been too much work to build up this army to lose it in a single day."

So he lacked trust too, Alex thought. Or perhaps it was the nature of generals to wish to preserve their armies lest they cease to remain generals.

"We'll fight." Wayne smiled at him. "Something on their rear. Greene and Lafayette are against too much caution. And I think the General is pulled this way and that. We'll fight. You'll see."

As Wayne rode away, the General came out of the house and stared up at the maple leaves hanging limply in the oppressive heat. He sucked in his thin lips thoughtfully and put on his hat. He took it off, then put it on again. Still wearing it, he walked back into the house.

Toward noon Tilghman gave Alex a message to take to Lee. He found him sprawled in the shade of a beech, surrounded by his dogs and reading an old newspaper. Raising his thin, ugly face to Alex, Lee took the message and broke the seal. After he'd read it, he said irritably, "That's all, courier, that's all."

As Alex walked Wanderer back to Headquarters, Lee passed him at a gallop, his dogs loping after him.

Alex waited all afternoon in the shade outside Headquarters. The entire army was waiting, it seemed.

In the evening, when he was freed of duty, he went in search of Micah. But the 7th Pennsylvania had been ordered east somewhere.

The sun trembled at the rim of the rolling plain, and then the earth turned from it. Micah believed he actually could feel the earth moving under his feet. In the stifling evening heat there was sudden, profound silence. Somewhere in the scrub pine an owl hooted mournfully. It broke the evening spell, and the army stirred, sighed, murmured.

Summer now, as violent as the winter past, and they were lost in another season of walking. It seemed a year ago when they had swung gaily out of Valley Forge, hoping never to see it again. But only ten days had passed; some said twelve or twenty, though he knew positively that it was ten, for this was the evening of June twenty-seventh. Now he remembered the snow and cold of Valley Forge with longing. He remembered the bursting of the spring when the freshets sang and the breeze poured through the green groves, when the Schuylkill turned cool blue and the fat shad ran.

"Where *are* we?" Tom asked sleepily.

"Around Englishtown," Micah said.

"I know that." Tom sounded angry. "But where's Englishtown at? I'm all lost."

And so am I, thought Micah.

The days since they left Valley Forge were like a bad dream of damp morning fog followed by burning sun, of sudden lashing rains that steamed the sandy earth and turned dust to mud. Nothing was constant except discomfort. The sun always burned through the rain clouds, parching mouths, rusting metal, raising a stinking vapor from the wet clothing of the trudging column.

The plan seemed simple enough: Head off Clinton's column creeping toward New York, strike it, defeat it—and win the war. They could do it. This was Jersey, their old fighting ground. They were the new army, strong and eager. But the summer land was not with them and they could not get with it. They were strangers to it, for some reason that baffled Micah. Why did the land and its rivers always go with them in retreat and turn against them in the advance?

Somewhere in the growing darkness a voice chanted, "Wa—ter! Fresh, cool wa—ter!"

"Bilby again," growled Macaroni Jack. "Hope it ain't all gone before he remembers his friends."

"He's been acting like the sun tetched him on the head," Tom said.

"Don't you talk so," Mrs. Munger said sharply. "He's a fine, good Christian gentleman since he's been saved."

Maybe that was what was wrong with him, Micah thought. He'd gone and got himself saved.

"It ain't his being saved that whets me," Macaroni Jack said. "It's what bad thing he done to make him go and get saved."

They often speculated on what he'd done during the year while he'd been absent from the army. No one knew for certain, except that he'd gone privateering again. One day in April he'd appeared at Valley Forge, his left leg severed at the knee and a handsome mahogany peg fastened to the stump. He wore a suit of plain dark broadcloth, like a wealthy Quaker, and he drove a two-wheeled cart laden with fresh beef. Captain Bilby a sutler? Micah could not believe it. But then Bilby went about the camp, seeking the most needy, and *giving* them the meat. And with each chunk of meat he offered a blessing and an urgent plea to shun evil and do good.

Macaroni Jack said that although he'd never known the man before, he must have lost his mind. No, said Mrs. Munger, he'd just been saved, and it was time all of them pondered the blessing of salvation. They realized that he must at last have made his fortune, for only a rich man could act so, disappearing for days at a time and returning with a cartload of food and clothing that he gave to those he considered the neediest. He did not give money or rum; in fact, he no longer drank anything stronger than sassafras tea.

When Micah asked him how he'd grown so wealthy, Bilby raised his hands to heaven and cried, "I'm poor in spirit! I've sinned a great sin I can't never bear to mention, God save my mean soul. *He* knows, God does, and may He have mercy on me." It was a pity that Bilby could not enjoy his money for some mysterious reason, and it was aggravating not to know what enormous and interesting sin he'd committed.

Bilby and John Tout led the cart out of the darkness now as men milled around with cups.

"Where'd you find fresh water, Cap'n Bilby?" asked Macaroni Jack.

"A revelation." Bilby smoothed his eyepatch. "The rod of the Lord smote the wilderness and a spring gushed forth. Drink your fill. I'll go load the barrels with more when these are empty. The spring's three mile from here toward the British camp."

The water was fresh and cool. Although they were grateful to him, he made Micah vaguely uncomfortable. For, as always since he'd appeared in April, he was disposed to sit down and talk about good and evil, salvation and damnation.

At times, when he remembered how Bilby used to be, Micah felt downright unnerved. Bilby made him remember things he'd rather forget: all the evil, and not one good thing that he could recall. He didn't like to think about it. He wanted to think ahead, to the end of the year when his time would be up. Then he'd go back to Philadelphia and ask Philly to marry him. She would; he was certain of it. What a fool he'd been not to ask her two years ago. He'd marry her and they'd take Liberty and Tom and go off west, far west into the deep woods to live forever in peace and solitude.

Seeing that Tom had fallen asleep on the ground, he pulled a blanket around him. Tom started awake.

"You sleep," Micah said gently. "Orders are there's no taptoo for you to beat tonight. Tomorrow you'll have plenty of drumming."

He slept fitfully that night. Clinton's army was encamped a few miles ahead of them around a hamlet called Monmouth Courthouse. Surely the General would order an attack in the morning. If they weren't going to attack, why had they bothered to make this long, hard march into Jersey? Did the General aim merely to follow the British to New York and wave them good-by across the river?

He awakened Tom in time to beat reveille when the distant headquarters signal drum rolled at five o'clock. They were in formation by six, but it was after seven before they moved out toward Monmouth Courthouse through the hot, still Sunday morning.

The long column wound into the glare of rising sun through rolling country coursed by marshy creeks. Now, surely, they would attack. But about eight o'clock they were halted and waited restlessly for half an hour. Then they went on, only to be halted again.

"Are we fightin' today or ain't we?" complained John Tout. "If we ain't, let's unhitch and get out o' this sun."

"We ain't," someone said. "Not if Charlie Lee has his way."

"Then why'd we come here?" demanded Tom.

"That's a bright young un," someone called. "Sergeant Heath, send him to ast it of the General."

They went on hesitantly, crossing a bridge over a marshy creek, and, a mile farther, passing over a swamp by a causeway. Firing rose ahead and died away. They halted again. There was no sound except the hum of insects in the heat. Officers clustered in knots in the shade, talking and swatting at horseflies.

"Where's the officers at?" someone asked.

"Yonder in the shade."

"Hell's teeth, I don't mean *them*. Where'd Wayne go to? I mean an *officer*."

One came, pounding up the road, with aides streaming behind him. "Lafayette."

Another galloped toward the rear.

"Woodford. He's goin' the wrong way."

"You ask me," said John Tout, "they can't make up their minds if to fish or dig bait."

Macaroni Jack strolled to Micah and remarked on the obscene command.

"Wa—ter! Fresh, cool wa—ter!" Bilby led his cart along the road behind them, with men swarming around its tailboard. "A cup apiece, boys, one cup to a man."

"You fightin' today, Bilby?" someone called.

He wiped his sweating face with a purple handkerchief and smiled wanly. "Him that takes up the sword dies by the sword."

"And how d'you aim to die, Bilby? In bed? *Alone* in bed?"

Ignoring the jeering laughter, he called, "Tom, a cup of water for you, lad." Limping around his cart, he struggled through the milling men. "Give the boy a cup of water, you wild wolves!" he cried.

But by the time he'd wrested a wooden cup from a man, the last water barrel was empty. For a moment Micah thought that both Bilby and Tom were going to burst into tears.

"Never you mind, Tom," Bilby said. "I'll fetch more from the spring."

"Take him with you," Micah said. "Tom, you go—"

"I *won't*."

"That's an order, boy. I *command* you to—"

"I *won't!*" Tom sat down in the dusty road, curled his legs around his drum, and glared at Micah. "I'm goin' to *fight*—"

"Mutiny!" someone cried. "Heath's got him a mutiny!"

Before he could seize Tom and lift him into Bilby's cart, a dust-covered horseman galloped from the east, shouting hoarsely to the officers.

"Captain Alex!" Tom cried.

Alex waved to him and then gesticulated to the officers, telling them something, as he wheeled Wanderer and dashed away again.

They moved at the double, off the road and across fields. No one knew where they were going, but Micah reckoned that since Alex carried the orders they should make some sense.

The orders made little sense, Alex realized with growing horror. He was groping through a nightmare with a badly disturbed man named Charles Lee.

The trouble began with the General himself, who seemed unable to make up his mind. At first he had seemed to accept Lee's advice not to fight. Then Hamilton told Alex, privately and joyfully, that the General seemed to want an all-out fight. Finally, at Wayne's insistence, he appeared to agree to a fight with less than his total force.

Meanwhile, Clinton had changed the direction of his march. Instead of coming on to Cranbury he had turned east at Allentown. Now his eight-mile column was creeping exhaustedly toward the protective guns of the British fleet at Sandy Hook. As best Alex understood the orders that poured from Headquarters on the twenty-sixth, the General aimed to commit about four thousand men to an attack on the British rear near Monmouth Courthouse.

First the General offered the command of this force to Lee, who rejected it. Then he offered it to Lafayette, who accepted it eagerly. And then Lee said he wanted the command after all. And the General gave in to Lee's demand, thereby committing the extraordinary error of giving a command to an officer who had refused it once and never had believed in the plan he now was required to execute.

Engage Cornwallis's rear division as soon as it is in motion tomorrow morning, the General told Lee on the twenty-seventh. Work out the details of the attack yourself. But, as Alex learned from confused and worried officers the next morning, Lee had not worked out details.

Tilghman aroused Alex from exhausted sleep about ten o'clock on the evening of the twenty-seventh to carry a message from the General to Lee directing him to place an advance force close to the British camp and give warning of any movement. It was a strange order from one who had told Lee to work out his own plans, Alex thought. Certainly it clearly indicated that the General was beginning to have doubts about Lee. Yet he left him in command.

It was one o'clock in the morning when he found Lee. He was pacing his tent and muttering to his aide, Captain John Mercer. Lee read the General's order, then turned to Alex. "You'll stay here," he said testily. "I'm understaffed, and I must be kept informed."

He stayed, though he could not believe that he was of much use.

Lee started his force toward Monmouth Courthouse from Englishtown at seven o'clock in the morning. But he halted it frequently, first when he received word that the British were not yet moving, again when he heard firing, and a third time for no discernible reason.

Sweat poured down his face as he stared ahead. "You," he said to Alex, "bring up Wayne and tell him to go ahead and take command of the scouting forces."

"Just Wayne, sir, or Wayne and his men?" Alex asked.

"You idiot," Lee shrieked, "I said Wayne, didn't I? Did I say Wayne and his men?" He cursed Alex and turned to Mercer. "Did I say Wayne and his men or did I say Wayne?"

Alex galloped back and brought Wayne to Lee, who gesticulated wildly and cried, "Forward, Wayne, you're in command. You, whatever your name is—March—ride with him and report to me what's happening."

As they galloped forward, Wayne said, "I don't know what we'll find, Alex, but I can tell you my order to that goddamn madman will be to bring up the goddamn army."

They found the advance forces under Colonel Grayson retreating. As Wayne rallied them, Alex galloped back and found Lee shrieking at General Philomenon Dickinson, who bellowed angrily in reply.

"General Wayne requests the full force forward, sir!" Alex shouted at Lee.

"What? What?" Lee blinked at him. "Yes, forward, and to the left."

Alex, Mercer and two other aides spurred back along the road, ordering the unit commanders to push forward at the double.

The army flowed east toward the Courthouse and then north, between a ravine and a road north to Middletown while the British rear formed on the farther side of the road.

Now Lee, smiling confidently, seemed composed. "The rear guard of the enemy is ours!" he cried and sent his couriers galloping to Scott, Jackson, Wayne and Oswald with orders to dispose their men in line of attack. He must have a plan, Alex thought. But what was it? No one knew except Charles Lee.

Then he sent Alex to Lafayette with orders to take three regiments of Wayne's men and what artillery he could and attack the British left. Lafayette nodded when he received the order and rode with his aides toward Wayne.

The army swarmed like ants through the fields and scattered woods sloping down to the Courthouse. Each well-drilled unit moved in good order, Alex observed, but none knew what the others were doing. There was firing on the right and firing on the left. A new regiment swung into line and waited. It advanced and halted, waiting for others to cover its flanks. Then it withdrew and waited as the British opened a heavy cannonade.

Lafayette's force moved forward under a hail of grapeshot and hesitated. Its ranks stood firm, but men and officers were looking to left and right for other units to cover their flanks.

"Are there orders to cover General Lafayette's flanks, sir?" Alex demanded.

"What?" Sweat dripped from Lee's face again as he stared at the British lines stirring through the rolling smoke. "How's that?"

"General Lafayette's flanks!" Mercer roared. His face contorted with rage, he lifted a big hand as if to spin Lee around by his thin shoulders. *"Are there orders?"*

"Tell him—" Lee's voice was lost in the crash of a cannon.

But Lafayette, recognizing his position was untenable, had begun moving his regiment to the right. Alex saw Maxwell on the left rise in his stirrups and gesticulate wildly. Understandably, he believed he would be cut off against the ravine as a result of the opened center.

"General Maxwell!" he shouted at Lee. "Will you cover him?"

But Lee, sitting rigidly in the saddle, seemed not to hear.

Maxwell was withdrawing, and so was Scott.

"You." Lee plucked at Alex's sleeve. "Tell Lafayette to retire. His position's no good out there, no good."

But Lafayette already was withdrawing. And then, Alex saw incredulously, everyone was retiring. There was no panic at first. The regiments simply marched away while Lee babbled, "Impossible situation. Impossible, impossible."

Alex stared at him, silently cursing him.

Men began to run. A regiment broke and slammed into the regiment in front of it.

Drawing his saber, Alex rode into the fleeing men, cursing them and begging them to hold. Mercer and others rode with him, but the men could not be held. They swept everyone with them along the road toward Englishtown, panting, cursing, sweating, shouting hoarsely in a white cloud of dust.

Then Alex saw the General, mounted on a big white stallion in the middle of the road, as he'd seen him at Germantown and Brandywine when the panic of feeling leaderless had seized the army. He saw Lee, his face rigid, his expression abstracted, borne along by the mob. The General saw Lee too and his eyes blazed, his thin lips worked.

In the din Alex could not hear what the General said. It didn't matter now; it was too late for a victory and possibly it was too late for a withdrawal to safety.

Pressing Wanderer off the road, he glimpsed Micah, a hand on Tom's shoulder, being pushed along past the General and Lee. Touching his spurs to Wanderer, he rode back toward the sound of heavy firing.

As in the past, Micah thought grimly, the army flowed around the General. But this time it began to hesitate. Men who had been running slowed to a walk. They went on, across the bridge, and then they halted, gasping for breath and staring around.

"Sound that drum, Tom!"

Tom gave the long roll and Micah shouted, "Com—pany!" Macaroni Jack's voice echoed his and Captain Newman shrilly ordered them off the road. They obeyed, but they had no faith in him as they looked around for a leader.

Then many leaders were riding among them. Steuben came, laughing at them good-naturedly and shouting, "Vere was going my dear poys?" Knox followed him, bellowing that guns were coming up. The General rode back across the bridge, talking to Hamilton and pointing to the left and right. Wayne, with Alex riding beside him, galloped across the bridge as heavy firing resumed beyond it.

Now, Micah thought, we'll do something.

They did. Moving up a slight rise, they formed behind a hedge which enclosed a small orchard and barn. The 3d Pennsylvania filed after them, and then the 3d Maryland, followed by a regiment from Virginia. The 13th Pennsylvania, firing methodically as it retreated across the bridge before a force of grenadiers and carrying its wounded colonel, Walter Stewart, moved off the road and took positions behind the hedge.

Wanderer, coat flecked with lather and flaring nostrils red, halted suddenly in the orchard, his legs spreading and head sinking. Alex leaped to the ground as the big stallion tottered and fell on his side. Dropping to his knees, Alex spoke to him and rested a dusty hand on his neck. Flanks heaving, Wanderer tried to raise his head and then let it fall.

Swinging to his feet, Alex shouted, "Give me a musket!"

Micah snatched up someone's musket and pouch and powder horn and raced to him.

Alex stared at him in surprise and then he grinned. "Thanks, Micah. It's the way we began."

As they hurried to the hedgerow together, Wayne rode along the line, bawling, "They can't budge us, boys! Damn their souls, we won't budge!"

Tom, his expression rapt, rolled his drum and trotted after Wayne. Turning in the saddle, Wayne smiled at him and shouted, "That's my own bonnie lad! Roll the drum, boy! Roll it and follow me!"

Tom, beating his drum frantically, danced behind him as he rode on.

Micah groaned. "I told him to flatten out in the grass," he muttered. "If anything happens to him, I—I can't ever face Philly."

Alex looked at him strangely as he loaded his musket. "I know," he said. "But Wayne told him, 'Follow me.' Philly would understand that command."

Heavy firing burst on the left and grew in intensity. A voice called from the road and Bilby led his cart into the orchard, chanting, "Wa—ter! Fresh, cool wa—ter!"

Tom ran toward him. There was a rattling in the apple trees above them and green leaves fell in a hail of grapeshot as the crash of cannon carried from the woods below.

Micah heard Tom shriek. Whirling, he saw him holding up his shattered drumhead angrily and Bilby leaping forward to drag him under the cover of his cart. He did not have time to look longer, for out from the woods below there flushed a green line followed by a scarlet line of grenadiers.

"Steady! Hold it!"

Wayne rode behind them, roaring, "Wait the order!"

Micah's voice rang clearly as the light infantry and grenadiers came on. "Poise your firelocks! . . . Cock your firelocks! . . . Present! . . ."

When the red, straining faces of the trotting British line were fifty yards away, Wayne roared, "Fire!"

There was a flaming blast. As the smoke rolled away, the men behind the hedge cheered at sight of the broken ranks running down the slope where many lay motionless and others were trying to crawl away.

Re-forming quickly, they came again, but again they broke before a hail of bullets and grapeshot.

A familiar voice was swearing steadily nearby in a strangled tone. Bilby had snatched up the musket of a wounded man and stood, reloading, his face contorted with rage.

"If it's hell for me," he shouted, "it's hell for some other son of a bitch too!"

Beyond him Macaroni Jack turned his powder-blackened face and yelled delightedly. John Tout pounded Bilby's back, laughing and shouting, "I got me one, so help me God! I seen him fall. I got me one bloody Englishman!"

"They're forming again," Alex shouted. "They have a new leader."

They were forming only a hundred and fifty yards from the hedge, their sergeants bawling the orders as the officers paraded before their lines.

A tall officer in a gold-braided scarlet uniform marched alone toward the American line, pulling on white gloves as he came. His gloves adjusted, he took a light stick from under his arm and tapped his thigh.

"It's Monckton!" called Macaroni Jack. "Monckton of the 45th, the Sherwood Foresters." Raising his voice, he yelled derisively, "Monk! Monk! The devil's Monk! The devil will get his Monk today!"

Monckton halted, faced about in a high stomp, and stood at attention with his back to the hedge. His high, clear voice came to them. "Grenadiers! . . . To the charge—for—hard!" He marched backward toward the hedge, his stick beating time to the British drums.

"Hold it! Hold!" Wayne cried. "Pick me some king-birds, boys!"

"Monk!" yelled Macaroni Jack. "Face about, you dirty Monk! Can't you bear to face it, Monk? He's mine, boys, all mine! I've still got the scars of your whippings, Monk! Face about, I say!"

Stepping high and in time to his drums, Lieutenant Colonel Henry Monckton of the 45th Foot faced about and advanced, smiling.

"Fire!"

Shadows came on through the moiling smoke.

"Fire!"

Micah saw Monckton staggering, his face twisted and looking green in the smoke. But he came on, his standard bearer staggering beside him with the colors of the 2d Battalion of Grenadiers. Then Monckton pitched forward.

Macaroni Jack and Bilby leaped through the hedge. Macaroni Jack grasped Monckton's body and dragged it in as Bilby, shouting, seized the colors. He turned, grinning, and there was a sound like a loud slap. He fell. John Tout snatched the British colors and Micah and Alex dragged Bilby behind the hedge.

Bilby stared up at them, his single eye wide. He muttered, "Tom—" His head slumped forward.

Tom? Micah and Alex stared dully at each other.

"They've got reinforcements," Newman shouted. "They're forming again."

Tom?

"They're extending beyond our flanks," Wayne called cheerfully. "We'll retire in good order. They paid today."

Micah glimpsed Wanderer struggling to his feet, as if the stallion had heard and understood the order to retire. Then he and Alex were running to the cart. Tom lay under it, his chest drenched with blood, his eyes open sightlessly.

Sobbing, Micah lifted his body. They placed it gently across Wanderer's saddle and took it with them as the regiments withdrew from the orchard.

Book Five

BIG LAND YONDER

XL

No one loved her, Kathy thought constantly. She was barely tolerated in Philadelphia now. Old friends such as Sally Mifflin would not speak to her. More recent friends like Becky Franks turned cool after Papa began making a great display of being a patriot again. Worst of all, she felt that Philly no longer was her friend.

She could not forget the day in July when someone delivered a letter for Philly. After reading it, Philly, face pale and lips tight, silently handed it to her.

It was from Alex. Addressed to "My dearest Philly," it told her that Tom had been killed at the Battle of Monmouth Courthouse. He had died in an orchard where they fought under Tony Wayne, and that evening they'd buried his body with Captain Bilby's in a field nearby. Alex expressed grief and sent condolences from all of them—Micah, John Tout, Macaroni Jack and Mrs. Munger. Alex never writes me, she thought dully, but he writes *my dearest Philly*.

"I'm sorry, Philly," she said in a low voice. "Terribly sorry."

There should be something else she could say. Yet what would it be? She would like to say, "It was so unnecessary." What good had been accomplished? The Philadelphia rebels claimed a victory by their army, but it appeared a British victory to Kathy. The rebels had attacked, but the British had repulsed them and marched on to safety in New York. Now Tom was dead. All these deaths, this grief and suffering, were the result of a madness called a desire for liberty.

"I'm sorry," she repeated, and Philly turned from her, eyes glittering with tears.

He calls her *my dearest Philly*, Kathy thought, and he does not write me at all. I never want to see him again.

She was determined now to leave Philadelphia and join Gordon in New York. But how would she manage it?

Bad as life was, she knew it would have been worse if General Benedict Arnold had not been appointed the military governor of the city. He protected Papa and her and others from the vindictiveness of

Reed and his followers. He did so not because he liked them, she realized; Arnold liked no one much. Rather, he saw in Papa and some others the opportunity to make money.

It was surprising anyone believed Papa's protestations that he was an ardent patriot who hated the British and had been maligned by former friends. Yet some seemed willing to believe him after he actually gave a large sum of money to the War Board. Although Reed called it a bribe, others said that money spoke louder than words.

Papa was in business again, and from the way he was shopping about for a suitable country seat on the Schuylkill it was obvious to her that he was making a great deal of money. She did not know exactly what his operations were, but she knew they involved Arnold and John Livingston and Army Clothier General James Mease and Mease's deputy, William West, Jr. Hated by some and mistrusted by nearly everyone, Papa went his way with surprising cheerfulness and optimism under the protection of General Arnold.

She grudgingly admired Arnold, who still hobbled about on crutches as a result of the painful leg injury he'd suffered at Saratoga. In his bright, piercing gaze and lean, strong face she saw an adventurer of the sort she always found interesting, whatever his cause. From the way he sometimes flirted with her she believed that he saw similar characteristics in her. He was too shrewd, however, ever to make serious advances toward the wife of a captain in the army he served; he'd cocked his hat to catch Peggy Shippen, who was greatly taken with him.

As the most recent conqueror of Philadelphia, Arnold had taken over the residence of its former conqueror, Sir William Howe. Although the radicals complained bitterly about the parties he gave in the Penn Mansion, Kathy thought them dull affairs compared to the great dinners and brilliant assemblies of the previous winter. She always went, of course; it was virtually the only place she and Papa were invited now. Even Tony Wayne treated her most coolly at one of Arnold's supper parties. She doggedly told herself, however, that she would rise again some day. But not in Philadelphia.

One night in September a letter from Gordon was slipped mysteriously under the front door. He begged her to join him in New York and to write him a letter which she should leave at the Crooked Billet Tavern in the name of a Simon Jones. She wrote the letter and left it at the Crooked Billet, but she could not discover a means of getting to New York.

Congress had revoked Arnold's authority to issue passes through the American lines drawn around New York and had placed it in the hands of the Pennsylvania Supreme Executive Council—*Reed's* Council, as

Papa called it. Arnold, the radicals angrily complained, abused his authority by issuing passes for all sorts of nefarious personal and business traffic with the British.

Yet she was determined to find a way to go. She didn't care whether, as Papa said, the British would lose the war as a result of the French alliance with the rebels. For she would not linger in New York. She would leave this miserable little country forever and go with Gordon to England, a big, happy, prosperous land.

There was no sense, she realized, in wailing to Papa that she hated Philadelphia now and wanted to run away with Gordon. It was the one wish he never would grant her. Sometimes she could scarcely abide her father; sometimes she wanted to interrupt his perpetual talk of money and cry, "I'll leave you and this miserable place if it takes the rest of my life!"

But she shrewdly kept her own counsel. Twice, when he timidly asked her if she ever heard from or thought of Gordon, she laughed and replied, "Heavens, no! A passing folly, Papa. I really *detest* him—and all of 'em."

He was such a fool to believe whatever he wished to hear, she thought contemptuously. How great a fool amazed her one evening early in December after they returned from supper at Arnold's mansion.

Closing the front parlor doors, Papa began to pace, hands clasped behind him, wattles quivering with each heavy step. He paused, looked at her sharply, and asked, "You never want to see Renshaw again?"

For an instant she was tempted to cry, "Yes! Yes, I do, and get away from this awful city forever." Watching him guardedly, however, she replied, "No. How many times must I tell you, Papa? I wouldn't glance out the window for a look at him."

He began to smile. "Good. I knew it. But what *would* you like? Perhaps a ruby necklace I've had my eye on?"

It's not what *I* want, she thought; what is it that *you* want? But she smiled and said, "That sounds very nice."

"Good." He almost rubbed his hands together. Then he frowned. "I'm going to ask you if you wish to do me a favor—a very big favor. You needn't do it. I don't really *want* you to do it, but Arnold—" He bit his lip and his frown deepened.

So Arnold was in his plan too, whatever it was.

"It's urgent, Kathy, it's *imperative* that a message be got to Thomas Ridgeway, the New York merchant. Arnold—and I'll tell you secretly that he's deeply involved in this business matter with us—doesn't trust the usual means. Somebody's been tampering with letters and the radicals are trying to make trouble for us. Well, Arnold insists that *you* are the only person he'll trust. Says he's observed you're a young lady of mettle . . ."

She scarcely heard him as she stifled a cry of joy. They wanted *her* to deliver the message in New York. What an incredible fool Papa was. Perhaps all men were fools when they began to scheme; the vision of wealth blinded them to obvious things and made them forgetful of the past.

"Neither I nor Barnaby dare leave the city," he was saying. "We're watched constantly—and as for either of us getting a pass from the Council, that's impossible. Philly must go with you and you can take my coach. Arnold will arrange for a regular courier to accompany the coach to Elizabethtown in Jersey. So you'll be *safe*—"

"But how am I to get a pass?" Kathy demanded. "I'm in no better odor with the Council than *you*. And I know Philly never would consent to go to New York."

"She *must*," he said heavily. "I won't let you go under any circumstances unless Philly is with you."

Her hands fluttered agitatedly and she swung to her feet. To be so close to freedom and then see it begin to fade was unbearable. Trying to control her tone, she asked, "For what reason would the Council give me a pass?"

"Well—I don't know yet." He fingered his chin and smiled weakly. "But Arnold said you'd think of a better reason than any he can imagine . . ."

Arnold! That man must have looked into her deeply.

". . . he expressed great respect for your—uh—cleverness, Kathy. . . ."

That shrewd but maddening Benedict Arnold! "My dear God in heaven," she murmured. And Philly must be brought into it too? My dear Philly. *My dearest Philly*.

"Why are you looking at me so oddly?" Papa demanded.

She began to smile. "I just thought of something . . ."

". . . something, Philly, that I must tell you and a great favor to ask."

"What is it, Kathy?" Philly saw her tense, watchful expression in the mirror. Why, if Kathy had something important to say, didn't she face her?

"I've just seen a list of prisoners published today by General Arnold's Headquarters." Kathy's tone was almost inaudible. "Alex's name is on it. He's a prisoner in New York."

For an instant the room seemed to tilt, and then Philly found herself gripping the back of a chair, thinking, I must not cry. I'm far past tears.

But it's *my* fault. I wanted him to go back to the army and now—he'll die. He never can stand imprisonment again.

Her gaze locked with Kathy's in the mirror and Kathy's eyes wavered. "The published list of prisoners is here." She gestured vaguely toward the escritoire.

Philly let go the chair and stepped uncertainly to the desk. The name seemed to leap up at her. *March, Alex, Captain, Philadelphia.*

"By coincidence," Kathy said, "Papa received word only today from a merchant acquaintance in New York that Alex was a prisoner again. The list there confirms it."

Thomas Ridgeway, Philly thought dully. And the jailer's name was Devore. And the bit of doggerel began, *The maggot agent moves in season . . .*

"Philly, there's only one thing I can do." Kathy kept her head averted. "I'm going to New York and plead for his freedom. I think I can arrange it."

With Renshaw, Philly thought.

"Papa is willing. But he insists you must go with me." Kathy faced her. "Will you do it?"

"Yes." Kathy did not love him, yet she was willing to make this effort. "Oh, *yes,* Kathy, of course I'll go with you." Her eyes burned and she moved toward her, arms outstretched.

But Kathy moved quickly, her eyes dry, her expression abstracted, and Philly's arms fell.

"I'm going to call on Reed today. When he sees Alex's name on the list of prisoners, he'll *have* to give us passes. No matter what he thinks of me, he can't forget who Alex is. I'll get us passes and we'll leave day after tomorrow."

"I'd forgotten Liberty," Philly exclaimed.

Kathy gestured impatiently. "Leave him with somebody."

"There's nobody—except Mother March. Will you let me—"

"Yes, yes, Philly. I'll speak to Papa and he'll lend you a phaeton tomorrow."

Philly had seen Mrs. March several times in August when she was staying at the City Tavern while a couple of men she'd hired were raising a cabin at the farm. "I'm going to build up the farm again if it kills me," Mrs. March had told her. "Come stay with me when you can."

As Philly drove one of Murdoch's old phaetons toward the farm with Liberty beside her, she recalled numerous times when she'd been tempted to leave Kathy and go to Mrs. March. But for an inexplicable reason she'd felt rooted in Philadelphia, as if she were waiting for something to happen.

When Micah wrote her, expressing sorrow over Tom's death and saying he was leaving the army at the end of the year, she'd wondered if she were waiting for him. For she knew that he would come to Liberty and her. She believed— She *knew* now, without his telling her, that he loved her and wanted to marry her. She was willing to tramp off west with the man she loved. But was Micah the man? She did not know.

Wondering about herself and the future, she had waited in Philadelphia for an ending or a beginning of *something*. Now it had happened, she thought despondently. As always, however, it was an unexpected something for which she was unprepared. Why were mortals forever faced with problems too big and strange for them to manage?

When she turned the phaeton into the March lane, she stifled a shocked exclamation. Mrs. March had told her that the house and stables were destroyed, the stock driven off, and the hired hands drifted away. But she was unprepared for the sight of the charred, roofless stone house and the burned-out stables against the bleak December fields. In the center of the ruins, where the flower garden once had flourished, stood a squat log cabin and small shed.

The cabin door opened and Mrs. March came out, waving. She was gaunt and her shoulders were bowed, but she was smiling and she cried heartily, "Philly, darlin'! I hope you've come to stay. Look how that Liberty has grown."

Liberty laughed as Mrs. March lifted him from the phaeton and hugged him.

"Land sakes, get down," Mrs. March said to Philly. "Ain't you took with my fine cabin? It's a snug one. Come along and see the two cows and old horse I bought. I butchered the hog, but see how I'm making this place *grow* again. Come spring . . ."

Come spring were the words Mrs. March constantly repeated in December as she showed Philly what she had done and told her what she planned to do. Money wasn't worth much in these times, but she was saving the little she had in order to accomplish a hundred things. The big south field would be plowed and sowed to wheat. She'd get a brood of chicks and a couple of weaned pigs; she'd hire a bull to serve one of the cows and grow the biggest mess of vegetables in Chester County. She'd find a strong hand to work with timber and together ("You'd be amazed how tough I am, Philly") they'd prod and raise new beams on the indestructible fire-blackened stone shell of the house. It would be a sturdier house than ever and she would live the rest of her days in it. *Come spring*.

Listening to her and looking about at the dreary December land, Philly knew how it would be. There would be a day late in March when the wind shifted to the south and died. A stillness would press on the land and the land would yield softly. Mud time and the faint murmur of water everywhere while killdeer cried and red-winged blackbirds answered mockingly.

"Come spring," Philly said and paused.

They were in the cabin then, seated on stools before the fire while Liberty played between them on the hard-packed floor. In this crude cabin they might be on the frontier, Philly realized. And then she thought, This *is* the frontier of *something*.

"Come spring," she said quietly, "I'd love to stay a spell and work with you."

"Good." Mrs. March rocked her body contentedly. "We'll make it *grow* again."

Then Philly told her that Alex had been captured and explained Kathy's plan of going to New York and trying to arrange his freedom.

Mrs. March stared into the fire and brushed a hand across her forehead. At last she said, "My boy is a strong boy, stronger than I ever knew till this war came. I ain't at all certain he'd want *her* arranging his lot. Fact, I'm certain he wouldn't."

She looked at Philly. "She's *up* to something, Philly, you mark my words. 'Course you should go and Liberty'll stay here with me till you get back. But I don't like *her* trying to *arrange* something for Alex. You watch her, Philly. . . ."

Philly, observing Kathy in the following days, could not understand why Mrs. March or anyone should think ill of her. Kathy was emotionally shaken, but that was understandable. So am I, Philly thought, and maybe I have as good a reason as she.

Kathy was determined to win Alex back, she believed. Although Kathy had not disclosed her plan, she doubtless intended to beg Alex's release from Renshaw and others with influence. Knowing Renshaw, Philly thought that he would arrange it for her. Although he was an enemy of the cause, he was a gentleman with a sense of kindness; and what gentleman could resist Kathy's plea? After Alex went free and learned what Kathy had done for him, he'd realize that she *did* love him—and he would love her again. To think of Alex free was cause for joy. But after he's free and they're together again, Philly told herself, I must go away some place and never see him or even think of him again.

"Don't be upset," Philly kept telling Kathy. "Everything will be all right."

However, Kathy acted as if nothing would be right again. Even trivial kindnesses brought tears to her eyes.

Reed issued their passes readily and, swallowing his obvious distaste for Kathy, wished her good fortune in anything she could do to arrange Alex's release. They might have left the day after Philly took Liberty to Mrs. March if Kathy had not been so slow in packing. She tried to cram so much clothing into her little trunk that Philly had to remind her she was going away for two weeks, not two years.

On the cold, dark Thursday morning when they rose very early to wait for Murdoch's coach, she found Kathy in the front parlor taking down Mr. Peale's portrait of her.

"Kathy! You can't take *that!*"

"I know it." Kathy stared at her dully in the candlelight. "I'm putting it in the pantry. If anything happens to me, the portrait is not for Papa."

"But nothing's going to happen!"

"Things do," Kathy muttered. "Coaches overturn and people are killed—"

"For heaven's sake—"

"It's *not* for Papa to have."

Philly blinked. "Then who—"

"It's for *you.*" Kathy's eyes shone with tears as she looked at her. "Would you have it, Philly? Would you hang it on your wall some day and remember I was your friend?"

"Oh, Kathy." Philly swung to her, arms outstretched.

Seizing her, Kathy held her tightly and sobbed.

"Kathy, Kathy." Philly stroked her shoulder gently. "Why do you carry on so?"

"I don't know," Kathy gasped. "I don't know why. I always have and always will. I can't help the things I do." Letting Philly go, she stepped back and dashed a hand across her eyes. "But if anything happened to me, I'd like to think that—that you . . ." Her voice trailed off as she stared at Philly. "Would you tell me something honestly?"

"Yes."

"Do you love Alex?"

Flushing, Philly lowered her head.

"You *do*. Does he love you?"

"Not that I know of, Kathy." Her voice was almost a whisper. Then, raising her head, she cried, *"No!"*

"But if anything did happen to me," Kathy said in a dull tone, "I think you would marry him and—"

"Kathy—"

"You *would* marry him, Philly, and it wouldn't be very pleasant for either of you to have my portrait looking at you from the wall."

"Kathy, you're talking insanely. I—"

"Help me hang the portrait again, Philly. Like everything else, it belongs to Papa."

On a cold, rainy morning six days later the coach pulled away from the General Washington Tavern in Elizabethtown and took the muddy road that wound four miles through marshland to Elizabethtown Point. From the box Billy called, "To the right, ladies . . . Now to the left, ladies," as the coach sank into potholes and skidded in the mud. Philly, clinging to a strap-hang, flung her aching body to one side and then the other with Kathy at Billy's directions in order to balance the coach.

It seemed a month ago that they had left Philadelphia and lost themselves in the infinite stretch of wind-swept land where rutted, muddy roads meandered purposelessly and rain and snow flurries lashed the coach from a dirty gray sky. It seemed even longer since they'd commented on anything more personal than weather and physical discomfort and the bad food and sanitary conditions at inns along the way. After Kathy had guessed that Philly loved Alex, they had been like strangers thrown together in a coach swaying toward an unknown destination.

Kathy seemed drained of emotion. Tears had welled in her eyes when she kissed her father good-by in front of the house. Again, as they left the city by the Old York Road and bells clamored seven o'clock, she had leaned from the coach and gazed tearfully at the spires of Philadelphia rising in the gray winter dawn. Then she'd flung herself into the seat opposite Philly's and folded her arms tightly. On the box Billy called with a cheerfulness that eventually became depressing, "Potholes ahead, ladies. Please hang to them straps."

So they had lurched, swayed, bounced and sometimes walked across Jersey on a mission that became increasingly unreal to Philly. If Kathy truly loved Alex, why didn't she ever mention him? But since she wanted to free him, must she not love him? Why had her father let her make this altogether hazardous trip to aid a son-in-law he obviously did not like? What was the letter he'd given her which she carried pinned to her chemise? Above all, Philly asked herself, what am I doing here?

Kathy did not want her company, Philly had quickly realized. She was locked within herself, as never before, contemplating some mystery that Philly could not fathom. It was Murdoch who had insisted on her coming and admonished her never to let Kathy from her sight.

The courier, an ineffectual man who was drunk much of the time, had turned off to Middlebrook before they reached Elizabethtown. Now they were alone, jolting beyond Elizabethtown toward the unknown end of the strange journey.

A man shouted somewhere and the coach swayed to a halt. Lifting the end of a wet leather curtain, Philly stared out at the bleak country in the rain. Men carrying logs sloshed slowly through the mud. Wet, hairy, ill-clad, dirty, they reminded her of gray rats. One stumbling alongside the coach grinned up at her, his lips curling back on yellowed, broken teeth.

Sammy opened the door, dropped the step, and handed them down into the mud.

"Carry you, ladies?" a hairy creature called mockingly.

"They call themselves soldiers," Kathy murmured, gazing around contemptuously at the ragged men who had gathered to stare at the splendid coach and four and the handsome lady with attending maid.

A pole was stretched across the road. Beyond a small blockhouse Philly glimpsed a muddy redoubt and a cannon covered with tarpaulin. "Go yonder," a man said, pointing to the blockhouse.

They slithered through the mud and entered a dimly lighted room that stank of wet clothing and dirty men. A thin man raised his scarred face and studied them sharply as they placed their passes on a barrel before him. After examining the passes closely, he put a ledger and quill and inkpot on the barrelhead and told them to write the numbers of their passes, their names, and their purpose in entering the British lines.

Kathy wrote: *Mrs. Alex March, Philadelphia—to visit husband, prisoner of war in New York.* On the next line Philly wrote: *Miss Philadelphia Twillow—servant to Mrs. March.*

"You'll walk from here," the man said in a weak, hoarse voice. "It's about two mile to the British outworks."

"Indeed we'll not walk," Kathy replied indignantly. "Not in this weather. And who's to carry—"

"Ma'am, I'm Captain VanZandt, in command of this post, and when I tell you—"

His voice died at the unmistakable *tunk* of coins as Kathy thrust a hand in a pocket of her cloak. And then, *tunk-tunk-tunk,* gold coins poured from her slender hand onto the barrelhead. VanZandt ran his pale tongue along his underlip.

"For the *indigent* in your company, Captain," she said acidly. "My coach will take me to the galley at Elizabethtown Point landing. I'll expect it to meet me there evening after tomorrow."

VanZandt coughed and pocketed the coins. "You'll ride to the Point," he said. "But thank God the regiment leaves this sink-hole of hell today and another comes in."

"Then you'll leave word to let my coach come to the Point Friday evening?"

"Oh, sure." VanZandt waved them out.

"Barnaby warned me how corruptible these soldiers are," Kathy said loudly as they returned to the coach.

The ragged soldiers pressed close, muttering and gaping at Kathy and Philly as Sammy handed them into the coach and closed the door.

"Let 'em pass!" VanZandt shouted from the blockhouse doorway and the coach lurched forward.

Philly could not control a shiver. It seemed to her that she was growing smaller until her feet would not touch the floor and her hand could not reach the strap-hang. She had strayed too far from home into a world she hadn't bargained to see.

Kathy felt the same, she realized. Her face was pale and she could not seem to keep her balance in the rocking coach. Kathy never had been so far from home either. Once she had been a great Philadelphia lady, but what did that signify in the enemy world of New York?

"Philly"—Kathy sounded breathless—"Philly, I want you to know this. You can go back with the coach if you want to."

Philly smiled at her, thinking how kind and brave she was to be willing to go on alone even though she obviously was frightened. "I'd not think of it." She reached out to pat Kathy's hand.

But Kathy withdrew her hand and frowned. "If you're determined, I'll have you understand this. You are to do exactly as I say and ask no questions of me or anyone."

"Yes'm," Philly said and sighed.

At last they were halted again and stepped down among well fed and clothed British soldiers who stared at them as curiously as had the Americans. They were conducted into another blockhouse where they confronted an officer who growled that a rebel pass was of no consequence to the British Army. Again Kathy poured gold coins from her hand. The officer slipped the coins in a pocket and ordered a sergeant to issue them passes to New York. This time, however, Kathy did not remark on corruptible soldiers as she returned to the coach.

When they reached the moored galley which left for New York at ten o'clock each day, Sammy and Billy carried their luggage aboard. Kathy reminded them to return to the landing Friday evening at five o'clock and gave them money to feed themselves and the horses in Elizabethtown.

"Until Friday," she called after them as they started ashore. "And Sammy, you mind that Billy doesn't spend his money on rum."

They grinned and waved to her. Philly noticed that she started to wave in reply before she recalled that a lady never waved to her slaves. Turning her back to them, Kathy said, "That reminds me, Philly," and handed her a heavy purse. "Keep this. You may need it."

"But—"

"Keep it and be still, Philly."

They did not speak as they sat in the small cabin with a few other passengers, listening to the cries of the boatswain and the grunts of the oarsmen.

Around noon Kathy rose and looked ahead at New York. Smiling, she said, "Just listen to it, Philly."

The clattering, rumbling turmoil of the city was frightening, Philly thought.

But it seemed to elate Kathy. "Noisier than Philadelphia," she cried. "It's not bigger, but it's a deal more important."

The noise grew as the galley curved toward a wharf at the tip of the city. Locked somewhere within its confusion was Alex, Philly thought. This was the city the army had lost and this was the great river pouring from the north which Micah had swum. She chilled at the thought of the vastness and turmoil of land and water and the amazing strength, the incredible suffering, of the men who fought to free it.

"What?" she asked vaguely, realizing that Kathy had been speaking to her.

"Listen to me." Kathy lowered her voice. "When we land we'll hire a carriage if there's no one to meet us. We'll go first to the office of Mr. Ridgeway, the merchant. There's a letter Papa wanted delivered to him since I was coming here. You'll take it in and give it to him personally. It requires a reply that won't be ready for at least a day, and it contains instructions for you—and me—to stay at Ridgeway's house. Go to his house, as he'll tell you, and wait for the reply to the letter."

"But, Kathy—"

"*Listen* to me!" She gripped Philly's arm tightly. "You want Alex free, don't you? That's what I must be about. You'll see me or hear from me at Ridgeway's house."

"Yes, Kathy."

As they walked up the gangway, a pale, thin man with a big nose shaped like a hawk's beak stared down at them. Resting his arms on a pier piling, he called, "Mrs. March?"

"Yes," Kathy replied uncertainly.

"My friend, Barnaby Falco, sent word you'd be along." He strolled to the head of the gangway and bowed. "Mr. Devore at your service, ma'am."

Philly, knowing that he was the man who had caused Alex so much suffering in prison, stared at him with horror. But Kathy did not seem to remember, for she was smiling pleasantly and saying, "So kind of you to meet us, Mr. Devore."

"A pleasure, a pleasure." Devore took out a large gold watch, opened it, and smiled faintly. "I see you're right on time, Mrs. March."

XLI

THE rain passed and a winter hush settled on the land. Under gray skies the depleted regiment drifted east and occupied the outer works beyond Elizabethtown.

Snow tonight, Micah thought as he stared west at the low line of mauve-colored hills. Clearing tomorrow, with the bleak marshland frost-rimed. Another cabin to build, another winter to begin. But he, thank God, had only two weeks left.

He did not like this low, gray country. His mind traveled west, springing over the hard winter hills and silent valleys, thinking how it would feel to be in a mountain hollow. Over yonder silent jays waited for snow in swaying aspens and thrifty squirrels rustled in damp leaves; along the hard blue western waterways deer and moose fed at evening while bear lumbered up the slopes to winter dens.

To think of all the big land waiting yonder made his heart beat faster as he leaned against the uncompleted cabin in the marshland, and he no longer felt tired.

"Dead beat from being dead" was the way Macaroni Jack described the feeling.

They had not fought since Monmouth. All summer and fall they had marched the familiar roads and camped in the familiar places. Brunswick, Scotch Plains, Pompton, Paramus, Kakiat, Aquackanock, Haverstraw, West Point, Middlebrook. They had been strong in summer, but they had not fought. And now their winter weakness was setting in again.

The war was over, most said. It had not been won, but neither had it been lost. It simply was dying away, like a brush fire that had run its course. The British held New York and Newport. You could not exactly say that the rest of the land was held by *us,* Micah sometimes thought; rather, *it* held us.

There was something puzzling about a war so formless. Only last week, when he'd complained to Alex at Middlebrook about the long inactivity, Alex had said that the French Alliance was the cause. The British had shifted men to protect their interests in the Indies; without reinforcements they could do little except hold New York. And the Americans lacked the strength to storm the stout New York defenses. They waited for the French. The revolution they had made no longer was theirs alone.

Then whose revolution was it? The question often baffled Micah. He had served this cause two and one-half years. He had fought, marched, starved, frozen. He had endured. Yet what did he have to show for it? Even his paltry pay was nine months in arrears. Had he received it, the pay scarcely would have provided him one big meal in a proper tavern because of the inflated value of the paper currency. The rich were growing richer while the General and the politicians grew more famous. But what about the walking, waiting men? It was no wonder so many were embittered.

Yet he was not. He did not want wealth or fame. Let those who desired it seek and find it. All he asked for himself was to go free. When his time was up, he would go. He'd walk to Philadelphia and see Philly. Surely she would marry him. And then, come spring, they'd take Liberty and head west. . . .

Later that evening, sitting on his heels beside a fire with John Tout and other members of the company, he heard Mrs Munger calling his name excitedly.

She stumbled out of the darkness, crying, "Micah, the devil's work, I vaw it is. Come and—"

"Simmer down, Mrs. Munger." He rose. "What's wrong?"

"It—it—" She led him from the fire. "The officers all went off drinking in Elizabethtown and left Jack in charge at the blockhouse. I went there to sit with him and get out of the cold and—"

"What's *wrong?*" he demanded.

"You come and see for yourself."

When he flung open the door of the blockhouse, he found Macaroni Jack fingering his scarred face and scowling at a ledger.

"What's the uproar, Jack?"

Macaroni Jack handed him the ledger and said, "You read this and tell *me*. Them names was entered today by the 13th before they pulled out and we come in."

Mrs. Alex March, Philadelphia—to visit husband, prisoner of war in New York. Under it, *Miss Philadelphia Twillow—servant to Mrs. March.*

"It's Philly's hand, sure enough," Micah muttered.

"That it is," cried Mrs. Munger. "What *I* want to know—"

"Pipe your yelling, Martha," Jack said. "It's what we all want to know."

Micah had a strange sense of dread. It was like fear, he realized, for his neck felt cold. Had Philly taken Liberty with her? Alex was not a prisoner; he was assigned as a courier and part-time secretary at Headquarters at Middlebrook. Kathy surely knew he was not a prisoner. But what did Philly know?

"For certain they didn't *walk* through here today," he said slowly. "They must have been riding, but what did they ride?" He rubbed his chin. "I'm going into Elizabethtown and speak to the stage master at the General Washington. If I learn it really was them, I'm going on to Middle-brook and tell Alex."

"Middlebrook's twenty miles away," Jack said, "and—"

"I'll hitch a ride, or walk if I must."

Macaroni Jack frowned. "And have Captain Newman set you down as a deserter?"

"He knows me better than that. Tell him you had to send me as a guide for a wandering Congressman or something. Tell him what you please. But whatever's going on here ain't funning. A fine officer like Alex listed as a prisoner. His wife, if that's who it is, scampering off into the enemy lines. I tell you he should *know* about it and—"

"It's Kathy, I vaw," Mrs. Munger said. "She's up to something again. She—"

"Another thing," Micah said sharply. "If Philly comes this way before I get back, you tell her to stop right here. You say I *told* her to wait here for me. I want to have a talk with her."

Turning, he hurried out into the darkness.

It was long after midnight and the candles had burned low on the paper-piled tables of Headquarters at the John Wallace house in Middle-brook when Tench Tilghman leaned back, sighing, and wearily passed a hand across his eyes.

"There it is, Alex," he said. "Thanks for your help and for staying so late."

"There it is." Alex grimaced at the piles of worn, water-stained regimental returns which he'd been poring over for two days. "But where are we?"

"Afloat on a sea of uncertainty and doubt as usual." Tilghman's tone was surprisingly cheerful as he tonged a coal from the fire and lighted his long pipe. Drawing on his pipe and casting back the coal, he said, "It will help the General deflate some of Congress's wild dreams of further adventures in Canada when he goes to Philadelphia on the twentieth."

"I wonder, Tench. We're a strange people. We talk and dream so vastly of freedom and every man—nearly every man—gives so little of himself to achieve it."

Tilghman pointed his pipestem at the report they had prepared for the General. "By your computation, which I don't question, about fifty-one thousand men have given time to the army this year—most of 'em very little time, not over two months with the militia. That's seventeen thousand fewer than we had last year in '77, and thirty-seven thousand fewer than we had in '76. No less a Tory than Joseph Galloway himself, who would like to be pessimistic on the subject, estimates there are two hundred and fifty thousand Americans capable of bearing arms. I accept his figure—and so does the General. What has happened to the revolution?"

"Let the General himself tell you." Alex rose and took a manuscript sheet from another table. "I took this dictation from him three days ago and he told me to lay it by. Wanted to cool off, no doubt. But I hope he adds to it and sends it to Congress. He was angry, Tench, very angry, pacing the floor and working his lips while his big hands clenched. Have you read it?"

"No."

"Then listen. I haven't embellished it, not even his grammar." Holding the manuscript close to a flickering candle, Alex read the words the General had dictated.

> "If I was to be called upon to draw a picture of the times and of men, from what I have seen, and heard, and in part know, I should in one word say that idleness, dissipation and extravagance seem to have laid fast hold of most of them— That speculation— peculation—and an insatiable thirst for riches seems to have got the better of every other consideration and almost every order of men— That party disputes and personal quarrels are the great business of the day whilst the momentous concerns of an empire—a great and accumulated debt—ruined finances—depreciated money—and want of credit (which in their consequences is the want of everything) are but secondary considerations and postponed from day to day, from week to week, as if our affairs wore the most promising aspect. After drawing this picture, which from my soul I believe to be a true one, I need not repeat to you that I am alarmed and wish to see my countrymen roused."

Alex looked at Tilghman. "That's what has happened to the revolution."

Tilghman nodded. "It's a true picture indeed. The General is angry, and well he might be. I think he's at his best when angry."

"It's a pity he's not angry more often," Alex said.

Tilghman smiled and shook his head chidingly. "He's angry more often than you know. A lesser man would reveal it. Since we captured you for service here at Headquarters I've observed a subtle change in your view of the General. You seem less—impatient."

"The more I learn of men and affairs, Tench, the less impatient I become with all of 'em. Considering the massive indifference every man faces when he undertakes the slightest endeavor, I sympathize with any man who undertakes a great and noble endeavor."

"Then you understand." Tilghman leaned toward him. "Despite everything, despite a slothful, selfish and often cowardly people, *we*—the army —will continue to exist. If we cease to be, these quarreling, chevying, unconfederated states will cease to be, and that will be the end of the dream—or whatever it is—of freedom. But *we*, the army, will continue. The General will last to the end of it all—and so shall I. How about yourself?"

"But of course." Alex looked at him in surprise. "Did you ever for a moment doubt it?"

"Not doubt you, Alex." Tilghman smiled suddenly and rose. "Good night—and thanks."

As he stepped into the cold morning, the sentry piped in a boy's high voice, "Captain March, I reckoned you'd left a long while back. There was a soldier just come lookin' for you, important, he says, an' I sent him to your quarters."

Snow began to fall as he walked through the grove to the cabin he shared with three other officers. Micah was knocking on the cabin door.

"Alex—excuse me, Captain March—"

"Something wrong, Micah?" He felt vaguely alarmed.

"I just rode in from Elizabethtown. Can we talk private?"

"Not in the cabin. The White Swan Tavern's still open across the way. Let's have a toddy—and something to eat. You must be hungry after that ride."

When they were seated at a corner table with hot rum toddies and bread and cheese, Alex asked, "What is it?"

Micah leaned toward him. "Are you listed in Philadelphia as a prisoner of war?"

"Yes." Alex smiled. "Somebody at Headquarters noticed it yesterday in a batch of Philadelphia orders. They made quite a joke of it. March a prisoner at Headquarters and all that. Another clerical error. Arnold seems to have more than his share of 'em down there in Philadelphia. I got off letters to my mother and Kathy—and Joe Reed, too—reassuring them I was merely a prisoner of the General's Headquarters."

"Kathy won't get your letter," Micah said.

"How's that?" Alex frowned at him.

Then Micah told him that Kathy and Philly had passed through the lines to New York less than twenty-four hours ago, stating that their purpose was to visit him, a prisoner of war.

"It *can't* be they!" he exclaimed. "It must be somebody else on some—"

"It's *them* sure enough," Micah said gloomily. "I found Billy and Sammy, Murdoch's Negroes, in Elizabethtown. They drove Philly and Kathy from Philadelphia to Elizabethtown Point and put 'em on the galley for New York. Kathy told them to come back for 'em Friday evening. Billy and Sammy were sure enough happy to hear it was all a mistake and you weren't a prisoner again. Said they always shined to you, and Billy lent me one of the coach horses to come and tell you what had happened." Micah scowled. "Maybe it's a mistake, I don't know. But I reckoned I should let you know—"

"I'm very glad you did, Micah." He added slowly, "And I don't think Kathy's action was the result of mistaken information."

"That's a feeling I've got, Alex—sir. But what do you mean?"

Why shouldn't he tell him what he was thinking?

"I mean, Micah, that if Kathy thought I were a prisoner in New York she wouldn't do anything about it. She'd think it good riddance and I got what I deserved. But she *might* use that as an excuse to take her to New York for some other purpose."

That was all he could tell him. He could not say what he believed true: Kathy had run off and joined Lord Renshaw.

"The person I'm worried about is Philly."

"Philly?" Micah looked at him sharply. "You're worried about Philly?" he asked slowly.

"Yes." Alex studied him calmly. "I don't love my wife, Micah, and she doesn't love me. I believe that she has a great capacity for—uh—getting what she wants. Taking care of herself, she'd call it. But I fear Philly being an innocent victim of Kathy's—uh—designs."

"So do I," Micah growled. "Since you put it so, I'll make free to say I don't trust Kathy. What I want to know is can you get me permission to try to get into New York—sir? I'll do any army business that needs doing, and while I'm there I'll—"

"No." Alex shook his head and smiled faintly. It was curious that they should have the same thought simultaneously. "And don't you try to go off half-cocked on your own." Was he speaking to Micah or to himself? "They'll be back Friday evening. I'll get permission to come down there myself and we'll greet 'em together."

We'll greet Philly, he thought. At least I hope we'll greet Philly.

Micah slept in the cabin for a few hours and Alex sent him back after breakfast with a vague message to Captain Newman explaining that he had been detached overnight for special Headquarters duty.

Toward noon, unable to stop worrying about Philly, he casually asked

Tilghman if anyone had volunteered recently for an intelligence mission into New York.

"No," Tilghman replied shortly. "And no one from this Headquarters will ever receive permission. The General has his own methods and his own people and it's no concern of the staff."

Tilghman at least gave him permission to ride to Elizabethtown on Friday afternoon.

He waited beside the road with Micah, Macaroni Jack, Mrs. Munger and John Tout late that afternoon as the coach disappeared into a whirling snow flurry. Time passed interminably as they paced and stamped cold feet.

It had been dark for more than an hour before they heard the squeak and rattle of the returning coach. Then Billy wailed to them from the darkness, "They ain't there. They ain't nobody there at all. What we do now?"

Micah said, "Alex—"

"No. There's another way to handle it and I'll tend to it."

"But—"

"No," Alex said sharply. "You're too big and command too much attention. It's not like slipping out of camp to visit a tavern." Besides, he wanted to tell him as he mounted Wanderer, you've spent too many years in prison.

Presumably the perfect man in these times buried his personal interests and was concerned only with the public good, Alex thought as he rode back to Middlebrook. Yet who was perfect? For the public good seemed unimportant when you were worried about one you loved.

He tried to tell himself that Philly had been delayed in New York for some valid reason and that he was acting like an old woman to worry about her. But it did not help; he could not overcome the conviction that Kathy had selfishly placed her in danger. Then he tried to tell himself there was nothing he could do about it. But that did not help either.

Considering what he would do if he went into the city, he could think of only the vague beginnings of a plan. Kathy surely had gone to Renshaw. It would be simple to learn where Renshaw lived, watch his quarters, and follow him to Kathy—and Philly. But what then? He did not have a plan at all. He merely had the worrisome notion that all was not well and the foolish notion that he was the man to set things right. He should forget it.

But he could not stop thinking of Philly, and early the next morning he asked Tilghman's permission to speak to the General about a personal matter.

Tilghman looked at him guardedly. "No," he said. "Too many people want to speak to the General about personal matters." He smiled wanly. "You can speak to me about it."

"You'd be no help, Tench. This involves a matter of personal honor that only the General can help me with."

"Personal honor?" Tilghman sighed. "There's so much personal honor rife these days—and damned little public honor." He picked up his quill and resumed writing.

Half an hour later, however, he came from the General's office and said, "He'll see you for a moment."

The General had finished his breakfast of toddy and tea, cakes and honey, and stood with his back to the small room staring out a window at a bleak field.

"You wished to speak to me, Captain March?" He did not turn.

"Yes sir. I want to volunteer for an intelligence mission into New York."

The General turned and studied him with an inscrutable expression. "Why? I understood you wished to speak about a personal matter."

"The two are related, sir. That is, I would like to make them related. I have an urgent personal reason for going into New York. I thought in trying to accomplish it I might also serve you—the army—in any matter of intelligence that's important."

The General slowly raised his right hand and rubbed his left shoulder. He grimaced. Whether his shoulder or Alex's remark pained him it was impossible to tell.

"Captain March—" He sank stiffly into the chair behind his desk. "I've yet to see the stone that killed two birds. And I doubt that you have. We can't let personal considerations jeopardize the—whatever sources we have in New York."

Alex felt his face flushing.

The General saw it. His cold gaze shifted and returned. His lips worked.

"I don't question your courage or skill, Captain March," he said at last. "I only say they should not be wasted on work that is being adequately performed by others. Is there a personal matter you wish to speak of?"

"Yes, sir." He hesitated. "My wife appears to have become disaffected with the cause. She passed through the lines into New York three days ago."

The General stirred. Taking a ruler from his desk, he stared at it expressionlessly. "And you want to go after her and bring her back." Twisting the ruler in his big hands, the General gripped it tightly. "I understand your—mortification," he said in a low voice. "I understand your desire to—to rectify the situation. But when a woman— When— It can't be done, March. I can't give you permission to go into New York."

"Yes, sir." Alex turned on his heel and started toward the door.

"March!"

He faced about as the General swung to his feet quickly, without stiffness. Leaning toward Alex, fists clenched on his desk and eyes fixed on him piercingly, he suddenly looked younger.

"March, I commend a man who would go back to the place where he faced the gallows."

Alex stared at him in amazement. He never had mentioned the incident, yet the General knew about it. Long ago some unknown eyes of the General's enigmatical intelligence system must have observed and reported his brush with the gallows. And the General not only remembers what happened to a rather unimportant member of his army, Alex thought; he understands how I felt then and feel now. Although the General sometimes vacillated in weighing an idea, he did not hesitate to measure a man. He observed, he remembered, and he judged only after long and painful recognition of natural human frailty.

Perhaps Alex was looking more deeply into him now than the General wished any man to see. For, he sensed, the General was withdrawing into the high, cold country of his mind from which he chose to view and be viewed at a distance. His body stiffened and he stood very straight as he gazed over Alex's head.

"I've heard of your wife's disaffection, Captain March. It's regrettable. But it in no way affects my respect or that of others for your loyalty and devotion to the cause."

Presumably the General had finished. Often it was difficult to know when he had completed a thought or terminated a conversation; withdrawing himself, he never made it easy for another to know when to withdraw.

But he had not finished. "I recall many instances of your meritorious service. I'm sure there are other examples I know nothing of."

Now his struggle to express himself surely had ended. This childless man who sometimes seemed to wish to be an Olympian father to many mortal men had patted him on the head and wished him to run along.

"Thank you, sir." Alex turned away.

"March!" The General's tone expressed distress, not with Alex, but with himself for having failed again to express unfalteringly what he wished to say. "March, you're understandably troubled. In light of your long service I recommend you request a month's leave—in writing—to put your personal affairs in order."

Sitting down, the General drew a stack of papers toward him to indicate to Alex, and perhaps to himself, that his concern with the matter had ended.

XLII

"TEN minutes more, Mr. Deakins," the old man said to Alex, striking his cane on the deck. "Ten minutes more and the city'll wrap us in a warm embrace. What's your errand there?"

A fool's errand, Alex thought, standing with his back to a stinging northeast wind and watching the galley oars flash in the lemon sunlight of that Monday afternoon.

"A title search," he said to the old Tory who had scarcely stopped talking since they left Elizabethtown Point.

"Eh?" The old man cupped an ear against the wind and peered up at him.

"Property," Alex said. "The rightful title to my property."

"Oh, property." He nodded wisely. "You're from Brunswick, you say. I'm pleased to know there's still loyal subjects in Brunswick who defy the damned rebel laws and seek the King's sanction of property."

"What other sanction is there?" Alex demanded and turned away while the old man babbled on.

His plan had worked with surprising ease—thus far. Think nothing of a little lying and forgery, he told himself wryly, and think nothing of apparently going against the General's wishes. In fact, it now seemed certain that the General was quite human behind his cold façade. Otherwise, why had he granted him a month's leave? The General surely had not expected him to return to Philadelphia and sulk morosely in taverns. Obviously the General had assumed he loved his wife, and there had been no point in trying to explain that he loved her maid.

After his leave had been granted on Saturday, he'd committed forgery over no less an impressive name than that of Joseph Galloway, now a resident of New York. Writing as Galloway, he had created Edward Deakins, an attorney of Brunswick, loyal to his King.

Micah had taken him through the American lines without difficulty on Monday morning. Then, carrying an old valise he'd borrowed from Tench Tilghman and fingering a few coins he'd borrowed from Harry Lee, both of whom believed he was going to Philadelphia, he'd walked to the British lines. Clearly there was magic in the word *property* to members of an orderly society. For, although the British soldiers at the outpost had not understood the legal phrases in the letter he'd forged in Galloway's name, they had been impressed by his aggrieved air and determination to have the Crown's sanction of his property. He received a pass.

"We're nigh there, Mr. Deakins," the old Tory said.

For some time he'd been aware of the rumble of the city, and now he faced it with dread. Even the gulls that mewed and swarmed along the wharves looked bigger and fiercer than the gulls of the Delaware, he thought vaguely. The boatswain shouted an order and the oars were still as the galley glided along a wharf. There were cries and the gangway was lowered.

"Passes in order," a voice called. "Four from Elizabethtown Point . . ."

He was hurrying up the gangway, trying to rid himself of the old Tory. Safe now, he thought. Safe thus far. In a moment he'd be lost in the teeming anonymity of the city.

Glancing up, he saw a man resting his elbows on a piling and staring down at him. He caught his breath. Devore! The predatory beak was turned toward him, the dark eyes watched, as in the North Church prison so long ago— He raised a hand, fingering his hat, trying to cover his face, and hurried faster.

Now he was on the wharf and swinging past Devore, head averted.

"You, there!" Devore called.

He walked faster, his heart racing. A dozen yards and he'd be off the wharf and among longshoremen who swarmed around wagons.

"You!" Devore whistled shrilly.

Faster, though he must not run.

"That man's name!" Devore shouted to someone on the galley. "What's his—"

Ducking around a wagon, Alex started to run. Then he halted, staring aghast at Philly descending from a phaeton. Turning, she faced him. Her eyes widened and she clapped a hand to her mouth.

There were shouts behind him. His heart pounding, he swung to the right between two huge piles of lumber and shrank into a recess.

"A man off the galley!" he heard Devore cry. "Stop him! Did you see—"

And then Philly's voice, shrill and anguished: "Yes! A man hurried down that way to the left—"

"Miss *Twillow*," Devore said heavily, "you won't be boarding the galley for Elizabethtown. Stay here. I want words with you."

Then, presumably, he was gone. Alex moved out of the lumber recess. To the left, Philly had told Devore. He turned right toward carts which rumbled over cobbles.

"Alex!" Philly whispered behind him. "I'm coming with you."

Wheeling, he gripped her by an elbow. "If you're certain Devore will let you go after questioning, don't come. If I'm caught—"

"I'm certain of nothing except I'm going with you." Her face was pale, her jaw set determinedly.

"Then walk slowly," he muttered, taking her by an arm and gripping his valise tightly in the other hand. "Once beyond the traffic there, we're safe—for a time."

But only for a time, he thought, and cursed himself as a bumbling, impatient fool. If only he had waited one more day, she would have returned safely through the lines.

Listening tensely for sounds of pursuit, resisting the impulse to look back, they finally passed beyond the line of carts which rolled slowly toward another wharf.

"You've no luggage?" he asked.

She hesitated. "Not much. I'm leaving it."

They walked faster south along the Battery. By following the waterfront thus, he thought, they merely paced the edge of a cage, with south becoming east and east becoming north on this cursed island. But if they turned into the city, the center of this cage, they'd quickly be caught now that he'd been recognized.

"Alex, what—"

"Don't talk," he said.

"But Kathy—"

"I didn't come to find Kathy. I came to find *you.*" He gripped her arm more tightly. "If we ever get out of this, you must constantly remind me that I suffer from impatience. Because of it I've caught us both in an absurd and monstrous— Has Kathy gone to Renshaw?"

Philly almost halted as she exclaimed, "Then you know!"

"I've known for a long time. She's gone with him?"

"Yes. I—I tried—"

"You're in good health, Philly? You're strong?"

"Of course."

"Thanks to my bumbling impatience you'll have to be strong now. Devore will have both our passes revoked at the lines when he finds you've disappeared."

His voice trailed off and he halted, gazing down at a jetty where the small boats of hucksters to the fleet were moored. "I've only a little money, Philly. Have you any?"

"Yes." She handed him a purse from under her cape.

A few men moved among the boats. He studied their faces, thinking, God help me choose a man of romantic, corruptible mind. His gaze lingered on one with a weathered, ageless face.

"Stay here," he told Philly. Descending to the jetty, he spoke to the man.

His situation was desperate, Alex explained. Up there stood the girl he loved and across the river in Bergen waited a parson who would marry them. But her father objected violently and even now was pacing the Bergen ferry wharf to stop them from eloping. The boatman's blue eyes lighted as he gazed up at Philly. So he was of a romantic turn of mind. But he had his share of human avarice, an extra coin because he'd row against an ebbing tide, and another because he'd face a northeast wind returning.

Alex beckoned to Philly. "Hurry," he told the boatman.

Darkness had fallen when they started up the rutted, frozen road toward Bergen.

"Safe," Philly said exultantly.

"Not yet." He caught and held her hand. "It's British country to the Hackensack. But luck seems with us."

"Darkness too. I feel safer in the dark." Abruptly she let go his hand.

"What delayed you in New York?" he asked.

"Kathy." She hesitated. "I don't want to cause you pain, Alex, but I suppose you must learn in time—"

"And you must understand now, Philly, that Kathy no longer can cause me pain."

"I—I wasn't certain. She *is* your wife."

"She *was* my wife."

Behind them he heard a horse approaching at a trot. He drew her off the road and they waited in the darkness until the horseman had passed.

As they walked on, he explained how Micah and he had learned they'd gone to New York and had become worried about her. Then he asked, "Did Kathy really believe I was a prisoner?"

"She acted like she did, Alex, and Murdoch wouldn't let her go to New York unless I went with her. That awful Devore was waiting for us when we arrived. He's an ally of Murdoch's in some way. Takes a great pleasure in meeting the daily galley from Elizabethtown Point."

"And seeing all his old friends," Alex said drily.

"They put me off at Ridgeway's, the merchant, to deliver a letter from Murdoch." Philly's tone became angry. "I'm certain Murdoch's trading with the enemy again."

That, Alex thought, was Murdoch's purpose in letting Kathy go to New York. And her purpose in going was obvious now.

"I went to Ridgeway's house to stay," Philly continued. "Kathy had said she'd come there or send me word. I reckoned at first she was trying to set you free. But she didn't appear on Wednesday or Thursday. Come Friday I went around to the prisons myself. A jailer acted real decent and sent me to the Liberty Street Sugar House where they have the full list of prisoners. A man there showed me your name wasn't on the list. When I got back to Ridgeway's there was a letter from her. She carried on about loving Gordon—that's Lord Renshaw—and loving me and dreading to leave Philadelphia. But she must go to London and all that nonsense."

"What sort of fellow is Renshaw?"

She hesitated. "Well—if he wasn't a lord, Kathy wouldn't pay him any mind.

"I'd never been so put out with Kathy as I was then. It tempted me to pack off to Philadelphia, as she told me to in her letter, and just leave her there. Still, she *was* Kathy and I'd promised Murdoch to take care of her. Next day, Saturday, I inquired where Renshaw lived and I went there. They were out somewhere. All those British do is *play*. I waited on the steps for her till dark and I was nigh frozen, and then I went back to Ridgeway's. He was upset because I wouldn't hurry back to Philadelphia. But I wouldn't leave till I'd talked to Kathy."

Alex restrained an impulse to hug Philly to him. How had she managed still to care what happened to Kathy?

"I went there again on Sunday," Philly said, "and told Kathy to pack her things, we were going home. Well, it was a scene. Kathy crying and Renshaw yelling at me and me yelling back at him. I tell you, Alex, it fair wore me down. And it wore them down too, until we just sat there, too tired to argue. I reckoned that then Kathy'd get her things and come home."

"But Philly, did you think I wanted her back?"

She walked silently for a while. At last she said, "I wasn't thinking about what you want, Alex. I knew—I know now—that Kathy doesn't really want to go off to London with Renshaw or anybody else. She's done wrong, but that doesn't mean she can't go home and do right again. I sat there looking at her sharp. After a spell she told me to go and take the galley today. I reckoned I'd lost her. But there were tears in her eyes when she kissed me and she said she couldn't bear to tell me good-by. I wondered then if she might still leave on the galley with me. But she didn't appear. Ridgeway was there, waiting to give me his precious letter to Murdoch once I was aboard. And then I saw you and never did take the letter from Ridgeway."

"Ridgeway would have seen you safely aboard the galley, Philly, and his friend Devore wouldn't have given you any trouble. You shouldn't have come with me."

She turned her head in the darkness and said in a surprised tone, "Of course I should have, Alex. I couldn't leave you there alone."

There was a moment, as they walked toward Bergen, when she was certain he was going to say *I love you, Philly.* But she spoke quickly before he could, telling him that she'd left Liberty with his mother.

"Your mother's well and determined to build up the farm again come spring. It's what she lives for—building up the farm again in the spring."

"Come spring," he said abstractedly. "I'd like to be at the farm myself come spring. But I shan't. I'm staying in the army till we've won."

"We *will* win," she said, and thought, Lord make it soon. "I'm glad you'll stay with the army till it's ended."

"Are you really, Philly?"

"Of course," she replied indistinctly. "If enough good men do, it will be won sooner."

The wind, rising steadily since they left the river, bore stinging snow as they entered Bergen.

"Can you go on, Philly?" he asked. "I'm afraid Devore may have revoked our passes at all outposts by morning, but it's a long way and will take us all night. Can you do it?"

"I surely can, Alex."

She'd walk all the way to Philadelphia with him if he wished her to, she thought. For she loved him and would love him forever. Yet she told herself that she was closer to him now in the cold darkness than she ever would be again.

After eating at a tavern in Bergen, they took the road to the New Bridge across the Hackensack. Once across the bridge, they'd be free, she knew. Free? A vague dread of the future grew in her as they bent their heads into the stinging snow. She almost wished they could walk together thus forever and never reach freedom.

But freedom, whatever that would mean for them, came quickly. At the bridgehead a British officer studied their passes by lantern light. At first he was suspicious of them, a man and a maid plunging off into the swamps at midnight. When he found their passes in order, however, he said his chief concern was with Hessians who were deserting this winter in the hope of starting new lives out there—the fools! The officer glared at them, as if they were fools too, and then they walked on across the bridge.

As they left the bridge, Alex caught her arm and said, "We're free, Philly!" In a moment he asked, "What do you want most in this freedom?"

She wanted much, she thought. She wanted children, to beget and to bear and to raise. She wanted her strong family in a stout house set in abundant fields. She wanted to spin and weave and cook and do without fear of a coming season. There should be much laughter to compensate for the inevitable tears. Not wealth, but neither should there be poverty. Fame never, but a book to read at the end of a day and a garden or chimney corner in which to read it. Above all, a man whom she loved more than anything else. Wars, politics and society never could supply these wants of hers. She and a man must do it themselves.

But she told herself she could not mention these things now without sounding as if she were asking him for them. And these things were not his to give.

When she did not speak, he said, "I look forward to victory—and hard times. Hard, *interesting* times. I want the farm to prosper and I plan to start my own practice in Philadelphia. That's the future. But now—" He hesitated. "I'm taking you back to Philadelphia in Murdoch's coach, and then on to the farm to stay with Mother. I'm starting proceedings for a divorce."

"Divorce?" She looked up at him quickly as he halted.

"Yes. I love you, Philly. I want to marry you."

"And I love you, Alex. But you aren't *free* with—"

"I told you I'm getting a *divorce*." He leaned toward her and she turned her face, fearing he might kiss her at the same time she wanted to draw him to her passionately. "Of course there will be a little scandal, but—"

"Scandal's not the trouble, Alex." She raised her voice against the wind. "What's proper isn't the trouble. The trouble is with what's *right*. Don't you see?"

"No! I have legal grounds for divorcing a woman who deserted me, a woman I don't love. I—"

"If you don't see, then I can't explain it." She started on, and he walked beside her.

Some day he'd understand, she thought. If he divorced Kathy and married her, he'd bear a flaw that distracted others from seeing his true fine character, Alex March, Philadelphia gentleman, who divorced his wife and married her maid. Philly Twillow, woodsy, bound girl, servant, and finally—only by virtue of Kathy's defection—the wife of Alex March. She would seem a wench who climbed the ladder rung by scheming rung. So much for scandal. They could live down scandal, which was a property of small minds and so of short memories.

Yet they never could live down the memory of Kathy, who was a property of both their hearts. For Kathy still *lived*. Being human, they judged her; but only God had the right to punish her. If Alex broke the sacred vows of marriage and divorced her, he punished her—and himself.

For Kathy will want to return some day, Philly thought. I saw that in New York. She's wanton and selfish now. But I couldn't live with the knowledge that Alex's divorce prevented her from coming home and being true and selfless.

"Philly, I don't understand you." His tone was angry.

"I told you that I love you, Alex."

He cried, "Then why in heaven's name—"

"I always will love you." Her voice trembled and she clenched her hands tightly as she walked faster. "But another wrong won't make everything *right*. Some day you'll know I'm not a fool."

"Fool!" Ridgeway had exclaimed. "You're being an arrant fool, Mrs. March!"

Kathy had realized it for several days. But not until Ridgeway confronted her in Gordon's quarters that Monday afternoon had she seen a way of ceasing to be a fool.

Fortunately Gordon was absent on duty when Ridgeway came to the house with an aggrieved and self-righteous air.

"I've finally learned the whole story, Mrs. March," he said. "Mr. Devore has informed me. I can't believe that a daughter of Timothy Murdoch, a married woman, should come to—this." He gestured disdainfully to the tiny parlor.

"*This,*" Kathy said coldly, "is the quarters of Lord Renshaw. As a loyal subject of the King, you might bear that in mind, Mr. Ridgeway."

"And you might bear in mind, Mrs. March, that I'm also a loyal subject of decency, with a daughter about your age. Sit down."

"I shall stand. I suppose my servant sent you here."

"Your servant, Miss Twillow, never mentioned—this. You might be interested to know she's disappeared. And your husband has been observed in New York."

Kathy sank onto a chair. "Philly—disappeared? Alex— Didn't Philly take the galley today?"

"She did not," Ridgeway said heavily. "Nor did she take with her this highly important letter for your father. Be quiet, Mrs. March, and listen to me."

At first she listened intently, but soon she heard only her own echoing thought: *It's not too late.*

Ridgeway confirmed sorrowfully what Gordon and his friends said angrily: The Crown could not hope to win the war now. Ridgeway said angrily what she already had confirmed sorrowfully with Banastre Tarleton and Gordon's other friends: There was no way for her marriage to be "set aside" and for her to become Lady Renshaw. Even if she could, she was not at all certain now that she would want to be Lady Renshaw, bride of Gordon, a most childish earl. Furthermore, if the rebels actually won this war, Alex possibly would be more powerful than a dozen earls.

Alex, Alex. She did not love him. But what was love except the fancy of a naïve young girl who looked through a farmhouse window and tried to see her future in a man? So Alex, the fool, had come into the city. Did he know? Was he searching for her? It didn't matter. It only mattered that she was Mrs. Alex March. She was a Philadelphian, the daughter of Timothy Murdoch. She enjoyed the protection of General Benedict Arnold, the lasting loyalty of Philly Twillow. She could explain to everyone that she'd gone to New York to help her imprisoned husband, only to find she'd made the journey as a result of a clerical error.

There, in Ridgeway's hand, was the letter to Papa that justified her return. As she reached for the letter Gordon, New York, the gaiety of these recent days, seemed to fade into the remote past and she was home again in Philadelphia.

She could not reach Philadelphia quickly enough and start a *present* life that would blot out the past. Not that she was ashamed of anything. What, indeed, was there to be ashamed of? She had tried something that had turned out to be—inexpedient. Now she would try something new, something—expedient.

The minutes flew as she threw things into her little trunk and Ridgeway waited. If she could be gone before Gordon returned, she'd avoid his inevitable tears and recriminations. When, in a brief time, she was ready, Ridgeway himself lugged her trunk into his waiting carriage and she hurried after him without bothering to write Gordon a note of farewell.

Then, in the privacy of a room at Ridgeway's house, the hours crept. She paced the floor, wondering what had become of Philly and what Alex was doing in New York. Perhaps Devore had mistaken someone else for Alex. But perhaps not. Perhaps he'd be hung as a spy if he were caught. She didn't care. She should, but she didn't. She did care, but she shouldn't. How—expedient that would be. Shivering suddenly, she wished that she believed in God as Philly did. God might stop her shivering. But it was more—expedient to ring for a servant and ask her to build up the fire.

The hours of Tuesday crept more slowly until, at last, Ridgeway knocked on her door and said his carriage was ready to take her to the galley. She rode beside him through the crowded streets with eyes closed tightly behind her dark veil. When they reached the wharf where the galley waited, she opened her eyes wide, threw back her veil and smiled at the bay glittering in the sun. The shores, white with snow, were like arms opened wide in welcome to her. South now, she thought, south and west at all possible speed toward the spires of Philadelphia.

She scarcely heard what Ridgeway said. Yes, she had the precious letter for Papa. Yes, yes, yes. Then he left the galley and she huddled in a corner of the small cabin, thankful that she was the only passenger.

The boatswain sang an order and oarlocks creaked. They were moving at last, gliding away from this city she never wanted to see again. She turned her head for a last look at it, and found herself staring into Devore's face.

"Mrs. March." He strolled into the cabin, his expression bemused, and closed the door behind him. "I must see you safely on your way."

She started fearfully to her feet. "That really isn't necessary, Mr. Devore. I—"

"But it is." His face, so like an ax blade, seemed nicked by a smile. "And I've brought us some punch, a bite to eat, to while our time to Elizabethtown Point." He placed a hamper on the cabin table.

She shrank from him as he sat down on the bench beside her and took a jug and two cups from the hamper. No, she was not hungry, nor did she want any punch. He shrugged and poured himself a cupful.

He was talking in a low monotone. She could not understand what he meant. Something about a net drawn tightly about the city. No one could escape it. But her pass was in order, she exclaimed.

Then he did smile at her and pressed his knee against her leg. "Not you, Mrs. March. Your husband."

She shrank farther from him. "What are you going to do with him if you catch him?" Her voice sank to a whisper.

Devore did not reply. Instead, he slowly drew a gold watch from a pocket and let it hang and turn slowly on its gold chain. He smiled at the watch and then at her. At last he said, "That should be—convenient for you."

"No!" she cried.

Grinning, Devore asked her to examine his watch and see if she recognized it. She paid no attention to the watch as she babbled, almost incoherently, that Devore misjudged her. Interrupting her finally, he said that he never misjudged anyone—least of all her.

She realized dimly that he wanted something. But it took her a while to comprehend that he wanted her. At first she was furious that such a low, common man should act so brazenly toward her, a lady. Then, as he made her understand that he never misjudged anyone, she was terrified. He seemed to have some kind of a bargain in mind, something involving Alex.

Leaping to her feet suddenly, she fled from the cabin. The wind knifed her sharply as she tensely paced the deck. She glimpsed Devore in the cabin, chewing on a chunk of meat and sipping his rum punch. He seemed to think that he *had* her, she thought frantically. He was like a loathsome spider that took a trapped fly from its web at leisure.

Eventually, despite her determination not to return to the cabin, the numbing cold drove her in. As she stood inside the closed door, shaking with cold and fright, Devore refilled his cup and suggested that she be reasonable. Truly now, she wished her husband dead, didn't she? In a voice so calm that it surprised her, she told him no. Very well, Devore said, then she wished him to live. That could be arranged too. He took out his watch, smiled at it, and said they were nearing Elizabethtown Point where there was a house in which they'd discuss the arrangements.

Her heart raced in fear as the galley approached the wharf at the Point. Be sharp, she told herself. Devore was powerful, but she held some strong cards too. He might be able to revoke her pass temporarily, but he'd have to reckon with Ridgeway later. And he couldn't assault her physically in the midst of the British garrison at the Point.

As she walked up the gangway, with Devore following, a horse whickered in the gathering darkness. The coach would be waiting—over there. "Billy!" she called. "Sammy!"

There was no answer.

She hurried through snow toward a fire. A couple of British soldiers who were warming themselves by the fire told her that no coach had come through the lines to the landing today. As she turned away distractedly, she saw Devore. He called to her, saying something about having her trunk taken off the galley. She strode away from him toward the outworks, clutching her British pass inside one mitten and her Continental pass inside the other. Hearing him following her, she went faster. She was almost running as she approached the blockhouse.

Suddenly he gripped her painfully by an arm and spun her around. "Mrs. March! You've come the right direction. The house is there." He nodded toward a cabin.

"My pass!" she gasped. "I want my pass through the lines approved before—before anything else."

He let go her arm: "Then take it to the officer of the day in the block-house yonder," he said slowly. "You'll find you're free to leave the lines. But you won't want to use your pass yet, Mrs. March. You see, I've just learned your husband has been captured."

She caught her breath as he turned away. "I'll wait for you there," he said, walking toward the cabin.

Be sharp, she thought numbly. Be sharp! Devore might be lying. But if he weren't, how did she know that he could or would release Alex? Yet he clearly believed now, in spite of everything he knew about her, that she wanted Alex free. She did, of course. She truly did. Devore was shrewd enough to see that—despite everything. So her only remaining weapon against him was his own shrewdness.

Whirling, she hurried into the blockhouse.

It happened with incredible ease. The officer accepted her pass and she was outside again, looking about fearfully for Devore. Then she was past the sentry and fighting the impulse to run into the darkness.

As the flickering British fires grew smaller behind her, she thought that she heard shouting back there. She ran. Once she stumbled off the road and fell. Struggling to her feet, she ran again until she was breathless and her heart ached. She paused, panting and listening. There was no sound except wind rustling the frozen marsh grass.

Free, she thought, and started on. It didn't matter what had happened to her trunk and Papa's coach. It didn't matter what had happened to Alex, or even to Philly. She'd walk all the way to Philadelphia if she had to. It didn't matter. *At last I'm free.*

She'd forgotten how far it was to the rebel lines, and she never had realized it could be so cold on a winter night. But it didn't matter. Each step took her farther from Devore and nearer Philadelphia.

A sound on the road ahead made her pause. And then she believed she heard shouting behind her. She ran again, brushing away tears of cold and staring into the white darkness of the swamp ahead. Something moved on the road. A figure, two figures. They must be rebel soldiers. She slowed until she thought vaguely, Not rebels, but friends.

She called wordlessly to them, but they seemed not to hear her, for they did not turn back. Instead, they disappeared, so that she believed she must have imagined she had seen them. She ran on, nevertheless, trying to make her cold lips form words her mind refused to summon.

Suddenly a blinding flash seemed to light all the marshland as a gigantic hand struck her breast and flung her around in an echoing roar. It bore her to earth and pressed her down, holding her. Her arms flailed, but she could not touch the hand that was crushing life from her. Screaming and writhing against the invisible hand, she dimly glimpsed a white moon rising swiftly in the sky. There were two moons now against the darkness. They were human faces looking down at her. She tried to scream at them to wrench away the awful hand, but the pressure crept upward on her throat and no sound came from her twisting lips.

Slowly, then, she was lifted toward the sky and borne forward into darkness.

XLIII

MICAH came from the frozen swamp that Tuesday evening, clutching three dead rabbits by stiff hind legs. As he entered the bivouac area of dark and smoking cabins, he halted and gazed west for a spell at the distant low hills which flung black wooded crests against red clouds. Then he went on to the fire Mrs. Munger had started outside her and Macaroni Jack's cabin.

She scowled at him and whispered, "You be quiet. Philly's still asleep in the cabin yonder."

As if he didn't know. He hadn't been able to think of anything else since Philly and Alex had stumbled, dead beat, into the lines that morning.

Looking at the rabbits, Mrs. Munger began to smile. "Leastways you didn't come empty-handed. Them rabbits is a blessing. The beef's spoiled again and there ain't a mortal thing in hand but hard bread."

Laying a rabbit on a log beside the fire, Micah nicked the point of his knife under the pelt at the breastbone and slit it to the crotch. He made slits down the legs, cut off the pads, and peeled the skin off over the head. After carefully examining the skin for worms and finding none, he cut off the head and gutted the rabbit.

"One thing that ails this army," he muttered, "is that it stays in *rabbit* country."

Lord take us out of the swamps to a high country where the deer browse, he thought. He fancied he could see them now, hundreds of winter deer in the western hill meadows, following their beaten trails and feeding on low-hanging cedar.

"I just can't get over Kathy running off with a British *lord,*" Mrs. Munger said. "It's all John Tout's talked about all day, and no wonder . . ."

Micah paid no attention to her. He didn't want to hear or think of Kathy. The only important matter was how would he speak to Philly. He'd certainly sounded a fool this morning, saying to her severely when she and Alex came into camp, "Well, Philly, you passed a mortal long time in New York."

Now the frost-starched grass had lost its white sparkle. Night loomed in the east and purple shadows stretched across the snowy plain. The drum rolled retreat and he got to his feet as the flag slowly fluttered down the staff on the little blockhouse.

Behind him Philly said, "Micah."

She stood in the cabin doorway, smiling at him. My memory's no good, Philly, he wanted to say to her. I always forget how beautiful you are at the time I should remember. You'll look just so in our mountain meadow cabin when I come home at evening.

But he said in a voice as dry as ashes, "Well, you slept the day away." Then, clenching his hands tightly, he said, "Philly, would you stroll with me for a spell?"

"Why—yes. Certainly, Micah."

They walked silently toward the road while he tried desperately to remember how he'd decided to say it. But all he seemed capable of doing now was to suck at a chapped knuckle. The wind was rising and it was almost dark. What he needed was a fence or wall to lean against while he talked to her, but there wasn't a leaning place in this swamp, nor even a place to get out of the wind.

At last he heard himself saying in a remote tone, "Philly, I aim to quit the army in eight more days when my time's up. The war's all but over. Like some other Continentals, I've been smart never to sign their three years or the duration papers. A year at a time I always told them, and they had to take it at that if they wanted me—and they did."

What could she possibly care about that? Yet she was saying, "I don't blame you, Micah. I reckon the army still needs you, as it does plenty of others. But you've more than done your time. You've certainly earned the right to—to go free."

He nodded, glad that it finally was dark and she could not see his face. "Philly, I'd like to come and fetch you after I'm out and—and ask you to marry me. We'll take Liberty and find us a place a little ways west where I'll work for wages or on my own. And some day when the frontier's quieted down and it's safe for you, we'll go on west. I—I ain't much, but I can do anything I lay my hand to."

I ain't much, he thought. Hell, I'm nothing. I've broken all the Commandments and betrayed everybody and everything. Except the cause of freedom.

"What I aimed to say—" He swallowed. "I love you, Philly."

Why didn't she say something? If he could at least see her face in the darkness he'd know—

"There was a time, Micah," she said unsteadily. "There—"

"I *know,*" he said quickly. "Don't think I haven't cussed myself for—"

"There's nothing to cuss yourself for, Micah. I say there was a time when I loved you best in all the world. But now I love you—only second best. And that's not good enough for you. It's not the way you—or I— should be."

He rubbed his jaw. "You mean?"

"I love Alex."

And Alex loves you, Micah thought dully. What was there to say?

He spoke slowly. "Alex is a good man, Philly. A gentleman who's brave and smart. An honest-to-God gentleman like they don't make many of. And you, Philly— Well! Sometimes when I so much as think of you I feel like jelly that won't set. I remember you a wild little woodsy with hair so tangled you couldn't run your haw-comb through it. I brought you east, and what a fine, beautiful woman you've grown to be. By God, Philly, if you don't see fit to marry me, I'd be proud to see you the wife of Alex March."

Maybe she was crying in the darkness. Maybe, if he weren't a man, he'd cry too.

"But I'm not going to marry Alex," she finally said in a low voice. "No matter what the law provides for divorce and such, I can't marry the man who's wedded to my dearest friend."

"Your dearest friend!" he exclaimed. "Now, Philly, you listen here—Wait, do you mean that since you won't marry Alex, you'd consider me—"

"No. You and I—and all of us—are always trying to get by on what's less than *best*. This time I—I want what my heart tells me is *best* or—or—"

"Nothing. See here, Philly—"

"I'll always take care of Liberty for you, Micah," she said, "but I can't marry you. Let's go back now."

She didn't make sense, he thought glumly, as he followed her.

Alex had come from Micah's cabin, where he'd slept since morning, and was sitting beside the fire. He nodded absently as Micah hunkered down on his heels near him and they stared into the fire while Mrs. Munger and Philly prepared a rabbit stew.

"I vaw there's mouths enough to feed tonight," Mrs. Munger said after a long time. "Jack halted Billy and Sammy with the coach at the blockhouse and told 'em there's no point in—" She glanced at Alex and cleared her throat. "They'll be along with Jack. I mind the time I was above eatin' with slaves, but now I reckon they's just as free as we are in this swamp. And then John will be coming. And— Ain't you men anything to do but sit there starin' at a fire? It's 'way late for feedin'. Go to the blockhouse and bring Jack and t'others."

They got to their feet and strolled slowly and silently through the camp. As they approached the blockhouse, they heard shouting and saw men milling around its open door.

"What's the trouble?" Micah asked a soldier coming toward him.

"Two more Hessian deserters," the man replied. "They're honest or fools or maybe both. Seems they thought they were being chased and one of 'em fired a shot. Turned out it was just a woman coming behind them. They carried her into the lines."

"Is she badly hurt?" Alex asked.

"She don't hurt at all," the man said. "She's dead."

Micah walked from the swamp again on Wednesday evening, his hands empty of game. Skirting the little cemetery where they'd buried Kathy that morning among the army dead, he went slowly toward Macaroni Jack's cabin.

His walk in the frozen swamp had cleared his mind somewhat of the things they'd said and of other things they'd left unsaid. Tomorrow Philly would leave for Philadelphia in Murdoch's coach and from there go on to the March farm to stay. Alex would escort her on Wanderer. But he would be back, he said. He was staying in the army to the end, even if the army stayed here in a swamp to the end.

Pausing, Micah took a last look at the dim red western light beyond the hills. Here in a swamp, he thought. Some, like Macaroni Jack and Mrs. Munger and John Tout, were here because there was no place else to go. And others, like Alex, were here because they wanted to be.

The sun had disappeared and now must be fading fast across the wide western land. He would not go with the sun next year, nor maybe the year after. But he would go some day.

Stepping around the cabin, he smiled at the faces of his friends about the fire. He wanted to call out, especially to Philly and Alex, and say that he had something important to tell them. But there was no sense in making a speech. For they'd learn in time that he would stay with them till everyone went free.